Midnight Harvest

Also by Chelsea Quinn Yarbro

Hôtel Transylvania

The Palace

Night Blooming

Available from Warner Books

Chelsea Quinn Yarbro

Midnight Harvest

ASPECT®

WARNER BOOKS

An AOL Time Warner Company

Copyright © 2003 by Chelsea Quinn Yarbro
All rights reserved.

Aspect® name and logo are registered trademarks of Warner Books, Inc.

Warner Books, Inc., 1271 Avenue of the Americas, New York, NY 10020
Visit our Web site at www.twbookmark.com.

An AOL Time Warner Company

Printed in the United States of America
First Printing: September 2003
10 9 8 7 6 5 4 3 2 1

Library of Congress Cataloging-in-Publication Data
Yarbro, Chelsea Quinn
    Midnight Harvest / Chelsea Quinn Yarbro.
        p. cm.
    ISBN 0-446-53240-1
    1. Saint-Germain, comte de, d. 1784—Fiction. 2. Viticulture—Fiction.
3. Depressions—Fiction. 4. California—Fiction. 5. Vampires—Fiction.
I. Title.
    PS3575.A7M53 2003
    813'.54—dc21   2003045089

Book design by Mada Design, Inc. / NYC

This one is for

Irene Kraas

agent extraordinaire

author's note

The 1930s, although still in living memory, are as remote as the Civil War for many Americans, especially those born after 1960, whose contact with those times—if any exists at all—tends to be through grandparents; the combination of the Dust Bowl and the Great Depression put the country into dire straits of a kind that has, fortunately, not been seen since. The impact of those privations touched every part of society, and the reforms undertaken by the government to address the appalling conditions that prevailed can still be seen in public buildings in almost all American cities to this day, and in the ongoing debate over Social Security.

The Roaring Twenties in America—themselves a frenetic reaction to the aftermath of World War I, or the Great War as it was then called—had come to a screeching halt with the Crash of 1929 and the catastrophic plummet of the stock market that led to the Great Depression. Europe had already endured financial hardship, most notably in Germany in the mid-Twenties, and the political instability that resulted from the disastrous inflation eventually led to the rise of the Nazi party, which used not only the vindictive terms imposed on Germany at the end of World War I to incite the populace, but the economic crisis as well. America may have lagged behind the Europeans in money problems, but eventually the same difficulties cropped up in the United States, and some of the same political unrest.

The wild card—and wild is the appropriate word here—in the American situation was the general air of lawlessness that developed during Prohibition. By making drinking alcohol illegal, the government created an environment that encouraged tolerance of lawbreakers as acceptable behavior in the general society more unobjectionable than had been the case since the great westward expansion of the nineteenth century. For many Americans, turning bootleggers was an irresistible temptation; and with others taking advantage of the situation, their daring and media exposure made them into mythic figures, like buccaneers or Robin Hoods, braving incompetent and unfair authorities on behalf of the common folk. In many ways this preoccupation with the exploits of criminal gangs engaged in circumventing the Volsted Act diverted the general social malaise into the single issue of booze and the escapades associated with it. By the time Prohibition ended in 1933, its impact had touched almost every aspect of daily life in America, and its impact was not only on issues of law enforcement: among the many victims of Prohibition were the American wine, beer, and distillery businesses, although a few distillers made a spectacular recovery at the end when the aged whiskeys they had made could finally be released for sale. Wine and beer producers did not generally fare so well, for only a handful had the financial resources to ride out the thirteen years of Prohibition, although few religious Orders continued to make sacramental wines, which were excluded from the terms of the law, but otherwise most of those industries suffered, many of them—already burdened with the flagging general economy—beyond remedy.

Yet a few industries prospered in these hard times, most notably in America the entertainment industry. As vaudeville breathed its last gasp, the 1930s saw the rise of major motion picture studios and expanded distribution of movies that in turn rode on technological advancements—many of which originated in Europe but moved across the Atlantic to escape the war-ruined economies and the political unrest that came with them. Radio became ubiquitous, in part because of an ambitious program of bringing electricity to all of the country, not just the cities. Thousands of theaters were refitted from stage to screen, for movies became the most popular form of escapist entertainment outside pulp magazines. Another industry that did well in the Twenties and Thirties in America was transportation: the burgeoning airline business, the ambitious expansions of roads and similar public works projects that were as much a means of creating jobs as opening the country to trucking, and the railroads all profited in the harsh financial climate that followed the Crash. By extension, the oil industry—although far more volatile than many other endeavors—expanded and, when it succeeded, succeeded handsomely; as more and more applications for petroleum products were developed, the greater the profits were in the oil business. All of this was not enough to offset the Depression, but as Will Rogers so succinctly put it, "All that money went somewhere"; these are some of the places it went. The free-falling downward monetary spiral of 1929 continued to wreak havoc in America right up to the first stages of World War II, when the demands of the arms industry finally got the American economy into high gear again.

In Europe, where conditions were harsher, the solutions tended to be more extreme: in Germany the Nazis came to power; in Italy and Spain, the Fascists rose, and the polarization of right-wing authoritarian governments (Nazis, Fascists) and left-wing authoritarian governments (Communists) became entrenched and the seeds of World War II—or, more accurately, World War I, Part II—were sown. With the demands of economic and material recovery making such stringent demands on Europeans, the unilateral might of authoritarian governments was not only tolerated, it was generally welcomed by the various countries in which that authoritarianism flourished; those who did not support the regimes were pressured into silence or removed from society, reinforcing the hold of the governments in question. As German belligerence increased through the Thirties, it found echoes in many other countries, including Britain and America, although the general return to isolationism in America kept Nazism and other authoritarian systems from establishing more than a minor toehold. But that did not mean Americans were immune to the appeal of extreme politics.

Extremist political groups sprouted up in all parts of America, from far right, racist organizations, such as the Ku Klux Klan and the notorious Black Legion, to the far left, such as the United Workers of the World, with every stripe and inclination in between, for although there was political unrest in the United States, it did not become fixated on one aspect of the country's many problems—the issues of Prohibition notwithstanding, for those had been preempted by organized crime—and as a result the responses were more varied and diffuse than was the case in Europe, and never had the opportunity to become entrenched in the centers of political power as was the case elsewhere in the world. There was also—especially in rural areas—an upsurge in revivalist religion, some of which went big-time, anticipating the televangelists of the present. Such preachers as Aimee Semple McPherson, who in 1923 dedicated her 5,000-seat Angelus Temple in Los Angeles, set the tone for spectacular, theatrical histrionics, a kind of showmanship that has remained in popularized religion to this day. The Fundamentalist farmers of the Midwest, uprooted from the Dust Bowl, took their faith with them as they moved—usually westward—in search of a living. It was a dicey situation that could only deteriorate as the problems escalated.

The middle to late 1930s brought increased tensions to Europe as the buildup to war began to pick up speed. This increasing conflict was known in America, but for the most part deliberately ignored as part of the desire of America to remain aloof from what was hoped was just more European squabbling. Many Europeans shared that hope of American isolationism, leaving their homelands for America in anticipation of coming conflict. Starting early in the 1920s, a number of successful businessmen and academics came to the United States—

and to South America as well—looking for an opportunity to avoid becoming caught up in the coming hostilities; most of them brought their families with them—parents, children, aunts, uncles, cousins, all were included whenever possible. As hostilities worsened, more Europeans left the Old World for the New: North and South America both experienced an influx of immigration in the Thirties. Shortly before World War II broke out at the end of August 1939, what had been a trickle became a flood.

Not all Americans were pleased with this situation, for in an already damaged economy, there were many who saw these newcomers as economic spoilers, bent on taking what little employment there was away from the "real" Americans. This served to fuel the various hate groups that battened onto the old organizations or cropped up as new ones from one end of the country to the other, and although the European arrivals created as many jobs as they took, the perception of many longtime unemployed was that they were being shoved aside in favor of the newcomers.

Unlike several of the other books in this series, this one doesn't lack for applicable information on the time and its events: there are newspapers, books, newsreels, radio broadcasts, magazines, and all manner of personal documents readily obtainable; in fact, the trick here is not to find out specific information, it is to winnow out the material essential to the story from all the data available. In that capacity, I have had the advantage of speaking to a dozen men and women who lived through these years as young adults, two in Europe, two on the East Coast, three in Chicago and the Midwest, and the rest in California. I am grateful to them for sharing their memories, diaries, and other material with me, for their personal reminiscences have provided me a wonderful window on the decade of the story. So: Anne, Claude, Durandarte, Elihu, Frank, Louise, Patti, Petronella, Renee, Silvain, Sol, and Yoshiko, thank you for all your time and generous conversation. If in making my selection I have left out some incident, person, or development that is your favorite, I apologize, and plead exigencies of narrative line for my omission, and I offer the same mea culpa to my readers whose view of that period may not be the same as the view of this novel. Also *California: The Guide to the Golden State,* published by the WPA in 1937 through 1938, proved extremely useful, particularly in details about roads and other travel conditions of the period.

There are also others who deserve a thank-you here: Elizabeth Miller, Stephanie Moss, and Sharon Russell of the Transylvanian Society of Dracula and the Lord Ruthven Assembly; to Mia Delancy, Jim Russ, and Jeanne Keagan, who read the manuscript for clarity, and to Anne, Sol, Yoshiko, and Claude, who read it for accuracy. To Lindig Harris for her newsletter *Yclept Yarbro*, available from lindig@mindspring.com; to Wiley Saichek for all his tireless promotional work; to Tyrrell Morris for keeping my machines and Web site (www.ChelseaQuinnYarbo.com) running; to Robin Dubner, who continues to look after Saint-Germain's legal interests; to Libba Campbell; to Maureen Kelly, Gaye Raymond, Alice Horst, Randall Behr, and the Luckes, just because. On the publishing end, thanks to the good people at Warner, including Larissa Rivera and Jamie Levine, who have taken Saint-Germain under their respective wings, and to Laurence J. Kirshbaum, Chairman of Warner Publishing, along with Stealth Press, for giving Saint-Germain such a splendid opportunity to rise from the grave of the out-of-print. And finally, thanks to my readers, new and longtime, for your continued support of this series.

Chelsea Quinn Yarbro
May 2002

part one

Doña Isabel Inez Vedancho y Nuñez

San Francisco, California, USA
October 21, 1935

Franchot Ragoczy
c/o Sunbury Draughton Hollis and Carnford
New Court
City of London, England

My dear Count,

I suppose I may still address you as such, though it has been a long time since I took pen in hand to write to you, a decade at least, and I am fully aware that you may have gone far beyond my ability to reach you via any address I have in my records. I trust your solicitors may still find you, wherever you are, and whatever name you are using now, for I must assume you have changed that as well as your address.

As you may guess from the letterhead, I am still in California, and still living in the magnificent fifteen-room house my grandfather bequeathed to me, and I am still painting. I employ a housekeeper-cum-cook—a sensible woman named Clara Powell, whose husband is incarcerated for bootlegging and whose three children are being raised by his parents in Michigan—and a gardener—Cedric McMannus, a Canadian from Saskatchewan who came here fifteen years ago to work at the Ralston Mansion—neither of whom live in; occasionally I hire a carpenter-handyman for more strenuous work, a great change from the staff of servants at Longacres. I have turned two of the parlors into a large studio where I work, and I have added a north-facing bay window to it; I have also improved the bathrooms and the kitchen. To hear my English relatives' reaction, you would think I were living in a tent in the middle of the wilderness. Yet, all in all, I have become, in my own way, quite staid in my life, though it is not the life my family would have chosen for me. They all thought me hopelessly wild when I came here, back in 1911, and nothing I have done since has changed their view of me, since I am continuing to pursue art instead of establishing myself as someone's wife and someone else's mother. In fact, my work has developed a fairly good reputation in the West, and I have had several shows, a few of them one-woman shows, the result of which has been that I have recently been approached by a gallery in New York to handle my work. I am giving their offer close consideration, for although I am fortunate enough not to have to worry about money—my grandfather left me handsomely provided for, and not even the Great Depression has diminished my holdings to a marked degree—I do have to consider the realities of the artistic world and make some accommodations. So it may be that I shall have to journey East and do the pretty to the ever-so-cultured New Yorkers. I am not wholly resigned to the prospect, as should be apparent. I left England to get away from just the kind of snobbery that the New Englanders have determined to enshrine, and I am disinclined to deal with such aggrandizement unless it becomes absolutely necessary.

You may be surprised to learn that I have become an American citizen, taken Saxon as my legal name, and voted for President Roosevelt, all much to the distress of my sister. Do you remember her? She was a precocious child when you met her. Penelope achieved her dearest wish and married Rupert Bowen in 1922, and I know you must remember him. She is a widow now, and living at Longacres, with her two children. I have seen my nephews three times—once in England, twice here in America—but not in the last five years; they were very young then, now they are eight and eleven. Rupert died in 1931, quite suddenly, and Penelope has made his memory into a hallowed one. You would scarcely recognize him in the paragon he has become in Penelope's remembrance. I have ceased to try to remedy her fiction, for it brings me nothing but her rancor and I already have a quantity of that to deal with.

On May 10, I turned fifty, and I have spent the last five months thinking over my life, and I have found myself recalling the time we spent together, your many kindnesses to me, and your love. Since my parents are dead, and my brother, and I find I cannot discuss these matters with my sister, I am appealing to you to read this with the compassion you have always e xtended to me, and which I am persuaded you must still possess. I hope I have not erred in this conviction, and that I do not intrude upon you in sending you this letter, but I am certain that you are cognizant of all I am presently encountering. You, of all people, must know the weight of mortality, as well as the burden living imposes. How capricious it all seems to me, the twists and turns of events, the bizarre whims of what some would call fate, but I can find no word to express. I thought the Great War had inured me to the uncertainty of life, but now I realize that there is another understanding that is part of age and comes only when one's contemporaries begin to fall away. In the last two years, my mother has died—which was painful but not unexpected—a childhood friend has succumbed to cancer, and a couple who have been my close friends here have been killed in a terrible automobile accident. Now I am distressed to learn that a longtime associate has suffered a stroke and is bedridden, unable to speak or walk. I went to see him yesterday, and I was shocked and saddened, he was so changed, like an echo of himself. I begin to feel the shadows gathering, as my grandfather used to say. He died in the Influenza Epidemic, early in 1919, when so many others perished. That was a dreadful calamity, coming as it did in the wake of the Great War. How much suffering shaped those years! At the time, I could not mourn for my grandfather, there being so many others dying all around me, and the grief of war still fresh. So I shut it away as best I could and decided that I would not be overwhelmed by the losses I had sustained—as so many others had elected to do, too. Only since the more recent deaths and misfortunes I mentioned have I come to appreciate how much I miss my grandfather, and to understand what I have lost. I begin to wonder if I shall ever reach a point when the mourning is eased, and I begin to suspect that I shall not. If I find myself so haunted by a mere five decades, I cannot imagine how it must be for you.

Your letters, though few, have been treasured. I regard each one as precious. I apologize again for my long silence, but after the death of your ward, I could think of nothing to say to you that would offer even a modicum of comfort, so I took the coward's way and said nothing, for which I am most heartily ashamed of myself. It was unconscionable of me to turn away from you in your grief, and I am distressed still that I could not summon up sufficient courage to extend you my sympathy at such a terrible time. You never treated me in any way that deserved such shabby behavior on my part, nor can I offer any explanation for my lacking that doesn't sound paltry. At the time, I told myself it was the Great War and my father's death that made it too difficult for me to try to console you, but over time I have realized that I felt inadequate to the task, and yielded to my qualms as a means of sparing myself pain. As I look at this paragraph, my chagrin returns in full force. I hope you can find it within you to forgive me, and that you will permit me to write to you as time goes on.

Recently I did some watercolor studies of the Golden Gate Bridge. It is being built across the mouth of the bay, a splendid enterprise that changes day by day. You would find it fascinating, I would think. Everyone in the area is excited about it. It will connect the north counties of the bay—Marin and Sonoma most particularly, and the highway that runs into Oregon and

Washington—with San Francisco, and allow much of the traffic to travel by road instead of ferry. They say it will be finished in two years, but that seems impossible to me. There is so much more to be done, I cannot see how it can all be accomplished in two years. Nevertheless, it is an awe-inspiring enterprise, no matter how long it takes to complete. To see those tremendous cables looming out of the fog between those tall towers is a most impressive experience, and one I have tried to capture in my work, not nearly so successfully as I would like. I haven't yet decided if I will show these works or not. They are somehow too personal, as are the two sketches I did of you, all those years ago, in Amsterdam, after your oil portrait was destroyed. I still have those sketches, and the watercolor study I did after I arrived here. I keep them on the wall of my library. I could never bring myself to send one on to you, as I said I would do. So they remain as my private icons: you and a fine bridge— what a perplexing combination. I don't suppose I'll ever part with any of them, unless, of course, you should want one of them, in which case you may choose which one you prefer, for, even after all these years, I cannot.

There is so much I want to tell you, but I don't want to fling everything at you at once, although I think I may have done just that, for which I apologize. I'd never realized until now how much I had pent up within me. So I will close for now, and hope that when your solicitor forwards this to you, you will read it kindheartedly, and tell me where I can find you without going through Sunbury Draughton Hollis & Carnford. If you cannot do this, I will understand, although I will be saddened.

Let me send you my love with this, and my thanks for all you did for me, when I was still too young to fully value it, and assure you that I no longer take such kindness as my right, but a treasured privilege.

Rowena Saxon

P. S.

If it isn't presumptuous for me to say so, my house is always open to you, and in the event that you ever come to San Francisco, it will be my pleasure to have you as my guest for as long as you wish to stay. I continue to keep those crates of Transylvanian earth that you sent at the outbreak of the Great War; they are in my basement, untouched, and at your disposal should you ever fetch up in this city.

chapter one

One of the shutters banged open, buffeted by the wind; it left a wedge of brilliant sunlight across the bed, making the sheet celestially luminous in the cool, shadowed room. On the bed, Saint-Germain moved out of the brightness, leaving Doña Isabel Inez Vedancho y Nuñez wrapped in the sheets. He rose and went to secure the shutter and looked out at the shining Atlantic edging the city of Cádiz. From here he had a view of the harbor, and he saw the clusters of soldiers near the warehouses and customs sheds, seemingly small as mice and as busy. In the bright, chilly winter sunlight they appeared preternaturally sharp and defined.

"Amor, come back to bed," murmured Doña Isabel. She rolled onto her back and stretched out her arm. Her face was still softened by the aftermath of passion and her dark auburn hair was a glorious tangle.

"In a moment," Saint-Germain said as he fastened the latch, restoring the dimness that had made their time together so private. Unlike the naked Doña Isabel, Saint-Germain was still dressed in slacks and an open silk shirt, though his feet were bare; he made his way across the lotus-patterned carpet, his movements measured, almost as if he were pacing out an ancient dance. "We still have an hour more before siesta is over. There is no reason to hurry."

"No, not to hurry, but I don't want to"—she let the sheet slide down her body, exposing more of her flesh—"neglect anything we might enjoy."

He smiled fleetingly. "Nor would I," he said softly.

"And I have no wish to waste this opportunity," said Doña Isabel, who was known as Isis to her friends for her love of all things Egyptian as well as the slightly exotic cast of her features. Her room reflected her taste with a pair of golden sphinxes flanking the door, a chair upholstered in appliqué linen that was a copy of a temple frieze at Luxor, and a small statue of a crowned Pharaoh on her nightstand—she called him Rameses, but Saint-Germain read his name in the cartouche as Khafre—as well as golden hieroglyphic motifs in her wallpaper. "It isn't just that siesta won't last forever: I have to attend a reception at the British Consul's residence this evening, and I'll need two hours to get ready. It's very formal—white-tie." She continued to watch him. "Will I see you there?"

"Very likely," said Saint-Germain. "But probably not until midnight; I doubt I'll appear at the beginning of the evening."

"You aren't going to attend the dinner, then, just the concert to follow," she said shrewdly; at thirty-two she considered herself very much a woman of the world, and in the last two months had become accustomed to Saint-Germain's eccentricities. "You don't like to have to avoid the food."

"A sad necessity, hermosa, or at least an exercise in forethought; you know how awkward it can be to have to account for such quirks," he said as he came back to the bed. "In any case, I prefer not to draw anyone's attention to it."

"It's probably for the best, though I would truly welcome your escort." She sighed, wrapping a stray tendril of hair around her finger. "I would be the envy of half the women there, I daresay, but I don't want tongues to wag about us."

"Nor I," he said, knowing his reticence was for vastly different reasons than hers. "So we must continue to be circumspect. And not simply because I do not dine as most others do." He sat on the edge of the bed and leaned over her, kissing her deeply and slowly, feeling her desire reawaken as her lips parted.

"Ah, Comte," she whispered as he stretched out beside her. "I am so glad you have decided to spend this time with me, no matter how brief it may be. It is little enough to brighten my life. But if Ponce," she went on, making a moue of distaste at her husband's name, "insists on remaining in l'Argentina for years on end with that German mistress of his, he cannot expect me to pursue a nun's existence." She slipped her hand into his hair. "Not that Ponce ever treated me so well as you have done."

"I have done nothing that would compromise you," he reminded her as his lips grazed the rise of her small, pointed breasts.

"I don't think Ponce would agree," she said with a quick, delicious smile. "If the well-born ladies and gentlemen of Cádiz knew what you and I have been doing with our Friday afternoons, they would be shocked, and scandal would follow. I have no liking for being an object of defamation." She ran one finger along the edge of his jaw. "But at least you have done nothing that would truly disgrace me. Or endanger my marriage. What a perfect lover you are, Comte: attentive, insouciant, and incapable of impregnating me. And so very discreet— if there are rumors, I can still deny them believably. "

"No, I would not put you in any danger that can be avoided. Nor would I expose you to ostracism, if I could prevent it," he promised her as he did something quite wonderful to her nipples.

She sighed again, luxuriously, and arched her back. "That's . . . that's . . . keep doing that," she murmured.

He obeyed, and slowly began to work his way down her body, his touch finding new sources of arousal as he went. When he discovered some especially intense response, he lingered, expanding on her excitement until she was almost shivering with anticipation. He parted her legs and caressed the soft folds that were already moist.

"Not yet. Not yet," she said, her hands in his hair. "Make it last longer." She drew his head down to kiss his mouth, releasing him slowly.

"Very well," he said, and slowly worked his way up her body, still learning new ways to excite her. "If this is what you want."

Her smile was subtly feline, deeply satisfied. "Most lovers would be vexed with me," she said softly as he kissed her shoulder. "But you don't mind at all."

"Why should I? My enjoyment is commensurate with yours. The greater your fulfillment, the greater mine is." He supported himself on his elbow and looked down into her face. "Why would I deprive myself of the full release of your passion?"

She laughed low in her throat. "Of course."

Saint-Germain kissed her again. "Still, we should be careful." He began to stroke her body through the sheet.

She held on to his neck, keeping their faces close together. "It isn't just Ponce who worries you, is it?"

"No," Saint-Germain admitted.

"The soldiers trouble you; I see you watching them when you're out in public," she said, knowing she was right; she pressed herself against him in languorous abandon. "You think they're going to be more aggressive."

"I fear so," said Saint-Germain, and swept her hair back from her forehead and bent to kiss the arch of her brow. "Soldiers often are, particularly when there is tension in the country as there is now in Spain."

"Should I be worried, do you think?" Doña Isabel asked, some of her attention straying to what his hand was doing to her hip. She half-closed her eyes and allowed her senses to drift. "Do you reckon I'm in jeopardy?"

"Not yet, but in time you may be. My risks are more imminent. Our situations are not the same," Saint-Germain reminded her, and kissed her upper lip, and expanded the exploration of his expert fingers.

"You mean because I'm Spanish and you're in exile," she said, beginning to pant. "Oh, that's just . . . lovely."

"Then enjoy it," he whispered, caressing the line of her thigh while he continued to elicit new bursts of pleasure from her awakened flesh.

"It's . . ." She managed to open her eyes to look deeply into his. "Can you do more?"

He did not bother to answer her, putting all his attention on rousing her totally. He stroked her hip down to her knee through the fine linen, and pushed the sheet aside so that her pale olive body was wholly accessible to him. "You're glorious," he whispered, running his hand lingeringly along her flank and onto her hip, duplicating his last caress. He curled over her, moving with care as he shifted his position. Gently he kissed the back of her knee and began to work his way up her leg, maneuvering to the inside of it as he went. By the time he reached the apex of her thighs, she was trembling, and as he touched her clitoris with his tongue, she jerked and let out a little cry, anticipating the splendid paroxysms that were building within her. Slowly he slid his fingers into her, and as he felt the first muscular contraction, he moved so that he could reach the marvelous curve of her neck as she gave herself over to her gratification; the intensity of her orgasm shook them both, and for a long moment it was as if they had removed themselves from the world.

The slow chiming of her boudoir clock caught their attention. Doña Isabel was the first to move. "Siesta will be over in a quarter hour."

"Then I must go," said Saint-Germain, sliding to the edge of the bed, one hand still resting on the rise of her shoulder.

"I wish you didn't have to," she said, laying her hand over his as if to keep him with her a little longer.

"And I," he said, and bent to kiss her fingers before drawing his hand away; then he rose and sought out his shoes and socks, and sank into the Luxor-decorated chair to don them. "You have been most generous, Doña Isabel."

"Oh, Comte. How can you be so formal, after all this? Doña Isabel indeed! Call me Isis. Please. I really do prefer it." She was trying to banter now, but not quite succeeding. "I wish you could remain with me all afternoon."

"That would be lovely," he said, continuing to deal with his thick-soled shoes. "But the results would please neither of us."

"You mean my servants would notice?" She almost pouted at the thought.

"At the very least," he said, tying his laces.

She sighed, this time in resignation. "You're right, of course." She sat up, pulling the sheet over her as she did. "I should bathe and summon Solita to do my hair."

He rose and reached for his waistcoat of black superfine wool. "It wouldn't do for her to see me." He reached out and took her free hand, bending over it to kiss the back of her fingers. "I will look for you tonight, at midnight, at the British Consul's."

"I'll try not to count the hours," she said, watching him fasten the eighteen buttons on his waistcoat. "The next time will be the last, won't it?" She spoke before she realized she had given voice to her thoughts.

He paused in the act of pulling on his jacket. "Yes," he said, his voice low and still.

"Because any more than five times and I will be at risk to become like you," she said, hating herself for repeating his warning. "And the next time will be five."

"Yes," he said again.

"I cannot think that would be so dreadful," she said, trying to keep the plea out of her voice.

"But it would be demanding in a way you have already said you're unwilling to accept," said Saint-Germain, securing the Windsor knot on his burgundy silk tie. "It isn't something you can alter once you accept it."

"How do you *do* that?" Doña Isabel wondered.

"Do what?" Saint-Germain asked as he smoothed his hair.

"Dress without a mirror," she said. "I know you have no reflection, but even then—"

"That is the sum of it," said Saint-Germain, starting toward the door that led to the small patio off the bedroom. "I've had centuries of practice."

She gave a single, disbelieving laugh, then cocked her head. "Be sure you aren't watched."

"I will," he said.

"More centuries of practice?" she teased as he reached for the door-latch.

"Yes," he said, and slipped out the door into the windy afternoon. The patio snuggled into the shoulder of the hill; Saint-Germain was over the low fence and up the steep slope with remarkable strength and ease, his powerful, compact body moving swiftly along the rocky face, grateful now that his native earth in the soles of his shoes could keep the worst of the sun at bay. It took a little more than a minute to reach the roadway above, where his automobile was parked. Neatening his clothes, he climbed into his Minerva cabriolet and drove off down the hill he had just scaled. As he reached the bottom of the slope where three roads came together, he saw a small group of soldiers blocking the way; he frowned as a sergeant motioned him to pull over.

"Papers," said the sergeant as Saint-Germain came to a stop beside him.

"My passport," said Saint-Germain, pulling this from his inside breast-pocket. It was one of four he had, and at present he used it preferentially.

"Hungarian," said the sergeant as if finding damning evidence, and examining the leather cover before opening it. "You travel a great deal, Señor Ragoczy," he remarked as he thumbed through the stiff pages, looking at the various stamps and seals.

"Yes; I do," Saint-Germain agreed without mentioning that the sergeant had erred in calling him Señor instead of Comte.

"Do you make a long stay here in Cádiz?" The question was sharper than it needed to be, and it was accompanied by an accusing stare.

"My visa allows me a total of three years," Saint-Germain pointed out. "I have been here ten months, as you see."

"And you are staying at the Hotel della Luna Nueva," the sergeant remarked, pulling a residency slip from the back of the passport. "Very expensive, very private."

"It came well-recommended," said Saint-Germain in a tone that suggested his housing arrangements were his own business.

"Such a place, yes, I would think it would," said the sergeant, smiling mirthlessly, and, after a brief hesitation, handing the passport back to Saint-Germain. "If you move, you must notify the police."

"Yes. I am aware of that," said Saint-Germain, and moved to put the Minerva in gear.

The sergeant laid his hand on the door-handle. "Do not think you can move about unnoticed. We will be watching you, Señor. We are watching all foreigners in Spain." With that, he stepped back and motioned Saint-Germain to drive on.

Proceeding along the widening road toward the Calle del Sol, Saint-Germain had to fight down a sense of unease; the encounter with the soldiers troubled him, and he kept watch for similar groups of soldiers on the road, in case he should be singled out again. He reached the Plaza de los Pescadores without further incident, but he could not rid himself of the notion that he was being followed. Turning into the Avenida Fantasma, Saint-Germain shifted down into second gear, maneuvering along the steep, narrow street with deceptive nonchalance, for he was surreptitiously checking the windows and roofs of the buildings around him; approaching the entrance to the Hotel della Luna Nueva he finally spotted a man in uniform in the upper window of the three-story house just across from the wrought-iron gates standing open for hotel guests. He made the turn rather abruptly, the tires squealing on the cobblestones.

"Welcome back, Conde," said the doorman in Spanish as Saint-Germain pulled into the parking area. He hurried up to get the door for this illustrious gentleman.

"Thank you, Cornelio," said Saint-Germain in the same language, handing over twenty francs; he knew Cornelio Liebre preferred foreign coins to Spanish ones. "Is Rogerio in?"

"Yes, Conde. He is in your front suite." Cornelio stepped back to allow Saint-Germain to pass. "Or," he added conscientiously, "he was half-an-hour ago. He may have gone out the north door. I wouldn't have seen him."

The Hotel della Luna Nueva was a handsome building that had once been the mansion of a wealthy merchant who had profited from New World trade three hundred years before. The style was the restrained Spanish Baroque, four stories high, with three wings, one of them added in the last century when it was changed from a private residence into a hotel. Saint-Germain went up the five broad steps and entered the lobby; he nodded at the manager as he turned toward the north wing where he had engaged three four-room suites for his use and one for his manservant, Rogerio. "Good afternoon, Señor Echevarria," he said.

"And to you, Comte," said Señor Hernando Echevarria, his French meticulous, with a politeness that bordered on the obsequious. He was perfectly attired and he supervised the lobby as his glorious fiefdom; it was a gracious and elegant place: the settees and chairs were upholstered in a damask of olive-green and turquoise, the carpet was a dull gold, the walls were a lighter olive-green than the furniture, and the pillars were the same dull gold as the carpet. Five large urns sprouted extravagant palms and two large vases contained cut flowers.

"Have you any messages for me?" Saint-Germain asked, looking toward the registration desk.

"Nothing today, Comte. But the afternoon mail hasn't been delivered yet," said the manager, as if apologizing for the lateness of the postman.

"If something should come, will you have it sent up to me, if you please?" Saint-Germain requested, and without waiting for an answer passed on through the lobby to the corridor that led to his suites. He arrived at the front suite and knocked twice, waited, and knocked twice again.

Rogerio answered the second pair of knocks promptly, greeting Saint-Germain without ceremony. "I was beginning to worry."

"You may have had cause to," said Saint-Germain lightly as he closed the door; when he spoke again, it was in Byzantine Greek. "Something has happened."

Rogerio took care to close the door. "Tell me," he said in the same tongue.

Saint-Germain shrugged. "We're being watched. At least, I am." He took off his jacket and changed the subject. "Will you draw me a bath?"

"Yes." Rogerio was not yet willing to abandon the matter. "Who is watching you?"

"The army, I believe. Perhaps the police. It may be both of them." He looked directly at Rogerio. "We have suspected this for some days, old friend. All that has happened is that the suspicions are confirmed."

"That is scarcely a minor matter," said Rogerio. He studied Saint-Germain's face. "Do you think perhaps we should leave for France sooner than we planned?"

"I see no reason why, and I can think of several reasons not to," said Saint-Germain. "I don't think that leaving would improve my situation."

"That may be so, but you are unwilling to leave—what reasons do you have for remaining?" Rogerio achieved a nice balance between respect and testiness. "It isn't because this is my native city. Gades," he went on, using the old Roman name of the place, "is long gone. This is just another Spanish port now." He studied Saint-Germain's face. "You don't like being forced to leave, do you?"

"That is the heart of it," Saint-Germain admitted. "But I have a few projects that haven't yet come to fruition. If it is possible, I would prefer to remain here until they are established enough for me to leave them in the hands of—"

Rogerio shook his head. "Your managers. Yes. All very well and good," he said sharply. "But they may not achieve the goals you seek in the time you anticipate. And some of them may be influenced by the political climate."

"Of course they are," said Saint-Germain, removing his jacket and handing it to Rogerio. "I'll want my tails for tonight. White-tie."

"At the British Consul's," said Rogerio, still not willing to set aside his concerns quite yet. "Will you at least reconsider your position if the surveillance is increased? If the risks change, perhaps you should as well."

"Yes, I will," Saint-Germain said. "You have my Word." He glanced toward the bathroom. "Not too warm, but not too cold." He spoke in Spanish again.

"I have drawn baths for you one way and another for two thousand years," Rogerio reminded him, also in Spanish. He went to hang up the jacket, saying as he did, "Do you know why you're being watched?"

"I have a few ideas," said Saint-Germain dryly. "I have three businesses the government may want: the fuel-processing plant near Bilbao, the shipping business here, and the airplane-manufacturing company in Córdoba. They may also want the chemical company in Valladolid, but it is a less obvious prize, and, at the moment, not especially profitable." He put two fingers to his brow. "They are becoming greedy, these new-style politicians, and they have enlisted the generals in their greed."

"Is that limited to Spain?" Rogerio asked as he went to turn the spigots for the deep, rose-marble bathtub. As the water began to rise, he went and adjusted the venetian blinds so that the bathroom was in shadow.

"Among other places. Look at Germany." Saint-Germain glanced toward the window. "And Russia is in a terrible state."

"A bad situation," said Rogerio, adjusting the temperature of the water.

"And getting worse hourly," said Saint-Germain, shaking his head slowly. "The Great War settled nothing."

Rogerio tested the water one more time. "What will you do if we must go?"

"I suppose we'll go to Montalia, as I promised Madelaine I would do." Some of the severity of his expression softened as he spoke her name.

"Is she still in Peru?" Rogerio asked.

"As far as I am aware. She has discovered an Incan tomb and plans to excavate it." He removed his tie and draped it over the back of a chair.

"For whom?" Rogerio came and gathered up Saint-Germain's shirt as he removed it. "Is it a private or a formal dig?"

"The university in Lima is her sponsor, if I remember correctly." He had a swift recollection of Lima as he had seen it in 1641 on his way to Cuzco; he knew it had changed a great deal since then but he could not change his memory of it. "They have an arrangement with one of the museums in France—I think it is in Provence, or perhaps the one at Lyons; she has done a great deal of work for them recently." He looked toward the tub. "I'm going to rest when I'm through with my bath."

"For how long?" Rogerio inquired. He took Saint-Germain's singlet, hardly noticing the broad swath of scar tissue that reached from his employer's sternum to his belt; it no longer shocked him to see it.

"Probably an hour or two. If you have any errands to run, perhaps they will wait until I rise?" He unfastened his belt and opened his fly to step out of his slacks.

"Certainly," said Rogerio. He took the black wool slacks and folded them over his arm. "Need I do anything to these?"

"You may sponge them when you press them, if you would; they don't need anything more than that," said Saint-Germain as he walked into the bathroom and stepped into the tub, getting onto his knees as he reached for the washcloth and began to rub a bar of Pears soap on it, watching the lather build up before he began to wash; he was quick and efficient, and soon had rinsed the soap off his skin, added a little more hot water to the tub, and prepared to relax. He had just settled back in the water, his head resting on the edge of the tub, supported by a folded hand-towel, when the telephone in the sitting room shrilled.

Rogerio answered it, and after a few quick questions in oddly antiquated Spanish, he called to Saint-Germain, "A Colonel Senda is in the lobby and would like to talk to you."

"Colonel Senda?" Saint-Germain repeated, trying to place the man; he made no move to get out of the tub. "I don't believe I know a Colonel Senda."

"My master says he doesn't recognize your name," Rogerio said to the telephone, and waited. "He tells me you haven't met."

"Then I will gladly arrange an appointment for him," said Saint-Germain.

Rogerio put his hand over the mouthpiece. "Do you want to provoke him?" he asked in an under-voice.

"No, I don't," said Saint-Germain. "But I don't want to be too accommodating, either. That would be as suspicious as too much resistance." He opened his eyes enough to shoot a knowing glance at Rogerio.

"Very well," said Rogerio, and addressed the telephone again. "I am sorry, Colonel, but my master is preparing to go out for the evening; he has a pre-existing engagement. There is a reception at—Yes, the British Consul's residence. Perhaps you can call again in the morning—say at half-ten?" Whatever the Colonel's answer was, Rogerio stood more stiffly, his face set in hard lines. "I will convey your remarks to my master, and I will tell him to expect you at ten in the morning." He waited a moment. "And thank you for calling," he said in a tone that was barely polite before he hung up.

"What does Colonel Senda want?" Saint-Germain asked, lifting his head to watch how Rogerio responded.

Very meticulously Rogerio said, "The good Colonel has asked me to inform you that he has some urgent questions to ask you concerning your contracts with certain Italian and French industrialists. Apparently he seems to think you are using them as a cover for political activities Generals Mola and Franco and their supporters do not support." His disapproval was so pronounced that he could hardly speak.

"They're in Spanish Morocco," Saint-Germain said, wanting to dismiss them.

"Their influence is everywhere, even in Madrid," said Rogerio. "And Cádiz is a garrison city. The army matters here." He began to pace. "If they can make an example of you, they can put the entire international community on notice."

"Yes; so I think." Saint-Germain closed his eyes again, settling back for the luxury of a long soak.

"What are you going to do?" Rogerio asked, recognizing this attitude of withdrawal; he had seen it many times in the past and knew there was little he could do to change Saint-Germain's mind once he entered this state.

"I'm going to consider the implications of what Colonel Senda tells me—tomorrow at quarter past ten." He sank a little deeper into the warm water. "Until then, I will do my utmost to keep from jumping to unfounded conclusions."

"What about well-founded ones?" Rogerio asked, an edge in his voice.

"When I know which is which, I will decide what is to be done," said Saint-Germain in a tone that seemed almost bored.

Knowing there was nothing more he could do, Rogerio left Saint-Germain to his bath and went to set out his evening clothes.

TEXT OF A LETTER FROM ARMANDO PRADERA IN CÓRDOBA TO CRISTOBAL
LAS TRUCHES IN MADRID.

> *17, Avenida de los Feos*
> *Córdoba, España*
> *9 January, 1936*

Cristobal Las Truches
Departamento de los Extranjeros
Madrid, España

Señor Las Truches,
   In response to your letter of December 14, I am delighted to answer your
inquiries in regard to Ferenc Ragoczy, le Comte de Saint-Germain, who is the
principal investor in this company, and for whom I serve as accountant in
regard to Eclipse Aeroplano Industrias. I write to you from my residence, for
it would be awkward to explain our correspondence to those who work with
me. I ask that you will be similarly discreet.
   As you are already aware, the Comte has been the head of this company in
all but name for the last five years. When he bought La Mancha Aeroplano
Industrias, the business was failing. He renamed and reorganized the business
from the sort of airplanes we manufacture to the way in which we sell them. He
has also enabled us to appeal to markets in France, the Netherlands, Belgium,
and Scandinavia. Under his guidance, the company has not only recovered, it
has prospered and expanded. This has meant that we have been able to double
our production in the last two years and to sell every airplane we produce.
   Our most successful airplane is the Scythian Type 44, which has been
used to deliver mail and other lightweight shipping purposes. It has two
engines, can seat up to four, and has a range of 590 kilometers under normal
flying conditions. Last year this plant produced fifty-eight of these airplanes,
as well as sixteen of our Spartan Type 29, which is designed for the private
sportsman. It also has two engines, can seat up to six, and has a range of
720 kilometers. Our Moghul Type 17 is currently undergoing redesign, the
Type 18 will be available early next year. It has four engines, can seat ten,
and has a range of 680 kilometers, making all three airplanes among the
best in their respective classes. The Comte has said he would like to add
another two models to our production in the next three years, and he has
been searching out engineers to help us improve our designs. It is his goal to
produce an airplane that has a range of 800 kilometers, can carry a dozen,
and can be used for service to smaller cities where airfields are more primi-

tive than most modern airplanes require. He offers good pay and fine working conditions, which has made it possible for him to select the most skilled technicians and designers currently working in Europe.

You ask if any of his airplanes have military potential—I am not a designer and so I have no opinion beyond telling you that he has never attempted to see his airplanes go to any military force anywhere in the world. He has made it his policy to avoid entanglements with the military, for he cannot engage in strategic enterprises so long as he is in control of the company: as a foreigner, he has said his situation is such that he should not put himself in the position of having to support one regime more than another. Some of our staff have tried to persuade him to make an exception for the Spanish government, but so far he has not relented. He is determined—he has said—to keep developing airplanes for peaceful uses, and thus far, his desires have prevailed. Of course, if the government should require him to provide military aircraft, I am certain he would not refuse to manufacture them. He must have acquaintances among Spanish industrialists who would be willing to take over the running of this company, to accommodate the laws of Spain. It would be worse than folly for him to remain obdurate in the face of a governmental mandate. I say this because if what you seek is his cooperation in such an endeavor, you would do well to present him with irrefutable demands, not polite requests.

As you must be aware, the Comte employs men from five nations, including Italy, France, Belgium, Denmark, and Poland, but he has shown no preferential inclination to any of them; the men were hired for their expertise. He has also employed a Czech woman, a mathematician, who has been developing calculations for improving fuel consumption for his engines. It is a bit irregular to employ women, but she is a spinster without family or expectations beyond her ability to find gainful employment, and so it may be a kindness on the Comte's part to offer her a position of a sort. She has done diligent work, but I doubt she could find so accommodating an employer elsewhere. Druze Sviny is very loyal to the Comte, and rightly so. She will undoubtedly side with him in any decisions that bear on this company. It is possible that the others may, as well, but they may also support the government, should there be a contest of wills. If you assure his staff of continued employment, only la Sviny is likely to refuse to go along with any changes in production that may be undertaken.

I am enclosing a full and accurate copy of our production records for the past eighteen months, and our projected production for the next eighteen months, along with copies of our ledgers for you to review for costs and supplies. If you have any questions in regard to the material, I hope you will ask in such a way that you do not compromise my position with this company. If I am dismissed for revealing this information to you, I will not be able to assist you again, if you should require more material from this company.

In this and in all things, I have the honor to be
Eternally at your service,

Armando Pradera

AP

chapter two

February had turned bitter in Spain, the cold wind slicing down from the central plateau, sending ribbons of sleet to ruin the roads and break the fragile electrical lines that had finally begun to crisscross the country. Córdoba was miserable, bleak, and sere; as Saint-Germain got out of the Minerva in front of his factory, he had to steady himself to keep from falling on the slick pavement.

"Dreadful," said Rogerio, emerging from the other side of the auto with exaggerated care, hunching his shoulders against the cold. "Almost as bad as when the Visigoths were here." He hoped Saint-Germain might find this amusing; his faded-blue eyes crinkled at the corners in what passed for a smile in his austere demeanor.

"Hardly," said Saint-Germain. "The streets are properly paved, for one thing. And the houses are better heated."

"I'll give you those points." Rogerio made a gesture of acknowledgment, adding, "The last half-hour, I thought we'd take a fatal skid for certain."

Saint-Germain shook his head. "The auto is well-designed. We weren't in any real danger, except perhaps from other vehicles." He patted the roof of the Minerva in much the same way he might have done to a strong horse. "We had nothing to fear: not on the roads, in any case; there may have been other dangers, of course," he said wryly, pulling the brim of his hat down to protect his eyes from the icy rain.

Rogerio assumed this was an oblique reference to the unpleasant second interview Saint-Germain had had with Colonel Senda four days ago, when the officer had again called at the Hotel della Luna Nueva without warning for another so-called discussion of Saint-Germain's equivocal circumstances; Rogerio had heard the Colonel's harangue two rooms away from him, and had noticed that Saint-Germain was not eager to discuss what had transpired. He came around the front of the auto and started toward the main entrance of the Eclipse Aeroplano Industrias office building, a large structure only four years old, a masterpiece of contemporary style in glass and brushed aluminum. Two long car parks flanked the building, and a broad road led to the more utilitarian assembly plants behind the office edifice. "I'll come back and move into one of the parks when you've gone inside. Would you prefer the east or west side?"

"No need," said Saint-Germain. "Our followers know where we are. We might as well accommodate them. Leave the Minerva where it is."

"If you like," said Rogerio, stepping up to the thick glass doors with a four-foot-high rendition of Saint-Germain's eclipse acid-etched to center on the opening. He grabbed the brushed aluminum handle, glad of his gloves in this biting cold, and pulled the door open as he stood aside, allowing his employer to enter the building ahead of him.

The two-story lobby was not large but its glass walls, even on this grey and gloomy day, provided so much luminescence that it appeared vast. The light, faintly green from the thick glass, gave an impression of being underwater, an impression that was enhanced by the celadon walls. A reception desk of polished teak in a modernistic wedge-shape dominated the main floor of the lobby, and acted as a divider for the double staircases that curved up the inner walls to the gallery on the second floor; behind the stairs was an alcove where the building's telephone switchboard was located, five women handling all the connections. Two well-dressed young women manned the reception desk, each wearing a welcoming smile that did not extend as far as their eyes.

"Buenos días, Señor Conde," said the taller of the two, not quite simpering. "I'll tell Señor Lundhavn you're here."

"Gracias, Estrellita," said Saint-Germain as if perfectly satisfied with this suggestion; he removed his hat and held it by the crown-crease as he looked about the lobby, barely pausing as he caught sight of two soldiers standing on the far side of the eastern staircase. "Tell him I'm on my way," he said, and started up the western staircase, Rogerio right behind him.

The second floor, with its three corridors leading away from the lobby gallery, was primarily devoted to office space, and Elias Lundhavn occupied one of the two largest at the end of the main corridor. He came to the door just as Saint-Germain knocked on it, saying, "So good to see you, Comte" in Danish, and repeated himself in French. He was middle-aged, stocky, brown-haired, and blue-eyed, with a square face that just now seemed wooden, although he did his best to force a welcoming smile. "If I'd known you were coming, I would have arranged a full turnout for you. The staff are always eager to be included in your meetings."

"Not this one, I think," Saint-Germain said lightly.

Lundhavn blinked. "Should I send for my secretary to take notes?" He tried to cover his sudden edginess by lighting a cigarette.

"No need for that," said Saint-Germain. "This isn't a progress call. I have a few matters I have to discuss with you, and I would prefer to do it without fanfare. I suppose you would prefer that, as well." He crossed the office to the larger of two visitor's chairs and sat down; Rogerio remained in the hallway. "Do sit down, Elias. This may take some time."

Lundhavn coughed nervously and removed a silver cigarette case from the inner pocket of his suit jacket; he offered this to Saint-Germain, and when it was waved away, took out one for himself. "Is something the matter, Comte? You seem somewhat troubled. Is there anything amiss?" He bustled back behind his desk as if to barricade himself against the well-mannered black-clad Saint-Germain.

"That is what I hope you will tell me," said Saint-Germain, and paused; when Lundhavn said nothing, he went on. "I have been receiving some rather alarming memos from—well, it doesn't matter whom—that have troubled me, and I have decided that it is time I addressed the issues with you." He sat wholly at his ease, his hat dangling from his fingers. "And now I find soldiers in the lobby of this building. Why is that?"

"They arrived," said Lundhavn. "They have orders to keep guard over this plant, because airplanes are strategically important—that's what their orders stipulate."

"I have no wish to be caught up in a civil war," Saint-Germain warned.

"No; who'd want that? It wouldn't be good for business to have to take sides," said Lundhavn, and laughed nervously. "We're not part of the conflict, thank goodness." He lit his cigarette and blew out a long cloud of smoke, but kept his lighter in his hand, as if anticipating the need to light another.

Saint-Germain nodded, frowning slightly. "And yet it seems that we have been dragged into the matter. Why is that, do you think?"

"I don't know what you mean," Lundhavn protested, clearing his throat.

"But you have made comments on the issues at stake here, or so the memos tell me." Saint-Germain watched Lundhavn as he fumbled with his lighter.

"What issues would they be?" Lundhavn asked, his manner defensive and his chin coming up sharply. He stubbed out his cigarette.

"It would appear that someone from this company has been negotiating with the military to adapt our Scythians for combat." He raised one brow. "I have proof that the information provided to the army came from this office, Elias."

"How could that be?" Lundhavn said as he stared at the pen-stand on his desk; he avoided looking at Saint-Germain directly, but watched him from the tail of his eye.

"That is what I am here to find out," said Saint-Germain.

Lundhavn rubbed his chin. "Are you sure your informant knows as much as he claims? It would be to the advantage of some of the smaller companies—Aero Madrid, for instance—to see us have to sell out this company. That could be what's going on. And your informant may be trying to make it appear he has more reliable information than is actually the case."

"He is very familiar with the workings of Eclipse, and must have enlisted more than one man on the staff to supply him crucial information." He said it bluntly, watching Lundhavn, his dark eyes narrowed.

Lundhavn did his best to chuckle. "That's absurd," he said.

"Alas, it is not," said Saint-Germain, his posture unchanged. "I have received several visits from a Colonel Senda who seems to be of the opinion that the arrangements have all been made. He chastised me for not signing the contracts that have been prepared. I don't think he believed that I knew nothing about them." He leaned forward and put his hat on the edge of Lundhavn's broad rosewood desk. "The Colonel informed me that you had agreed on the terms of the contract, and that some of my staff had helped you. Why would he say that if it were wholly lies?"

"Don't be ridiculous," said Lundhavn, his face darkening to a blotchy shade of plum. "It must be—"

"I knew that our financial information had been obtained by authorities in Madrid. I might have thought one of the men working on aircraft assembly had passed on what he saw in constructing the airplanes, but my informant had access to new design modifications that haven't yet been incorporated into the current airplanes being prepared for delivery," Saint-Germain said thoughtfully. "But the contract was the stumbling block for me. It implied the collaboration of the managerial staff."

"Why should anyone—?" He waved at the air as if to banish a nightmare.

Saint-Germain sat back and studied the Dane. "I know this kind of industry is under pressure to cooperate with the generals, but surely you haven't forgotten that foreigners are specifically forbidden to participate in strategic industries? That stricture isn't limited to ownership of such companies; it encompasses the design staff as well." His half-smile was gentle. "Do you know what would happen if the changes you so willingly endorsed were put into effect? To begin with, the government would seize Eclipse, and then all non-Spaniards would be dismissed." He let Lundhavn have a long moment to consider this.

"There have been exceptions to that rule," Lundhavn said at last, his neck so stiff that he seemed propped in his chair like a puppet.

"A few, a very few," Saint-Germain pointed out. "And you, Elias, would not be one of them. Colonel Senda has a nephew who is earmarked to assume your position as soon as the contract is signed." He saw the shocked expression that Lundhavn could not completely mask. "Ah. You had been given assurances, hadn't you?"

"Of course not," Lundhavn blustered.

"Elias, please," Saint-Germain said patiently. "I am not so shocked as you might suppose; I will admit to being disappointed, but what man in my position would not be?" He did not add that he had seen this sort of maneuvering many times in the past. "The country is preparing for war; it would be remarkable if there wasn't some attempt to control and exploit this technology, and because of my ambiguous status, Eclipse is especially vulnerable to manipulation."

Lundhavn stared toward the window. "How am I to respond?"

"Truthfully, I hope," said Saint-Germain. "If you are unwilling to tell me what has been going on here, then I cannot allow you to remain in your present position, and that," he went on less emphatically, "would be unfortunate, for you have done your work well, and I am loath to lose you unless I must."

"You will have your joke, sir," said Lundhavn. "If you are so convinced that I have worked against your policies, why should you keep me on?"

"You are a fine engineer," said Saint-Germain. "You do superior airplane designs, and this is what I hope you will continue to do here at Eclipse."

"And that is enough to mitigate any questions you have about my loyalty?" Lundhavn let out a single bark of laughter. "Of course you will dismiss me."

"I may remove you from your present position," said Saint-Germain resignedly. "But I would prefer to continue to employ you if you are willing to be forthcoming with me now."

"Why would you do that?" Lundhavn demanded, anger suddenly awakening within him. "Do you think you can force me to capitulate?"

"No, I don't. I'm not interested in your capitulation: this isn't a contest of wills." Saint-Germain made an exasperated gesture.

"Why should you accommodate me? Since you think I have betrayed you to the generals." His anger was beginning to fade and turn to petulance. "Why haven't you dismissed me?" Lundhavn asked.

"Because, as I have already told you, you are very capable, and I would just as soon keep your abilities here at Eclipse than send you out to peddle what you know to the generals. I am the more reliable employer, Elias, little as you may think it." He saw Lundhavn's cynical expression, and said, "If you are willing to accept my terms, it would please me very much."

Lundhavn glowered at a place outside the window only he could see. "What terms?" His voice was flat.

"I will appoint another member of the staff to run the company; you needn't concern yourself about whom I will select; I am not going to take your recommendation for your successor. Rest assured I have considered this carefully and it will take place immediately. You will stay on in the engineering design department, in charge of your three projects, but under supervision; I will only reduce your salary by ten percent. But there will be certain restrictions on you: you will not be permitted to take any plans or papers home, so if you wish to work past the usual hours, you will have to do it here. I am aware that the schematics are all in your head and I cannot compel you to forget the work you do when you leave, but I ask you to honor the terms of this agreement and devote yourself only to Eclipse." He gave Lundhavn an opportunity to speak, and accepted his silence as an inclination to consider his offer. "You will keep the auto Eclipse provides. You need not give up this office, or your secretary. But you will relinquish all your developmental records not presently in development to me. My attorneys will draw up a revised contract for your signature and you will sign it without revision."

"You could put anything in such a contract, and claim that my refusal to sign would excuse your dismissing me." He propped his elbows on the desk and steepled his hands above them. "It would let you be rid of me without allowing me any recourse."

Saint-Germain nodded once. "I have already explained why I would prefer not."

"You want me to be grateful to you," Lundhavn said with conviction.

"Gratitude can be very unreliable," said Saint-Germain apologetically. "Say rather that I am hoping you might wish to keep most of what you have enjoyed rather than try to depend on the . . . loyalty of the generals."

Lundhavn tapped his fingers together. "You mean to tell me that because I haven't been as steadfast as you would have liked, I might be paid by the same coin?"

"It is a possibility," said Saint-Germain. "And given your talents, you might not find it easy to leave Spain for another country, as you might intend to do." It was only a guess, but the flicker of Lundhavn's eyes told him he had been right. "So. You are planning to go elsewhere."

"I have received a flattering offer," said Lundhavn, a bit too nonchalantly. "The terms are quite favorable."

"If you cannot leave Spain to accept it, the flattery means little, and you may discover that the generals will not be willing to let you go as long as they have work of their own for you," said Saint-Germain with a wry turn of his mouth.

"I am a Dane. They can't keep me here," Lundhavn insisted.

"You may find that they can, unless you are planning to fly out in one of our test airplanes, leaving your wife and children behind. And do not assume that they would hold your family blameless." He studied Lundhavn's face. "You think you can elude the government? Just where were you planning to go?"

"I have received an offer from . . . a company in Dresden." He set his jaw. "I have already agreed to start work there in May."

"Then I see my visit is useless." Saint-Germain rose, picking up his hat. "Very well: since you will not relent—you will not be allowed to take any blueprints or files out of the building, Elias. And since you are so determined to put yourself at a disadvantage, you may do so at once. I will have a check carried to your home by messenger before the end of the day. You may consider yourself dismissed. I will draft a letter to that effect before I leave this afternoon." He turned toward the door. "You may have your secretary assist you in gathering your things; I will expect an inventory of what you have removed from this office, signed by you and your secretary, to be left on your desk when you leave."

"And now you'll tell your Colonel Senda about my plans," Lundhavn goaded him.

"No. I doubt that will be necessary. There are others in the company who report to him regularly." Saint-Germain pulled the door open. "I will go to the accounting office now. When I return I will expect you to be gone."

"If you are determined, I will go," said Lundhavn in a tone of ill-usage. "I trust I may be permitted to telephone my wife to tell her I am going to be home early?"

"Why should I object to that?" said Saint-Germain as he closed the door.

Rogerio had been standing near the end of the conference room door, and he turned around to face his employer. "It went badly."

"Yes; is it that obvious?" Saint-Germain inquired politely. "He has an offer from a company in Dresden and I believe he supposes helping the generals will smooth his departure."

"More fool he," said Rogerio, falling in beside his master. "Where are we bound?"

"To accounting, first. I need to authorize a final payment for Lundhavn, and then I need to have a word or two with Armando Pradera. Then I want to talk to Druze Sviny." He started down the stairs to the lobby, apparently unaware of the attention he was attracting among his staff, or the sharp surveillance of the two soldiers. "I dislike having my hand forced."

"And that is what's happening," said Rogerio.

Saint-Germain said nothing as he descended to the main floor. "Is the house ready for us, or do we need to find a hotel for the night?"

"Lazaro has said the house is ready," said Rogerio, accepting this change of subject as a matter of course. "If the electricity is working, then we'll have a pleasant evening."

"That may be uncertain," said Saint-Germain as he went toward the north hall; he saw a man pull back from his doorway.

Rogerio sensed the tension and curiosity in the building. "Have you decided how long you want to stay in Córdoba?"

"Three days at least. It will depend upon what I find out during my inspection here tomorrow." He stopped in front of the frosted glass door of the accounting department. "This shouldn't take long." He tapped on the glass lightly before stepping inside, once again leaving Rogerio in the corridor.

"Conde," said the young man behind the counter, trying to seem at ease. "We were told you were in the building."

"No doubt," said Saint-Germain. "Is Señor Liston in?" He lifted the counter-bridge and came up to the young man's desk. "Or Señor Pradera?"

"Señor Liston will be back in a few minutes," said the young man uneasily. "He is with Señor Pradera and someone else in the small conference room."

Saint-Germain wondered with whom Liston had gone to confer, but said nothing of this, remarking only, "I will wait in his office. Will you be good enough to ask Señor Pradera to come in when he returns. Señor Liston will not be required to join us."

"Certainly," said the young man, a bit too quickly. "Anything you like."

"Thank you, Raimundo," said Saint-Germain, noticing that the young man was surprised that his employer remembered his name. He went into the nearer office and sat down in the visitor's chair, once again putting his hat on the corner of the desk; he guessed he would not have to remain alone long.

It was less than five minutes later that the door opened and Armando Pradera came into the office; he was in a fashionable suit of navy-blue wool with a navy-and-dull-gold tie over his crisp white shirt. With care he adjusted his tie-clasp in order to do something that looked suave. Satisfied with the result, he ducked his head and stood nearly at attention. "Good afternoon, Señor Conde," he said, his voice tight.

"Good afternoon, Señor Pradera," Saint-Germain responded. "Thank you for coming so promptly." He indicated the straight-backed chair by the wall.

Pradera drew the chair away from the wall and sat down, very like a truant schoolboy. "What do you want?" He knew that came out badly. "I'm at your service, of course." That was a bit better, he decided.

"I need a final check for Señor Lundhavn—all that is due him, plus three months' pay. It is to be carried to his house." He studied Pradera's features. "And then we will negotiate how much you are to receive in your final payment."

"What?" Pradera looked up sharply. "What sort of jest is this?"

"No jest at all, I fear," said Saint-Germain.

"But . . . Why should you terminate my employment because of Señor Lundhavn? If he has disappointed you, why should you demand satisfaction of me? I am not privy to his work, or anything else." Pradera set his jaw and tried to summon up his indignation. "How do you . . ." His voice dropped away as he saw Saint-Germain pull a carbon copy of a letter from his waistcoat pocket: it was the letter he had sent to the Departamento de los Extranjeros a month ago. "Madre de Dios," he whispered.

"Well might you pray," said Saint-Germain, his expression unchanged. "This is most distressing, Armando. I am not dismissing you for what Señor Lundhavn has done—I am dismissing you for what you have done. Do you have some reason for your disloyalty? I hope it wasn't simple caprice." He folded the letter and slipped it back into his waistcoat pocket.

"Saints save me," said Pradera as his predicament sank in.

Saint-Germain studied him. "Can you tell me what you wanted to accomplish with this?"

Pradera had large, big-knuckled hands, and he knotted the two of them together. "I don't know if I can explain it to you."

"Armando: try," said Saint-Germain.

"Oh, God. This can't be happening." He looked about as if his sentiments were innovative and not the same protestation Saint-Germain had heard countless times over the centuries. "I was assured that no one would learn about what I've done." He bit his lower lip.

"You were misled," said Saint-Germain, his voice gentle but his dark eyes keen.

Pradera nodded. "Yes. Yes. You're right. I was." He steeled himself to meet Saint-Germain's dark eyes. "But how did it come about that you received a copy of the letter? I didn't make one, not that I recall, and I never had it in the office." He fretted, working his hands more tightly. "How did you manage to get your hands on it?"

"There are those whose task it is to monitor those in responsible positions, in industry and in government; you should not be surprised that you come under scrutiny as well as I." Saint-Germain stared toward the high windows that provided light with privacy for the office. "I don't employ spies, if you think I do."

"But it seems you have them nonetheless," said Pradera humorlessly. "You aren't going to tell me, are you?"

"No; I'm not," Saint-Germain told him. "Suffice it to say that it has become known that a few of my employees have made a point to try to gain the favor of certain political factions and will now have to reap the rewards of their efforts."

"This is dreadful," said Pradera.

"I would agree," said Saint-Germain, and went on at his most urbane. "I am saddened to have to lose you, Pradera, but a man in your position must maintain the confidence his position demands, or he cannot be worthwhile. You have divulged too much that isn't yours to impart to others. " He rose slowly. "You have compromised my company, Armando. You have put me in a position where I must divest myself of this company or have to enter into a pact with the government that will only be to my disadvantage."

"You overestimate the importance of this company, Conde; it cannot be so significant as you seem to think it is. I have been told that interest in it is only cursory," said Pradera with a forced smile. "The airplanes we make are not what the government is seeking. I sent the information to the Departamento de los Extranjeros so that they would know your company isn't anything they'd want."

"Of course," said Saint-Germain, coming to stand directly in front of Pradera's desk. "So you must be shocked to know that I am now being forced to deal with the military."

"I didn't intend that anything of that sort could happen. I was assured . . ." Pradera sighed. "No. No; I was hoping they would be grateful for my help and do something to show their appreciation." He looked up at Saint-Germain and did his best to plead his case. "You're in exile. You should be eager to cooperate with the government. Consider what you can offer. You could do yourself a great deal of good."

"Do you think so?" Saint-Germain regarded him, his expression revealing nothing of his ruminations. "I trust you don't believe that." He picked up his hat and smoothed the brim. "If you want to resign, you may have six months' pay when you leave. If you insist that I fire you, you can have half that amount." He waited a moment. "In any case, you will be gone by the end of our business day."

Pradera dropped his head. "Very well. I will resign."

"And you will leave this office forever by the end of business today," he repeated. "You may take your own property with you, of course, but nothing from this company beyond your final check. Prepare your check and Lundhavn's; I will sign them, and I will stipulate they are final payments." He took a step back from Pradera's desk. "I'm sorry it came to this, Armando."

"So am I," said Pradera, then added in a note of forlorn hope, "I can't say anything to persuade you to reconsider."

"No, you can't," said Saint-Germain.

"But you must know that the government will know about this. The soldiers will make their reports." He rubbed his hands together. "There must be a way to—"

"I've had too much experience with the wishes of governments to become party to their plans," Saint-Germain interrupted him, and did not add that his cognizance of governments stretched back four millennia.

Pradera was not familiar with the implacable note in Saint-Germain's voice, but he realized what it meant. "Exiles are at a disadvantage, I suppose."

"In many ways," said Saint-Germain, and started toward the door.

"You won't provide a recommendation, I suppose," said Pradera.

"Would you, were you in my position?" Saint-Germain countered, and left the office.

Raimundo stared at Saint-Germain, his big eyes wary. "Is there anything wrong, Señor Conde?"

"Not now," said Saint-Germain. "Señor Pradera is leaving. At once. And there is a check to be messengered to Señor Lundhavn's home at the end of the day. Use a company courier to carry it." He could see that Raimundo was shocked, so he added, "I rely upon you to make sure the check is delivered."

"Yes, Señor Conde," said Raimundo, staring at the large blotter pad on his desk.

"And do not worry, Raimundo. None of Señor Pradera's mistakes redound to you, or to Señor Liston." Saint-Germain reached out and lifted the counter-gate and let himself out of the accounting office.

"I've spoken to Señor Liston, and apprised him of Señor Pradera's departure, and Señor Lundhavn's," Rogerio said as Saint-Germain came up to him. "I suggested he might want to give you some privacy while you dealt with Señor Pradera. Do you still want to see Señor Liston?"

"Yes, but not today, I think. Tomorrow will be time enough. I'll return after siesta tomorrow. Raimundo Orgullo will tend to taking care of the final checks; Señor Liston won't have to be part of any of it." Saint-Germain glanced toward the accounting-office door. "I suppose there is no way to keep the staff from speculating on this."

Rogerio shrugged. "You know the answer better than I," he responded.

For a long moment Saint-Germain said nothing. "I think it would be prudent for us to remain here for at least a week. There is more to be done here. I cannot rid myself of the notion that Lundhavn and Pradera are only the tip of the iceberg." He glanced down the corridor. "Where are the soldiers?"

"In the lunchroom," said Rogerio. "With Lundhavn's secretary."

"Should I be troubled by that, do you think?" Saint-Germain inquired with a wry twist of his mouth.

"I doubt it," said Rogerio. "I gather they flirt often."

Saint-Germain began to walk toward the lobby. "I'm almost through here for now. There are two checks I still have to sign, and I need to make sure that Lundhavn has left. His office will have to be inspected tonight."

"And Pradera?" Rogerio asked.

"He will be gone by the end of this day," said Saint-Germain. He stepped into the lobby and noticed that the receptionists were watching him covertly, whispering together. "I don't think it would be wise to linger."

"I'll bring the auto to the front door," Rogerio offered.

"I will be with you shortly." He started to climb the stairs, wishing as he went that he did not feel as if everyone in the building were watching his progress.

TEXT OF A LETTER FROM HORATIO BATTERBURY IN WINNIPEG TO LEANDRO DE GUZMAN IN MADRID; WRITTEN IN ENGLISH.

> Compton House
> 658 Selkirk Road
> Suites 4–9
> Winnipeg, Manitoba, Canada
> 22 February, 1936

Leandro de Guzman
Ministerio de Guerra
Madrid, Spain

My dear Mr. de Guzman,

I am in receipt of your letter of 10 February, and I thank you for your kind inquiry into Manitoba Chemicals, Ltd. Yes, this business does have international clients, and you are correct in your assumption that Ferenc Ragoczy, le Comte de Saint-Germain, sits on our Board of Directors, albeit in a purely honorary capacity, for he has never, in fact, done more than supply the company with formulae, which, given the efficacy of his work, is more than enough. In fact, as far as I am aware, he has not visited Canada. I have only met le Comte once, and that was in Brussels, four years ago, when I went there to finalize our dealings.

I must congratulate you on your thoroughness, but I am baffled as to why you should be interested in this company. Surely there are chemical companies in Spain that are producing all that you require. Manitoba Chemicals, Ltd. does have certain proprietary compounds that may have application to your work, and if this is the reason you have contacted us, I will, upon your request that I do so, pass on your solicitations to our legal department to arrange for any applicable licenses sought.

However, your questions suggest that you are attempting to catalogue le Comte's foreign holdings; while it may be appropriate for you to do so in your capacity as a member of the Ministry of War, I cannot offer more to you than that which is public record. For that reason, I will stipulate that we at Manitoba Chemicals, Ltd. have no direct contractual obligations with any company in Spain, for such information is undoubtedly within your purview, but I will offer you nothing more about other arrangements we have with other countries.

I regret any inconvenience this may cause you.

Cordially,

Horatio Batterbury

Chairman, Manitoba Chemicals, Ltd.

HB/lm

chapter three

Mercurio Zapatilla spread the contents of the brown accordion file out on his desk, thumbing his way through the array of onion-skin carbon copies, good quality bond letters, clipped newspaper articles, and a dozen photographs. Carefully he read through two of the letters, shaking his head as he perused them, disliking what he saw. He pursed his lips, making his small mouth look even smaller. Finally he picked up the telephone and spoke a few words to the man who answered. "And bring me the file on Doña Isabel Vedancho y Nuñez," he added, an afterthought.

"In addition to the file on Eclipse Aeroplano Industrias?" Zapatilla's assistant asked.

"Yes. I need to have all our information on this man and his associates; this file on el Conde de Saint-Germain is sadly lacking," said Zapatilla, a slight impatience in his voice as he gathered these all together and put them back in the large accordion envelope that had contained them. "What I have here isn't nearly enough.

It doesn't matter if the records are not in Spanish." This was a subtle little boast; Mercurio Zapatilla had risen to his present post in large part due to his linguistic abilities—he spoke nine foreign languages: French, German, Italian, English, Dutch, Swedish, Czech, Russian, and Greek, and had a nodding familiarity with an additional five—which he liked to remind his underlings of from time to time was the reason for his promotion to his present position.

"Of course," said his assistant, and rang off.

Zapatilla sat staring into the dull morning light that filtered into his office through the gaps in the draperies; he was growing perplexed with the very visible but strangely elusive Conde de Saint-Germain. Fussily he smoothed the waves of his thinning, greying hair, and then touched the ends of his meticulous, narrow mustache, as if seeking to make himself more presentable for any visitor he might have; he had a slight resemblance to Claude Rains, which he carefully cultivated, combing his hair as the actor did, and affecting the elegant manner that was Rains' hallmark. A small clock on his desk delicately chimed eleven, and, as if reminded of a forgotten engagement, Zapatilla rose from his leather-upholstered chair and paced the length of his tall, oaken bookcases, pausing by the window to lift the edge of the deep teal velveteen draperies the better to look at the bustle on the floor beneath him in the busy street. He felt himself remote from the activity below, which both saddened him and made him proud of his position. Eventually he would be posted to Madrid, but for now he had to be content with Sevilla. A discreet tap on his door halted him in his tracks. "Come in," he rapped out.

His assistant was a slender man of about thirty wearing thick glasses that magnified his black-brown eyes to the point that they resembled those of frogs. Aside from this, Esteban Pasotorpe was a good-enough-looking fellow—fashionably lean, clean-shaven, and as well-dressed as his salary would allow. "I have the files you asked for, Jefe." He used the title with an air of jest that was just enough to keep it from being insulting. "Eclipse Aeroplano Industrias and Doña Isabel Vedancho y Nuñez." He held the two thick envelopes for Zapatilla to see.

"Put them on my desk, Esteban, and send down for two cups of coffee," said Zapatilla. "Bring them in when Liebre gets here—not just at once; wait five or ten minutes."

"Of course, sir," he responded, and did as he was told, withdrawing from the room quickly.

Zapatilla went back to his desk and sat down, unfastening the string closure on the uppermost file. He took out the various papers and photographs, spreading them out, the better to contemplate them. His concentration made him tense as he scanned the material from the file. Eclipse Aeroplano Industrias was a thriving firm, that much was certain: well-financed and successful, meeting its contractual obligations in a timely manner. The Scythian airplanes were the best-selling of their models, and had been sold all over Europe. He studied the information on the assembly plant and the level of production it maintained. "Most commendable," he muttered as he reviewed the records. No wonder the generals were interested in the business. He looked at the most recent additions to the file—copies of the resignation letters of Elias Lundhavn and Armando Pradera, both signed on the same day. He contemplated them. Lundhavn had been offered work in Germany, so his desire to leave was understandable. But Pradera was a bit of a puzzle. His letter cited personal reasons for his departure, with no hint as to what they might be. The pay records showed both men had received handsome closing checks, so it seemed unlikely that they had been forced to resign. But that they left on the same day continued to trouble him. He would have to get to the bottom of it. The letter from Colonel Juan Enrique Senda was a masterpiece of understated indignation, implying all manner of nefarious motives for Saint-Germain's actions, all of which were unsupported by any reliable evidence. Still, the Colonel's animus might reveal something that deserved closer attention. He put the material back in the file and wound the string to close it. Then he took the second file and opened it. The uppermost photograph showed Doña Isabel in a lovely formal gown of pale silk under an elaborate lace jacket with a tulip hem; her head was turned slightly away from the camera and showed the elegant line of her forehead, nose, and cheek to advantage. Zapatilla stared at her, struck by her beauty; he could find it in his heart to envy her absent husband: the woman was a prize of the highest order. He moved the photograph aside, placing it where he could look at it. A tap on the door disturbed his concentration, and he stacked the papers on top of the photograph. "Who is it?"

"Señor Liebre is here," said Esteban.

"He's early," Zapatilla complained as he squared off the sheets of paper and put the file envelope on top of them. He sighed as an indication of the concession he was making. "But you might as well show him in." He paused. "And I suppose you should bring in coffee in ten minutes. Ask Señor Liebre what he would like in his."

"Yes, sir," said Esteban, and, after an exchange of barely audible words with the visitor, opened the door, admitting Cornelio Liebre; in his neat business suit, he did not much resemble the parking attendant at the Hotel della Luna Nueva, which was his intention—he seemed older and more solidly built, with a hint of menace in his walk that was entirely lacking when he was at the Hotel. "Señor Liebre," Esteban announced.

"Good morning, Señor Zapatilla," said Liebre, extending his hand as he came up to the desk. "It's good of you to admit me early. I'm sorry if I intrude."

"Nothing of the sort," said Zapatilla, scowling as they shook hands. "If you will take a seat?"

Liebre pulled up one of the wing-back chairs and set it directly in front of Zapatilla's desk. "You have received my reports, I believe?"

"Yes, I have, and I thank you for providing them." Zapatilla sounded stiff, but he was unconcerned. "It is your duty to do so."

"Of course," said Liebre.

Zapatilla tapped the desk with the end of his pencil. "It is my understanding that you have kept special files on this Conde de Saint-Germain?" He inclined his head. "A pretentious name, don't you think—presumptuous at least?"

"I couldn't say," Liebre replied, uninterested in what the foreigner called himself.

"Well," Zapatilla conceded. "And what have you learned about him? I have some information here already, but I am told your records are more complete."

"I have kept special files. I was asked to do so," said Liebre in the same stiff tone as Zapatilla favored. He settled into the chair with a degree of comfort that Zapatilla found insulting. "I am more than willing to share my information with you; it is why I am here, at the behest of the army. I have been assured by my superiors that it is permissible for me to provide you with as much information as you may want from me." His hauteur was subtle, but enough to annoy Zapatilla.

"We are all pledged to the same purpose," he reminded Liebre. "You and I have an obligation to preserve España from her enemies."

"When we can be certain who they are," said Liebre.

This was more than Zapatilla was willing to tolerate. "If you have any reason to question my loyalty, do so. Otherwise I expect you to remember the position I occupy, and to honor it." He tapped his finger on the desk next to his telephone. "We are in dangerous times, Señor Liebre. Our fighting has been fairly confined, but it may yet erupt in open warfare. You must keep in mind that if you fail to do what you are sworn to do, many of your countrymen will die."

"Many of them will die no matter what you or I do," said Liebre, then adjusted his posture so that it was more attentive.

"You're cynical," said Zapatilla, disapproval radiating from him like body heat.

"I am experienced," Liebre corrected.

Zapatilla was about to take issue with this when there was a rap on the door and Esteban, not waiting for a summons from Zapatilla, let himself in; he carried a tray with two steaming cups of coffee on it, along with a jug of milk and a small jar of sugar cubes. "Oh. Yes." Zapatilla motioned to the place on his desk where the tray should be set. "Do you want milk or sugar?"

Liebre leaned forward and poured in a generous dollop of milk, then took the tongs and dropped three cubes of sugar into his coffee. He selected one of the small spoons on the tray and began to stir the contents of his cup in a negligent manner. "Thank you, Señor Zapatilla. It is most gracious of you."

"It is my pleasure," said Zapatilla in a tone that implied the opposite. He put one cube of sugar into his coffee and gave it a perfunctory stir. "You may go, Esteban."

His assistant withdrew promptly, taking care to close the door with a final sound that made it apparent that they would be private.

"And now, about this Ferenc Ragoczy," Zapatilla prodded. "You have had the opportunity to observe him. What have you found out?"

"That you aren't the only official looking into his activities," said Liebre with a smug little smile. "The army is curious about him, too. I am proof of that. And I am not the only one assigned to monitor his activities."

"Yes," Zapatilla muttered. "I had heard something of that."

"His actions are watched and his professional dealings are observed most carefully, particularly his correspondence, as I suppose you are aware."

"Yes. I have received notice of this," said Zapatilla. "And what have you discovered from your inquiries in this regard?"

"There have been letters from Germany and England and Russia. Most of the English letters come from a firm of solicitors and barristers, I believe they are called." Liebre let this information sink in. "There have also been letters from Canada, and from a university in Peru, apparently from a woman with a French name. There may be more: I haven't checked the letters for myself and that is all the desk clerks have told me. I cannot seem too curious, or Señor Echevarria may put me to work in a less convenient place than in the car park."

"Wouldn't you learn more at the desk?" Zapatilla inquired.

"I might, and I might not, but I am not yet sufficiently trained—in Señor Echevarria's opinion—to do that work, nor am I in a hurry to learn." He managed a little chuckle to indicate how ridiculous he thought this. "It is as useful for me to tend the autos as to go to the registration desk—more useful, in fact." He tasted his coffee and set it aside. "I can learn all I need to know without appearing to . . . to snoop."

"Do you mean to say you are watched?" Zapatilla asked. "You?"

"Of course I am. All the employees at the Hotel della Luna Nueva are." He looked mildly amused. "Do you suppose that I receive any undue attention? I do not; I am a nonentity, less to be noticed than the autos the guests drive. If I behave well, no one pays any attention to me. But chambermaids have been known to pilfer, and desk clerks from time to time take bribes that are compromising to the hotel. Everyone has to be careful of clerks and maids. Not so much so with cooks and waiters, but they see very little of the guests, and what contact they have is very formal, limited to meals in the dining room. A parking attendant? I hear the same gossip as all the others, and I am practically invisible so long as I do nothing to draw attention to myself. I would be a fool to steal an auto, or to damage one; everyone knows that. As an attendant, I can see what the patrons bring with them, and I am in a good position to discover where they go, for they often ask for directions. Even Saint-Germain's manservant occasionally asks me how to find certain streets, though he claims to be a native of Cádiz. His hair is tawny-and-white and his eyes grey-blue so it doesn't seem likely that he is. Still—who knows? he might be." He studied Zapatilla for a long moment, keeping silent.

Zapatilla hated being forced to ask questions, but he acquiesced. "And thus you are unnoticeable as so many servants are, and you use that to your advantage," he said heavily. "What has this allowed you to discover about this Ferenc Ragoczy, Comte de Saint-Germain?"

"I must suppose you know he is from the Carpathians and travels on a Hungarian passport. The government has such things on record, and I know you have been given access to the files," said Liebre, his attention drifting slightly after his brisk beginning. "I also suppose you know Saint-Germain is wealthy. That is obvious to the meanest intelligence. His suits are some of the best I've ever seen—very subtle, very understated, but highest quality, made by the best tailors, English and French. All his shirts and ties are silk. He has the manner that comes with long-held riches." He picked up his coffee-cup and took another sip. "According to Señor Echevarria, Saint-Germain has a great many business investments, in many countries."

"Yes, yes," said Zapatilla impatiently. "You aren't telling me anything that we are unaware of." He tapped the desk with his spoon. "If you have nothing more to add, this conversation is useless."

Liebre stiffened. "I know more, of course. I wanted to show you I know what you would expect me to know—" He stopped, and leaned back. "I have learned that le Comte has a mistress in Cádiz; he has visited her privately five times that I am aware of, although it may be more. He has been giving her his attention since last October, so far as I am cognizant of his actions. I have seen him take her flowers, even in January. He is very discreet, for the lady is married."

"And this is not new information." Zapatilla put down his spoon. "I would think that every intelligence service in España knows that."

"He has been away from Cádiz for almost a month, though he continues to pay for his suites, which is an expensive gesture if it is only intended as a ruse. His manservant goes with him; his rooms at the Hotel are empty, but paid for for the next five months. Saint-Germain drives a Minerva cabriolet and owns a Riley Monaco—"

"An unusual auto," said Zapatilla.

"He keeps it at the Hotel," said Liebre. "He may have another auto in Córdoba; I haven't been able to ascertain that. His manservant has a Voisin C14. Not many employers have an auto for their servants."

"We have already determined he is wealthy," said Zapatilla.

"That we have," said Liebre. "It is real wealth, not the flash display that is seen so often with the newly rich. No high airs for le Comte. He tips handsomely but not foolishly." He paused. "He doesn't eat in the Hotel dining room."

"He likes his privacy, and he has a good-sized suite, does he not?" Zapatilla interjected.

"He has three four-room suites on the second floor—almost half the wing. He has another four-room suite for his manservant. They say he brought his own bed and it is as simple as a monk's—just a thin mattress atop a chest." Liebre shook his head in disbelief.

"Some men are like that; the Kaiser slept in an iron soldier's bed all through his youth," said Zapatilla, doing his best to show indifference to this new and perplexing information. He reminded himself he would have to confirm the information about Saint-Germain's bed for his records.

"No doubt they are," said Liebre. "But le Comte doesn't appear to be one of them: he's elegant, not puritanical."

Zapatilla decided not to pursue the matter with Liebre. "What else have you observed? Is there any event that stands out in your mind, or any detail, no matter how small, that might reveal important information about the man? What has caught your attention about him?" He laid his forearms on the desk, his thumbs just touching. "And keep in mind that I'll be sending a report to your superiors."

Liebre hesitated for an instant—a tactical error with Zapatilla—and attempted to mask it by having a bit more coffee. "I don't think he likes going out during the day. Whatever he does in his suites, it occupies him until sunset."

"He never goes out in the day?" Zapatilla asked, instantly suspicious of Liebre.

"I didn't say that. He does it less frequently than most of our patrons at the Hotel," Liebre told him, still uneasy.

"Many Spaniards prefer to go out during the night," Zapatilla pointed out. "Most of the entertainments of life happen after sundown."

"So they do," Liebre agreed, a little too quickly. "But le Comte is a foreigner, and many of them are not accustomed to our ways. It is unusual for a foreigner to—"

"That doesn't mean that he isn't able to live as we do," Zapatilla interrupted, beginning to count this interview as a waste of time.

"No, it doesn't," Liebre conceded. He finished his coffee and set the cup down. "But there is something I have noticed that may be of interest to you." His early cockiness had faded and he seemed subdued, tentative. "It's what he keeps in the Hotel safe."

"And what would that be?" asked Zapatilla, prepared for almost any outrage from this self-important young man. Still, he was curious enough to want to find out what Liebre was prepared to vouchsafe him.

"He keeps jewels. Many jewels. More than a hundred, I should guess; perhaps as many as one hundred fifty. A considerable fortune, in fact." Liebre's voice dropped to a whisper.

"And how do you know this?" Zapatilla demanded.

"The night clerk showed me, at the end of last month." It was a stunning admission, and, if true, a potentially alarming circumstance, for the lapse in confidentiality this indicated was troubling.

"Are you certain the jewels are genuine?" Zapatilla asked smoothly.

"According to what Señor Echevarria told the night clerk, all of them have been examined by jewelers of the highest repute and they have certified the quality of the stones, which is very, very high." Liebre cleared his throat. "They were astonishing to see, like bits of the rainbow sitting in a metal box."

"And has he done this before, the night clerk, with other patrons' possessions? Shown you what they kept in the safe?" Zapatilla almost held his breath for the answer.

"Yes," said Liebre as if offering up an obtuse apology; he volunteered nothing more.

"How often?" Zapatilla asked. "And which patrons?"

"Only the foreigners," said Liebre, as if this made such behavior more acceptable. "He never interferes with any property of our Spanish guests."

"Oh, very good," said Zapatilla with heavy sarcasm, his head lowered and his hands spread out. "He does not break the law for Spaniards—only the foreigners are afforded that privilege," he scoffed; but even as he spoke, it occurred to him that the night clerk might also be working for one of the governmental offices, which would account for his behavior. "Who is this most accommodating clerk?"

Relieved to be able to shift some of the error away from himself, Liebre said, "Eduardo Deshielo. He comes from Asturias."

"Which accounts for something, to be sure," said Zapatilla at his driest, just as he supposed Claude Rains would say it.

"I thought you'd want to know," Liebre said, a suggestion of sulkiness in his attitude. "If I erred—"

"And so I do," Zapatilla allowed hastily, then paused to consider what he had heard. "I need to know more about this Eduardo Deshielo. He has broken the law, and that may make him useful to me." He was thinking aloud, and he did not invite any response from Liebre.

An uncomfortable silence settled between them that lasted for the better part of two minutes. Finally Liebre said, "I have found out that le Comte has property in Córdoba. There is a house that has been in his family for some time, according to what his manservant told Señor Echevarria. The house is supposed to be in the old part of the city, built on the foundations of another house that was torn down centuries ago. His manager, Lazaro Flojasilla, sends regular reports to the Hotel. Also, he often has letters from England, from a firm of solicitors."

"So you mentioned," said Zapatilla. "As to the property manager, we have already spoken to him. The house le Comte keeps in Córdoba sustained some damage in a recent bombing incident—nothing very bad, but enough to require repairs—that accorded us an opportunity to learn a bit more about the holding." He said nothing more, savoring the frustrated expression Liebre tried unsuccessfully to hide; Zapatilla decided to drop a crumb for Liebre. "The house is a minor matter. His business there is my primary concern: I have been reviewing his airline assembly plant's records; he is very up-to-date on innovations. And he has a head for business, I will give him that."

"It could be . . . he may convert his earnings to jewels," Liebre ventured, making an effort to smile; he wanted to restore Zapatilla's good opinion of him.

"It is possible," said Zapatilla.

"And prudent," said Liebre. "Just consider the advantages. He can carry the jewels anywhere, they will not diminish in value, no matter what becomes of the currency, they have value everywhere in the world he might decide to go, and they are less conspicuous than cash, and more reliable than bank drafts."

"This is so," said Zapatilla, who was not so convinced by his own argument as he pretended to be. "You may be on to something."

Glad to be able to improve his standing with Zapatilla, Liebre enlarged upon his thoughts. "If he has jewels enough, he could travel without difficulty, and establish himself with minimal effort."

"I wouldn't go so far as that," said Zapatilla.

"He could leave España easily, and most countries would be glad to have a rich industrialist settle inside their borders. Some of the other countries may be offering him favorable conditions to move." Liebre was being more confident again. "Never mind his title, his riches make him useful for any nation."

"It is a sad commentary on our modern world," said Zapatilla, dismissing the issue with a turn of his hand just as Claude Rains might have done it. "Have you any reason to suppose he may be planning to leave? Has he said anything, or his manservant?"

"I can't recall any such suggestion," said Liebre, becoming a bit more animated. "If you like, I can try to find out as soon as he returns."

Zapatilla considered this. "I think it may be more important to watch him. If he is going to leave, he may do so without warning." He achieved a dry chuckle. "He manufactures airplanes—who is to say he won't fly out of España?"

"I have no reason to believe he is a pilot," said Liebre.

With a little sigh that his humor was unappreciated, Zapatilla said, "No, he is not. We have that on the testimony of his two pilots—Blaz Riosalado and Raul Telas—who have already told me that Saint-Germain dislikes flying; he claims he doesn't want to be far from the earth." This observation was accompanied by an overly ingratiating smile.

Liebre managed to laugh this time. "He may be wise."

"His airplanes have excellent reputations. I don't think he would have any reason to hesitate to fly in one," said Zapatilla austerely. "And no one can claim he isn't aware of the quality of his company's products."

"Very true," said Liebre quickly. "But it does seem that Saint-Germain dislikes flying. There are any number of people who do."

"Surprising, that he should be one of them—don't you think?" Zapatilla asked, observing Liebre closely.

Liebre smirked. "He probably watched dogfights during the Great War. He's old enough. That would make anyone think twice about flying." His face paled a bit. "Airplanes were less reliable then, of course."

"Of course," Zapatilla echoed.

"But he has also said he dislikes traveling by sea," added Liebre.

"When did he say that?" Zapatilla asked, thinking he had never had a report on Saint-Germain expressing such sentiments before.

Aware that he had finally hit upon something Zapatilla wanted to hear, Liebre lost a little of his stiffness. "He was going to some kind of affair at the concert hall, a gala for some sort of occasion, and he happened to mention that some of the guests had arrived by yacht. I made some comment about his lack of one— just a joke, you know how you do—and he told me he becomes seasick far too easily for sea travel." He smiled a little. "A man as polished as he, turning green and puking over the rail!"

Zapatilla was not amused; he laid his hand on the files on his desk. "Still, a most interesting admission, if it's true."

"Why shouldn't it be?" Liebre asked. "It isn't the kind of thing one says of oneself if it isn't."

"Unless he intends for us to think of him as incapacitated by sea travel, and thereby misdirect our attention." Zapatilla tasted the last of his coffee; it was cold and turning bitter.

"But you are not misdirected," said Liebre, making the most of his opening; he felt his confidence begin to well again.

"No. There is no reason I should be," said Zapatilla. He wanted to make notes but would not give Liebre the satisfaction of seeing him do it. "In fact, I will take this as an indication that I should alert the army to the possibility that Saint-Germain may have access to a ship—not necessarily at Cádiz, but there are many other harbors in Spain, and in Portugal, for that matter." He looked down at the files again. "It is a worthy precaution, I think, watching where he doesn't expect to be observed. He may yet betray himself."

"Then you anticipate trouble," said Liebre, a bit too eagerly.

"Always, in all things. I do not limit myself to le Comte de Saint-Germain." He directed his best stare at Liebre. "And you would do well to do the same."

Liebre tried to remain comfortable. "I will. Of course I will."

"You are in a most opportune place to take advantage of the post you have." He gave Liebre a long, thoughtful stare. "I think you may count yourself fortunate. If you are able to acquit yourself well, I believe you will be assigned to more rewarding work than what you currently have."

"I am eager to serve," said Liebre. "Tell me what you want me to do."

Satisfied that he had engaged all Liebre's attention, Zapatilla leaned forward and lowered his voice. "I have it on good authority that Saint-Germain is returning to Cádiz in a week or two. If you take the time to make a record of all the letters he receives between now and his return, I will put your name forward at the Ministerio de Guerra for advancement. I can see you're ambitious and dedicated, both of which should serve you well in the Ministerio."

Liebre seemed to grow sleeker before Zapatilla's eyes. "You are most generous, Señor Zapatilla. I am grateful to you."

"It's a bit premature for that," Zapatilla said quietly.

Again Liebre smiled. "Still, I am grateful." He rose. "I shall report to you in a week, or sooner if there is something of importance."

"I would appreciate it," said Zapatilla at his most daunting.

Liebre proffered his hand, then, when Zapatilla did not take it, awkwardly withdrew it. "It's been a pleasure, Señor Zapatilla."

"The pleasure is mine," Zapatilla assured him.

Stepping back, Liebre tried to recover himself as he left. "Yes. Well." He all but bolted for the door.

Left alone, Zapatilla sat still for some little time. It was almost time for the noonday meal and the siesta, but just now neither had any appeal for him. He considered everything he had heard and tried to evaluate it. There was little doubt in his mind that Liebre was a willing tool, but one he must not abuse. Getting up, he went toward the door, then stopped, and began to pace. He had said he would do his best to advance Liebre's career, and he would have to find some means to do it in order to keep the eager young man acting on his behalf. "Best to do this now." He returned to his desk and sat down, lifting the receiver, then holding it while he heard the operator ask him what number he wanted. Recalling himself, he gave the exchange for Madrid and asked for Leandro de Guzman. "You have his number in your files."

The operator agreed that she did and rang through to the operator at the Ministerio de Guerra, requesting connection to de Guzman. There was the sound of ringing, and after six rings the telephone was answered. "Leandro de Guzman's office."

"This is Mercurio Zapatilla. May I speak to Señor de Guzman?" He was very polite but firm.

"Señor de Guzman has left for the afternoon. He should be back after siesta. I am his secretary, Pablo Robleseco. May I help you?"

"Ah," said Zapatilla. "I need to speak to Señor de Guzman. Is there any way we can arrange this? I would prefer not to wait until this afternoon."

Robleseco paused. "I believe he is lunching at El Caballero Negro. I can call him there. If you will give me your number, he'll get back to you."

"You're most accommodating. I'll remain in my office until I hear from him," said Zapatilla, and left his number. "On the Seville exchange."

"Of course, of course," said Robleseco. "I'll telephone him at once."

"Gracias. Then I'll ring off," said Zapatilla before Robleseco could hang up on him. But as soon as he had put the receiver down, he wondered if he had been too abrupt, for he was relying upon Robleseco to contact de Guzman for him, and that meant that he needed to maintain cordiality with the secretary. He walked the length of his office and once again looked down onto the street, noticing the bustle had increased as businesses prepared to close for luncheon and siesta; he saw four men in laborers' clothes approaching his building, one of them holding a short pipe in his hand. They moved cautiously, threading their way along the narrow sidewalk, breasting the tide of office workers who hurried out the doors of the government offices. As Zapatilla studied them, he began to feel uneasy. What was it about these men that so unnerved him? He could not bring himself to identify any single element about them, but he was increasingly certain that they were up to no good. Then it struck him. "A bomb," he said, and repeated it more loudly. "Esteban! They have a bomb!" he shouted as he ran toward the door and pulled it open, only to find that the outer office was empty. "Esteban! Where are you?" He lost precious seconds in looking about, then started out into the hallway when a loud noise thundered up from the floor below. Zapatilla staggered back and reached for the nearest chair to hang on to it, only to find it and himself on the carpet.

A siren was howling somewhere in the building, and two alarm bells shrilled; there were cries and screams of dismay and pain. Zapatilla struggled to his feet, and almost fell when his ankle turned under him. He kept from falling by leaning heavily against Esteban's desk. Where was he? Zapatilla tried to call out again and ended up coughing.

In the next office along the corridor someone was sobbing—a woman by the sound of it—and Zapatilla decided to make his way to her. Taking care to put as little of his weight as possible on his ankle, he limped down the hallway, blinking at the dust and smoke that filled the air. "Just a moment!" he did his best to shout. "I'm coming."

The woman's voice crescendoed, prayers mixed with sobs.

A groan of wood and plaster went through the building like the death-throes of a wounded behemoth; Zapatilla listened to this ominous sound with misgiving. He very nearly turned and went toward the stairs, but the renewed keening of the woman brought him a renewed sense of purpose, and he kept on in her direction, doing his best to ignore the sounds of the building. He had almost reached the door—marked by a swath of shattered glass—when there was a loud crack, and the floor canted at a dangerous angle as, with a howling moan, the upper part of the structure began to collapse in on itself.

For an eternity of twenty seconds Zapatilla imagined he had escaped, was free of any danger, was, in fact, delivered from harm. He began to smile just as the ceiling fell in on him and carried him down to be entombed on the ground floor amid broken beams and rubble.

TEXT OF A LETTER FROM COLONEL JUAN ENRIQUE SENDA TO LEANDRO DE GUZMAN.

> *Edificio del Puertomaestro*
> *Calle Atlantica*
> *Cádiz*
> *9 March, 1936*

Leandro de Guzman
Ministerio de Guerra
Madrid

Señor de Guzman,

In answer to your inquiries, no, I have received no further information from Sevilla; the attack on your building there seems to have destroyed all the records kept in the offices within. No one could be more distressed than I am at the loss of intelligence and records that are so essential to the protection of España. I am willing to set aside men for the task of reconstructing the files that the Ministerio de Guerra has prepared and has lost as a result of that treacherous explosion. To further that end, I will answer the questions in your letter of 23 February; I ask you not to hesitate if anything I and my men can do may additionally assist you.

As regards the journalist Hector Iglesias, I have only had passing contact with the man, as he has not stayed in Cádiz for more than a week. I have it on reliable authority that he is now in Lisboa, in Portugal, and planning to go to Bilbao within the month. Whatever reports he makes will be reviewed and scrutinized for disloyal sentiments. I have already spoken to Carlos Santiago, who has assured me that no seditious material will be published in La Tarde, and I am convinced that he is sincere in his assurances. Many other newspapermen throughout España have given you similar guarantees, I have been told.

You ask about the artist, Martin Teodorez, and I must inform you he is a bit problematic. His paintings are controversial, but they are also very abstract, and much of what has been said of them has been read into them, rather in the manner of those inkblots the Austrians use to determine madness. To be sure, Teodorez is perplexing, for he thrives on contention and actively seeks out confrontation regarding his work. I have said that this man is an exploitive and outrageous poseur, but that does not mean that he is politically subversive. For the time being, I will have my men continue to watch him and to report on those whom he sees. We may yet learn some-

thing in regard to his opinions, and should that happen, I will inform you of all I discover as promptly as possible.

The questions regarding Silva Brancato are another matter; Brancato not only has a formidable international reputation in his field, he is Portuguese, and therefore not to be trifled with, even though his condemnations of the growing hostilities in España are embarrassing. I cannot even keep his books from being sold, not without specific authorization. I wish to remind you that if such censoring is commanded, we will be subject to the world's denunciation for attempting to silence an author of such a distinguished career. Also, Brancato is welcome in any civilized country, and could leave España without hindrance if he decides he is the object of disapprobation here, or anywhere. I believe it would be wiser to leave him alone for the time being, and take a position that his fears of our struggles spreading across all Europe are alarmist.

Some of our files on Ferenc Ragoczy, le Comte de Saint-Germain, were destroyed in the blast, as you have been informed. I am doing all I can to reconstruct the material that Mercurio Zapatilla assembled. This is more difficult than it might be: Saint-Germain is a foreigner and as such has certain protections that we would be ill-advised to contravene. I have spoken with him five times, and although he is not uncooperative, he is not particularly forthcoming, either, which has created certain problems between us. If I make a point of renewing my inquiries, he may very well liquidate his Spanish holdings and depart, taking his engineers and patents and his wealth with him, which could be unfortunate for us at this crucial time.

On the other hand, I have two days since conferred with Cornelio Liebre, who is employed at the Hotel della Luna Nueva; he was the last to meet with Zapatilla and he has told me that he will do his utmost to fulfill those instructions Zapatilla gave him, and do it for our benefit. He is well-placed to surveil Saint-Germain without bringing attention to his activities. I am going to order the army watchers to make a point of withdrawing from their posts. This, I trust, will ease Saint-Germain's mind, which may, in turn, cause him to be less careful in his dealings, and that we may turn to our advantage. I have also had some success in questioning Señor Hernando Echevarria, the manager of the Hotel della Luna Nueva, who has been willing to tell me as much as he can without violating what he perceives as a trust he has with his patrons. The rest of the staff is less informative, although the meat chef, Gustavo Perez, has told me that Saint-Germain has his meals prepared by his manservant, who procures fresh meat for his use, and occasionally goes so far as to bring live chickens into the Hotel della

Luna Nueva; there is a small kitchen in the manservant's suite, and it is there that the meals are made, according to Perez. Señor Echevarria has confirmed this, and we may assume that he will not deviate from this practice.

I will need to have the use of two or three more operatives here in Cádiz if I am to maintain a reasonable level of usefulness for those we must watch. I know it is difficult just now, with all the demands of the increasing conflict arising in so many parts of our country, but I am sure that with a few more well-placed intelligence officers, we can gather the information that is crucial to our work, and to our ultimate conquest of those who stand against us. This may be seen as an imposition, but I promise you, it is not. We must keep our minds on achieving victory, and prepare to do whatever we must to attain our goals. If we do wrongs now, we can right them once we have triumphed. It is essential that we maintain our resolve, for in the face of the adamant opposition of the rebels, we must be prepared to do everything and anything our cause necessitates.

You may wish to extend your attention to Servetus Valencia: he is currently at Salamanca and his publisher is in Barcelona. He purports to be a scientist, and has written three books on his theories about social evolution. He has lately been challenging the whole conduct of our hostilities, saying that it is a sign of social regression, a step backward that is likely to push España back into the patterns of the last century instead of embracing the growing internationalism of the present. You cannot overestimate the damage some of his writings can do, for they stir up the educated who are inclined to accept his notions without any consideration of the ramifications of what he espouses. You may dismiss my apprehension as futile—and you may be right—but at this time we need the support of the intelligentsia to make our positions acceptable not only in España, but throughout Europe. We need our professors and theorists to endorse our goals, not undermine them. I cannot be comfortable with the possible outcome of his activities, especially now, when we have seen such an escalation of fighting all over the country, and the attention of Europe turned on our squabbles.

I look forward to hearing from you at your earliest convenience.

Most respectfully,

Juan Enrique Senda, Colonel

JES/mll

chapter four

"I think the soldiers are no longer in the building across the street," Rogerio observed as he came into the room in the second suite of the four Saint-Germain occupied in the Hotel della Luna Nueva that had been relegated for use as his study. It was nearing the end of siesta and Cádiz was unusually silent as most of the inhabitants took advantage of the hour to stay indoors, not to avoid the heat of the day, which was still moderate, but to escape the attention of the army; squads of soldiers were everywhere, patrolling the streets, demanding food and drink from cafés and private houses, stopping persons at random and taking money and other valuables from them, supposedly to pay for their ordnance and materiel.

"Oh?" Saint-Germain looked up from the Dutch newspaper; he had been reading an article on recent events in Germany that the Dutch reports viewed with mixed admiration and uneasiness, sentiments Saint-Germain thought were insufficiently alarmed. "Perhaps they are observing siesta."

"The windows are shuttered and I'm told no soldier has been in the building since midnight," Rogerio said; the Latinate language he spoke had not been used in España for more than sixteen hundred years, before the Moors had come, or the Visigoths. "Neither Cornelio, the auto attendant, nor Gustavo, the meat chef, has seen a soldier go into that house today, or come out. I made it a point to ask both of them if they had noticed anyone, and both said they had not."

"Is it a holiday of some sort? Could they have been posted to another location, one that hasn't been detected yet? Are there military maneuvers or a parade that require their attendance? Has fighting broken out in the countryside?" Saint-Germain asked in the same tongue, skeptical of this news.

"There is no fighting I have heard of, and no parade. It is not a holiday, not so soon after Easter," said Rogerio.

"I know there are concerns for the first of May," said Saint-Germain, folding the newspaper and setting it aside.

"With good reason," said Rogerio. "The Left and the Right have been itching for an excuse to fight, and on the first, they will have it." He went to the windows to adjust the shutters so that no sliver of sunshine penetrated the room, though it was light enough for Saint-Germain to read.

"In ten days," said Saint-Germain.

"Ten days," Rogerio echoed. "You're expecting trouble."

"Certainly," said Saint-Germain. "The way the army is behaving, I should think that the populace would be disappointed if nothing happened. The intrusion the army has made into everything will be resented if there isn't something to show for it, and fairly soon; the army will be held responsible if the unrest continues unresolved: without doubt Generals Mola and Franco will be held similarly accountable, as they should be." He sighed. "It's a pity that Eclipse Aeroplano Industrias has been designated a strategic business producing objects with tactical implications; the government doesn't want to have it controlled by an owner living outside of España. They don't much like it being owned by a foreigner who lives *in* España, either. They have intentions that include turning all the airplanes into fighting ones, the very thing I would like to avoid."

"If you sell Eclipse Aero, you could leave without hindrance, according to Colonel Senda," Rogerio reminded him. "You wouldn't have to see how they use your airplanes."

"So I could, and as things are going, I probably should; it is the prudent thing to do," Saint-Germain agreed at his most genial. "Yet, I would like to save Eclipse Aero from becoming another instrument of war; I cannot think of what the Germans have done with the petroleum business I had in Munich, ten years ago, without becoming slightly ill. I would prefer not to see that happen here: so long as I can hold on to control of the company, it should be possible to keep some limits on what the army may do with the assembly plant and the airplanes. I may be fighting a rear-guard action, but I must make the attempt. It is a flaw in my character." He managed a quick half-smile. "You needn't remind me again how often I have had to answer for my intractability—I don't like having my hand forced." He held up his hand. "I know; I know—stubborn pride and obstinacy. Yes, you're right: I should know better."

Rogerio made a gesture of capitulation. "You leave me nothing to say."

"Except that you are worried," Saint-Germain added for him. "You are afraid I will mull too much and act too little."

"That, and I am concerned for your lethargy." He regarded Saint-Germain levelly. "I sometimes feel you are daring the world to have done with you."

Saint-Germain shook his head. "I am not so far gone as that, although perhaps five years ago I might have been tempted . . ." His voice trailed off; when he spoke again, it was with renewed purpose. "Still, I am grateful for your reminder, little though I may show it, and I do heed what you say; in principle I agree with you." Saint-Germain reached for another newspaper—this one

German—and opened it slowly. "España is becoming dangerous, no doubt of that. Not that I like what I see from the rest of Europe."

"No; nor I," said Rogerio, accepting this shift of emphasis without exasperation; he was relieved that Saint-Germain had perceived so much.

"Russia is worse than Europe," Saint-Germain went on. "China isn't much better, what with the Japanese wanting to control the north."

"And the New World? Aren't conditions somewhat better in the Americas?" Rogerio cleared his throat. "Mr. Tree could advise you where you might be most comfortable." His mention of the American journalist was a deliberate nudge.

"You mean among the gangsters in the North and the peon revolts in the South? And the economic troubles they're having, North and South." Saint-Germain folded a page back. "Even America might not be safe: no one can say that the European strife will not spread, even to the Americas, eventually."

Rogerio hesitated, familiar with Saint-Germain's saturnine state of mind; he had seen it many times in their long years together. "Where would you like to go?"

Saint-Germain uttered a single, sad chuckle. "I would prefer not to go anywhere, though that may not be an option any longer. I agree that we may have to go a long way to find a modicum of peace." He waited a moment and added wryly, "At least we need not have a month at sea to get across the Atlantic." He read a few lines, then added, "If the Great War is starting up again—and it may well be—it may be prudent to put the ocean between us and the fighting, gangsters and peons be damned." His words were gentle and his eyes were sad.

Rogerio managed not to reveal the relief that went through him. "Shall I make some discreet inquiries?"

"No, not yet." Saint-Germain shook his head. "I want to try to negotiate a reasonable solution to the present impasse; ideally, I'd like to keep Eclipse Aero if I can find a way to do it. It is not very likely that I can prevent all military applications of the airplanes, especially the Moghul, in spite of the design limitations, but if I make no push to stop it, most certainly the business will end up a wholly military operation, and that would be dreadful. You must pardon me for trying to swim upstream. I still have to try to do all that I can to prevent the worst from occurring." He uttered a single chuckle: his antipathy to water made him a very poor swimmer and they both knew it. "Nevertheless, I will give you my Word: if I fail in my efforts, then I will make whatever arrangements are necessary to leave, however I have to."

"Do you suppose you'll have to give up the aircraft business?" He knew this was the crux of the problem.

"It may come to that, but I assume there must be some way I can save it—I hope it is not too late," said Saint-Germain. "I have only two aliases to use here in

España, and neither one will tolerate close scrutiny." He shrugged disconsolately. "If I am wholly frank, I suppose I may have to part with the company completely, as little as I want to give it up. I believe that once the company is out of my hands the airplanes will be used for war. But it seems it may no longer be an option, given the state of the country, in which case, I would like to minimize the extent to which Eclipse Aero becomes dedicated to killing." He turned the page of his German paper. "I will have to make up my mind what to do to protect the business."

Rogerio looked down at the floor. "It would be wise to decide soon, I think. I may be overcautious, but I cannot help but wonder if there will be any way for us to leave España, or Europe for that matter, if we wait much longer. I have no wish to dwell on the matter, but with violence escalating—"

"I understand your concerns," Saint-Germain said, "as I always do when you warn me." His smile was swift but sincere.

"Very well, I will have to be content with this for now, but if matters get worse, I will speak with you again," said Rogerio, preparing to leave the study. "Is there anything you need me to do in the next hour or so?"

"I don't think so: why?" Saint-Germain responded.

"I have a fresh shoat being held at the butcher's shop on the Avenida Santa Cajetana. I was thinking I would call in there as soon as siesta is ended." He saw Saint-Germain nod. "Thank you. I will not linger."

"With the army making a pest of itself, it is a good idea to provide them as little opportunity to impose as is possible. Be careful while you are on the street, for you know the army is to impose its will on everyone." He tapped a card that lay on the table beside his chair. "Colonel Senda is still paying close attention to everything I do. But more than my predicament troubles me." He took up another newspaper—this one from Milan—and opened it. "This arrogant popinjay Mussolini, for instance: he troubles me. The continuing persecutions in Russia trouble me. The unrest in China troubles me. The aftermath of the Great War troubles me. The fate of the Armenians troubles me. The difficulties in the Middle East trouble me. The confusion in Britain and her colonies troubles me. The vindictive complacency in France troubles me. We won't even speak of the NSDAP." His voice tightened at the mention of the ruling party in Germany, whose followers had killed his ward in Munich a decade ago; he still mourned Laisha, her memory as tender as the half-healed wound it was.

"The Nazis have many supporters outside of Germany," Rogerio reminded him gently, using the nickname of the National Socialist German Workers Party that had already made itself infamous among certain groups.

Saint-Germain contemplated the page in front of him. "They will come to grief over it," he said at last, very softly.

"That is my point," said Rogerio as he opened the door. "May I get anything for you while I am out?"

"I don't think so," Saint-Germain said after a moment's hesitation.

"Will you see Doña Isabel?" Rogerio asked, his hand on the door-latch.

"No, not tonight," said Saint-Germain, a certain distance in his tone telling Rogerio far more than words about the current state of the affaire. "She has an engagement with her aunt at the Ballet Catalonia. They are planning to spend a few days together."

"I see," said Rogerio, and hoped he did; he closed the study door and went into the principal sitting room, where he took up a canvas shopping bag and hung it over the scrolled door-latch in anticipation of his errand. He busied himself for the next half-hour with the mundane task of putting the room in order to receive any visitor who might call, and then, at the conclusion of siesta, took the shopping bag and went out to the butcher's, where he paid for the newly slaughtered baby pig, put it into his bag, then returned, watched but unhassled, to the Hotel della Luna Nueva to find that Colonel Senda had called and was still with Saint-Germain.

"Ah, Rogerio," said Saint-Germain as Rogerio came into the sitting room. "As you see, Colonel Senda is here."

"I see that," said Rogerio, and added with utmost politeness, "May I get you a drink, Colonel? We have an excellent Burgundy, and a tolerable Sangue di Christi nel Vesuvio. If you would like something stronger, a very good cognac as well as a single-malt scotch. There is also a little grappa left, if you would prefer a digestif." He regarded the Colonel as if he were glad to see him, although he was inwardly alarmed by Senda's presence so soon after his last visit.

"Cognac, in a balloon snifter," said the Colonel, snapping out the order as if Rogerio were a green recruit in need of training.

"As soon as I put this in our kitchen," he said, indicating his canvas bag. He left the sitting room and went about his work.

"He's been with you a long time," said Colonel Senda. "Your servant."

"Yes; half my life," said Saint-Germain accurately, not adding that he and Rogerio had met in Roma when Vespasianus was Caesar.

"Such loyalty is rare," said the Colonel with a languid wave of approval. "Not many of us find that in our lives."

"I know I am fortunate," said Saint-Germain, wondering what Colonel Senda intended by his remarks.

"It would be a shame to repay his devotion with hardship," said the Colonel with a slow, malicious smile.

His expression did not change, but Saint-Germain felt a surge of anger at this threat. "Why should he have to fear hardship, Colonel?"

"You cannot be unaware of the increasing violence that daily desecrates our streets and countryside," said Senda with a false display of sorrow. "A man such as your manservant, unused to our ways, and often abroad, who knows what might happen to him?"

"In other words, your men would target him and any misfortune he suffered could be laid at the door of those whom you wished to blame." Saint-Germain folded his arms. "Why not abandon your pretext of civility, Colonel? You have made it clear that you want something of me, and that you are prepared to exert any pressure you can to gain what you seek."

"You make it all seem so uncouth," Colonel Senda complained. "I'd prefer to think of it as adapting to exigent circumstances."

"Of course you would," said Saint-Germain with world-weary amusement.

The Colonel heard the condemnation in Saint-Germain's observation and he reacted sharply. "I have been patient with you, it may be I am too patient. I think you may consider yourself fortunate that I haven't put you in prison—I have the authority to do so, you know." He showed his teeth in a furious smile. "I don't think you'd like being in prison. No more fine clothes, no more suites, no more manservant, no more autos, no more pretty mistresses, just a small cell, an army cot, and a bucket for slops."

Saint-Germain nodded. "Yes. I know what prison can be." He had been in many of them in his four thousand years, and found one to be much like another; some were a bit more comfortable, some more uncomfortable, but in the end, all of them were containers for the unwanted.

"You have been in prison, then?" The Colonel all but pounced on this.

"In Russia, some years ago. Many European industrialists were." It was his most recent incarceration. "My primary crime was being rich; my secondary one was having a title. Add to that my foreign origins, and my ties to banks and shipping, and my doom was sealed." The corners of his mouth lifted for an instant. "For since I am an exile with no government to complain of my incarceration, there was no embarrassment for the Bolsheviks. I should imagine the same realization has crossed your mind, as well."

Colonel Senda did his best to look shocked. "I would not resort to anything so unpleasant unless you make it necessary."

"That is what the Bolsheviks said, too," Saint-Germain approved. "They were certain that they could achieve their goals by depriving me of property, wealth, and at last, food and warmth. They put me in a monk's cell outside of Krasnoye Selo and did their utmost to forget about me. They very nearly succeeded." He inclined his head. "But as you can see, I am still here." He recalled his escape as he fled westward on a stolen horse, and knew he would not have such an opportunity in España.

"But here is España, not Russia," said Colonel Senda.

"No; not Russia," Saint-Germain agreed.

Whatever Colonel Senda had been about to say, it was silenced as Rogerio came back into the room carrying a tray on which stood a very large balloon snifter of fine Austrian crystal, with a pool of cognac in the bottom. "I trust this is to your satisfaction."

The Colonel took the snifter, gave the contents a swirl, and sniffed deeply at the vapors that rose from the wild-honey–colored liquid. "Very good. Not the best I have had, but very good." He took a generous swig of the cognac, then sighed with satisfaction. "How much of this do you have?"

Saint-Germain glanced at Rogerio. "A case or two. There is more in Córdoba."

"A case or two," the Colonel mused. "Quite an investment for a house where you do not live for years on end."

"The servants who maintain it cost a great deal more than the cognac," said Saint-Germain, a sardonic light in his dark eyes.

"Tell me," said Colonel Senda, "do you think you can influence me with good drink? On such an important matter?" He nodded his dismissal to Rogerio; he stared at the servant as if he wanted to annoy him. "You needn't listen at the door."

Rogerio paid no attention to this studied insult, but stepped back from Senda's chair. "Will there be anything else?" he asked Saint-Germain.

"Not just now, thank you, Rogerio" was his reply. "Perhaps you could look in on us in half-an-hour or so? If I need you before then, I'll ring."

"Very good, Comte," he said, and withdrew.

"He's very old school, isn't he?" Colonel Senda said as he took another generous sip of the cognac; he paid no attention to the sudden eruption of gunfire in the street below.

"I suppose so. But then," Saint-Germain explained, "so am I."

Colonel Senda laughed immoderately. "Oh, how apt," he said as his mirth ceased. "You are that, no doubt." A second volley of shots caught his attention, but he said nothing more.

"And, in my old-school way, I am not yet ready to be coerced into surrendering all control of Eclipse Aeroplano Industrias to you, no matter how much it would please you to have me do it. My corporation is not in violation of any Spanish laws, and I have maintained the company along the recommended governmental lines." Saint-Germain stood up slowly. "You know my conditions for releasing control of the firm to the army, or any other group."

"You've spelled them out: adaptation for surveillance only, no weapons to be added to the airplanes, or alterations in design that would accommodate the use of weapons," said Colonel Senda as he swallowed a third mouthful of the cognac.

"I am sorry to inform you that I cannot agree to any such limitations as you would impose on the army: my superiors will not allow it. Surely you must know they will not accept any such conditions."

"Will they not," said Saint-Germain, walking to the window and opening the louvers of the shutters enough to permit him to look out. He could see a few frightened pedestrians emerging from doorways along the Avenida Fantasma clutching their belongings as they cautiously resumed their progress down the street; there were no autos in sight other than the dozen in the Hotel's car park, and most of the windows facing the street were still firmly shuttered. "It is a lovely afternoon," he said, more to himself than the Colonel.

"No, they will not," said Colonel Senda, belligerently sticking to the previous topic. "You must know it is ridiculous to impose such limitations on the army. Let me reiterate our position: constraints imposed by industry are dangerous just now, and cannot be tolerated. We are on the brink of war in España: why do we want airplanes, but to use them for fighting?"

"Why, indeed," said Saint-Germain, and was just turning away from the window when the crack of a rifle sounded as the wooden louvers shattered and a bullet ploughed deep into Saint-Germain's right shoulder. He staggered, dropped to his knees, then fell onto his side; the pain had not hit him yet, only the impact of the wound, as heavy as a blow with a stone. It was an effort to breathe, as if the air itself had become weighty.

Colonel Senda was on his feet, shouting something Saint-Germain could not quite make out. "Your master is shot! A terrible accident! He is shot!" he repeated at the top of his lungs, and came to Saint-Germain's side, bending over him, not quite touching him. "Where were you hit?"

Saint-Germain blinked as if to clear his thoughts. "Shoulder," he said at last.

Lips pursed, Colonel Senda got down on one knee. "No blood pumping. Your artery is spared." He still held the snifter in his right hand, and he emptied the little bit of cognac remaining over the spreading patch of blood on Saint-Germain's jacket. "You may even live. If you have good care." He was struggling to his feet when Rogerio rushed into the room, an apron still tied around his waist. "He's shot in the shoulder: the right one, by the look of it," the Colonel informed him, then went back to his chair to sit down. "An outrage."

Rogerio knelt beside Saint-Germain. "My master," he said in a quiet tone that demanded attention.

"The bullet's . . . still . . ." Saint-Germain muttered; the pain had struck now, and left him breathless in a way the initial shock had not.

"In the wound. I will remove it as soon as I can be rid of the Colonel," he said in an under-voice in Greek, then spoke up, in Spanish for Senda's benefit. "I must telephone his physician. If you will excuse me?"

"Will you not take him to hospital?" Colonel Senda inquired as if he were discussing primroses.

"If his physician so orders, of course: to the hospital of his designation," said Rogerio. "If the streets are safe enough to travel just now."

"Very well," said the Colonel. "If you should prefer, I can order my men to transport him to San Gil's; they will take very good care of him there." When Rogerio did not seize the opportunity, Senda shrugged. "No? Then I will not linger. I should report this; accidents like this are on the rise, and care must be taken. Random shots are as dangerous as intentional ones, aren't they?" He put the snifter down and stood up. "I leave you to it. Do let me know how he fares." With that, he went to the door and let himself out.

As soon as he was gone, Rogerio went back to Saint-Germain and again knelt beside him. "Are you still—"

"I am . . . conscious," said Saint-Germain. His voice was thready, and his skin was paler than usual. "How bad is it?"

"I will have to dig out the bullet," Rogerio said apologetically. "I don't think it would be wise to go to hospital."

"I agree," Saint-Germain managed to say.

"Can you get to your feet?" Rogerio put his hand on Saint-Germain's wounded shoulder.

"With help," said Saint-Germain. He prepared to push himself with his good left arm; his whole body felt wobbly.

Rogerio put his arm over Saint-Germain's back and helped to pull him upright, then shifted his position so he could lever Saint-Germain to his feet, letting his master lean against him as he did. "This is a very bad wound. You should be on your bed." He spoke levelly, though his faded-blue eyes were filled with trouble.

"Yes," Saint-Germain said, his head ringing from this simple effort. He swayed, his vision swimming. "It's deep."

"Can you feel it?" Rogerio asked as he adjusted his hold on Saint-Germain, wedging his shoulder against Saint-Germain's chest as he began to guide him out of the room and toward the corridor; as they went, he saw a ribbon of blood following them. He said nothing of this ominous sign, but did his best to make Saint-Germain move a little faster.

"Yes . . . I'll let . . . you know where . . . it is." He took an uneven breath and went on. "Use the pansy paste."

"Will it help?" Rogerio asked, knowing that few analgesics or anesthetics worked on Saint-Germain.

"A little." He grunted as he almost tripped.

"Colonel Senda said this was an accident," said Rogerio, doing his best to keep Saint-Germain awake and alert.

"Hardly," said Saint-Germain. He made an effort not to drag his feet.

"So I thought," said Rogerio as he guided Saint-Germain into the anteroom to his bedroom. "I am going to remove your jacket and your shirt." The room was shadowed, being on the north side of the building, and the windows still shuttered against the brightness of the day, and Rogerio made no attempt to change this.

"Carefully," Saint-Germain admonished him, wanting to sink into the nearest chair and knowing that he must not. "Bed," he murmured; he needed the annealing presence of his native earth in the chest upon which his bed was made. Sitting on the chest, he could feel the first anodyne touch of his native earth seep into him; stoically he permitted Rogerio to remove his jacket and, more gingerly, his shirt. "Ruined," he remarked as Rogerio dropped the white silk into the hamper.

"So is the jacket," said Rogerio.

Now that his skin was exposed, Saint-Germain almost shivered, although he was rarely cold; in a remote part of his mind he knew this was a sign of shock. "Fetch a blanket," he made himself say, then lay back, allowing Rogerio to pull a blanket from the closet over him as far as his bleeding shoulder. At first this made no difference, but then the combination of the blanket's warmth and his native earth combined to shield him from the worst of his shock.

Rogerio left Saint-Germain for a short while, going to the makeshift laboratory in the third suite; he opened Saint-Germain's chest of medical tools and medicaments and selected three small, specialized knives not unlike scalpels, and put them into a neat, metallic container that began to hum as soon as he closed the lid. Then he took two vials of heavy glass filled with various substances and fitted with glass stoppers, closed the chest and locked it, retrieved a stack of bandages and a sling from the shelves near the inner door, picked up half-a-dozen sheets of spongy cotton, then hurried back to Saint-Germain.

"Do you . . . have everything?" Saint-Germain asked, his eyes opening a little.

"I think so," said Rogerio; he opened the writing desk and set out all he had brought. "I'll get distilled water from the kitchen and I'll be ready."

"Good . . . I'm weakening," Saint-Germain told him as he closed his eyes again.

"I'll get this over as soon as possible. I'll need your help," said Rogerio, and went to the kitchen for the distilled water. When he returned, he could see that Saint-Germain's pale olive skin had an ashen hue. He forced himself to be methodical, setting out his instruments and putting all he would need in proximity to Saint-Germain. As soon as he was ready, he went to the side of the bed and gently touched Saint-Germain's hand. "My master?" he asked in the Latin of Imperial Rome. "I will have to begin."

"I'm almost . . . ready," Saint-Germain answered in the same language.

"It is going to be painful," Rogerio warned, looking at the sluggishly oozing blood on his shoulder; the wound was a messy one, with bits of wood and fabric embedded in it, and would require careful cleaning.

"I expect so," said Saint-Germain through clenched teeth.

"Can you tell me where the bullet is?" Rogerio asked as he reached for the knife with the slight curve in its blade.

"It's lodged just . . . behind my . . . right scapula, about a . . . a thumb-joint below . . . my clavicle . . . go between the . . . deltoid . . . and trapezius." He took a long, unsteady breath. "Both of them . . . must be torn."

"There's a fair amount of damage," said Rogerio at his most neutral. "The trajectory seems fairly straight, and the entrance not too badly torn."

"Nothing as bad as . . . the road to . . . Baghdad," Saint-Germain said with a rictus smile.

"No, nothing like that," Rogerio agreed, and brought up the little knife. "I am going to start now." The low light did not particularly bother him, and his hands remained steady as he began to probe for the bullet, listening for Saint-Germain's instructions as he proceeded. Finally he located it, and reached for the small tube that contained four tiny grapplers that could extend to take hold of the bullet and help to remove it. The process was slow and painstaking, and Rogerio was constantly aware of the pain he was causing Saint-Germain, though the Comte remained doggedly silent. Rogerio went on with meticulous care, removing all the bits of cloth and wood he encountered even while he tried to locate the bullet; he did not bother to apologize but kept at his work with steady purpose, his hands as steady as a glass-carver's. Once he had the bullet out, he took care to remove all the fragments of cloth and wood that he could find, wiping each of these on the remnants of Saint-Germain's shirt, and then sluiced the wound first with the distilled water, then with the contents of one of the vials, absorbing the blood and other matter with one of the spongy cotton cloths. "I am almost finished," he told Saint-Germain.

"Good," Saint-Germain muttered. "You know . . . what to do."

"I'll make sure the wound is as close to closed as it can be made; I will put bandages to hold it in place; then I'll bind the wound. You'll have to wear a sling for a month or so." He had the bandages at the ready; at least, he thought, he did not have to stitch the wound closed. That would have been hard to take just now.

"I'll do . . . it," Saint-Germain said, sounding exhausted.

"And," Rogerio went on as he began to wrap the shoulder with broad strips of linen, "it will not heal immediately."

"But . . . it will heal," said Saint-Germain, and let himself drift off into a dreamless state that was more than slumber and less than unconsciousness. When he wakened, a single light burned on his writing desk and he had been given another blanket to keep warm. The carriage clock on the single large chest-of-drawers indicated that it was 3:49, and the silence of the night made the ticking of the clock loud by contrast. As he took stock of his surroundings, the injury that had sent him to bed came back to him in vivid detail. He attempted to rise, and was stopped at once by a bolt of agony that went through him like a hot iron. Lying back down, he tested the bandages that enveloped his shoulder and crossed his chest, trying to determine how incapacitated he was. He was deciding that this was not as bad as he had expected, when he realized that he was not alone in the room.

Rogerio rose from the chair he had pulled in from the sitting room, anticipating Saint-Germain's need of assistance. "You're awake."

"In a manner of speaking," said Saint-Germain, waving him back.

"I reported the incident to the police. I told them you had received private care here, since there was shooting in the streets." He had been reading the newspaper, but he now set it aside. "According to *La Revista del Cádiz,* nine people were killed and twenty-six wounded in yesterday's outbreak of gunfire."

"Did they say who is responsible?" Saint-Germain asked, unable to keep a degree of cynicism out of his question.

"'Unknown groups of anti-military insurgents,' according to this; the usual diatribes about Basques and Communists," said Rogerio, putting his hand on the paper. "The editor is calling for a stricter enforcing of the laws, and more severe punishment to those who are caught causing public mayhem," he added.

"In other words, he is playing into the army's hands." Saint-Germain used his right hand to pinch the bridge of his nose. "Is that the sum of it?"

"There is also a long piece on General Franco," said Rogerio. "You would find it interesting, I think."

"Oh? What does he say?" Saint-Germain knew Rogerio well and recognized this remark as an indication that there was more to the article than was immediately apparent.

"More of what he has been saying all along," Rogerio told him. "But what he does not say is particularly interesting."

Saint-Germain closed his eyes. "I'll have a look at it in the morning, when I wake up."

"Do you want more sleep?" Rogerio asked, relieved to hear this.

"Want it or not, I need it," he said, preparing to drift off again. "And remind me: tomorrow I must spend some time . . ." He yawned.

"Some time?" Rogerio prompted.

"What?" Saint-Germain blinked. "Oh. Yes. Some time finding out who ordered me shot, and why." With that, he let his attention fade as sleep overcame him again.

TEXT OF A LETTER FROM DRUZE SVINY OF ECLIPSE AEROPLANO INDUSTRIAS TO ESTANISLAO MENENDEZ Y MORRO.

> 729, Calle de las Piedras
> Córdoba
> 11 May, 1936

Estanislao Menendez y Morro
Mininsterio de Carretera
Departamento de Desarrollo
Madrid

My dear Señor Menendez y Morro,

I have in hand your inquiry of 29 April, and I have read it over carefully. As acting Chairman of Eclipse Aeroplano Industrias, I am willing to answer your questions, except those that I deem unsuitable by reason of confidentiality, which I am legally required to maintain. I am sure you understand, and will not intrude further into such issues as those I cannot and will not now answer, and I thank you for respecting my decision, and honoring the obligation under which I make it.

First, as you must know, Eclipse Aeroplano Industrias is well-funded. You have access to banking records, and all transactions regarding this company have been subjected to the usual scrutiny. But let me assure you that should Eclipse not sell another airplane for two years and continue its production at the current rate, the company would not be in financial trouble for at least four years. I think you will agree that this is adequate for the projected output of this plant. Additionally, as you have certainly found out, the company is privately held by Ferenc Ragoczy, le Comte de Saint-Germain, who is a registered resident alien, just as I am, and who has been most careful to observe all governmental regulations imposed on the airplane industry since he acquired Eclipse Aeroplano Industrias. No doubt you can find the specific terms of that agreement in public records, along with the articles of incorporation.

How much has been paid can be found out from a careful inquiry into the banking arrangements that were part of the purchase of the business. You need not get such information from me, unless you suspect fraud; if that is the case, I would require a subpoena to release our records as part of your investigation. I cannot confirm any link with Eclipse Shipping for the same reason.

Your question about the use of our planes for surveys I can answer. Of course the airplanes can be used for such work. In fact, the Scythian can be fitted with cameras for the purpose of filming newsreels and motion pictures from the air. The cost of this adaptation is minimal, and depending on the number of airplanes ordered, can be adjusted to your advantage. The Moghul is not as versatile, but can be fitted out with cameras as well; it has the greatest carrying capacity of our present models, and as such, may be the most potentially versatile of our airplanes. The Spartan is not adaptable for cameras, but it can be given pontoons for water landings.

I am not at liberty to divulge the reasons for the dismissal of Señor Lundhavn; I am not certain he was dismissed, for there is a letter of resignation in his file which presupposes he left voluntarily. If, as you say, he has accepted employment in Germany, you may have hit upon the reason for his leaving here, for undoubtedly the Germans are offering excellent salaries to engineers. I can propose no reason why he should not be granted permission to accept the offer of work, for all the designs of Eclipse Aeroplano Industrias remain here with us, under the terms of our contracts with the company.

How can you ask that this company divert our work from that which we are chartered to do? We could lose our business license if we fail to produce airplanes for nonstrategic use: you are as aware of the terms of our corporate grants, and you must know we are under specific mandate regarding the use of our airplanes.

It would be improper for me to provide you with our production schedule without the express permission of le Comte de Saint-Germain. I doubt he would refuse to tell you what he has arranged in that regard, but the information must come from him, not from me, or any other employee of this company. I will be pleased to forward your request to him if you would prefer I do so.

None of our employees have been the subject of governmental scrutiny, at least not to my personal knowledge. If such inquiries have been made, no part of the investigation has been revealed to me. Your interest in le Comte de Saint-Germain is well-known in this office. If suspicion has fallen on any other men, or upon me, I am unaware of it; if there is any such inquiry being made, I ask you to make a formal statement of such probes to this office as soon as is convenient for you.

Our test pilots are not currently available to train military personnel to fly reconnaissance missions in our airplanes, nor do I think you would find their techniques appropriate. If you would like to interview them, I ask that you arrange to do so through this office so that even the appearance of duplicity is avoided.

There are no plans at present to develop a new model of airplane, so your questions in that regard have no significance. However, if you mean to ask if we are able to develop new models, then I must tell you that of course we are. This company has five of the best airplane-design engineers working in western Europe, even with Señor Lundhavn gone. Our staff is second to none; le Comte has made it worth their while to work here, and unless the government should force a change in company policy, I cannot believe that you will find any other designs superior to ours.

In the hope that this will allay your fears and promote a cordial relationship between Eclipse Aeroplano Industrias and the government,

I remain

Most sincerely,

Druze Sviny

Acting Chairman
Eclipse Aeroplano Industrias

～

DS/jp

chapter five

"I still can't believe I'm actually leaving tonight," Doña Isabel said, not looking directly at Saint-Germain. "I must thank you again for arranging for me to lease that fine house fairly near London. Does it have moors and heaths? When next you have contact with the owner, tell him I am grateful to him." She was dressed for the theater, in a long, drapey, sleeveless and backless silk dress the color of poppies; a fox wrap was negligently thrown around her shoulders—although it had been quite warm during the day, there was now a brisk wind off the Atlantic, and besides, the fox set off her lovely arms and back to spectacular advantage—and she carried a small, beaded bag worked in an Egyptian motif of jackal-heads. "It is Solita's night off and she will not come until after siesta tomorrow. I should be well out of España by then."

"The servants know you're going out tonight, don't they? And they know it's likely that you will sleep well into the morning." Saint-Germain wished he had thought of some other way to get her safely out of the country, but the ships were very closely watched and the trains could be stopped anywhere between Cádiz and the French border. "It is unfortunate that we must employ such a ruse, but better a little deception and you safe than prolonging your danger."

"I feel foolish, resorting to this ruse to leave the country. It's like a bad motion picture." She managed a frangible smile for a long moment, then looked away, fright catching up with her again.

Saint-Germain reached out his hand to her. "I am sorry." The action made his half-healed wound ache but that hardly mattered to him now.

"Oh, don't be. I am grateful that you are willing to do so much for me. So you have nothing to be sorry about: there is no reason to be. You aren't to blame for the hostilities, are you? You didn't begin them, and you cannot stop them. You needn't apologize for helping me." She did her best to look brave and very nearly succeeded. "I didn't have to leave—I might have decided to remain here, mightn't I?"

"Yes, you might have done that," Saint-Germain said, a tinge of dubiety in his voice.

She pursed her lips. "You are the most infuriating man, Comte," she said in mock frustration. "Of course I cannot remain here, not with everything I do subject to scrutiny."

He made a gesture of apology. "I am sorry it came to that."

"Oh, don't be. Without your warning, who knows what foolishness I might have committed? Most of my friends think I am indulging in histrionics when I tell them all that has happened in the last month." She pressed her perfectly made-up lips together. "You said I would have to be careful because my mail might be being read, and it was. You said my telephone calls were being overheard, and they were. You said they would question my servants, and they did. They questioned Solita twice. How dare they? As if I could do anything disloyal to España, or if I were, that I would tell my maid about it. They have subjected me to indignities that I wouldn't demand of a felon. Having my letters read! Yet I feel as if I am a criminal, and I'm not. *I'm not!*" She turned her back on him and strove to gain control over her emotions. "They did the same to you, too, didn't they?"

"Yes." Saint-Germain took a turn around the sitting room. Old-fashioned gaslights provided the illumination, golden and glowing; the very modern furniture with the Egyptified decor seemed shockingly futuristic in this gracious traditional chamber. "If it helps you, I don't think you're being foolish, or overly dramatic: you are in danger—there are those who would stop you if they suspected you wanted to leave."

"Is that why you're driving me to that secret airport of yours? So no one will know I've left?" She wanted to be playful but ended up feeling forlorn; her mouth trembled and she pressed her hand to her lips to stop it.

"That is part of my plan, and it is known that we're going to the theater tonight. Who would guess that you are going to be on your way to an airplane journey while the audience is sitting through the last two acts," said Saint-Germain. "A diversionary tactic, attending the theater, to throw our followers off the scent, and that should buy us an hour or so. We'll watch the first act and then we'll depart, after the second act has begun. This will probably mean speculation about us, but that is preferable to being dogged by spies. I've already told Rogerio to let it be known that I'll be away for a few days, and that, too, will buy you some time."

Her laughter was more brittle than amused. "You must have anticipated everything."

"I have some experience in these matters," he said, and thought of Franksland and Fiorenza, of Russia and Saxony, of India and China, of Baghdad and Shiraz, of the Viceroyalty of Peru and Spain, of places forgotten or never recognized that he had flown, as he would shortly fly España again. How many times he had been forced to escape in his forty centuries! The memories might have overwhelmed him if he had not been giving his attention to Doña Isabel. "At least you have a little time. You will not be entirely without resources. The transfer from your bank went through without difficulty; fortunately your husband transfers monies all the time, so yours attracted no particular attention. Your goods will arrive in England in a week or two. The ship left yesterday afternoon, the crates addressed to the house. I think you'll like it; Copsehowe is a lovely old manor, and Briarcopse is a beautiful little village, Tudor and Georgian for the most part. The villagers are a bit insular, as are most English villagers, but they will find a Spanish woman, especially one so young and beautiful as you, a prize. You will not be ignored or neglected, nor will you be imposed upon: the Earl of Copsehowe keeps a house in London where his grandson lives; his two sons died in the Great War. The Earl himself is in a nursing home, for he is quite old. His grandson, Peter—who acts for him in all his business now—has no interest in Copsehowe, preferring to raise his family at their London house, and so Charles and his grandson are both glad to find a tenant for it."

"You say the lease is for twenty years," Doña Isabel said, although she knew the answer; she was comforted by reviewing the arrangement, as if that made her future more definite. "Isn't that a long time?"

"Yes, it is, but it can be to your advantage: Peter Whittenfield, Charles' grandson, suggested the terms himself, to encourage a long tenancy; my solicitor handled all the arrangements, and will carry out any dealings you need to undertake about the property," Saint-Germain answered, hoping to reassure her. "You also have the option of buying the property once you have lived there a decade, or any year thereafter until the twenty years are up. You may decide you want to remain there, and if you do, it would be prudent to buy the place." He smiled at her, hoping to lessen her apprehension. "You won't have to live in isolation; you can motor to London in little more than two hours, and there are four trains daily to Victoria Stati—"

"I only wish this weren't necessary," she exclaimed. "If you hadn't been shot, I would never have considered leaving. But that bullet—" She stopped, staring at his right shoulder as if she could make out the fading pucker of his injury beneath his elegant dinner jacket and pin-tucked silk shirt. "I hate it that you were hurt."

"I know," he said.

"That scar is a constant rebuke to me," she said in a muffled voice.

"It needn't be," he said gently. "You did nothing to cause it."

"You can't be sure of that." She shook her head slowly.

"In another three months it will be gone," he assured her.

She shook her head. "Not a wound like that."

He touched her cheek, and held her eyes with his. "It will be gone," he repeated; every injury he had received since he first came to his present life had left no marks on his body.

"I don't like leaving you here; Ponce will be furious when he learns I have gone, and he will blame you if he learns anything about what you've done," she admitted. "I feel ashamed of myself for abandoning you when you are risking more than I am."

"Don't fret on my account, Isis. I am making arrangements of my own. I'll let you know as soon as they're completed what I have done." He took her hands and drew her close to him. "I will miss you, querida."

"And I you, Comte; but I think it would be best for you to leave España, just as I am doing. We are at war, no matter how unofficially, and it is only going to get worse; it is becoming more evident with each passing day. Say what they will about seeking peace, the generals want war and they intend to have it. Isn't there another house in Hampshire where you could go? It would be wonderful to have you as a neighbor." She pressed her head against his shoulder. "How could they have allowed things to get so out of hand?"

"Because they—both sides—believe it will secure them an advantage, or assuage their fears," said Saint-Germain with sudden weariness. He had heard such promises more times than he could easily recollect, and he had seen the same results in every case: ruin, misery, famine, destruction, displacement, and devastating loss. He would have stroked her hair, but it was sleekly and carefully coifed, held in place by two elaborate combs, and he did not want to disarrange it, so he caressed the nape of her neck instead.

"I can't see how. Shooting people in the street. Blowing up buildings. Bombing villages. What are they thinking?" She had summoned up her indignation to bolster her flagging spirits and was now sufficiently outraged and frightened that she became embarrassed.

"You are sensible to go now, before there is more escalation of trouble." He felt her shudder against him. "It isn't easy to leave your native earth: no one knows this better than I. You have courage, Doña Isabel."

Her laugh was shakily close to tears. "How can you say so? I feel as if I were made of aspic." She moved back from him. "I shouldn't be so restive, should I? I'm going to be safe soon, thanks to you: at least you have been willing to help me. Ponce has done nothing, just nothing. So far as he is concerned, I might remain here until the country is in flames. In fact, he may hope I will burn with it."

"Perhaps he's afraid," Saint-Germain suggested.

"Everyone's afraid," she said, dismissing this.

"And I cannot dispute that," he said, then offered her his left arm for support, adding in his most urbane manner, "Shall we go?"

"We will arrive early," she said.

"So much the better. People will see us and remember that we were at the theater, which is what we want them to do." It was awkward to open the door for her, but he managed; he escorted her across the lanai that served as the house's inner courtyard, then out to the street where the Minerva waited. He settled her into the passenger seat, then went around to the driver's side and slid in.

"I can't believe I'm leaving for good," she said, tittering nervously. "Nothing so much as a toothbrush with me."

"Then don't think about it," Saint-Germain recommended as he pressed the starter and engaged the choke. "I have a Gladstone bag in the boot that will carry you through the next day or so. It has a heavy woolen coat as well as your puce suit and your ivory organza blouse, along with shoes, underwear, silk stockings, and toiletries you may need. I also took the liberty of purchasing mascara and lipstick for you, and a small flagon of scent; I thought you would like to have them."

She gazed at his profile. "How providential you are," she said at last, and sat back against the padded leather.

In a short while the engine was humming, and he turned on the headlights, put the handsome automobile in gear, and started down the street toward the center of the city and the cluster of buildings devoted to public use. Cardinal among them, El Teatro de las Artes Clasicas was a splendid structure, about seventy years old, and beautifully maintained from its nineteenth-century baroque columns to the bas-relief of dancing Muses over the main entrance. It boasted seating for 984 persons and three tiers of boxes all of which faced a cavernous stage that was the largest in the city. Tonight the resident company was performing *Juana la Loca*, a new play about the unfortunate sixteenth-century mother of Charles V and grandmother of Felipe II; it dealt with her obsessive passion for her dead husband, casting him as a malevolent character bent on her destruction. The work had already generated a great deal of controversy, which had resulted in an extension of its run.

"I love this place," Doña Isabel said wistfully as they drew into the car park behind the theater. "I'm going to miss it."

"No doubt; it is your home," said Saint-Germain as he turned off the engine and set the hand-brake. "But there are theaters in London, and the ballet, and the opera. You will not have to languish."

"So you say," she rebuked him lightly. "My English isn't very good. I may not be able to follow the performances."

"I imagine you will discover new friends to explain them to you," said Saint-Germain as he got out of the auto and went around to help her from her seat. "You are an attractive woman of intelligence and charm with much to recommend you to anyone. You'll have willing escorts in no time."

She smiled up at him winningly. "You are so reassuring, Comte."

"Thank you," he replied, and bowed over her hand before securing the door behind her and offering his arm to her for the walk along the side of the theater to the broad steps in the front, where the first of the evening's crowd was beginning to gather under the festive lights that adorned the elaborate facade. He took the tickets from his inner breast-pocket and presented them at the door.

"The second floor, the third box on your left," said the bored usher, and gave his attention to the next patrons coming into the building.

"Conspicuous seats," Doña Isabel whispered as they headed for the grand expanse of the stairway.

"So I hope. It is to our advantage to be seen. Let us stop in the gallery above; I will order champagne to be delivered to our box." He smiled slightly. "That will also make it seem we will be here all evening."

She lifted her hand to her lips as if to remind him of their precarious situation. "Don't."

"No one is listening," said Saint-Germain as they began to climb the broad curve of the stairs. "If we converse as the rest do, we'll be safe for now."

"But—" She did her best to look amused but there was a shine of fear in her eyes. "There are . . . you know . . . *listeners* everywhere."

"So there are, but not in this theater, not yet. The audience is too sparse—spies stand out in thin crowds. In fifteen minutes, yes, we will have many persons mingling with the audience who are not here to see the play; just now, we are safe enough. You may speak freely, but softly." He nodded to a stocky man in a well-tailored dinner jacket who was leaning on the gallery rail above them. "Buen' anochecer, Señor Gusanavispa."

"Buen' anochecer, Conde," the man replied. "A pleasure to see you."

"And you." The two men exchanged half-bows and Saint-Germain continued on toward the bar, murmuring to Doña Isabel, "He will tell everyone that he saw us tonight. Be cordial to him."

Doña Isabel inclined her head to Señor Gusanavispa, saying quietly to Saint-Germain, "He's a friend of Ponce's."

"I know," Saint-Germain responded and put his attention on the bar at the far end of the gallery. "Do you want something to eat?"

She shook her head. "I don't think I could keep it down," she confessed. "Champagne will be sufficient."

He squeezed her fingers with his free hand. "As you wish: champagne it will be."

"How can you be so . . . so nonchalant?" she asked him, astonished at his composure. "Surely you must know that what we're going to do is perilous."

"It is a sensible thing to be; most of the audience is nonchalant, and we wish to be part of them," he said, and raised his voice a bit. "Champagne for Doña Isabel," he ordered, and saw one of the waiters at the bar jump to obey.

"French?" the man asked.

"Of course. The best you have. Set it up in the box before the play begins." He took a roll of banknotes from his pocket and peeled off three of them. "This should cover the cost and leave something for you, as well."

"Comte," whispered Doña Isabel, flattered and embarrassed by this display.

It was a handsome sum; the waiter grinned and pocketed the money. "Where are you sitting, sir?"

"Third box on the left," Saint-Germain told him, and held out his ticket-stub. "Two glasses and a plate of canapés."

Doña Isabel plucked at his sleeve. "Comte . . ."

"You may find you want a bite to eat, later on," said Saint-Germain, and bowed slightly to an elderly couple in elaborate formal dress a decade out of style.

There were more than twenty men and women in the gallery, most of them eager to see one another and to exchange the latest rumors of the day; the buzz of their conversation echoed through the ornate corridors and over the expanse of the lobby. Doña Isabel looked about, half-curious, half-apprehensive. "Do you think there are going to be military men here for the play?"

"Certainly; very high-ranking ones," said Saint-Germain without any loss of equanimity. "It is a grand occasion."

"Doesn't that trouble you?" she whispered.

"No, it reassures me," he said. "Don't fret, querida. It is to our advantage to be seen and watched just now."

"Do you think they won't notice when we leave?" Her question was urgent.

"No; I am going to half-draw the curtains on the box, and it will be assumed we are having an assignation, and when we leave—if anyone should notice—everyone will believe that we are going to indulge our passion. I am sorry to have to impugn your reputation, but I suppose it is better to have gossip circulating than to be arrested." He lifted her hand to his lips and added gallantly, "I am the envy of half the men here tonight, I think."

She accepted the compliment with a practiced smile. "You needn't offer such fulsome praise, Comte. I may be nervous, but I know how to hide it."

"That was never my concern," said Saint-Germain, and turned to greet the formidable Señora Acerespada and her two handsome daughters.

Doña Isabel did her best to enter into the spirit of the evening, but it was an effort and by the time the chimes rang to summon the audience to their seats, she was feeling exhausted. "I don't know what's wrong with me: I hope I can stay awake," she whispered to Saint-Germain as he guided her to their box.

"I'll wake you when it's time to leave," he said, nodding to another acquaintance who was en route to a box farther on along the corridor.

"You would, wouldn't you?" She stepped into the small chamber and found an ice bucket with a bottle of champagne in it waiting for them; two flutes stood on the minuscule table, a plate of canapés precariously balanced on the edge of it. "I'd almost forgot about this."

Saint-Germain pulled the door closed and tugged one of the curtains half-way across the front of the box. "Sit down, Doña Isabel. Let me pour you a glass of champagne."

"You won't have any, will you? You never do." She expected no answer and got none as she chose the seat on his left, and sank into its brocaded embrace with real appreciation. "This is very comfortable."

"Then make the most of it," he recommended as he loosened the guard on the champagne cork, took it off, and gave the cork a single, expert twist. He eased it out of the bottle and poured out the pale, foaming liquid into one of the flutes. "Here you are," he said as the houselights began to dim.

She took the flute and sipped at it once, watching Saint-Germain as he put the bottle back in the ice, then sat down as the theater hushed. The champagne was very good; it lightened her heart just enough to make it possible for her to enjoy the performance. On impulse she took one of the canapés as the curtain rose on the court of Charles V. By the end of the act, she had eaten all but two of the delectable tidbits and was on her third glass of champagne, though she hardly felt its effects at all. Over the welling applause, she said, "It's engrossing, isn't it? And well-written."

"It has a certain appeal," Saint-Germain answered, and poured more champagne for her. "This will have to be the last: we will be leaving in half-an-hour."

"The intermission is twenty minutes," she said, a bit disappointed, for they were often longer.

"And ten minutes after the second act begins, we will leave," he reminded her.

Doña Isabel's face changed, taking on sad purpose. "Yes. Of course. As you say, once the play resumes, attention will be directed elsewhere." She brushed imaginary crumbs off her skirt and adjusted her fox wrap. "I'll be ready." She struggled to keep her smile bright, then gave it up and drank half the champagne in her flute. "I'll be ready," she repeated as if to convince herself.

"Do you want to stroll in the gallery? Or visit the rest room?" He had risen and was looking out into the theater, where a rush of conversation had begun.

"I suppose I should, but I don't think I can. I might start weeping, or who knows what," she said, and finished the champagne. "I probably shouldn't have any more of this." Her stare revealed her unslaked thirst.

"If you would like some, you have only to tell me. There is a third of it left," he said, and took the bottle from the ice.

She shook her head. "No. We're going to be on the road soon and I don't want to be too much the worse for drink."

"It is going to be a long night, and you're nervous," he warned her. "You may want to nap along the way."

She considered this, and held out her flute. "Just a little more, then," she said, watching him pour.

"Enjoy it," he recommended as he put the bottle into the ice bucket again. "Once we leave, we will not stop until we reach our destination, unless the army decides otherwise."

"Where are we going?" She had not dared to ask this until now, and it took all her courage to speak. "You don't have to tell me."

"We are going to meet an airplane. It may be just as well if I don't mention the place, in case we are stopped." He looked directly at her, his compelling gaze holding her entire attention. "I will tell them we are bound for Sevilla."

"Sevilla," she repeated. "I'll remember."

"When I return, I will leave the Hotel della Luna Nueva and move into a house on Avenida de las Lagrimas. I will supply you with the address when you arrive at Copsehowe. I have received permission for the move already, so there should be no difficulty." He gently brushed her cheek with his fingertips.

"So many changes," she murmured. "And we're going to Sevilla."

"Um." He sat down again. "Have you ever been in an airplane before?"

"No, I haven't," she admitted. "I've always wanted to, but that's not the same as doing it. Do you think I'll enjoy it?"

"You may. You may not," said Saint-Germain, who disliked flying only slightly less than he disliked traveling by boat. "It is fast. Much faster than dirigible."

"It's exciting, I should think, being up in the air, with the clouds all around you." She put her flute down and sat a bit straighter. "I'll be ready," she assured him a third time, then lapsed into uneasy silence that lasted until the chimes rang for the second act.

He reached out and laid his hand reassuringly on hers. "You have no reason to worry about me, Isis."

"At least you've stopped calling me Doña Isabel," she said, trying to hold her emotions at bay, for she was afraid they would overcome her if she gave them opportunity.

The curtain went up, sparing Saint-Germain the necessity of answering her; the two of them allowed themselves to be captivated by the action on the stage until, ten minutes later, Saint-Germain moved his chair back and rose. "Come; it's time to go."

She looked up at him, a bit startled, and swallowed nervously. "Of course," she said with a sangfroid she did not feel. "I'm ready," she insisted, although now that the moment was upon her, she was not. Clutching her beaded purse as if it were a life-belt, she followed him out the door, hearing the soft snick of the latch as if it were a clap of thunder, utter and final.

The waiters were not at their stations on the gallery, and there was only a single usher near the door as they descended the sweep of the staircase. Once outside the theater, Saint-Germain led her to the Minerva and helped her into it, taking a lightweight lap-rug from the backseat and spreading it over her knees. "It's going to be chilly once we get on the road. You can wrap up in this."

She pulled the lap-rug about her. "Thank you," she whispered.

Saint-Germain got into the Minerva, pressed the ignition, and adjusted the choke, waiting as short a time as he could before putting the automobile in gear and heading out onto the street. "It is going to be a long night, Isis. Sleep if you can."

"All right," she said; she huddled down in the seat trying to find a comfortable position; much to her surprise, in half-an-hour she was dozing.

They left Cádiz without incident and swung onto the road to Sevilla; there were few autos on the highway, and only two lorries, their headlights standing out against the darkness in long cones. Dust sprayed up from their tires obscuring the road ahead much as a bank of fog would do. Saint-Germain kept at a steady, moderate speed, and in three hours was almost alone in the vast expanse of the night. Six kilometers from Sevilla, he turned southeast toward Utrera, onto a narrow, unpaved lane that wandered between fields. "We haven't much farther to go."

"Good," murmured Doña Isabel, and yawned.

"Go back to sleep," he recommended, skillfully avoiding a series of potholes the size of bathtubs.

"Your Minerva will get damaged on such a road," she murmured in a tone of real regret; she shifted in the seat but could not bring herself to sleep. She looked out at the shadowy landscape. "Is it far to go from here?"

"It is roughly two kilometers," he said.

"Roughly. Yes, roughly," she said, glad of a little amusement. She took a deep breath. "How long will it take me to reach London?"

"Well," Saint-Germain said, "you will fly from here to Burgos, where you will refuel at my airfield there; you will not leave the airplane at Burgos. If possible, no one should see you. As soon as the pilot is ready, you will fly on to Nantes, where refueling has already been arranged. You will change clothes and have breakfast there, and then you'll go on to London, and should be there shortly after noon, if all goes well." He wanted to reassure her, but was aware that she would not be consoled by anything he said just now.

"Noon. So quickly," she said. "Less than twelve hours."

"If all goes well," he reminded her; he was worried about Burgos, with its soldiers and spies, and the increasing tension of a region about to burst into war, but he decided to make no mention of it, for she would become more anxious than she was if she knew there could be trouble ahead. He had filed the appropriate forms for a test run of the new Spartan Type 30, and he hoped that would ensure a minimum of fuss with officials.

"Yes. Of course," she mumbled as she pulled the lap-rug higher up her chest. "It's getting cold."

"And the airplane will be colder still," he reminded her. "Take the lap-rug with you when you get aboard." A dip in the road demanded his full attention on his driving, and so he did not quite hear her remark. "Pardon?" he said as the way smoothed out.

"I think I should call someone, just to let them know I'm safe," she said.

"Do that when you reach London. Send telegrams to all your friends," he suggested. "You will be safe then, and you'll be able to be more candid than you can be here in España."

"But—" She stopped herself. "You're right; you're right. I'll wait until I am out of the country. It seems craven, but I know it's the sensible thing to do."

"Good." He gave her a quick smile.

She huddled into the lap-rug. "I hope so."

He reached over to touch her shoulder. "I know this is hard, querida. Being forced out of one's home is never pleasant."

She was very still. "No," she said at last. "It's not."

He reduced his speed, knowing his turn was not far ahead. "We're almost there."

"Oh." She had to quell a frisson of apprehension. "So soon."

"It's almost one in the morning," he said, turning off onto a single-lane track that led off to the east between two fenced fields, one of which lay fallow, the other bristled with corn. "Hold on," he warned her as he turned into the fallow field at the open gate in the fence. "Look. There. Up ahead. You can see it, under the lights." A single airplane stood at the far end of the field near a small shed where two large bulbs blazed.

"Oh. Dear," said Doña Isabel, one hand to her cheek.

"That's our new Type 30 Spartan," said Saint-Germain. "Two engines, seats six," he went on. "This model has improved speed, or so we hope. Your flight will demonstrate whether or not the engines are indeed faster than the Type 29." He pointed to the man emerging from the shed. "The pilot, Raul Telas. He'll be taking you to London."

She stared through the windscreen with new intensity. "How old is he?"

"Twenty-six," said Saint-Germain, and braked to a halt.

"Isn't that young?" Doña Isabel asked, though she was only five years older than he. "He has so much responsibility."

"He's very experienced. Flying is a young man's work, Isis." Saint-Germain turned off the engine.

"When do we leave?" asked Doña Isabel.

"As soon as we get you and your things aboard." He opened the door, stepped out, and went around to the boot, removing the Gladstone bag before he went to help Doña Isabel out of the automobile. "Take my arm."

Raul Telas was coming toward them. "Comte. You're here promptly." He slapped the front of his leather aviator's jacket. "I'm finishing my supper. Would you like some broiled pork?"

"No, thank you," said Saint-Germain. "Here is your passenger." He brought Doña Isabel up to the wide runway that ran the length of the field.

"A pleasure," said Telas, staring appreciatively at Doña Isabel. "I'll be ready in a few minutes. I'll let down the stairs."

"Thank you," said Saint-Germain.

"Yes," Doña Isabel echoed. "Thank you."

Telas trooped over to the airplane and pushed the release, then stood aside as the stairs dropped down with a section of the side of the airplane. "There. Go aboard. Take any seat you like. They're none of them fancy, and there's not much to choose among them. There's a small chemical toilet, if you need to use it." He laughed at Doña Isabel's look of dismay. "It is a real improvement. In the old days, we had to carry cans."

Saint-Germain helped Doña Isabel into the airplane, ducking over in the small cabin. "You'll be comfortable enough sitting down," he said as he put the Gladstone bag on the nearest seat. "If you want the coat, you should take it out now; Telas will stow the bag in the compartment between the cockpit and the cabin."

"Yes. The coat," she said distantly. "I'd like that." She still held the lap-rug, and she looked about for somewhere to put it. "Should I keep this with me?"

"Certainly," said Saint-Germain. "Anything that will make you comfortable." He guided her to the seat across from the one where he had put the Gladstone bag. "Tell me, do you want something to drink on the flight? Telas will have a jug of tea. It won't be very hot, but it will be yours to drink."

She closed her eyes for a long moment. "So tell me, Comte, will you come to see me in England?"

"I may," said Saint-Germain. "We shall see." He helped her fasten her seat-belt, then kissed her forehead. "I have put my solicitor's card into the pocket of your coat; he's expecting to hear from you as soon as you arrive in London. If you need to reach me, he will always know where I am," he said as he opened the Gladstone bag and pulled out the heavy iris-blue coat of fashionable cut; he handed it to her. "Use it as a blanket if the lap-rug isn't enough."

"You've anticipated all my concerns," said Doña Isabel.

"To the best of my ability," said Saint-Germain, and stepped back to the door. "Bon voyage, Isis. Have a pleasant flight." Saint-Germain climbed down from the airplane and turned toward the shed, where he saw Raul Telas hurrying out, a small valise in his hand, a peaked cap on his head at a rakish angle. "Send a telegram from Burgos and one from Nantes," he told the young pilot.

"I will. I have your instructions with me," he said, hefting the valise as if offering proof. "I'll make a full report when I return." He laughed. "I've never been to London before. Would you dislike it very much if I spent the night there? I'd like to have a look at the place while I'm there."

"If you like," said Saint-Germain as Telas reached the airplane and got aboard, closing the drop-down door behind him. In a matter of minutes the two engines had sputtered to life and the Spartan Type 30 began to taxi to the farthest end of the runway before sprinting down the hard-packed earth and rising into the night, eclipsing the brilliant display of stars. The Spartan wheeled to the north, gaining speed and altitude. When he had lost sight of the airplane, Saint-Germain went into the shed and turned off the lights.

TEXT OF A LETTER FROM MILES SUNBURY OF SUNBURY DRAUGHTON HOLLIS & CARNFORD IN LONDON TO FERENC RAGOCZY, LE COMTE DE SAINT-GERMAIN, IN CÁDIZ; WRITTEN IN ENGLISH.

SUNBURY DRAUGHTON HOLLIS & CARNFORD
SOLICITORS AND BARRISTERS
NEW COURT
CITY OF LONDON, ENGLAND

29 June, 1936

Ferenc Ragoczy, Comte de Saint-Germain
Avenida de las Lagrimas
Cádiz, Spain

My dear Comte,
I am pleased to inform you that Doña Isabel Inez Vedancho y Nuñez has taken up residence at Copsehowe, in accord with the terms agreed upon with Peter Whittenfield, and that she has declared the arrangement to be to her satisfaction, although she has arranged to have three of the rooms repainted, a request well within the contract with Whittenfield. In accordance with your instructions, I have arranged for Doña Isabel to have protection around the clock, although I still believe you are being overly protective of the lady; she may have been in danger in Spain, but I would be astonished to learn that she faced any threats here in England. Hampshire is not Catalonia. Still, your instructions were specific and I have put them into action just as you specified: two men who are ostensibly gardeners and occupy the gatehouse of Copsehowe are retired army officers with experience in intelligence work. They keep watch over Doña Isabel and make notes on all comings and goings from Copsehowe. I must tell you that they, too, believe such precau-

tions are excessive, but they will keep at the work as long as you are willing to pay for it. I have paid them out of your miscellaneous account, in accord with your orders, and will continue to do so as long as you would like, and are satisfied with the terms of their employment.

Your own house in London is still kept ready for your occupancy; I have, in the last year, retained three new servants to occupy the house and maintain it for you. Your previous servants had reached the age of retirement, and have accepted your very generous pension. Your new housekeeper is Ernestine Bell, your steward is Desmond Reeves, and your cook is Hilary Shoemaker; Mrs. Shoemaker does not live in, Mrs. Bell and Mr. Reeves do; Mr. Reeves' wife is also in service, and spends the night with him at your house, an arrangement that has proven satisfactory. Mrs. Bell is a widow with a ten-year-old daughter who lives with her aunt and uncle in Gloucestershire. I am enclosing copies of all their recommendations and references for your files, and copies of the terms of the pensions you have provided for your former staff.

I am also enclosing four brochures, as you asked, on airlines flying across the Atlantic, along with their schedules. If you decide to undertake such a journey, I would be pleased to purchase tickets for you from here, in order to avoid questions in Spain, as I take it you wish to do. Tell me your preference and I will comply.

I have arranged the transfers of funds you have requested, one to the Credit Lyonaise office in Avignon, one to the Bank of America in San Francisco, California. I have included the certificates of transfer as per your instructions. I hope I will have the pleasure of seeing you in London, although I suspect that you are once again going to Montalia in Provence. Your dealings with the vintner in California continue unabated, and are finally beginning to show the promise of profit. My father thought it Quixotic of you to support such a venture during the time alcohol was illegal in the States, but now that they have rescinded that absurd law, you stand to do very well by your investment; you chose well when you took on that enterprise, there can be no doubt about that now.

You have expressed concern for your airplane company, and I share that concern. I would be remiss if I did not tell you that you may be forced to give up control of your company. I do not know if I can do much to prevent any claims the Spanish government may make upon your manufactory, but if you authorize me to undertake a suit, I will be willing to find counsel for you in Spain, and work with that advocate to protect your interests to the best of my ability.

If there is anything more you require of me, you have only to inform me of it and I will do my utmost to carry out your wishes.

Most sincerely at your service,

Miles Sunbury, Esq.

MS/jnp
enclosures

chapter six

Your waxwork is ready," said Rogerio as he came out of Saint-Germain's study in the house on the Avenida de las Lagrimas. "I have your camera set up as well." He was beginning to show signs of strain as he looked across the room to the two trunks waiting to be carried down to his automobile.

"I'll take the photographs," Saint-Germain told him. "And I'll process them as quickly as possible. It will be enough to get us the visas we need." He paused. "It is inconvenient to be unable to leave an image more precise than a smear on film."

"You have remarked on the hazards of the present age before." Rogerio did his best to smile, but his strain was evident in the pull of his mouth. "This is just another one."

"So I have, and never have I felt it as I have these last few months. To be under constant scrutiny in such a way that not even the Emperor of China or the Doge of Venice—let alone the Inquisition—could have imagined in the past; it is most disquieting. Binoculars at the window, interceptions on the telephones . . ." He started toward the study. "Give me an hour-and-a-half. Then I'll carry down the trunks; I'll make it seem they're empty, in case anyone should see us at this time of night."

"Do you think it's wise to leave at such an hour? Mightn't it look suspicious?" Rogerio was keenly aware that they were still under observation by various government agencies and the military.

"We have permission to travel, and it makes sense to go as early as possible, given how hot the days are. Burgos is a long drive," he reminded Rogerio. "We have a meeting there, and the bureaucrats know it. But it will be best to be cautious." He was quiet for a long moment, then added, "Once we're there, we will know how best to proceed."

"So I hope," said Rogerio.

"The military wants my airplanes," Saint-Germain said with annoyed determination. "If I must surrender them, I intend to do it with as much protection as I can warrant. I will not be complacent about this, no matter how much the army may wish me to be."

"So I understand," said Rogerio with a hint of exasperation in his manner. "It is probably no longer in your hands." This reminder made both men uncomfortable.

"You're right," Saint-Germain allowed after a short pause. "All the more reason to leave while we can."

"So, if you will take your photos . . ." Rogerio said in a tone that made it clear he would not question anything Saint-Germain had decided to do.

"I will," said Saint-Germain, and went into the study where he set up his waxwork, taking care to adjust the wig to conform to his present haircut; he adjusted the shirt and jacket to look more natural; then he put this against a plain, light turquoise background and lit it as most official photographs were lit, snapped four photos of it, shifting the position of the waxwork a little each time, hoping to achieve an illusion of animation. Satisfied, he took his film into his small laboratory that also served as a darkroom, rolled up his sleeves, donned protective gloves, poured out the chemicals under the glare of a red bulb, then went to work developing his film. He was pleased with the results; the waxwork had cost him a fair amount of money, made by Madame Tussaud's best image-makers, but it was worth the price in these photograph-driven days. He made several copies of the four photographs in a number of sizes, then cleaned up his laboratory and stepped out into the study to dismantle and pack the waxwork, which, disassembled, fit nicely into a small steamer trunk.

Rogerio came into the study. "I have packed the Voisin, as you ordered. Are you sure you want to leave the Minerva here?"

"I would rather not, but it is the prudent thing to do; it gives the illusion that we are going to return—that, and your Voisin handles bad roads better than the Minerva; we will certainly have to use bad roads," said Saint-Germain with a slight chuckle as he slipped his photographs into a manila envelope. "I am going to assume the military has read my letter to Charles Whittenfield, and will take it to mean that we will be here for a while yet." He shook his head once. "I hate having to use old acquaintances for such a ruse, but I doubt he will mind."

"If he understands at all," said Rogerio.

"There is that," said Saint-Germain sadly. "Do you have your copies of your photos?"

"In my valise." He looked at the small trunk containing the waxwork. "You're taking that with you?"

"Of course. I will undoubtedly need it again, and it isn't the sort of thing I want found. It would create too many suspicions." He rolled down his sleeves and reached for his jacket of black, tropical-weight wool. "Did you put in the containers of extra fuel? We're likely to need it before we're out of Spain."

"Yes. They're in the boot." He lowered his head for a moment. "It is sad to go."

"It is," Saint-Germain agreed, going on in a kindlier tone, "Possibly more so for you—this was your home."

"Two thousand years ago," Rogerio pointed out. "Gades is long-gone. Cádiz is as foreign to me as Lo-Yang."

"Still, you may feel a pull," said Saint-Germain as he prepared to carry the small steamer trunk down to the courtyard.

"That is more for your blood than for me," said Rogerio. "What do you want me to bring?"

"I have two leather suitcases in my sitting room. If you'll fetch them?" He was already at the door.

"Yes." He went toward the hallway, turning off the lights as he reached them. Slipping into Saint-Germain's sitting room, he picked up the two suitcases and turned out the reading-lamp on the small desk. The house was beginning to feel empty already, so he turned the light back on, to give the appearance of occupancy. He went down the rear stairs, pausing at the door to the kitchen to put the door keys onto one of the hooks, where the cook would find it in the morning.

The Voisin stood near the back door, its boot and one of the rear doors open. The auto was fairly well-laden, the various chests and cases tied down and braced, the small steamer trunk set in the boot. Rogerio put the suitcases in the backseat and pulled a strap across them, securing it under the seat so it would not shift. He closed the door and went around to the passenger side, where he stood waiting. When Saint-Germain reappeared, he had one of the large chests in his arms; this he worked into the boot, then closed the lid.

"Is everything in place?" Saint-Germain asked.

"I think so," said Rogerio. "If you have your chests of native earth and your other supplies, we should be ready."

"Then there is no reason to wait," said Saint-Germain.

"It is a pity to give up an entire year's lease on this house," Rogerio remarked, looking back at the building.

"A small price to pay for the protection it provides us," Saint-Germain said. "With the lease paid in advance, the military will assume we're returning, as our travel plans would indicate. If they thought we were leaving, they would take steps to stop us."

"Are you certain of that?" Rogerio asked, then answered his own question. "Yes, I know. Colonel Senda has been busy, and as soon as Eclipse Aero is taken over, you will be arrested and held as a suspicious alien, just as those five Italian engineers have been."

"They've almost vanished," said Saint-Germain, "for no reason more than they designed ships' hulls."

"The generals have uses for ships," said Rogerio bluntly.

Saint-Germain nodded. "As soon as I heard about the Italians, I knew it was time to go. Thank all the forgotten gods, I heard about it almost as soon as it happened."

"They have kept it out of the press," said Rogerio.

"Another ominous indication," Saint-Germain agreed.

"Yes, it is," said Rogerio. "Are you carrying your pistol?"

"No, of course not. All the army would need is an excuse to detain me, and then I would be in prison for who knows how long." He suppressed an inward shudder at the recollection of the various cells he had occupied over the centuries. "You don't have one, do you?"

"No," said Rogerio regretfully. "But there is one in the compartment behind the rear seat, the hidden one. There are cartridges for it as well." He looked directly at Saint-Germain. "In case we need more than money and words."

"We are taking a chance," said Saint-Germain.

"Always," Rogerio concurred. "At least it doesn't look deserted," he decided aloud as he looked back at the house.

"I left four lights on," said Saint-Germain as he stepped into the driver's seat. "And there is the lamp at the kitchen door."

"I left one," said Rogerio, doing his best to contain the apprehension he felt.

"Very good," said Saint-Germain as Rogerio got into the Voisin; the engine rumbled to life and warmed up quickly. Saint-Germain released the hand-brake, eased the clutch into first gear, and drove out of the courtyard onto the Avenida de las Lagrimas. When he reached the first cross-street, he turned on the headlights and turned south toward the main road out of the city.

"Do you think the military will believe you have gone to Montalia?" Rogerio asked when they were safely beyond the limits of Cádiz.

"I hope so. I'm doing my best to make that the logical conclusion," said Saint-Germain as he turned onto the road leading to the main highway to Sevilla, Madrid, and Burgos.

"And you think they will be satisfied?" Rogerio could not contain his uneasiness.

"They may or may not be; that doesn't concern me just now." He looked at his wristwatch. "We should be at Sevilla shortly after dawn. A pity we can't go through Córdoba, but that would be reckless."

"You intend to go to Mérida from Sevilla, and then on to Madrid," said Rogerio, repeating what they had decided two days ago.

"Yes. At Sevilla, you can take over driving; I'll get into the boot for the duration of daylight." He gestured to show that this was acceptable to him.

"I still worry about what could happen—it is so hot during the day, and the boot is an oven," Rogerio remarked.

"I'll lie on my chest of native earth, and we have rigged those two air-screens. I shouldn't be too uncomfortable." He sounded more convinced than he was. "If we have to break our journey, we should do it in Toledo; we don't want to spend any more time in Madrid than we must. There is too much military activity around Madrid."

"We're agreed on that," said Rogerio.

They went on for another ten kilometers in silence as the eastern horizon began to glow; in half-an-hour the sun was rising. Saint-Germain pointed out a sign indicating five kilometers to Sevilla. "I'm going to pull over and get in the boot."

"A good idea," Rogerio seconded. "Once we reach the city, someone might notice and wonder why such a well-dressed man wants to ride there."

"You're worried, old friend; not that I can fault you—I am, too," said Saint-Germain as he pulled out into a small lay-by where a single lorry was parked. He pulled the brake on and put the gears in neutral. "Are you ready?"

"I think so," said Rogerio, opening his door and going around to the rear of the auto; he opened the boot and waited for Saint-Germain to get in. "If you become too hot, you know the signal."

"I do," said Saint-Germain as he ducked his head and climbed into the boot, atop the large chest of his native earth. He took the inner latch and pulled the lid closed.

Rogerio waited a moment, then went to the driver's side, got in, and put the Voisin in gear as he released the brake. Soon he was barreling down the road into Sevilla, his faded-blue eyes narrowed against the brilliant morning sun; he kept unobvious watch on everything around him. He passed more autos and horse-drawn carts as he entered the city where the first activities of morning made the streets crawl. Four times he passed armed soldiers in lorries, and he felt a twinge of apprehension; he drove steadily on, and, to his surprise, he was able to motor out of Sevilla without being stopped. An hour later, he purchased fuel at the village of Huelva, then went on toward Mérida, where he saw half-a-dozen lorries filled with armed soldiers drawn up at the side of the road; they watched all the vehicles passing, as if searching for a particular auto or person. He did not stop for siesta, pressing steadily on while many autos and lorries pulled off the road; with the highway all but empty he was able to increase his speed to one hundred kilometers per hour, making a great deal of progress by the time traffic again picked up as the day waned. At sundown, they were four hundred kilometers from Cádiz and Rogerio was beginning to feel tired. He pulled off the highway near Mijadas and went to open the boot.

"Ah. At last," said Saint-Germain as he climbed out; he brushed his clothes, smoothing out the wrinkles he found. "It was not as bad as I feared it might be."

"Are you . . . uncomfortable?" Rogerio asked.

"If you mean, am I hot, the answer is yes. But I am not baked. I have certainly endured worse. The air-vents helped a great deal. It was certainly preferable to riding in direct sun." He gave Rogerio a steady gaze. "I am grateful to you for your concern."

Rogerio put down the lid of the boot and locked it, then handed the key to Saint-Germain. "We'll need more petrol soon. We have only one full spare container left."

"Then I will look for a station; they usually have pumps at the post offices, and a few of the general stores," said Saint-Germain. "Has there been any difficulty?"

"I haven't been stopped," said Rogerio. "But I have seen soldiers in lorries and autos on the road. More than I expected to see," he added.

"Not a good sign," said Saint-Germain. "We'll need to be more alert." He got into the Voisin and looked at the fuel gauge. "We can always use that extra petrol we're carrying, but I would prefer not to do that until we're beyond Burgos. In fact, I'd like to fill up our extra containers again."

"I understand," said Rogerio, getting into the passenger seat.

"If you want to rest, go ahead; I'm quite refreshed." Saint-Germain put the auto into gear and rolled onto the highway. "Thank goodness España doesn't fold its tents once the sun goes down, as so many northern countries do; it's still too hot to sleep." He managed a quick, wry smile. "We should be able to purchase fuel in Talavera de la Reina, which is up ahead."

"My thought as well," said Rogerio, leaning as far back as the seat permitted. "I may rest my eyes a bit."

"A fine idea," said Saint-Germain cordially as he switched on the headlights and drove eastward into the dusk, keeping a good speed until the outskirts of Talavera de la Reina, when he came upon a barricade across the highway manned by soldiers. He pulled into the rear of the line of waiting automobiles, carts, motorcycles, and lorries, taking his travel documents from his small leather portfolio on the seat beside him; Rogerio continued to drowse, not quite sleeping but far from awake, apparently unaware of what was happening at the barricade. Slowly he advanced to the inspection point, watching all that transpired ahead of him; by the time he arrived at the front of the line, he had seen four vehicles—

two lorries, an auto, and a motorcycle—pulled over and taken away from the road, which struck him as ominous.

"Name?" The officer in charge snapped out the question as Saint-Germain rolled down his window.

"Ferenc Ragoczy, le Comte de Saint-Germain," he said, handing over the small portfolio. "My documents."

"Not Spanish."

"No, not Spanish," said Saint-Germain.

"Um," said the officer, holding up a grimy lantern to read the various authorizations and permissions. "You have a private airfield near Burgos?"

"My company does," said Saint-Germain carefully.

"You have two houses, I see: one in Cádiz, one in Córdoba." He made this sound like an accusation.

"Yes. My assembly plant is in Córdoba. I have other business interests in Cádiz." He made his answer flat and to the point.

"But you are not Spanish." He reiterated as if confirming something nefarious. "Where do you come from?"

"My home is far from here, in the Carpathians. My passport, as you can see for yourself, is Hungarian." Saint-Germain gave a little diplomatic cough. "I am no longer wholly welcome in my native land."

"Many of you aristocrats from the East have battened on the West; you stole from your own people and live on the spoils," the officer said condemningly.

"Many have, more's the pity. Yet, I believe I have not been so ungrateful to this country," said Saint-Germain. "My businesses are approved by the government."

"For the time being," the officer muttered. He held the portfolio for a short time, staring down at the various documents in it. "Who is with you?"

"My manservant. You have his passport there, an Italian one; you will see that it is totally in order." He made no effort to tell the officer that Rogerio had been born in España. "Rogerio has been with me a very long time."

"And you think that is something to be proud of?" The officer regarded him, his lip curled in scorn.

"No; I am thankful for such loyalty," said Saint-Germain with utter sincerity.

"Huh!" the officer scoffed. Then, abruptly, he handed it back to Saint-Germain. "Well. Everything seems to be in order. Drive on."

Saint-Germain took the portfolio, saying, "Muchas gracias," then did as he had been ordered, noticing in the rearview mirror that the auto that had been in line behind him was pulled over and the occupants removed at gunpoint.

"Trouble?" Rogerio asked without opening his eyes. "I listened."

"Indeed. As to the trouble, we'll have to wait to find out," said Saint-Germain, putting his attention on the street ahead, for he was now entering Talavera de la Reina and saw soldiers everywhere; most of the population remained indoors, those few on the streets were either outrageously reveling or careful and furtive, avoiding the soldiers who gave the streets the appearance of an army camp. "I think we had best not stop here," he remarked as he heard the rattle of gunfire nearby.

"On to Madrid," Rogerio said dryly. "As soon as possible."

"No. Not Madrid. Not with the military already spreading through the country. If Talavera is so filled with soldiers, Madrid will be worse, and more dangerous because of it." Saint-Germain began to read the various road-signs as he passed them. "I think we'll take another way. There is a road to Escalona. If you will look for it?"

"Escalona. Certainly," said Rogerio, sitting up and beginning to take notice of the activity around them. "This is very troubling."

"Yes, it is," said Saint-Germain as he reached the Plaza de Santa Maria de las Estrellas, where a small sign pointed the way to Escalona. He made the turn, pausing to let a squad of soldiers cross the plaza in front of him. "They are getting ready for something."

Rogerio peered down a side-street where the first bright streamers of fire were beginning to rage. "We'd best leave here soon."

"My thought exactly," said Saint-Germain, and continued down the street toward the road to Escalona. "Let us hope we can depart without incident."

"Are you expecting an attempt to stop—" Rogerio began, stopping himself before he said too much.

"I am trying to expect nothing," said Saint-Germain as his memories crowded in upon him. "I want to keep my attention on what happens now, not what might happen."

"Just as well," said Rogerio.

Saint-Germain said nothing, but there was a glint in his dark eyes that warned Rogerio that his master was in a state of heightened awareness. Finally, as they left Talavera de la Reina behind, he relaxed a little. "A discouraging turn of events."

"The army being in Talavera?" Rogerio asked.

"The whole of it. I thought it would not escalate so quickly. I suppose the generals are becoming impatient." He sighed and drove awhile in silence. "If you will watch for a place we can purchase fuel?"

"I have been doing," said Rogerio. "How much do we have left?"

"A bit less than a quarter tank," said Saint-Germain, glancing out the window to the mountains rising sharply on their left. "I doubt there are any villages off this road that would have petrol to sell."

"Most won't have petrol at all," said Rogerio. "I think San Juan el Monje is up ahead. There is a post office there."

"I hope we're not too late," said Saint-Germain.

"It's not quite midnight. We should be in time," said Rogerio. "I hope there aren't so many soldiers." He looked down at the portfolio. "We may have to pay a high price."

"That is no problem," Saint-Germain said. "The banknotes are in the map-pocket on your seat. There's enough there to fuel half-a-dozen airplanes."

"Weren't you worried the soldiers might find it?" Rogerio inquired, trying not to sound worried.

"No. If they had taken us from this auto, money would have been the least of our problems." The line of his mouth was grim.

Rogerio nodded, then pointed. "San Juan el Monje. There are some lights burning."

"Any sign of soldiers?"

"None that I can see," Rogerio answered carefully.

"Then we'll see if we can buy some petrol. The post office should be in the central plaza," he said calmly. "If there is fuel in this place, it will be there."

"We'd best buy as much as we can," Rogerio said, worry in his voice.

A few gaslights shone to mark the central plaza; at the east end stood the old church of San Juan el Monje; to its right was the Officina del Pueblo; to the left were the post office and bank, which then became an arcade for shops and eating establishments. A pair of soldiers stood in the plaza where a few late-dining citizens were lingering in an outdoor café; the soldiers kept a casual eye on them, then turned their attention to Saint-Germain as the Voisin came into the plaza and rolled toward the petrol pump in front of the post office.

One of the soldiers ambled over to the petrol pump and put his arm around it. "You looking for something, señor?"

"I am," said Saint-Germain.

"And would it be petrol for your auto?"

"It would."

The soldier smiled without any humor. "If it is fuel you want, it is under the control of the army."

"I am prepared to pay," said Saint-Germain.

"How can I ignore my orders, señor?" the soldier asked in mock dismay. "You expect me to make an exception of you?"

"I think you wouldn't turn down a great deal of money," said Saint-Germain.

"A great deal of money?" the soldier echoed. "What would that be?"

"Do you know what gold coins are worth?" Saint-Germain asked.

The soldier laughed. "You cannot tell me you would pay gold for petrol."

"I would, if you want gold."

"How will I know the coins aren't base metal with a thin coating?" The soldier wagged a finger at him. "There are many offering such counterfeits."

"What would you consider, then?"

"Oh," said the soldier with exaggerated nonchalance, "I don't know. Suggest a sum."

"Do you want pesetas as bills, or old-fashioned reales?" Saint-Germain kept his voice level.

The soldier looked about as if he were afraid of being overheard. "Reales? You have them?"

"They are gold coins," Saint-Germain reminded him.

"But stamped and . . ." His voice trailed off. "How many reales will you pay?"

"For a full tank of fuel, and two full extra containers, five reales," said Saint-Germain, who, a century ago, had paid that amount for a superb Andalusian stallion.

The soldier swallowed. "Is this a joke?"

Saint-Germain pulled the coins from his pocket and held them out for the soldier to see. "Examine them. Satisfy yourself that they are genuine."

With trembling fingers, the soldier took the five gold coins. "Heavy," he remarked, and bit one of them, not knowing what it should reveal but aware that it was proper to bite gold. "I suppose these must be genuine."

"They are," said Saint-Germain, who had made the gold and poured the ancient molds himself, a month ago.

"A goodly amount." The soldier regarded Saint-Germain with avaricious speculation.

"I must reach Burgos in time to show the army a new airplane my company makes," said Saint-Germain without any outward indication of the anxiety he felt. "I am expected there, so it is worth extra money to me to be timely."

The coins clinked in the soldier's hand. "Five gold coins."

"For a full tank of petrol, and two containers," said Saint-Germain, "you may have them."

The soldier continued to stare at the coins in his hand. "All right," he said at last. "But I could simply keep these and order you to go along."

"Yes, you could," said Saint-Germain. "But you are a man of honor." There was no suggestion of sarcasm in his voice.

"That I am," he said, and cranked the pump. "You will have to fill it yourself," he announced.

Rogerio got out of the Voisin. "I'll attend to it," he said, and went to take the nozzle from the soldier. He filled the tank as quickly as the pump would allow, taking care not to look directly at the soldier. When he was done, he thanked him and got back into the passenger seat.

"Where are you bound, again?" the soldier asked.

"We have authorized passage to Burgos, as I told you," said Saint-Germain.

"A long way. Perhaps you should rest for the night." There was a crafty angle to his brow now, as if he had hit upon another way to get more riches from this stranger.

"Thank you, soldier, but we still have a way to go tonight, I fear." He put the auto in gear.

"There may be fighting ahead," the soldier warned.

"Thank you for telling us," said Saint-Germain before he rolled up the window.

"Don't blame me if you're stopped again!" the soldier yelled after them.

A short distance out of San Juan el Monje the road ran parallel to an old railway line; Rogerio relaxed a bit as the tracks and the road began to rise into the hills. "They usually maintain roads that give rail access," he said after a few kilometers of silence.

"They also make excellent targets," said Saint-Germain, a frown beginning to accent his brow.

"Surely you don't think there will be an attack at this hour," said Rogerio. "It's almost midnight."

"I think anything is possible," said Saint-Germain. "There is so much at stake, for all the sides in the conflict."

Rogerio nodded sadly. "But out here, in the mountains, what would be the point?"

"There is always intimidation," said Saint-Germain, and slowed down as he caught sight of a peasant in a goat-cart on the road ahead. "What do you think?" he asked Rogerio.

"A farmer who stayed late in town," said Rogerio as they came abreast of the goat-cart.

"Or a partisan carrying weapons to guerillas," said Saint-Germain. "The cart is empty but the goat is straining."

The peasant paid no attention to the auto; he stared ahead as if completely unaware of the Voisin and the men in it.

"It has been a long day; the animal is tired," said Rogerio, no longer as certain of this as he was a moment before.

"Perhaps," said Saint-Germain as they left the goat-cart behind. "I hope the soldiers don't find him, whatever the case. They might not be willing to leave him alone." He shifted gears and picked up speed once more.

By dawn they had reached Alcobendas; they sought out a repair shop where Saint-Germain purchased and replaced two tires, commenting as he did, "The roads are very rough, here in the countryside."

"Yes, señor, they are," said the mechanic who changed the tires. "Pray God they do not improve, or my children will starve." He grinned.

"Then I will also pray that no one will improve the tires," said Saint-Germain sardonically, as he paid him and tipped the man ten pesetas for his work.

"Gracias, señor," he said, nodding acknowledgment. He wiped his hands on a tattered bit of toweling and added, "If you are going far, they say there is trouble in Basque country."

"There is always trouble in Basque country," said Saint-Germain, recalling how Karl-lo-Magne had made just such a complaint, and the Visigoths before him.

"No; real trouble. The army is going after them, they say." He crossed himself. "A bad thing."

"Yes," said Saint-Germain, preparing to help roll the Voisin out of the repair garage.

"The fighting gets worse and worse; they promise each fight will end it, but then there is another one and it never stops," the mechanic said, and took the other side of the car to push it outside to where Rogerio waited. "You don't want to be caught in it."

"Truly," said Saint-Germain.

"You were wise to buy fuel now, as much as you can. You may not find any as you go north," the mechanic told him. "You could be left by the side of the road if you did not fill your tank now."

"I would prefer not to be," said Saint-Germain. "And I appreciate your warning."

"It is my privilege, señor," said the mechanic. "If you are thirsty or hungry, there is an excellent cantina in the next street. My brother-in-law runs it." He winked at Rogerio as if he knew that working men shared a secret unknown to their employers. "You will get a good meal there, and wine at a reasonable price."

"Another time," said Saint-Germain as he opened the driver's door.

Rogerio got into the passenger seat. "Thank you for telling us."

The mechanic shrugged; he had done his best. "As you wish, señor. Buen' viaje," he said, waving them away.

Saint-Germain started the engine and listened to the sound of it. "It's running well," he told Rogerio as they drove out of Alcobendas.

"That's a relief," said Rogerio, his austere features set in stern lines. "We need only concern ourselves with insurgents and soldiers." He did not expect Saint-Germain to reply, and he went on, "Where are we bound now?"

"Lozoyuela," said Saint-Germain. "Then Burgos."

"Assuming all goes well," said Rogerio.

"Yes; making that assumption," said Saint-Germain as he shifted into third gear and began to pick up speed.

Text of a report submitted by Colonel Juan Enrique Senda in
Córdoba to the Secretario de Seguridad Fortunio Morales y Seto
in Valladolid.

83, Calle Arruga
Córdoba
19 July, 1936

Fortunio Morales y Seto
Secretario de Seguridad
La Plaza della Sagrada Corazon
Valladolid

Dear Secretario Morales y Seto,
It is my duty to report to you my discoveries at Eclipse Aeroplano
Industrias, formerly owned and financed by Ferenc Ragoczy, el Conde de
Saint-Germain, and to that end I submit this to you. This is the sum of the
information I have been able to garner in his regard, and I offer it to you.
Ten days ago, this Conde de Saint-Germain left the city of Cádiz. He
had valid travel documents for Burgos, and apparently went there, for
there is a reliable report that he and his manservant were there for the tri-
als on the new design of the Eclipse Aeroplano Industrias' Spartan
airplane, this one with increased range. He watched the whole official tests
of the airplane, and then said he was going to leave for the night. He did
not return the following day, and, from all I can discover, he did not spend
the night at any hotel in Burgos. It is always possible he had friends in the
city, but if so, they have not come forward and he, himself, along with his
manservant, is missing.
It may be that since he was wounded by random gunfire, he has decided
to isolate himself, which is understandable, for he is a foreigner and inclined
to avoid direct conflict. It may be that his injury was more serious than any-
one supposed and he has gone to seek appropriate medical help. He may
have encountered an enemy from his past and decided that it was wiser to
disappear than fight. Whatever the case, his absence is to our advantage just
now, for with the generals finally making their move, we will not want to
have to gain the approval of this foreigner for all we need this company to
provide us. We have only to declare him an enemy of the revolution, and then
claim his business.
The woman presently acting as Chairman of Eclipse Aeroplano

Industrias, a Czech woman named Druze Sviny, who is a mathematician, tells me she has had no instructions from Saint-Germain, either by telegram, telephone, or letter, since his appearance in Burgos. She has no notion of where he can have gone, although she says he has planned to visit a blood relative in Provence, and may well have gone there.

I have busied myself the last four days trying to learn everything that I can about the condition of his company, and, I must say, it appears to be in excellent financial and design health, and the worth of the airplanes has been proven many times. This company is going to be a real asset to the army as soon as we can take possession of it. I have already filed the papers of military acquisition to claim this business as strategically necessary for our eventual triumph over the guerillas who so plague our country. The Junta will need all the support we can provide them: with Cádiz and Seville rising in their favor, we must have victory, and soon.

The various airplane designs that we have seen here may be adapted to military purposes without adding significantly to weight or fuel consumption. I believe there are men here who are willing to stay on and aid us—not all are Spanish, but they live here and have some interest in seeing the country stable once again. I will enclose the names of those I recommend for employment.

I was relieved to discover that Saint-Germain had stockpiled steel and aluminum; this plant can continue to produce airplanes for another ten months at the current rate without requisitioning more materiel, which is to our advantage with the possible shortages we anticipate being part of our coming struggle. These stockpiles are an unanticipated asset, and one that we should make a gesture of recompense to Saint-Germain, to show that it is not our purpose to strip him of his company entirely, for that would be seen as plundering a business, which would not be to our advantage at this time. A settlement for the supplies should soften the blow of our laying claim to this fine manufactory.

The financial records I have seen indicate that this company has been turning a profit for the last two years, and that those profits are increasing, and therefore we will have no debt that we would have to discharge. This, too, is good news. I don't suppose you can authorize any accountants to inspect the books, but from my cursory inspection, you will not find hidden debts or other indications of mismanagement.

If you have any specific information you wish me to provide, it will be my pleasure to comply with your request as quickly as possible. Most devotedly at your service,

Juan Enrique Senda, Colonel

JES/ay

chapter seven

C herbourg was warm and breezy, the morning limpid in its newness. Saint-Germain stood at the edge of the airfield, hatless and shading his eyes as he looked up at the airplane that was coming in for a landing on the private airstrip that was flanked with open fields basking in the rising summer sun. Behind the two, the control tower rose up, topped with an octagonal cupola of glass. "Is that our—" he asked, turning to Rogerio.

"Yes; it is our airplane," said Rogerio from his place by their chests, crates, trunks, and suitcases. "You chartered it and it will carry us to America." If he was disquieted, he gave no indication of it. "You can stay with your native earth all the way."

Saint-Germain nodded, saying apologetically, "I'm sorry to fuss so, but being high in the air, over water . . ." He stepped into the shadow of the control tower.

"I am cognizant of the problem," said Rogerio with a trace of humor. "I have explained that you are terrified of flying, and that you have been given a calmative by your physician so you will sleep for the whole journey. You are so wealthy, the pilot thinks you are indulging a foolish eccentricity."

"And so I am. Clever as always, old friend," said Saint-Germain as the airplane touched down and rolled down the long paved stretch toward the shine of the English Channel, three kilometers beyond the fence at the end of the airfield.

"The pilot and his assistant pilot are both accustomed to dealing with very rich customers—their business depends upon them. They boast of the oddities they have to accommodate; by comparison with some, you are quite tame. He said one of the Rockefellers demanded a half-sized table be brought on, for table tennis, so he and his friends could amuse themselves playing the game all the way to Boston. It was a fairly smooth crossing, so they actually played awhile."

"I shan't need anything so athletic." Saint-Germain patted his pocket. "All our papers are in order, so there is no reason to stay here much longer; once our things are aboard and the pilot is satisfied, we should be ready." He squinted at the sky. "It will be hot before noon."

The airplane turned and started back up the runway toward the control tower and the two waiting men.

"It is a good-sized airplane," said Saint-Germain, studying it with narrowed eyes.

"It has four propellers, and it can accommodate seventy-eight passengers in its usual commercial set-up, but it has been modified for private charter use, with sofas and a lounge in front, and sleeping cabins behind, instead of rows of seats. Very luxurious. You will be accommodated in one of the two sleeping cabins. It's all arranged." Rogerio patted his leather portfolio. "I have everything here. Mr. Dylan has assured me that the pilots have made this crossing many, many times, very successfully."

"Mr. Dylan is the agent for the airline?" Saint-Germain asked.

"Yes; the man Miles Sunbury suggested we contact; his offices are in Paris, but the company is Irish," said Rogerio. "He has been very helpful in making our arrangements."

"I thought I recalled the name," said Saint-Germain, mildly distracted.

Rogerio knew Saint-Germain was growing more nervous—a rare event for him—and wished he could allay his discomfort. "You have survived a month in the hold of a ship; twelve to fifteen hours in an airplane should not be intolerable. The speed is worth the discomfort, or so you've said. You have had a few days to recover from our rapid journey to France, so you are not as exhausted as you were."

"You mean that I visited that young dancer in her sleep, yes; and it did somewhat restore me," Saint-Germain admitted.

"And you're prepared for this journey, as much as one of your blood can be," Rogerio reminded him.

"So I try to tell myself, and I recall other journeys in other times that were more arduous for both of us," said Saint-Germain, coming as close as he would to admitting his unease.

"Truly," said Rogerio, raising his voice to be heard over the roar of the engines as the airplane swung around and came toward them.

Saint-Germain pressed his lips together in thoughtful silence, then said, "You have done very well; I know I have been a trial."

"We have left Spain behind," said Rogerio, "and that is more urgent than any of these arrangements."

"Yes. Spain is no longer safe in any way, not with the turn events have taken.

Still, I dislike having to slip away as I did, but I gambled and lost." He looked off toward the Channel again.

"You got Doña Isabel out," Rogerio reminded him.

"Hardly significant in light of all that has transpired." Saint-Germain shook his head once. "The war is well and truly begun there, and nothing will stop it until one of the combatants has been defeated. The generals are pressing their advances from every garrison. Cádiz is already in their hands, and Zaragossa, and Burgos will be next, and Sevilla, then Barcelona, and then they will take Madrid. And, of course, Eclipse Aeroplano Industrias."

"A foregone conclusion," said Rogerio. "But you have left other things behind in Spain."

"Many times, as have you," Saint-Germain agreed, recalling the past with an intensity that made him wonder if Csimenae was still alive, and if she was, where she was hiding during this latest upheaval.

The airplane halted, the propellers ceased their rotations, and two men rolled out a tall flight of stairs; slowly the door in the side swung open and a young man in a blue-grey uniform stood aside as the pilot, his second in command, and the navigator came down the steps. When they were on the ground, the young man came after them, leaving the door open for the ground staff to deal with the airplane.

"You mustn't worry. The crew will be with you shortly," said the young man. "They are allowed forty minutes between flights to recruit themselves, so they are going to have breakfast. While they dine, the fuel tanks will be filled again, as they were in Paris, and your belongings will be put aboard, and then, as soon as the crew is ready to leave, we will be on our way to Ireland, then on to Newfoundland."

"Very good," said Saint-Germain.

"I'll tend to your needs during the flight. I'm your cabin steward." The young man added, "My name is Ange."

An unreadable expression flickered across Saint-Germain's attractive, irregular features, but all he said was "Thank you, Ange" as the young man continued on toward the ground floor of the tower.

"Is this all you're taking with you?" a man in overalls asked, his French that of Cherbourg laborers, as he and two companions came up behind Saint-Germain. "We're loading up now, while the crew is in the café."

"Yes. This is all of it," said Saint-Germain; his French was educated, with a slight, unidentifiable accent.

"Then we'll put it aboard," said the man, and signaled to the others; a portion of the airplane's belly swung down, giving access to the storage hold.

Saint-Germain stood very still, watching the workers move his bags, chests, and luggage; he said nothing, not wanting to attract too much attention.

The assistant pilot stepped out of the tower, a cup of coffee in one hand, a croissant in the other, to look at Saint-Germain, sizing him up. "I can see you are anxious, but there's no reason to worry. The weather is fine. You'll have a fresh crew; don't worry. We aren't tired after the flight from Paris," he remarked in French, but with an Irish lilt to it, before going back into the lower part of the control tower where the café was located.

"That is our agreement," said Rogerio, although he doubted the man heard him. He looked over at Saint-Germain. "It's a shame you've had to leave so many autos behind."

"Better autos than . . . many other things," said Saint-Germain obliquely. "We have lost much more at other times."

As the loading continued, one of the workmen stopped as he was lifting the last remaining chest onto his dolly. "This is going into one of the sleeping cabins?" he asked, clearly doubting that this could be correct.

Saint-Germain turned toward him. "Yes. Be good enough to put it there."

The workman shrugged. "All right," he said in a tone that showed he thought it was a ridiculous thing to do.

"It is not yours to question what the charter asks, so long as it doesn't endanger the airplane, as we both know this will not," Rogerio said firmly. "You are being well-paid to do this, and you will not debate your instructions."

"Servants are more haughty than their masters," the man declared, and spat before consulting his work-order. "In the second sleeping cabin, then. There won't be much room for you to move around once I put this in place." He shoved the dolly ahead of him and went back toward the airplane.

"He thinks I'm a fool, or worse," said Saint-Germain in third-century Greek. "No matter, so long as he stows the chest in the sleeping cabin."

"He'll do that," said Rogerio. "He wants the bonus promised for obeying instructions. It is enough to convince him to make an extra effort."

"Thank goodness for that, although it will also make him recall us, and where we are bound," said Saint-Germain in French as his gaze followed the workman to the airplane. He paced a short way down the runway, then came back, his features schooled to a self-possession that did not reflect his state of mind. "I am not usually so nervous. I will be less apprehensive once we are under way."

"Yes," said Rogerio.

He stood still for a short while, then managed a rueful smile. "I'm sorry I have been so uneasy. If you can pardon my lapse in—"

Rogerio shook his head. "You have no reason to apologize."

Another silence overtook them, this one more companionable. Finally Saint-Germain said, "I may sit up until we leave Ireland."

"You don't have to," said Rogerio. "If you like, then do."

Saint-Germain chuckled once. "I may have to: I'm still restive, and I may remain so for a while, even after we are in the air."

"That is apparent." Rogerio glanced at his watch. "We have half-an-hour until the crew is supposed to return. Do you want to step into the waiting room now that all our chests and luggage is aboard?"

"That might be best. We'll be out of the sun. There should be newspapers in the waiting room." He lifted his head and squinted up at the sky, searching as if for signs. "Let us hope for a smooth flight."

"Certainly," said Rogerio as he followed Saint-Germain into the small waiting room where three modern sofas made up the furnishings, two of them standard-length, the third noticeably longer. There was a magazine-rack on the far wall and under it an occasional table stacked with newspapers; Rogerio picked up the top newspaper. "Two days old," he said.

"Nothing more recent?" Saint-Germain asked while Rogerio flipped through the stack.

"No; the others are older." He held out the copy of *Le Jour*. "It's Cherbourg. There are two pages of shipping news."

"It will do," said Saint-Germain, taking the paper and beginning to read it. "There are more developments from Germany, I see."

"Yes," Rogerio said as he sat down and selected a magazine.

"The Belgians are worried about Hitler's move to reoccupy the Rhineland," said Saint-Germain as he read. "I would like to hope their fears are unfounded."

"But you don't," said Rogerio.

"How can I? I have seen what the NSDAP have done in Germany, a few short years ago, and they have only grown stronger and more belligerent. They have become so cocksure, it isn't likely that they will rein themselves in." Saint-Germain turned the page. "The Italians are continuing their advances in Ethiopia. Ever since they took Addis Ababa, they have become more and more pugnacious."

"A sadly uneven match," said Rogerio.

"It appears the young Egyptian King may have been able to strike a bargain with the British," Saint-Germain went on as he turned another page. "A sixteen-year-old boy: Farouk. I can recall Pharaohs that young."

"He has much to deal with," said Rogerio.

"That he has," said Saint-Germain, and turned the page again. "There is more speculation about Stalin and his Purge. Poor Russia—the Soviet Union," he corrected himself. "Matters there grow worse by the hour." He put the paper aside.

"Is the news too upsetting?" Rogerio asked.

"There is so much of it," said Saint-Germain, turning back to the front page. "Look at it all. A century ago it would have taken months to accumulate the information in this single edition of the newspaper. Since the telegraph, the telephone, and the wireless, all this has changed, and the news arrives within two days of the events—three at most—to be assimilated over morning coffee." He tapped the pages he held. "The next issue will have as much again, and possibly more. It is the quantity and rapidity of it all that is occasionally . . . overwhelming."

Rogerio kept his opinion to himself, but he studied Saint-Germain closely. "It isn't the news that bothers you; it is something else."

"You know me too well, old friend," Saint-Germain responded after a brief silence. He lowered his head for a long moment of contemplation, then said, "You are right, of course."

"But you will not tell me," Rogerio guessed aloud.

"Not until I have a better understanding of it myself." He shrugged as if making sure he had not offended Rogerio. "I do apologize for my untoward behavior."

There was a tap on the waiting-room door and Ange leaned in. "You may go aboard now, if you like." He glanced down at the clipboard he was carrying. "You made no food selection for your crossing. Is there something you would like to have aboard?"

"No, thank you," said Saint-Germain quickly. "I prefer not to eat while flying."

"So," said Ange sympathetically, "you have sickness in the air."

"Something of the sort," Saint-Germain admitted.

Ange turned to Rogerio, his manner subtly less pleasing. "And you? You have made no selection other than steak tartare."

"That will suffice," said Rogerio. "As simply made as possible. You need not add capers and onions." He could bear to eat a little of such ingredients, but they always gave him indigestion.

"Just pepper and eggs?" Ange asked, clearly disappointed.

"That would be most suitable," said Rogerio.

"And no wine or spirits?" Ange consulted his clipboard again as if he could not believe what he saw.

"No, thank you. I like to keep a clear head while traveling," Rogerio said.

The steward lifted one shoulder in eloquent French indifference. "Then I shall only include what the pilot and crew wish to have. Your steak tartare is in a refrigerated chest and I will be able to serve you whenever you wish." He studied the two men for an intense few seconds, then withdrew.

"Well," said Saint-Germain, resigned. "I suppose we should get aboard." He got to his feet and slowly made his way to the door.

"It might be wise," said Rogerio; he followed Saint-Germain out of the waiting room.

The airplane was parked in the same location, the boarding-stairs pulled up to its side; the drop-door in the underside was closed and only one workman remained near the airplane. As Saint-Germain emerged from the tower-building, he came forward.

"You carried out our orders?" Rogerio asked him.

"Just as specified," said the workman, and blatantly held out his hand. "You owe me my bonus."

"So I do," said Rogerio, and took his wallet from his inner pocket, then counted out the money promised. "One hundred fifty," he said as he laid down the last bill. "It is the amount agreed upon, isn't it?"

The workman folded the money and slipped it into a pocket in his overalls. "Merci," he muttered before stalking away.

Saint-Germain had already begun to climb the stairs, but he paused to stare after the workman. "Not very forthcoming, is he? I wonder what he thinks of all this—so large an airplane, and only two men bound westward."

Rogerio shook his head. "He has his view of the world."

"As have we all," said Saint-Germain, resuming his upward progress. "Never mind. He will boast to his friends how he was able to hoodwink an aristocrat and his unctuous servant, and that will mean more to him than the money."

Behind them, the pilot stepped out of the tower-building and started toward the airplane; he carried a valise and a cup of coffee in his left hand.

"Very likely," said Rogerio, and smiled, his austere features transformed by amusement. "It's what I would have done, when I was first in Roma, had I been given such an opportunity." He made no mention that he was first in Roma during the reign of Nero.

Saint-Germain had reached the top of the steps; he stood for a long moment before ducking into the airplane, where he looked about with a slow, appreciative nod. "Yes. Very well done."

Rogerio came into the airplane. "Just what Mr. Dylan described," he said. "The design has the two sleeping cabins behind the lounge of the airplane, with toilet facilities all the way to the rear."

"Very likely; it is a sensible arrangement, given the room." Saint-Germain went to the longer of the two sofas and patted the full roll of the back. "This is very pleasant; considerably less Spartan than Eclipse Aero's Spartan." The clumsy pun received a wince from Rogerio; Saint-Germain looked abashed. "Sorry for that."

"If it eases your state of mind," said Rogerio, "say anything you like."

"So you will indulge me?" Saint-Germain countered, shaking his head. "I am nervous, but not yet an idiot, I hope."

"Hardly that," said Rogerio.

"Um," said Saint-Germain. "It is necessary that we leave: I am certain of it."

"If only it didn't have to be in the air," said Rogerio, his voice dropping.

Saint-Germain nodded ruefully. "Yes; if only." He stepped around the end of the sofa and sat down. "Comfortable."

"Do you want to see the sleeping cabin?" Rogerio asked. "Or would you prefer that I check it?"

"If you would, please. The workman said the second cabin, didn't he?" He glanced toward the window. "The fields are in good heart."

Rogerio went back to the sleeping cabins. The one on the right was labeled "A," the one on the left, "B"; he opened the "B" door and saw the chest full of earth shoved up against the bed. He stepped inside and pulled the mattress and covers off the bed and laid them on the chest, then set the pillow at the fore-end before returning to the lounge. "All attended to," he reported.

Ange was securing the outer door, and the hatch to the cockpit was standing open.

"The crew is aboard," said Saint-Germain.

"So I gather," said Rogerio.

"Then we'll soon be airborne," said Saint-Germain.

"Off to Ireland," said Ange in fairly good English.

"To Ireland," said Saint-Germain, doing his best not to sound dismayed.

"There are seat-belts in the sofas, if you will use them for take-off and landing; just pull them around and buckle them, not too tight, but enough to hold you in place while we reach our cruising altitude," said Ange, sounding slightly bored. He went on, his delivery almost sing-song; he had given this information so many times before that he no longer thought about what he was saying. "Once we're in the air, you can retire to the sleeping cabin, if you like. The bunks are ready for use. We'll wake you for our landing. We need you seated and buckled in for landings, just to be safe. The rest of the time, provided it isn't stormy, which is unlikely today, you may walk about the cabin or retire to the sleeping cabins, as you wish." His smile was as practiced as it was insincere. "It's helpful for nervous fliers to have a chance to become accustomed to being in the air before they attempt to rest."

"I'm sure you're right," said Saint-Germain, listening intently as the engines revved; in a very short while they began to taxi. "We're under way."

Rogerio smiled his encouragement. "The engines sound excellent."

"Like four well-tuned autos," Saint-Germain agreed critically as he listened more intently. "Just as they should."

Ange all but smirked. "We take very good care of our airplanes. We have our own crews of mechanics on the ground, and we contract directly with the fuel suppliers." He had strapped himself into a jump-seat between the cockpit and the alcove that served as a galley. "The assistant pilot can explain our policies to you after we're in the air, if you like."

Saint-Germain considered the offer. "If I don't take a nap, I would like that."

"He will make it very simple for you," Ange assured him. "Airplanes aren't all that mysterious, you know."

This was too much for Saint-Germain. "He needn't bother. I have—or I had—an aircraft design company and assembly plant in Córdoba; I am familiar with airplane engines and the principles of flight. I am much more interested in how your charter company is run, and how well it has done as a business." His testiness ceased and he went on more urbanely, "I have invested in many shipping companies, over the years, and it may be that a charter service, such as this one, can prove to be another opportunity."

Ange looked distressed, and his polished demeanor slipped a bit. "I didn't mean . . . no disrespect intended."

"None assumed," Saint-Germain said, wholly regaining his composure as the airplane picked up speed. "But in future, don't jump to conclusions so readily. I may be a skittish flier, but I am not unaware of what is transpiring."

"No," the young man said hastily.

The airplane began to rise; thirty meters before the end of the runway, it was ten meters off the ground, aimed directly at the English Channel. The sound of the landing gear being retracted silenced the three men in the main cabin.

"Well," said Rogerio as the land fell away behind them, "a fine day for flying, just as the assistant pilot told us."

"The winds are light," said Ange, "and this is especially good." He unbuckled his seat-belt and stood up. "I have an insulated carafe of coffee. Do you want some?"

"No, thank you," said Saint-Germain.

"Nor I," said Rogerio.

"Then I'll offer it to the cockpit crew," he said, and went to tap on the hatch.

The airplane climbed higher; soon the water beneath them looked like an expanse of blue-green pebbled silk crepe spreading from the green-and-tan expanse of Europe to the greener expanse of England; the Channel Islands were smears on the clear water. Cherbourg melted away behind them into the general smudge of clustered buildings that marked the edge of the Channel. Rogerio looked out the nearest window, remarking, "It is surprising how much the same all the land looks."

"Why shouldn't it?" Saint-Germain asked with a hint of amusement. "It isn't marked in colors or with boundaries; human beings do that. Think how often you have seen frontiers change over the years."

"I wasn't expecting blocks of color," said Rogerio, the corners of his eyes crinkling.

Saint-Germain ducked his head. "I know, old friend. I didn't mean to suggest anything."

"It is your edginess," said Rogerio.

"Yes. Indeed." Saint-Germain fussed with his seat-belt.

Ange came back from the cockpit hatch and said, "If you would like to smoke, you may do so now; it's safe now we're in the air. We should be landing in Limerick in roughly two hours forty minutes. We'll cross over a bit of Cornwall, and then go on to Cork, from there to Limerick, where we will land to take on fuel." He recited this much the same way he might have recited the tide-table.

"Neither of us smokes," said Saint-Germain. "Two hours forty minutes?"

"Possibly a little sooner," Ange replied.

"Then I will stay here in the lounge until we depart for America," said Saint-Germain, and caught a sharp glance from Rogerio.

Ange shrugged. "Suit yourself, Comte." He took a cigarette from a pack in his waistcoat pocket and, after a brief hesitation, took out a lighter and began to smoke.

For the next twenty minutes no one spoke; the engines droned on, steady as a swarm of bees. Ange smoked a second cigarette as if to alleviate intolerable boredom. Rogerio occupied himself looking out the window while Saint-Germain sat as if in a trance.

The cockpit hatch opened and the assistant pilot came out, a cup of coffee in one hand; his peaked cap was worn at a rakish angle. "We'll be crossing over Cornwall shortly. You'll see our progress more easily from the right side of the airplane than the left, if you want to watch." He spoke in English, his Irish brogue even more apparent than when he spoke French. "You do understand me, don't you?"

"Yes, I do," said Saint-Germain in that language.

"Just as well, if you're going to America; most of them talk English," said the assistant pilot. "Rory Yeats, at your service, and no, no relation that I know of."

"To the poet," Saint-Germain guessed.

"The same," said the assistant pilot. "The captain is Dennis McInnis; he's a Canadian, from Halifax—been flying since he was fifteen. He's the best we have." He lifted his cup in salute. "The navigator is Conrade Ensuite, from Rouen. And you've met Ange."

"Yes," said Saint-Germain.

"We'll be with you all the way to Boston," said Yeats.

"I should hope so," said Saint-Germain with a little of his customary urbanity returning.

Yeats laughed. "Good point," he exclaimed. "So far everything looks fine; if there's any change, I'll let you know," he assured them before returning to the cockpit.

"Encouraging," said Rogerio after a brief silence.

"I would expect no less," said Saint-Germain. "It wouldn't be in his best interests to contribute to our apprehensions."

Rogerio knew of old that when Saint-Germain retreated behind elegant vocabulary that he would reveal little of his inner thoughts, so he replied, "No. I should imagine they would like their passengers calm."

"Or possibly comatose," said Saint-Germain. "As soon as we leave Ireland, it is my intention to accommodate them." He closed his eyes as the airplane bounced a bit. "Yes," he said as steadiness returned, "I am sure that would be best."

"It's going to be—"

"Fine," Saint-Germain finished for him. "I know. But I can't rid myself of the agitation I feel. I don't want to burden you with it, but—" He shrugged.

"You have no need to apologize," said Rogerio.

"But I do, you know," Saint-Germain corrected him gently. "And I thank you for putting up with me."

"You can see Cornwall," Ange informed them from the entry to the alcove that was the galley.

"At least it is quick," said Saint-Germain.

"Not like that voyage to South America," Rogerio reminded him.

"Three centuries past," Saint-Germain added. "Not too long ago, all things considered." He pointedly looked away from the nearest window.

"And certainly preferable to the voyages across the Arabian or Black Seas," Rogerio said.

"True enough."

Cornwall passed beneath them, and then Saint George's Channel. Ireland lay ahead, its intense green relieved here and there by the green-gold of planted fields. The engines changed pitch subtly as the airplane began its descent into Limerick.

"Keep your seat-belts buckled until Captain McInnis turns off the engines. If you intend to leave the airplane for any reason while we're refueling, please make sure to tell me where you can be found—we will not be here long."

"I think we'll stay where we are," said Saint-Germain, adding to himself that if he left the airplane he might not want to return.

"As you wish. I am going to get a few meat pies and potato wedges for the Captain and the crew; that and if you've changed your minds, anything you may like to eat?

We can't offer the fine fare of dirigibles, but we don't take as long to get across the ocean, either." He received head-shakes for answers, so he sat on his separate short bench and buckled himself in; the airplane was dropping lower and lower, and the scenery below seemed to be moving faster the closer they came to the ground.

Saint-Germain closed his eyes and fought off the queasiness coiling within him. He sat very still until the airplane had taxied and stopped. As the engines shut down, he opened his eyes and tried to give an encouraging smile. "Very good," he said.

Ange unbuckled and stood up. "I won't be very long," he announced, then went to open the door in the side of the airplane. A moment later, steps were rolled up, and Ange hurried down them; a few minutes later, Rory Yeats ambled out of the cockpit and stepped out onto the landing, his peaked cap shoved back on his head, shading his eyes with his hand. After a short while he sauntered back into the cockpit without stopping to talk to Saint-Germain and Rogerio. There were shouts and bustle as the ground crew hurried to top off the fuel tanks, and just as the flurry of activity began to diminish, Ange returned with a canvas bag held daintily in front of him. The preparations for departure were made quickly and efficiently, and in what seemed to be too brief a time the airplane engines started again.

"Newfoundland," said Saint-Germain as the airplane taxied to take-off position.

"Newfoundland," Rogerio seconded as the airplane began to pick up speed over the ground.

They had just begun to rise into the air when Ange said with elaborate nonchalance, "There was a man, a Spaniard, looking for you. At the airport. He had on a Colonel's uniform. Not bad-looking but much too gruff for my taste."

Saint-Germain did his best to conceal his dismay. "What did he want?"

"He didn't say," Ange reported primly. "But he did say a Spanish court is going to take control of your Spanish businesses. He had some sort of official notification with him, very official by the look of the envelope. It had a seal on it."

"So you talked to him?" Saint-Germain asked, a bit too quickly.

"Just a bit," said Ange. "He knew that your manservant chartered this airplane. I couldn't deny that, could I?"

"Probably not," Saint-Germain told him, his self-possession returning. "Did you learn anything else?"

"Only that you're in trouble about some woman—she vanished after spending the night in your company." Ange's brow went up speculatively.

"Going to England is hardly vanishing," said Saint-Germain.

"Just as you're going to America," said Ange, apparently satisfied with the answer he had been given.

"Exactly," said Saint-Germain as the airplane headed out across the Atlantic Ocean.

Text of a letter from Miles Sunbury in London to Ferenc Ragoczy, le Comte de Saint-Germain, held at General Delivery in Boston, Massachusetts.

SUNBURY DRAUGHTON HOLLIS & CARNFORD
SOLICITORS AND BARRISTERS
NEW COURT
CITY OF LONDON, ENGLAND

22 July, 1936

Ferenc Ragoczy, le Comte de Saint-Germain
General Delivery, Central Post Office
Boston, Massachusetts, USA

My dear Comte,

I have enclosed copies of all transactions I have undertaken on your behalf in the last ten days: I trust you will find that all is in order and done to your satisfaction; if you have any questions, I will be pleased to answer them promptly. I am, in accordance with your instructions, sending this via air mail, special delivery, to General Delivery in Boston, Massachusetts.

The sum of ten thousand pounds (£10,000) has been transferred to the Mercantile Bank of Massachusetts where you will find cheques waiting for you upon your presentation of the agreed-upon identification. Also the amount of fifteen thousand pounds (£15,000) has been wired into a new account for you at the Bank of America (formerly the Bank of Italy) in San Francisco, California, along with another two thousand pounds (£2,000) to the account of Mr. Carlo Pietragnelli of Geyserville, California, at the Bank of America in San Francisco, as per your annual instructions. You will find enclosed the receipt for all three transfers, as well as the exchange rate currently prevailing: five dollars fifty cents to the pound. I could have improved upon that, had I had more time to negotiate; as it is, I took the best rate I could get in the last forty-eight hours.

While I share your concerns over various European currencies, I do not necessarily think that the dollar is much safer than the franc or the lira, given the state of affairs in America. Little as I may like the German regime, I must say the mark is holding very strong, and I would be astonished to see it devalued again for the rest of the decade. The Germans learned a lesson a decade ago, and they're not likely to forget the trouble inflation caused them then. If you wish to transfer more of your wealth to dollars, that is, of course, your decision, but I must say that I would be remiss if I did not advise strongly against it.

I have received the annual report from Horatio Batterbury for Manitoba Chemicals, Ltd. and I am pleased to say that they have turned a modest profit for the second year in a row; I have transferred twenty-five thousand pounds (£25,000) from your development account, as you instructed me to do in 'your telegram of 9 June, and I have Mr. Batterbury's assurances that the company will continue on sound footing.

If you decide to increase your investments while in the United States, let me recommend the services of Messrs. Bradley, Hunt, and Shumaker; they are Wall Street brokers who have survived the dreadful Crash and are still able to do business successfully. They have excellent reputations and their probity is beyond question. I will be pleased to make any arrangements with them you may wish if you would prefer to draw upon your resources here in England rather than transferring funds across the Atlantic.

Also, I can recommend attorneys in Boston, New York, Chicago, Denver, St. Louis, and San Francisco if you find you have need of such services. You will find many American attorneys to be more flamboyant than many English barristers: incidentally, they do not separate their solicitors and barristers as we do, but put all under the blanket of attorneys. They deal with this by allotting specializations to partnerships or members of the partnerships. You may find it confusing at first, but they insist it works as well as our system does. In Boston, Hiram Jaynes of Jaynes Jaynes Fleming & Gries will be happy to serve you; in New York, Morton Putnam of Guilifoyle Avery Putnam Jones & van der Hoovn; in Chicago, J. Harold Bishop of Horner Bishop Beatie Wentworth & Culpepper; in Denver, Willard Powell of Latimer Trace Dawson & Powell; in St. Louis, Timothy McGregor of McGregor Little & Moulin; in San Francisco, Oscar King of King Lowenthal Taylor & Frost. I can personally vouch for every one of these men and their firms. I know you will find them discreet, attentive, well-informed, and meticulous. Each firm has been in business for more than thirty years and has proven its integrity many times over.

I have given your written instructions to your staff here in London, and they will continue to keep your house in readiness for your return. The standards you have set forth for maintaining the house will be strictly observed unless you should amend them in future. I must tell you that your generosity, given the ease of their circumstances, seems excessive, but I will, of course, comply with your orders in this regard, as I have striven to do in the past. I have also ordered the new roof you have requested, with reinforced beams beneath and double-thickness of slates above. In my opinion this is exces-

sive, but, as you have already said, this is your house and it will be fitted out in accordance with your specifications. When the work is completed, I will inform you at whatever address you would like me to use.

With the assurance of my continued dedication to you and your enterprises, I am

Most sincerely yours,

Miles Sunbury, esq.
Sunbury Draughton Hollis & Carnford

MS/jnp
enclosures

chapter eight

It seemed impossible for the pounding to grow any louder; surely the door would break if it kept up one instant longer. Druze Sviny put her square, blunt-fingered hands to her ears to shut out the worst of it, and very slowly rose from behind her desk to make her way across the room to the door. "Stop! I am going to open," she shouted, hoping the soldiers would hear her. She waited two seconds, then turned the key in the lock, and pressed the handle down, allowing the door to swing inward. Warily she moved aside, but not far enough to permit the soldiers to enter easily. From beyond her office, she could hear autos coming into the parking lot, and she feared what it might mean—that Eclipse Aero was finally in the hands of the army. It was almost five in the afternoon of a hot summer day; after siesta, the streets were becoming noisy again as the people of Córdoba tried to hang on to a semblance of normality in their daily lives. Druze knew their efforts and shared them.

Four young men in rumpled army uniforms stood in the corridor, one still holding his rifle up, ready to pound it on the oaken door again; dents and scrapes in the wood showed the hard use the door had already been given. Behind them was an officer, his uniform much neater, his hair well-cut, his nails trimmed, and his manner so disdainful that Druze itched to slap him: she had seen enough of haughty men since she entered the university to study mathematics; the faculty had been full of them, intellectual popinjays all, treating her more like a clever dog than another human being with a gift for numbers. The soldiers regarded the plain, middle-aged woman with faint surprise, as if they were surprised to see her.

"Señora Sviny," said the officer, stumbling over the unfamiliar name and favoring her with a hint of a bow.

"I am Druze Sviny," she said, knowing it must be obvious. She stood a little straighter, not wanting to appear intimidated by the soldiers. "No one else is in my office, and my name as Acting Chairman is on the door."

The officer made a face to express his annoyance at her and her manner. "Naturalmente. The title speaks for itself. So. If you will let us in? We have documents to present to you."

"Of course you do, and you must do your duty," she said with patently false cordiality but not wanting to provide the soldiers with an excuse to be more aggressive. "Do come in." She stood aside and managed not to add another sharp comment to the one she had already made.

The officer entered first, fingering his mustache nervously. "I don't want to make this any more unpleasant than it has to be."

"How considerate," she said as neutrally as she was able.

"I am certain," he said as he motioned his men inside, "that this can be accomplished with a modicum of difficulty." He took an official envelope from inside his tunic and smirked. "This transfers ownership of this company to the Spanish Army. You will see it has been properly signed, sealed, and endorsed. This is a strategic industry, and has been operating in accordance with the regulations set down for strategic industries, but now that your owner is gone, it has been decided that authority over this business must remain in España." He made this recitation as if it had been carefully rehearsed.

"Señor Ragoczy is gone because he is under order of arrest," said Druze sharply. "You know as well as I that he would have been thrown into prison had he remained here."

"Yes," the officer conceded. "He would have been, and no doubt it was a necessary thing to do." He smiled slightly. "We cannot have airplane assembly plants in the hands of foreigners, not at a time like this."

Druze bit her lip, keenly aware that she was as much a foreigner as Saint-Germain was. "What are you going to do?"

"Colonel Roberto Clavel will take over the running of this assembly plant effective tomorrow morning. He has been foreman for an automobile factory, and knows how such things should be run. And Colonel Jaime Manguera will review all designs and assembly specifications in preparation for their adaptation to our purposes." He gave a single nod. "You will be here in the morning to help the transition to this new chain of command, and you will make it your business to encourage the others working here to accept the changes we will institute with a minimum of fuss. España is at war, Señora Sviny, and no one at Eclipse Aeroplano Industrias should forget that." He pointed directly at her, making no apology for this rudeness. "You're said to be a sensible woman. Well, now is the time to keep your wits about you."

"Señor Ragoczy is my employer," she said, maintaining a fierce formality with the officer. "I have an obligation to him."

"Señor Ragoczy, as you call le Comte de Saint-Germain, is a foreigner, already condemned as working against the policies of España. Your obligation to him is over." The officer glared at her.

"So you tell me," she said, doing her utmost to hang on to her fading courage. "But I have a contract with him—"

"It is null and void," said the officer, patting the envelope he carried. "It is all spelled out here. Perhaps you should read it before we go any further in this?" He handed her the envelope and folded his arms. "Go ahead. Read it. Take all the time you need."

She opened the envelope carefully, scrutinizing all the signatures and seals on the outside before she pulled out the six sheets of folded paper it contained; she smoothed the pages flat and began to peruse the documents, doing her best to control her anger and her fear. How on earth would she explain this to Señor Ragoczy? The orders left her without recourse of any kind—she had to turn over the assembly plant immediately, as the orders stipulated, or risk being sent to prison. She read the pages twice, as if hoping the commands they contained might change before her eyes. When she was done, she looked up at the officer. "Are you Capitán Andreas Morales?"

"I am," he said, bowing very slightly.

"It says here that you are to be in charge here until Colonels Clavel and Manguera arrive," she remarked. "Is that your understanding?"

"It is."

"I see also," she went on in a harsher tone of voice, "that you are authorized to confine me to my home or a cell if I do not fully cooperate with you."

"I will do," he said, not quite smiling.

"Isn't that a trifle arbitrary?" She waited for him to speak.

At last he said, "I don't think so."

"No; I suppose you wouldn't," she said. "It also says here that you may order me escorted out of the country if you believe it would aid your country in more fully securing this facility."

"So it does. You are free to go, at least for a little while yet. And in case you supposed you could trade upon your work here, it also provides that you cannot take anything from this office." He took a cigarette from a small brass case in his breast-pocket and used a matching brass lighter to ignite it.

"Yes, I saw that." She took a deep breath, knowing that most of the important information contained in the office files already existed in her mind. "I think it would be best if I left España, all things considered."

Capitán Morales studied her with narrowed eyes as he exhaled a plume of smoke. "Is that what you want?"

Druze answered before she could consider the ramifications of her admission. "Yes. Yes, I want to be out of España." Now that the words were spoken, she felt recklessly free. "I am from Czechoslovakia; my interests in this war you are fighting is minimal, and I would just as soon not have to deal with it."

"Do you have someplace to go?" Capitán Morales asked, slightly amused at her temerity.

"That is hardly your concern," she said with the sinking certainty that she did not—all she had was the address of an advocate's office in London that Saint-Germain had left her; she hoped it would be enough.

"You're right." He studied the far wall as if the grain of the wood contained a hidden message; then he said, "Very well. I will see you have a pass to leave España, provided to take a train tomorrow."

"Must it be a train?" Druze asked.

"It is all I may do," he answered somewhat obliquely. "If it isn't to your liking, then I regret that you will be left to your own devices. You will find that ships leaving Spanish harbors will not take on foreign nationals without proper authorizations, and all airplanes have been commandeered for military use."

Druze gave this her quick consideration, wondering if she could still get passage on an Eclipse Shipping vessel, and decided not to chance it. "Very well. I will depart tomorrow on the train—for Toulouse and Burgundy," she added quickly. "From what I have heard on the wireless, there has been a flood of refugees through the southern passes of the Pyrenees, and I have no wish to add to their numbers."

Capitán Morales bit his lower lip. "I will arrange it," he said at last. "Be ready at half-seven in the morning and one of the soldiers will escort you to the train station." He glanced around the room. "This was Saint-Germain's office?"

"No—his is at the end of the corridor," said Druze, feeling uneasy at revealing so much, yet compelled to offer these men something to appease them. "His name is on the door. You can look for yourself. He did use this office occasionally, for certain meetings, but—" She was finally able to stop herself.

"He has records in his office?" Capitán Morales inquired.

"In his safe and in the filing cabinets. They're locked." This last pleased her.

"Do you know how to open them?" the Capitán pursued.

She shook her head. "I don't have the combination to the safe. The keys to the cabinets are in the fourth little drawer of his desk—just above the inkwells. There's nothing secret about the location of the keys. I'd guess that anyone in this building could tell you that." She picked up her purse and made sure the latch was closed.

Capitán Morales nodded. "As you say, Señora Sviny." He flicked his hand in the direction of the door. "Estanque, escort Señora Sviny from the building. In fact, drive her to her home, and see that she remains there."

One of the four soldiers ducked his head, then remembered to salute. "I will, Señor Capitán." He motioned to Druze with the barrel of his rifle. "Come along, Señora."

"Respect, Estanque, respect," Capitán Morales reminded him as he started toward the door, Druze falling in beside him. "Let her go into her house by herself. You stay outside, and watch. She isn't to telephone anyone, or go anywhere alone."

"Yes, Señor Capitán," said Estanque.

As she reached the door, Druze looked back. "May I go to the bank? I should like to—"

"I regret, Señora, that is impossible," said Capitán Morales, dismissing her with a wave of his glowing cigarette. "Take her home, Estanque."

"Yes, Señor Capitán," said the young soldier, this time with greater purpose.

"All right," said Druze, squaring her shoulders, resolved to leave with her head high, and all the while fighting tears. As she reached the top of the curving stairs that led to the lobby below, she noticed a tall, slender man of perhaps thirty-five with floppy, brownish hair and light, china-hazel eyes; he was wearing a nondescript navy-blue double-breasted suit with a white shirt and simple navy-blue tie. For some inexplicable reason, she shivered when he nodded at her as he climbed up the stairs.

Estanque laughed at her obvious discomfort. "They say he's Italian; he's called Cenere, in any case." He relished the look of dismay in Druze's eyes as she followed the thin man's steady progress up the stairs. "It means ash."

"I know," said Druze, wondering what it was about the man that so disturbed her.

"Keep going," Estanque told her, strutting a little as he noticed Estrellita glancing at him. "Cenere isn't the kind of man you want to notice you."

Druze did as he ordered, only nodding once to the receptionist as she walked to the heavy glass doors that led out of the building. The tightness in her throat was painful but she maintained her composure as she went out into the afternoon heat. "Which auto?"

"That one," said Estanque, pointing to the Benz tourer. He guided her by her elbow. "Get into the front passenger seat."

"As you like," said Druze, obeying him. She took a last look at the Eclipse Aeroplano Industrias building through the windscreen and was stricken with a sense of loss that would have staggered her, had she been standing. As it was, she murmured her farewells in Czech, glad for once that only she could understand.

From his vantage-point at the top of the stairs, the man called Cenere watched the Benz depart, then made his way down the corridor to the office where Capitán Morales awaited him. He paused in the doorway as if uncertain of his welcome. "Capitán?"

"Ah, Signore Cenere," Capitán Morales exclaimed. "The very man I have been looking for. Come in, come in." He had taken the chair behind the desk and was relishing the position.

"You have work for me?" If Capitán Morales' position intimidated him, he disguised his apprehension very well.

"Yes, I do. With the full approval of the generals." He smiled, showing his teeth.

"I should think so," said Cenere, a world of disagreeable implications in his tone. "Very well. Who am I to find, and what am I to do with him?"

Capitán Morales sighed; he had hoped to milk their conversation a bit more, but he knew enough about Cenere not to press his luck. "You are to find a foreigner—one Ferenc Ragoczy, le Comte de Saint-Germain—"

"An auspicious title," Cenere said, sneering.

This remark was lost on Capitán Morales, but he went along with Cenere anyway. "Yes, it is."

"He is the one you want me to locate for you? Is that all?" He looked about the office. "I should think you would prefer to have him gone, out of reach."

"It will not serve our purposes. He could make claims in court that would prevent our use of his company for months, if not years, and we cannot have that." Capitán Morales pursed his lips in distaste.

"Ah. I understand why you summoned me, Capitán. You would prefer to have this Comte de Saint-Germain truly gone, completely out of the picture," said Cenere. "No embarrassing protests to deal with."

"Yes. You have it precisely." He paused, hoping to add impact to what he was about to say. "You are to find him and you are to kill him—unobviously. This is to be an entirely clandestine operation. Nothing of his death is to redound to us in any way, but he must not vanish, or his estate will have to wait the required seven years to settle. He is rich enough to demand attention, so his death cannot rouse questions."

"So an unobvious murder that will leave no questions. A lamentable accident, in fact," said Cenere with spurious sympathy.

"Yes. A lamentable accident."

Cenere flexed his long, thin hands. "Do you have any notion where this Ragoczy is?"

"No, not just at present. We know he isn't in España."

"That leaves a great deal of the world in which he may hide," Cenere observed, unimpressed. "Is there any information that could narrow the search?"

"That is what we are hoping to find out," said Capitán Morales. "His office should contain material we can use to locate him. I can appoint one man to help you."

"I'd rather use the receptionist. She'll know with whom he talks, and she should be able to provide us telephone numbers or street addresses. And if I speak firmly to her, she will want to tell me everything she knows." Cenere spoke flatly, completely confident that he would get what he wanted.

"Then you may use her," said Capitán Morales, disliking the way his statement came out. "I will appoint her to assist you." There. That was less sinister.

"Thank you," said Cenere, and took another turn around the office. "May I go inspect his files?"

"Certainly," said Capitán Morales as he stubbed out his cigarette in an onyx ashtray on Druze Sviny's desk. He would be glad to have Cenere out of the office. "If you wish to remove anything, tell me what it is, so I may give you a certificate allowing you to take it."

"Very good," said Cenere, and left Capitán Morales and his three remaining men in the Acting Chairman's office. He entered Saint-Germain's office and took stock of it: the room was paneled in mahogany; wall-sconces in the shape of sea-shells provided a soft lighting that was as quietly elegant as the burgundy silk draperies that covered the three tall windows, one of which was fronted by a trestle table made of glossy teak; three Oriental carpets lay over the polished wooden floor, their rich colors luminous; a handsome roll-top rosewood desk dominated one end of the office, facing three high-backed chairs upholstered in celadon damask; golden-oak file cabinets matched a set of glass-fronted book-cases on the west wall. In spite of himself, Cenere was impressed. He rubbed his chin with his forefinger and thumb, concentrating on what he did not see: there were no photographs anywhere. Perhaps, he thought, they had been removed and sent on to Saint-Germain, in which case he would have to find out where they had gone.

There was a tap on the door and one of the soldiers called out, "The Capitán has the receptionist with him, if you would like to speak with her." His accent was that of Malagá.

"Bring her to me when Morales is done," said Cenere, exasperated at having his hand forced.

"Sí, Señor Cenere." The soldier went away.

Cenere waited a few minutes, then went to test the drawers on the file cabinets. Finding them locked, he took a small tool—not unlike a toothpick with a little bend at one end—from his wallet and jimmied them open. He made a swift examination of the tabs and pulled out six of the files, spreading them out on the narrow table in front of the central window. He pulled a handful of onion-skin carbon copies from files, then stacked them, but did not return them to the files. With a hint of a smile, he folded the carbons in half and slipped them into one of the three large pockets in his suit jacket. Satisfied, he took a seat in one of the visitor's chairs, turning it to let him see the door as well as the desk. For twenty minutes he waited, smoking and thinking, and then there was another knock on the door.

"The receptionist, Señor Cenere," called out the soldier who had spoken before.

"Bring her in," said Cenere, rising with deliberate slowness to greet the much-subdued young woman who came through the door. "Buenas tardes, señorita," he said, his gallantry enough to make her skin crawl.

"Tardes," she murmured, staying near the door, her face slightly averted.

"Do come in and sit down." He indicated another of the visitor's chairs. "Here." Reluctantly she did as he ordered, sitting without leaning back on the upholstery, her hands clasped in her lap. "I trust you're comfortable?" Cenere said, knowing she was not.

"I am," she lied. "Capitán Morales said I am to answer your questions. I am ready to do so."

"Very good," said Cenere. "May I begin by knowing your name?"

"Estrellita Rocio," she said, giving an Asturian trill to the *ll*.

"I am Cenere," he said. "A pleasure to know you, Señorita Rocio."

"Tengo alegrarse de verlo, Señor Cenere," she whispered, her good manners not yet completely banished by her dread.

He chuckled. "Are you sure?" He lit another cigarette—his third since he entered the office—and peered at her through the smoke.

Estrellita shook her head in confusion. "I will tell you anything you want to know."

"I am certain you will," said Cenere, and leaned forward. "You are aware that the army is looking for Señor Ragoczy, aren't you?"

"Yes, I am," she said quickly. "Everyone in the company knows it."

"It is obvious," Cenere agreed. "And you must have more information about him than most do."

"I'm not sure," she said, her manner more guarded than ever.

"You're too modest," said Cenere. "You have a position of responsibility, of trust. You know those whom Señor Ragoczy telephoned, and who telephoned him, you received his telegrams and saw where they came from. You have been privy to a great many communications, and you know who all the visitors have been. Don't you?"

Estrellita shrugged, her tension making the gesture awkward. "I know some," she admitted.

"And you can remember a great deal more, can't you?" Cenere challenged.

"I suppose so," she said, her voice dropping again.

"Yes, of course you can," said Cenere as he reached out to pat her hand; she almost shrieked as he touched her, but was able to stifle it so that all he heard was a soft yelp. "Be calm, be calm. Gather your thoughts. We have plenty of time, Señorita Rocio. Do not feel pressured by me—take as long as you need."

She winced. "I will try to remember."

"Muy bien," said Cenere. "Now then, you must have seen mail from other countries sent to Señor Ragoczy—"

"Le Comte de Saint-Germain," she dared to correct him. "Most of his correspondents addressed him by his title."

"Of course, of course," said Cenere, taking another drag on his cigarette. "From which countries did his mail come?"

Estrellita thought a moment. "He had mail from everywhere, even Peru."

"Peru," said Cenere, mildly surprised.

"From a professor with a French or Italian name. I recall two letters but neither one came less than a year ago." She felt a catch in her throat.

"What others?" Cenere asked.

"Letters from a firm in Canada—a chemical factory of some sort, in Winnipeg—such an odd name for a city," she said quickly. "And letters from a place in Bavaria. Sometimes a letter would come from Greece from someone with a German name. Occasionally he has had letters from the Soviet Union, apparently regarding businesses his family had invested in back when it was still Russia." She glanced at Cenere to see if any of this was the information he sought.

"Bavaria and the Soviet Union," said Cenere. "Where else?"

"France, of course, and Italy, from companies interested in our airplanes." She could not keep from boasting a little. "Also from Sweden and Denmark."

"Very good," said Cenere, sounding a bit bored.

"There were letters from a publisher in Amsterdam," she went on, "and from a group of attorneys in London."

These two possibilities were more promising, Cenere thought, although he gave no outward indication of his interest. "What would Señor Ragoczy want with a Dutch publisher?"

"I don't know," said Estrellita primly. "I received the letters, I didn't read them."

"Just so," said Cenere, thinking of the carbons in his jacket; he would match them up with what Estrellita revealed when he was done with her. "How does it happen that you recall these letters? Was there anything unusual about them?"

"The stamps," she said at once. "My little brother collects them, and so I try to get as many for him as I can."

"Ah," said Cenere. "So it is a fortunate accident that you have such a clear recollection of the letters. And you would not let one slip your mind, would you?"

"If it was delivered when I was on duty, no, I would not," Estrellita said. "I had permission to remove the stamps, you see," she added self-consciously.

"I do see," said Cenere. He got up and came around behind her chair. "What more, Estrellita? What can you tell me?"

She went more pale. "I . . . I can think of nothing more."

"What of visitors?" He waited a long moment. "Tell me who came to see him."

"Do you mean non-Spaniards?" Her hands were shaking; she knotted them together in an effort to steady them.

"Yes, that is what I mean." The edge in his voice made her jump.

"Well," she said, struggling to concentrate, "there was a man from Egypt who wanted four airplanes. He is some kind of nobility there and said he preferred airplanes to camels." She attempted a smile without success. "There were two men from Germany, but le Comte refused to see them. He had a policy not to use his airplanes for military purposes. That's changed now."

"So it has," said Cenere. "Who else?"

"An American journalist called once, but le Comte was in Cádiz. He left no message." She shivered as if the room had abruptly turned cold.

"No message? Are you sure?" Cenere asked.

"If he did, I never saw it, and he was only here for a few minutes." She huddled in on herself as if she hoped to escape Cenere by vanishing. "A pilot from Hungary came once, hoping to get work, but he left before he flew any of the airplanes. He said he had a better offer from a company in France."

"Do you remember any other foreigners?" Cenere's manner suggested only slight curiosity, but he was keenly alert to her answer.

"No, no, I don't." She pressed her lips together. "That's all I can think of."

"Um-hum," said Cenere. "Well, then I think you had best return to your duties." He saw the startled look in her eyes and permitted himself a hint of amusement. "I'll be here tomorrow, in case you should think of something more during the night."

The dismay on her face was almost comical. "That's all of it, Señor Cenere. I promise you, it's all."

"Yes, yes. But something may occur to you, and it would be worthwhile to tell me. I won't fault you because something slipped your mind." His geniality made her queasy. "You can let yourself out, can't you?"

"Yes." With that, she all but bolted from the room, leaving Cenere to take out the carbon copies from his vest pocket and begin to look for letters to a Dutch publisher and an English attorney.

Text of a letter from Horatio Batterbury in Winnipeg, Manitoba, Canada, to Druze Sviny in Toulouse, France.

> Compton House
> 658 Selkirk Road
> Suites 4–9
> Winnipeg, Manitoba, Canada
> 27 July, 1936

Druze Sviny
c/o Hotel Belvoir
47, Rue des Bergers
Toulouse, France

My dear Doctor Sviny,
I thank you for your letter of the 23rd which has just arrived via air mail. You were very right to send it to me, and I appreciate your timeliness in making this contact. Our current contractual schedule would make your addition to our work deeply appreciated, and we're looking forward to a long association.

I hope this will put any anxiety you may have to rest at once; yes, I am interested in employing you. I already received a sterling recommendation from Ferenc Ragoczy, le Comte de Saint-Germain, who has been your employer and our investor, and who has given me his personal assurances that you would be a true asset to Manitoba Chemicals, Ltd. I have reviewed your curriculum vitae and I am as impressed as Saint-Germain said I would be. Your credentials are truly remarkable, and I know you will fit into our company most suitably.

While I realize that moving across the Atlantic is not a venture to be undertaken lightly, I think I can assure you a handsome salary, starting at $6,500 a year with the potential of increasing to $10,000 in five years, rates that are more than competitive with any other business in Canada that might offer you a position, and certainly as good or better than any salary

you could command in Europe or the United States. We will also include
$1,500 for moving expenses, which should make the upheaval less of a bur-
den for you. If you have chests or crates you would like to send on ahead, we
will be pleased to supply storage for you.

I am looking forward to your answer; if you agree to come to work here,
we would like you to begin on 1 September, if that is convenient. I am aware
that the political situation in Europe just now may make travel problematic.
Should you need more time to make arrangements, please let me know as
soon as possible and I will adjust your starting date to suit your travels.

Incidentally, we can provide you an apartment in Winnipeg until you find
housing to your satisfaction, so that need not hamper your plans regarding
your work here.

In anticipation of a happy outcome, I will extend a welcome to Canada.

Most sincerely yours,

Horatio Batterbury
Manitoba Chemicals, Ltd.

HB/cd'm

chapter nine

"I have the train schedules, and costs for private cars; we can make arrangements by the end of the week and be away early next," Rogerio told
Saint-Germain as he came into the hotel suite sitting room that overlooked the
Charles River. It was a muggy summer day, and Boston was dragging toward
evening, men on the street walking slowly; even the laborers were wilting, and
the horses drawing wagons amid the automobiles and lorries plodded, leaning
into their collars and sweating. Rogerio had removed his jacket and waistcoat
and had rolled up his shirtsleeves but the heat still weighed upon him.

Saint-Germain held out his hand for the glossy, printed pages Rogerio carried, holding them up and flipping through them. "It will be good to leave. It's
stifling," he remarked as he indicated the open window. "I saw heat-lightning a

while ago." He was wearing a black linen dressing-robe over black linen slacks, and although there was no trace of moisture on his face, he was unusually pale, a sure sign that the sultry weather was taking a toll on him.

"This has been a difficult few days," Rogerio agreed. "But we can be gone by Tuesday, if the contract is accepted."

"I hope there will be a break in the weather before then." Saint-Germain turned away from the window.

"Yes, that would be welcome." Rogerio opened the contract he had finally got from the attorneys. "If you will sign this, Hiram Jaynes will make all the arrangements."

"It's just as well that Miles Sunbury recommended this firm to me; I would not have known how to approach one of these Boston firms without an introduction." Saint-Germain set the brochures aside, took the contract, and read it through, stopping now and then to scrutinize a particular clause. "The law is its own language, no matter what language it's written in," he said as he sorted out one especially convoluted provision. "But I surmise I will not have to pay for any damage to the private car if it is damaged as the result of a train-wreck or other external causes."

"It seems fair that you should not have to," said Rogerio.

"I see there is insurance I may purchase for the duration of the lease," said Saint-Germain as he read further. "That will pay for any damage that I do or cause to have done. What, I wonder, do they think I am planning to do while I travel?"

"Hiram Jaynes recommends the insurance, at full value," said Rogerio.

"No doubt," said Saint-Germain. "It would be less conspicuous to have it, wouldn't it." He had already made up his mind.

"Yes, that was Jaynes' thought." Rogerio went to the window and lowered the venetian blinds.

Saint-Germain finished reading the contract, a slight frown between his brows as he considered the contents. "I'll telephone Jaynes in the morning."

"Not this afternoon? He'll be in his office for another hour," said Rogerio.

"No; that would give the impression I haven't thought about the terms, and a man as methodical as Hiram Jaynes doesn't respect mercurial decisions. The terms and specifications suit me well enough, and any additional changes I might want at this point could draw attention to . . . certain aspects of my life I would as soon keep private." Saint-Germain went to the old-fashioned writing desk near the door. He took out his fountain-pen and initialed each page, then signed on the designated line; he held out the pen to Rogerio. "To witness, if you will."

Rogerio took the pen and signed on the witness line, then blotted the two signatures. "Do you think there could be an objection to me as a witness?"

"Why? You have a vested interest in this travel, but that shouldn't preclude witnessing the contract. You are in my employ, of course, but you have money of your own, and so you aren't dependent upon me; there can be no concern in that regard. Besides, whomelse do I know in Boston to vouch for my character? I've corresponded with two professors in Cambridge, but they know nothing of me beyond my work with chemicals. No, old friend, you are the obvious choice— anyone with an ounce of sense would see that, and agree you are an appropriate witness." He folded the contract and put the cover around it. "Tomorrow it will go to Jaynes." Slipping the blue-covered pages into one of the desk slots, Saint-Germain sighed. "I should go out tonight."

"Late?" Rogerio asked, knowing the answer.

"Yes. I may not return until shortly before dawn. I am still enervated from the airplane journey." He disliked the admission, and he quickly changed the sub-ject. "The contract stipulates that the car has sleeping accommodations for four in two bedrooms."

"That is my understanding; a full bedroom and a second, smaller one," said Rogerio, unfazed by the shift in conversational direction. "And a sitting room, a small dining room, and, of course, appropriate water closets." He smiled at this. "Not that either of us have need of one."

"If they provide baths or showers, we will have," Saint-Germain reminded him.

"Yes," said Rogerio quickly. "Baths and showers."

There was a mutter of thunder but the lowering, pink-tinged clouds did not open.

"Tell me," said Saint-Germain a moment later, "is the summer so fierce all the way across the country? The wireless—the radio," he corrected himself, "cer-tainly would make one think so. Yet I find it hard to imagine that the weather is uniform, given the size of the land. This isn't the Year of Yellow Snow."

"That was cold, not heat," Rogerio reminded him.

"So it was." He mused a long moment. "Madelaine told me San Francisco was chilly in the summer."

"That was eighty years ago," Rogerio reminded him.

"Do you mean it might have changed?" Saint-Germain asked, then went on, "They say the drought in the middle of the country has made everything differ-ent in only three years; there were dust-storms that made the drought worse, last year and the year before. The devastation is reported on the news twice a day even now. So your point is well-taken; San Francisco may no longer be foggy in the summer. We will not rely upon the weather." He regarded Rogerio with curiosity. "Will that have a bearing on our travel, do you think?"

"As much as the weather ever does," said Rogerio.

"Such a circumspect answer," Saint-Germain chided him gently. "Very well; I won't plague you with any more questions neither of us can answer; my Word

on it. We will be on our way by next Tuesday and we will find out for ourselves."
He checked his new wristwatch, saying, "As I have already mentioned, I plan to
go out shortly after sundown."

"Have you a destination in mind?" Rogerio asked.

"I think I will begin with the Commons and then go where my steps take
me." Saint-Germain smiled a little. "There must be someone in this city who
will let me visit her in sleep."

"There must be hundreds, if only they knew," said Rogerio, and regarded
Saint-Germain with some concern. "They say the police here are vigilant."

"I'll keep that in mind," said Saint-Germain. "I have no wish to end up in an
American prison cell. Or a psychiatric ward," he added with distaste.

"Surely it wouldn't come to that," Rogerio said.

"Because I am foreign and rich?" Saint-Germain asked sadly. "At this time, I
think both those things might well count against me here, and Americans, like
the Germans, have taken to using the mental hospitals as de facto prisons for
those who prove too awkward for them." He took a deep breath. "You needn't
worry. I will be discreet."

"And good thing, too," said Rogerio with a touch of asperity. "What shall I
lay out for you?"

"My tropical-weight wool jacket, I think, with the red-and-black lining. No
waistcoat, not in this heat. A white linen shirt and the deep red tie in silk brocade."

"As you wish," said Rogerio, and went to attend to sorting laundry in preparation for their coming departure.

It was after eight in the evening when Saint-Germain strolled out of the hotel
and into the warm, close summer evening. There were occasional flashes of lightning, but no rain had yet fallen, and the whole city seemed breathless in
anticipation. Four blocks brought him to the Commons, and he walked across
it, admiring the old trees and watching the autos doing their best to negotiate
the narrow streets around the Commons. He gave a half-dollar to a man in a
ragged overcoat and advised him to buy something to eat with it, for the man
was dreadfully thin. Walking farther, he noticed a tavern at one of the corners, a
sandwich board standing in front of it advertising food and drink, its doors standing open more in hope of a breeze than invitation to patrons; a group of men
were bustling into the low-ceilinged establishment, one of them propounding
emphatic political opinions. Realizing this was no place for him, Saint-Germain
went on, following the street past the church and winding up a hill. A few of the
buildings were dark, but most were alive with activity, their lights shining against
the night. Saint-Germain stepped aside as a small procession of autos went past
him: a Hudson, a Packard, two Studebakers, a Buick, a Cadillac, a Lincoln, a

Hupmobile, and a Pierce Silver Arrow; their headlights were dazzling in the deepening twilight; the occupants of the autos were apparently all bound for the same function, for they kept in their formation for as far as Saint-Germain could watch them go, their taillights marking their progress down the curving street. When the autos were out of sight, he resumed his walk, coming at last to a cluster of larger houses with gardens and lawns, and the general look of prosperity, although one had overgrown hedges. He stopped at the fence and studied the house beyond, noticing that it was kept up but without any excesses or obviously new work. The lights were on in half of the rooms, judging by the windows, but there was little sign of much activity, although there were faint sounds of a radio on the second floor.

A large black dog—a mastiff with something else in the mix—bounded up to the fence where Saint-Germain was standing, barking ferociously while wagging his tail.

"Max! Max! Cut it out!" The voice was young and female, and in a little while she came out of the rear of the house, calling, "Max! Stop it, now!" as she hurried toward the fence. She caught sight of Saint-Germain and stopped. "Oh. Sorry."

"He's protecting you," said Saint-Germain.

"Yes," said the young woman. She stared at him, a bit wary, and patted her thigh to call Max to her side. "The tail isn't very frightening. I guess he doesn't think you're dangerous." She spoke with a flat Boston accent and possessed the angular prettiness that promised charm and chic in later life. She had lively blue eyes and slender hands; her dress was of good quality but at least three years old and her light brown hair was in need of cutting; she regarded Saint-Germain with a mixture of chariness and curiosity.

"How good of him," said Saint-Germain.

She smiled at the dog. "Good Max. Good Max." She patted him on the head as he sat beside her.

"He is a good dog," said Saint-Germain, his praise accompanied by a new, louder roll of thunder. "He pays attention to you and he guards your house."

Apparently aware he was being praised, Max flattened his ears and thumped his tail on the ground.

"We're saying *good* a lot," the young woman said, her smile now more relaxed. She came to the fence. "You're not from around here, are you?"

"Alas, no. I am from Europe, only recently arrived on your shores. I have been looking about your beautiful city." He held out his hand as he had seen Americans do. "Ferenc Ragoczy, at your service."

She took his hand and shook it once. "What kind of a name is Ferenc?" she asked, a bit apologetic for her lapse in manners; she folded her arms as lightning spangled almost overhead, followed in less than two seconds by a sharp thunderclap.

"Hungarian," said Saint-Germain. "The English version is Francis, I believe."

"I'm Bronwen O'Neil." They shook hands and she blushed. "I don't think I've ever met a Hungarian before."

"A pleasure to meet you, Bronwen O'Neil." Saint-Germain took a step back.

"Are you moving to Boston, Mr. Ragoczy? Or are you visiting?" She stumbled over the unfamiliar combination of syllables.

"No; I am traveling through," said Saint-Germain.

"Oh," she said, sounding disappointed.

"I want to see more of America while I have the opportunity." He gave her a quick, one-sided smile.

"There is a great deal to see," she said as if indulging in dinner conversation. "Have you plans for your explorations yet?"

"I leave for Chicago early next week," he told her.

"Chicago." She stared into the distance. "My father went to Chicago, two years ago, looking for work."

"And you've remained here," said Saint-Germain.

"Mother said it was best, until something was settled." Her frown revealed that this had been more than an inconvenience.

"That must be difficult for you, having him in Chicago and you remaining in Boston," said Saint-Germain, speculation in his voice.

"He . . . didn't get the work he wanted. He told us he had to look elsewhere, so he left Chicago last year, or he said he did. We haven't heard from him for months." She was so forlorn that Saint-Germain could think of nothing to say to her; she recalled herself in a fluster. "Oh, dear. Listen to me! I am so sorry. I shouldn't impose upon you." She smoothed her hair back from her brow. "I hope things go better for you in Chicago, and wherever your travels may take you."

"I'm sorry to hear about your father," said Saint-Germain.

"Well, at least the house is paid for, and there's a little money left. We're managing. A lot of my friends lost much more than we did." She looked away. "In the Crash."

"I heard something about it, in Europe, which had its own economic problems," said Saint-Germain, recalling the catastrophic inflation that overtook Germany just over a decade earlier, and the privations it brought.

"Muffy Collins' father killed himself. His company was ruined and he couldn't stand the shame of it. At least my father's alive," said Bronwen. "Just missing."

"A terrible time for you," said Saint-Germain, aware that her distress was still very much with her.

"It was, and it isn't finished yet," she said, not quite understanding, then turned to him, shocked with herself. "I'm so sorry. I didn't mean to say so much."

"You have no reason to be sorry," he assured her. "You have had much to contend with, and those burdens are not always easily borne."

"But I shouldn't have said anything. It isn't seemly. And certainly not to . . . you . . ." She faltered. "What must you be thinking?"

"Nothing that would disquiet you," said Saint-Germain, continuing tranquilly, "I have found it is often the way when strangers meet—they exchange confidences they would never impart to nearer acquaintances."

Bronwen put her hand to her cheek. "Oh. Yes. I suppose it is like that. How kind of you to say so." She flashed a look of gratitude at him, even as she addressed him with utmost propriety. "You have been very kind, Mr. Ragoczy. Thank you for listening to my ramblings. But I really must go in now. It's getting late, and I have chores to attend to. I'll wish you a good evening now." She hooked her fingers under Max' collar. "Come along, Max," she said crisply, and went back toward the looming house. "It was a pleasure to meet you," she called over her shoulder as she paused before she went in through the rear door.

"And you, Bronwen O'Neil." He watched her go, and decided to return to this house later that night. He walked away from the fence, setting a leisurely pace for his reconnoitering. At the crest of the hill he turned to look out over the city and the water. It was a handsome setting, he thought, good for commerce and nicely situated. Another volley of lightning and thunder drove him away from the heights to lower elevations, where he saw more closely packed housing and heard a more volatile mix of voices than he had before. He recognized Italian and Portuguese mixed with English; he moved with care in these streets, knowing he was more alien here than he had been on the hill. His clothes and manner set him apart from the residents of the area as surely as his accent would, so he was guarded, avoiding darkened side-streets, for although the night did not hamper his vision, he was aware of the danger such places could harbor. For the same reason he gave a wide berth to two rowdy groups of young men.

At midnight, the chimes from a Victorian Gothic church startled him, and he stopped, looking about him. It would take half-an-hour to walk back to Bronwen O'Neil's house if he went directly there. He looked at his watch, and decided to start back in that general direction, but not to move too quickly; he wanted to arrive at the house about one in the morning when, he hoped, Brownen would be asleep. There were fewer people on the streets now, and they were furtive, exhausted, or tipsy. Saint-Germain watched as the lights in the taverns winked out, and the windows of the houses went dark. He saw occasional autos on the streets, their numbers lessening steadily.

Saint-Germain reached the O'Neil house shortly after one in the morning; there was a single light glowing beside the front door, but other than that, no other illumination shone. He stood by the fence for a short while, his whole attention on the place, sensing the state of the occupants. When he was satisfied that the three inhabitants were asleep, he vaulted easily over the fence and stepped behind the hedge so he could not be seen from the street. As he started toward the house, Max came bounding up to him, tail swinging eagerly, tongue lolling, uttering low whuffs and half-barks to greet a welcome friend. He reached down and stroked the dog's big head, scratching him gently and reducing Max to imbecilic happiness. When Max was willing to release his guest, Saint-Germain continued up to the back door and tested the door; it opened with a soft complaint from the hinges. He entered a narrow hallway with a pantry on one side and a mudroom on the other. He went on into the kitchen; it was not modern but everything was in fine order. There was someone asleep in a room just beyond the kitchen, and Saint-Germain assumed that there was still a housekeeper on the premises. He stood still, deepening the woman's slumber, and then continued on down the corridor to the front of the house. There was a handsome entry in what he recognized as the Federalist style, with a curving staircase leading to the floor above; he climbed it quickly and silently, reaching the gallery without incident. He stood for a moment, expanding his senses: there was someone asleep to his left, and to his right; the sleeper to his right was in the grip of a drug of some sort, locked in the arms of Morpheus with such intent determination that Saint-Germain supposed the woman would remain so until well into the morning; he supposed this was Bronwen's mother. The sleeper on his left was dreaming, and that was much more promising. Saint-Germain went to the left, silent as a shadow, and paused outside the door to take stock of what he perceived. Then, very slowly, he eased the door open and slipped into the room.

Bronwen O'Neil lay under a satin comforter, her sheet turned back by her arm. She was on her side, facing away from the door, and her hands moved in little, restless starts as she responded to her dream. A few bits of words came from her, nothing truly coherent. Gradually her motions subsided and she lapsed into the stillness of deep sopor, her body still, her breathing slow and regular.

Saint-Germain stood very still, all his concentration upon her as he lulled her into a kind of trance; only then did he speak. "You are dreaming, Bronwen, dreaming happily. Your dreams are filled with delight, with every joy and delight that you can summon up." He moved a few steps nearer to her bed. "You are in a place where all your worries have vanished, and all your sadness has ended. You have nothing to distress you, nothing to mar your contentment." Very carefully he sat beside her on the bed, taking care not to disturb her in any way. "You have put all distress behind you and you have embraced gladness. Your heart is light; you have only that which gratifies your senses and uplifts your heart." He touched her cheek, as lightly as a feather landing on a soap-bubble. He felt more than heard her sigh, and he moved his hand again. "You are achieving the abiding elation you have sought for so long." His lips brushed hers as ephemeral and intense as morning mist. He would do nothing that would waken her, and so limited his arousal of her desires to words and insubstantial caresses.

This time a half-uttered name rode on her breath: "Brad . . ."

Her wistfulness told Saint-Germain more than the name itself. He touched her brow lightly, lightly, then said, "Brad is yours again. Everything that stood between you has gone. There are no more doubts, no questions, no reasons left to keep you apart. You are ready to embrace each other, to have the fruition of your devotion." His voice dropped lower, became more musical. "You have Brad and he is everything you hoped he would be. You have nothing to hold back from him; everything you are is euphoric for him, and that thrills you. He is overjoyed to be with you at last, to love you as he has wanted to love you for so long." His fingers strayed along the line of her neck, the motion so delicate that it hardly disturbed the lace edging of her nightgown. "You are rapt, blissful. Everything about you is a manifestation of your love, and Brad's. You relish each moment spent together, and you take courage and strength from your passion."

Bronwen's sleep-softened face flushed as her body responded to her inner visions; her torso arched slightly as if in response to the memories of Brad that had coalesced in her mind.

"You want to touch Brad, to know him to the limits of your being." He moved close to her, feeling her emotions well and near their crest. "You will reach what you seek, and you will keep that fulfillment with you as long as you remember this dream." His lips grazed her neck as she shivered and sighed at the culmination of her dream-induced ecstasy. Then Saint-Germain moved carefully back, whispering, "You will be rested when you wake, and your delight will sustain you. As you face the demands of your life, you will be confident and happy, and you will not be lost in grief, or troubled by what has happened to you in recent times. You will know your bravery and you will trust it." He got to his feet and went to the door, watching Bronwen as he moved. Going out into the corridor, Saint-Germain took stock of the house before he swiftly and silently descended the stairs and went out through the kitchen, as he had come in.

Max came up to him, giving happy little yelps that gave way to happy moans as Saint-Germain scratched his head.

A cough from the housekeeper's room alerted him and Saint-Germain made for the back door, slipping out into the night to be greeted by a peal of thunder that brought no rain.

At the first intersection, a policeman approached Saint-Germain, swinging his nightstick and looking narrowly at the black-clad stranger. He stood under the streetlight, his whole attention on this stranger. "Ho-there," he said with a Boston-Irish brogue as he moved to block Saint-Germain's progress. "You're a face I don't know."

"Good evening, Officer," said Saint-Germain, making no effort to push past him. "I'm pleased that you've found me." His urbane manner did nothing to lessen the policeman's suspicions.

"I'm wondering what you'd be doing out at this hour." He tapped his pocket-watch for emphasis. He appeared to be forty or so, a solid, experienced police officer.

"I'm afraid," said Saint-Germain, "that I've managed to get myself lost in this fine city."

The policeman peered at Saint-Germain. "You're not from here?"

"No. I arrived from Europe not long ago and I am making arrangements to go to Chicago," he said, his manner unrelentingly cordial. "I didn't have the foresight to bring a map with me, nor a torch—a flashlight."

A bell somewhere not far away rang three.

"Where are you staying?" asked the policeman, clearly doubting almost everything about this stranger.

"I'm at the King Charles Hotel," said Saint-Germain, knowing its reputation for excellence.

"The King Charles, is it?" said the policeman. "Well, sir, if that's the case, I can escort you back to the King Charles, if you like."

"That would be very kind, but I am willing to take myself back if you will give me instructions how I am to find it," said Saint-Germain.

The policeman shook his head. "No. I'll be wanting to see you safe, you being a foreigner newly come to Boston and all."

Saint-Germain ducked his head slightly, recognizing the steely intent beneath the genial assurance. "That's very good of you. I appreciate your concern, but I don't want to keep you from your duties."

"Watching after people in Boston is my duty, sir," said the policeman most pointedly. "The citizens depend upon me and those like me to keep them safe." From the tone of his voice, this was intended to warn as much as to inform.

"And it is fortunate for your city that there are such men to defend them," said Saint-Germain, adding, "In many cities in Europe the police are more the plunderers than the protectors of the populace. I have been in Spain, where their Civil War has turned the police to bandits; there the people fear the police and flee them."

"I read about that," the policeman admitted grudgingly. "All the more reason to be shut of the place, I'd say."

"Well, as you see, I am here," Saint-Germain said with a hint of an amused smile lurking at the corner of his mouth.

Thunder trundled along the sky, strong enough to rattle a few windows along the dark street.

"But, begging your pardon, it could be that you've learned a trick or two about spoils. It is a thought peculiar to have a foreigner making his way through the streets at this hour." The policeman slapped his palm with his nightstick to add emphasis to his point.

"If you mean you're worried that I might do something to compromise your citizens, I assure you that is not my intention. If I need someone to vouch for me, Hiram Jaynes will probably do so. He is handling my legal affairs just at present."

The policeman looked at Saint-Germain in mild surprise. "Hiram Jaynes, you say?"

"Of Jaynes Jaynes Fleming and Gries," Saint-Germain finished for him. "Yes. A man of some repute in Boston, I gather." Saint-Germain smiled. "He's expensive enough."

"Isn't that the way of it?" said the policeman. "Lawyers! Shakespeare was right—we should kill them all. They're nothing but trouble."

"A necessary evil," Saint-Germain said, matching his tone to the policeman's. "I don't know about you, Officer, but I wouldn't want to have to find my way through the law without one."

The policeman nodded. "There's much in what you say. Turn left at the next corner."

Saint-Germain was aware of the shift in attitude on the part of the policeman. He thanked the man, then said, "It's been a hard time in this country, from all I have learned; I can see that many of your people are enduring real hardship."

"Bad, yes, it's very bad," said the officer. "I don't know that I didn't prefer Prohibition to this dreadful Depression. At least during Prohibition we didn't have businesses closing and able-bodied men out of work. They might be drunk on bathtub gin but they had jobs to go to." He watched Saint-Germain carefully. "We don't want what work we have taken over by foreigners running away from the mess in Europe."

"I doubt you have to be too worried about that," said Saint-Germain. "Most of the people in Europe can't afford to come here, not with work so scarce." He went on a few strides in silence, then said, "I gather your parents or grandparents came from Ireland—during the Potato Famine, perhaps?"

Lightning zigzagged overhead, followed by a drub of thunder.

"Grandparents it was; came over in '87 from Cork," said the policeman proudly. "Settled in Boston and been here ever since. We've done well. My father was a builder and my uncle was a customs officer. They worked hard for us. My brother Gabriel's an important man in the ward."

Although Saint-Germain was unsure what that meant, he gave a sign of approval. "So America has been good for you, though your family came from Cork fifty years ago."

"Yes, it has. That's why we don't want to see it overrun with foreigners," the policeman said, unaware of Saint-Germain's ironic smile; he indicated the trees of the Commons not far ahead, waving shadows against the few streetlights. "There, you see? About half-a-mile to go. We'll be at the King Charles in ten minutes or so."

"Very good. Thank you for your help. I should have been wandering until dawn if you hadn't come along," said Saint-Germain.

"No reason to thank me, sir. I'm only doing my duty." The policeman showed no inclination to leave, keeping pace with the stranger beside him. "There've been a spate of break-ins of late, all through the city. We're on the lookout for the perpetrators: most are men out of work looking for anything they can take to wear or sell or eat. We've got to be careful."

"Your diligence is admirable," said Saint-Germain, "but in my case, misplaced. I am not out of work, and I have no need to steal from anyone. Believe this: I have money enough in my pocket, and I have . . . dined this evening. Still, if it will put your mind at ease, continue along with me. I am relieved to have your protection as well as your directions."

"Very understanding of you, I'm sure," said the policeman. "And I'll put myself to the trouble of escorting you to the hotel. If they know you there, all's well and good. If they don't, you'll want Hiram Jaynes first thing in the morning."

"As you wish, Officer," said Saint-Germain, and turned as he heard the sound of an auto horn.

"Damn foolish kids," the policeman muttered as a Cord went by, six young men crammed into it. The vehicle skidded as lightning ripped the clouds, then vanished with a crescendo of thunder.

"They will learn, in time," said Saint-Germain, and looked up in surprise as large, wet drops fell on him. In the next instant the downpour was upon them, as noisy as gunfire. He looked for an overhang to provide shelter, and heard the policeman swear comprehensively. "If we wait ten minutes, the worst should have passed."

The officer joined him under the eaves of a narrow shopfront. "The rain's welcome, but damned inconvenient."

"My sentiments exactly," said Saint-Germain, and peered out at the sheeting water; he was glad that he had taken nourishment so recently, and that his soles were newly lined with his native earth or he might have felt queasy with so much rain in the streets.

"A pity neither of us has an umbrella," said the officer, and cleared his throat. "When it lets up, we'll go along to the King Charles."

Saint-Germain listened to the tempest and told himself it would end shortly. "Yes. We'll do that," he said, wondering if the policeman spoke for all Americans in his distrust of foreigners; he raised the collar of his jacket to keep any stray drops from sliding down his neck as the thunder beat a tattoo over Boston.

TEXT OF A LETTER FROM DOÑA ISABEL INEZ VEDANCHO Y NUÑEZ AT COPSEHOWE IN HAMPSHIRE, ENGLAND, TO FERENC RAGOCZY, LE COMTE DE SAINT-GERMAIN, SOMEWHERE IN AMERICA; WRITTEN IN ENGLISH.

> *Copsehowe*
> *nr Briarcopse,*
> *Hampshire*
> *England*
> *11 August, 1936*

Ferenc Ragoczy, le Comte de Saint-Germain
c/o Miles Sunbury
Sunbury Draughton Hollis & Carnford
New Court
City of London, England

My dear Comte,

I trust Miles Sunbury will know where to send this letter, for I do not imagine addressing it to Le Comte de Saint-Germain, America, would allow the postal services to find you. I apologize for not writing to you directly; I trust you will understand, and make allowances for our current situations.

How glad I am that my mother made me learn English as well as French and Italian. All my friends at school studied German, but I learned English instead, and now I am relieved that I did. The library here at Copsehowe is quite wonderful; I am making my way through it by fits and starts, and slowly the tongue becomes less strange to me.

You were quite right to recommend this house to me. And Hampshire is a very lovely region, quite unlike Spain; I am determined to explore it thoroughly. I could not ask for a pleasanter place to live, nor a more well-situated one. It is quite charming, pleasantly laid out, and with gardens that, even neglected as they are now, are delightful; with a bit of effort, they could be truly splendid. Yet, now that I am settled in, I find the manor so large that I fear I will have to take in lodgers if only to make the rooms less empty. Twenty-six rooms! I have closed off the south wing, leaving myself seventeen rooms, but that is still a bit overwhelming. I have, in fact, considered extending my hospitality to two or three expatriate Spaniards who are presently living in London, but I am not yet satisfied that they are persons I want to have under my roof. I realize I may have to amend the terms of our lease if I bring others into the house, but that is the least of my concerns at present.

The people of Briarcopse are hospitable in their way. They think me exotic, but that makes them proud of me in some way I cannot entirely grasp. They treat me with profound respect, but with a kind of caution as if they suspected I might go up in flames at any moment. I have made it a point to take my tea in the local tea-shop twice a week, and that seems to be a prudent decision, for the ladies now nod to me, and the hostess asks me about the weather when I arrive, which, I am told, is an indication of acceptance.

Last week I drove up to London and visited some of my countrymen as well as the shops—my clothing does not suit this climate and I realize that I must stay warm when winter comes. No doubt Ponce will be annoyed at the expense of my wardrobe, but that is the price he must pay for remaining where he is. While I was in London I used part of the afternoon to visit the British Museum, and had a glass of sherry at the Museum Pub, which was very good, but made me homesick. That same afternoon, I was able to claim some of my belongings that have been shipped from Cádiz, and to make arrangements for them to be sent on to Copsehowe. I know it will be good to have my own things with me once more, and they will give the villagers something more to talk about: I doubt they have seen much of the Egyptian fashion in furniture outside of the cinema.

Speaking of my husband, I have had a letter from Ponce, who is both satisfied and irked that I am living here now. He is satisfied because three of his friends in Spain who own important businesses have been imprisoned, along with their families, so that the generals may take over their companies, much as has happened to your Eclipse Aeroplano Industrias. I have heard of more than a dozen such men. So Ponce knows his companies remain (albeit precariously) his, since I cannot be held as a virtual hostage in a prison cell. But he is irked because I am in England and he has no say in my being here. He tells me if I had waited two months, he would have been able to move me to whatever city in South or Central America I wished—so long as it is not where he is. To make it worse, you were the one who took the trouble to get me out of Spain, which must reflect poorly upon him. I have told him that if I had waited so long as Ponce liked, I would not have got out at all. If he has an answer to that, I have not received it yet.

My staff here—two groundsmen, a gardener, a cook, a housekeeper, a butler, a chauffeur, and three maids—are all paid by the family; Charles tells me that they would be here if I were here or not, and so the expense should not fall upon me. I have made a counter-offer: that I should pay half their wages, since I am reaping the immediate benefit of their presence. I do hope the family will agree, for I cannot be comfortable with the present arrangement; I can certainly afford to do this, but so far, Charles will not consider it. It is most perplexing, to have a landlord who is so generous. I feel crushed with kindness, and I know that in time I must strike a more equitable arrangement with them, for all our sakes.

A reporter from the local paper is coming to speak with me tomorrow, to get my opinion on the European situation. I almost declined his request, but then I thought that since I am living in self-imposed exile, it is incumbent upon me to express my reasons for doing so. I am trying to decide what to tell him, for I know that the English are hopeful that war can be avoided no matter what Germany does, and it is Germany that worries them, what with all the rumors of their military buildup and their forced-labor camps. But the Great War took a heavy toll on England, and no one here wants to consider another war, except perhaps that man Churchill, but no one listens to him. There are a few others in the government who, along with Mr. Churchill, share my concerns; they, too, are becoming unpopular because of their doom-saying. I am more troubled about Spain than England or Germany, but I know there is danger of war breaking out, no matter how much they may wish to avoid it: that may be out of their hands. It is surprising to me that these English will listen to the opinions of a woman on such matters, but I will do my best to explain my worries and I will trust I will not be too egregiously misquoted.

Let me thank you again for all you have done for me. My correspondence with my friends tells me that the situation in Spain is grave and growing more so by the day. I can only pray that when the war is over the country will not be so devastated that it will not recover, for no matter who is head of the government, it is the people who must make the country, or it is nothing. I occasionally feel guilty, to be living here in safety and comfort while my country is ravaged. But my presence in Spain would change nothing, so I must believe that I have not failed my homeland by leaving it in such a time of trial.

I would be happy to receive you here for any occasion, or none. Perhaps when you return from America you may take the time to call upon me so that I may more fully demonstrate my gratitude to you. I send you my best wishes until then, and my hopes for your safe travel and early return.

Your most affectionate

Isis

part two

ROWENA SAXON

8581 Barrington Avenue
Chicago, Illinois
August 17, '36

Ferenc Ragoczy, Count Saint-Germain
c/o Hotel Montgomery
774 Lakefront Blvd.
Chicago, Illinois

Dear Count Ragoczy,

Thank you so much for your kind letter of the 14th which arrived yester-
day. I must tell you it was something of a shock to read Simeon's name on
the envelope, for, you see, he died last January, on the 2nd. He had been
unwell for the last year-and-a-half with a complaint that the doctors were
never able to diagnose, but which they reckoned had something to do with
his heart, and when he contracted pneumonia in December, there was noth-
ing left in him to fight it, and he failed rapidly. His final days were spent at
home with a nurse to care for him and all but one of the children home again
to see him before the end. He slipped away quite easily just after sunset, his
hands in the hands of those who loved him. Although his health had not
been robust, at least he wasn't condemned to months and months of agony,
or to the isolation ward in the hospital, both of which he dreaded.

As I am sure you are aware, he suffered greatly after his first wife was
killed, and his baby. At the time it was more shocking than now, given how
the Jews are being treated in Germany. I know you were of true help to him
then, but nothing you, in your kindness, nor anyone could do was enough to
relieve him of the anguish which consumed him. I also know you provided
him with funds to travel, for the bank would not release his money because he
was Jewish, and even then, the NSDAP had a long arm. I believe it may well
have been your support that made it possible for my husband to begin his busi-
ness here, for it was not easy for him to solicit funds from strangers for such an
enterprise as he wanted to undertake. If I am mistaken, then I apologize, but
someone was kind enough to advance him the money, and of all his clients,
you were the most loyal to him after his family was so ruthlessly damaged.

When he left Germany, he did it with a heavy burden on his soul, con-

demning himself for being gone when it happened, and convinced that he could have prevented the killing, had he been there. Since that tragic day, the NSDAP has been ever more aggressive against Jews, as I am sure you know, and Simeon had come to see that he saved his older children and himself. Of late, the few letters he had from Germany made him certain that the dreadful whispers one hears from Jews leaving Germany are all true, and Jews are being put into labor camps and their property seized by the government. It seems impossible as I write it here, but I have relatives whom I can no longer reach by letter, and that concerns me deeply. What occasionally is shown in the newsreels brought Simeon nothing but distress, as it must to all of us.

For all his pessimism, I was happy to be his wife and to raise his surviving children as best I could, but I had no illusions of the place I held in his life; ours was an arranged marriage, and neither of us expected grand passion from it, which suited us both. He was in many ways caught in the past, and the past never completely released him. I hope that his death has finally ended his anguish. I have to say that he was always good to me, and our life together had genuine contentment, and I cannot fault Simeon for his loyalty to Amalie and Dietbold—had I been his first wife and his murdered child, I would want him to remember, too.

You inquire after the family, so I will do my best to fill you in on what has happened in the last dozen years. I am enclosing Bruno's business card: as you can see, he is practicing psychology here in Chicago. He graduated summa cum laude from Northwestern and has his Master's and Doctorate from there; he is on the staff at the H. T. Smith Institute, as well as having his own practice and offices, all of which pleased Simeon immensely. He is engaged to a wonderful girl—Rachel Fishman—and they plan to marry next spring. I know he would be glad to hear from you, if you have the time to call upon him.

Olympie married in '34, and she and her husband now make their home in New York. Eli Rosenblatt is a junior executive for Intercontinental Insurance, specializing in insuring commercial property and large construction projects. So far they are doing fairly well, which, given the nature of the times, is most encouraging. She and I maintain a regular correspondence, and from time to time, she telephones me. Olympie expects a baby in October, which would have delighted Simeon; he wanted—no, longed for—grandchildren so much, but he didn't live to see one; Olympie plans to name the child for him if they have a boy, and for her mother if she has a girl, and Eli is in complete agreement with her. I think this is a lovely tribute.

Emmerich is a lawyer now, and has a practice in Detroit, and for a young man only a short time out of law school, he is doing very well for himself. He already has a house of his own, and a Buick. Some of his clients are shady, and Simeon worried for his boy, doing business with such men. The firm he joined has made a reputation defending all manner of men associated with organized crime, and, as is often the case, the reputation of the clients has rubbed off on the attorneys defending them. Emmerich is young, and he may still realize that the excitement of taking on the cases of crime lords is not compensation enough for the damage to his integrity, no matter how much they pay.

You know that Hedda saw the men kill her mother and brother and was never quite the same afterward. Her affliction has only gotten worse over the years. She has spent a considerable amount of time in the care of an excellent psychiatrist, and has received the best therapy available, but nothing seemed to help. She even spent some months in a hospital, but with little improvement in her condition. Then, five years ago, she converted to Catholicism, which grieved Simeon greatly, and three years ago, she became a novice at the Poor Clares' convent, Holy Redeemer, in Menomonee Falls, just outside of Milwaukee. She is Sister Eustochium now, named for an obscure saint who lived in the Holy Land in the early days of the Christian religion, or so she told us when she entered the convent. Simeon was heartbroken over her joining the Order, and for almost a year wouldn't even mention her name, or accept anything she had done; toward the end he became resigned to her decision, saying that if it gave her peace, then he would have to consider it a blessing for her. She isn't allowed to write to any of us except at Christmas, and so I don't know very much about her that I can tell you, but that she says she is happy for the first time in her life. I was never able to get close to Hedda while she lived with us, and I sometimes feel I failed her when she had the greatest need of me. Of course, Simeon never made such a suggestion, but I can't help but think it must have crossed his mind now and then.

Simeon's architectural firm, Schnaubel & Wood, has done very well. Simeon has left his family comfortably off, and not even the Crash eroded the greatest part of the wealth he accumulated over the years. You may see his work in buildings throughout the Midwest, which the firm continues, with his founder's shares still providing a little money each year, and should continue to do so as President Roosevelt continues his policy of public works to bolster the economy. The investments Simeon made in land have proven to be of some worth, as well, so neither I nor his children need ever be in want, provided a little good judgment is exercised. As you may know, Simeon distrusted stocks after the German currency underwent such outrageous inflation a decade ago, and for that reason, he put his money in land and jewels. At the time I believed that he was being too cautious, but events proved him right, and I am grateful to him for his decision. So many of our friends have sustained appalling losses and may not have the opportunity or time to earn it all again.

I would be happy to have you visit, if you decide you have time to come by. If you can't, I do understand the problems travel imposes, and I will pass on your greetings to as many in the family as you would like, except Hedda, since she isn't allowed to receive mail from any of us, and will not be until her vows are final. I have heard the family speak of you many times, always with a kind of clemency and a shared sorrow for the death of your ward. Simeon called you merciful once, and although that was a strange choice of words for him, from what I have learned of you, it is singularly apt. On his behalf, and on behalf of his family, I would be glad to receive you any afternoon but Friday, if it suits your schedule to drive out to our house. Simeon designed it and it is easily recognized. You will know it when you see it.

In your note you say you are leaving for the West in a few days. If this precludes time for a visit, then let me take this opportunity to thank you for all the graciousness you showed my husband in Bavaria, and the help you provided in his time of greatest need. Many others have turned their backs on the plight of the German Jews, but you were not willing to set aside your humanity so readily. Without your help, he would probably not have made it to America, and he and his family would be facing who knows what problems in Germany, and my life would have been a great deal lonelier. If you cannot spare the time to call, then let me wish you a safe and pleasant journey. From all I know of you, it would be richly deserved.

Most sincerely yours,

Sarah Schnaubel

(Mrs. Simeon Schnaubel)

~

chapter one

This is a Packard Twelve," said the salesman. "The '34 model, the last year they made them. A truly fine piece of machinery. It's as good as anything

Rolls-Royce turns out." He patted the automobile on the hood, taking care to buff the light tan finish when he had done. "Hand-made, only two thousand of them in existence."

"What if it needs repair?" Saint-Germain asked, stroking the small black leather valise he carried under his arm. He looked around the showroom, a vast hall half the size of an airplane hangar, but with Corinthian columns and a few improbable murals of buxom Greek maidens in brightly colored but inaccurate chitons and hymations performing unlikely athletic feats. Three large fans hanging from the ceiling stirred the air but provided little alleviation from the heat.

"But it won't, not this car. It's as close to perfect as a car can get," the salesman insisted, his voice becoming edgy; he was in his late thirties in a summer-weight suit that had once been expensive but had seen better days. His shirt was spotlessly white but there was a beginning of fraying at the collar and cuffs, and on this feverish afternoon, he was sweating heavily enough to need to wipe his brow every five minutes or so. "And Packard's part of Studebaker now, and Studebaker's everywhere. If anything happens to it, you can get it fixed. Don't worry about that. Not that it's going to need fixing, just regular servicing."

"How much do you want for it?" Saint-Germain asked, knowing that Americans expressed real interest by asking about price.

"We're asking four thousand five hundred." The salesman mopped his brow.

"A considerable amount," Saint-Germain remarked.

There was a long pause, and the salesman cleared his throat. "We can't lower the price—it's a rare car. It's held its value and it will continue to do so."

"I was not asking for a lower price; I am only commenting that this is an expensive auto," said Saint-Germain.

"The former owner paid a much higher price for it," the salesman said, a bit defensively.

"And disposed of it within two years of buying it," said Saint-Germain.

"He suffered some business reversals," said the salesman with a quick gesture that he had made a great many times before. "The car's a real classic already, and a bargain at the price we're asking."

"If you say so," said Saint-Germain. "Do you think you would take four thousand three hundred for it, if you had the amount today, in cash?"

"Well," the salesman stalled nervously, "it's possible. I'll have to ask my supervisor to—" He stopped talking.

"If you need approval from someone else, then please, submit my offer. It's quite serious, I assure you." Saint-Germain seemed unaffected by the heat; his clothes were elegant and unrumpled, and his face was completely dry. "Four thousand three hundred dollars in cash by three this afternoon."

The salesman was flustered. "That's a considerable sum," he said nervously.

"Is it," Saint-Germain said as if without interest. "I will take your word for it. It is an amount I have to hand; if you will accept it, we can conclude the negotiation this afternoon, and you will enjoy your commission."

The salesman coughed. "I'll talk to my superior as soon as he returns from lunch." He put his hands together, rubbing the palms as if to start a fire.

"When will that be?" Saint-Germain asked.

"Two o'clock?" The salesman lowered his voice. "He sometimes takes a late lunch, and he did today. If you don't mind waiting twenty minutes? He'll be back and then I can submit this offer to him. If it were up to me, I'd say yes right away, but . . ."

"But?" Saint-Germain prompted when the salesman faltered.

"Any sale over a thousand dollars has to have his approval." He swallowed deeply. "I don't know what to say besides wait."

"Twenty minutes, you say?" Saint-Germain inquired.

"Thirty at the most." The salesman patted the Packard fondly. "It's a really wonderful car. If you want to take it for a test-drive, you may, but I have to ride along. You understand, a car this valuable, it can't be let out without someone from the dealership to keep track of it, and to vouch for it in case anything happens." He tried to show an ingratiating smile and only managed to look as if his feet hurt.

"I do understand," said Saint-Germain, only a hint of irony in his voice. "And I am willing to leave a surety deposit with you—say five hundred dollars?—while I take it for a test; alone." He let the salesman consider his offer, then went on, "I will endeavor to have the auto back here in fifteen minutes, twenty at the most."

The salesman, who made three hundred dollars in a good month, stared at the black-clad foreigner. He hadn't seen anyone handle money the way this fellow did since before the Crash, and it took him aback. "Five hundred?"

"Toward the purchase, of course," said Saint-Germain at his blandest.

"Of course," said the salesman, recovering himself enough to behave as if such offers were common occurrences. "Five hundred surety and you'll be back in fifteen to twenty minutes."

"You may ride with me, if the amount isn't sufficient." He managed to appear more willing than he was.

"Five hundred is a lot of money," said the salesman, again wiping his brow.

"Well and good," said Saint-Germain. "It should persuade you: I am sincere." He looked at the auto again. "It is elegant."

"Servo-assisted drum brakes on all four wheels, semi-floating rear axle," the salesman agreed, misunderstanding the compliment. "Top speed is just over one hundred miles an hour. Passenger windscreens, as well as for the driver. Eight coats of paint, each hand-polished. Same with the chrome. Six-volt electrical system. It weighs around two tons. Two spare tires. You can almost put a piano in the trunk. And the backseat compartment is thirty percent larger than in most cars." His recitation seemed to steady him a bit and he took a deep breath. "It's the best we have on the floor."

"I don't doubt it," said Saint-Germain, his attention directed to the overhead fans again. "I do want to drive it before I spend all this money on it." The money meant little to him, but it clearly meant a great deal more to the salesman.

The salesman laughed a little. "Leave your five hundred here and I'll explain it all to my boss if he gets back before you do. Just remember, we have all the paperwork here. You can't drive very far without proof of ownership." As a joke it fell flat; as a warning it was a great success.

"I have no wish to abscond with such an automobile—it is far too conspicuous." Saint-Germain opened the driver's door and got in, noticing how well-appointed the interior was. "Very nice," he said as he noticed the salesman looking at him nervously.

"For a car like this, we recommend insurance," the salesman added. "It's a good-sized investment and you want to protect it."

"I gather it can carry fairly heavy loads," said Saint-Germain as he pressed the ignition and heard the engine purr into life. He put his valise on the seat beside him.

"It can. As you see, the passenger compartment is larger than most. They like these cars for grand occasions." He coughed a bit nervously. "The five hundred?"

"Oh," said Saint-Germain as he took his black Florentine-leather wallet out of his inner breast-pocket and pulled out five 100-dollar bills; the salesman clasped them to his chest as if he feared a sudden wind might blow them away. "And here," he added, giving him a card for J. Harold Bishop of Horner Bishop Beatie Wentworth & Culpepper. "My local attorney's card. In case anything should happen."

The salesman took the card gingerly, and read the name. "Pretty classy lawyers; they handle all the bigwigs," he said.

"So I understand," Saint-Germain responded without concern. "Where may I drive out? Is there a special door?"

The salesman motioned toward the large, double-glass doors in the front of the building. "This way. There's a driveway just beyond."

Saint-Germain had noticed it coming in, and he nodded as he eased the big auto into gear. It moved forward with stately grace and a rumble of power that he found reassuring. He drove very slowly, so that the salesman could get ahead of him and open the doors while he got a feel for the auto. As he eased his way out into the street, he waved to the salesman, then rolled down the window so he could raise his arm to signal for a right turn, waiting for a gap in the vehicles on the street. The big Packard responded smoothly, and as Saint-Germain changed gears, he was reassured that he did not need to double-clutch. It was hot in the sunlight, and Saint-Germain was grateful for his native earth lining the soles of his shoes; there was a hint of the stockyards in the sluggish breeze that shoved at the heavy air. Joining the flow of traffic, he headed toward the lakefront, matching his speed to that of the autos around him. The pace was alternately slack and brisk with occasional snarls at major intersections, in spite of or because of the traffic lights, and Saint-Germain took care to make the most of the movements of the autos and lorries around him, maneuvering in the European fashion through the Chicago streets. He paid close attention to the way in which the Packard turned, how quickly it picked up speed, what amount of sway it had on corners: he was quickly satisfied with the auto. Glancing at his watch, he decided it was time to head back toward the showroom, and he signaled for a left, crossing the thoroughfare on the light just ahead of a Chevrolet; its rumble-seat was filled with four children in party clothing.

The salesman was pacing nervously, his collar noticeably wilted, as Saint-Germain drove back in through the open doors. He did his best to smile ingratiatingly, and looked uneasily at his watch. "Not quite twenty minutes."

"Just as we agreed," said Saint-Germain as he brought the Packard to a halt and set the hand-brake, then picked up his small valise.

"Well?" The salesman could not contain himself any longer. "What do you think?"

"It's an excellent vehicle, and handles very well, particularly for being such a heavy automobile. If you will let me inspect the motor and read the rest of the specifications for it?" He got out of the auto and closed the door. "I want to know what manner of machine I'm purchasing, and what modifications are possible."

"Modifications?" the salesman exclaimed. "To this car?"

"Yes," said Saint-Germain.

"Why would you want to modify this car?" The salesman was looking warily about, as if he suspected Saint-Germain of nefarious intentions.

Saint-Germain gave a little sigh. "I would like to add a second fuel tank; I am planning to drive extensively and I have no wish to be caught miles away from any gasoline simply because the tank could not contain sufficient—"

The salesman smiled again. "Oh. Well, yes. I think there is a standard augmentation still available for the car. I don't know what it would cost, or how long it would take to install, this being a hand-made vehicle and all. But I'd be happy to find out."

"If you would, please," said Saint-Germain as he watched a globose fellow with a sweating, pumpkin-shaped head trundle toward them; he assumed this must be the supervisor, finally back from his lunch.

"Good afternoon, good afternoon," the fat man said, holding out a massive paw. "I hear you're interested in our piece de resistance." He pronounced the words as if they were English. "I'm sure Ronweicz told you what it costs. Daniel Hirshbach, at your service."

"Ferenc Ragoczy." They shook hands. "That he did, and it seems a reasonable price," said Saint-Germain, noticing that the supervisor was startled, a response he quickly concealed. "I can give you cash today for the vehicle, providing I can arrange for a minor modification in the automobile."

"Modifications can be expensive," said the supervisor. "And they often take time to get done."

"The price of what I would like added to the auto is what Mr. Ronweicz is finding out for me now," said Saint-Germain, his urbanity unruffled but with an underlying decisiveness that impressed the supervisor and silenced him. "I will make the arrangements for the alterations as soon as I have title to the Packard."

"If you insist," said the supervisor, unable to conceal his disappointment, for he would have liked to have been able to charge a service fee for arranging the changes made to the Packard. "So," he went on with forced geniality, "you really want to buy this baby?"

"Yes. Mr. Hirshbach, I do." Saint-Germain favored the man with a direct look. "I also wish to arrange for registration and insurance for it, which I trust you may do for me?"

"We have an insurance agent on the floor, yes," said Hirshbach. "The state forms are all in my office. We can attend to this as soon as you like." He lifted his bushy eyebrows as if he were still uncertain that Saint-Germain would go through with the purchase.

"That suits me very well; I am prepared to conclude the . . . ah . . . deal now," said Saint-Germain, slipping his valise under his arm again, and glancing toward the offices at the rear of the showroom. "If it is convenient?"

"Oh. Yes." He started to walk, then slowed. "Don't you want to wait until you find out how much the alterations are going to cost?"

"It's immaterial to me. I only want some sense of the price," said Saint-Germain, continuing toward the office.

Hirshbach shook his heavy head. "You Europeans. You don't know how hard it's been here in America."

"As you don't know what Europe has endured of late," said Saint-Germain, then added, "Why should you."

"Yes," Hirshbach agreed, not understanding Saint-Germain's intent. "America has her own problems to solve. It doesn't do any good to get involved in the rest of the world's troubles." He reached ahead to open his office door, and indicated a ladder-back chair facing the big desk that occupied most of the room. "Sit. Sit. I'll just get out the papers . . ." For a large man he was very light on his feet; he glided behind the desk and dropped into the big oaken chair and opened one of the drawers, taking out papers with carbon sheets attached between them. He rolled these into his large Royal typewriter and hit the carriage return until he was at the right line. "Your name, please, last name first, and spell it."

"Ragoczy: *R-A-G-O-C-Z-Y*, Ferenc: *F-E-R-E-N-C*," he responded, watching Hirshbach's sausage-like fingers work the keys as delicately as dancers. "It's Hungarian."

"Address?"

Saint-Germain used his Chicago attorney's office—which he had arranged earlier—as his registration address. He was about to open his valise when Ronweicz tapped on the door.

"The Studebaker dealer on Michigan says the second gas tank will run you about two hundred twenty-five dollars, with installation. He can do the job day after tomorrow. I told him that would be okay?" He did his best to maintain his affability, but his nervousness was apparent; he was afraid he was going to lose the commission for this sale to Hirshbach.

"Thank you, Mr. Ronweicz. If you will provide me the telephone number, I'll confirm the appointment today." Saint-Germain looked directly at Hirshbach. "You must be pleased to have such an industrious salesman working for you."

Hirshbach's smile was sour. "Yes. Ronweicz is a good man on the job." He scowled at the paper in the typewriter. "Now, where were we?"

"You have my address; you have still to fill out the specific information on the auto itself, and then you will have to calculate the cost of the vehicle." Saint-Germain inclined his head. "Then I should speak with your insurance agent."

"Yes. Of course," said Hirshbach. "You're an alert fellow, Ragoczy. No doubt about it." The way he said it, this was not entirely complimentary.

Saint-Germain chose to ignore the unpleasant undertones of Hirshbach's remark. "Thank you. I find it incumbent upon me, as a foreigner, to be on the qui vive."

"Of course," said Hirshbach, taking an index card from a drawer made for them. He very carefully copied the information from the card onto the paper in the typewriter, and was about to put it away when Saint-Germain stopped him.

"I know you're a diligent man, Mr. Hirshbach, but I think it would be wisest to compare your record here with what is on the Packard itself, if you don't mind. I'm probably being overcautious, but I know how easily numbers can be transposed in a long string." He spoke so blandly that it was impossible for Hirshbach to protest. "A man in my position—a foreigner in your country—is under constant scrutiny."

"As you say, such things can happen, and it would make things difficult for you," he muttered as he shoved himself out of his chair and made his way around the end of the desk. "Let's go make sure this is all accurate—engine number and car serial number. Better safe than sorry."

"Exactly," said Saint-Germain, following him out into the showroom and over to the Packard.

Hirshbach shoved up to the Packard and opened the driver's door. "There is the registration number." He read it off, comparing it to the card he held. "Oh," he said as he came to the last two numbers. "I reversed them."

"An easy thing to do," said Saint-Germain smoothly. "Shall we correct the form?"

"Yes," said Hirshbach, moving away from the Packard and back toward his office. "How astute of you, Mr. Ragoczy." He plunked himself down and xed out the inaccurate number, typing in the corrected one above it. "There. I'll need you to initial this when I'm done."

"Fine." Saint-Germain opened his valise and took out an envelope filled with hundred-dollar bills. "What is the total?"

"Just a moment," Hirshbach said, and turned toward his large adding machine. He punched in numbers and cranked them up. "You told Ronweicz you'd pay four thousand four hundred—"

"Four thousand three hundred," Saint-Germain corrected gently. "Plus all other required fees." He counted out four stacks of ten bills each. "Four thousand. What is the balance?"

Hirshbach cranked in another sum, and said, "With state license fees and all applicable taxes, it comes to four thousand four hundred seventy-eight dollars and thirty-six cents." He tore off the adding machine paper and handed it to Saint-Germain. "Check my calculations, if you like."

Saint-Germain glanced over the figures. "They appear accurate to me," he said, and counted out five hundred dollars more. "I believe you owe me twenty-one dollars and sixty-four cents in change."

"Just a moment," Hirshbach said as he took the money and counted it. When he was done, he nodded. "I'll get your change." He pulled a key from his trouser-pocket and opened the middle drawer of his desk where a change tray sat. With great deliberation he counted out the change and handed it to Saint-Germain.

"My bill of sale?" Saint-Germain asked politely.

"Just a moment." He rolled the completed transfer of title form out of his typewriter and put another one in. This time he filled it out quickly and gave one of the carbon copies to Saint-Germain, along with a pen so he could provide his signature. "Sign on the lines I've indicated, and initial where the number is corrected. This is all you'll need. Between these two documents, you have undisputed and unencumbered title to the Packard Twelve." As soon as the forms were completed, he held the two pieces of paper out to Saint-Germain. "Congratulations, Mr. Ragoczy. It's a wonderful car. I know you'll enjoy it." These practiced sentiments were recited as if by rote. "You may talk to Brendon Shelly about insurance."

"Thank you. I'll attend to that at once." He folded the papers and put them into his inner breast-pocket. "When will I receive the official documents from the state?"

"In ten days or two weeks, or thereabouts. In the meantime, carry those two papers with you in the car at all times." He pressed his mouth closed, then asked, "Is there anything more?"

"Oh; yes, there is," said Saint-Germain as he got to his feet. "The surety deposit I left with Mr. Ronweicz? Five hundred dollars."

"Of course," said Hirshbach, very nearly pouting. He reached into his drawer again and counted out the five hundred. "What would you have done if the Packard weren't to your satisfaction?" he asked as he handed the money over. "What better were you going to buy?"

Saint-Germain gave a quick smile. "Fortunately the auto suits me very well, so neither of us will know the answer to that." He tucked the envelope back into his valise and slipped it under his arm.

"Do you always travel with so much cash?" Hirshbach asked, trying not to sound too curious.

"When it is necessary, I do." He opened the door and stepped back into the showroom, where he caught sight of Ronweicz hovering near the Packard. "Thank you for all your help, Mr. Ronweicz. I hope you will not have to give up too much of your commission on this sale."

The wry tone in Saint-Germain's voice caught Ronweicz's attention. "I hope the same thing," he said in a lowered voice.

"Then I will provide you a recommendation, should you want it, for seeking out a less greedy employer," Saint-Germain said, and saw Ronweicz blink in astonishment. "You did well for me; the least I can do is return the favor. I will give my attorney a letter for you in the next day or two, and you may call for it at any time you wish."

"That's very kind of you, Mr. Ragoczy," said Ronweicz, becoming flustered.

"I have had some fluctuations of fortunes in my life," Saint-Germain told him as his thoughts filled with remembered images: his father's enemies in the Carpathians; the Temple of Imhotep; the Roman arena; a riot in Antioch; the Huns attacking on Greek hillsides; a frost-blighted summer in Mongolia; Spain, Franksland, and Saxony; the lamasery in Tibet; Heugenet's castle; Delhi besieged;

Fiorenza and Venezia; the mountains of Peru; Russia and England; Italy and France. "I know how difficult they can be to endure."

"It's still real nice of you," said Ronweicz. "Even to think of it."

"I will do as I've said: my Word on it," said Saint-Germain, offering his hand. After they had shaken, he asked, "About the insurance?"

"That door," Ronweicz said, pointing. "Brendon Shelly's the agent here. He'll explain it all to you."

"Very good." He turned away, then said over his shoulder, "I wish you every success, Mr. Ronweicz."

"You too, Mr. Ragoczy." For the first time Ronweicz looked at ease.

"Thank you," said Saint-Germain, and continued on to the desk of the insurance agent. Their conversation was brief and to the point; at the end of it, Saint-Germain handed Shelly fifty-six dollars for a full-coverage policy for one year, took the copy of the policy Shelly had filled out for him, and put it into his inner breast-pocket with his other papers, thanking the agent as he did. He glanced at his wristwatch: it was two forty-one. He had purchased the Packard before three, just as he had intended to do.

Now that the auto was his, he got into it and drove to Horner Bishop Beatie Wentworth & Culpepper. He parked in the lot next to the building and went inside, taking the elevator to the sixth floor, where a receptionist in a heat-rumpled linen suit kept him waiting for ten minutes before admitting him to J. Harold Bishop's tome-lined office, where the attorney was waiting, a cigarette in one hand held the same way Franklin Roosevelt held his, but without the ivory holder. He was wearing a three-hundred-dollar navy-blue, pin-striped, double-breasted suit that was admirably tailored to conceal a slight paunch; his shirt was white linen and his tie was blue-and-red–medallion foulard silk. Bishop had well-barbered hair cut like Cary Grant's, and manicured nails that had been buffed to a subtle shine. Only his pocket handkerchief—pale blue silk—could be said to be a bit overdone, but for Chicago, Saint-Germain recognized that Bishop was conservatively dressed.

"Good afternoon, Comte," Bishop said, rising to shake hands. "Have a seat. I guess since you're here, you bought a car?"

"A Packard Twelve, the '34 model," Saint-Germain confirmed.

"That's a swell car," Bishop said, his enthusiasm kept in check by his contained demeanor. "You're registering the address as this one?" He sat down as soon as Saint-Germain had chosen a chair for himself.

"I have done so, as we agreed," said Saint-Germain. "I will tell you where to send the registration when it arrives. Shall I allow five weeks?"

"That should be about right," said Bishop, then conscientiously added, "If you take up full residence in another state, you'll have to re-register the car there."

"I understand that," said Saint-Germain. "But I don't know yet what my long-range plans will be." He ducked his head as if to imply an apology for any inconvenience this might cause.

"Just as well to have this as your address of record, then." Bishop leaned back in his fine leather chair.

"I accept your advice in this regard," said Saint-Germain, and reached into his breast-pocket, removing the copies of the registration, the transfer of ownership, and the insurance policy. "Here. Your secretary may use these to make your file on my affairs current."

Bishop opened the pages and perused them swiftly. "All standard. And the most thorough insurance available on the open market." He pressed a button on his desk, signaling his secretary to come in. "Miss McAllister will take care of this for you, Comte."

Miss McAllister, middle-aged and plainly dressed, came into the office. "Yes, Mr. Bishop?"

"You know the pertinent data we'll need. Take them down, if you will. The Comte will wait for his documents." Bishop handed them over and motioned Miss McAllister away. "She's the most efficient woman on our staff."

"How fortunate for you to have her services, then," he said.

"You can have no idea what a difference she makes," said Bishop, then resumed his most professional manner. "Do you know yet when you plan to head West?"

"A week at most, three days at least. I'll leave a message with you when I depart." Saint-Germain smiled at him. "I have obtained a driver's license, and so has my manservant." He had not wanted to supply a thumbprint, but it was required, and so he had done so.

"Very good," said Bishop. "Do you have your temporary copy?"

"In my wallet, as you advised me," said Saint-Germain.

"Excellent. Make sure you keep your registration and your insurance information in the car at all times. The registration certificate must be fixed to the steering column." The attorney did his best to be cordial. "I'm sure similar laws prevail in Europe."

"In certain countries, yes," said Saint-Germain.

Bishop coughed delicately. "I have your memorandum about inquiries regarding your whereabouts. I am authorized to only reveal that information to inquiries coming through the attorneys you provided for me on your list, from Manitoba Chemicals, and from duly authorized governmental agencies. No one else is to be given any information I may have on your location, of which you will keep me apprised by telegram every two weeks." He paused. "Have I understood your instructions correctly?"

"Yes. And you are to inform me of any inquiries made in regard to me," Saint-Germain reminded him. "You will have up-to-date information through which to notify me." He looked up as Miss Dorothy McAllister, Bishop's secretary, came back into the office with a large manila envelope in her hand.

"This contains your documents, Mr. Ragoczy," she said.

Saint-Germain took the envelope. "Thank you, Miss McAllister."

She looked at him in surprise; she was unused to being thanked, especially by clients. She nodded to him as her cheeks flushed. "You're welcome, I'm sure." With a glance at Bishop, she turned and left the office.

"So," said Bishop. "I think this will take care of everything for the time being." He rose and held out his hand. "It's a pleasure serving you, Comte."

"Thank you," said Saint-Germain. "I'll settle my current bill on the way out."

"Your retainer is more than sufficient to cover it," Bishop assured him.

"Still, I would prefer not to have any ends dangling, as the saying goes," said Saint-Germain as he started to the door.

"I'm not one to turn down money. Miss McAllister will take care of the bill for you." Bishop laughed theatrically. "I wish I had more clients like you."

"Do you," said Saint-Germain with an irony that was wasted on the lawyer as he went out of J. Harold Bishop's office to pay his secretary for the man's opinions and time.

TEXT OF A LETTER FROM DESMOND REEVES IN LONDON TO FERENC RAGOCZY IN AMERICA, CARE OF MILES SUNBURY IN LONDON; SENT AIR MAIL TO CHICAGO AND FORWARDED TO OSCAR KING OF KING LOWENTHAL TAYLOR & FROST IN SAN FRANCISCO.

> *London, England*
> *22 August, 1936*
>
> *Ferenc Ragoczy, Count of Saint-Germain*
> *c/o Miles Sunbury*
> *Sunbury Draughton Hollis & Carnford*
> *Solicitors and Barristers*
> *New Court*
> *London*
>
> *My dear Count,*
> *I make bold to approach you on this most disturbing matter that Mrs. Bell, your housekeeper here in London, has brought to my attention, or more properly, to the attention of my wife, who has correctly mentioned*

the incident to me, and which I now recount to you: on the 19th of this
month, when I was out of your house attending to making arrangement
for a few minor repairs, a man called and was received by Mrs. Bell. He
was a foreigner going by the name of Ash and claimed acquaintance with
you from your days in Spain, and expressed a desire to know where he
might find you. Mrs. Bell is an excellent woman in many ways, but she is
not inclined to guard her tongue, and so she told this gentleman that you
had gone to America. He ventured a guess that it was New York that had
been your destination, but Mrs. Bell took it upon herself to correct him,
and told him you had gone to Boston. The man said you must have
changed your plans from what they had been before, thanked Mrs. Bell,
and departed.

Would that was all there was to it, for I have come to find out that this
Ash person has returned yesterday, ostensibly to give a token of thanks to
Mrs. Bell, but I fear that was only a ploy to attempt to learn more from her
in regard to your travels. Thinking this Ash was an associate of yours—he
apparently knows about your airplane business in Spain—she gave him tea,
as it was late in the afternoon, in the back parlor and fell to chatting with
him. I have not determined how much she revealed, but it is apparent to me
that she has said a great deal more than she should. My wife came upon
them less than an hour later, at which time Ash took his leave, but not
before my wife had the opportunity to size him up, and to learn about the
two visits. She has correctly informed me of the two incidents and I have
now reported them to you.

If it seems to you that Mrs. Bell has overstepped herself, you have only to
let your solicitor know you want to terminate her services. If you believe she
is deserving of another chance, you may rest assured that I have chastised
her for her poor judgment, and she has promised most faithfully not to forget
herself again. I have asked the cook, Mrs. Shoemaker, to be a bit more alert
when Mrs. Bell is here alone. Mrs. Shoemaker leaves at half-eight every
night but Sunday, which she has off. I can pledge to be here after eight in the
evening, which will not provide Mrs. Bell the opportunity to speak to this
Ash again, even if he should call here again. I believe Mrs. Bell liked the company of this Ash fellow, and in spite of the trouble he has brought her, she
might be inclined to speak with him. I have reminded her that she is a
widow with a child to provide for, and it would be preposterous for her to
put her livelihood in danger for a smooth-speaking foreigner. I think she has
taken my warning to heart.

I have given a full account of this to your solicitor, Mr. Sunbury, and on his advice, I will inform you of any other incidents of untoward behavior, as well as any attempts to obtain information in regard to your travels, and whatever your instructions may be in regard to this or any other household matters, I will obey them on every point to the limits of my abilities.

Your most devoted,

Desmond Reeves

chapter two

Doña Isabel stepped out of her mallard-green SS Airline saloon auto and looked around Cross Street in Uxbridge as a nearby church clock chimed one. She read the various signs and finally walked toward the St. Andrew Hotel and Public House, the invitation she had received the week before held in her hand. She was handsomely turned out in a dark teal suit of woolen crepe with a fox wrap negligently tossed around her shoulders; her hat was a feminine navy-blue version of a trilby with a pheasant's feather and a wisp of a veil that held the sleek roll of her dark hair pulled back and anchored with a small, bejeweled comb; artfully applied make-up set off her lovely mouth and fine eyes; her gloves and clutch bag matched her suit, the seams of her silk stockings were absolutely straight, and her shoes were navy-blue with three-inch heels and a fashionable ankle-strap. Had she been in Bond Street, she would have turned heads; here she attracted a great deal of attention as she made her way into the pub and went up to the bar. "I am supposed to meet Mr. Sunbury here," she said.

"He's expecting you. In the lounge, by the settle, ma'am," said the publican. "Can I send anything in to you? We aren't strictly open yet—won't be for an hour—but given as you've come a distance and Mr. Sunbury is an old acquaintance, I think I can make an exception for you—"

"A dry sherry, if you would," said Doña Isabel, and swept into the lounge where she saw Miles Sunbury seated, as the publican had said, by the settle, a small table in front of him. "Mr. Sunbury," she said, starting toward him, her hand out.

"Doña Isabel," said Sunbury, getting to his feet and taking her hand to kiss. He was dressed for London in a handsome three-piece suit of charcoal wool, a white linen shirt, and a claret-colored silk tie. His hat lay on the bench next to where he had been sitting. There was a pony of sherry on the table in front of him. "Thank you for coming to meet me." He slid around the end of the table and held the chair out for her.

"I was glad to, Mr. Sunbury; it's given me a chance to get out and do a bit of exploring. I enjoyed the drive over very much. Such wonderful little villages you have in this part of England: Addlestone, Laleham, Aldershot, and dozens more. As I drove in from Hampshire, I found so many of them," she said, taking her seat and crossing her legs the way Marlene Dietrich did. "Why did you want to meet with me in this place? You could have come to Briarcopse if you wished to visit a pretty little town, though it is farther away from London."

"Well, you see, I didn't want to call upon you at Copsehowe, because there are those who would make note of such a visit, and if you were to come to my chambers in London, it would be equally obvious. Also, I have reason to think I might be observed, and I would not want to put you at risk by leading my follower—whoever he may be—to your door. If there is such a follower." He gave a subtle emphasis to *you* and smiled uncertainly. "I know this may seem overly cautious, but I believe it is better to be prudent than to be lax in this case." He resumed his seat. "It's about Saint-Germain, you see."

"Ah," said Doña Isabel. "Is there trouble?"

"There may be," said Sunbury. "I thought it best to tell you of this, in case it is as serious as I fear it may be."

"Gracious," said Doña Isabel. "This sounds dire." She liked the way the word *dire* sounded, almost Latin, but with more edges on it.

"It may not be so very dreadful. Not that I want to make light of it, but I have no wish to distress you." Sunbury laid his hand on hers for a moment. "I want you to know that my concerns are more of an anticipatory nature than an actual—" He broke off as the publican came into the lounge, a pony of sherry on a wooden tray. "I'll pay for the lady's drink," Sunbury said as Doña Isabel reached to open her purse.

"That's very good of you, Mr. Sunbury," she said, smiling at him.

"You've done me the honor of coming here; the least I can do is buy your sherry." He handed a half-crown and sixpence to the publican.

Although this was nothing more than what Doña Isabel expected, she found herself flattered. "How nicely expressed."

Sunbury looked a bit nonplussed. "Thank you." He motioned the curious publican away. "Let me put you at your ease as much as I can, which is difficult for me to do, under the circumstances. I may be jumping at shadows, but who knows—where Saint-Germain is concerned, there are so many problems . . ."

When Sunbury did not go on, Doña Isabel asked, "Has this anything to do with what is happening in Spain?"

"I think it may," said Sunbury. "I'm not entirely sure, of course, or I would say so, but it certainly is possible."

Doña Isabel looked directly at him. "What do you feel?" She saw him falter. "Not think, Mr. Sunbury: feel."

"I'm a lawyer, Doña Isabel, and I am paid to think. I am asked for assessments and opinions." He saw the slight distress in her eyes, and went on, "I tend to distrust my feelings."

"That must be very trying for your wife," said Doña Isabel.

"I am not married, Doña Isabel," said Sunbury huffily.

"I did not mean to insult you, Mr. Sunbury," said Doña Isabel, noticing his stiffness. "But whatever your marital status may be, *I* cannot rely wholly on thought in such circumstances. Thought can be very misleading when there may be trouble brewing. You may not have experienced the gathering storm, but I have, and it has made me appreciate my emotions, and listen to their promptings. The only reason I got safely out of Spain was that I put more faith in my feelings than in thought, for thought would surely have made my departure seem capricious." She was not as self-possessed as she wanted to be, and she could feel color mounting in her face. "If there is hazard here, I want to know what your sense of it is."

"That is why I am meeting with you now, Doña Isabel, if I may say so," said Sunbury.

Doña Isabel took her glass of sherry and offered a silent and rueful toast to Sunbury while she gathered her composure. "Then tell me what has happened that has alarmed you so much that you asked me to meet with you away from your chambers and my house. I must suppose that it was more than your logical interpretations of events that led to this meeting." She tapped the edge of the glass with one perfectly lacquered nail.

Sunbury coughed diplomatically. "Desmond Reeves, who is Saint-Germain's steward at his London house, has recently reported to me that a man has been to the house asking for Saint-Germain's present location. He implied acquaintance from Spain, and was able to glean enough information to know he has gone to America. The man's name, he said, was Ash." He regarded Doña Isabel. "Ash. Do you recall a man of that name?"

"Ash? No, no one comes to mind. Nor anyone called Ceniza," she said, translating the name to Spanish. "But I did not know everyone he knew in Spain. He had associates in cities other than Cádiz, and they may be able to identify this man. Of course, the government has seized Saint-Germain's businesses, as they have the businesses of many Spaniards as well, and I may not be able to contact any of these—"

"I've already sent a telegram to Eclipse Aero, and received notice that only the government can provide answers in regard to the business or the persons employed by it," said Sunbury. "All connection to Saint-Germain has been officially severed."

"Then I begin to understand why you may want to speak with me. This person named Ash is the cause of your concern. You suspect he may be intending something against Saint-Germain, and seeks to do it through those who know him." Doña Isabel took another sip of sherry. "Do you suppose he will find me, and seek to learn more from me?"

"It may be unlikely, but I cannot rule out the possibility," said Sunbury.

"And you think this man might be dangerous to me as well as to Saint-Germain?" Doña Isabel's voice caught in her throat.

"I would hope not," said Sunbury, once again putting his hand over hers. "But it would be remiss of me not to warn you."

"You haven't met this Ash, have you?" she guessed aloud.

"No, but I have reason to believe that he has called at my chambers—at least a foreigner matching his description has done so, and was turned away when he refused to disclose the reason for his call to my clerk. But I have to assume he is aware of who I am." He sighed apologetically. "When I telephoned you, I was relieved to hear that you had not yet been visited by him, and I hoped that meant he was unaware of your residency in England."

"But you have changed your mind," said Doña Isabel.

"Yes. After a night's sleep, I realized he might well have more than one set of clues to follow, and that it was incumbent upon me to warn you." He lowered his gaze to the tabletop.

"How very kind of you," said Doña Isabel most sincerely. "I truly appreciate your concern, Mr. Sunbury, and your effort on my behalf, but I cannot think that this man will know how to find me. Why should he?"

Sunbury nodded. "I do agree that it is doubtful that he is aware of you, but I could not take the chance that it was wholly impossible."

"Of course you could have, Mr. Sunbury," said Doña Isabel. "It is very good of you to let me know about this man, though I may have no reason to be troubled. I would prefer to be alert to something that doesn't happen than asleep to something that does. It is very sweet—and very English—of you to extend yourself on my behalf. I count myself fortunate to have so scrupulous a guardian." She had another sip of sherry. "My stay here would be much more difficult if not for you. I thank you for all you have done."

"In spite of all my thought?" Sunbury said, one eyebrow arched. He had more of his drink, liking the warmth it spread through him.

"And because of it," Doña Isabel conceded.

"So you are willing to grant that deduction has its place in the world," Sunbury said, liking the smile this remark brought to her face.

"I am willing to allow that it has its uses," she said, and sipped her sherry again. "They may not be applicable now, however."

Sunbury took his watch from his waistcoat pocket. "It is half-one. Would you object if I asked you to join me for luncheon?"

She finished her sherry. "I am thankful for your invitation," she admitted. "I had coffee for breakfast and the drink could easily go to my head if I don't have food to offset it." Looking around, she asked, "Would you like to eat here? Have they a dining room?"

"They serve pasties and meat pies and sandwiches in the taproom. Not quite what you would like, I reckon. There is a tolerable dining room in the hotel across the way," said Sunbury. "I should think we could get something suitable there." He rose, picked up his hat, and came to help her up from her chair. "I imagine you might find English food rather tame after what you have been used to in Cádiz."

She took his hand as she got up. "Thank you." As she slipped her arm through the crook of his elbow, she remarked, "Fortunately, I know my way around a kitchen, and so I've been able to prepare dishes from my own country. I wish I could find a better supply of peppers, though."

He held the pub door open for her and indicated the hotel on the opposite corner. "Peppers." He considered this. "There are some Chinese markets in London that might have what you're looking for, or something close enough. I know there are a number of peppers the Chinese use in their cooking."

"So there are," said Doña Isabel. "If you will tell me where I ought to go to find these markets, next time I'm in London, I'll look for them."

"They aren't in a part of town where you should venture alone," said Sunbury as they crossed the road together. "If you want to go pepper-shopping, let me know when you would like to do so and I'll arrange to escort you."

She looked at him, so startled that she almost stumbled on the curb. "You're a busy man, Mr. Sunbury. I can't impose upon you in that way."

"I'm not so busy that I cannot find an hour or so to make sure you don't get into anything unpleasant in your shopping. In fact, I would rather enjoy such a lark." He opened the door into the small lobby of the hotel and removed his hat. "There may also be something to your taste in the few Indian markets we have, as well." He nodded in the direction of the dining room, and started that way.

"Your proposed escort is turning into quite an expedition," said Doña Isabel. "And I will accept your kind offer before it becomes so disproportionate that I must ask you to bill me for your time." She laughed lightly, hoping he would not be offended by her jest; Englishmen could be so very prickly about such things.

"There is no reason you should trouble yourself on that account," said Sunbury, looking a bit awkward as he told the maitre d' that they would like a table for two near the garden window; four of the other fifteen tables were occupied, and a few of the dining patrons turned their heads to look at Doña Isabel as she crossed the dining room with Sunbury.

"But surely you won't put yourself at an inconvenience," she said.

"Coming to Uxbridge in the middle of the day to have a meeting with—if you will allow me—a beautiful woman could be seen as an inconvenience by some; I find it a most delightful interlude, and you the most stimulating company," he said, a hint of color in his cheeks as they were seated at a table in the corner near the garden window. He put his hat down on the edge of the table, opposite the place she put her purse.

"How very deft you are at turning compliments," she said, sitting down and taking the proffered menu.

"I bow to the better . . . person." He was suddenly inept, as if this reminder that she was a woman troubled him.

"Hardly that, Mr. Sunbury," she said, and opened the menu to give him a chance to recover. "Is there anything you recommend?"

"I am partial to their Welsh rarebit. I think the cook here has a knack for it," said Sunbury.

Doña Isabel looked around the menu at him. "You know this place, then?"

"Oh, yes," he said. "My father had a good many friends living in Buckinghamshire, Berkshire, Hampshire, and Surrey. The Wainfords near Slough, the Tissinghams at Maidenhead, the Pearce-Mannings at Chalfont Saint-Giles, and the Byreleighs near Ockham. When I was a young man, I think my brother and I spent half my holidays with these families. Our family came originally from Sunbury, of course, although we have been Londoners since the first King George. Still, we have cousins in and around the town. When we visited our friends, we would come here to Uxbridge from time to time, and it has remained in my memory. I am nostalgic every time I visit."

"Do you ever come here with your brother?" She saw his expression change, and said at once, "I'm sorry. What have I—"

"My brother, and my mother and sister, died in the Influenza Epidemic. It quite devastated my father, who was never the same after that." Sunbury shook his head. "We're hardly the only family to have such losses."

"True enough," said Doña Isabel. "My husband lost his first wife and his daughter to the Influenza. And my grandfather—who raised me—died of it, leaving me with only my widowed mother. Fortunately, she sent me to school where I learned English, among other things. It has proven the most useful of my studies. My mother said that because of the Great War, husbands would be in short supply for years to come, and I would need to be well-informed to attract a man able to support me in the manner to which I had become accustomed, or, failing that, to have some means to make my way in the world, such as commercial translation." She wished she could turn the conversation to something more pleasant, but her mind seemed unable to shift its focus. "I don't know what . . . I'm sorry I've brought back such painful losses, Mr. Sunbury."

"It is not your fault, Doña Isabel," he said, squaring his shoulders. "I think all of us lost someone dear to us in that tragedy." He looked up. "I hope you will not think the less of me for my lapse."

"How could I? I do not believe that honoring the dead is a lapse, Mr. Sunbury." She did her best to look encouraging, to hearten him again.

"It is hardly appropriate luncheon conversation, I agree." He pretended to scrutinize the menu. "I recommend the soup. They do a very good puree of peas with heavy cream. Also, their baked onions make an excellent side-dish. The mushrooms with soft cheese is also quite a good dish, if a little bland."

"The soup sounds delectable," said Doña Isabel, allowing herself to be distracted; it actually did sound better than a great many English dishes. "I'll have some, and, I think, the breast of chicken with chutney sauce." She doubted that the chutney sauce would be as flavorful as she hoped, but it was more promising than the lamb chop with mint sauce or the filet of plaice in bread-crumbs with butter, and the thought of something called shepherd's pie filled her with apprehension. "Yes. The breast of chicken will do very well, after the soup. And perhaps a glass of white Burgundy to lend it savor?"

"Shall I order a bottle? They have a tolerable cellar here." He was calmer now that he was back on safe conversational ground.

"That would be lovely," said Doña Isabel, relieved at the very idea.

"Very good, then." He signaled for a waiter and placed their orders, adding a side-dish of baked onions. "If you have Meursault '32? The Leroy?"

"Very good, sir; I believe we have a bottle or two left," said the waiter, and left them alone.

For the greater part of a minute the two were silent, then Sunbury said, "I am going to notify the men guarding you to be on the alert for this Ash fellow."

"Do you think that's necessary?" she asked. "I would have supposed that the need for all this protection was diminishing, not increasing."

"Last week, I would have agreed with you. Now, I would prefer to take the extra precaution, in case you are in any direct danger. I would not like to have to answer for any harm that could come to you." He reached into his jacket and pulled out a gold cigarette case and a matching lighter. "Would you like one?"

"Not before a meal. Perhaps afterward," she said.

"All right," said Sunbury. "Do you mind if I smoke?"

"Of course not," she said, and gestured to him to go ahead.

He selected a cigarette, tamped it on the gold case, and lit up. The faintly acrid odor of burning tobacco wafted over their table. "I have to admit I thought the Count was overdoing it when he said you should be guarded, even out at Copsehowe, but I can see it was a wise decision."

The waiter returned with a bottle, which he presented to Sunbury, who read the label and nodded; the waiter took out a corkscrew and began to open the wine.

"But who would want to do me an injury? This Ash person may be dangerous, but what can he want of me?" She felt restless, and her patience began once again to fade. "I know nothing that could interest anyone. I don't know where Saint-Germain is, other than in America. My husband has a life of his own in l'Argentina"—she pronounced it in Spanish—"with his mistress; I haven't seen him for nearly five years now, and I can reveal nothing about his business, or anything else, for that matter, not that he has ever told me much about his dealings in any case. What could anyone want with me, that he would seek me out? He would have to be desperate indeed to think I could provide any useful information." She waved her hand in dismissal while she watched Sunbury taste the wine and examine the cork.

"Still, the Count was very specific in his provisions, and I am obliged to tend to his instructions." Sunbury signaled the waiter to fill their glasses.

"When do you reckon the guards will no longer be required?" Doña Isabel asked, cocking her head.

"I can't say; it will depend on Saint-Germain's orders. You understand that he is my client, not you, and that I am bound to honor his behests so long as they are legal, and in this case, it is my sincere pleasure to do so. There is no illegality in his current provision for you, and so, no matter what you may think, it is incumbent upon me to do as he tells me." He looked away, as if embarrassed by his ethics.

"I do understand that. I only hope you will assess my situation and advise Saint-Germain that his stipulations are overly stringent and need not be followed quite so rigorously as they have been." Doña Isabel paused to remove her gloves; she laid them down on the top of her handbag. "If that is, truly, your opinion, of course."

He gave her an appreciative smile. "I will review your situation as soon as I am assured that you stand in no danger from whoever this Ash is, or may represent. If I find there is still reason for concern, I will say so."

"I accept this," said Doña Isabel. "And if there is anything I can do to assist you in your deliberations, I'll be pleased to do it. All you need do is ask."

"I'll keep that in mind," he said. "Perhaps when you come to London to shop for peppers, we might discuss this further."

"That would please me," said Doña Isabel. She put her serviette in her lap.

"Then all that remains is to set a date for the expedition," said Sunbury, and lifted his glass of white Burgundy in pledge.

She did the same. "Perhaps in the third week of September? That isn't too distant a time."

"That suits me, as far as I can determine," said Sunbury. "I'll have to ring you up to confirm, of course."

"Of course." She put her glass down, seeing a waitress approach with a basket of rolls and a ramekin of butter-curls.

"And any change in your current arrangement rests with the Count." He said nothing while the waitress put the rolls and butter on the table. "Made at the local bakery," he said as he selected a roll for himself.

"They smell fresh-baked," said Doña Isabel. She chose a roll, broke it in half, and put it on the bread plate.

"Yes, they do." He tore off a wedge of bread and buttered it. "Do you have any letters or small packages you want me to forward for you to the Count? I'd be delighted to do it for you, if you like."

"Not just at present," she said, then hesitated. "Would you be willing to send a letter to Ponce for me, or let me use your chambers for my return address? I would prefer not to give him my present direction."

"Yes, of course. Is there some difficulty that you feel requires this?" He seemed genuinely concerned.

"I would simply prefer to have a lawyer's office for my correspondence with Ponce," she said. "Ever since I left Spain, matters have been badly strained between us, and I cannot feel it wise to give him too much information. He knows I have moved out of London, but nothing more, and I would prefer to keep it that way."

"That is a bit evasive, if you don't mind my saying so," Sunbury told her.

"I know it may seem that way," said Doña Isabel. "It is not my intention to . . . I would just as soon Ponce understands that I have the advice of a lawyer."

Sunbury nodded. "I can certainly understand your concerns," he said, although he was baffled. "I will recommend that Alex Carnford handle this for you. I don't want to present any appearance of conflict of interest, as that might be the case if I do this for you while Saint-Germain is my client." He stopped talking as the waiter brought them two large plates of soup. Chopped scallions were sprinkled on top, and steam rose from the surface of the plates; the aroma was light but promising.

"Is there a little pepper I might put into it?" Doña Isabel asked.

"In the shaker, by the bread-basket," said Sunbury as he picked up his soup-spoon and gently brushed the surface with it. "Just as wonderful as I remember," he said to Doña Isabel. "I know you'll like it."

She was busy sprinkling pepper into her plate of soup, a bit disappointed at the fine-grind the shaker contained. "I'm looking forward to it. *Bon appétit*," she said, and sank her spoon into the pale green liquid. They ate in silence for a short while, then Doña Isabel dabbed her serviette at her lips and said, "A fine dish for a starter." She put her spoon onto the charger and dropped her serviette back into her lap. "If I have any more, I won't be able to eat the chicken."

Sunbury smiled. "I hope you won't go away hungry."

"I think not," she said, and sipped her wine, then buttered half her roll and took a bite out of it. "This is excellent." Spots of her red lip-rouge marked the white roll where she had bitten; they stood out bright as new blood, and seemed oddly tantalizing to Sunbury.

He almost finished his soup, and used a little bit of his roll to sop up the last of it. "I imagine our English cuisine seems fairly tame to you, Doña Isabel. I know your Spanish dishes are a good deal more lively than ours."

"I am becoming used to it," said Doña Isabel. "The bakery goods are quite wonderful. I particularly like scones."

"For afternoon tea," said Sunbury.

"And breakfast, with coffee," said Doña Isabel. "I don't know how you can face baked eggs and sausage first thing in the morning."

Sunbury almost choked on his wine. "There's more of me to maintain than you, and England can be quite cold, as you'll find out in a month or so."

"I have had some hint of that already. My housekeeper flings open the windows when she thinks the day is warm; that is when I put on my jacket or find a lap-rug." She touched the stem of her wineglass but did not lift it. "If you could advise me: I think I would like to purchase a pair of dogs—not hunting dogs, companion dogs. There are three cats in the house, and they are all very well in their way, but they are hardly . . . gregarious."

"Did you have dogs in Cádiz?" Sunbury asked, hoping to discover what manner of animal she was used to.

"No. Ponce dislikes them, and even after he went to La Plata, I never went against his instructions." She stared down at the soup-plate as if there were answers to be found within it. "But my grandfather had a . . . I think you call it a lurcher—thin, rough-coated, clever. Others had greyhounds, but not my grand-father. He said his lurcher was worth a dozen greyhounds any day."

"A lurcher?" Sunbury repeated, and moved a bit so the waiter could more easily remove their soup-plates. "Would you like me to see if I can find such a dog for you?"

"Mr. Sunbury, that would be such an imposition," she said, startled by his offer.

Four women who had been dining on the far side of the room now rose, gath-ered up their things, and departed, leaving Sunbury and Doña Isabel more isolated than before.

"Nothing of the sort. It will be easier for me than for you to find out about it, I dare say. The English love dogs; someone must breed lurchers. I'm sure one of my chums in the dog show circuit can point me in the right direction." He had only one school friend who actively participated in dog shows, and he had no idea how he might approach George Bridgewarden, but at the moment, he wanted nothing more than to give himself another reason to spend time with Doña Isabel. A warning voice within him reminded him she was a married woman and a Catholic, but for once in his life, he paid no heed to the voice.

"That would be truly splendid, Mr. Sunbury," Doña Isabel exclaimed, impul-sively touching his hand. "Would you be willing to do that for me? Really?"

He flushed at this effusive praise. "It will be my pleasure. Do you want one dog or two, puppies or grown, and what training would you like in a grown dog?"

She held up one hand in mock surrender. "So many things to consider," she protested. "I suppose it would be wiser to have grown dogs—two of them—trained to walk next to me, to sit and come on command, and to stand guard if necessary."

"So you have given this some thought," said Sunbury.

"For the last two weeks, I have thought about it every day. Country life leads me to think of such things." She was relieved. "I can't tell you how much I appre-ciate this. I haven't the least notion how to go about this, and now—You're doing so much for me, Mr. Sunbury."

"Nothing of the sort. I am doing what the Count would expect me to do, as his deputy." He fell silent as the waiter brought their main courses, not speak-ing again until that worthy was out of earshot. "If there is anything you require of me—short of breaking the law—I am yours to command."

"I can't think of a single law I would be likely to break," she said, "except perhaps the speeding laws."

Sunbury laughed softly. "I think I can vouchsafe to find you excellent defense if you should be cited for speeding."

"That's very obliging of you, Mr. Sunbury." She looked down at her plate, and decided the chicken did not look as uninviting as she feared it might. "I'll contrive to keep within the limits where they are posted."

"I thank you for that, Doña Isabel." He saw the waiter coming with the baked onions and nodded, indicating that he might approach them.

She looked at the onions and wished they were prepared with tomatoes and garlic, not just topped with butter. "I wouldn't express gratitude just yet, Mr. Sunbury; you have no notion what may happen."

"You're very right," he said, and picked up his knife and fork.

"Still," she said, as she, too, prepared to eat, "I am the one who should thank you for looking after me."

Admiration shone in his eyes. "It is a privilege, Doña Isabel," he said with more feeling than he intended. "A privilege."

Text of a letter from Carlo Pietragnelli in Geyserville, California, to Ferenc Ragoczy Saint-Germain, care of General Delivery, Salt Lake City, Utah.

> Geyserville, Sonoma County, California
> September 9, 1936
>
> Ferenc Ragoczy Saint-Germain
> General Delivery
> Main Post Office
> Salt Lake City, Utah
>
> Most honored patron,
> I cannot express what delight I feel in learning that you will soon be in California, and will visit my family home and my winery—surely both have much to be grateful to you about. Without your investments over the years, our business and our home must surely have failed, as so many others have. As it is, thanks to you, we are thriving when only a few others are just getting back on their feet.
> It seems we will begin the crush at the end of this month if the weather holds, and that will allow you to see us at the peak of our operations. I will take on extra help for this month and next, so that we may harvest, crush, and begin the fermentation for this vintage. It is a most exciting time, which no doubt you will enjoy.
> Yes, we do have a telephone. The number is Geyserville 899; the exchange is open around the clock until November, and from November until March, it is open eighteen hours a day. We are on a four-party line, which is occa-

sionally inconvenient, but it should not keep you from reaching us if you are persistent. I'm up until ten, so you can call late, if you like.

It will also be a great pleasure to welcome Mr. Rogers to our winery. In the years that he has served as your intermediary in our dealings, he has been a steadfast supporter of all we have done, including the purchase of the six plantations on the east side of the town, with the possibility of more to come. I am sorry that my neighbors were so near bankruptcy, but at least I was able to buy half their land and vines for a good price, high enough so they could hang on.

We have a family dinner on Sundays, at two in the afternoon. They are not the busy affairs they once were, with my children grown and my wife long-dead—may God rest her soul—but they are happy times, for all that. I will be glad to see you join us at table on any Sunday that suits you, for as many Sundays as you like.

I will contact Oscar King in San Francisco, so that, as you suggest, we may know as soon as you arrive there. I hope there will be many opportunities for you to come to Geyserville. The roads are much improved of late, and with the Golden Gate Bridge opening next year, travel into Marin, Sonoma, and Napa Counties should be much easier than it is now, although the ferry service is quite good. All you need do is find Route 101 and drive north; the Redwood Highway, as it's called locally, goes right through the middle of town.

Confirmation has arrived from the Bank of America in San Francisco of another transfer from you into my business account, for which I thank you— they also provided me with the address where I could contact you. I am planning to enlarge my winery yet again, expanding south and east into Napa County, where I have three plantations already, and I have just ordered oak barrels from France and an improved bottling machine. These things would not be possible without your investment, which has enabled me to do so much more than I had thought possible twenty years ago.

I should mention that we have been somewhat troubled by men taking midnight harvest—coming into the vineyards in the dead of night and carrying off large baskets full of pilfered grapes. They sell these to unofficial jobbers for a dollar or so for each basket they bring. A number of wineries have been hit by these thieves, but they are hard to catch and the sheriff doesn't have the men to patrol all the wineries in the valley. I have given my workers shotguns and put them on guard, which should decrease midnight harvesting, or at least discourage any more than what has already taken place.

Vineyards are not the only places where midnight harvesters have struck, of course. I have read in the papers that the orchards of San Jose have been raided with some regularity, and there have been rewards offered by farmers in the Salinas Valley for information on the men taking lettuce and tomatoes and squash in the dead of night. It is all due to so many men being out of work, but the thefts only make the situation more difficult for everyone. I know everyone is afraid of Bolsheviks and fear that FDR is leaning in that direction, but if men cannot work, then they will steal, no matter what kind of government they have.

This does not mean that my business has been deeply compromised. I would rather not have such losses, but they will not bankrupt me, in large part because you have sustained this winery for so long. I know half-a-dozen families who are badly hurt by these raids. I have offered to send my men to the vineyards that have been hardest hit, but so far no one has accepted my offer of help.

Until the day when I can shake your hand, may your good angel watch over you.

Sincerely,

Carlo Pietragnelli

chapter three

ake Tahoe was a startling, vivid blue set in a bowl of deep pine green, the tall peaks rising to the west reflected in the water, mirroring the beautiful, imposing barricade to the hills and valleys beyond. Two motorboats were cutting white swaths across its surface, and even from the road, Saint-Germain and Rogerio could hear the whine of the engines as they swerved closer to the shore.

"Do you suppose they're playboys, out there?" Rogerio asked with a gentle smirk.

"To go with the divorcées in Reno?" Saint-Germain suggested, whose drive through the Biggest Little City in the World had been made memorable by a group of women who had crowded around the Packard at a stoplight, one of them pretending to swoon on the hood and then calling out, "Come back in four weeks—I'll have my final decree then."

Rogerio ignored that remark. "It's two in the afternoon. Shouldn't they be busy indoors, or working somehow, if they can?" He held a road atlas open on his lap turned to the Sierra Nevada North page.

"In this place? This is a playground. There may be loggers in the forest and workers on the roads, but the lake is for entertainment and recreation," said Saint-Germain, opening the window of the Packard a little wider, for it was hot, and not even the altitude put much of a damper on the clear day. They were eastbound on the north shore of the lake and it was beautiful, warm, and balmy. Although the two-lane road had been graded and oiled recently, there were uneven stretches so that driving required concentration. The Packard was dusty, showing the demands the miles had made on it; the large backseat and the trunk were crammed full of chests and trunks all held in place by broad leather belts, and the enlarged fuel tank showed as a hump behind the rear seat. In spite of the dust and grime, the Packard attracted stares, and a few envious glances from those occasional groups of people taking the sun at the water's edge.

"It is a fine place for entertainment," said Rogerio, his faded-blue eyes glinting appreciatively. "They say Hollywood stars come here to relax."

"Not you, too," Saint-Germain lamented with a quirky smile.

"No, not I," said Rogerio. "But you saw the sign on the road outside of Reno: *Lake Tahoe—where the stars come out to play.* There must be some attraction in that."

Saint-Germain could not help but laugh. "Thank goodness we found petrol—gas—in Truckee, while we were on US 40, or we might have had to spend more time here than either of us wanted; we were down to three gallons when we filled up. Without the fuel, we would have come to a stop somewhere on this road. Not that this isn't a pleasant place; and at least there seems to be work for most of the men, unlike what we've seen in the cities." He thought about what he had said. "Or the men without work may have left and gone elsewhere to look for jobs; we've seen a lot of that, too. The opportunities here must be limited. At least I haven't seen any hobo camps in the mountains. I know that doesn't mean they're not there. But they may be nearer Truckee, or Reno, or in the forest, at least until the snows come." He glanced away from the lake toward the pines around it, and the swath of the road ahead of them. "This is the road to Crystal Bay; as soon as we pass King's Beach, there should be a sign for the Ponderosa Lodge in the next three miles, about a mile from the lakeshore, if what the postman told us is correct. Look for Ponderosa Road. It should be coming up." As the road meandered along the north shore of Tahoe, he glimpsed the lake again.

"I'll watch for it," said Rogerio, ignoring the two boats as they hurtled back across the water.

"Very good," said Saint-Germain. His black linen jacket was only slightly wilted, and he had loosened his dark red silk tie, but other than those two considerations, he was as neatly groomed as when he had got into the Packard shortly after dawn that morning in the small, dusty Nevada town of Elko. The sun was beginning to bother him, but not enough to cause him to climb into the trunk. "It will be easier once we're over the summit. The road should be fully paved all the way to the ferry pier."

"Do you think we'll be there by tomorrow?" Rogerio asked.

"I surmise that will depend on how many delays we encounter. And we may decide to stay at the lodge for a day or two, if it is a promising place. We have been driving for six days without interruption, except for those stops where the road-builders were working—we've done far more rigorous journeys in the past, and may do so again, but this time we have the luxury of setting our own pace in a mode of transportation that is truly pleasant, and I can see the advantage of taking a short break. Once we cross the pass, there might well be more road-crews out working, it may be that we'll have to stop short of our goal in Sacramento or Vacaville. But if the way is clear and we depart in the morning, then I have no doubt that we'll reach San Francisco tomorrow night. It should be a seven- or eight-hour drive, all things being equal." Saint-Germain swerved to avoid a rut in the road.

"Where do you plan to stay? Have you made up your mind yet?" Rogerio was curious. "You telephoned a San Francisco hotel from Elko, didn't you?"

"Yes," said Saint-Germain. "I decided upon the Saint Francis, on Union Square. The name appeals to me." The first time he had used Sanct-Francisus as his principal name, Heliogabalus had been Caesar; most of his memories from that time caused him acute chagrin even now: Rogerio knew Saint-Germain well enough to realize that this choice had been ironic. "I told them we would arrive in the next four days and I will pay for those days whether we occupy the suite or not; I have booked the suite for at least a month, and referred them to Oscar King and the Bank of America for surety." If he considered this an extravagance, he did not say so. "Ponderosa Road." He took a left turn away from the lake down a single-lane graveled road flanked by ponderosa, sugar, and lodgepole pines. "I think the road we'll want is ahead on the right."

"I'll look for the sign—the postman said there is a sign, didn't he?"

"Yes. A wooden one, about four feet high and six feet wide, just before the entrance to the resort's grounds," Saint-Germain recited from what they had been told.

Rogerio nodded. "Very good."

Saint-Germain held the steering wheel as the road curved, keeping the big car from fishtailing; a plume of dust rose behind the car, rolling like boiling water. The Packard slithered as Saint-Germain double-clutched down into second gear; the transmission whined as the big car slowed down.

"There!" Rogerio said, pointing to the Art Nouveau sign about thirty yards ahead. "And there's the arch over their road."

"Fine," said Saint-Germain, and slowed down still more to make the turn onto the dirt road leading up to the Ponderosa Lodge. The Packard held the road and slowed down to ten miles an hour as it went up the long, sweeping drive through the pines, dust swirling behind them, hanging on the still mountain air.

Ponderosa Lodge sat in a broad clearing, a handsome building in the Arts-and-Crafts style that had been in vogue twenty-five years ago but now seemed a little passé. The front of the building opened onto a wide, flagstone patio framed by Japanese arbors around which tea roses grew; just down the slope from the lodge, a swimming pool glinted, three deck chairs close to it, one of them occupied by a woman in a fashionable bathing-suit. On the far side of the parking area, a half-dozen small paddocks fronted a handsome stable that was in need of a new roof; four horses stood in the paddocks, tails swishing. Paths went in many directions, to cabins located out among the trees, and an access road looped around the back of the cabins. There were half-a-dozen autos pulled up at the side of the lodge, and Saint-Germain took the next space along, then shut off the engine.

"It looks satisfactory," said Rogerio. "If a trifle out-of-fashion."

"I agree," said Saint-Germain, and got out of the car. He had not been wearing his hat and he did not bother to put it on now. Giving a tug to his black linen jacket and straightening his tie, he started toward the door marked *Office*. The lobby was not large but it had eight big windows, all open, and the quality of light in the wood-paneled room gave it an impression of size that spoke well of its design. Saint-Germain went up to the registration desk and rang the service bell set out where it could easily be seen.

"Good afternoon," a middle-aged woman of medium height, her short-cropped, dark hair just turning to grey, said as she came out of the inner office behind the registration desk, donning a welcoming smile with the ease of long practice. "What may I do for you?" She was dressed in what Saint-Germain had learned from travel magazines was California equestrienne style: loose, coffee-brown slacks tucked into tooled-leather boots, a long-sleeved ivory cotton shirt—just now with sleeves rolled up to the elbows—under a short, open bolero jacket in dull red canvas with elbow-length sleeves. She looked over the new arrival appraisingly.

"My name is Ferenc Ragoczy," said Saint-Germain. "My associate and I would like to arrange for accommodations here for tonight, and possibly tomorrow night as well." His demeanor was cordial but not familiar.

The woman looked flustered. "Oh. Well, I have three doubles here in the lodge; I could let you have one for seventeen dollars a night—"

"What about your cabins?" Saint-Germain asked when she stopped.

"They're . . . more expensive," she said. "A single-room—studio—cabin goes for thirty a night, a one-bedroom for forty-five, and a two-bedroom—our largest—for sixty-five." She stared down at the countertop as if she knew the prices were outrageous. As she brought her head up, she added emphatically, "The cabins are all Maybecks, just like the lodge."

Saint-Germain was unfamiliar with the name, but he nodded. "Which is your best two-bedroom cabin?"

She coughed. "That would be the *Tuolumne*. It has a full fireplace, a good view of the lake, and a balcony."

"Is it occupied?" Saint-Germain inquired politely.

"N-no," she faltered. "Not just at present."

"And it's sixty-five dollars a night?" Saint-Germain pursued.

She flicked a glance in his direction, and then away. "Yes."

Saint-Germain reached into his jacket for his wallet. "Shall we say two nights, then? In your *Tuolumne* cabin?" he asked as he peeled out seven twenties and held them out to her. "Paid in advance, of course."

The woman stared at the bills in disbelief, unable to move for a full thirty seconds. Then she snatched the money and shoved it into her cash drawer, handing him back a ten. "It isn't ready yet. You'll have to give my staff an hour to make it up. We don't like to keep the cabins fully . . . They get musty so quickly when they aren't in constant use." This admission caused her some perturbation; she was talking too quickly, moving her hands as if unsure of what to do with them. Finally she took the guest register and turned it around to him. "Your name, place of residence here, please. Also your car's make and license number. I'll fill in the rest." She read as he wrote, having no difficulty with the upside-down letters. "You have a Packard Twelve?" she marveled.

"Yes. Do you need my associate's name as well? And his identification?" Saint-Germain asked as he wrote *Ferenc Ragoczy* in his small, meticulous hand. He noticed from the other entries on the page that since the end of August, occupancy had dropped off sharply; surely the beginning of the fall semester could not account for all of it. He also noticed that among the length of stays indicated in the register, none was longer than a week.

"Oh. Yes, please. And I need to see your passports, if you're foreign." She had become aware of his accent, and belatedly remembered that she needed to make note of it. "The government requires it. Not that we have to submit the information, or anything like that—not yet. But I have to have it in case there is an inquiry later. Bureaucracies! There's more of them every day. You know how these things are." She shrugged as if to apologize for this intrusion.

"Yes; I know." Saint-Germain pulled out his Hungarian passport and showed it to her, holding it open so that she could copy the necessary information. "It is much the same everywhere these days." He did not add that his recollection of travel stretched back four thousand years, and, from his experience, passports and bureaucratic hassle were minor inconveniences compared to some of the trials he had encountered.

She took a second record-book out from under the counter and began to write down the data it contained. Half-way through she put her finger on the line under his name. "What is this? It isn't part of an address, is it?"

"No," said Saint-Germain diffidently. "It is my title."

"Title?" She blinked.

"I'm afraid so," he said.

"Oh," she whispered, and then said, more loudly, "Oh!" as her cheeks reddened. "Then you're a—"

"Count, not that it has any bearing in this country," he said, and held out his hand. "I am pleased to meet you . . . Though you have the advantage of me."

She took his hand and gave it a firm shake. "Everyone calls me Mrs. Curt. It's Curtis, actually, and I'm a widow, but you know how things stick." Then she let go of his hand. "My first name's Enid. Good to meet you, Count."

"I am delighted to know you, Mrs. Curt," said Saint-Germain. "Shall I call my associate in? His name is Mr. Rogers, originally from Cádiz, but currently an English citizen."

"Okay. I'll need to get his passport number, too," she said, now in greater possession of herself. "I'll send Beryl and Grace up to the cabin. They'll have it ready in an hour."

"Take as much time as you need," said Saint-Germain as he went to the door to signal Rogerio to come in. "Bring your passport."

Rogerio got out of the Packard, the road atlas still in one hand, his wallet in the other. As he passed Saint-Germain, he asked in an under-voice, "Spanish or English?"

"English, Mr. Rogers," said Saint-Germain, raising his voice just enough to be heard, "The manager is Mrs. Curtis, called Mrs. Curt."

"Owner," she corrected as she pointed out the line where Rogerio was to sign. "My late husband left it to me, free and clear. His life insurance is what keeps us going. The lodge was the whole legacy, and I'm lucky to have it. There's many another with less." There was both pride and anxiety in her tone. "Now that gambling's legal in Nevada, we hope business'll pick up here, as part of it. Not that California's going to allow gambling any time soon, but this place has been a resort area for eighty years."

Rogerio finished signing his name, using Saint-Germain's London address, and handed over his English passport.

"It can't be easy, the country being in the state that it is," said Saint-Germain gently, remembering the economic devastation of Germany just over a decade ago, when a pound of butter could cost a wheelbarrowful of banknotes, and inflation was so precipitous that the value of money would half in a day.

"You can't imagine," she said, trying to laugh to make light of it, but botching it. "I'm going to send the girls up to *Tuolumne* right now. If you'd like to wait in the bar, or take a stroll around the place? If you'd prefer to rest up from your travels, the bar is open and I can send my nephew in to tend bar. If you'd like to take the sun, there are chairs on the patio, and Paschal, our cook, can make you up some sandwiches, if you're hungry. On the house."

"No need to go to such trouble, Mrs. Curt," said Saint-Germain. "I'm sure we can find something to occupy us until the cabin is ready." He gave her a genial nod as he reclaimed his passport and gestured to the outer door. "I think I'd like to have a look around your lodge, if you don't mind."

"Look away," she said, and turned back to her inner office, tapping a button on her desk there; a buzzer sounded in a distant part of the lodge.

Saint-Germain and Rogerio stepped outside into the dusty sunlight. Shading his eyes with his hand, Saint-Germain said, "I paid for two nights."

"I assumed you would," said Rogerio, and started in the direction of the stable. "I also assume you want to have a look at the place as a possible investment."

"You know me too well, old friend," said Saint-Germain, and went with him toward the stables. The interior was pleasantly dark, smelling of horses, hay, and pine. The box-stalls fronting the long, wide aisle were no more than half-full.

"They could have taken some of the horses to winter pasture," Rogerio suggested doubtfully.

"In September? While the weather is still pleasant and the roads are open? If so, why keep so many behind?" Saint-Germain asked. "No, I think Mrs. Curt has been selling her stock in order to keep this place open. She has accommodations for thirty horses in these stalls, and there are only sixteen. With another four in the paddocks outside, she must have cut back her herd pretty drastically."

"Perhaps some of her guests bring their own horses," Rogerio said, unpersuaded.

"Some may, but I doubt they could fill the stable," Saint-Germain said.

"I wouldn't have thought it was a good time to sell horses," Rogerio said.

"No, nor I," Saint-Germain agreed.

Rogerio looked toward the far end of the stable. "Tack room and feed storage, there on the left," he surmised.

"Two of these horses are Percherons," Saint-Germain observed. "Why would she keep draft horses?"

"She must use them. Perhaps in winter, if the roads become too muddy, or too snowy for autos," Rogerio said. "You might want to ask Mrs. Curt about them."

"I will," said Saint-Germain, and continued on to the tack room. He looked in the door, screwing the light switch to turn the overhead bulb on. "All in good condition, but none of them new," he said as he made a circuit of the room. "Mostly Western saddles, but three English, on that end rack. Bridles enough to match the saddles."

"And racks for several more of each," Rogerio said.

There was a small coach-house just beyond the stable, a little in need of upkeep but well-built. Inside were three vehicles: a large buckboard wagon, an elaborate sleigh, and a small, Western-style coach, all recently polished, as were the three sets of harness hanging on racks in front of them. "Well," said Saint-Germain. "Now we know what the Percherons are for."

"It makes sense," said Rogerio.

They left the coach-house and ambled along the nearest path toward a cluster of cabins, all of them of a type, but each different from the other. Each had a plaque over the door with the names of the cabins on them: *Nevada, Amador, Placer, El Dorado, Alpine*. The proportions of the cabins were satisfying, and the steeply slanted roofs reminded the two men that winters here were snowy. Passing the five cabins, Saint-Germain noticed that only two were occupied, and wondered how much longer, at this rate, Mrs. Curt could hang on. The next group of cabins was in a grove of large rhododendrons: *Angel's Camp, Auburn, Sonora,* and *Placerville*. They, too, were small but individual, *Sonora* having a little patio that gave out onto the extensive lawn behind the dining room of the main lodge, *Placerville* having a well-kept walkway that led toward what seemed to be tennis courts below the lodge terrace.

"How many cabins, do you think?" Saint-Germain asked, looking along the trail toward the next group.

"Over thirty," Rogerio said, pointing to the slope opposite where they stood. "There are at least five more groups of them: you can see them through the trees. Even if not all of them are guest cottages—I would guess that some are for staff—they must have a minimum of thirty for guests."

"So it seems to me," Saint-Germain agreed. "A good deal to keep up, even in prosperous times, with an adequate staff. But now—" He stopped as he looked around again. "What do you think? Perhaps four or five in the kitchen, and six waiters. They might also do room maintenance, so that would mean another seven or eight for housekeeping tasks, but I would imagine they are currently getting by with three, possibly four. A waiter in the bar, as well, I would think. A carpenter and two gardeners for the upkeep of the buildings and the grounds. Someone to run errands. Someone to take the guests up and down the hill to the lake. A—what do they call it in this part of the country?—a wrangler for the horses, and a groom or stable-boy, and a farrier. Then someone to maintain the pool and similar facilities." They began walking again and came upon a flume, water running along it from a source somewhere farther up the hill. Another six cabins were strung out along the flume like over-sized beads, all with names of writers who set stories in California. One of the cabins, *Jack London*, had a damaged roof, but otherwise they seemed to be in fairly good repair, although by their appearance, none of them was occupied at present.

Rogerio pointed to the roof. "That happened recently."

"So I think," Saint-Germain said, and pointed to the sugar pine standing next to it, where the scar of a broken limb was apparent. "Probably early in the spring, at the thaw. That's when the branches break."

"Very likely," said Rogerio. He lengthened his stride and went on down the path, where another path crossed the one they were on. "Which way?"

"Up the hill," said Saint-Germain.

They had passed three more gatherings of cabins before they got to the crest of the rise where two of the large cabins stood: *Yosemite* on the north side of the path, *Tuolumne* on the south; it did indeed have a patio, a balcony, and a chimney, and the car road skimmed the edge of the lot on which the cabin stood, offering easy access to a parked car. The cabin had two walls of huge windows, one on the south side with French doors built into it, facing the lake; the other expansive window was on the west side of the building, giving an excellent view of the lodge itself. The patio wrapped around the south and east flank, near the front door, and the balcony was on the east. From the inside came the sound of a carpet-sweeper being operated.

"It will have a great deal of light," said Rogerio.

"I can see that," Saint-Germain agreed. "I think I'll bring in one of my chests. My native earth will counter-act the light from the windows."

Rogerio made a gesture to show he understood; then he looked down the hill. "Four more cabins just below us. And it looks as if one of them is occupied."

"I'll be careful," Saint-Germain assured him, adding, "There is no reason to be reckless, not here."

"You are not often reckless," said Rogerio as if to remind himself of that. "Not when you have any choice in the matter."

"Yes. I prefer not to be," Saint-Germain said as they started down the slope toward the four cabins. "But think of the excellent investment the spa in Austria has turned out to be. It took thirty years to pay off, but it has been earning money steadily since 1872. This place has just the same potential. By 1955, I would think it would be flourishing."

"This isn't Austria," Rogerio reminded him. "And, given the politics in Austria, you may not be able to hold on to the spa much longer."

"Even if I lose it, it has returned handsomely on my investment," said Saint-Germain. "Unlike the living, I can afford to wait."

Rogerio had no answer for this. He glanced back over his shoulder at *Tuolumne*. "It is a pleasant site."

"The whole resort is—that is what I like about it." They had reached the next group of cabins. "*Sutter Creek*, *Yuba River*, *Feather River*, and *Mokelumne River*. I sense another theme here. *Yuba River* has at least two guests in it."

"The theme is regional, as with all the rest," Rogerio said, picking up his pace to keep up with Saint-Germain.

"I do like this place. I can see why it isn't doing well just now—very few people can afford to come here, or anywhere, for that matter. But when the country finally emerges from its financial woes, I should think this would be just the kind of resort where many families would want to come on holiday. With the improvements on the roads, it should make Lake Tahoe an easy destination for many." Saint-Germain walked past the four cabins to another group of eight; unlike the others, these were all of the same design and large enough to house four or five people; they were numbered instead of named. "This must be for the staff. The cabins are simpler—no patios, no balconies, no picture windows—but the look of them is still a handsome one. And in another decade, they will not look out-of-fashion, they will have regained their charm in the public eye." He continued on, closely observing all he saw. When they reached the last group of cabins— *Mono Lake*, *Cathedral Lake*, *Loon Lake*, *French Meadow Lake*, *Silver Lake*, *Gold Lake*—just below the terrace where the swimming pool was located, Saint-Germain announced, "I will make arrangements through the attorney and the bank to invest in this place."

"Was that in doubt?" Rogerio asked.

"Probably not," Saint-Germain conceded. "But it will require finesse. Unless I have erred in my assessment of Mrs. Curt, she does not want to be beholden to anyone, for fear of losing what she has. Tact will be needed, and an ironclad contract that gives her autonomy in running the place for as long as she is willing and capable."

"And it will give you a place to go to ground," Rogerio said knowingly. "In case you should need one."

Saint-Germain hesitated before he answered. "What better place than a resort? It has worked in the past." He looked around again.

Rogerio nodded twice. "That it has."

Satisfied that they were in agreement, Saint-Germain changed the subject. "I'll drive the auto up to the cabin; if you'll check out the lodge for me?"

"I will," said Rogerio. "And I'll report on what I find."

"Thank you," said Saint-Germain. "Do you mind walking up to the cabin when you've done? It isn't a long way."

"Of course not," said Rogerio.

"I need not have asked; pardon me for being maladroit." He lowered his head as an acknowledgment. As Rogerio walked away toward the patio, Saint-Germain went around the front of the lodge to the entrance to the registration lobby, where Mrs. Curt was waiting, a key in her hand. "Is that ours?"

"Count Ragoczy—" she began.

"Count Saint-Germain," he corrected her kindly. "Mr. Ragoczy will do very well, Mrs. Curt."

She flushed. "I didn't mean to offend you."

"Nor did you," he said. "But my native earth is far away, and yours is officially an egalitarian country, so Mr. Ragoczy will suffice." He took the key, noticing that she was disappointed. "You have a beautiful resort here, Mrs. Curt."

She ventured a smile. "We've got a hayride planned for tonight, starting at eight. I don't know if you like that kind of thing, but—"

"I have no idea: what is a hayride?"

"Oh, we harness up Davy and Joe to the buckboard, fill the bed with hay, and load the guests in on top of it, and then go off for a moonlight ride down to the lake, and then up the back way, along the eastern edge of the lodge's land. It takes a couple of hours." She paused, then plunged ahead. "We're having a bon-fire when we get back, down in the fire-pit on the far side of the parking lot. Marshmallows and hot dogs for everyone. Beer and coffee for the grown-ups, apple juice for the kids."

Saint-Germain had learned in his long drive from Chicago that marshmal-lows were a kind of soft meringue and that hot dogs were sausages, so he could say without hesitation, "It sounds charming, but I believe Mr. Rogers and I are in need of rest. We've been traveling hard for ten days, and, to be candid, we're both ready for a little sleep." He did not add that his sleep was more like a coma and lasted, at most, four hours.

"Well, hayrides aren't everybody's cup of tea." She gave a little sigh.

"But tomorrow," Saint-Germain went on, "I wonder if you could rent me a pair of your horses? I am an experienced rider—you need not fear I will do anything foolish—and I would welcome a few hours in the saddle."

She brightened. "I'm sure we can arrange something. You'll have to take a guide with you. That's our policy—it won't do to have guests lost in the forest. It's happened in the past, and the sheriff insists that all rent-strings have guides."

"Good enough," said Saint-Germain. "Shall we say seven in the morning? I prefer to ride before the day gets hot."

"All right. I'll have Mickey or Julian meet you at the stable at seven. I guess you'll want English saddles?"

"Yes, if you don't mind." Saint-Germain smiled slightly. "An old habit."

"We have English saddles as well as Western." She turned as a young woman came in from a door at the far end of the registration lobby, which Saint-Germain assumed, by the aroma filling the air, led to the kitchen. "Yes, Grace?"

"Excuse me, but Paschal needs you, Aunt Enid," she said, and ducked back through the door.

Mrs. Curt gave Saint-Germain an apologetic gesture. "I'll have to take care of this, whatever it is."

"How many family members do you employ?" Saint-Germain asked quietly. "Do you mind me asking?"

"No, I don't mind. Six in winter, as many as ten in summer. It's the only thing I can do to help. I'd give them all jobs if I could. God knows there are men who are willing to work. Women too. Grace has four younger brothers and sisters, and she doesn't want to be a drain on the family; my brother-in-law's been out of work for four years. Their oldest boy's going into the CCC, to plant trees up north, but the others are too young; two of them have little jobs, and everything helps, but it's hard." She said this as if she were reciting a lesson or something she had repeated many times. "We all have to pitch in. I can't pay a lot, but I can give Grace a place to stay and three squares a day, and I make sure she goes to school."

"How old is she?" Saint-Germain asked.

"Seventeen. She'll graduate from high school next May, and she'll be off to college. She's got applications in at Cal Davis and College of the Pacific in Stockton. She'll have to work her way through, wherever she goes, but at least she'll have some job experience behind her, and that should help." She waved to indicate her departure. "Dinner starts at five-thirty. This time of year we don't worry about seatings. Come when you like between five-thirty and eight. And let me know if you change your mind about the hayride."

"I will," he said as Mrs. Curt went through the kitchen door.

Slipping the key into his pocket, Saint-Germain went out to the Packard, got in, and started toward the access road, heading up the hill past the lake cabins toward the staff residences and on up the hill. He pulled into the parking space on the northeast side of the cabin and set the brake as he turned off the motor. As he got out of the Packard, he looked around with his usual care, then went to the door and turned the key in the lock, opening the door onto a large central room with a river-stone fireplace, a pair of sofas in the Arts-and-Crafts style—just now in need of reupholstering—a coffee table with a Mission-style lamp on it, two occasional chairs. An Indian rug was spread on the flagstone floor, its colors vivid in the slanting afternoon light that flooded in from the wide picture window. The stairs to the second floor began next to the fireplace, rising to the gallery leading to the balcony. One door on the gallery, standing open, showed a room with a double bed. Under the gallery, two doors opened on another bedroom and a bathroom done in peach-and-green tile. Saint-Germain made a quick inspection of the cabin, and was pleased with what he saw.

"Oh, very nice," said Rogerio as he came through the door.

"It is, isn't it?" Saint-Germain said.

"If the other cabins are as nice as this one—" Rogerio began.

"Mrs. Curt says this is her best," Saint-Germain interjected.

"Still, it is a great deal more promising than the Austrian spa was when you bought your half-interest in it." Rogerio sat down on the nearer of the two sofas.

"My thoughts exactly," Saint-Germain said. "I'll take the upper room, I think. The bathroom can mean running water, and I would rather not have to deal with any more of that than necessary." He angled his head so that he could look out the southern window without having to stand in front of it. "By the way, I've reserved horses for us for tomorrow morning at seven."

"In case you want to buy adjacent land as you've done with your resorts in Austria and Bavaria," said Rogerio, being careful to keep his tone neutral; Bavaria was still a painful memory for Saint-Germain.

"Truly," said Saint-Germain at his most matter-of-fact.

Rogerio went to the fireplace, where kindling and short logs had been laid. "Do you plan to light this later?"

"It will depend on how cold it gets. It would raise suspicions if we make no effort to keep warm." He went and tried the latch on the French doors; they opened easily, and Saint-Germain stepped out onto the patio. "This is very nice."

"A good place to go to ground?" Rogerio suggested as he had earlier.

"As I said before, that had occurred to me," Saint-Germain said, a touch of irony in his voice. "This is new territory to me, and it would be prudent to have a safe haven nearer to San Francisco than Chicago."

"Just so," Rogerio said.

"I'll make any necessary arrangements with Mrs. Curt tomorrow, and we can leave the day after." He pressed his small, well-shaped hands together. "I won't do anything so foolish as lease one of the guest cabins—that would draw too much attention. There are advantages to having resorts for vampires, if we're careful. But tomorrow morning, when we ride, be alert for other buildings. I would like to be able to leave at least one chest of my native earth here in a protected place."

"Speaking of chests, when should we bring in our luggage? And how much should we bring in?" Rogerio asked from his comfortable place on the sofa.

"Shortly; no more than twenty minutes. Otherwise we might attract attention," Saint-Germain said in the Latin of Imperial Rome.

"All right," said Rogerio in the same language. "Your leather suitcase, and my Gladstone bag. You'll bring in one of your chests of earth—"

"The smallest," said Saint-Germain. "I have no desire to cause any more speculation than I must." He came back inside, closed the door, and slid the locking bolt into place. "So I will go fetch my chest and carry it up the stairs."

Rogerio got up. "I'll manage the suitcase and the bag." He followed Saint-Germain out of the door to the Packard, where they found a boy staring at it.

"That's some car, mister," he said, as if summoning up his nerve to speak at all.

"Thank you," said Saint-Germain.

"I saw you drive it up to your cabin. We're down in *Yuba River*." He was nine or ten, wearing dusty cotton trousers, a plaid shirt a size too large for him, and canvas-topped shoes.

"Your whole family? How nice for you." Saint-Germain made no mention of the school year, which had already begun.

"Dad says it's the last vacation for a while and we better make the most of it. We go home next Sunday." He turned on his heel, calling over his shoulder, "It's a real fine car" before he bolted, running off down the path.

"What now?" Rogerio asked.

"We unload the things we need," said Saint-Germain. "What else?" He unlocked the rear door and unfastened the leather strap that held the cargo in place. Pulling out a small chest, he stepped back and went toward the open door, knowing that Rogerio would attend to the other bags.

TEXT OF A NOTE FROM MILES SUNBURY IN LONDON TO DOÑA ISABEL INEZ VEDANCHO Y NUÑEZ AT COPSEHOWE.

> 43C Siddons Lane
> City of Westminster
> 14 September, 1936

Doña Isabel I. Vedancho y Nuñez
Copsehowe
nr. Briarcopse
Hampshire

My dear Doña Isabel,

Forgive my presuming upon our acquaintance to write to you so informally, but after our luncheon in Uxbridge, I hope I may count you as much a friend as a benefactor of my client's concern for your welfare, which I have come to share.

As you will recall, you expressed a desire to own a pair of lurchers. I have spoken to a reputable breeder who has assured me he has a pair that should be suitable: both are a year old, and are half-brothers, properly trained and generally suitable. If you will deputize me, I'll drive out to Surrey and collect these lurchers and bring them to you on any day that will suit you.

I must tell you that I was delighted to see you have settled into the English way of life so well. I know you will become more accustomed to our society as time goes by. It would please me very much if you would be willing to permit me to help you make this transition.

Believe me,

Most sincerely at your service,

Miles Sunbury

chapter four

"S o what do you think of San Francisco?" Rowena Saxon asked Saint-Germain as they strolled along the Marina Green toward the Palace of Fine Arts, where he had left his Packard parked. It was a chilly afternoon, the fog just beginning to blow in through the Golden Gate past the incomplete bridge, suffusing the light; the warm September sunshine could make no headway against the wind and the thickening haze.

"One of my blood was here almost a century ago; this is much-changed from what she described to me," he said; Madelaine de Montalia had reported a new, raw, bustling place of wooden buildings, muddy streets, and tall ships: today San Francisco was a true metropolis, boasting handsome avenues, commerce and culture, a diverse population, vast numbers of houses, and a thriving port. "Except for the weather, of course. It is just as she described it."

Rowena laughed, her golden eyes shining with more than merriment. "I should imagine so," she told him. She was no longer the same young woman he had last seen in Amsterdam, before the Great War; she was middle-aged and her strawberry-blond hair had faded to what she called "light roan," a kind of pale, pale shade between peach and coral. There were lines in her face that showed her character clearly, unlike the slightly unfinished look he remembered, and although she was still trim, her body had taken on the contours of maturity. She wore a casual suit in dark ochre wool over a silk blouse of rich chocolate-brown, both of which she had bought at the City of Paris on Union Square; she had not bothered to put on a hat, and her shoes were more comfortable than fashionable. Her clutch purse of oxblood leather was tucked under her arm and her gloves matched the purse. She picked up her pace. "Come on. It's only going to get colder." Unlike a great many expatriate British who rigorously maintained the language of England, her accent had blurred and faded over the years, and she now spoke a curious hybrid, no longer entirely English, nor yet quite American.

"As you wish," he said, lengthening his stride. "Does it ever get truly hot here?"

"We have a couple of beastly days each year—often one or two in early summer, and then in October, of all things. The hottest day I can remember was in October. It was stifling. But that comes to an end quickly, and by the end of the

month it's chilly. The rains usually start in early November, and last until March."
She folded her arms to help stay warm. "It's going to be sere tonight."

"Sere: what a fine choice of words," he said, smiling at her.

"And appropriate," she said as they neared the Packard. "You can't see much
of the yacht club just now, but there are some lovely sloops and ketches there. Last
week the most splendid schooner was visiting the Saint Francis Yacht Club." She
indicated the fog at their back. "I'll bring you down here one day, when it's clear."

"Thank you, but ships and such have little attraction for me, though I have
owned a great many in my time," he said, reminding himself that he still did.

"Why? I thought it was only running water that caused you problems," she
said, a bit surprised.

"And what are the tides, if not running water? Add to them the currents of
the ocean—in this bay, a river-current as well—and I am guaranteed misery," he
said. "Even still water can be uncomfortable. It interferes with my contact with
the earth, you see."

She nodded. "I hadn't thought." She went around the rear of the car with him.
"Then Amsterdam must have been quite unpleasant for you."

"I had my native earth lining the foundation of my house, and that provided
relief." He had his key out of his pocket.

"Would crossing the bay by ferry make you—"

"—seasick?" he finished for her. "It might, but I'll take reasonable precautions. I managed the trip from Berkeley to San Francisco without too much
inconvenience; that bridge over the Carquinez Strait is an impressive piece of
engineering, and mercifully we were over it in less than two minutes: even then,
I could feel the enervation of the current below. The airplane flight over the
Atlantic was far more . . . disquieting." He offered a half-smile. "Still, it was better than lying for days—or weeks—in a sealed chest in the hold of a ship."

She considered all this thoughtfully. "Then, if you don't think you'll be too
uncomfortable, we'll plan to drive up to Geyserville next week, if that's all right
with you? Can you endure to ride the ferry as far as San Rafael?"

"That will be fine, particularly if we go at slack tide, assuming the ferry runs then,"
he said, unlocking the passenger door for her. "You've taken to this place, I see."

"I certainly have," she said, relieved to have a change of subject. "Thanks to
my grandfather." She slid into the seat and nodded for Saint-Germain to close
the door.

"He truly did his best for you," he said as he got into the driver's seat and
started the car.

"Yes, he did," she said, a distant look in her eyes. "I miss him still, and he's
been gone for more than fifteen years."

"So you said in your letter last year." He halted at the entrance to the street and checked the traffic before turning left.

She smiled tentatively. "I hope I wasn't too presumptuous."

"Certainly not," he said, then added in a different tone of voice, "You'll have to tell me how to find your house. I am still unfamiliar with the streets."

"You can take me back to the Saint Francis, if you'd rather," she said. "I can hail a cab to go home, just as I called one to take me to the hotel."

"If that is what you prefer," he said, his tone carefully neutral.

"Oh, dear. How awkward this is becoming," she said as if thinking aloud. Then, putting her purse squarely in her lap, she said, "I would love to have you come to the house, today or anytime. But I didn't want you to feel that I *expected* anything of you other than the pleasure of your company."

"As I am enjoying yours right now," he said.

She gave a snort of exasperation. "Are you making this difficult on purpose?"

"No; that wasn't my intention," he said, and went on, "I would be honored to take you to your house. But as you don't want me to feel as if you expected anything of me, so I would like you not to feel that I expect anything of you."

Her cheeks suddenly reddened. "I thought I couldn't blush at my age," she said, abashed by her lack of composure.

"It is very becoming," he said.

"Because it's blood?" she challenged, and regretted saying it the next instant. "Oh, dear. That came out badly. I'm sorry, truly."

"Rowena," he said lightly, "I am not some overgrown mosquito, interested only in corpuscles and hemoglobin, nor am I a seducer who seeks to suborn your will to mine; that would benefit neither of us." Then his tone deepened. "If you are afraid I will make importunate demands of you, I give you my Word I will not. If you believe I sought you out for only one thing, you demean yourself, and me. If you fear I would not desire you because of age or any other factor, I assure you it is not youth or anything so fleeting as prettiness that intrigues me; it is your self, the whole of you, and that totality commands my respect in every way I can express it. When you have lived as long as I have, you learn to treasure all life gives you as it gives it to you."

She was now as pale as she had been rosy. "I'm making a mull of this," she said to her hands locked together on top of her purse.

He slowed down for a stop-sign. "Which way shall I turn?" he asked her.

"Go up to Lombard and turn left," she said. "I'll tell you how to find the house." So saying, she leaned back against the leather-covered seat. "This is a wonderful auto. I thought my Chancellor Miller Speedster was the bee's knees, and the cat's pyjamas, as they said ten years ago—but this . . . I bought it in the summer of '29 and it is still running perfectly. I'll hate to give it up when the time comes, which I hope won't be for a while yet. Cedric—my gardener?—has very real talent as a mechanic, and keeps it in perfect condition."

"The bee's knees?" Saint-Germain repeated, amused and puzzled at once.

"You know: swell, spiffy, top-notch. It's a compliment that implies being up-to-the-minute as well as good quality. Or it meant that a few years ago. It seemed so important then, to be at the leading edge of everything. The bee's knees." Rowena laughed, a little sadly. "How dated it sounds now. And how fresh it seemed before."

"I am aware of the phenomenon," said Saint-Germain as gently as he could. "When do I turn?"

"Cross Van Ness and go to Larkin, then cut over. The house is on Taylor Street," she said.

Although he knew the address he said, "The fourteen hundred block, as I recall."

"Between Jackson and Pacific," she said. "It's a beautiful house. You'll see." She smiled in spite of herself. "Oh, dear. I don't want to seem house-proud."

"It won't trouble me, even if you are," he said, slowing to get around a milk truck stopped for deliveries. There were a number of pedestrians on the side-walks, a few of them already huddled into jackets or coats, the others moving briskly in an attempt to keep warm. There were a few men in worn clothing with hand-lettered signs offering apples or day-old bread for sale, and every few blocks, a newspaper boy shouted out the day's headlines for *The Chronicle* or *The Daily News*. In counterpoint to all this, Saint-Germain heard the first moo of the foghorn, a deep, lugubrious pair of notes mixing with the bustle of the city.

"I think you'll like the house. Grandfather chose a very good architect after the fire in '06. That's what did the damage, you know, much more than the quake." She was doing her best to make the kind of small talk she had been taught to do as a child.

"In a city made of wood, that's hardly surprising," he said, thinking back to Moscow when Ivan Grosny ruled there, and the building components that were all pre-cut and ready to be assembled quickly. California was a far cry from Russia, but the hazards of wooden buildings pertained in both places.

They had reached Larkin. "Turn right and go over to Pacific and then turn left," said Rowena as if registering a final wish.

Saint-Germain heard the reticence in her voice and slowed down. "You may change your mind, Rowena, if you would prefer to postpone this."

"It's like getting into a swimming pool—better to jump in and get it done all at once than to ooze in bit by chilly bit," she said, and then looked at him, dismayed with what she just said. "Not that you are anything unpleasant—what worries me is that you may be too pleasant. That is a bit troublesome."

"An excellent recovery," he approved, then, seeing that she was still uncomfortable, softened his voice, "I took no offense; why should I?"

She gave a diplomatic cough. "Well, I can't tell you that you should be offended—where would that leave me?"

He sounded the horn at a bicycle rider who had cut in front of him as he turned. "You needn't feel importuned, Rowena."

"I don't," she insisted, then said in a rush, "I haven't had to deal with a man, not sexually, for six years. I'm out of practice." She laughed a little. "There. I've said it."

"I hadn't thought that intimacy was a sporting event," he said, sad amusement in his dark eyes.

"It may not be," said Rowena, "but—" She stopped herself before she became too mired in this conversational morass.

He gave his full attention to driving so she could sort herself out. Finally, as they neared Pacific, he said, "Shall we agree that this visit is something of an experiment? It will end whenever you would like it to, and will be in accordance with your wishes from start to finish."

"But I don't know what my wishes are, and they may change," she said. "Oh, Lord, I sound like a schoolgirl."

"Nothing is writ in stone, Rowena," he promised her. "You needn't fret about that. You aren't committing yourself forever through this one afternoon in each other's company."

"Now you sound just like the psychiatrist I saw, some years ago, talking about mutability." She paused. "It was after my last trip to England, and I was feeling restless and out of sorts, dissatisfied and discouraged. My work suffered, and finally my friends convinced me to see a psychiatrist; most of them had done so: it was a fashionable thing to do, if you could afford it, and I could." Folding her arms, she went on. "I don't think he helped very much, but at least I didn't say anything too hurtful to Penelope; I said it all to Doctor Motte instead, which I guess was a good thing. After all, Penelope is my only immediate relative still living, and I don't want to alienate her any more than I already have."

Saint-Germain nodded to show he was listening, but his attention was on the street ahead that was being veiled by fog. "Did you find Doctor Motte insightful?" He stopped at Broadway and waited for a break in the traffic before crossing.

"About some things, yes, but generally, he seemed too dogmatic, too eager to conform my perceptions to Doctor Freud's neat little pigeonholes, whether they actually fit or not, as so many of them seem inclined to do. *I* don't think a paintbrush is a displaced phallus, or a painting a substitute for a child, though Doctor Motte certainly thought so. He thought the affaire I had then was a validation of my femininity. I thought it was a mistake." She looked around at the thickening gloom. "It's going to be a miserable night, all pea-soupy."

"Should I turn on my lights?" Saint-Germain asked.

"It's probably a good idea," she said. "I would."

He did as she suggested and saw the mists brighten in the beams of his headlamps. "How much farther?"

"Two blocks; we just passed Leavenworth." She cocked her head as the echoing clang of a trolley-bell sounded among the buildings. "That's the Hyde Street line, on its way to the pier, or back from it. Foghorns and trolley-bells, the two sounds that I will always believe are the voice of this place."

Saint-Germain did not challenge this diversion. He slowed and signaled a turn onto Pacific. "Mayor Rossi has plans for the city for the coming World's Fair, doesn't he?"

"He certainly does," said Rowena, seizing this new topic fervently. "He's a clever politician, and he knows the value of a World's Fair suits his ambitions down to the ground. Treasure Island, as they're going to call it, is going to be a triumph or he'll know the reason why." Her tone changed. "We're almost there."

"These hills can be a bit daunting," Saint-Germain said calmly. "They're steep enough to be a trial."

"Yes. This isn't a city where you want to neglect your brakes, or your tires. Sometimes I wonder how horse-drawn carriages made it up and down them in bad weather, or even good weather, if it comes to that." She glanced out the window as he signaled for a right turn onto Taylor. "Up ahead on the left," she said, a bit distractedly. "There should be a parking space on this side of the street."

"If you see one, tell me. The fog is getting worse." He noticed an approaching car materializing out of the mists ahead of them, coming slowly as if groping its way toward the intersection; it was almost in the middle of the roadway, and Saint-Germain pulled the Packard to the side to give the other driver room to maneuver.

"There's a space, there. In front of the next house along. You can fit in there." Rowena pointed with one hand and touched his sleeve with the other.

Saint-Germain pulled into the parking space, curbed the wheels, and set the brake. "Well, here we are," he said, getting out of the Packard and coming around to open the passenger door for Rowena.

She got out of the car with practiced ease. "Gee, it's cold," she exclaimed, folding her arms, her purse pressed against her breasts as if to shield her from the chill. "I should have brought a coat with me."

"I'll get you inside quickly, so you can get warm," he said, offering her his arm as he squinted into the fog, hoping to get them safely across the street; even his night-seeing eyes could not penetrate the blurry mists around them. "How dangerous is it?"

"I can't tell. The corner won't be any safer—it could even be more risky because of traffic turning. Best to take our chances here." She took a step out into the street, and as quickly stepped back; a moment later, a Cadillac loomed at them, passing on to the intersection. "I think we'd better listen, and when it sounds clear, make a run for it. That's what I usually do." She shivered, as much from apprehension as from the cold.

"As you wish," he said, and stood silently, trying to hear the approaching rumble of car engines. Three cars passed before they sprinted across the road, slipping between a Pierce-Arrow and a Lincoln tourer to the sidewalk.

"Not that you can see it at its best, but that's it, two doors down," said Rowena as they started toward the house. They walked toward it, and gradually it became more visible, a large house in a style that combined elements of the Edwardian and Queen Anne, with a touch of Orientalism thrown in. The windows were good-sized and three of them were fronted by trellises upon which wisteria grew. "Not Gingerbread Gothic, but still . . ." She used the knocker, which was a flying brass bird, over which was the elaborately lettered motto *And lo! the bird is on the wing.* "Clara should still be here. She's supposed to be at the house until five, more than an hour from now."

"Your housekeeper—yes, I recall." He stepped up onto the porch beside her, under the broad eaves that sheltered the front door.

There were footsteps inside the house, the distinctive sound of heeled shoes, and then the snick of a lock, and the door opened inward, revealing a woman of about thirty-five in a plain dress of dark blue; her hair was done up in a simple bun and she wore only a touch of lipstick. "Good afternoon, Miss Saxon," she said, glancing toward Saint-Germain with veiled curiosity. "The mailman arrived at one, and I put your letters on the table. There's one from your nephew." She indicated the small taboret under a framed painting of deer grazing at the edge of a meadow; the impression was pastoral, but with an underlying unease, as if the deer were being watched by a predator.

"Thank you, Clara," said Rowena, maintaining her composure as she and Saint-Germain stepped into the foyer. "We're going into my studio." She smiled. "The Comte here was one of my first patrons. He and I met in England, before the Great War."

Clara regarded him narrowly. "Do you say so? He must have been very young."

Rowena looked a bit startled; she picked up the envelopes on the taboret and began to sort through them. "Yes. We were both much younger then, and our lives were very different."

"I should think so," said Clara. "Is there anything you want of me just now, or shall I go back to making dinner?"

"Oh, yes, please," said Rowena. "A tray with tea and English muffins—you know what I like—and a snifter of brandy," she said. "We'll be in my studio." She put all the envelopes but one back on the table. "I'll take care of the mail later. Come along, Saint-Germain. I want you to see what I've been working on." He followed Rowena after favoring Clara with a nod; Rowena opened the pocket-doors on the left side of the foyer, and motioned to Saint-Germain to come along. "These used to be parlors, and could be opened up to make a small ballroom; my grandfather often entertained fairly lavishly. They make a fine studio, and you can see the windows I had put in at the far end for north light," she said, pointing these things out, a bit of her nervousness returning. There were paintings on almost every foot of wall-space, some of them finished and framed, others in various stages of completion. "That group I did on a trip up to Mendocino, a little town about a hundred sixty miles away. The coast north of here is still fairly remote and the road is not an easy one, but the town—you can see the sawmill in this view—has a beautiful location, and the isolation makes it unique. The painting in the foyer is part of the series I did there. I did twenty watercolors and nine oils." She put down her purse on a trestle table and pulled off her gloves. "And these are my studies of the bridge being built. This one is the Oakland bridge—as you see, it's further along than the Golden Gate—and the—" She stopped abruptly and put her hand to her mouth. "Oh, dear. I am rattling."

"No. I don't think so," Saint-Germain said. "I think you're trying to compress more than two decades into ten minutes."

She managed a bit of a chuckle. "You've always been kind."

"Not always," he said, suddenly reserved. Then he looked directly into her golden eyes and offered her a fleeting smile. "You needn't bother trying to tell me everything in an hour. I would prefer not to leave for a while, unless you ask me to go; and there will be other times for us to talk. I am very much enjoying your company, and your art. You may take your time telling me whatever you'd like me to hear, or you can say very little, and allow me to study your work." He indicated the pictures on the walls. "I didn't know there was much interest in representational art."

"Oh, not in some circles," she said, waving her hand in dismissal. "But a few people still like artwork they can understand directly, and, although they may admire large abstractions, prefer something a bit more . . . familiar for the walls of their homes." She pointed to a place high on the wall in the front half of her studio. "That's one of the studies I did from memory."

He looked at the watercolor portrait that was, as far as he could tell, a good likeness of his face; Rogerio could tell him more confidently. "I'm flattered."

She studied it. "I don't know. I've missed something; I think it's your eyes, but I'm not certain. That color: blue so dark, it's black. I've tried to capture the depths, but so far . . . That's hard to achieve. But your presence is even harder. It is strange that you are unchanged, although you warned me you age very slowly." She looked away and began to pace. "I have the two sketches I did as studies for that upstairs, in my bedroom." She suddenly went quiet again.

"How very good of you," he said as if he did not notice her silence. "If you would like to show them to me at some time . . . Bring them down, if you wish . . ." He let the suggestion hang in the air between them.

"Not today, I think," she said, suddenly prim; she made another turn about the studio. "At least, I haven't made up my mind."

"Whatever you wish," said Saint-Germain, and nodded to a small settee in the Edwardian style, covered in faded burgundy velvet. "Do you mind?"

"Go ahead. Sit down. You needn't stand on ceremony—literally or figuratively," she told him brusquely, but remained on her feet, walking back and forth, the sharp sound of her heels marking her progress.

He did as she recommended, making himself as comfortable as the old furniture would allow. Looking around at the various sketches and paintings, he said, "I like your subjects; your ability to make implications not apparent at first glance is quite remarkable."

She nodded, a bit distracted. "Thank you. I'm glad you like them."

"Oh, I do," said Saint-Germain. "You've developed a strong . . . voice of your own. I suppose I can call it a voice, although we're discussing paintings?"

"Yes, you can," she said, warming in spite of her growing restiveness. "I'm glad to hear you like that about my work: it's what I like about it."

He was about to say something more when the side door opened and Clara Powell came into the room, carrying a tray in her hands. There was a large porcelain teapot, two cups-and-saucers, a covered plate, and two snifters of brandy on it, along with a pot of milk and a sugar-bowl, as well as silverware and napkins. She shot a single look in Saint-Germain's direction, then set the tray down on a small table near the wide rear window. "Just as you ordered, Miss Saxon."

"Thank you, Clara," she said, coming to a halt at last.

"Do you want me to stay? Dinner's in the oven, a leg of lamb stuffed with onions and wild rice, and there's a salad in the refrigerator; it'll be done at seven. I've set two places at the dining table, but if you'd rather I clean up tonight . . ." She let the suggestion trail off as she glanced again at Saint-Germain. "You don't have to be alone."

"Thank you, Clara; I think I can manage," said Rowena, smiling at this display of protection.

"I'll be here another fifteen minutes, if you change your mind," she said, and withdrew.

"I think she's prepared to throw me out bodily," said Saint-Germain, a wry smile touching the corners of his mouth.

"As if she could," Rowena scoffed.

"She is ready to try," said Saint-Germain, and nodded toward the tray. "But she is also willing to encourage me."

"Goodness, yes," said Rowena. "She has hoped I would find a—she calls it a *beau*, or sometimes a *suitor*. Can you imagine a suitor? At my age?"

"Not a swain?" Saint-Germain asked.

Rowena actually laughed. "No, not a swain." She drew up a chair to the table, where the tray waited. "I don't imagine I can tempt you with tea or English muffins."

"Thank you, no," said Saint-Germain.

"I didn't think so," said Rowena, and lifted the cover from the plate, revealing two split, buttered English muffins. She picked up one of the halves, dropped a napkin in her lap, and bit into the crusty, white pastry, taking care not to let the melted butter run down her chin. Then she set the rest of the muffin down and went about pouring herself a cup of tea, putting a little ornamental strainer over the cup to catch the leaves. "These things might not be English, but I do love them," she said as she stirred milk into her cup and picked up the muffin again.

"You're hungry," said Saint-Germain.

"I'm ravenous," she exclaimed. "If I have to wait until seven to eat, I'll gobble the table linens."

He watched her devour both halves of one English muffin and go through three cups of tea. "Do you miss England?"

"Occasionally," she said. "But not nearly as much as I thought I would." She wiped her mouth with the napkin—most of her lipstick came away on it.

"What do you miss the most?" He leaned back, crossing his ankles and studying her.

"The smallness," she said at once, as if she had thought this out some time ago and was satisfied with her answer. "Here everything is vast—you travel for hours and hours and still you're far away from your destination. In England, nothing is that far away, and although the heaths and dales are wonderfully wild, they aren't remote in the way things are here; the scale is entirely different. It's a cozy place, England. California, while beautiful, isn't cozy, and America is huge. When I came across the country in my grandfather's private railway car, all those years ago, I was astonished by the size of it." She poured herself a fourth cup of tea and stirred in milk. "At first, the amalgam of people perplexed me; now I've come to like it, and I'm sorry for all the artificial divisions that remain."

Saint-Germain regarded her thoughtfully. "The amalgam—do you ever paint that?"

"Oh. Yes. Ten years ago I did a series of street-scene studies, looking for places that had the greatest variety of subjects in them. There was a total of nineteen paintings in the suite. I did three in North Beach, along Columbus Avenue, where the Italian part of the city almost touches Chinatown. I did another out on Geary, where the Japanese and Russians have settled, and two around Mission Dolores, where the Irish and Spanish tend to live. I did a couple at the crest of Nob Hill, at the front of the Mark Hopkins, and studies of passengers on the trolleys, fishermen at the Wharf, the Cliff House in the fog. They were fairly well-received in a one-woman six-week show I had in '28. Most of the paintings sold, and the reviews were better than I had expected." She smiled with a touch of embarrassment at her pride. "It was probably the best one-woman show I've had so far; I haven't had one on my own since. I'm almost afraid to try another, in case it doesn't go as well."

"It must please you to get recognition for your work," he said, contemplating her changing expressions.

"Most of the time," she admitted. "But it can be awkward; it depends on the circumstances." She reached out and turned on one of the standing lamps in the room, casting back the shadows that had begun to thicken in the fog and fading day.

"I can imagine," said Saint-Germain with a hint of irony. "Successful women, especially those in the arts, can be—"

She interrupted him. "Men don't know how to deal with me, and women worry that I'll take their men away from them. There. Now you know." She put down her teacup with a bit more force than necessary. "It happens less often now that I'm over fifty, but from time to time I find it difficult to mix in certain circles. A woman on her own can be a social liability, and that doesn't change as one gets older. And I'm not inclined to spend my time with the groups of widows one sees everywhere—not that most of them would have me. My friend—the one I wrote you about, who had the stroke?—he used to be my escort to social events, which suited us both down to the ground. We enjoy many of the same things, and he's been very good company, with no complications. I think I made things easier for him, as he did for me. Now that he isn't able to leave his bed, I try to visit him once a week, but he is . . . so unresponsive, I don't know if it does him any good." Reaching for one of the snifters of brandy, she said, forcing herself not to dwell on her friend's misfortune, "I haven't gone out much since Greg was stricken."

"Poor man," said Saint-Germain; over many centuries he had seen many of the ills that could blight the human body, but the isolation imposed by stroke seemed to him one of the cruelest. "He must be suffering."

"Yes," she said, and pinched the bridge of her nose as she held the snifter. "On many accounts. And there is nothing very much that can be done for him." She looked away from Saint-Germain. "He had a companion for years, who tried to care for him, but after a while had to hire nurses for Greg."

"I gather your friends are homosexual," said Saint-Germain.

She looked up at him sharply. "Yes. They're very discreet, of course. If you didn't know, you wouldn't know. Penelope was horrified when she found out that I was willing to be seen with such a man, though I reminded her I was perfectly safe with Greg; which she should have found reassuring, but she didn't, as if she thought something perverse might be communicated to me. She believes in the stigma associated with such men, as if they wore brands, or—"

"There was a time, not so long ago, when many did, if they were caught: wore brands, and worse," said Saint-Germain.

Rowena took a deep breath. "Not that Penelope knows only heterosexual men, as much as she may think that is the case." Her features softened. "You don't seem surprised."

"I'm not," said Saint-Germain.

"Why do you say that?" She was deeply interested.

"Because it's a pattern I've seen before, in many guises," he replied, thinking back to Ettore Colonna in Rome, not quite three centuries ago, and all that he had endured. "At least they don't kill homosexuals anymore, though there are still some hard laws against it, and a great deal of blame and fear; much the sort of things vampires have endured, and for similar reasons." He paused. "There have been times and places when homosexuality was openly exalted and privileged, but those were few, and circumscribed. For the most part, except in very specific circumstances, there has been intolerance at best and persecution at worst—centuries and centuries of it."

She fiddled with her napkin. "Have you ever—? I mean, with men?"

"Of course, but rarely. Among other things, men are not so willing as women to accept my impotence." He saw the question in her eyes. "Just as I have come to think that most of those who love their own sex are born with that predisposition, so most of those who love the opposite sex are also predisposed. I was a man long before I was a vampire, and I have found that I have a greater inclination to love women than men; not wholly exclusively, but preferentially." His candor spared her the distress she had begun to feel.

"And you still feel something for me?" She brought up her chin as if daring him to let her down.

"Most certainly," he said. "I have tasted your blood and I know you; how can I not love you?"

"There is so much I want to say to you," she said as she put the snifter down, its contents untasted. "I don't know how to begin."

"There is plenty of time, Rowena. I have no plans to leave yet awhile," said Saint-Germain. "You needn't do anything that troubles you, not now, not at any time. I don't expect you to offer yourself to—"

"But I may lose my nerve," she admitted.

"You make being with me seem dire," he said lightly, but with an underlying note of sadness.

"No, not dire. Anything but that. I remember so well how it was in Amsterdam."

"It will be different now," he told her gently.

"Because I'm older and you aren't?" she asked, a little downcast.

"Because time has passed and our lives are different than they were," he said with such utter kindness that the breath caught in her throat.

She was silent for the better part of a minute. "Would you like to stay to dinner?"

His dark eyes lingered on her. "You understand that this would mean you would be in danger of becoming like me when you—"

"—die?" she finished for him. "Yes. I know that. But just now I am more concerned with my life than my death." She rose, moved her tray aside, and came toward him where he now stood ready to take her into his arms.

TEXT OF A LETTER FROM CENERE IN LONDON TO COLONEL ANDREAS MORALES IN MADRID.

> *Browns Hotel*
> *London, England*
> *29 September, 1936*
>
> *Colonel Andreas Morales*
> *22, Calle Real*
> *Madrid, Spain*
>
> *Dear Colonel,*
> *First, my congratulations on your promotion. No doubt it is highly deserved and one of which you can be proud. The eyes of your superiors must be on you.*
> *This is coming to your home address in order to spare you—and me—any difficulties regarding the errand on which I am embarked, on your behalf. I am convinced that this mission on which you have sent me exceeds your*

authority, but I will not hold that against you as long as you continue to support what I am doing to promote your agenda. Like you, I am a professional, and I have certain standards to maintain if I am to preserve my reputation and continue in my chosen occupation. For this reason, I will endeavor to complete my assignment to your satisfaction in all regards, just as I will anticipate your upholding our agreement. You may have questions put to you that you would prefer not to answer officially, which this private communication will make it possible for you to do; you can still deny my work, which undoubtedly suits us both.

I have, in accordance with your wishes, continued to try to locate Ferenc Ragoczy, le Comte de Saint-Germain. As you may recall, I had traced him as far as Cherbourg, but after that, I had drawn a blank, so, as you know, I went to England, where, as you can see, I still am now. I have been busy attempting to get information, but without much success. His household staff were not forthcoming, although I have managed to get a little from one of them, which I have attempted to confirm, for to run off across the Atlantic on only the word of a servant would be irresponsible.

To that end, day before yesterday I had occasion to accost his attorney, one Miles Sunbury, in his flat in Siddons Lane. Sunbury had been avoiding me for some little while and I decided to approach him directly, and press the urgency of my inquiries. He was not inclined to impart the information I sought willingly, so I was forced to make my argument more physically. It took me longer than I expected, and required more stringent measures than I had anticipated; Sunbury turned out to be stubborn and I am afraid our interview became harrowing for him. He was alive when I dropped him off just outside of a large local hospital. I did not bother to get the name of the institution. If he received prompt care, he will probably recover, although he may need to walk with a cane, and his face isn't quite what it used to be.

I have learned that Saint-Germain has indeed gone to America, and Sunbury at last provided the names of a number of law firms to which he referred the Comte, the most prominent of which is a firm in Manhattan. I propose to take the next ship to New York and begin there, for I don't think the servant who said he had gone to Boston knew what she was talking about. New York is a much more obvious place for a man like Saint-Germain to go, and it would amaze me if he was foolish enough to confide his intentions to a servant. I will hope to find him without much delay, and I will do as you have charged me. You needn't fear that any of my efforts will be traced back to you. I have been able to keep your name out of this and will continue to do so.

However, once I reach New York, I will need additional funds if I am to continue this chase. You will have to wire money to me at whichever bank you use in New York. Let me know which bank and the account number so I can use the money promptly. If you fail to provide me with what I need, I will return to Spain and make you regret what you have neglected to do: the very questions you seek to avoid would have to be asked and neither of us would acquit ourselves well in such an eventuality.

I anticipate a complete resolution to your problem no later than the end of the year, if all goes well. It may be that I will not find the Comte as quickly as I anticipate, and if I require more time, I will so inform you. I will keep you abreast of my progress as I have the opportunity to do so.

Yours to command,

Cenere

chapter five

It was sunny to the north of San Rafael, a golden, early-autumn morning that was warm except in the shadows, where the chill in the air was a reminder that winter was coming. The Packard rolled along Route 101 past the cemeteries at a steady fifty-five miles per hour until they reached Novato, where they slowed down to twenty, having been warned about the eagerness of the local police to ticket speeders passing through their town. Once beyond the city limits, they resumed the higher speed and continued on up the highway. There were dairy farms along the road, and the fields were filled with grazing cattle. At Petaluma the dairies were replaced with poultry farms and large, hand-lettered signs advertising fresh eggs for sale. Beyond Petaluma the farms were bigger, with sheep and goats as well as cattle out in the fields. The morning grew warmer as they traveled.

"We couldn't ask for nicer weather," said Rowena as they reached the outskirts of Santa Rosa and slowed again to pass through the small city.

"It is quite beautiful," Saint-Germain agreed. "Geyserville is not much farther, is it?"

Rowena laughed. "You saw the map."

"Yes, but you have actually been here," Saint-Germain reminded her. "You know what's ahead because you've seen it."

"Not for a couple of years. They've been improving the road. Another one of FDR's projects, I believe." She pointed to the line of hills ahead of them on the left. "There are still many stands of redwoods as you go along this highway."

"We have passed logging trucks in the south-bound lane," he said as they stopped for a traffic light. "Not much farther."

"Do you know how to find the winery once we get there?" Rowena asked. She had taken stock of the dry, khaki-colored, velvety hills that framed Santa Rosa, with their occasional clusters of trees, and knew that once they were out of the town, they would be a long way from the usual comforts she was accustomed to have around her. This did not trouble her; she was prepared for roughing it a little.

"I have the directions he gave me on the telephone last night, and he said, if we need better instructions, to call from Healdsburg. There's a café in the middle of town with a telephone booth just inside the door, according to Pietragnelli," said Saint-Germain. "Why are you so nervous? I hope you don't regret accompanying me."

"No; it's not that. You said he knows I'm coming," she said. "I'm not the kind of surprise most hosts like to have." She smoothed her tan twill slacks and touched her natural-leather handbag; she looked casually elegant, sleek, and informal at once, in the fashion made popular by Hollywood, her roan hair tied with a long scarf of soft, brocaded silk in a bronze shade that almost matched her dark gold eyes and complemented her olive-green linen blouse.

"I don't think you have anything to worry about. I arranged to bring you with me this time; he knows you're an artist specializing in land- and cityscapes. He was quite impressed. I'm fairly certain he'll be delighted to have you visit." Saint-Germain looked down at his gas gauge. "I think we should fill up the tank at the next opportunity."

"Shall I look for a gas station? There must be one along this stretch of road, for travelers. Out here in the country, they often have them at general stores or garages." She adjusted the side-wing so that the dusty wind did not blow directly on her.

"If you would, unless you recall where one was," he said, starting ahead on the green light.

"I'll keep an eye out," she said.

They found a Texaco station on the north side of town, and Saint-Germain ordered the scruffy young attendant to fill the fuel tank. After paying for the gasoline, they got back on the road, continuing on up the Redwood Highway. Thirty minutes later they entered Geyserville; Saint-Germain began looking for Geyser Creek Road, and turned right onto it, following out along a graveled two-lane way for three miles. The only signs of humanity were the road itself, the barbed-wire fences, and the telephone poles.

"He really is out in the middle of nowhere, isn't he?" Rowena asked, then pointed. "Look. Grapes. We must be getting close."

"These vines have been recently harvested," Saint-Germain observed. "If they are picking, it must be in another plantation."

"Then we must be getting near the place," said Rowena, looking around more carefully.

Saint-Germain nodded. "There should be a gate in the next half-mile." He could see in the rearview mirror the boiling dust behind the Packard.

"Which side of the road?" she asked.

"The right," said Saint-Germain, braking as a covey of quail burst from the weeds at the roadside and scurried across their path.

"There's the gate. It's flanked by two stone lambs, just as he said it would be," said Rowena, pointing. "Shall I get out and open it?"

"I'll do it," said Saint-Germain, pulling the Packard to cross the cattle-guard that fronted the gate. He set the hand-brake and put the transmission in neutral, then got out and went to open the metal-framed gate. Returning to the car, he drove through, then braked again and went back to close the gate. "He said it's half-a-mile to the house. It's in a stand of oak, on the far side of the rise."

"With this one road, and the telephone poles, we can't miss it," she said, with an amused glance toward him, so nattily dressed in his black linen suit and immaculately white shirt; even his perfectly knotted dark red bow tie belonged more to a resort than a winery.

They crested the rise and saw, almost directly in front of them, tucked into a hollow of the rising hill, a sprawling, two-story house painted a pale terra-cotta shade with white trim built in an Italianate version of Carpenter Gothic, an L-shaped structure with a broad flagstone terrace in the bend of the L. It was shaded by a half-dozen scrub oaks that hovered around the house like huge, anxious, dark green hens. There was a small barn a short distance from the house, and a cluster of small cabins on the far side of the barn. The winery itself was off to the side of the house on the side opposite to the barn, a large stone building built up against and back into the hill. From somewhere a short distance away came the sound of machinery and occasional imperative shouts.

Saint-Germain pulled up in the circular drive in front of the house and stopped the Packard. "I assume we're here," he said to Rowena, and got out of the car.

As he opened her door for her, she looked around her. "What a wonderful place. Just look at that house! I'm surprised *Sunset* hasn't done a piece on it."

"They might not know it exists," said Saint-Germain, cocking his head toward the road they had just driven. "It is not exactly on the beaten path."

"No, it's not," she said, and reached back into the car for her sketch pad. "Do you think Mr. Pietragnelli would mind?"

"I have no notion. You will have to ask him when he comes." Saint-Germain checked his watch. "We're almost on time." He started toward the front door, only to be stopped by a stentorian shout.

"Il padrone!" A man in work-clothes surged across the yard between the winery and the house; he had a fringe of disordered, greying curls that made his pate all the more obvious; his eyes were small and black as raisins, very animated beneath his tufted brows. His face showed years of use, leaving it rumpled and friendly as an unmade bed. "Il signor' Conte! Benvenuto a la casa mia!" He clapped his hands as he came, his grin infectious.

"Signor Pietragnelli," said Saint-Germain, for surely it was he. "Che piacer. I am delighted to meet you at last."

"Ed io lo stesso," enthused Carlo Pietragnelli as he reached Saint-Germain and laid claim to his hand, shaking it vigorously. "You come in good time." His English was excellent, almost without accent, but the cadences in which he spoke it were entirely Italian.

"Your instructions were very clear and there were only two delays on the road." He extricated his hand. "This is a fine place you have here."

"É tanto bene. It is well enough," he said with required modesty belied by his stance. "But it will be better. I have bought a new plantation in Knights Valley, to the east of here, and another near Calistoga, in Napa County." He pointed to the southeast. "My daughter Sophia and son-in-law, Ethan, live in Calistoga, and he is presently running that operation for me. So I have the best of the region—Sonoma and Napa Counties. In ten years, who knows what will be possible?" He bounced on his heels. "But enough of such matters. Let me welcome you to my house as if to your own; for without you, I would no longer have it." He turned to Rowena. "And this is your ospide—your guest?" His smile found a way to broaden. "It is a real pleasure to welcome you, Signora Saxon, to my home. It is an honor to have you here. I am told you are a fine artist. I look forward to seeing your work and to the joy of your company."

Rowena held out her hand to him, and had it kissed. "You're very gracious, Mr. Pietragnelli." She indicated her sketch pad. "I hope you won't mind if I do a few studies of your marvelous home?"

"Why should I mind to have such a kindness done for me?" he asked the world at large. "You must sketch to your heart's content, cara doña."

"Thank you," she said, a bit nonplussed by his relentless cordiality.

"Well, come inside. It is time for lunch, in any case, and my men will be taking their hour of rest." He stumped up the four broad steps onto the covered verandah and made for the front door. "Come in. Prego."

The interior was cool and comfortably worn, nothing shabby, but everything having the unmistakable look of appreciative use. Most of the furniture was older, but the carpet in the entry hall looked newer than most of the furnishings. There were framed pictures on the wall, and a cluster of photographs on the Chickering cabinet grand piano in the parlor, which stood on the left side of the entry hall; the parlor had two sets of French doors leading to the terrace, but Pietragnelli led them straight ahead, past the broad staircase to the upper floor, and into a sunny dining room.

"This is a beautiful room, Mr. Pietragnelli," said Rowena, setting her sketch pad down on the window seat and looking at the fine bay window that made everything so luminous. Fine lace curtains filtered the light, making the room seem slightly hazy, and softened the three place-settings in white stoneware and good glass that were laid at one end of the long dining table.

"It is the heart of a house, the dining room, don't you think?" He went to hold a chair for her. "If you will be seated, I'll bring you some wine in a moment. I have soup and bread and cheese for lunch. And, of course, wine. I hope you will join me for the meal." After a short hesitation, he said, "My workers get soup, as well, and bread. On days like this, they are served in the field. When it is cold, I serve them in the winery."

"That's generous of you," said Rowena. "In these times, many employers require their workers to bring their own lunches." She had read the arguments in the newspapers about such demands, and tended to favor the workingmen's positions, especially now when money was so hard to come by.

Pietragnelli shook his head vigorously. "I do not hold with such things. I was taught that if I hire men, I must feed them while they labor for me. And," he added, "many of them cannot afford to feed their families unless I provide lunch for them. It is not an imposition for me. I have a large vegetable garden, and what I do not grow, my neighbor does; also, I trade wine for meat with my neighbors, so it is not difficult for me to offer good, simple meals."

"An admirable tradition," said Saint-Germain. "I applaud you for it."

"I do not do it for applause," Pietragnelli announced. He shot a questioning look at Saint-Germain. "Would you like to have me turn on the radio? Or show you to the piano and the sheet music? Our meal is almost ready. We're going to eat, and if you—" He broke off and resumed in a slightly more conversational way, "Mr. Rogers informed me that you do not eat or drink in company. Can't I persuade you to make an exception so that we can continue to become acquainted?"

"I mean no offense, Signor Pietragnelli, but I fear I must decline the food and drink," said Saint-Germain. "But do not let my eccentricity keep you from having a proper meal. And if it will not trouble you, I would like to sit with you while you eat. If you don't find my abstention awkward, I won't, either, for I am accustomed to doing this. So, if this is acceptable to you, there is no need to offer me other entertainment. And I do agree with you that the room where you dine is the heart of any home."

Pietragnelli sighed. "Very well." He turned his attention to Rowena. "You will not refuse me, will you, signora?"

"I have been looking forward to a good lunch," said Rowena promptly. "Soup, bread, cheese, and wine. What could be better?" She put her napkin in her lap.

"A woman of taste as well as art. Com' è bella," approved Pietragnelli. "If you will excuse me, I will ask the cook to bring our food and I will get a special bottle from my own cellar." So saying, he bustled out of the dining room, calling as he went, "Mrs. Barringstone! Serve our meal, if you would!"

Saint-Germain sat down opposite Rowena, leaving the head of the table free for their host. "It seems that they are still harvesting grapes."

"Apparently," said Rowena. "Look at these soup-bowls! They must contain a quart at least. Does he serve as much to his workers, I wonder. They work hard, of course, and would need an ample meal. But—" She stopped speaking as Mrs. Barringstone came into the dining room carrying a large covered tureen; she was a raw-boned woman probably no more than thirty-five but with skin and hair and worry-lines that made her look ten years older. She said nothing as she put her burden down, wiping it carefully with a dish-towel. "Thank you," Rowena told her.

"I'll bring the rest in a minute," Mrs. Barringstone said in a flat Oklahoma twang. She went back to the kitchen.

Rowena lifted the lid on the tureen and sniffed deeply. "She may not be forthcoming, but the soup smells delicious." As soon as Mrs. Barringstone returned with a large loaf of bread in a basket, a tub of butter, and a round of cheese, Rowena complimented her on the soup.

"It's Mr. Pietragnelli's recipe. Thanks anyway." She put the rest of the meal on the table and left them alone.

"The cheese is local, according to the impression on the rind," Saint-Germain remarked. "All those dairy cattle must provide the milk."

"There are probably goats, as well," said Rowena. "Not that this is goat cheese."

"Or sheep," said Saint-Germain.

Pietragnelli came bustling back into the dining room, a wine-bottle in one hand, a corkscrew in the other. "This is eight years old, a blend of Cabernet Franc and Cotes Sauvage, for the wine, a good year, but—Eight years ago was a hard time for us. Prohibition was the law, and if I hadn't had contracts with Saint Laurence's and Saint Thomas More, I couldn't have stayed in business, no matter what you did for us, Conte. The government would have shut us down, as they did so many others—those who didn't go bankrupt." He held up the bottle, a happy grin returning to his face. "Still, it was a good year for reds."

Rowena tried to think of something to say as she watched Pietragnelli wield the corkscrew, and finally commented, "You must be proud of what you've accomplished here."

"Proud?" He set down the corkscrew and twisted the cork off it, sniffing it critically before pouring a little out into his glass. "We shall see."

"The color is intense," said Saint-Germain.

"A pity you cannot have any of it," said Pietragnelli as he swirled the wine in his glass, inhaling deeply.

"I must concur," said Saint-Germain, watching Pietragnelli take a first, critical taste. "The smell is ambrosial."

"It will do," he decided. "But it will need about fifteen minutes to open up fully." He filled Rowena's glass and then his own. "It will go well with the soup. If the food is the verse, the wine is the music." He remained standing as he reached for the ladle and filled Rowena's soup-bowl, and then his own. "Alla tavola non s'invecchia," he said as he finally sat down and reached for his wineglass.

"At the table, we never age," Saint-Germain translated. "An excellent motto."

Rowena shot him an intense look, then lifted her glass to endorse his sentiment. "Thank you for having me, Mr. Pietragnelli."

Pietragnelli took the loaf of bread and tore off an end; he offered this to Rowena, then pulled another for himself. "You will pardon us, Conte, but we will eat now."

Saint-Germain inclined his head. "Please; don't let me stop you enjoying your lunch."

"It is lamentable that you cannot join us," said Pietragnelli as he buttered his bread. "I think you must miss a great pleasure in life."

"Oh, I agree that taking nourishment is a very great pleasure," Saint-Germain said, and saw Rowena almost choke on her first taste of soup.

"This is very good," Rowena managed to say to Pietragnelli. "What is in it, besides chopped beef and onions?"

"Beef stock, of course. Then zucchini—as you say, Italian squash—two kinds of bell peppers, chopped spinach, mushrooms, string beans, oregano, thyme, summer savory, basil, garlic, lemon peel, a little ginger, black pepper, salt, and, of course, wine." He reeled off the ingredients easily. "It is simmered for five hours, and that gives it body and a good flavor. I have often made it myself. But now I have Mrs. Barringstone to manage the kitchen during the day. Her husband runs the crusher and so is busy today, with the current—"

"The crusher? You don't stamp the wine with your feet?" Rowena asked, oddly disappointed.

"No, signora, we do not. In the early days we did, but as soon as I could afford it, I bought a crusher. The crusher does the crushing better and faster than feet can, and the men don't get as drunk on the fumes as they do if they tread on the grapes themselves. With as large a harvest as we have here, every one of the crew would be drunk if we had to crush by feet." He picked up his glass and took a sip of his wine. "It is improving."

"But surely, with the grapes just harvested, there would not be enough alcohol to cause drunkenness," said Rowena.

"The fermentation begins at once. There is sugar in the grapes, and it starts to become intoxicating as soon as the skin is broken, but it is raw, very raw." He smiled. "In time, and with proper care, the rawness goes away, and the wine is ready."

Rowena tasted the wine and smiled. "The rawness is certainly gone from this. Very, very good, Mr. Pietragnelli."

He beamed. "It thrills my heart to please you." He drank a little more, then turned to Saint-Germain. "My children will be sorry they missed you. When you come again, it must be on a weekend, so you may meet them. They, too, want to thank you for preserving our business and our family."

"I would be delighted to meet your family, but thanks aren't necessary: believe this," Saint-Germain said with conviction.

"I will have to disagree with you, Conte," said Pietragnelli. "But not while I'm eating." He pinched a bit of bread off his portion and dipped it into the soup. "Country manners, signora; I know. But we are in the country."

Rowena laughed and did as her host had done. "This is very good bread. What's in it?"

"It is pugliese, Italian country bread. Chopped ripe olives and pine nuts are kneaded into the dough." Pietragnelli smiled at her. "I used to make this, too; before Mrs. Barringstone came. I still do occasionally, but my daughter Adrianna makes it for me when she and Enrico come on Sundays."

"This doesn't taste three days old," Rowena observed.

"No; it was baked this morning, for this occasion." He took some more of it and dipped it in his soup.

Lunch went along pleasantly enough, the conversation steered artfully away from politics and other vexing matters. By the time it was finished, both

Pietragnelli and Rowena had eaten most of their soup and had had a second glass of his excellent wine and a good wedge of cheese. Pietragnelli had summoned Mrs. Barringstone from the kitchen and ordered coffee.

"It was a superb meal, Mr. Pietragnelli," Rowena approved as she finally put her napkin on the table.

"I am glad you found it so," Pietragnelli said, and looked over at Saint-Germain. "No coffee, either, I suppose?"

"No, thank you," said Saint-Germain. He was so much at ease that Pietragnelli was convinced of his sincerity.

"Perhaps another time?" Pietragnelli suggested.

"It is kind of you to ask, but probably not," said Saint-Germain.

Rowena drank the last of the wine in her glass. "This is so good."

"I will provide you some to take home with you," Pietragnelli exclaimed. "You will do me the honor of taking it with you."

Trapped by her good manners as much as her liking of the wine, Rowena nodded. "Thank you, Mr. Pietragnelli. I will appreciate every drop of it."

"Well and good!" Pietragnelli said, pushing back from the table. "You must excuse me. There is a car coming—" He went off toward the front door.

Rowena was a bit startled. "Goodness. Do you think anything's wrong?"

Saint-Germain shrugged but there was worry in his dark eyes. "I don't know. He wasn't expecting anyone, was he?"

"He didn't mention anyone," said Rowena cautiously.

"No." Saint-Germain rose and went toward the entry-hall. He paused under the arch of the staircase and watched as a small Oriental man came in through the front door with Pietragnelli.

"—if you won't go to the authorities," Pietragnelli was saying.

"But they do nothing! Nothing!" the Oriental man insisted in disgust. He was wiry, shorter than Pietragnelli, and about forty. His clothes proclaimed him a farmer as much as his hard, chapped hands. His English was slightly accented; he had obviously spoken the language most of his life.

"If you keep at them, they will. I'll come with you," Pietragnelli said, going on forcefully, "They can't ignore these thefts forever."

The Oriental man laughed bitterly. "And why not? Why should they listen to a Japanese or an Italian? They don't want us here in the first place."

"Well, perhaps they don't, Hiro, but they have to enforce the law. Otherwise there can be trouble." Pietragnelli looked up and saw Saint-Germain watching them. "Come in. I want you to meet my guests."

The Japanese farmer stopped still. "I didn't realize you weren't alone," he said, attempting to back out of the room.

Pietragnelli would have none of it. "You can speak in front of these people. They won't think the less of you." He propelled the newcomer forward, saying as he did, "This is my neighbor Hiro Yoshimura. He raises vegetables, about half-a-mile up the road. He's been losing his crop to the midnight harvesters. I believe I wrote to you about the problem?"

"That you did," said Saint-Germain, holding out his hand. "I am Ferenc Ragoczy."

Yoshimura bowed. "A pleasure," he said, looking as if it were anything but.

"You have to excuse Hiro. He has had a hard month, and it is only getting worse." By now he had guided Yoshimura into his dining room; Saint-Germain offered the chair he had occupied and took the one next to it. "Was it the Leonardi boys again?"

"I don't know," said Yoshimura miserably. "I didn't catch them. It could have been men from the hobo camp outside of Windsor." He made a gesture of futility.

"We have some youngsters who like to commit mischief," Pietragnelli explained. "They also know the jobbers who take stolen produce. I think they're the ones who made off with sixty pounds of my grapes three weeks ago, but I didn't see them do it. But they are the ones who would be most likely to do such a thing, and know how to do it, and are inclined to do it. So I have no proof. All I know is that Sam Petrie bought grapes from Oliver Leonardi, and they weren't from the Leonardi vineyard."

"They are criminals," said Yoshimura.

"They probably are," said Pietragnelli as he filled Saint-Germain's unused wine-glass with the last of what was in the bottle. "Have some of this. You'll feel better."

Yoshimura scowled but did as Pietragnelli ordered. "I can't afford another midnight harvest. I've lost a third of my crops already."

Mrs. Barringstone came in from the kitchen with a tray on which stood a cof-feepot, a creamer, and a sugar-bowl and three mugs. Seeing Yoshimura, she put the tray down and, with an expression of distaste, withdrew to the kitchen.

"You see?" Yoshimura said as he watched Mrs. Barringstone depart. "They all hate me."

"No, they don't," said Pietragnelli. "They think you're strange, and they're troubled because of it." He sat down in his chair again. "Signora Saxon, would you be good enough to pour the coffee?"

"Of course," said Rowena, and set about doing it.

"What can I do, Carlo? I can't afford men to guard my fields. It's all I can do to pay my two hands." He took a long drink of wine. "If they continue to raid my fields, I won't have money enough to keep Tochigo and Junimoto on."

Pietragnelli put his large hand on Yoshimura's shoulder. "We have to report this to the sheriff. If it's happening to you, it's happening to others, and something must be done to stop it." He turned to Saint-Germain. "Don't you agree . . . Signor Ragoczy?"

"Yes. I do, if the police are supposed to protect you." He took a deep breath. "There are places in the world where that is not what police do, but in this country, as I understand it, they are required to enforce the law."

"If I were one of their own," said Yoshimura. "None of them is Japanese."

"But most of them know farmers, and that is the most important thing," said Pietragnelli. "Just now, it is the farmers who are keeping this region alive. You more than I, because you grow vegetables, not grapes." He took the mug Rowena held out to him. "I don't have to tell you how important vegetables are."

"Most of those who buy them are Orientals, too, and that doesn't mean anything to the sheriff." Yoshimura sighed. "I still have my Chinese cabbage, but none of the other cabbages. I should be grateful for that."

"Tell the sheriff, or his deputies. You can telephone them from here. The telephone is in the kitchen, on the wall by the pantry." Pietragnelli rubbed his chin. "There has to be some way to keep your fields from being ransacked."

Yoshimura drank the last of the wine. "If times were better, I'd sell out and go down to South San Francisco, to join my wife and children. But raising flowers is less profitable than raising vegetables just now." He coughed once.

"Let them run the greenhouses, as they've done from the first," Pietragnelli urged. "In time, they'll pay off. But you can't give up your farm. You mustn't. Not because of thieves and troublemakers, but because it is yours and you mustn't give up what is yours, not to a gang of rascals." He slapped his palm on the table; the noise was loud enough to bring Mrs. Barringstone in from the kitchen.

"Is there anything more you want, Mr. Pietragnelli?" She was stiff with disapproval.

"No, not now, grazie. Go back to the kitchen, Mrs. Barringstone." He waved her away with a hint of impatience.

Rowena poured her own cup of coffee and glanced at Saint-Germain before she held out the third mug in the direction of Hiro Yoshimura. "Would you like some?"

He hesitated, then said, "If you would. With sugar." He braced his elbows on the table and dropped his head on his hands. "What is there for me to do?"

"Look, I can call Will Sutton in Healdsburg. He's the nearest deputy. His mother's Thomas Leonardi's sister, and he knows what kind of boys his cousins are. If Oliver and Arnold are behind your midnight harvest, you can bet Will can talk sense to them. It's in the family's interest to avoid scandal." He waited while

Yoshimura thought about it. "Besides, Sutton isn't the kind of man who lets the law slide for his kin's sake. He knows that leads to trouble."

Slowly Yoshimura lifted his head. "If you want to talk to the deputy sheriff, go ahead. But I don't want to have officers all over my place."

"I understand," said Pietragnelli. "I'll do my best to make sure Will sees the problem we have here."

"It is good of you to do that," said Yoshimura in a discouraged tone.

"I'll explain it to him. He'll know something must be done," said Pietragnelli. "He is no fool, and he is not depending on rich men to support him. There aren't enough rich men in the area to support the sheriff and his deputies as well."

Yoshimura's smile was cynical. "No. The deputies must fend for themselves."

If Pietragnelli understood this as Yoshimura intended, he gave no indication of it, saying only, "Will has to uphold the law. He knows it and I know it."

"Naturally," said Yoshimura sarcastically, and gulped the sugared coffee Rowena had provided.

"You will see, Hiro," Pietragnelli told him. "If you will give Will Sutton a chance, you will see."

"Very well," said Yoshimura. He turned a haggard face toward Pietragnelli. "I will try to guard my fields awhile longer, but if I sustain more losses, I may have to sell out, in spite of everything."

"I hope not," said Pietragnelli. "It would be sad to have you gone."

"You're probably the only one who thinks so," said Yoshimura, and downed the rest of his coffee. "What terrible stuff this is."

"It will help you stay awake tonight, if you drink more of it," said Pietragnelli. "Would you like to borrow a few of our geese? If you let them out in the fields, they'll eat snails and bugs and they'll make a racket if anyone tries to get into your fields."

"They'll just fly back to your pond," said Yoshimura. "I appreciate your offer, though."

Pietragnelli sighed. "All right. I can't offer you anything more. I'm sorry."

"You've lost grapes to the midnight harvest, too," Yoshimura said. "You have had a lot to endure."

"That's why I make sure the geese have the run of the property. Although the last raid took two of the geese as well as grapes." Pietragnelli addressed Saint-Germain. "Do you have any recommendations to make, Conte?"

"I?" He considered the matter. "I don't know the scope of your problem, so I don't think I can come up with anything useful, not right now. In a day or so I may have a suggestion or two, if you would like to hear them."

Rowena refilled Pietragnelli's and Yoshimura's mugs, and said, "If you can find a way to sound the alarm for all of you, so that no matter where the thieves strike, both of you can answer the signal—that might help."

"We both have telephones," said Pietragnelli. "But going through the switch-board could mean that the robbers could be warned as well. The operators listen, and the lines are shared, so everything is public. We can use the fire-whistle, but some of the neighbors might say we were wrong—since there would be no fire."

"Yes," she said. "That's possible. But it is also likely that these raiders cannot be warned any more quickly than either of you can be, whether you telephone or use the whistle or anything else."

Pietragnelli got to his feet and paced down the length of the dining room. "I can spare you two men to guard your fields beginning next week. I've told my workers that if they have children they can stay on through the winter and into the spring, so their children can go to school. But once the harvest is in, many of them will have less to do, and I can send them to your farm."

Yoshimura shook his head. "No, Carlo. That would be too much. And your men might not want to work for me."

"They want to work, period," said Pietragnelli. "Most of them have already lost all they had. They will not sit by and see another man lose all he has."

"They may resent me for having it," said Yoshimura. "They may want it for themselves."

Saint-Germain spoke up, cutting into what promised to be a fruitless wrangle. "You may want to ask your men, Pietragnelli, if any of them are willing to do extra work for Mr. Yoshimura. That way, you should be able to avoid any disgruntlement."

Yoshimura stared at Saint-Germain. "If no one volunteers?"

"Then you will find another means to achieve the end you have in mind," said Saint-Germain. "But why not try this first? Let the men decide for themselves."

Pietragnelli nodded slowly. "Yes. The crush is our busiest time, and I've had to put men into the vineyards late at night, to watch my grapes. But some of them will be glad of more to do. For the additional pay, if nothing else." He bustled back to the head of the table. "I'll put it to the men directly, as soon as their noon break is over." He turned his bright little eyes on Saint-Germain. "Who would think that you—a financier—should come up with such a solution."

"I haven't always been a financier, as you call me," Saint-Germain said dryly. "And I know it is folly to ignore those who work for you, particularly when they have nothing more to lose." He had a fleeting recollection of the French and Russian Revolutions, and the chaos in Germany little more than a decade ago, and what had come from them.

A clock in the parlor sounded the hour, a hollow sound on a note that was not quite F.

"I must go back to work," said Pietragnelli, ducking his head apologetically. "I have to excuse myself. I labor alongside my men."

"Of course," said Saint-Germain. "We will not get in your way."

"I shouldn't mind if you did," said Pietragnelli, casting an uneasy glance at Yoshimura. "Will you have something to eat while you're here?"

Yoshimura tried to summon up an answer and finally managed to nod.

"You will not leave until you've eaten?" Pietragnelli pursued.

Rowena saw the trouble in his gaze, and said, "Go speak with your men, Mr. Pietragnelli, and tell Mr. Yoshimura the results while he is still here. You'll both feel better."

He clapped his hands. "Yes. Yes. You wait here, Hiro. I'll bring you news in a quarter hour. Have some soup if you like—there's plenty in the kitchen." With that, he hastened out of the dining room and into the kitchen; the rear door slammed a moment later, leaving Rowena and Saint-Germain alone with the dejected Yoshimura.

TEXT OF A LETTER FROM J. HAROLD BISHOP IN CHICAGO TO FERENC RAGOCZY, LE COMTE DE SAINT-GERMAIN, IN SAN FRANCISCO.

HORNER BISHOP BEATIE WENTWORTH & CULPEPPER
ATTORNEYS-AT-LAW
7571 MICHIGAN AVENUE
SUITE 602
CHICAGO, ILLINOIS

October 10, 1936

Ferenc Ragoczy
le Comte de Saint-Germain
The Saint Francis Hotel
Union Square
San Francisco, California

Dear Saint-Germain,

Enclosed please find copies of your vehicle registration as well as all copies of all correspondence dealing with the process in question. You already have your insurance policy, and appropriate proofs of ownership, copies of which I have in my files, should you require such records.

If you are going to be in residence in California for more than six months, you will have to secure California registration for your Packard. The Department of Motor Vehicles will handle such a change. I ask for copies of all papers having to do with such reregistration, when and if you apply for it.

In accordance with your wire of September 28, 1936, I have begun negotiations with Mrs. E. Curtis of Ponderosa Lodge in California with the intention of establishing a partnership for the resort she currently owns. I am puzzled why you should prefer a Chicago firm to handle this when the resort is in California, but I will, of course, abide by your instructions in regard to this, and all ventures, so long as no law is violated. A copy of the first response from Mrs. Curtis is enclosed, and I think you will find that she is a very cautious woman. I understand that she is apprehensive because what you are proposing might endanger her title to the property in question, and that is not wholly unreasonable of her, given the rate of foreclosures that currently occur in this country. Your offer is more than generous, and I am certain her attorney, and her banker, for that matter, would be inclined to support your proposal, particularly since you make no demands for changes beyond specific upkeep, and you provide funds for that which you require. Such generosity may well account for her apprehension, which I will strive to address to her satisfaction, with safeguards for her included in the contract, so long as they meet with your approval. I will, of course, keep you informed of all developments in regard to this project, and alert you to any difficulties that arise.

I have your power-of-attorney for your bank accounts at the Illinois Trust Company, for which I tender the first statements. As you see, no charges have been made. I am also including the interest rates currently being paid by the ITC, and recommend that you transfer $2,000.00 (two thousand dollars) from your checking account into your savings account in order to accumulate interest on the money. That will leave $1,000.00 (one thousand dollars) in your checking account, which is more than sufficient for most routine charges. That would mean you have $24,500.00 (twenty-four thousand five hundred dollars) in the savings account. Let me know what you decide in regard to this recommendation.

Additionally, I have sent to King Lowenthal Taylor & Frost in San Francisco copies of all correspondence with Mrs. Curtis, so that they may advise me in any aspects of California law that may pertain in this negotiation. Oscar King has confirmed he will give his opinion as I may need it from time to time.

I have received your check for $700.00 (seven hundred dollars) paying in full all current charges for services from this office. I will submit monthly bills to you, in accordance with our agreement, and I thank you for your promptness in payment.

Please do not hesitate to notify me if there is any additional service I and this office may provide you. Particularly in these difficult times, your business is appreciated by my colleagues and me, and rest assured we will perform our duties with due diligence and dispatch.

Most sincerely yours,

J. Harold Bishop
Attorney-at-Law

⌒

enclosures
JHB/dmca

chapter six

R ogerio looked around the empty house on Clarendon Court, taking stock of the space and contemplating how it could be made liveable for Saint-Germain; he consulted the notes he had made during his tour of the whole house. "Yes," he said to the agent who had been taking him around San Francisco and showing him a number of houses for sale. "I think this may be satisfactory. Certainly better than the others I've seen."

"The view out the back of Golden Gate Park is especially nice, and Sutro Forest so close, you might well think you're in the country. You'll find it very pretty, very quiet," said the agent, still determined to sell the place as if he had not heard what Rogerio had told him. "I know thirteen thousand is a lot to pay for a house, but this location is—"

"I said I think it is satisfactory," said Rogerio. "If you will, tell me when it was wired for electricity?"

"The gaslights still work," he began, and consulted the papers on the clipboard. "The house was electrified in 1916, and the wiring expanded in '27. The kitchen stove and the water-heater—a twenty-gallon one—are gas-powered. The present roof was put on in '24, and it is considered a twenty-year roof." He did his best to make the sale immediate. "If it's a question of financing—"

"That's no immediate concern. My employer will pay cash," said Rogerio, and pretended not to see the agent's astonished goggle. "It is a good thing that there is a full basement."

"Completely finished, as you saw," said the agent proudly as if he had arranged all of it. "And with a pump in case of flooding. It's the second-oldest house on the street, built in 1902. It had only moderate damage in '06, which was repaired, and the addition was put on in 1910."

"I'm sure this will suit him very well." Rogerio went into the living room and looked out at the street. "This is, as you say, a pleasant location," he remarked.

"Yes, it certainly is," said the agent, his agreement verging on obsequiousness. "I think you'll be more than satisfied with this situation. Private though it is, you aren't far from shopping, and the streetcar line is just down the hill. If you have any need of schools, I can tell you—"

"No, thank you." Rogerio kept his tone level.

"Well," the agent said, trying to get back on his track. "It is good-sized, with all the modern conveniences—or at least, provision for them."

"So it has," said Rogerio. "I will inform my employer that this is the most suitable house of those you have shown me, and we will arrange the purchase and occupancy within the next two weeks, if that is time enough for you?"

"It's more than suitable," said the agent as if he had to make all his points twice; he was almost shaking he was so relieved. "I will inform the owners of your offer and I will let you know what their answer is as soon as I have it." He had gone a trifle pale. "Will your employer want to see the house for himself?"

"Of course," said Rogerio. "I was hoping you would agree to let me have a key so I may bring him here this evening, when he is able to inspect the house. If this isn't acceptable, perhaps you will be able to meet us here at—shall we say eight this evening?"

The agent frowned, from the lines in his face a habitual expression with him. "I have to attend a meeting this evening; I won't be able to join you. Technically we aren't supposed to let anyone in without—" He paced into the dining room, the empty house echoing his steps. "I suppose you will not do anything incorrect while you're here?"

"Incorrect? Why should either of us do that?" Rogerio asked. "If you have any doubts, I will provide a bond for the night. Would one hundred dollars be sufficient?" He reached for his wallet as he spoke.

"Oh, no," the agent said, embarrassed at the very notion. "I don't think it's . . . Fifty should be more than enough, and it will be applied to the purchase price, assuming no harm is done to the house. The owner needs some sort of assurance until the sale's complete. You know how these things are."

Rogerio dismissed the matter as he handed over five ten-dollar bills. "You can give me a receipt later. Where are the owners living now?"

"They are living south of here," the agent replied, deliberately vague in his reply. "They have taken over the family farm now that the wife's parents are getting too old to manage for themselves, and the Waggoners' children are grown. And his work became . . ." He stopped, as if he feared he had said too much.

Rogerio filled in what he supposed the agent might have said. "They must be relieved to have the house sold, then, given the state of the—"

"Yes. The taxes and the upkeep are a drain on them; the house has been on the market for almost a year." It was as much as he would admit. "They've paid to keep the power on, so we can show the house in the evening. It's not a large sum, but it adds up. The account would have to be shifted as soon as your employer gets the title."

"All upkeep and taxes would be a drain for almost anyone," Rogerio agreed. "And even in better times, they would be an imposition."

"Not that they're without means or have been less than diligent in their obligations," said the agent hastily. "They aren't arrears in any payments, and there is no mortgage; that was paid off four years ago."

"I'd assumed it was paid off," said Rogerio.

"As of '32," said the agent, flipping to the third page on his clipboard. "Not an easy thing to do, pay off a mortgage, not in these days, no matter what Roosevelt tries to do."

Rogerio nodded. "That must be a load off their minds. There must be many who aren't so fortunate."

"A great many; you see them on the streets and in Hoovervilles and hobo camps everywhere. Some wives go back to their families when their husbands can't support them anymore, and some of them end up in shanties. Some of them send their kids to relatives, if they're lucky enough to have someone to take them, and some kids go on orphan trains, even though they aren't really orphans." Now that he had said so much, and with suppressed emotion, the agent tried to change the subject. "Not that any of that concerns us now."

"I hope the family has remained intact," said Rogerio, who had himself been separated from his family not quite two thousand years ago.

"Their oldest son is a printer, right now with the WPA," the agent volunteered. "He works here in San Francisco and lives with his uncle, on Rincon Hill. His brother's at college in Los Angeles on scholarship, and their daughter is still in high school. She's with them on the farm, in King City. Out here, we've got families going back to the farm, just the opposite of what's been happening in the Midwest. Of course, the farms aren't blowing away in a drought, either."

He tried to assume the demeanor of an old family friend. "They were hoping one of the kids could take over the house in a few years, to keep it in the family, but it doesn't look as if that's going to happen. The sensible thing is to sell it and get some money out of it. They don't want to lose the farm now, as so many have done. But the Dust Bowl has put a lot of farmers looking for work, a lot of them in California. I don't mean to rattle on."

Rogerio understood the pressure the family had been under, and he felt a surge of sympathy for them. "Then I must assume the purchase in cash will be acceptable to them, at their full asking price, as a hedge against drought or other trouble."

"Yes. I think so; I can't imagine why not. The taxes on the sale won't be too high, and once they're paid, they're paid," said the agent.

Rogerio went to the fireplace and got down on one knee to look inside it. "Has the chimney been cleaned recently? Or inspected?"

The agent resorted to his clipboard again. "The last cleaning was four years ago."

"Then it should be cleaned again before it's used," he said, dusting the soot from his hands. "Is there a service you recommend?"

"I can give you a list once we get back to the office," said the agent. "There are a couple very good services."

"I'd appreciate that," said Rogerio, rising again.

"Very good," said the agent, fussing a bit with the pages on his clipboard. "If you're ready, we'll go back to the office and get the paperwork started."

"By all means," said Rogerio. "I must assume a cashier's check will be an acceptable form of payment, assuming the Waggoners agree to the sale."

"It will be fine," said the agent, and started toward the door.

"I have no doubt." Rogerio looked about before following the agent out onto the covered porch. As soon as the agent had locked the door, Rogerio held out his hand for the key. "I'll be sure you get it back tomorrow."

The agent hesitated, then held out the key. "See that you lock up when you leave. There are folks about who look for empty houses where they can squat," the agent admitted as he got into the driver's seat and reached across to open the door for Rogerio.

"Have Roosevelt's policies been any help?" Rogerio asked as the agent depressed the starter.

"For some, yes, but it is a bargain with the Devil, if you ask me," the agent admitted grudgingly. "There could be other ways to help out, that wouldn't be so reckless, ways that are more American than what he's done. He looks like he's a Socialist, and that's too near being a Communist for me." He drove to the corner and headed down Stanyan Street. "He should know better. He's not a fool from the docks, or one of Harry Bridges' cronies."

"What else could he have done?" Rogerio asked.

"He could have done what the Germans have done—restored order, strengthened the army and navy, built up our people—instead of his alphabet soup services, and coddling the workers." He continued down the hill, turning at Kezar Stadium and driving into the next block, where he found a parking place. "This won't take long."

"I am at your disposal," said Rogerio, and got out of the DeSoto.

The real estate office was a small store-front with six desks, each with a telephone and a typewriter. File cabinets were ranked along the back of the room. Just now, three of the desks were occupied, two of the agents reading the *Bulletin*, the other scowling at a stack of manila file-folders.

The agent with Rogerio pointed him to the second desk. "I'll be with you in a moment."

"Take all the time you need," said Rogerio, watching the agent take a folder from one of the file cabinets.

"Here," said the agent, bringing the file back to his desk. "We can get started." He took a form out of a tray on the edge of his desk, rolled it into the typewriter, hit the carriage-return, and began to type the address of the house they had just left.

Forty minutes later, Rogerio was out of the office and in his Auburn, going along Haight Street toward Masonic. He was timing the drive out of habit, familiarizing himself with the rhythm of the traffic. He had the contracts in his pocket, and knew Saint-Germain would be prepared to sign and have his signature notarized at the bank the next morning.

Saint-Germain was at the dining table in their suite at the Saint Francis when Rogerio arrived; he was writing letters, but looked up. "So you've hit upon a place."

"I believe so," said Rogerio. "You can see it this evening, if you like."

"Oh, yes. Very much," said Saint-Germain. "Not that I do not trust your judgment."

"Still, it is a formality worth maintaining," said Rogerio.

"Tell me about the house," said Saint-Germain, moving his letters aside and giving his whole attention to what Rogerio had to say.

"It is thirty-four years old, has a full basement, four bedrooms, a small study, an attic accessible by stairs, a living room with a fireplace and a wall of built-in bookcases, a good-sized dining room with a hutch, two bathrooms, a kitchen with a rear enclosed porch with a laundry and a pantry. It is handsome but not conspicuous, and the street—Clarendon Court—is easily reachable but not heavily traveled. There is a police station at the foot of the hill, near the stadium. The location is an attractive one, on the side of a hill at the edge of Sutro Forest with the east end of

Golden Gate Park visible from the dining-room window, and other parks nearby, if the forest isn't an attraction. It has two electric outlets in each room, three in the kitchen and three in the living room. The living room is approximately fifteen by eighteen feet, the dining room thirteen by fifteen, so you will not be cramped. The attic is twenty-three by twenty, or twenty-one. There are also three outlets in the attic, and two in the basement, which is twenty-six by twenty-two. There are sockets for a washing machine and an indoor clothesline in the basement for doing laundry in inclement weather." He paused. "The walls in the living room and the dining room are wood-paneled, in need of refinishing, but otherwise in good condition. The kitchen and bathrooms have tile floors and surfaces. The largest bedroom is about fifteen by twelve feet, the smallest about twelve by ten, part of an addition to the second floor. The power is on, so the ceiling fixtures can be lit, but there is nothing else in the house; it's completely empty."

"It sounds ideal," said Saint-Germain when Rogerio stopped speaking. "I take it this is the best of the houses you inspected?"

"Oh, yes," said Rogerio. "I told the agent that we would provide full payment in the form of a cashier's check as soon as the owners accept the offer." He very nearly smiled. "The poor man looked almost dizzy."

"It is a hard time for men in his profession, for all sales are not readily come by," said Saint-Germain. "And it carries over into many other professions and trades." He rose from the table, looking at the paper Rogerio had held out to him. "How long do you think we will need to furnish the house and make it liveable?"

"From the time we gain occupancy?" Rogerio thought the matter over. "Two weeks, assuming what we purchase can be delivered quickly, and we can get draperies ready-made, and carpets that fit the rooms."

"I'll go to Gump's tomorrow or the day after and have a look at their furniture," said Saint-Germain. "I'll arrange for as many household items as possible from there—lamps, draperies, china, ornaments. If I don't find what will suit me at that store, I will get a recommendation for an antiques dealer to consult, and a mercer for fabrics. I'll need the dimensions of the windows as soon as possible. You can take care of the other necessities. I'll authorize as much as you need to pay for what you may need to purchase." He touched his fingertips together. "I should arrange for another transfer of funds from London."

"The bank can help with that," said Rogerio.

"Yes. When I go to get the cashier's check, I'll make the necessary arrangements." He walked into the sitting room. "It will be good to have my native earth under my feet again."

"Miss Saxon has crates of it, doesn't she?" Rogerio inquired.

"Yes. Though when I sent them to her, I didn't actually anticipate needing them so soon." He looked at the stack of four newspapers, all with that day's date. "I've finished reading these, if you'd like to review them."

Rogerio shrugged. "I gather Mayor Rossi is pushing his Treasure Island project again. He keeps saying he's creating jobs as well as a setting for the World's Fair, and the San Francisco Airport. That seaport is expected to expand, and soon. He intends the China Clippers to take off from there."

Saint-Germain shook his head. "If air travel grows as much as some think it will, having an airport at the edge of the shipping lanes could interfere with maritime trade, and having airplanes so near the Bay Bridge could be hazardous in bad weather."

"Then you don't think it's going to turn out the way the Mayor wants," said Rogerio.

"No, I don't; and by the end of the World's Fair, I should think that the Mayor will see the disadvantages, too. Mills Field is a more reasonable place for an airport, I would have thought, though it has no facilities for water-landings. That may be the single most telling factor: not all planes will be amphibious. The Mayor's assuming development will go in one way only, and development is rarely so biddable." Saint-Germain looked out the nearest window, down toward the bay where the towers of the Bay Bridge rose beyond the buildings of the city. "The bridge will be open in another month, and that will mean Oakland will be as accessible as South San Francisco."

"And the Golden Gate will open next spring, if it remains on schedule," said Rogerio. "What a change it will make to the region."

"I wonder if anyone here has any idea how much those bridges will change the city?" Saint-Germain mused.

"Probably not," said Rogerio.

Saint-Germain turned away from the window. "I assume you have the key to the house—when do you propose we go look at it?"

"Around sunset, or a little after. I would recommend going over to the house while most of the neighbors are eating dinner. We'll be less apt to attract attention."

"You have an excellent point, old friend," said Saint-Germain. "And I'll inform the front desk that I'll be leaving in two weeks."

"Best wait until the offer is accepted." He reached into his jacket-pocket and drew out the terms of sale, which he handed to Saint-Germain. "If the agent says the price is acceptable, then you can deal with this at the bank tomorrow."

Saint-Germain took the papers and began to peruse them. "What is this clause about only selling the house to Caucasians?"

"The agent said it was one of the owners' stipulations. The courts have upheld such terms in the past."

"Astonishing. I would expect that in Europe, but here?" He continued reading. "The Yellow Menace," Rogerio suggested.

"Perhaps; it may be a measure against all outsiders," said Saint-Germain, a world-weary note in his voice. When he had finished reading, he put the papers down, and said, "I don't see anything too unreasonable, aside from that one proviso."

"I suspect you'll find it or something similar in most conditions of sale; the contracts for Sea Cliff had the same clause in them," said Rogerio. "The agent left me with the impression I should expect it in most of the city. It's supposed to preserve the character of neighborhoods."

"Ah," said Saint-Germain, an ironic smile on his lips. "Well, let us plan to leave here at six-forty. That should put us at the house around seven."

"Very good," said Rogerio. "I'm going out to the butcher; I have two ducks on order. I've been feeling hungry today."

Saint-Germain gestured his dismissal and went back to the dining table to resume work on his letters. By the time Rogerio returned, he had finished all but one, and while Rogerio went about preparing a meal, Saint-Germain carried his letters down to the front desk, sending four of the letters by airmail—two to England, one to Canada, and one to Peru—and two by regular post—to Chicago and Truckee—then he returned to his suite and took down his black camel-hair overcoat and gave it a good brushing.

At six-thirty, Rogerio came out of the kitchenette and said, "Which car shall we use? Yours or mine?"

"Yours, I think. An Auburn is less remarkable than a Packard Twelve." He sighed once. "I suppose I would be well-advised to purchase something less conspicuous; it attracts far too much attention."

"I'm sure a dealer would give you a good price on it," said Rogerio as he held the overcoat for Saint-Germain.

"Let me think about it, at least for a day or two." He went to the door and took his key from the occasional table just inside it. "Perhaps Rowena has recommendations she'd like to make."

"Ask her," Rogerio suggested as he stepped out of the suite behind Saint-Germain, and after the door was locked, he followed his employer to the elevator and rode down to the black-and-gold columned lobby. "The car is at the garage on Mason," he said, stepping out into the gathering dusk and the busy activity around Union Square.

They drove out Geary to Masonic, went left on Masonic to Haight, retracing the route that Rogerio had traveled earlier that day. As they climbed the hill to Clarendon Court, Rogerio pointed out the various features in the area. As he parked in front of the house, he noticed that the front curtains in the main window of the house across the street moved. "Someone's watching," he said to Saint-Germain.

"Probably more than one someone," said Saint-Germain as he got out of the car. "I like the look of the place."

"I thought you might, it's elegant without being conspicuous; I saw some of that sort over near the Presidio," said Rogerio as he went up the three shallow steps to the front door and opened the lock. "They have the new push-button switches rather than the twists." He demonstrated this by punching on the light in the entry-hall; a low-wattage bulb came on overhead. "All the switches are like this. Half the sockets have provisions for two plugs."

"We might want to ascertain how much power these sockets will support," Saint-Germain said as he went into the living room. "Very nice."

"The dining room is on the left," Rogerio said. "With the kitchen through the swinging door. One of the bathrooms is on the other side of the inner dining-room wall. You reach it from the study or the kitchen." He nodded toward the stairs that rose in the juncture between living room and dining room. "The bedrooms are upstairs, and the attic is above them all."

"Conventional but sound," Saint-Germain approved as he went through into the kitchen. He saw the stove, noting it was more than ten years old, and the refrigerator, also an older model. "We'll need new appliances, I think."

"As you say," Rogerio remarked.

"And I see there is a floor-heater. I suppose the unit is in the basement?"

"Yes. And there are three registers. One in the living room, one in the break-fast nook, and one just outside the bathroom. Each is operated by a key, and a match," said Rogerio, who had followed him into the kitchen. "With all three registers on, the whole house can be heated efficiently, including the upstairs."

"Very good," said Saint-Germain, and looked about for the way to the basement.

"You go to the left. There's a door that opens on to the stairs down. The other door leads to the pantry and porch, and the stairs down to the garden," Rogerio explained.

Saint-Germain opened the door and prepared to descend. "You say it is finished?"

"Yes. The floor is in sections and the sections can be lifted. The intention was for easy repair in case of earthquake, but it serves your purposes quite well." He punched on the light at the top of the stairs. "I think you'll see it can be—"

"Yes. I see. There's a door to the outside?"

"On the right, at the back. The enclosed porch steps are immediately beside it," Rogerio told him.

"I think it is suitable. Let me see the attic," Saint-Germain said, climbing the basement stairs and turning out the light as he reached the top. "This door locks, I see."

"So does the pantry door," said Rogerio as he held open the swinging door.

The second floor was nicely laid out around the lightwell that went down through the center of the house. "Not lavish, but far from inadequate," Saint-Germain said, and looked toward the attic stairs. "You said there are sockets in the attic, I recall—three of them."

"Yes; three, and an overhead light," said Rogerio. "Climb up and see."

The attic occupied one side of the lightwell, and stood over three of the bedrooms on the floor below; the fourth bedroom and a small sunporch had been added after the house was built, but the style was the same as the rest of the building and created an expanse of roof next to the attic, which had two fan-shaped windows, one at each end of the room, and a door that gave access to the roof.

"Oh, very good. Yes. I can see why you preferred this house," said Saint-Germain. "This will make an admirable laboratory for me. I thank you for finding it." He tested the roof door to make sure it was locked, then turned out the lights and shut the door before going down to join Rogerio on the second floor. "We've certainly lived in less convenient places."

"And given the reasonable price, it can be made to accommodate your needs without dramatic alteration," Rogerio observed. "Or without attracting undue attention."

"A very good point," Saint-Germain concurred. "I am beginning to share your enthusiasm for this place."

"There was that very nice house on Divisadero near Broadway, but it was a trifle . . . grand," said Rogerio. "And the one in Sea Cliff was much too near the water."

"At another time, they might be preferable to this, but in this country at this time, it is better to choose a less arresting place," Saint-Germain said.

"Then the offer goes forward," said Rogerio. "I'll call the agent this evening. And tomorrow we can take care of matters at the bank. Once we have title, it should be an easy matter to occupy the premises."

"Yes. It is more than time to be gone from the hotel; we're much too noticeable there. I am thankful to Rowena for allowing me to store some of my chests of earth and other possessions at her house, where they attract no unwanted attention, but I would prefer not to abuse the privilege."

"I'm sure she doesn't mind," said Rogerio.

"Possibly; but I do. I think removing my native earth from her house would be prudent." He went down the stairs and out into the living room. "Yes. This will do very well."

Rogerio waited. "Is there anything more?"

"Not that occurs to me just now." He went to turn out the light in the dining room, then did the same in the living room. "I suppose the street is not busy."

"Hardly," said Rogerio. "The whole neighborhood is quiet." He opened the front door. "You should find a good deal of privacy without too much effort."

"Which was less likely in the other houses you saw," Saint-Germain suggested lightly.

"Yes. I'd have to say privacy was the deciding factor. Sutro Forest is a real asset. If you need to leave the house without being noticed, the forest will provide superior cover." He took care to lock the door and went back to his Auburn, letting Saint-Germain into the passenger seat once he was ready to drive.

"Wise, as always," said Saint-Germain. "I hope the promise of cash will speed up the acquisition of the house."

"You seem uneasy about it," said Rogerio as he started to drive away from Clarendon Court.

"I am," said Saint-Germain. "I can't get the notion out of my mind that I am under scrutiny, and that troubles me."

"But who would be watching you?" Rogerio wondered as he turned onto Stanyan Street.

"I have no idea; that is the most perplexing aspect of it all." He had not worn a hat, and now he ran his hand through the close-cut waves of his dark hair.

Rogerio had enough experience of Saint-Germain's sensitivities not to dismiss this example as unfounded. "If not the hotel staff, who, and why?"

"That is what I can't determine," said Saint-Germain, trying to make himself comfortable in Rogerio's car. "I would like to be convinced I am being foolish, but—" He stopped speaking suddenly.

"But?" Rogerio prompted as he turned onto Haight Street, the Auburn's headlights picking out three ragged men holding up a sign offering to work for a meal.

"I don't know. It may be nothing more than the general air of concern in the area regarding the new bridges, for there are rumors that they won't be safe, or that they will be the objects of demonstrations. The Mayor certainly doesn't want another Bloody Thursday on his hands, nor does Governor Merriam. That may be what bothers me, remembering Saint Petersburg and Munich, but it may be something more specific and current." His voice dropped, as if weighted down by his memories.

"I'll see if the agent can move quickly on this purchase," said Rogerio, honking his horn at two young boys on bicycles hurtling across the street without regard to traffic.

"Thank you. I admit it reassures me to know that we'll be a bit less visible than we have been." He lapsed into silence, and a while later he said, "It isn't that most of these people fear my nature—the vast majority of them think vampires are creatures of legend and cinema, something to shudder over but not to fear.

But there are scientists who would be intrigued by my longevity, if nothing else, and they would like nothing better than to subject me to study and experimentation that would shame a Grand Inquisitor, but in the name of knowledge, not God. I would just as soon avoid such a development."

"Do you think anyone suspects anything?" Rogerio changed gears a bit too abruptly and nearly stalled his car. "You haven't visited any of the women at the hotel in their sleep, have you?"

"There is no reason. Rowena has been everything I could possibly want." He watched a van laden with bundles of newspapers lumber across the street.

"She wouldn't reveal anything crucial about you," said Rogerio.

"Not willingly," said Saint-Germain.

"Could it be the news from Europe?" Rogerio suggested. "It isn't very encouraging."

"No, it isn't," Saint-Germain agreed. "And I am uneasy about what I have heard. I should have had a letter from Sunbury a week ago, and it is disturbing that I haven't, but there may be a perfectly innocent, mundane reason for the delay. I may be responding to a totality of minor uncertainties, but it may be more serious than that." He glanced out the window again, his thoughts preoccupied.

Rogerio said nothing more, driving to the garage on Mason Street and getting out with Saint-Germain. They went into the Saint Francis, stopping at the desk for messages before getting onto the elevator and telling the operator which floor they wanted. The elevator car rose at a dignified pace and was brought to a halt at their floor. Rogerio wished the operator a good evening and followed Saint-Germain down the corridor to their suite.

As Saint-Germain put the key in the lock, he felt the door give, and then it swung open. Saint-Germain turned to Rogerio. "I locked this door, didn't I?" Saint-Germain tapped the door as if to alert any occupant. He had no need to turn on the lights to see that the parlor and dining room had been ransacked. Very calmly he looked back at Rogerio. "Will you go down to the lobby and ask the manager to telephone the police?"

Rogerio could not conceal the dismay he felt. "Immediately," he said, turning and retracing his steps to the elevator, anxiety gnawing at his thoughts like rats; whatever Saint-Germain had sensed, he had been right that they were under some kind of scrutiny. He saw an expression of annoyed inquisitiveness on the elevator operator's face, but he paid no attention to it as he put his thoughts in order while the elevator descended to the lobby.

TEXT OF A PRIVATE REPORT TO MAYOR ANGELO ROSSI OF SAN FRANCISCO
FROM DETECTIVE INSPECTOR JAMES O'NEIL OF THE SAN FRANCISCO POLICE
DEPARTMENT, PRESENTED PRIVATELY AND IN PERSON.

October 19, 1936

Angelo Rossi, Mayor
City Hall
San Francisco

Your Honor,

As you know, I was called to the Saint Francis night before last to investi-
gate the pilfering in the Commodore Suite, which is presently occupied by
Ferenc Ragoczy, a Hungarian with a French title: le Comte de Saint-
Germain. This Ragoczy has a sizeable amount of money in deposit at the
Bank of America, and is about to purchase a house in the Sutro Forest dis-
trict of the city.

I and two officers arrived at the hotel at eight thirty-three and were
escorted up to the suite by the assistant manager of the Saint Francis and
Ragoczy's manservant, a fellow named Rogers. We found Ragoczy standing
at the door, saying he had not gone inside once he realized that the parlor
was in disarray. The assistant manager—a young fellow named Fisher—
was the first man to enter the suite. The upholstery of the chairs and the
two settees had been slashed and the stuffing pulled out of them. All drawers had been pulled out and their contents overturned at random onto the
carpet. In the two bedrooms, the dressers, armoires, and nightstands had
received the same treatment, and the mattresses had been pulled off the
beds, the bedding removed, and the mattresses slashed. There is a kitchenette in the suite, and all the drawers and cabinets there had been
similarly dealt with.

My men and I kept Ragoczy and his manservant out of the suite until we
had thoroughly examined the damage. I then summoned them into the suite
to determine what, if anything, was missing. They conducted a complete
search, and indicated that so far as they could determine, approximately nine
hundred dollars in cash was gone, along with a portfolio of documents and
letters of no particular value beyond a personal one. There was also a small
case of uncut jewels, unappraised as to worth but of considerable potential
value, which Ragoczy claimed he preferred to cash when traveling, being
gems and gold hold their value more consistently than currency.

I took Ragoczy into one of the other suites that is presently empty, and I

questioned him at length about his presence in San Francisco and his immediate past. He explained that he had left Spain the very day their Civil War
began, that his company there had been taken over by the government, and
that he had decided that it was prudent to put Europe behind him for a
while. He has business ties to Sonoma County, and has had for twenty years
and more; he offered to provide proof of this through Bank of America if we
should require it. He told me that he wants to expand his dealings there.

He also claims to be an old friend of Rowena Saxon, the artist, and took
advantage of his travels to visit her as well. He says she will vouch for him.

In regard to the house he has offered for, he said since it appears he will
be in California some time, he believes purchasing a house is money better-
spent than in renting a hotel room or an apartment. I must admit, I see his
point, and the bank confirms that he can afford the purchase and a great
deal more.

I am not quite satisfied with the answers this Ragoczy has given me. He
has referred me to Oscar King, the lawyer, who Ragoczy says represents him.
That's high-powered legal muscle at King Lowenthal Taylor & Frost. I can't
help but ask myself why a Hungarian businessman would need such a firm
to represent him. Oscar King isn't saying anything one way or the other
except to confirm that Ragoczy is his client.

There's no way we can trace the cash or the jewels—if they actually exist,
and I'm not satisfied they do. I've assigned Patrolman Angus Murchison to
keep an eye on this Ragoczy, at least until the Golden Gate Bridge is open,
just in case. It might be a good idea to continue the surveillance beyond that
date, if Murchison turns up anything suspicious. You know what these foreigners can be, no matter what claims they may have to titles and money.
Many confidence men pose as displaced aristocrats.

The hotel staff is being questioned, but so far no one seems to have
noticed anything untoward in the Commodore Suite yesterday afternoon. I
don't like to think that this was an inside job, but it could be, and I'm proceeding with my interrogation of the room service and housekeeping staffs. It
could be that one of them is trying to shore up the family finances through
theft, or has desperate relatives who have turned to stealing. It wouldn't be
the first time. If I can get any kind of break in this case, I'll let you know—
confidentially, of course.

If circumstances should require it, I'll assign more men to the case; if not,
I'll leave well enough alone unless you should ask me to reconsider. These
kinds of things will happen from time to time, and it makes no sense to let

them become too important. Until we see a repeat of this crime, I will not rank it as high priority.
  Sincerely,

James O'Neil
Detective Inspector, SFPD

⌒

chapter seven

"Come in, come in!" shouted Carlo Pietragnelli from his porch as Saint-Germain pulled into the driveway curve in his new silver-grey Pierce-Arrow; steadily falling rain gave the whole house a drowned look, fading the color to a pale sepia, turning the windows to dark sockets, and making the trees seem darker by contrast. "Mille grazie per quest' favor'. But I should never have asked you to come."

Saint-Germain got out, and rushed toward the house, Rogerio close behind him. Water splashed with every step, and by the time they were in the shelter of the porch, their shoes and trouser-cuffs were soaked. In spite of feeling a bit queasy, Saint-Germain preserved his genial demeanor. "How do I find you, Signor Pietragnelli?"

"Very well, and then again, not so. I am restless in spirit. The power is out, so I cannot listen to the radio; the telephone is still working, which is a blessing. I have spoken to my son, Massimo, already." He held the front door wide. "Your company is very welcome. Yours too, Mr. Rogers."

"Thank you," said Saint-Germain, tugging out of his overcoat and taking off his dripping hat. "What appalling weather."

"It's hard to believe it was over eighty-five yesterday. October is often thus. It may be warm again one more time before winter. Thank my good Saints, all my harvest is in and the crush complete. Now all I have to do is watch the progress of fermentation and aging." Pietragnelli indicated the parlor. The house was dim, glowing in the pale light of kerosene lamps, and the fireplace was stacked with logs merrily alight. "I have a fire going. You'll warm up quickly. The house isn't cold yet." He helped Rogerio out of his raincoat and hung it beside Saint-

Germain's on the coat-tree near the front door, and placed his hat on the rack next to Saint-Germain's. "I have some mulled wine in the kitchen. Would you like a mug of it? It's warming and delicious, if I say it myself." He glanced at Saint-Germain. "I will not offer any to you; you will only refuse it."

"Alas," said Saint-Germain.

Rogerio sighed. "I must also decline," he said. "But don't let us keep you from enjoying the drink yourself."

Pietragnelli lifted his hands into the air to show his helplessness. "Why do you invest in my business if you don't drink the product?"

"Ah, but many others do, and you make it so well. I admire quality, whether I actually use it or not," said Saint-Germain, and went to the Chickering cabinet grand; he touched the keys and was surprised to find it properly tuned. "Would you mind if I play? I haven't had much opportunity recently, and I miss—"

"Ti prego," said Pietragnelli gallantly. "I will have Mrs. Barringstone bring in a carafe of mulled wine, and perhaps Mr. Rogers will change his mind." He rocked back on his heels, then headed for the kitchen, calling for his cook.

Saint-Germain sat down on the piano-bench and ran a series of arpeggios to limber up his hands. When he was satisfied, he began with an ambitious little *Rondo* by Czerny, then moved on to a Chopin *Ballade*. When he finished, he turned to see Pietragnelli sitting on the edge of an overstuffed chair, his face rapt. "Thank you for permitting me to play."

"You need not cease on my account," said Pietragnelli. "I do not play, although my daughter Angelina does. She visits once a month—she has a job in Oakland— and I keep it tuned for her. It is a pity she hasn't more opportunity to play, but she has no desire to be a professional musician, not in these times." He made a troubled gesture, revealing more complex emotions, and poured more mulled wine into his mug. "Music is the solace of the soul."

"Yes, it is," Saint-Germain agreed, and played a progression of chords. "It's a very nice instrument," he said sincerely, then studied Pietragnelli's face more narrowly. "Why did you want me to come today? Do you have more trouble?"

"You mean midnight harvesters? No; all the grapes are in, thank God, and I have men to guard my cellars at night. No one has been bold enough to try to steal a barrel, not yet. No, it isn't that." He drank a bit of his mulled wine. "I have been receiving complaints from the Leonardis." He pointed in the direction of their land. "I know I've mentioned them before. They're very inclined to blame me for their troubles, and to suspect everything I do as having an ulterior motive, although I have done my utmost to be a good neighbor to them. They are always looking for something to say about me that discredits me, and never more so than now."

"You bought some of their land a few years ago, didn't you?" Saint-Germain asked. "I recall you said something about that in one of your letters."

"Yes. It was the only thing I could do to help them at the time, since they wouldn't accept a loan, much less a gift. They were about to lose everything, so I paid as nearly top dollar as I could afford for a third of their acreage and they were able to keep their vineyard and the remaining vines, and the winery. I didn't expect gratitude, but I hoped they would not resent me for doing it." Pietragnelli's bright little eyes clouded briefly. "The boys are especially bitter about what I did."

"They have boys? Didn't you mention them before?" Saint-Germain asked, and went on, "How old are these boys?"

"Oliver is nineteen, just a year out of high school; Arnold is seventeen, and he'll graduate next spring. They are both still with their parents, and are supposed to be helping out with their wine-making, but they don't do much work that I can see." He frowned. "They call themselves Leonard, not Leonardi. They say that Italians are a bastard people, even though they are half-Italian themselves. They shame their father."

"And what is their complaint just now?" Saint-Germain watched Pietragnelli squirm before he summoned up an answer.

"They—as we have all done—have lost some of their grapes to the midnight harvest, and they say I have caused the thefts. They are convinced that their losses have been greater than mine, and nothing anyone can say has changed their minds. The thefts have been the same for all of us, but they believe that they have been more deeply wronged. They say my policy of employing only men with families has led to more theft on their property, since unmarried men are as desperate as married ones, and more inclined to break the law. I do not offer work to such men, so they are more inclined to rob, or that is what they are saying." He had been speaking very rapidly, and now he forced himself to slow down. "I don't know if you can do anything about this trouble. The Leonardis are not going to listen to any opinion that does not agree with theirs, and you would be considered tainted because you have done business with me for so long. They say I have brought trouble to them, that if I employed single men as well as married men, they would not steal. They claim I can afford to provide jobs for dozens of men, although I cannot, even if I had work for dozens of men to do. And some of the thieves are no more than criminals in any case, and they do not seek jobs, only opportunities. So the Leonardi sons say I have left them and all the farmers around Geyserville without protection from the midnight harvesters. They are very angry."

"But that's foolishness," said Saint-Germain. "If they are worried about idleness, do they have any idea how you are to afford to employ all these men, and keep them busy once you have employed them?"

"I don't know," Pietragnelli exclaimed, turning his eyes upward. "I have tried to do as much as I can. The Leonardis employ only three men, and they do not give them a place to live—they cannot afford it. They have no accommodations for wives or children." He glowered in the direction of the nearest lamp. "I don't expect them to do what I do, but I wish they would not carp about what I do, whether they agree with it or not. I mean them no harm."

"I gather something has happened to make the situation worse, or you wouldn't have called me," said Saint-Germain.

"Something has happened," Pietragnelli said, and took a long moment before going on. "Thomas Leonardi has filed a grievance with Will Sutton—the deputy sheriff in Healdsburg?—claiming that I am deliberately creating trouble so that I can compel my neighbors to sell their land to me for reduced prices; I had a call from Will yesterday about it. He said he thinks it's nonsense, but he's afraid it could mean problems, all the same. I asked him what he has to do now. He isn't willing to do more than file the papers with the sheriff, and he warned me that it could lead to court appearances, to defend my actions, or show that the grievance is without merit." He took a long sip of mulled wine. "I fear Sutton may be right."

Saint-Germain considered what he had heard. "Have your neighbors been harder hit by thefts than you have?"

"Hiro Yoshimura certainly has, and Alphonse del Castro, but they are not vintners—they grow vegetables, and there is a greater demand for vegetables. Neither of them has complained about my policy, but that means little." Pietragnelli sighed heavily. "I have talked to them both, and I have sent my men to help guard their fields, but the thieves are patient, and they strike late at night. We've routed some of them, but not nearly enough."

"And you say it is the Leonardis who are complaining, not Yoshimura or del Castro," Saint-Germain remarked. "How odd."

"They believe they must speak against me," said Pietragnelli. "That is what I have come to realize, little as I want to. What man likes to think his neighbors wish him ill?"

"Most of us would prefer to have it otherwise," Saint-Germain said, his memories filled with painful reminders of when that had not been possible for him.

"So I have said, many times," Pietragnelli declared. "I have tried to make the most of my good fortune, yes, but I have wanted to share it with my family and neighbors, as an honorable man should. Thomas Leonardi used to be my friend; not so much his wife—she is from Scotland and thinks men should be taciturn. But I do not find her as objectionable as she does me."

"That's unfortunate," Saint-Germain said, and attempted to discover where this was leading. "You have intimated that the Leonardi sons bear you a grudge. Do you think they are inclined to be more belligerent than they have been in the past?"

"I am afraid so. They have been attending meetings somewhere near Santa Rosa of a group of men who claim to be protecting the white race from corruption. They don't consider Italians white, of course, or Russians, or Spaniards, or Frenchmen, or anyone they decide is not one of them. They advocate running off anyone they don't approve of, in the name of racial purity." He barked out a laugh. "They have been feeding on shared misery."

"Do you suppose they are planning to do more than talk? If they are behind the grievance, they could damage you." Saint-Germain had a sharp recollection of the Militia Christi in his palazzo in Fiorenza, and all that had come of their zeal; this was the same mentality cloaked in a different cause.

"It's possible," Pietragnelli said heavily. "I hope I am wrong, but after what they said to me last week, I can't be blind to their ire, though it was their father who made the charges."

"Have you spoken to the deputy about this?" Saint-Germain asked. He heard the wind change direction, sending the rain spattering on the French doors; he knew the drive back to San Rafael would be slow and wretched with water running on the road; luckily, his native earth was under the springs of the seat, which would reduce the vertigo running water caused him.

"Certainly. When he called me about the complaint, I told him what I knew, but I probably sounded as if I wanted to retaliate for their grievance." He shrugged to show his frustration. "I don't know what more I can do beyond calling you."

"I'm glad you did," said Saint-Germain. "It is not in your interests or mine to be bogged down in all manner of legal posturing. I don't suppose this can be readily resolved, not as complicated as it seems to be. " He got up from the piano and went over toward the wide doorway into the entry-hall. "I wonder what we could do to lessen the animosity."

"If you can think of something, I would be grateful," said Pietragnelli. "I am prepared to deal with all manner of trouble, but I would prefer not to have to. I am sorry I must draw you into this, but you have a share in the winery, and if it is damaged, you will feel it as well as I." He stared down into his mug. "I have struggled to do what I think is right. Because I have had more opportunities than some others, I have wanted to extend as much help as I could to those with fewer; when I decided to employ only men with wives and families, it was because I thought that the salary I paid would do more good that way. Thanks to you, I am able to do this, but not even your resources are infinite; I can't afford to hire every man out of work—not even the government can do that—but so long as I can pay a hundred dollars a month, I want the money to benefit as many as possible. Am I wicked to do that?"

"You are asking the wrong man. In your shoes I would probably do the same." Saint-Germain put his fingertips together. "But that isn't the issue, is it: what you believe you have done correctly?—the problem is what others think you ought to have done, and how they believe it has affected them."

"Veramente," said Pietragnelli. "Nothing I have been able to say has persuaded the Leonardis that I do not mean them injury. And now that the midnight harvests have increased, it has only made matters worse." He set his mug aside and rose.

"Have you spoken to any of the Leonardis since they filed their grievance?" Saint-Germain observed Pietragnelli closely.

"It was my first impulse, but I decided not to," he admitted.

Saint-Germain nodded. "Certainly a prudent decision," he said.

"I thought it best to talk to you first, and in person. I don't want the switchboard operators telling everyone what we discussed. They love gossip, and as you know, they listen to everything." Pietragnelli swung around to face Rogerio. "You have said nothing."

"I've been listening," said Rogerio.

"That's all well and good," Pietragnelli grumbled, "but something more is needed."

"Yes, it is," said Rogerio. "I am trying to decide what I might be able to do that would not make the situation worse."

"As are we all," said Saint-Germain. "This may require very careful negotiations."

"Per sfortuna," Pietragnelli muttered.

"Possibly," said Saint-Germain. "But we should be able to avoid the worst if we plan carefully."

"I am sorry to impose upon you so; I wish it weren't necessary," Pietragnelli said. "But I could think of no one else to turn to who would be in a position to help. You have an interest in the winery, and so if there is trouble, you will have to bear some of its burdens, or so you have told me. Will Sutton won't be able to do anything, and so it seemed to me—"

"You needn't apologize," said Saint-Germain.

"This isn't your battle," Pietragnelli exclaimed, suddenly chagrined. "I could not think of anyone else to call; still, I know I should not ask you to be part of this."

"But it is, you know," Saint-Germain told him. "It is my battle."

Rogerio recognized the resolve in Saint-Germain's steady voice, and said, "What do you need me to do?"

Saint-Germain shook his head. "I'll decide that once Signor Pietragnelli and I have agreed upon a strategy." He went and drew up one of the chairs to where Pietragnelli sat. "You tell me the Leonardi sons belong to a group in Santa Rosa: what do you know about it, and what can you tell me about what the members have actually done?" He sat down and motioned to Rogerio to join them.

Pietragnelli rubbed his chin with his thick, blunt hand. "I believe they call themselves the White Legion, or some such grandiose name. They blame the terrible state of the country on all those they consider non-white. They send insulting letters to the *Press-Democrat* and post derogatory notices on the windows of stores and other businesses owned by those they dislike. They run advertisements saying that thus-and-such a business or farm or company is owned by non-whites. They paint mailboxes with yellow or black to warn people in the county that they have non-white neighbors. They have claimed that they have wrecked a fruit-stand run by a Spanish family. Whether it is true or not, the fruit-stand was certainly wrecked. They also claim to have forced Mr. Wu to sell his restaurant and move back to San Francisco. Mr. Wu is gone, and, as far as I know, is not planning to return. It is a pity. His was the only good Chinese restaurant in Santa Rosa. He served wonderful food, and his prices were reasonable. You could get a whole dinner—an ample dinner—for less than a dollar a person."

"So this White Legion may do more than talk," said Saint-Germain. "They may actually do real damage." He thought of the men in brown shirts in Munich, and, for a terrible moment, Laisha dead. "Groups of that kind are dangerous."

"I fear so," said Pietragnelli. "They also say that they will chase all non-whites out of Sonoma County. I don't know if they will, but it is their admitted intention: everyone they decide isn't white enough for their standards must be gotten rid of. I know this because I have read their tracts, and I know what they advocate. They had a booth at the County Fair, and they had posters saying that, with copies of their advertisements about non-whites. The men all wear blue trousers and white shirts, and they march about as if they were soldiers. Oliver Leonardi was working at the booth, handing out material and collecting donations, some as much as a dollar. A lot of men stopped at the booth and took their pamphlets."

"That's unfortunate," said Saint-Germain. "I don't suppose they can be stopped from—"

"No. They have a right to their opinion: I understand. It's in the Constitution, as they point out in all their literature. And many of the police agree with them, so they do not watch them too closely." Pietragnelli caught his lower lip in his teeth. "I don't know what I am to do if the Leonardis turn their associates against me."

"You must make sure they don't have that opportunity," said Saint-Germain. "And you must employ their tactics against them."

"How am I to do that?" Pietragnelli asked, sounding dreadfully tired.

"You say they advertise in the newspaper; they may have overstepped themselves," Saint-Germain began, his dark eyes lit with purpose. "If they can do so, you will, too." He held up his hand to stop Pietragnelli's objection. "You must run a notice every day that yesterday the White Legion did not attempt to run you off your land. Don't worry about the cost: I'll pay for it."

"But won't that goad them? provoke them?" Pietragnelli cried in dismay.

"It will. And on the day that they do anything against you, you withdraw that notice from the paper—for that day. You must be scrupulously honest in your notice, and if you are, the stratagem will succeed." Saint-Germain saw a glimmer of mischief in Pietragnelli's worried scowl. "If others will join with you, the notices will have more power."

"They will be furious," Pietragnelli said, almost relishing the prospect.

"Very likely. But so long as you are scrupulously truthful, the White Legion will be held up to scrutiny and ridicule at once. Movements of that sort can endure anything but derision. Provided there are more people to stand against them than support them, they stand to lose far more than you do, and you alert the community to the menace they are without providing them an aura of power." This last, he thought, was the most crucial element, and the one thing that could tip the balance away from the White Legion.

"Do you think they will try to retaliate for such notices?" Pietragnelli asked.

"It is a possibility, and you must not ignore it," said Saint-Germain. "How many of your neighbors have been harassed by this White Legion?"

"Yoshimura and del Castro, of course, and Hooperman—he is a farmer about two miles away—and Giovenezza, who has orchards south of Cloverdale. There are probably others, but I don't know of them specifically," said Pietragnelli. "I will ask the ones I know to recommend others."

"Do most farms and vineyards in this region take the *Press-Democrat*?" Saint-Germain asked.

"Oh, yes. From Petaluma to Ukiah, it is the most frequently read paper. They boast of that," said Pietragnelli.

"Good. That should suit us very well," said Saint-Germain. "If the editor is any kind of a journalist, he'll welcome your notices."

Pietragnelli considered this carefully. "Do you really think that the paper will accept such notices?"

"If you are willing to pay for them, why not? They are not libelous, and they are of public service, and they imply an interesting story," said Saint-Germain.

"The more of you who will do the same, the better effect your notices will have."

"I'll do it!" Pietragnelli clapped his hands, almost upsetting his mug. "And I'll ask my neighbors whose mailboxes have been painted to meet with me. I'll try to convince them to take out notices of their own. I suppose the *Press-Democrat* is the most useful paper—it's a daily. The Healdsburg paper is a weekly."

"You will need a daily paper," Saint-Germain concurred. "If the White Legion has notices in it, ask if yours can run alongside theirs." This could prompt a more immediate response, but it was also the most direct counter-attack that could be made.

"I will ask. Most of the advertisements and notices are on the same pages of the paper," said Pietragnelli.

"I'll also make sure you have extra protection," said Saint-Germain. "I'll hire guards for you, and pay their wages, through you, to ensure their loyalty to you."

"You needn't," said Pietragnelli, abruptly reticent. "It would appear—"

"I won't leave you exposed to the kind of trouble these men can bring," said Saint-Germain. "It would be bad business to put you at risk and do nothing to reduce your jeopardy."

"I don't know that you need to do so much," said Pietragnelli.

"Better have the guards and not need them than need them and not have them," said Rogerio, giving Pietragnelli a sign of encouragement.

"Where is the Leonardis' winery in relation to yours?" Saint-Germain asked in new concern.

Pietragnelli pointed to the southeast. "Half-a-mile in that direction, as the crow flies; a bit over two miles by road. They are down a winding lane called Los Coyotes, the third drive on the right. There's a sign at the gate." He looked suddenly sad. "When I was younger, I would hitch my horse to our surrey and drive across the plantation to their house—that is the half-mile route. I'd bring along wines, and Thomas and I would compare his and mine. I am sorry those times had to end."

"Do you still have the horse and the surrey?" Saint-Germain asked.

"My daughter and son-in-law have both, in Calistoga. They give rides to the local children, and at Christmas, they take panettone to all their neighbors; when they have children, of their own, they will take them along. They have bells for the surrey at Christmas, very festive, and their children will have fun delivering bread and wine to the neighbors. Sophia and Ethan enjoy these occasions, and are planning to continue them for as long as they can. But the mare's almost twenty, and they're going to retire her soon, and they'll buy another horse to pull the surrey, probably in a year or so. The mare won't be sold: I'll bring her back here and put her out in the pasture." He shook his head to rid himself of his nostalgia.

Saint-Germain regarded Pietragnelli sympathetically. "It is always sad when friendships end, no matter when or how."

"Lo so," Pietragnelli mumbled, embarrassed by his remarks. "I know this."

"And it still troubles you, that the Leonardis have not continued their friendship with you," Saint-Germain went on. "No doubt the way in which the sons are behaving is hurtful to you."

"In some ways," Pietragnelli allowed reluctantly.

"It is to your credit that you care about them," Saint-Germain said. "A lesser man would have steeled himself against them, and refused to accept that there had been any loss."

Pietragnelli was becoming uncomfortable. "As you say. But it will do nothing for any of us to remember those times now. I should not let what is past keep me from doing what I must."

"True enough," said Saint-Germain.

"So." Pietragnelli rose and went to the fireplace, leaning against the mantel, his eyes focused on the medium-distance. "I will begin with the notice in the paper next Monday, and continue until something happens to me, or my land."

"Yes, basically that is it," said Saint-Germain.

"And once I have begun this, how long do I continue?" He stared hard at Saint-Germain.

"Until the White Legion withdraws their notices," said Saint-Germain. "Once that happens, continue yours for one more week, and then discontinue them. You don't want to keep them in the public eye any longer than necessary."

"I assume you have a reason for this," said Rogerio.

"Yes," said Saint-Germain, a bit grimly. "I know that making them appear absurd will do much to stop their spread, but continuing to mention them after they have been made ridiculous will undo some of the good done, and that might be enough to give them the power they seek." He closed his eyes, his memories nearly overwhelming him.

"You are a clever man, Signor Ragoczy," said Pietragnelli. "Very well, I will try your idea." He rubbed his hands as if bathing them in the heat of the fire. "These poor men—so many have lost everything: land, family, homes, and they do not want to lose anything more." He took a step back. "But that does not excuse their actions."

"No, it doesn't," Saint-Germain said, recalling the times he had lost land, intimate associates, and homes.

There was a canny light in Pietragnelli's small eyes. "You have endured more than most. I can see it in you." He nodded to the piano. "I heard it as you played."

"Then you are an astute fellow," said Saint-Germain in a tone that did not encourage further inquiry.

"I am as I am," said Pietragnelli.

"*This above all, to thine own self be true?*" Saint-Germain quoted.

"Veramente. And for that alone, I have to say I am more grateful than I can express to you for all you have been willing to do for me." He stared at Saint-Germain. "I'll call some of my neighbors and we will begin this campaign next week. I'll talk to them in person, so that the operators will not spread about what we plan to do. Is there anything else you would recommend?"

"I'll arrange for your guards." Saint-Germain swung around to face Rogerio. "Have you thought of anything more?"

"Not as such, no," said Rogerio. "But I do think the guards should not be too obvious; that may increase the animosity and perhaps alienate the very men you want to have join with you."

Pietragnelli nodded twice, very emphatically. "I know why you say this, and I am inclined to agree with you."

"I see your point," Saint-Germain said. He regarded Pietragnelli in silence for the greater part of a minute, and then he said, "I think you may find this a hard struggle."

"I am a vintner—I have struggled for years. I can continue to do so for a few more months." He lifted his chin. "I am almost sorry now that I bought the Leonardis' land—but I couldn't bear to see them lose all. It would have struck too close to home."

"It is no easy thing," said Saint-Germain knowingly.

The room was quiet but for the rattle of the rain and the rush of the fire. Then Carlo Pietragnelli shook off the gloom that threatened to envelop him. "I will begin my tasks soon. You and I will plan what the notice is to say, and we will decide how I am to approach the rest about this. At first, I assumed it would be all right to have a general meeting, but now I suspect that might be too conspicuous. I will arrange to call upon the others and speak with them privately, so as to draw less attention to what I am doing." He was speaking rapidly, as if he needed to keep the words coming or lose his impetus. "Then I will go in person to the *Press-Democrat* and arrange to place my notice with them. I will make sure they have the wording exactly right, and I will make some arrangement about withdrawing the notice on very short notice. That may require an extra charge."

"I'll pay it, if there is one," said Saint-Germain.

"You are a very generous man, and I may be taking advantage of that generosity, but I see how important it is that this be done." He went and picked up his mug again and refilled it. "I wish I could speak to Thomas Leonardi, but I know the time for that is past."

"You are probably right," said Saint-Germain.

"I spoke with him last spring, when Oliver first started attending his meetings, and Thomas was most annoyed with me for saying anything about his son. In its way, that is an admirable thing, but in another, it is far from praiseworthy." He folded his hands around the mug of cooling mulled wine. "A man who cannot examine his own is a man who has become blind." With an impatient gesture, he said, "I love my three daughters, but I have grave doubts about my son, Massimo, who is working in Davis at the university. Not that he has done anything reprehensible—or not that I know of. It isn't that. He has shown himself to be inclined to retreat into the world of his mind instead of seeking life. I am proud of what he has done, but I am also worried about what may become of him."

"What man doesn't fret about his children," said Saint-Germain, more images of Laisha, his dead ward, flooding his thoughts.

Pietragnelli was not actually listening. "I am pleased with my son-in-law, Ethan, but I am afraid my daughter is too ready to put his interests ahead of her own; many women do. And Angelina, though she has a good job and does it well, has made it into the center of her life, which makes me worried about her." He took a long sip of his mulled wine. "I know they have faults, and that their desires are not necessarily mine, but they are also my children, and I will stand by them. I share that with Thomas, but not to the exclusion of all other considerations. If my son had done as Oliver and Arnold have done, I would not stand idly by and approve of their—" He stopped, struck by recognition. "Perhaps Thomas feels as they do, and encourages them. He may be the starting point for all this."

Mrs. Barringstone appeared in the doorway. "Am I to make supper for your guests?"

With an effort Pietragnelli managed to smile. "No, thank you, Mrs. Barringstone. You have only to put the roast in the oven for me."

"That I will. As soon as the roast's in the oven I'm going to meet my kids at the school bus. I'll be back in half-an-hour." She tromped off to the kitchen.

"She is a good mother," said Pietragnelli. "And she follows my recipes. Her husband works hard, but without any feel for the wine. Still, he is industrious and doesn't complain. It is a pity she is so dour, but with all that has happened to them, I can see how she would not be jolly."

"At least you have given them a place to live," said Rogerio with a meaningful glance at Saint-Germain.

"It isn't the same as their own home," said Pietragnelli. "But this is the most I can provide." He looked aside, as if embarrassed. "They came from Oklahoma, and they didn't want to move. Their farm blew away on the wind, so they had to leave."

"There are many kinds of refugees," said Saint-Germain, remembering the Year of Yellow Snow, Spain and the Emir's son, Delhi after Timur-i sacked it, Florence when Savonarola came to power, Russia before the Revolution, and the chaos after the Great War.

"And all manner of wars," said Pietragnelli.

Saint-Germain ducked his head. "I am glad you called me," he told Pietragnelli.

"I hope you will say the same six months from now," said the Italian with a gloomy twist to his mouth that was meant to be a smile. "That will be the test." He looked up as the back door slammed shut. "I hope that isn't an omen."

"Of what?" Saint-Germain asked.

"Of all things coming to an end," said Pietragnelli, his face very serious.

"But all things come to an end," said Saint-Germain. "It is only a question of when, and how."

TEXT OF A LETTER FROM DOÑA ISABEL INEZ VEDANCHO Y NUÑEZ AT BRIARCOPSE, HAMPSHIRE, TO FERENC RAGOCZY, SENT CARE OF OSCAR KING OF KING LOWENTHAL TAYLOR & FROST IN SAN FRANCISCO.

> *Copsehowe*
> *Nr. Briarcopse*
> *Hampshire*
> *England*
> *31 October, 1936*

Ferenc Ragoczy
c/o Oscar King
King Lowenthal Taylor & Frost
630 Kearny Street
San Francisco, California
USA

My dear Comte,

It has been some time since I wrote to you, largely because I have been trying to gather my thoughts and present them to you in a way that will convey all that has taken place in the last several weeks. This has proven to be more difficult than I had anticipated, for which I apologize in advance of explaining all this to you.

Three days ago I went up to London to visit Miles Sunbury, who is in hospital recovering from terrible injuries he received just over a month ago, on 28 September, at the hands of a man who wanted information about your whereabouts. The beating he administered to Mr. Sunbury was truly ferocious. When I visited him, I was very much shocked at how drawn and pale he looked, as if he had aged a decade in a month. There are deeper lines in his face and white in his hair that was not there before. Mr. Sunbury will leave hospital in three days, providing he has no set-back, and he'll be confined to his flat in Siddons Lane for another month to recover. I may ask him if he would like to come down to Copsehowe to recuperate, so that he may have constant attention and the benefit of the guards you have assigned to me.

In spite of what has happened to me, I did not actually think I could be in any danger this far from Spain, but I see now that this is wishful thinking on my part, and that the precautions you urged upon me are not only appropriate but necessary. I am doing my best to follow your recommendations, however belatedly. It is also apparent that the danger extends to Mr. Sunbury and to all the members of your London household. Therefore I am asking you to help to the extent that you will engage more security than you have already, not only for us, but for you yourself.

Mr. Sunbury has told me a little of what the criminal did to him, and what he wanted to know, which Mr. Sunbury believes he was able to conceal to some degree. He tells me that he revealed that you went to America, and have the advice of several attorneys in that country, but he did his best to convince the man that you began your stay in New York, and intend to return there. He isn't certain how much more he was able to keep to himself, since he was no longer wholly cognizant of his speech. He said the man intended to cause him extreme pain without doing him irreparable harm.

Still, one of his knees has been destroyed, and his foot has been broken—three of the bones were shattered, and the physicians believe he will never again walk without a cane. In addition to this, three of his fingers were utterly ruined and his shoulder was dislocated and his earlobe was cut off. I understand you have authorized your London bank to pay for all his medical expenses, for which I cannot help but feel you have shown the same honor that has marked your conduct at all times. I know that Mr. Sunbury is grateful to you for all you have done, and so am I, for I have developed a fondness for Mr. Sunbury. It is not likely that it will go beyond fondness; I am still a married woman, although Ponce isn't one to remember that minor detail. Mr. Sunbury is the sort of man who will not cross the line, which is one of the things about him that I admire. This does not redound to your discredit, for you did nothing that could compromise me.

Which brings me to another matter: Ponce and, by extension, I have been declared enemies of the state, and convicted in absentia of treason. Our bank accounts have been seized, and the money confiscated by Spain. Luckily, this does not compromise me, thanks to your cleverness in moving my funds out of the country shortly before I left. Ponce, on the other hand, is not so fortunate as I, and he has lost more than half his fortune. What this will mean to him in his present dealings, I cannot guess, nor do I want to. But I know that unless I am legally compelled to do so, I will not part with one shilling to relieve him of any impecuniousness he may experience. I am not a vindictive woman, but he left me to fend for myself when he went to the Argentine, and now I will see that the same is done to him.

I know you will understand my decision in this regard, and whether you agree or not, you will not hold it against me that I will not extend myself on my husband's behalf. It is hard enough to be left as alone as a widow but with none of the possibilities a widow can have. To support the man who deserts me is intolerable, and I will do all in my power to insure this does not happen. Fortunately, Mr. Sunbury has promised one of his colleagues will be my advocate if it comes to that; he is confident that the greatest part of my money can be preserved with a modicum of forethought. I am grateful to be in his hands.

Shortly before he was so badly injured, Mr. Sunbury purchased for me a pair of lurchers, litter-mates, males, very well-trained and sweet-tempered. I am thrilled to have these dogs as companions, not simply because they assuage my loneliness, but because they are so protective and willing to serve as watchdogs as well as pets. The guards tell me that they are excellent creatures, inclining to patrol and to give the alarm at any questionable sound or presence. They are affectionate with me, and, once familiar with my friends, gentle as lambs with them, although they can be fierce with strangers. Considering all that has happened, I can only thank Mr. Sunbury for his concern. Contemplating what has happened to him, I find great comfort in having these dogs to keep me safe.

I hope you do not encounter this man who is searching for you. He is a most sinister and ruthless person, one who will do anything to achieve his ends. If you have any question about your safety, then let me urge you to go where you will be safe. Do not hesitate to take any measures you deem necessary in order to preserve yourself from him, for it is Mr. Sunbury's conviction that this man means to kill you, and, given how seriously Mr. Sunbury was injured, I have no doubt that he is more than capable of completing his mission.

This comes to you with my deep distress. Do not answer me directly, for *it may be that I am under surveillance, and that any communication from you may lead this assassin or his accomplices to you. After all you have done to save me, it would be inexcusable of me to do anything that might bring you into danger. I will hope that you can receive mail from me through Mr. King, and to that end, I will write to you again by the end of the year, unless I have reason to believe that such correspondence is hazardous.*

I hope in many ways that this finds you well and safe, and that you never have to encounter the man who tortured Mr. Sunbury.

With all my devotion,

Isis

chapter eight

"I'm sorry I'm late," said Dorothy McAllister as she came into the restaurant, an elegant, Viennese-style establishment with velvet-upholstered furniture, flocked wallpaper, and crystal chandeliers. It was not far from the offices of Horner Bishop Beatie Wentworth & Culpepper, walking distance from the Commodities Exchange; smiling apologetically, Miss McAllister left her raincoat and hat at the hatcheck booth and joined her companion for the evening at a table in an alcove booth far from the front door. "There were three letters I had to type over. I promised Mr. Bishop I'd finish them before I left."

"You didn't make any mistakes, surely? I can't believe you'd be careless," Cenere said solicitously as he rose to greet her. He favored her with a smooth smile and a courteous squeeze of her hand, but nothing more forward—that was for later, when he had her where he wanted her. "What did he require of you, your Mr. Bishop?"

"Oh, nothing to speak of. Nothing unusual: Mr. Bishop wanted to add explanations to the letters, and that meant typing them over." She was flushed and a bit breathless, but only a little because of the furious weather that slammed sleet along Chicago's streets and snarled traffic from one end of the city to another.

"Isn't that the way with lawyers, always lost in details," he said, shaking his head as he waited for her to slide into the booth before he sat down again, the very model of European good manners. He studied her face. "You're looking very fine tonight, Dorothy."

"Am I?" She put her hand to her throat, to her string of fairly good pearls that was her one bequest from her mother.

"You are," said Cenere in a manner that suggested warmth.

"It must be the company—I can't think of any other reason," she said archly, daring to look directly at him.

"You're being kind to me," he said with a slight smile, which revealed small, shiny teeth.

"Hardly," she said in a burst of candor. "Kindness has been in short supply these last few years."

He studied her face. "Has it been a difficult time for you? The Depression must make attending to the law especially taxing."

"No more so than Prohibition did, particularly here in Chicago," said Dorothy McAllister. "I went to work for Mr. Bishop back in those lawless days, in '27, to be precise. This time is sad, those times were dangerous."

"Danger can be more exciting," said Cenere, knowing how much the financial collapse of Germany following the Great War had spread trouble all through Europe.

"Danger breeds recklessness; this hardship breeds desperation," she said. "Both make their own demands on the law and the courts."

"Mr. Bishop is lucky to have you, if you'd like my opinion in the matter," said Cenere, aware that he would be foolish to underestimate her, at least while she was getting used to being in his company. "From what I could see, you're the very heart of his office."

"You're biased," she said with a suggestion of wary flirtatiousness.

"Biased doesn't mean wrong," said Cenere gallantly. "May I order a drink for you? They have good bourbon here, and real Scotch whiskey. Or would you prefer a mixed drink? Something elegant. What about a Sidecar, just to take the edge off?" He signaled a waiter.

"I don't usually drink spirits, but this *is* a special occasion." She beamed at him. "A Sidecar would be very nice."

"Good," said Cenere. "A Sidecar for the lady and some of your excellent Kentucky bourbon for me—no ice." He motioned the waiter away. "I'm glad you changed your mind and agreed to come out with me. I know the invitation was on short notice, and you've had to shift your schedule to accommodate me; it's very nice of you." Leaning across the table enough to speak very softly, he added, "I've been waiting for this opportunity all day."

Dorothy McAllister was a bit flustered. "I don't know what to say. You take me aback—not unpleasantly." This was more difficult than she had thought it would be. She had not been out alone with a man in more than six years—that had been with a visiting attorney from Minneapolis and had turned out to be a disastrous evening—and the experience now was a heady combination of exhilaration and jumpy nerves. She fiddled with the cuff of her suit-sleeve, wishing she knew how to behave in this situation. "I'm very glad you asked me to have dinner with you."

"I wanted to speak with you alone, away from the office. What kind of a gentleman asks a lady out without offering her something more than his company?" He reached for his cigarette case and removed one of the cigarettes, offering it to her; when she accepted, he handed it to her and selected a second for himself. As he lit them, he smiled into her eyes. "I know this is going to be a very special evening."

"Oh," she breathed, and did her best not to cough on the first inhale of smoke.

He sat back. "You know, I had resigned myself to this journey as a duty, nothing more, something that had to be done but not enjoyed. I was prepared to accomplish the tasks I have been sent to perform, to be pragmatic about my assignment. But I knew when I met you the day before yesterday, that I had been wrong to assume that there would be no aspect of this country that could engage me."

She put her hand to her throat. "You are too kind, Mr. Cenere." She pronounced the name properly—CHEHnehray—not SenEER as the receptionist at Horner Bishop Beatie Wentworth & Culpepper had.

"I would like to be more than that," he said boldly, looking directly through the wraiths of smoke into her eyes.

"Mr. Cenere," she said in mild rebuke to hide her sudden rush of panic. "You may find such extravagances succeed with European women, but it is not what I am accustomed to." She could not bring herself to admit how much she liked his extravagant attention; she sat a bit straighter.

"Of course not," he said at once, accepting her reprimand without anything more than a shift in his gaze. "I didn't intend any disrespect. I'm not wholly familiar with American manners, and if I have erred, it is because that after the Great War, things in Europe have changed a great deal, and are changing still."

This was much safer ground to be on, and she used it to shift the subject away from her. "I have heard that the fighting in Spain is getting worse," she ventured, tapping her cigarette ash into the crystal ashtray next to the table candle.

"It's very bad," he confirmed. "And the worst isn't over yet. In fact, I suspect the worst hasn't yet begun." He looked up as the waiter arrived with their drinks; he rested his cigarette on the edge of the ashtray.

"It must be dreadful. I can't imagine what the last decade has been like. Europe seems to go from one crisis to another, as if the Great War settled nothing." Her voice dropped. "My fiancé was killed in the Great War, like so many others. I read his letters from the Front, and they sounded so disheartening. I think it must have been terrible to fight in that war." She blinked as if to stop unshed tears; then she put out her cigarette and reached out for the glass that had been set down in front of her.

"War has always been terrible, and it becomes more so with every passing decade as the weapons become more lethal," he said. "But enough of such hideous things." He looked directly into her eyes and lifted his drink. "To unexpected meetings."

She touched the rim of his glass with hers. "To unexpected meetings," she seconded, and drank, feeling the cold heat of the Sidecar percolate through her.

He took a small sip of bourbon and set his glass down. "Still, I'm sorry to hear about your fiancé. It's very sad, how many valiant young men were lost in that war."

"I wasn't the only girl to lose a sweetheart," she allowed, drinking more of her Sidecar.

"No. Many women became widows much too early," said Cenere. "Enough of these gloomy thoughts. The War is long over and it cannot be changed or undone. I don't want to dwell on what is past, but to contemplate that which is to come."

Miss McAllister touched the corner of her eye, afraid she might be weeping, feeling embarrassed by the possibility. "I don't know what came over me. I haven't spoken of George Eastman for . . . it must be three years now. I beg your pardon."

"I'm pleased to have your confidence, Dorothy," said Cenere. "I hope I can help assuage your grief." He picked up his glass, and had another minuscule sip. "I know such wounds take many years to heal."

"I resigned myself to his loss fifteen years ago," she said.

"Still, a difficult burden for any woman to shoulder." He made his smile a commiserating one. "You have made something of your life, and that is to your credit."

"Please don't say anything more on this, Mr. Cenere. I'm a bit nervous as it is," Miss McAllister said as she took another drink; she began to feel a bit steadier. She managed a smile. "I hope you don't mind."

"I don't," said Cenere, seeming utterly genuine. "I know you haven't had an easy life."

"Oh, I'm not complaining. I have nothing to complain about—I have a good job at a time when many women cannot find work at all, and those who do are paid poorly for laboring long hours at menial tasks. Mr. Bishop is a wonderful boss, he pays a reasonable wage, and he gives Christmas bonuses as well. He's kept me on through thick and thin, and he's never once made me worry about where my next meal's coming from." She lowered her eyes. "My sister has had to take her family to Cleveland; they lost their house."

"Why Cleveland?" Cenere asked, wanting to keep her talking; he was looking for things he could employ to manipulate her into providing him the information he sought. "What happened to your sister's family?"

"They moved. Because her husband has finally got a job there. Nothing as good as what he had before, but at least it's work. He used to work for the railroad, but they fired him six years ago, and now he's finally working for a delivery service. The family suffered before he got work, but they managed to stay together somehow." She shook her head. "Oh, dear. You don't want to hear all about this. I didn't mean—"

"Say anything you want," Cenere encouraged her.

"Well, I don't want to bore you . . ." she faltered, and had the last of her Sidecar; she was a bit surprised to find the glass empty.

Cenere signaled the waiter to bring another. "You aren't boring me," he assured her.

Miss McAllister shook her head. "I really shouldn't have a second drink. I'm not used to it and this is a work night—"

"It is our celebration," Cenere corrected her. "And I cannot stay long in your city; I am obliged to continue my search. I must make the most of this marvelous opportunity, no matter how brief it may be." He laid his hand on hers. "Don't begrudge me the pleasure of your company, and our shared celebration."

This was more than Miss McAllister knew how to deal with: a good-looking Continental man was treating her as a fellow-sophisticate and lavishing the kind of attention on her that she had not experienced since George Eastman left for the Front. Her emotions were in turmoil, and so near the surface that she was unsure if she could continue to hold them in check, as she knew she must do, for lovely as this evening was, she was keenly aware it was only one evening, with no hope of more to come. She pulled her hand from under his and muttered a few disjointed words, finally managing to gather her thoughts enough to say, "I wish I knew what was on your mind."

He recaptured her hand. "You wouldn't believe me if I told you," he said, his manner laden with innuendo.

"That's a bit beyond the line." She glanced about as if she expected to find she was being watched by someone she knew, someone whose presence would be harmful to her. Finally she put her free hand flat on the tablecloth and dared to look at him. "You won't let me get tipsy, will you?"

He shook his head. "Of course not," he promised her as the waiter took her first glass and set down the second. "What gentleman would do that?"

"Perhaps we had better order our dinner shortly, so that I won't be tempted to forget my own intentions," she said, and sat back, trying to make herself comfortable.

"As you wish," he said as he let go of her hand and motioned for the waiter. "Menus."

"Of course, sir," said the waiter, a trifle too accommodatingly, as if he realized he was being deliberately slighted.

Miss McAllister had had one little sip of her second Sidecar and her good sense seemed to be reasserting itself, for her confidence was returning and she felt more keenly aware of her surroundings than she had been when she first arrived. "Do you make a long stay here?" That was too personal; she modified the question. "You have much to do while you're in America?" She liked the coolly professional sound of her voice.

"I have two, possibly three things I must attend to before I return home," he said, apparently unperturbed by her abrupt change in manner.

"Will they take long?" She hoped she didn't sound as desperate as she felt.

"That, Dorothy, depends to a great degree upon you," said Cenere at his most purposeful; he leaned forward and looked deeply into her eyes.

"Oh!" She could not bring herself to think of an answer to this.

He took advantage of her lapse. "You can help me, if you want to. It would make my task so much easier, but I have no wish to impose upon you, or cause you to do anything you would not like."

This was as intriguing as it was scary, and Miss McAllister wanted to spread her wings while she could. "What manner of thing might that be, Mr. Cenere?" she asked, and bolstered herself with a taste of the fresh Sidecar.

"This is a . . . bit awkward," he said, doing his best to appear perplexed. "I don't know how much I ought to reveal to you."

"I'm very good at keeping confidences—I have to be, in my line of work. I'm required to, you know." She put her elbows on the table and leaned toward him. "I pledge to keep your secret, whatever it may be."

He pretended to mull this over, all the while planning how he would manage the rest of the evening; so far he was very delighted by how willing the woman was to trust him. "The thing is, I don't want to put you into a difficult situation."

"How do you mean a difficult situation?" Miss McAllister asked, walking right into the trap he had laid for her.

"You see, the mission I am on is a delicate one. I am pursuing an enemy of Spain, a man who has been found to be a foe of the Revolution that is taking place now. I am supposed to return him to Madrid for trial, but as your government has not recognized our Generals as the leaders of Spain, I have no authority that your country recognizes, nor can I request local assistance. I am very much on my own, and that limits how I can handle my task." He stared at the chandelier hanging in the center of the dining room.

"How troublesome," she said, trying to follow what he was saying.

"It is, for this man is potentially very dangerous. You see, he had a business that has great strategic value, and he fled before he could—" He stopped abruptly. "I probably shouldn't tell you any of this."

"Why not?" she asked, her eyes dancing.

"I understand he is a client of your law firm, and that could make for . . . problems for you," he told her as if his hesitation was for her benefit. His cigarette went out in the ashtray.

"Goodness," she whispered, and drank a little more. This was turning out to be a most astonishing evening, one that made the rest of her life drab by contrast.

The waiter appeared and handed them menus. "I'll be back for your order in a few minutes."

Mentally cursing the waiter, Cenere said to Miss McAllister, "Order anything you like, Dorothy, even caviar."

She beamed. "I wouldn't do that. Not at such prices! Fifteen dollars an ounce-and-a-half—I ask you!"

"It is a bit expensive, but for you, it would be worth it. If it is what you want, you must order it, and enjoy it." He was afraid he had said too much, but she did not give any response that suggested he had gone too far. He studied the menu, finding the selection limited and the side-dishes mundane, but he assumed an enthusiasm for her benefit. "The duck looks promising, and so does the veal."

"But they're so expensive," said Miss McAllister, who rarely dined lavishly except at home on Thanksgiving and Christmas.

"The soups look tempting," Cenere said, wanting to distract her from the prices.

"So they do," she said. "I do like cream of tomato soup." She licked her lips in response, saying nothing more for a moment. "Would you mind if I had the soup and perhaps the duck as well?"

"Have what you like," he said, growing a bit tired of having to remind her that he could afford the meal. He restored his charming manner. "I'm planning to order champagne, if that might influence your choice."

She shook her head. "I don't think I ought to have any. I've had so much to drink already and . . ."

When she did not go on, he said, "I hope you'll have at least one glass, to toast our meeting. I'm sorry it could not take place under more propitious circumstances, but that doesn't mean that we shouldn't make the most of it."

"I suppose not," she said.

"What else can we do? We have so little time that we must pack as much into it as we are able." He took another small sip of bourbon and nodded to her to drink again.

She closed the menu and met his eyes. "All right. One glass of champagne, and I'll have the cream of tomato soup and the duck."

"Good for you," said Cenere, confident that with such rich foods, he could persuade her to drink more.

"Thank you so much," she said, mindful of her behavior. "I really appreciate this evening."

"Now you're the one being kind," he said, and summoned the waiter with a flick of his hand. "The lady will have the cream of tomato soup to start, and the duck. I'll have the consommé, and the pork loin stuffed with mushrooms. And bring us a bottle of your Roederer, the '24 or '26, chilled and in an ice bucket."

"Of course, sir," said the waiter as he reclaimed the menus and went off toward the kitchen.

"Foolish sort of fellow, isn't he?" Cenere asked.

"He's got a hard job, and he works at the library during the day," said Miss McAllister. "I have seen him there."

"That explains his demeanor," said Cenere, aware he had made a misstep and anxious to undo any damage he might have done. "He seems made of crumpled paper." He was disappointed when she showed no sign of amusement.

"Many men have to take what work they can get. Most of these jobs don't pay very well, and if he has a wife and family, or parents, to support, his library salary won't suffice." She drank down the last of her Sidecar; she was feeling a bit guilty to be here, having such a wonderful meal in a gorgeous restaurant, all the while aware that most of the people she knew could not afford to have anything half as nice as this.

"We know something of hardships in Europe," he said, his eyes lowered.

"And many of them worse than anything we endure here, I'm sure. The privations of war are much more destructive than the problems of economic woes—not that Europe hasn't had more than its fair share of those." She put her hand to her mouth. "I'm so sorry. I didn't mean to lecture you on what you must know far better than I."

Cenere schooled his features to an accepting partial smile. "You have a better grasp of these things than most of your countrymen, if you will forgive my saying so," he told her soothingly.

"I didn't mean—" she started to apologize.

"Your knowledge makes my predicament less complex," he interrupted her. "I should have known that you, working as you do for such a law firm, would be more familiar with European affairs than are most Americans." He touched her hand again. "I hope you will not be put off by anything I say, but if you are, you must tell me so."

"Then you *will* let me know more about this criminal you're pursuing?" she asked.

"I think you will appreciate my dilemma when I have done." He sandwiched her hand between both of his. "This man, who escaped from Spain on the very eve of his arrest, has been making his way across America. I was sent to deal with him, but to do so, first I must find him. I looked for him first in New York. I wasted four days in that city, and then I went to Boston and discovered he had reached your country there."

"And did you find him? How did he escape you?" The questions tumbled out of her.

"He had taken a train here, to Chicago. And something I learned in London led me to your office; I had reason to believe that he had had dealings with your firm. In fact, for all I know, he is still in this city." He set his half-finished bourbon aside, releasing her hand again.

"Gracious me," said Miss McAllister.

"The man was in Russia at the start of their Revolution—I find it suspicious that he has been so recently in Spain." Cenere had become aware of the American dread of Russia and Communism, and he decided to use that fear now, at least by implication.

"And you say he's here?" Miss McAllister queried, trying to keep her thoughts in order. "In Chicago? Are you sure?"

"I said he *might* be here. He may also have left the city. That is what I was hoping to find out when I called at your office. I was hoping to discover where he has gone." He admitted this as if he was expecting her to be shocked.

"For whom are you searching?" she asked, leaning forward as if to listen to a whisper. "And how urgent is your mission?"

He was spared the necessity of putting her off momentarily by the arrival of the champagne. "Now we can have a proper toast, and a promise for more and better times together, once my mission is over."

She blinked as if she had not heard him correctly. "Do you mean you might come back?"

"If there is reason to, I will," he said significantly, and watched as the waiter removed the guard on the cork. "I'm glad we can have this special occasion and mark it properly. Prohibition must have been as dreadful in its way as the Depression is."

"Some certainly thought so," said Miss McAllister in a slightly condemning tone. "Not that it truly worked; people continued to drink, but they did so illicitly, and that put a great deal of money into the pockets of criminals and politicians. There was a shocking disregard for law: ordinary citizens, who usually wouldn't dream of breaking the law, bought illegal alcohol and frequented speakeasies, and counted smugglers and moonshiners their friends, and mocked the police for trying to keep order." She was sitting very straight now. "Not that the criminals were always readily identified. My maiden aunt used to make elderberry wine; she served it on special occasions—New Year, birthdays, and such—even that was breaking the law."

"Then you must have some of this excellent champagne, now that it's legal," said Cenere, motioning to the waiter to fill her glass. "When we recall this evening, in times to come, I want it to be the most unforgettable night in your life."

She picked up her glass and looked down into the pale, fizzy liquid. "I've only had champagne twice before," she admitted.

"That alone makes this evening memorable, and there are many other reasons to mark it," he said, and lifted his own glass to be filled. They touched the rims of their glasses. "To memorable nights," he said.

"Amen." She gulped down almost half the champagne. "You're being . . . very nice to me. I'm having a wonderful time."

"It's easy to do, Dorothy, being nice to you," he said, a trifle too glibly; he had to make a recovery. "I'd begun to think that Americans only thought about money and movie stars. I was beginning to believe that it was impossible to find someone of substance in this country. And then I met you. You are an intelligent and sympathetic woman, and those are wonderful qualities to find in anyone."

"You are a flatterer," she said, the merest hint of a slur in her speech.

"I hope not. I may compliment you, which is only speaking the truth favorably; flattery assumes I am praising you for what does not exist." He let this sink in, and added, "I must assume all the men in Chicago are dolts, to leave you on the shelf."

There was just enough of a sting in his remarks for her to wince; she collected herself and managed to say, "Thank you, Mr. Cenere" before she drank more champagne. He carefully refilled her glass.

"I would like to think that you would not be entirely adverse to seeing me again, when I've finished with my mission." He let the suggestion hang in the air between them.

"Oh, Mr. Cenere, that would be . . . quite splendid," she said, knowing it was folly to let a man know you were interested in him so early in the acquaintance.

"Good. Then we should toast to that, as well," he said, lifting his champagne glass and prompting her to do the same.

Miss McAllister threw caution to the winds, and said, "I'll look forward to it."

The waiter arrived with their bowls of soup on polished brass chargers and set them in place. "Is there anything else, sir?"

"Not now," said Cenere, expecting the man to go away. He gave his full attention to Miss McAllister. "This looks very good, doesn't it?"

"It certainly does," said Miss McAllister, less than truthfully, for she was beginning to feel the impact of her drinks, and food seemed oddly unappetizing.

"Then enjoy your meal," said Cenere, and picked up his spoon.

Miss McAllister managed to finish about half her cream of tomato soup before it became too much for her. She began to wonder if she had been right to order the duck; her digestion wasn't what it was a decade ago, and this might prove too much, no matter how good it was. When her soup-bowl was removed, she had to fight the urge to ask the waiter to be sure the left-overs were given to a soup-kitchen or other service, so it wouldn't go to waste. She drank a little more champagne, as if that could make up for her leaving the soup. "I'm afraid I'm beginning to feel the alcohol," she said to Cenere.

This was precisely what he wanted to hear, but he managed to look concerned. "The food will sop it up. You don't need to worry, Dorothy."

"You're being so nice to me," she said, not wanting to appear ungrateful for all he had done for her.

"I'm glad I can do this," he said. "I only hope I can do something more to show you how much I value this evening."

This effusiveness would have alerted her, had she been more watchful, but her usual keenness was blunted, so she struggled to return the compliment. "It's very special to me, as well, Mr. Cenere. I wish I could tell you how much. You quite . . . overwhelm me with kindness." This seemed a bit too impersonal, but she could think of nothing more intimate to say. She wanted to learn his first name, but she knew that Europeans could be a great deal more reserved about such things than Americans were; Mr. Bishop insisted on a high level of decorum in the office, and for Miss McAllister, that tended to carry over into everything she did.

"Thank you, Dorothy; I'll try to be worthy of your high regard." He saw the waiter approaching with their entrees and fell silent.

She beamed at him, thinking things she had not dared to think for more than a decade, not since George Eastman had died in Flanders. To be treated so well—almost courted—was an experience she had assumed was lost to her. When the waiter set down her dinner, she tried to push those burgeoning hopes away, reminding herself that this man was a foreigner and a stranger, and she actually knew almost nothing about him, that his attention might not be anything but courtesy to a secretary who had been useful to him. Finally she murmured, "This is really superb," and trusted he would think she meant the food.

Cenere ate sparingly, finding the meal fairly ordinary, but he was careful to give no indication of this. He also refilled both their glasses. "Just in case," he said.

"I shouldn't have any more," she said as she fiddled with the half-duck; the skin glistened and she had to press down with the knife to slice it, an action that made her wince. The temerity she had thought was so enlivening a few minutes ago now seemed rash and ill-considered. "In fact, I probably shouldn't have had any."

"As you wish," he said, not pressing her, but he did not move her glass.

She ate less than half of what was on her plate. "I'm sorry, but I'm full; I can't manage another bite," she said contritely.

"They are generous in their servings," he said. "But you aren't compelled to do anything you wouldn't like, including finishing your entree."

"It seems so . . . wasteful. I ought to eat everything on my plate." She could feel color mount in her cheeks and she thought she should say something more. "It's wrong to leave so much behind."

"Perhaps they will let you take some of this with you," he suggested. "I'll ask the waiter, if you like."

Now she was very confused. "Would it be correct to ask? Doesn't the kitchen staff dine on the left-overs?"

"I don't know," said Cenere, who did not care what became of the unfinished dinners. "But if you want the rest of the food, you shall have it."

She shook her head, and, without meaning to, took another sip of champagne. "If you don't think I'll overstep—"

"Does it matter? The waiter is here to serve us. Let him do his job," said Cenere.

She dropped her eyes. "Whatever you think is best."

"I'll have him box up your food. You can get another evening's meal out of what's on your plate." He signaled the waiter and issued his orders. "So you see," he said to Miss McAllister as the waiter left, "it's done."

"Thank you," she said, admiring his air of authority. "I hope this isn't an imposition, but—"

"I do understand," he said, and paused for a long moment. "I hope, when I return from my mission, that you'll let me take you out again."

She hesitated, reminding herself not to read too much into this simple request, and at the same time longing to have it be a promise of something to come, and she spoke in a rush. "If you decide you'd like to see me again, I'd be delighted to see you. You could have a long way to go to find your criminal. I know you may not come back through Chicago, so I want you to know, whether or not I see you, I'll always remember this evening."

For a short while Cenere said nothing; then he said, "I don't know how long it's going to take me to find this Ragoczy." He saw Miss McAllister start at the name. "Do you know who this man is?"

"I think I may," she said carefully.

"The attorney I spoke to in London indicated as much," he said, "but your employer wasn't willing to tell me anything about him. If Ragoczy weren't such a dangerous man . . ." He let this dangle; he took care not to look at her.

"He is a client of the firm," said Miss McAllister, ignoring the uneasy sensation that niggled at her. "And he is no longer in Chicago."

Cenere turned an expression of gratitude on her. "Oh, Dorothy," he said in a manner calculated to engage all her compassion. "I don't know how to thank you for that. It makes my mission much easier, knowing he has left Chicago. I won't have to spend time here looking for him." He paused as if to weigh his options. "You probably shouldn't tell me anything more, but for as much as you have said, I am grateful. I hope it won't put you at a disadvantage with Mr. Bishop, but I must tell you: you've been very helpful."

She lowered her eyes. "I'm glad to help you, even though I probably shouldn't. I'm supposed to maintain Mr. Bishop's confidentiality, and generally I would. This is different. If Ragoczy is a dangerous criminal, as you say he is, I think it may be my duty to give you what information I—" Now that she thought about it, she began to wonder if it might not be imperative to help Cenere, if Ragoczy was an enemy of the state in Spain, and moving through America without any limitations on him.

"You know what these exiled aristocrats can be like—decadent, exploitive, treacherous," he said flatly, as if everyone shared his opinion.

Miss McAllister gave a shudder of dismay. "I wish I could tell you as much as I know. He bought a car here." That much seemed to be all right to tell him, since vehicle registration was a matter of public record.

"Did he?" Cenere said. "I assumed he was still traveling by train. But you say he has an automobile." He smiled at her. "I think you have simplified my search, and that may bring me back here sooner than I expected I would be."

"Oh," she said, trying not to look too pleased, in case his intention was not what she expected.

"Then you and I will have a wonderful time, Dorothy." He glanced at the waiter as he came up with the packaged remainder of Miss McAllister's dinner. "Do you want dessert, my dear?" he asked at his most chivalrous.

"No; I don't think I could eat another thing," she said, still amazed that he had called her *my dear*. She knew he might mean nothing by it, but it had been so long since a man had called her that, that she was stunned.

"Then will you let me take you to the movie theater? *The Petrified Forest* is playing at the Royale, and that is nearby. I must admit, I would prefer not to part just yet." He waited a long moment. "I do enjoy your company, and, I confess, so far from home, I get lonely."

She sighed, reluctant to let this magical night come to an end, but aware of her obligations. "It's a work night, and I really shouldn't, but I've wanted to see it; I understand it's wonderful. It's Humphrey Bogart and Leslie Howard . . ." With a sudden decision, she said, "Yes, please. I'd be delighted to go with you."

"Wonderful," he declared, reaching into his jacket for his wallet and pulling out a ten and a twenty. "Let me get the bill." He summoned the waiter with a snap of his fingers. "The check. Now."

The waiter offered a sour smile and went to obey the order.

While waiting for the waiter to return, Miss McAllister finished off the last of the champagne in her glass, so that something so expensive would not go to waste. She continued to try to sort out her feelings, which only confused her more completely. Finally, as Cenere sorted his change, rose, and offered his hand to help her out of the booth, she blurted, "You've been divine, Mr. Cenere."

He offered her his arm and went to collect their coats, their hats, and umbrella. Cenere paid the hatcheck girl and added a generous fifty-cent tip. He helped Miss McAllister into her coat, and then donned his own. "The storm's still going on. Do you think we should call a cab?" He had no intention of doing it, but realized he was expected to make the suggestion. "I have an umbrella." He held it up.

"Do we have time? To walk?" asked Miss McAllister, who clung to his arm. "It's only two blocks, and the weather isn't that bad. The cab would be too extravagant."

"Your wish is my command," said Cenere, and unfurled his umbrella as they stepped out of the restaurant and onto the wet sidewalk. Just as he had expected, the street was fairly empty. "Come, Dorothy," he said, putting his hand over hers in the bend of his elbow. Wind-driven sleet battered at them as they pressed close together in the shelter of the umbrella. They walked fairly slowly, Miss McAllister savoring their growing intimacy, Cenere seeking an opportunity. At last he saw a side-street, and directed her toward it. "I think this will save us half a block."

As much as she was reveling in this time alone with him, she was beginning to shiver, so she made no demur, and allowed him to turn her away from the well-lit avenue into the access alley. It was not very long; she could see the cross-street a short way ahead, the marquee of the Royale blinking its fine array of lights around the featured attraction: *Humphery BOGART Leslie HOWARD*

Bette DAVIS THE PETRIFIED FOREST. The thrill that shot through her was almost painful, and she found herself blinking back tears. She felt Cenere slow his pace, and her heart caught in her throat as she felt his arm go around her. "Oh, dear," she whispered as he took her chin between his forefinger and thumb and bent to kiss her. As she began to respond, his hand dropped to her neck.

He let go of the umbrella, and, keeping his mouth pressed to hers, he tightened his hands on her throat, strengthening his grip inexorably while her struggles diminished and ceased, until the pulse in her neck was still and she was a limp, dead weight in his embrace. Then he half-dragged, half-carried her to a cluster of garbage cans and shoved her body down behind them. That done, he retrieved his umbrella and went off into the wet, cold night.

TEXT OF A LETTER FROM LUCINDA BARNES OF THE SANTA ROSA *PRESS-DEMOCRAT* TO CARLO PIETRAGNELLI.

PRESS-DEMOCRAT

1561 MENDOCINO AVENUE

SANTA ROSA, CALIFORNIA

November 9, 1936

Carlo Pietragnelli
Pietragnelli Winery
Geyserville, California

Dear Mr. Pietragnelli,
I have in hand your check for the amount of $3.00 for continuing the notice you placed with us a week ago. As per your instructions, the text and contents are to remain the same, and the notice is to be subject to withdrawal on one-hour notice prior to press time (8:00 p.m.), the price of which is covered in the payment received. The date on each notice is to be for the immediately previous day, and the notice is to appear on the same page as the advertisement of the White Legion.

If you have any changes you wish to make, either in the notice itself or in the terms of its publication, please call me at your earliest convenience at the number at the foot of this page. Unless notified otherwise, the notice will appear as written, and as it has been run in prior editions.

My editor, Mr. Sharpe, would very much like to talk to you about the reason for this notice. I hope you will grant him an interview, for this may well be newsworthy as well as intriguing. If you are willing to answer his questions, he will set up a time within the next week convenient to you to call at your winery, or to speak to you here in Santa Rosa, as suits you best. He, too, may be reached at the number below.

Thank you for your continuing business,

Lucinda Barnes

advertising and classified listings director

∽

Santa Rosa 7-133

chapter nine

Two men in overalls were struggling with a rolled carpet, trying to position it in the living room so they could lay it out with a minimum of fuss. The older of the two was sweating in spite of the chill in the room; the younger was glaring in frustration.

"If you gentlemen would like a cup of coffee?" Rogerio offered, coming in from the kitchen carrying a tray with two good-sized ironstone cups on hefty saucers. There was a plate on the tray as well, with four doughnuts laid out on it.

"Oh, good," said the older man, glad to relinquish his burden. He looked around for something to sit on, and decided to make do with the floor. "When's the rest of the furniture coming?"

"Very likely next Monday," said Rogerio. "You have today and tomorrow to complete your work." He glanced toward the dining room and the fine Oriental carpet, which had been laid that morning. "You shouldn't need much more than an hour in here, and then the runners for the stairs and upper hall, and the carpeting in two of the bedrooms."

"It's a lot to do in two days," said the younger man.

"Aw, Stevie, don't complain. You got paying work, which is more than most of your family can say."

"My dad's going to work at Treasure Island," the young man grumped. "Building the dock for the China Clippers."

"Good thing, too. It's time he brought in some money instead of leaving it to your mother to earn everything from her nursing. Not that *that* pays enough for the five of you; if you weren't working, it'd be a lot harder on everyone. My brother's been useless for the last three years. It's good he's joining the Thirty-Niners." He chuckled at the designation given the workers building Treasure Island. "I hope he makes his fortune. Too bad he couldn't sign on with Tripp to build that hotel on that island—Wake, isn't it? Way out in the Pacific, anyway."

"You don't give him enough credit," mumbled his son. "He's not like you. Pop's been doing everything he can. But he doesn't like the union, so he has trouble getting work." He took a cup from the tray and reached for a doughnut. "Mighty good of you to do this for us; lots of people don't bother," he said to Rogerio.

"My employer believes in showing appreciation for work done," he said, and put the tray on the floor between the two men.

"Is he in?" asked the older man.

"He's upstairs," said Rogerio a bit vaguely; Saint-Germain was in the attic, turning it into his alchemical laboratory.

"Do you find him a good man to work for?" Stevie made the question a challenge. "Isn't he real Old World?"

"I have been with him half his life, which should make me somewhat Old World as well," said Rogerio, not adding that half of Saint-Germain's life covered over two thousand years. "I would not stay if he were not."

The two carpet-layers exchanged looks, and the older man nodded. "Not too many like that left these days."

"Uncle Albert's a romantic—he thinks the past was better than the future. He's saddened by progress. Says he'll never travel by airplane." Stevie met his uncle's gaze with the steadiness of long habit. "I think the future is going to be a lot better than anything we can imagine now. Look at the Bay Bridge. It opened just fine, in spite of the nay-sayers, and the party's still going on. The same will happen with the Golden Gate, you wait and see. And they're just the beginning. The country's going to turn around. FDR's on the right track, and this area is the proof. In ten years, you won't recognize this city."

"Stevie hasn't lived long enough to value the past," said Albert; their wrangle had the sound of a well-established family debate. "I tell him, he should keep an eye on Europe before he says the future is rosy. It looks pretty messy over there, if you ask me, and they're supposed to be making things so much better."

Rogerio prepared to leave the two alone. "Put the tray in the kitchen when you're through, if you would."

"Why? You going to be too busy?" Stevie asked sharply.

"No; because I'm going to be out. I have much to do today, probably almost as much as you do. As you see, this house needs a great many things, and they won't get done on their own. It's part of moving in." He paused. "Mr. Ragoczy will answer any questions you have. You needn't go upstairs to fetch him. There's a newly installed buzzer in the kitchen that will summon him if you press it." It had been put in two days ago, in anticipation of the arrival of various tradesmen.

"Where's this buzzer?" Albert inquired around a mouthful of doughnut.

"By the refrigerator. I'll just let him know I'm on my way out." He went to the stairs and climbed two floors to the attic, letting himself in after a single knock. "The dining-room carpet is done, and they are about to work on the living room. Just at present they're having coffee and something to eat. I'd check on them in an hour, if I were you; they work well, but they may need supervision. Their names are Albert and Steve, or Stevie. Albert's the uncle, Steve his nephew. Their last name is Morris. I suspect it was something more Slavic, a generation or two back." He paused, waiting for a response.

Saint-Germain looked up from his half-assembled athanor. "And where will you be, old friend?"

"I'm going out to pick up the linens I've ordered," said Rogerio. "I should be back here within two hours. I'm stopping by the drapers on my return."

"Very good," said Saint-Germain. "Do you have enough money?"

"Six hundred dollars in tens and fifties, and a pocketful of change," said Rogerio. "It should more than cover everything."

"I'd imagine so," said Saint-Germain. "But you needn't skimp; if you find something you like that you didn't anticipate, buy it. It will not be an imposition."

"Have you made another profitable investment?" Rogerio asked, only partly in jest; over the centuries, Saint-Germain had made and lost many fortunes through investing in local businesses. Some of those ventures—like Eclipse Shipping—were still paying dividends, centuries later.

"Nothing like that, or at least not yet. The transfer of funds came in from London, so there's more than enough in the accounts to last another three years and the purchase of an additional house. I've also put five thousand more into Pietragnelli's account. I don't want him running short of money just now."

"Is he buying more land?" Rogerio asked.

"No; he's employing three more men with families. That will cover their salaries—eighty to one hundred dollars a month plus room and board—for more than a year, with a little left over for emergencies." Saint-Germain achieved a hint of a smile. "He tells me he's going to need men to manage the new plantation and wants them to get started during the winter."

"He knows his business."

"As he's shown us so clearly," said Saint-Germain.

Rogerio started toward the stairs, but stopped before he closed the door. "Are you going out tonight?"

"Rowena Saxon and I are attending the opera. It's one of the Verdis: *Traviata* or *Trovatore*, or perhaps *Ballo*; I don't quite recall which. She has season tickets and wants a companion for the night, and I would be glad of some music." He volunteered nothing more, but was not entirely surprised when Rogerio had another question for him.

"Should I expect you back tonight?"

"Probably not until very late. I'll let myself in." He began to work again.

"Of course," said Rogerio, and went down to the first floor, where he saw that Albert and Steve were once again wrestling the rolled carpet. "I'll be back in two hours. Mr. Ragoczy knows you're here."

"Fine," said Albert, and shoved the carpet, trying to align with the oaken flooring.

Rogerio left the house and went to his Auburn and climbed in. The engine started promptly and Rogerio pulled away from the sidewalk, headed toward Stanyan.

It was roughly forty minutes after Rogerio left that a black Ford opera coupe pulled into the place his Auburn had vacated. A tallish, thin man got out, his hat worn low on his brow, his tie the wrong width, his suit showing the effects of years of wear; his walk was slow, revealing fatigue and perhaps an aching back. His long face had deep lines worn into it, although he was not old. He went up to the door and used the knocker. "Open up. Police." He was about to repeat himself when Steve opened the door.

"If you're police, do you have identification?" Steve asked.

The man produced a badge and a card that said he was Inspector John Smith. "I'm here to see Mr. Ragoczy."

"If you got nerve enough to say you're John Smith, I got nerve enough to let you in," said Steve, and stood aside to admit the inspector, a hard expression on his face. "Ragoczy's upstairs. I'll go let him know you're here."

Albert was just pressing the living-room carpet flat, but he rose uneasily. "Is something wrong?"

"Yes, but not to Ragoczy's discredit," said Smith. He watched Steve go into the kitchen and heard the distant buzz, followed shortly by a closing door and crisp steps descending the stair.

"Good morning," said Saint-Germain, coming down the last step into the space between the living and dining rooms. "What may I do for you—?"

He held out his badge. "Inspector John Smith," he said. "San Francisco Police Department."

Ragoczy made no comment on the name, only saying, "What may I do for you, Inspector Smith?"

"If you don't mind, I have some questions I have to ask you; I won't be here long," said Inspector Smith. "I should tell you this is in association with the break-in to your suite at the Saint Francis—part of our continuing investigation of the crime." He tightened his mouth in what might have been a smile, and deliberately loomed over Saint-Germain; this move usually made anyone cooperative. He had moved his hat farther back on his head, but did not take it off.

Saint-Germain was unimpressed; he offered Smith an urbane nod. "I think we should talk in my study," he said. "It's off the entry-hall, under the stairs." He started toward it, saying to the carpet-layers, "If you need me, knock on the door."

"Thank you, sir," said Albert, recognizing Saint-Germain's air of authority, and was ambivalent about his response; he was unused to being impressed by strangers unless they were prominent politicians or sports figures.

The study was not large, but it had a bay window that gave it plenty of light, and the window seat in the embrasure provided a place to perch among the cartons and smaller boxes that were everywhere on the floor. Indicating the window seat, Saint-Germain said, "If you'd like to sit, please do."

Smith hesitated, not wanting to give up the advantage of his height. "I'll stand, thanks."

"As you wish," said Saint-Germain, taking a seat on a large crate. "I thought you might want to give your back some relief, but if you'd prefer not to—" He saw the surprise in Smith's face. "You walk as if your back is sore, Inspector."

"Comes with the job, like sore feet," said Smith, trying to recover control of this interview. "I'm used to it."

"If you change your mind, don't hesitate to make yourself as comfortable as you can in this disorder." Saint-Germain studied Smith, his expression politely curious. "What progress have you made?"

"Not as much as I'd like," he admitted. "The thieves are still at large, and they've struck twice since they raided your rooms: once at the Sir Francis Drake and once at the Mark Hopkins. They targeted suites both times. The mayor is getting upset; with all the Bay Bridge opening celebrations going on, he doesn't want another such incident. It'd put a damper on a swell occasion." He hated to tell Saint-Germain so much, but the information had already been in the newspapers and it was likely that Saint-Germain had read some of the accounts.

"So I gather," said Saint-Germain, confirming Smith's suspicions. "You're sure they're the same perpetrators?"

"We have fingerprints at all three scenes. Thanks, by the way, for letting us take yours. It makes it easier for us in identifying the thieves'." He took a notebook from his outer jacket-pocket and thumbed through the pages. "There are three of them, or there are three sets of fingerprints, in any case—they don't belong to anyone working for the hotels, and they don't belong to any of the guests we've been able to fingerprint. The victims at the Mark left before we could fingerprint them, so we've got some questions there. They had to catch a train to Denver—it wasn't a suspicious departure. This isn't helping the hotels, having a ring of thieves breaking into their high-ticket rooms."

"I should think not," said Saint-Germain.

"I have to ask you—I know you were asked before, but you might have remembered something since you moved here—if you noticed anything out-of-place at the Saint Francis, anyone loitering in the vicinity of your suite, or the elevators?" He pulled out a pencil and prepared to add to his notes.

Saint-Germain thought carefully. "As I told Sergeant Roselli at the police station, I don't recall anything that might have been the criminals preparing their theft."

"Did you have any guests in your suite? There might be more fingerprints that we can eliminate." Smith held his pencil poised.

"I'm sorry to disappoint you, but aside from my manservant and the hotel staff, no one came into the Commodore Suite, other than myself. I haven't been in San Francisco long enough to do any real entertaining; I haven't met enough people." Saint-Germain took a long moment to consider. "I know this is not the answer you want, but it is the truth."

Smith did not respond to the last. "What about the items stolen? Have you anything to add to the list you submitted to us?"

"No; I've gone over everything, and the inventory I prepared is as complete as I can make it. There may be one or two dollars in change unaccounted for, but nothing more than that. I have a habit of leaving coins on the dresser, but I don't keep close track of them." He showed no sign of agitation in stating any of this, which surprised Smith.

"It's unusual, if you'll pardon my saying so, for a victim of theft to be so calm about it," Smith observed.

"Inspector Smith, I am an exile; my native country no longer exists, and I have moved about the world since then. I fled Spain not very many months ago, having to leave behind a flourishing airplane business and two good-sized bank accounts, which were taken over by the insurrectionists. The losses I have had here—while I would rather not have had them—are what you would call small potatoes compared to what I lost in Spain." He spoke flatly, adding, "Fortunately, most of my money is in the bank."

"Yes," said Smith. "We checked with Bank of America and found out that you're quite well-off."

"Luckily. It has not always been thus," said Saint-Germain, his memories of hardships long past intruding.

"So you don't have anything more you want to tell me? Nothing has occurred to you since you left the hotel?" Smith put an edge in his voice; this usually brought a quick response from the people he questioned.

Saint-Germain gave him an affable smile. "If not for your own sake, for mine, Inspector: do sit down. There's no reason for you to stand, and it makes good sense to spare yourself discomfort." He indicated the window seat. "Please."

Reluctantly Smith did as Saint-Germain asked. Little as he wanted to admit it, his back was aching more intrusively. Sighing, he settled himself on the upholstered bench; Saint-Germain was right: this felt much better. "All right. Now let me ask a few more questions."

"I'm at your disposal," said Saint-Germain, a hint of amusement in his dark eyes. "I will do what I can to assist you in your inquiries."

"What, if anything, did you tell the hotel staff about any valuables you had in your room?" Now that he heard himself, he thought he sounded foolish.

"I said nothing; I don't make a habit of imparting such information to strangers, let alone those who might be tempted by such knowledge," said Saint-Germain. "I also found no indication that anyone had searched the room prior to the robbery."

"That was going to be my next question," said Smith. "How can you be sure?"

"Because I have lived in many places far more dangerous than this, and I have become accustomed to taking precautions," said Saint-Germain. "My manservant will tell you the same thing, if you wish to ask him."

"And may I? ask him?" Smith turned the page of his notebook.

"Of course, as soon as he returns. He's out just now, attending to certain errands." Saint-Germain regarded Smith. "If you like, you are welcome to wait for him, or you can arrange a time to come back, whichever suits you best."

"I have to get back," said Smith. "Let me just finish up with this."

"As you wish," said Saint-Germain, completely unhurried.

"Thanks," said Smith dryly. "I'd like to review what you were doing while the suite was being robbed."

"Again?" Saint-Germain said. "All right. I had come here, to this house, anticipating purchasing it. We—my manservant, Mr. Rogers, and I—drove here. We were in this house about forty-five minutes or as much as an hour. I didn't bother to look at my watch." He stared at the opposite wall as if hoping to find a message there that would jog his memory. "No doubt someone on this street noticed us arrive and depart. If you talk to the neighbors, someone can probably give you accurate times on the length of our stay; that's my suggestion, in any event." He glanced at Smith. "If the thieves were watching us, I wasn't aware of it. They took a real chance. We might have returned much sooner."

"The other thefts took place while the victims were at dinner. I understand you went out in the early evening." He looked at his notes. "The thieves might have assumed you'd gone out to dine, and went in as soon as you were gone." That scenario certainly fit the other two break-ins. It was also a time the hotel staffs tended not to be in the guest rooms.

"We left the hotel around six-thirty, and we returned to the Saint Francis not quite two hours later." He paused. "I do remember saying to Mr. Rogers that I felt as if I had been watched. I had seen nothing, but . . ."

"I know what it is to get those impressions," said Smith. "Cops have to pay attention to those sensations or we get into trouble. Why would you—?"

"I left Spain the very day their Civil War broke out," said Saint-Germain. "If I had not paid attention to similar sensibilities, I would now be in a Spanish prison, or a grave."

"That would do it," Smith allowed.

"I was inclined to discount the feelings, thinking they were left over from Spain," Saint-Germain went on. "I am disinclined to mention them now, because I still reckon they are more connected with Spain than anything I have experienced in America. But Mr. Rogers may mention my remark to you, and I would just as soon bring it up myself. For what worth it may be to you, I did have an intuition that I and my manservant were being observed, but by whom, or why, or even if, I cannot tell you now." This was true enough in its way, but also intended to lessen the skepticism Smith demonstrated.

"Something like that could make a man jumpy," Smith said, closing his notebook. "Well, Mr. Ragoczy, that should do it for the time being."

"I'm sorry I couldn't be of more help," said Saint-Germain.

"Oh, one more thing," said Smith in what he hoped was an artless last thought.

"What would that be, Inspector Smith?" Saint-Germain asked with unruffled good-nature.

"It would be that the bank said you're a nobleman, with a title and all that. Do you think this robbery could have anything to do with that?" He levered himself to his feet, resigning himself to the pain in his back.

"I don't see how," Saint-Germain said.

"Okay," said Smith, and started toward the door.

"You don't think it has anything to do with the theft, do you, Inspector?" Saint-Germain asked as he rose.

"I don't know what I think," said Smith. "I don't know enough yet." He opened the door and stepped out into the entry-hall. "Thanks for seeing me, Mr. Ragoczy."

"You're welcome, Inspector Smith. I'll tell Mr. Rogers you'll be back to talk to him later on today." He was about to open the front door when Smith turned to the carpet-layers, who were now almost finished with their work in the living room.

"Did Mr. Rogers go out earlier?" The inquiry was deceptively mild, as if it was nothing more than an afterthought.

"Yes, sir," said Albert. "He'll be back in an hour or so, he said."

Smith nodded. "Thanks." He looked directly at Saint-Germain, trying to use his height against the smaller man, without success. "I'll call back before five."

"I'll make sure he's available, Inspector," said Saint-Germain, holding the door open for him.

"I'd appreciate that, Mr. Ragoczy . . ." He hesitated. "Just what is your title?"

There had been many of them over the millennia, but Saint-Germain answered promptly, with the one he had used most frequently for the last thousand years. "Count. Of Saint-Germain. Not that it means anything in this country."

"Um. Just so," said Smith, and stalked off to his Ford.

Saint-Germain watched him drive away; he closed the door, his demeanor thoughtful. He saw the two carpet-layers looking at him, and he said, "The police are investigating a robbery that took place in my hotel suite."

"Un-huh," said Steve.

"I requested that I be kept up-to-date on their progress," said Saint-Germain, "and I've offered to help them in any way I can," he added, looking at Steve.

"Cops!" said Steve, then looked away, as if he had revealed too much.

Saint-Germain stepped into the living room and looked down at the carpet. "You've done an excellent job." He started back toward the stairs. "Will you be working on these next?"

"Yes, sir," said Albert. "The runner is on the next floor, isn't it?"

"Yes. Next to the newel post at the top of the flight," said Saint-Germain.

"We'll take care of it, sir," said Albert with a warning glance at his nephew.

"I have no doubt," said Saint-Germain, and went up the stairs, all the way to the attic, where Rogerio found him almost two hours later.

"I'm sorry I took so long," said Rogerio as he shut the door behind him.

"No matter. I trust you made good progress?" His athanor was complete and he had set up two trestle tables. There were half-a-dozen boxes set under the tables. "It's times like these that I miss my red lacquer chest."

"It came through a great deal," said Rogerio.

"So it did, in wear and time." Saint-Germain cocked his head. "An Inspector Smith called earlier today; he had follow-up questions to ask, concerning the ransacking of the suite. He'll be back later this afternoon, to talk with you."

"Have they made any progress?" Rogerio asked, hearing the wary note in Saint-Germain's voice.

"It doesn't appear so," said Saint-Germain. "I wonder if they suspect the theft was arranged, possibly as an insurance fraud or something of the sort. There have been two more such thefts, as the papers reported."

"It's a pity that we had to give them our fingerprints," said Rogerio.

"Yes, it is," said Saint-Germain. "But refusal to provide them would have created more doubts than letting them take them. We must hope they will not keep them on file too long."

"So we must," Rogerio agreed.

"This compulsion to gather information on all manner of people—it could lead to problems in the future." Saint-Germain knelt to open a crate labeled *alembics*. "At least my waxwork is well-hidden."

"And you have an explanation for having it," Rogerio added.

"Yes. But I would prefer not to have to use it." Saint-Germain carefully removed the largest of the three alembics and put it on the table.

Rogerio watched him. "What bothers you?"

"I wish I could say," Saint-Germain told him slowly. "I continue to have this sense of being watched, of being pursued."

"Then be very careful," said Rogerio, who had come to trust Saint-Germain's intuition in their long association.

"I plan to be," said Saint-Germain. "Be circumspect yourself." He straightened up. "How is the carpeting coming?"

Recognizing this as the end of their discussion, Rogerio said, "They are almost through with the stairs. I'm going to prepare a tea for them—coffee and sandwiches—and I'll make sure they're paid in full. If they still return tomorrow, our carpeting should be finished by tomorrow night."

"Very good. Then the furniture can be delivered next Monday. I'll call the shops and make arrangements." Saint-Germain bent to retrieve another, smaller alembic. "In another day or two, I should be ready to work here."

"Then I'll leave you to your work, unless you need anything more?" Rogerio was almost to the door.

"One thing: will you let me know when Inspector Smith returns? I want to know what his secondary purpose is, if we can learn it without difficulty."

"Are you certain there is a secondary purpose?" Rogerio asked.

"No," Saint-Germain said.

"All right," said Rogerio with a slight smile. He opened the door and let himself out of the attic. He had to step over Steve on the lower stairs, and as he did, he asked, "When do you think you'll be done?"

"Half-an-hour, an hour—why?" he asked.

"Don't talk to him like that," Albert warned, going on to Rogerio. "You know how young men are these days. They see their chances gone before they have an opportunity of their own."

"Not without good cause," Steve grunted, using carpet-tacks to keep secure the runner to the stairs. The sound of his hammer punctuated his words.

"No, not without cause," said Rogerio, and got off the stairs, bound for the kitchen, where he put the coffeepot on the stove to percolate, then took a loaf of bread from the refrigerator and began to slice it for sandwiches. He put together an egg salad for filling, and cut off a few slices of summer sausage. By the time the coffee was ready, he had two sandwiches made and was preparing two more. Working swiftly, he set out a tray for the men, put out the food, coffee, sausage, cream, and sugar, then carried this into the dining room, calling out, "It's almost four. I have a tea—or a coffee—for you."

Albert looked up from his labors, letting out a long breath. "You're a very considerate man, Mr. Rogers, no doubt about that."

"My employer is," said Rogerio. "I'm sorry the dining table hasn't been delivered, and that there's no place for you to sit, but I hope you'll be willing to sit on the floor again." He set the tray down. "I'll come back for this in twenty minutes."

"Thanks," said Steve as if he hated to make such a concession to good manners. "Once we finish up, we'll get our equipment out of your way."

"No rush," said Rogerio, going back toward the kitchen to take the freshly killed and dressed chicken out of the refrigerator. This would be his supper; he took the only knife from the drawer by the stove and began to cut up the bird, then expertly sliced meat from the bones to eat. Being a ghoul, he ate only raw meat, but he disliked dining like a savage, so he sat at the small table and used a fork and knife. He took his time, and by the time he was done, he saw from the clock on the wall it was time to reclaim the tray.

"Doesn't it ever bother you?" Steve asked Rogerio when he had finished the last drop of his coffee and set the mug on the tray.

"Doesn't what bother me?" Rogerio asked.

"Always being at the beck and call of your boss," said Steve, ignoring the angry glance from his uncle.

"Why should that bother me?" Rogerio asked.

"Steve," Albert said in a warning voice.

Steve plunged ahead. "Because no time is your own. You can't go home at the end of the day, and do whatever you like. That's going to change in the future: you'll see."

Rogerio contemplated the earnest young man, and said in a level way, "It may change, but I will not." He considered his next words carefully. "I find it no imposition to serve le Comte. I have done it for a very long time, and I am used to it. I do not feel confined, for he is a very reasonable man. If I wished to find another place to live, he would make that possible: he has done so in the past. At present it suits him and me to share this house. At another time, in another place, it will be otherwise."

"And it saves him money," said Steve as if this clinched his opinion.

"It may do; I don't know, nor do I care," said Rogerio.

"I'll bet he does," said Steve. "Rich men always care."

"Steven Albert Morris, you'll hold your tongue if you know what's good for you." Albert turned an apologetic gaze on Rogerio. "I'm sorry. Ever since he started earning a hundred bucks a month, he's been acting as if he were Mr. GotRocks. Not that it isn't good wages, but it's not real money, is it?"

"It's as real as any," said Rogerio. "But if you mean it's a vast amount, no, it isn't."

Albert seemed relieved. "There. I told you."

"I'm making as much as Pop's doing at Treasure Island," said Steve, a bit defiantly. "And there's going to be more opportunity for men like me. It's going to be a better time ahead."

Before his nephew could launch into his favorite diatribe, Albert stood up. "We've got work to do yet, Stevie, and the sooner we get it done, the sooner we get to leave." He looked over his shoulder toward the stairs. "We'll be back in the morning, at eight. You don't have to worry about that."

"Then I won't," said Rogerio, taking the tray into the kitchen. He set the dishes on the sink-side counter to be washed, and disposed of the chicken-bones as well as the left-over bits of crusts from the sandwiches into the garbage pail out on the enclosed rear porch; the sky was almost dark and the wind had begun to pick up. He had tied an apron around his waist and was filling the sink with hot water and Ivory flakes when he heard the door-knocker, and a few moments later, Albert called out, "That policeman's back. He wants to talk to you." Rogerio turned off the water, wiped his hands, and went to meet Inspector Smith.

TEXT OF A LETTER FROM DRUZE SVINY IN WINNIPEG, MANITOBA, CANADA, TO FERENC RAGOCZY, CARE OF OSCAR KING, KING LOWENTHAL TAYLOR & FROST, SAN FRANCISCO, CALIFORNIA.

Compton House
658 Selkirk Road
Suites 4–9
Winnipeg, Manitoba, Canada
24 November, 1936

Ferenc Ragoczy
le Comte de Saint-Germain
c/o Oscar King
King Lowenthal Taylor & Frost
630 Kearny Street
San Francisco, California, USA

My dear Comte,

I trust this finds you well and flourishing, in spite of your recent misadventures in Spain. I cannot thank you enough for making it possible for me to emigrate to Canada. This has proven to be the best move of my life. I have never enjoyed myself as much as I have these last several weeks. Manitoba Chemicals, Ltd. is a wonderful company, and I have rarely felt so good about my work since I left Prague.

When I received the offer of employment that brought me here, I accepted it as a kind of last opportunity. To be frank, its distance from Spain was more important to me than the work that was going on here. I accepted the job because I was desperate. The terms were unbelievably favorable, the salary well beyond anything I expected, and I thought it would provide me the chance to recoup some of the losses I had sustained in Córdoba. This was not the best frame of mind to have to begin a new position, but it was mine.

You will be astonished to learn that I am delighted with Winnipeg, and Canada. It is a very genial city, well-designed and filled with interesting persons and places. The Canadians I have met have been hospitable and well-mannered, willing to extend a welcome to me no matter what my reason for arriving on their shores may be. I am purchasing a small house—not out of necessity, but out of choice, that is not far from the laboratory where I have been installed. The neighborhood is pleasant, the neighbors are kindly, and I have now two cats and a dog to keep me company. I cannot tell you how much I like the way I live. Even the prospect of a Canadian winter does not frighten me, although they tell me that three years ago, the conditions were as bad as anyone here can remember. I will hope that I will not have to sustain such a harsh season, but if I do, it is a small price to pay for all the benefits I have gained in coming here.

I have recently heard from my cousin in Brno, and the word from there is grave indeed. Say what they will about the Berlin Olympic Games and all the good-will Hitler is supposed to be showing the world (and I think Hitler's slighting of that American Negro runner was disgraceful), the Germans are readying for war, and unless the rest of Europe moves now to stop them, they will be running rampant again before the decade is quite over. I wish I had some good reason to contradict him, but even at this distance, I can feel the winds rising and hear the clarions sounding. My cousin told me that six of his colleagues are trying to get permission to go to America while they are able to, not wanting to be caught up once again in the toils of war. I cannot say that I blame them for wanting to leave; in fact, I hope to convince my cousin to join them in their move. So little of our family is left that I would be greatly saddened to see him go the way of so many of the others.

Of course, no one wants war, and everyone is terrified that it could all begin again. So many are willing to look the other way in the name of peace. But one must look: look at Italy, and all they're doing in Ethiopia. Calling deadly bombs blooming red flowers! What sort of sophistry is that? And the least said about Spain, the better. Mola and Franco are turning the entire country into a slaughter-house, and the loyalists are taking a beating that beggars description that no one outside of the country wants to admit. There are some idealists who have gone there to support the loyalists, socialists, and communists, and no one wonders that they are as much cannon-fodder as any peasant, and are important more to journalists than generals. But I fear that in seeking to maintain the illusion of peace, the cost of war may become monstrous before any resolution is possible.

It may be wrong of me, but I don't think there is much I can do to ease the hostility in the world. Not even a newspaper columnist can do much to move the public, no matter what one hears. So I have resigned myself to my happiness in this place, and in this work, all the while aware that it may be more ironic than unfettered. Still, I am able to do what I do best in a place that values my work and treats me far more generously than I have been treated by anyone but you. I hope in time I may find some way to thank you

*for making this possible for me. Manitoba Chemicals is a fine business, and
those who work here are very aware of their good fortune; I am first among
their number, and I hope it will always be so.*

 With utmost gratitude and my pledge of good-will,

 Sincerely yours,

    Druze Sviny

chapter 10

Do you have any plans for Christmas?" Rowena asked Saint-Germain as
she came back into her studio with a wrapped package in her hands. She
had changed from her puce-wool suit into a hostess-gown of golden-umber velvet, and had put on the tiger's-eye frog earrings he had made for her so many years
ago. It was a rainy December evening, and they had spent part of the day at the
Palace of the Legion of Honor, taking in the latest exhibits and avoiding the
downpour outside. "Or are you going to do something at Clarendon Court?"

"No," said Saint-Germain, mildly amused. "It isn't a holiday I usually celebrate, unless not doing so would generate suspicions I would rather not have to
sustain." He was meticulous in his three-piece black wool suit, his white silk shirt,
and burgundy tie; his hat and overcoat had been laid over the back of the settee
at the other end of the double room. "There have been times I have been very
diligent about observing it." The sardonic humor in his face vanished as swiftly
as it had appeared. He accepted the package and held a chair for her.

Rowena sat down in the fashionably low, rounded chair, tucking one leg up
under her. "Would you like to come here? For Christmas, I mean? I usually have
a tree and a proper dinner—not that you care about such things—but I would
be glad of the company. The friends I have often celebrated with are not available this year, and I know it will seem empty without some other guests. It used
not to bother me, spending the holidays alone, but now that I am over fifty, it
weighs on me. At least tell me you'll think about it." The light from her floor-
lamp cast its soft glow upon her face.

"I can do more than that." Saint-Germain turned on the table-lamp beside him, and sat down immediately opposite to her and put the package on his lap. "If you would like my company at Christmas, it's yours for as much of the holiday as you want." He said nothing about having been born at the dark of the year, on the day now reckoned as Christmas Eve; marking his birth after forty centuries struck him as hubris at the least, absurdity at the most.

"Thank you," she said, and held out her hand. As he took it, she went on, "I haven't known how to bring this up. I couldn't seem to find the right moment . . ." She looked to him for help.

"Christmas?" he asked, not following her thought.

"No," she said, smiling a bit self-consciously. "I had a call two days ago. From a policeman. An Inspector John Smith. Is there something I should know about?"

A flicker of disquiet went through Saint-Germain, but no trace of it showed outwardly. "No, I don't think so. He's the one assigned to the matter of my suite being burgled."

"So he said. But I can't think why he'd want to talk to me," she prompted, hoping he would have answers she had been unable to get from Smith.

"Nor I, on the face of it," he admitted. "I don't like that he bothered you."

"He wanted to know all manner of things about you: how long I'd known you, where we had met, your situation in the world, those you might know in the city." She pulled her hand back from his. "I was not pleased that he was so suspicious about you."

Saint-Germain considered this, becoming more alarmed. "How very odd."

"Isn't it?" she agreed. "I assured him that I had known you more than a quarter century, and that you had done diplomatic service in England. I was right to tell him, wasn't I?"

"Of course," he said.

"He was a bit surprised that you should have been given such a mission so young," she went on as if confessing a fault. "It took me aback, for I realized how he had assumed—quite naturally—that you must have been in your twenties then, given how you appear now."

"That is a bit awkward," Saint-Germain said, hoping to reassure her.

"I said you were older than you looked and left it at that. It seemed the only safe thing to do. But I thought I should tell you, in case you have to answer any more questions." She joined her hands over her knee. "I don't know why something so . . . so natural as years should bother me as it does. They didn't used to. But talking with the inspector brought it all into sharp relief. I never thought the years would weigh on me, but I've found out differently. It's not as if I've been a young woman recently, and my youth is slipping away, and I mourn its passing; it's been gone for more than a decade, and I usually think good riddance. So that's not it."

"It may be you feel that life is passing, and you are losing your chances," said Saint-Germain as kindly as he could. "That can be a far greater loss than youth."

"Does that ever happen to you?" she asked.

"Oh, yes. Constantly," said Saint-Germain with a wry smile. "I have become accustomed to it, but it still feels as if I'm standing in a cold wind that blows everything past me."

She shivered a little. "A powerful image," she said softly.

"I'd prefer not to dwell on it," he said lightly. "Don't let it trouble you."

"But I have to consider these things, if I am going to become like you when I die; I had better learn what I am going to have to deal with. You told me about your life, back in Amsterdam, but I haven't thought much about that since." She leaned forward.

"There are ways you can circumvent coming to my life, if that's what you prefer," he said, unable to keep the sorrow from his dark eyes as a sudden image of Tulsi Kil formed in his mind.

"I know; you told me: fire, severing the spine, prolonged exposure to sunlight. I am considering my options." She held out her hand to him.

Their fingers touched this time with the intensity of the blue heart of a flame. "Whatever you decide, I will honor it."

Rowena met his gaze with her own. "Thank you."

Her gratitude surprised him. "You seem to think I would impose my will upon you. Why would I do such a thing?"

"I may decide to reject your life," she said, as if this must be obvious. "You might see that as a deliberate slight."

"If you do not want to be a vampire, then you would do well to reject coming to my life," he said, and when he saw her confusion, he added, "I have known four women who came to my life and discovered it wasn't what they wished. Two of them died the True Death by their own hands, one by the hands of others, and one decided the Blood Bond wasn't what she wanted and cut off all contact with me and my kind." He smoothed the lapel of his suit with his free hand, using the motion to cover his need to think. "I have no desire to cause you anguish, nor the wish to compel you to act against your inclinations."

For several seconds she remained still, and then she said, "I have no idea what your life is like, not really, though I've been thinking about it a lot. I know it must be unlike anything I've known before, and that makes me uncertain. I realized I can't have an audition for vampirism, and that means that I must continue to debate with myself; how can I know if I want it, that life?" She pulled her hand back. "I know about the native earth, and the problems with sunshine and running water, and the lack of reflection, and the other matters you described.

But that's not the same thing as knowing—really *knowing*—what it is to be nourished solely by intimacy and blood."

"I wish I could describe it adequately, but I've never hit upon the words to depict the experience. I suspect it is one of those things that cannot be expressed in words." He regarded her, his eyes filled with compassion.

"But how then am I to know if it is a life I want for myself? How can I decide without knowing?" Rowena shook her head. "You mustn't be troubled by this; I am inclined to ruminate aloud—it comes from living alone."

"Is Clara in the house? Should I expect her to announce dinner, or supper?" Saint-Germain asked. "If she's going to—"

"No." She laughed a bit unsteadily. "I'm not so heedless as that. She's left for the day. I give her half-days for two weeks before Christmas, and the week between Christmas and New Year off. She has shopping to do and arrangements to make for her three children, who visit twice a year. She's been planning for their arrival for more than a week. She'll pick them up at the train station in two days, and I won't see Clara until after the New Year, after she's sent them back to their grandparents in Michigan." She was soothed by speaking of these very ordinary things; her edginess faded, and she relaxed. "So you and I will have time together—as much as you like."

"Thank you," he said, watching her. "I'm looking forward to it." He paid no attention to the expanse of windows in which the room was reflected; he had long since ceased to be disoriented by his missing reflection, although he was comforted by the realization that she could not see the windows behind her.

She got up and went to the cabinet to Saint-Germain's right. Opening the carved doors, she took out a bottle of brandy and a bubble-snifter and set them down on the wide lip beneath the doors. "If you don't mind, I'm going to have a drink." The color of her velvet hostess-gown almost exactly matched the shine of the brandy. "I've been wondering about my life a lot of late."

"As you like; drink what pleases you," said Saint-Germain, watching her, his eyes contemplative. "You know, Rowena, you have much to be proud of."

"Why do you say that?" she asked, stopped in the task of pouring the fine Mattei brandy.

"I think you often underestimate your accomplishments because you have not achieved all you have set out to do," he said at his most gentle.

"Well, you're right about that—I haven't; nowhere near," she said, judiciously gauging the amount of brandy in the snifter; she put the cap back on the bottle and returned it to the cabinet, closing the carved doors before lifting the snifter. "You don't know how much I haven't done."

"No; only you know that," said Saint-Germain. "All I have to go by is what you have done, and you have done a great deal."

"No, I haven't, not really; I should have done much more," she said. "I wish I hadn't wasted so much time." She sat down again, and again tucked one leg under her, the snifter resting in her hand. "Every year that passes, I can't help but compare what I've done to what I had intended to do. It seems to me the gap widens a little with every passing year. It troubles me that I haven't accomplished all I have set out to do. I could have done so much more if I hadn't spent so long at meaningless events that everyone said were important but turned out to be nothing more than a gathering of gossips. Thank God I was never in that group that takes tea at the Saint Francis, or it would be much worse." She gave a slow sigh. "I don't mean that it's wrong to have a social life, but so often that means—"

"No one can work every hour of every day, or night; all creatures need rest, or exhaustion sets in and stops all work, and thought," said Saint-Germain. He waited a long moment, giving her a chance to speak; when she said nothing, he went on, "If you had attempted to soldier on at all costs, you would probably have produced fewer works, not more, and you probably would have liked them less. Insight cannot be forced, Rowena, and it cannot thrive without stimulation, which includes reflection." He rose and went to stand behind her, his small, beautiful hands resting on her shoulders.

"That may be true, but I know I could have done so much more." She sounded mournful; her face grew more somber. "I keep thinking about it."

"You speak as if you are going to stop all work tomorrow, or run out of subjects to sketch and paint," he told her.

She turned and lifted her head so she could look directly at him. "I don't plan to, but it is possible. And what then?"

"The conundrum of all living things—and the undead. None of us know when it will end, or how." He bent down and softly kissed the nape of her neck. "Any of my blood could die the True Death at any time, just as you breathing people might perish. But I must assume—and so must you—that it isn't apt to be today."

Rowena sipped her brandy. "But it is growing closer, the end of life."

"For all living things," said Saint-Germain. "And all of us as well."

"Doesn't that bother you?" She sipped again, then put her snifter down on the end-table. "The knowing you'll die?"

"But I already have died, once. I was executed and left on a dung-heap." It still bothered him slightly to recall that horrible afternoon four thousand years ago, and how he had behaved for five centuries thereafter.

She made a face. "How can you talk about it like that?"

"How do you mean?" he asked as he half-sat on the back of her chair.

"You know, so calmly," she said.

"It happened a long time in the past," he said. "I cannot cling to it as much as I once wished to because it has vanished. If I searched for it, I would hardly be able to find the ruins. My people are long-dead, and they left the Carpathians many centuries before they disappeared from the earth. Some went east and some went west, but they abandoned Transylvania about three thousand years ago." They had not wholly gone from the West, for their name, in a reshaped form, still echoed in Tuscany. "It would be foolish of me to yearn for those times. They were harsh, as all men were in those times, and I was cut of the same cloth." He touched her hair, smoothing the tailored waves carefully. "You would not have liked that age."

"You aren't like that now," she said, aware of something in his manner that convinced her he was telling her the truth.

"No, not now. I learned, in time. That is the one thing those of my blood usually have: time." He bent to kiss the top of her head.

"Do you regret being what you are?" She had another sip of brandy.

"No. Once, a very long time ago, I did, so profoundly that it truly altered the course of my existence." He thought back to his early years in the Temple of Imhotep, and Hesentaton, frightfully burned and dying in agony. "And I have done things since I regret, at least in hindsight. I certainly regret I wasn't able to save Laisha; that failure still haunts me. There was so much promise in that child, and I miss her and all she might have become." He felt more than saw her frown of uncertainty. "No, Rowena, she was not of my blood. I couldn't have done that to her. She was my child, as much as if I had fathered her myself."

"But if she had wanted—" Rowena blurted out.

He shook his head. "No. I would not do this to my child; it's an unconscionable notion. It would appall me to attempt something so . . . contemptible." He lifted her face so she could see him. "What you and I share isn't for a father—or mother—and child. You have no reason to fear that there is an iota of incest in what is between you and me." The image of Csimenae and Aulutis came to mind; he winced.

"What is it?" She was troubled by his sudden change of expression.

"Another thing I regret. I'll tell you about it, someday. Not tonight."

"Why not?" she asked. "You don't suppose I'd be jealous, do you?"

He laughed shortly. "No. There is nothing of which to be jealous." He put his hand on her shoulder again. "It's not that; I am chagrined by what happened."

"I find it hard to imagine you chagrined by much of anything," said Rowena.

"Then you have an idealized impression of me." He was at once complimented and vexed. "No one can live a decade—let alone millennia—without having at least a few moments of mortification. If you think vampires are immune from being disconcerted, you have been taken in by film and Stoker."

"Oh, that's right. You saw my drawing of the Borgo Pass for *Dracula*, didn't you?" She put her hand over his. "Talk about chagrin."

"I told you I liked how well you had caught the spirit of the book." He could feel the tension in her shoulders. "How can that embarrass you?"

She pressed his fingers. "I thought at the time you were being kind."

"Had I done that, the way you imply, I would have said it was accurate to the place as well as the book, which—"

"—it wasn't," she finished for him. "I do remember that. So I absolve you of trying to sweeten a bitter pill."

"Thank you," he said solemnly.

"You shouldn't thank me," she said, turning in her chair so that her back was against an arm and she was staring up into his face. "I should thank you."

"For what reason?" he wanted to know.

"For taking me seriously when no one else did," she said. "You and my grandfather were the only ones."

"There was you," said Saint-Germain, his voice deep and stirring, like the base note of a 'cello.

She shook her head. "Not always, especially at first. Oh, I said I was certain, but in my heart I had many doubts, about the quality of what I had done, let alone what I could do. Occasionally I still do." She gazed dreamily across the studio, seeing events of twenty years ago. "When I first arrived here, I was sure I was doing the right thing, leaving England and living as an independent woman on my own, but then I knew my grandfather would support me, and so I never had to put myself on the line as so many others did, which gave me an advantage of a sort."

"Did that worry you?" Saint-Germain asked, perceiving it had.

"Not at first. It was hard enough just being a woman entering the world of artists. But over the ensuing years, my doubts reasserted themselves." She pressed her lips together.

"How much did they trouble you?" He spoke steadily, no accusation in his question.

Rowena took a long moment to answer. "I began to feel ashamed of my good fortune. I wondered if I ought to throw everything to the winds, go off on my own, and try to survive on my art, to prove myself, to earn my place." She ducked her head. "I might have done it if a woman I met here, another artist, who lived as much by her wits as her brush, wasn't killed by a man who was supposed to be helping her arrange for a show at a small gallery. I knew it could have been me, in her place."

Saint-Germain stroked her hand. "That must have been upsetting."

"Terrifying is more like it; it brought back everything that happened with von

Wolgast," said Rowena with a self-deprecatory chuckle. "That's the first time I went up the coast. I told myself it was to paint, but it was also to get away, to think. The first time I went with a guide, and we rode from the rail-stop outside of Ukiah. The road was hardly more than a goat-track, and it took two days to get to the coast. We both had a horse and a pack-mule, and we stopped at farmhouses along the way until we reached the old coach-road that follows the Noyo River; in many places it was little more than two wide ruts along the river-track. There was a train for the loggers, but it took no passengers. I think now we should have taken the coach-road all the way, but I wanted to see unspoiled territory." She shrugged. "Most of it had been logged over, and there were what they call stump-farms all through the hills." Picking up her snifter again, she swirled the brandy in it. "I don't know—I think I was trying to prove something to myself."

"And did you?"

"Who knows? I thought at the time I had, but now?" She sipped the brandy, taking her time, and at last she said, "I went back in '26, and in '28, and by then there were real roads, graded, some paved, and even a few hotels along the way. I could drive all the way without too much difficulty. For a while I considered buying a house up in Albion or Little River or Mendocino or Casper, but I realized I would be too much of an oddity in those towns, among those loggers and fishermen and berry-farmers, and I didn't think I could stand to be that much of a peculiarity." She set the snifter aside again, and looked up at him. "I'm glad we had an early dinner. Well, *I* had an early dinner, in any case."

"Why is that?" He remained very still.

"Oh, because . . . because I didn't want to have to cook tonight. You've spared me that."

He could sense this was not the real reason, but kept his reservations to himself. "Have you been back to the north coast again recently?"

"Three years ago; I went as far as Eureka, to see their Victorian houses. They have some very fine ones, though it is hard times there as it is everywhere else." She bit her lower lip. "There was trouble brewing—labor organizers trying to get the loggers and mill-workers to unionize. It's strange: most of northern California has been heavily union since before the Great War, and southern California not; but logging and lumber have lagged behind, and the struggles in some areas are becoming entrenched. I found the conflict interesting, I'm ashamed to say, and I followed it with some diligence for over a week. I did some of my best sketches of the loggers working on the Eel River until one of the foremen told me to get out of the area, and to keep my pictures out of the press if I knew what was good for me. They didn't want anyone making note of what was going on there. I left that day. I still have the sketches, but I haven't done anything more with them."

"Do you plan to?" Saint-Germain asked her, his compassion almost too much for her.

"I don't know," she said curtly. "It's one of the many things I intend to do, but haven't done yet; no specific plans yet."

"Perhaps you're getting ready to do those paintings," he suggested. "Many perceptions take time to become clear."

"That's the attraction of your life, of course," she said, impatiently pinching burgeoning tears from her eyes. "Having the time to do more."

"But this troubles you," Saint-Germain said.

"Yes. An artist's style is always distinctive, if he or she's any kind of an artist, and I'm afraid if I came to your life, I would eventually have to stop painting, or risk being found out utterly." Now that she had actually said it, she felt a burden lift from her.

Saint-Germain gave a single nod. "Of course. It is a problem."

"Do you have any solution?" She sounded precariously near weeping.

"I can tell you what I have done, and what others of my blood have done," he said. "I don't know if that would be sufficient."

"All right; other than travel, what do you do?" she queried.

"Yes, travel, that's the heart of it, and change. There are other forms of art you might pursue, and other applications of your talents," he said. "For myself, to make that less cumbersome, I have a number of identities established in various places."

"That is becoming more difficult to do," said Rowena.

"Yes, and it takes a bit more caution, but it can be done. It takes time and a little thought, and the opportunity to . . . slip through the cracks, as it were." He offered her a single-sided smile. "One of my blood always creates the impression she has a niece interested in following in her footsteps. She's an archeologist, and that is a very small world; those in the profession tend to know each other by reputation, and most of them have closer contact than that. So far she has been able to continue her work, supposedly from aunt to niece, but she has said it isn't easy." He could not convince himself that Madelaine de Montalia's methods would work for Rowena. "Others have had their own ways to deal with their lives."

"And none of them have ever been found out?" The angle of her chin suggested she would not believe a denial.

"All of us have, from time to time, and paid the price for the lapse," said Saint-Germain, recalling many of his own mishaps.

Rowena sighed. "This is what makes me hesitate. I don't know how I could manage to live as you and your kind must do. What I want to do is paint. I would love to have decades and decades more in which to do it, but I don't know if I can . . . I wouldn't be young again, would I? When I became a vampire."

"Circling back to this, Rowena?" he inquired, ironic and saddened at once. "Very well. You would stay the age you were when you died, as it is for all of us. Vampires do age, but very, very slowly, and some of it is the changes that happen around us, more than within us. I was a tall man in my breathing days—today I am short, although my height is unchanged. I was thirty-two or -three when I was killed, and now I appear to be in my mid-forties, or so I'm told. Whether I have changed, or the look of age has been pushed back, I cannot say. I haven't seen my face since I became a vampire, although I have seen portraits, such as yours." He had a distant memory of his features reflected in a mirror of polished copper, as foreign now as if they belonged to an utter stranger.

"That does alarm me, being the age of one's death for hundreds and hundreds and hundreds of years," Rowena admitted. "But what can I hope for, a woman in my fifties, getting older every hour? How long will I be a woman whom men will seek? What if I don't die until I'm seventy-five or more? How will I manage in the world once I become a vampire? I'm going to ask you about this again, you know, until I work it out."

Saint-Germain contemplated her pensively. "I can only tell you what others have done. What you decide to do is up to you."

She sighed. "You are the most provoking man! I want you to lay out a strategy for me, and you won't do it."

"Because I can't," he said. "To tell you otherwise would debase you."

"I know; I am glad of it, inconvenient as your scruples may be," she conceded, her confidence increasing. "And that's why I haven't been able to make up my mind. I haven't yet decided what I must do." She looked into his eyes, happiness softening her expression. "But I am sure that I want you to stay with me this evening."

He took her hands in his. "As long as you want me, I am greatly favored, and I thank you."

"You have nothing to thank me for," she said.

"But I do," he said mellifluously. "You have given me the gift of your self, and there is nothing more estimable in all the world. If only I could show you how highly I value you." His dark, enigmatic eyes rested on her.

"Another notion peculiar to vampires, all this valuing?" she proposed, enticing and defensive at once.

"Not peculiar to us, no, but necessary to us." He lifted her hand to his lips, kissing the back and then the palm; her mercurial state of mind did not trouble him, for he was aware of her growing passion, and her increasing yearning for coalescence.

"You are perplexing," she said, attempting to sort out her many emotions; she moved in the chair with unconscious sensuality, graceful and voluptuous.

"But I don't want to give up what you provide me; you're too sensitive to me for me to reject you—it would be like shutting off a part of myself."

"That is the nature of the Blood Bond," he said.

"You've tried to explain that to me before, and I still don't entirely understand it. Perhaps I can't so long as I'm one of the living." She pulled closer to him, as if willing herself to absorb his understanding by touch alone. "I may not decide to come to your life, but I don't want to turn you away from my life, or my bed. For now, I want you to continue to be my lover." The bluntness of her statement surprised her, and she blinked in confusion. "There should be a better way to say all this, but I—"

He bent to kiss her mouth, saying as she ended their contact, "It was a wonderful way to tell me. I don't mind if fondness isn't wrapped in respectable phrases."

She touched his leg that rested on the rolled back of her chair. "I am so happy to have this time with you. I was beginning to think that there was nothing left but work and the long, darkening path toward death. You restore my aspiration as the psychiatrist could only struggle to do, on his terms, not mine."

Saint-Germain laughed softly. "Hope is as necessary to life as blood: believe this."

She moved in her chair, rising onto her knees so she could press herself against him. "Then I hope we have a wonderful night tonight."

He took her face in his hands and kissed her tenderly, taking all the time they needed to feel the kiss to its full extent, to let it work its magic on them both. Slowly he slid his hands down her neck and over her body, his touch light and stirring. "You are sweet as honey and wine, nourishing as bread," he murmured.

"My blood?" she asked, intrigued.

"No, you, Rowena; you." He bent to kiss her a second time, and felt her arousal as he moved back from her.

She took a deep, unsteady breath. "Then let me be both to you." As she rose to her feet, she put her hands on his chest. "My room is ready, the sheets freshly changed. We have until seven-thirty tomorrow morning to ourselves."

His eyes were lambent, his voice was stirring. "You are the riches of my living, Rowena; never think otherwise." He ran his fingers down her face, his touch light and evocative. "How much you offer in your self."

"Come with me," she said, catching his hand in hers and drawing him after her toward the stairs leading to the second floor. "I've wanted to lie with you since we left Lincoln Park. And so I will."

Saint-Germain followed her up the stairs and, as they reached the top, stopped as she swung around to embrace him. "Nothing is urgent, Rowena. We have all night." Their kiss went on for some time, growing increasingly complex. When she finally took a step back, he brushed her lip with the end of his finger. "Why rush?"

"Because I'm afraid it will all be gone too soon, not just you, but everything—my work, my life, all of it; I'll be an old woman with nothing to show for my life but a nice house and a generous bank account to leave my nephews, and no one will know or care that I lived and painted," she said, starting toward her bedroom. "That policeman being here reminded me that you, because of what you are, cannot stay anywhere for very long."

"No more than twenty years at most," he said, following her through the door. "And often far fewer years than that."

"That's not what I mean, and you know it," she said somberly, stopping at the side of her bed and confronting him. "If matters become too difficult, or too perilous, you will depart, possibly with nothing more than a telephone call, if that. Then I'll have a letter from Venezuela, or Hong Kong, or Timbuktu, and that will be the end of it." Her expression dared him to contract her. "Well? Can you tell me it wouldn't happen?"

"No," he said calmly. "But it is unlikely." He paused. "And I doubt I would go to Timbuktu. I have spent very little time in Africa."

Momentarily distracted, she asked, "Why?" her curiosity outstripping her need.

"I have found it useful to be able to fit into the population around me: in Africa that is impossible."

"But you have traveled to the Orient," she pointed out.

"So have many from the Occident. I am an oddity but not an obvious one." He watched her consider this.

"There have been white men in Africa," she reminded them.

"Most of them exploiters, slavers and the like," he added with an air of contempt. "I want nothing to do with that pernicious market."

"But you have had slaves," she said, sensing that this was crucial to understanding him. "Haven't you?"

"Not since Heliogabalus was Caesar, and I always provided manumission for any slaves I owned. The Romans approved of that, at least for a time. Slaves were allowed under law to buy their freedom unless their slavery was a punishment under the law." He loosened his tie. "I have been a slave, more than once. I cannot put another human being into that despicable state."

She felt a rush of sympathy for him, and her ardor returned at full intensity. "You would not have anyone be subject to you that way, would you?"

"No," he said, remembering Tishtry and Kosrozd, and Nicoris.

"But you are bound to me for as long as you live? Through the Blood Bond." She stared into his dark eyes, wanting to sound the depths of him.

"I am, as I am to everyone who has knowingly had my love," he said, taking care to make this last clear without inflicting pain.

"I don't care about them—at least, I don't care tonight," she declared, and began to unfasten her hostess-gown with a pragmatic efficiency that was enticing. "For whatever time we have, I have you knowingly and I intend to make the most of it. Who knows when we'll meet again, or under what circumstances?"

He sat down on the opposite side of her bed. "I hope this isn't an act of desperation, Rowena."

"And if it is, what then?" She was in her underwear now, and starting to shiver for the room was chilly.

"It will be of little value to you and me," he said. "If you want me, let it be for love, or desire, or comfort, but not for desperation."

She regarded him thoughtfully. "I am not desperate," she said at last. "I am lonely. And so are you."

"Loneliness isn't the reason I love you," he told her as he removed his jacket.

"But it probably is for me, at least part of it," she said, and reached around herself to unfasten her brassiere.

"Let me do that for you," Saint-Germain offered, and wrapped his arms around her in order to work the hooks. The undergarment came away in his hands; he set it on the nightstand under the lamp.

She looked down at her body, and managed a little sigh. "I wish I were as young as when we first met."

"Why?" he asked softly as he kissed her shoulder.

"Twenty-five years of wear-and-tear," she said, indicating her breasts. "They were firmer before. All of me was."

"It is only a quarter century," said Saint-Germain, going on contritely. "For me, that is a very, very short time."

She stared at him, struck by his words. "I suppose it is."

He reached out and touched her breast. "Your skin is wonderfully soft."

"Oh," she breathed as the first quivering thrill promised greater rapture to come. She wriggled in an effort to get out of her garter-belt, stockings, and panties. "Clothes can be such a nuisance."

"So they can," he agreed, all the while caressing her breast.

"You're distracting me," she warned him, no hint of complaint about her remark. "Oh, that's wonderful."

"If you don't mind, I don't," he said, continuing what he was doing.

"How good that feels," she murmured as she finally struggled out of the last of her underclothes. "There. More."

Saint-Germain bent to kiss her nipples, taking the time to lavish attention on them both while he slowly, deliciously, slid his hands along her flanks. He was unhurried, relishing her heightened arousal. "What would you like, Rowena?"

"I want my bones to melt," she sighed.

"How would you like to have it happen?" He increased his ministrations, feeling her flesh mold itself to the movement of his hands.

"That's . . . lovely," she sighed, and opened her body more fully to him.

He increased his attentions to her breasts again while his explorations of her body continued.

"What more?"

"Anything," she whispered. "Anything you want."

"What you want is what I want," he reminded her, gently fondling her thighs, gradually easing them open.

"You've been with me enough to know," she urged him in an under-voice. "I don't want to have to choose."

He stroked the soft folds between her legs, then moved so that his tongue could take the place of his fingers; she sighed as he found the bud of her clitoris. As her craving for fulfillment began to gather in her body, he gradually made his way up her body to her throat, tantalizing and igniting her fervency to its utmost, and finally joining her in the sublime moment of her fulfillment, and for that ineffable time, knowing the whole of her, and embracing the entirety of her self as fully as he held her body.

"Oh, God," she whispered in fading ecstasy as she moved away from him at last, then reached out for him again. "Stay with me."

"All through the night," Saint-Germain promised as he drew her close to him once more, cradling her in his arms as she drifted off into jubilant sleep.

TEXT OF A LETTER FROM CENERE IN DENVER TO COLONEL MORALES IN MADRID; SENT BY AIRMAIL.

> *Denver Train Station*
> *Denver, Colorado, USA*
> *21 December, 1936*

> *Colonel Andreas Morales*
> *22, Calle Real*
> *Madrid, Spain*
> *My dear Colonel,*

> *I have only a short time to write as my train begins boarding in thirty minutes and leaves in forty-five, so you will pardon me if this is necessarily brief.*
> *I am on my way to San Francisco in California. Through the inadvertent good offices of a secretary in the Chicago firm that has been managing some*

of Saint-Germain's legal affairs, I learned he had purchased an automobile and had struck out for parts unknown. I was stymied when I discovered this, but I was then informed that he would have to re-register his auto in whichever state he settled. I have been in touch with the Department of Motor Vehicles for the state of Illinois and I have learned that his auto was sold in San Francisco, and so I am going there to learn as much as I can of his present whereabouts. He must have taken US Route 40 and gone as far west as it runs. I see no reason to duplicate his feat, and so the train will suffice to carry me to where he has been and, if luck is with me, may still be. I have the name of his attorneys in that city and I will call upon them shortly after my arrival. No doubt I will find a way to persuade someone at the firm to provide me the information I seek.

The secretary in Chicago need not cause you any anxiety: she will not be revealing anything to anyone. I felt it was best if she not be available to identify me. If I must, I will deal with others who provide me information in the same way. I am also making plans for the lamentable accident that will end Saint-Germain's life and spare you the trouble of trying him in absentia. As you say, there would be many difficulties in keeping his company without at least the appearance of respect for the processes of law.

I will be in San Francisco in less than two days, and I will begin my work at once. You need have no fear that I will waste time in sight-seeing or other tourist entertainments. Perhaps if I finish my work quickly, I'll permit myself an amusement of my own devising, but that will not be anything that need concern you. I am committed to completing your assignment—as irregular as it may be—and you may rest assured that I will not falter in it: this is just the sort of mission I most enjoy, and that, as well as my promise, ensures I will accomplish all I have undertaken on your behalf. I am assuming you will continue to support what I do in your name, and will continue to fund my search.

To enable me to do this, have $2,000 waiting for me at the Crocker Bank in San Francisco so I may recommence the work I am doing for you. Do not try to bargain with me or I will make known what has been done in your name, which will cause you more than embarrassment. $2,000 may be a fair amount of money, but for what it is buying you, it is more than reasonable, for it ensures my silence as well as the results you seek.

Yours to command,

Cenere

part three

FERENC RAGOCZY, LE COMTE DE SAINT-GERMAIN

7, Avenida del Templo Viejo
Cuzco, Peru
29 December, 1936

Ferenc Ragoczy
le Comte de Saint-Germain
c/o the Saint Francis Hotel
Union Square
San Francisco, California USA

My most-dear Comte,
At last I have an address that will find you! Since you left Spain I have been beside myself, wondering where you had gone. Thank you for your letter, which arrived a week ago, delayed for reasons I cannot fathom, that told me finally where you were. I have been able to sense that you were alive, but nothing more than that, which, I will tell you, is not reassuring, for I have been imagining such things as would make your hair stand on end. But now I know you are in San Francisco, and I know what a splendid place it is. If you have found a house to buy, as you say you are going to do, you must provide me that address as soon as you have it to give. I will correspond with you as much as I am able, but here in Cuzco, with a dig underway, I may not write as frequently as I would like.

Cuzco is a most fascinating place, as you said it would be, although it is very much changed from the time you were here—that was three hundred years ago, or nearly that, as I recall. The old Incan buildings are not as intact as they were then, and we have had a challenge, trying to reconstruct what they were like before the Spaniards arrived. Our efforts are not universally approved. There are some in this city who would be delighted to have our team gone from Cuzco and all of Peru. They believe that archeological studies will lead to social unrest. I cannot follow their logic on that account, but I do believe the descendants of the Incas have not received the regard their lineage would command had they been Europeans and not New World Indians, whom many of the Spaniards still consider ignorant savages. Ignorant savages, indeed! I'd use that phrase more to describe the Conquistadores than the civilizations they conquered. Not that I believe the Incas were models of humanism, for that seems very unlikely, given some of the things we have found. Rather, they lacked gunpowder and horses, not reason and society. Do not let me get on this soap-box or this letter will weigh more than the air-mail limits, and I will have to send it as air freight for ruinous amounts.

The Spanish Civil War has repercussions even here, some greater than I would have expected, others far less so. The war is heavily reported in the newspapers and the state radio station carries regular reports about it. I should think that you were wise to leave Spain and Europe behind for a while. I agree that the turmoil is likely to spread and the price paid by the people there will be high. The Great War was unresolved when the Armistice was signed, and the problems that caused it are still festering. You have said you think Spain is just the beginning, and that in time all Europe will be caught in the conflagration of war, and I am increasingly persuaded that you are right, and no matter how much I would like to think otherwise, I am preparing myself for the fighting to begin. Some of the results of the Spanish conflict may yet interfere with my work here and make it prudent for me to leave Cuzco, although I hope this won't come to pass, or will be postponed until I have another dig arranged.

In that light, I am concerned for Montalia. Provence might not be the most volatile place in France, but it is ideal for fighting, and I would hate to lose my home—my native earth—to the predations of war. Unfortunately (or it may be a fortunate thing), I am going to be in South America for several more years, and should war erupt, I will be in no position to go to defend my home. Now I know how you must feel as Romania, Turkey, Hungary, and Austria all lay claim to your Carpathian birthplace, and I sympathize with you as well as empathize.

How are you finding the United States? I have been told their Great Depression is a terrible thing, and that many people are suffering. Is that your understanding, or do you believe that President Roosevelt is doing some good with his many public agencies? Have you seen where I used to live, or is it all quite changed? The house on Franklin Street probably did not fare well in the 1906 earthquake and fire. I am curious about how matters are progressing in that country, because I recall the turmoil in Europe a decade ago, when Germany's currency became more worthless than the paper it was printed on, and I would like to think that Herr Hitler has not found the only solution to economic disarray, and a less drastic solution to the problems of a monetary crisis is possible. I hope the United States can achieve that and, perhaps in the process, show Europe another path to follow. A terrible thing for a Frenchwoman to say, but true, nonetheless.

I wish I could tell you how much I miss you, but as I try to find the words, they fail me. Suffice it to say that were I still breathing, I would miss you as I would miss air in my lungs. That does not sound as romantic as I intend it, but suffice it to say that it is heart-felt and as genuine as any more sentimental expression would be. I long for you, and I know it would be folly to be together. Since you kissed me in Berlin, I have accepted that, but I wish with all my being that it were not so—that those of our blood could be lovers as we love the living. Such hopes are futile, I know, but I cannot rid myself of them.

Enough of maundering; there is nothing to be done. I thank you again for all you have told me about your years in this city so many years ago. You have helped me immeasurably in my work, and I only wish I could give you credit for your information when I publish my papers on this dig. I will not, for, as you say, that would lead to questions neither of us would like to have to answer; I have concocted the tale that I came upon the journal of a European explorer who lived in Cuzco while I was researching another subject in a private library. Its contents spurred me to come to Cuzco and search out those places described in the journal. So far no one has doubted my story. Other, far more unlikely scenarios have brought all manner of academic fortune-hunters to this place. It is always possible that such a journal actually does exist in a private collection somewhere in Europe, and so my speculation is not so far removed from reality that it becomes fuel for gossip.

Among those accompanying me on this dig are two men from the University of Wisconsin at Madison. One is an archeologist, the other is a history professor specializing in Spanish colonialism, and between them, they have been very helpful. The archeologist is a former farm-boy, athletic and energetic. The historian is bookish with a droll sense of humor. They are good company, clever and hardworking, and they are eager to explore the dig. I have never heard either one complain about the weather, the food, or the many difficulties we have had with the authorities here. Both of them have a small grant to do this work, which they are in hourly dread of losing, for it is possible that they could be stranded here. Their university has had to cut many of its programs for financial reasons, and they know their work here might be seen as an unnecessary expenditure of funds already in short supply. I have informed them that if it is necessary, my aunt will buy them return tickets to the United States. I can afford such a gesture, particularly since it is well-known that this aunt is a primary sponsor of this dig, along with the Division of Antiquities of the Peruvian government. This aunt of mine has been very useful: she is now a recluse, living at Monbussy-sur-Marne; it was she who inspired me to follow in her footsteps as an archeologist.

*My most precious Saint-Germain, it is growing late and those in this
rented house are finally fast asleep. I am going to visit one of them in his
sleep, and I ought to be about it shortly, for I have more work to do tonight.
It will sustain me, but it does not provide the nourishment of the soul that I
have known with you, before I came to this life, and my two Americans
since; with you in the United States, I am doubly reminded of how much I
miss you—and them. I hope you are doing well in San Francisco. As I have
said already, I accept it is nothing like the city I visited eighty years ago, but
I trust you have found it beautifully situated and charming. I do hope all
those bridges will not ruin the lovely bay, though I comprehend the need for
them now that the area is more settled than when I was there. You tell me
that there are more than half-a-million people in the whole of the region, a
figure I find staggering. I think Proust may be right—that the past is a foreign
country where we can no longer go.*

*Know that this comes with my enduring love and my truly undying (if
unfulfilled) passion,*

Your Madelaine

chapter one

The blare of ships' and cars' horns greeted midnight in noisy cacophony, to usher in 1937. All along the Embarcadero sailors and fishermen formed impromptu parades, while in the fine hotels around Union Square and atop Nob Hill, dance bands played "Auld Lang Syne," the saxophones deliberately slightly flat, to make it easier for the singers on the dance-floor. At the Cliff House, diners threw lit sparklers into the Pacific Ocean and hoped for better times ahead.

In his fine three-story house on upper Broadway, Oscar King put another Strauss waltz on the phonograph and urged his guests to dance some more. He was holding another bottle of champagne in his hands, worrying at the cork guard in an attempt to get it open without sending the cork flying across the room. His concentration was less keen than it had been an hour ago, but he was a very determined man, and he kept at his self-imposed chore while his wife helped the cook set out roast turkey and ham for the midnight buffet. Most of the guests were in formal clothes, the women in gowns and jewels, the men in tuxedos, and the house was still decked out in its Christmas finery, making for a gala evening. Between the cigarettes and cigars smoked for the occasion, the air had a fine, filmy haze of smoke in it.

"Why don't you let me do that?" Saint-Germain suggested as he came up to his host. He was very grand tonight, even among such well-dressed guests, in tails with his sash and Order of Saint Stephan of Hungary blazing on it, and ruby studs in his pin-tucked shirt.

"I can . . . manage," King insisted, working the cork with his thumbs.

"You don't have to pry the cork that way. If you give it a half-twist, it will come out more easily," Saint-Germain assured him.

"Damned if I'll resort to that," King muttered, and finally levered the cork loose enough to pop. "Get a glass! It's foaming."

Saint-Germain obeyed, holding the glass to catch the spume that welled from the bottle. As the flow diminished, he set the glass aside and reached for another. "You're entertaining lavishly, Oscar," he observed.

"I can afford it. 1936 was good to me; I did twenty-two thousand in fees— not that I'm boasting—and I want to encourage 1937 along the same lines." He put the champagne bottle down. "I'll take that round when the record's finished."

"I'm sure you'll get plenty of grateful guests who'll be glad of a refill," said Saint-Germain, looking at the five couples attempting the Viennese waltz in a room not quite large enough for it.

"But not you," King said, his eyes narrowing. "I've been watching you. No drink and no food that I've noticed."

Saint-Germain nodded apologetically. "I'm sorry. It's nothing against you. I suffer from a tedious complaint that limits my diet severely."

"Diabetes?" King guessed. "You should have a little something to eat. Diabetics shouldn't starve themselves."

"Not diabetes. Something inherited." That sounded too personal for most people to inquire further, but Saint-Germain could see the spark of curiosity in King's bright-green eyes. "It is an affliction limited to those of my blood."

"Oh. Hemophilia, or something like that," said King knowingly.

"Something like that," Saint-Germain concurred, and poured more champagne into the two glasses, for the foam had subsided.

"I suppose that's why you're not married—you don't want to pass it on?" King was just drunk enough to pursue matters he would normally leave alone, but not so drunk that he could not make fairly sensible conversation.

"But I have been married," said Saint-Germain. "My wife was Russian. She didn't live long enough to have children. She was killed while we were trying to get out. There was an English ship waiting for us." He did not add that Xenya had married him on the order of Ivan Grosny, and that their escape had taken place in 1585, and that the ship, the *Phoenix*, was waiting at the port now called Archangel, but was then Novo-Kholmogory.

"Oh," said King, almost soberly. "I'm sorry, Ragoczy. I had no idea."

"It was many years ago," Saint-Germain said truthfully, and let King think what he would.

"Sorry to bring up something so unpleasant. It's New Year's. You should be positive, optimistic. That's why we toast the New Year, to bring us all good luck and good times." King forced jollity back into his voice. "Your companion, Miss Saxon? is having a good time. You should take a page from her book."

"Excellent advice," said Saint-Germain.

King winked. "I'll bill you."

"Do all attorneys jest about fees?" Saint-Germain asked, a sardonic lift to his brow.

"Most have to. I do it for fun." He laid his finger beside his reddened nose. "Sugar for a bitter pill."

"I'll keep that in mind," said Saint-Germain, and strolled away toward the dining room, where the buffet had been set out. Aside from the ham and turkey, there were two rice dishes, one with mushrooms and scallions, one with raisins and chestnuts; an aspic mold with crab and shrimp; a tureen of corn chowder; a large bowl of black-eyed peas—a dish that Luella King served every year for good luck; a platter of celery stalks stuffed with pâté and cream cheese; a bowl of mixed olives; sourdough French bread and a basket of dinner rolls, both with sticks of butter beside them; a deep dish of spaghetti and meatballs; a relish platter with three kinds of pickles, radish-rosettes, and toasted onions; a platter of deviled eggs; and a two-tiered display of petit fours and babas-au-rhum. An impressive feast, Saint-Germain thought, but one for which Luella King had made every dime count. The only excess for the evening was the champagne. Behind him, the phonograph stopped playing.

The cook and Mrs. King made a last survey of the table, and then, as the cook retired to the kitchen, Luella King rang a crystal dinner-bell to summon her guests to their midnight meal. "Plates and silver are on the left. Go around and help yourselves. If you want to sit down properly, there are coffee tables set up in the den."

Saint-Germain moved away from the table and slipped out the side door into the hallway. He went in the direction of the study.

Obediently the fourteen other guests began to file in, some of them showing the signs of overindulgence already. Millard Taylor, King's oldest partner, a white-haired man of sixty-two, was very ruddy, with bits of cigarette-ash clinging to the front of his tuxedo, and he slurred his words when he talked, much to the chagrin of his wife, who constantly excused his misbehavior to anyone who would listen. Rowena was next-to-last in line, Oscar King coming behind her.

"I wanted to tell you how glad we are that Ragoczy brought you tonight," he said, doing his hostly duty.

"Thank you for having me," said Rowena, equally good-mannered. "It's been a lovely evening so far."

"And the food's going to be great," King enthused.

"It really looks wonderful. And it smells delicious," she said, going along with him.

"I understand you've known Ragoczy a long time?" This was more than simple pre-dinner small talk, but he tried to make it seem so.

"We met some time ago, in England. At my parents' estate, in fact. He came down for the weekend," she said.

"Was he traveling with his wife?" King asked artlessly.

"No," she answered, doing her best to be unaffected. "He was on a mission for Czar Nicholas, as I recall. It wasn't a family journey." She picked up a plate and silverware.

"Oh," said King. "He must have been pretty young?"

"I didn't think so at the time, but you know how easily young people imbue persons in authority with age. I assumed at the time he must be . . . oh, at least thirty." She began to serve herself from the buffet, selecting carefully, and in smaller quantities than many of the guests had done.

"You don't need to be shy. Have all you want," King urged. "It's New Year's."

"That's what I'm doing. I've found, as I've got older, that I mustn't overeat in the late evening if I want to get any sleep at night." She smiled at him, to be sure he wouldn't read an oblique insult into her remarks.

"I know how that can be," he said, beginning to fill his plate. "But I'm making an exception tonight. As I've said, it's New Year's."

Rowena nodded to show she'd heard and took a stalk of pâté-stuffed celery. "Your wife has certainly done a splendid job, Mr. King."

"We're not in the office. You may call me Oscar if you like." He grinned, more avuncular than flirtatious, though he and Rowena were roughly the same age. "Luella is a fine woman, and she is a first-rate manager. I don't know what I'd do without her. She's been the best thing that ever happened to me."

"And a good thing that you know it," said Rowena. "So many men take their wives for granted these days."

"Not I," boasted King. "I tell everyone that Luella is a jewel."

"I'm sure she appreciates it," said Rowena.

King was taking another deviled egg and trying to find room for it on his plate. "She's a swell gal, my Luella. Finest woman ever to leave Alabama."

"How good of you to say it," Rowena told him as she stepped away from the table and threaded her way through some of the others to go—not too obviously, she hoped—in search of Saint-Germain. As she reached the corridor, she went down it toward the open door of what she supposed was the study and found him in the corner in an overstuffed chair, beside the big, square Stromberg-Carlson radio, his head bent as he listened to the news reports. The three other couples sitting at the card tables paid no attention to him, preferring their own conversation. Approaching him, Rowena asked, "Anything interesting?"

"I wish the radio here covered European events. All I have been able to find out is that there has been a fire in Seattle and that it was put out quickly." He dropped his head and continued to listen for a short while, then said, "No, nothing. I suppose I'll have to look at the newspapers in the morning, and hope they've given some space to European news."

"What about the *Voce del Popolo* or the *California Demokrat?*" Rowena suggested, referring to San Francisco's Italian- and German-language newspapers.

"You're right. I'll pick them up day after tomorrow," Saint-Germain said, turning off the radio. "Have I told you that you look smashing tonight?"

"Yes, but you can tell me again," she said, turning slightly to show off her mauve velvet long gown with the elbow-length bell-sleeves and draped cowl neckline. She wore this with a double-strand choker necklace of black pearls she had inherited from her mother, and a pillow-cut pink zircon ring set in white gold.

"You do look smashing," he said.

"Thank you," she responded. "Is there a place I can sit down in this room, or must we go out and find another spot?"

"It might be best to go out," he said, indicating the way so she could precede him. "Turn to the right down the hall."

"You're a perfect escort," she said lightly, and was about to pass along the hallway when she almost ran into Millard Taylor, who took up a stance in the middle of the corridor, glaring at the diamond star-burst on Saint-Germain's sash.

"Piece of nonsense, if you ask me," he declared, a bit too loudly.

"I beg your pardon?" Saint-Germain said politely.

"That ostentatious display on that red sash you wear. Who do you think you are?" He was swaying a little, as if his choler buffeted at him like a wind.

"Does my Order offend you, Mr. Taylor?" Saint-Germain asked mildly, regarding the taller man with an air of indulgence reserved for obstreperous teenagers and drunks.

"Order!" he scoffed.

"Of Saint Stephan of Hungary. It's given for service to the crown." He took a step forward, paying little heed to the warning glance Rowena shot him.

"Paste and rhinestones," said Taylor conclusively. "We don't have trumpery geegaws like that in America. No titles, no nobles."

"And it has suited your country very well," Saint-Germain soothed. "If I were an American, it wouldn't be appropriate for me to wear this, but since I'm not . . ." He bowed slightly. "If you will excuse me?"

"Excuse you? Ex-*cuse* you?" Taylor was shouting now, his face turning a dark plum color as he lurched a bit closer to Saint-Germain.

Saint-Germain lowered his voice, and although his stance did not change, there was an air of authority about him that he had not displayed until now. "Mr. Taylor, you are not sober, and so I will not protest what you are saying. You are also my host's partner, so it would not be appropriate for me to reprove you, particularly not here, on this happy occasion. I see that inebriation has made you uncouth, but it is pardonable, under the circumstances. If you will stand aside, I will consider this forgotten."

Taylor seemed about to bluster more, but something in Saint-Germain's steady gaze took the wind out of his sails, and he mumbled something about ill-mannered foreigners, and continued past Saint-Germain toward the open door to the bathroom.

"That was unpleasant," Rowena whispered as she and Saint-Germain entered the living room.

"He's drunk and wanted to show off," said Saint-Germain, indicating the sofa on the far side of the room.

"A fine way of doing it," said Rowena, shaking her head. "Some men ought not to drink, and he's probably one of them."

"Probably," said Saint-Germain, dismissing the matter. "Aside from that little display, have you been enjoying yourself?"

"Oh, yes, very much," said Rowena. "I hadn't thought this would be so much fun."

"I knew you had your doubts," Saint-Germain said, a trace of amusement in his eyes.

"So had you, as I recall," she countered. "But after I monopolized you for Christmas, it was the least I could do—and accepting an invitation to a party is hardly an imposition." She maneuvered her plate so that it rested fairly securely on the arm of the chair, and prepared to eat her supper.

"Would you like some more champagne?" Saint-Germain offered.

"Not just now, thank you. I don't want to start the New Year with a throbbing head, which I will do if I drink much more." She cut a wedge of the ham. "It has a pineapple glaze."

"Is that good?" he asked.

"It's not bad," she said carefully.

Saint-Germain was chuckling as Oscar King came up to him. "There you are." He had loosened his tie and was starting to look tired. "I just remembered something I should have told you earlier. A fellow came by my office yesterday afternoon, said he was a business associate of yours from Spain and wanted to look you up. I wasn't going to see him, but my secretary said he was most insistent, and I think he scared her a little. Since I understood you had left Europe in some haste, and that your situation in Spain is still unresolved, I said that I could do nothing more than forward a message to you, but he declined, asking only if you were still in the city. I'm afraid I wasn't quite honest with him and I said I didn't know." He noticed that Saint-Germain was frowning. "Is something the matter?"

"I don't know," said Saint-Germain. "I can't think of anyone I worked with in Spain who would have reason to look for me here who doesn't know I'm here already." He paused. "Can you describe the man to me?"

"Tall, lean, dark brown hair going grey, ears flat to the head. Not bad-looking, but something a bit . . . serpentine about him. That's all I noticed. He had an accent, but it didn't sound Spanish to me." He shrugged. "Well?"

"He doesn't sound familiar," Saint-Germain said after a brief moment of consideration. "No, I can't recall knowing anyone like that. Did he happen to mention how he knew me?"

King took nearly a minute to think. "I believe he said he had met a woman in Córdoba, at your plant. She had a foreign name. I can't recall it."

This troubled Saint-Germain more than all the rest, but he maintained his calm. "Strange."

"It is, isn't it?" said King. "He put me off, but I can't say quite why."

"Stranger still," said Saint-Germain. "It's disconcerting, at least, to have some unknown man from Europe asking about me here. I trust you'll do everything to keep him at bay?"

"I should think so!" King looked indignant, as if about to address a jury.

"He may be from the new government—assuming it actually prevails and remains in power. He probably has papers for me to sign," Saint-Germain said, though he doubted this inwardly. "If he comes back, ask him to leave the papers with you, along with an address to which they should be sent, and I'll review them with you."

"And what if he's not?" Rowena asked in what she thought of as her sensible English voice.

"Yes, she's got something there. What if that isn't his intention?" King asked, looking a bit worried.

"Then you and I will have to come up with some manner of plan to deal with him. For the time being, let's extend him the benefit of the doubt."

"Or rope enough to hang him," said King in grim satisfaction.

Saint-Germain gave a single nod. "Thank you for dealing with him with such dispatch. I hope you weren't put out by anything he said or did."

"No," said King, a bit reserved in his answer. "But let me make it plain: there was something about him—nothing obvious, but I had the feeling he could be trouble. Maybe it was just that serpentine head, but he struck an off-note with me."

"Did he leave a name?" Saint-Germain asked, aware that Rowena had stopped eating and was staring at him in dawning alarm.

"Something foreign, Latin-sounding. Just a second. I'll recall it." He looked up at the ceiling and tapped his fingers on his shirt-points. "Yes. I have it now: Cenere. I remember because I asked him if that was Italian for ash and he said it was." He achieved a little smile. "I've had Italian clients, in the past, and of course I know Mayor Rossi. In the process, I've picked up a bit of the language. You know how it is."

"Yes," said Saint-Germain. "I do."

King waited, as if hoping for a more complete response from Saint-Germain. "Do you know anyone named Cenere?"

"No," said Saint-Germain. "I don't recollect anyone by that name."

"Curiouser and curiouser," said Rowena, her face averted but her body no longer relaxed.

"That it is," said King. "Well, I'll tell my secretary that if he calls again she's to collect any papers he may have for you, and you'll return them by mail. Do you think that will do?"

"It sounds like just the thing," said Saint-Germain, infusing his tone with an ease he no longer felt. "Thank you, Oscar."

"Welcome," said King, and coughed once. "I'm sorry about Taylor. They just told me what happened. He's got a tendency to be belligerent when he drinks."

"You have nothing to apologize for, Oscar. I don't take the accusation of anyone gone in drink seriously." Saint-Germain cocked his head. "If anyone deserves an apology, it's his wife. The poor woman was beside herself."

"Oh, yes. Ivy always takes Millard's behavior to heart. You can't imagine the problems she had with him during Prohibition. Luella is talking to her now in the kitchen. Poor woman's in tears." King sounded slightly embarrassed by this revelation, but he went on, "Millard's probably going to want to lie down in a bit, and I'll send him up to one of the guest rooms. He won't bother anyone."

Saint-Germain's fine brows drew together. "Please tell his wife she has no reason to be upset on my account, if you don't mind."

"I'll wait awhile on that," King said. "Right now, it's least said, soonest mended, if you know what I mean."

Saint-Germain was sure it meant that King wanted nothing more to do with this contretemps tonight, so he let it go. "As you think best."

"Thanks," said King with more relief than seemed warranted. "I'm going to go open another bottle of champagne." Saying that, he toddled off.

"Good Lord, that poor man. How mortifying for him," Rowena said as soon as King was out of earshot.

"Mortifying: how?" Saint-Germain asked sharply.

"To have to deal with such a partner. What a liability to the firm; they must wish they had some way to be rid of him. And having the partner's wife weeping in the kitchen. Dreadful! He's probably wishing Taylor in the Polish salt mines, or Outer Mongolia. And you needn't tell me about either place, if you please. I presume they're both unpleasant." Rowena resumed her meal, but slowly, her attention on other things than food.

"The man's a trial, no doubt, and the Kings and the firm are dealing with him as best they can," said Saint-Germain, his frown returning as his thoughts took another turn. "What do you make of this Cenere?"

"More to the point," she said, "what do *you* make of him?"

"I don't know," he said, his voice lowered and sounding troubled.

"It could be just as you said—someone trying to get you to sign over your aircraft assembly plant to the government." She caught her lower lip in her teeth.

"No, I don't think so, either," he said when she stopped. "I'm beginning to wonder if I'm as safe here as I thought I would be."

"You don't think he intends you any harm, do you? Why should he?" She looked shocked, and had a brief but stunning memory of von Wolgast in her flat in Amsterdam, his vial of pitchblende in his hand.

"I don't know, and until I do, I will err on the side of caution." He gave her a reassuring smile.

"That's prudent," she said dryly.

"Yes," he said, mischief in his voice. "I think so, too."

She laughed and shook her head, and let the matter go for the time being. But later that night, as he drove her home in his Pierce-Arrow, she brought it up again. "Why not meet with the man? This Cenere?" she suggested, not quite seriously.

Saint-Germain gave a small, exasperated sigh. "Because, Rowena, if this man means me harm, the less I have to do with him the better. I'm glad he wasn't told I'm still in San Francisco, or that I have a house on Clarendon Court. That could be an invitation to trouble." He approached the intersection with Octavia carefully, narrowly avoiding a careening Chevrolet that came barreling down Broadway behind them, filled with young men whooping at the night.

"Do you think you're being overly circumspect?" She wanted him to dismiss her question as ridiculous, to reassure her that she was too timorous.

But he answered very seriously, "I hope so. But I can't afford to put it to the test. There's too much at stake."

"You're no help," she said, almost hitting his arm with her small, beaded handbag. "I want you to reassure me."

"I don't want you to get dragged into anything on my account. Once was enough." He stopped at the light on Van Ness, and watched the cross-traffic with interest.

"How long?" she asked after a short silence.

"How long?" he echoed.

"How long will you need before you decide how much of a risk Cenere represents?" She had opened her purse to search for her house-key. "I don't want to fight with you, and I don't want to be frightened."

"Neither do I," he said, turning onto Hyde Street. Behind them a church-bell rang four. "I didn't intend to bring you home so late."

"It's New Year's," said Rowena fatalistically.

"And January first is a holiday, isn't it?" He noticed two couples on the sidewalk, making their way unsteadily toward the corner. "Just as well, considering."

"You don't approve?" she asked, daring him to speak against the revelers.

"I neither approve nor disapprove," he said gently. "And I won't be goaded into bickering with you. I know you're troubled about Cenere, and you don't want to have to be on guard all the time."

"You'd think I'd be over that. It was so long ago, and so much has happened since," she said, touching her hair in a motion that briefly hid her face from him.

"You haven't been kidnapped and held as a captive, have you? That is not the sort of experience that one can forget," he said, remembering the remote cabin where she had been held, and the thick snow all around it.

"No," she said, and managed a single laugh. "Once was quite enough."

"Yes, it was," he said, touching his horn as a Buick shot out of a parking place without regard for traffic. "That's why I want to take every precaution so that you don't have to endure anything disagreeable again on my account."

She reached over and laid her hand on his leg. "You brought me safely out of that. No one else could have done it."

"Possibly," he allowed. "But you were there because of your association with me, and I will not let that happen here." He signaled to turn onto Pacific.

"It's very provoking," she told him. "You'd think there was a direct way to learn about this man."

"There may be, but it could mean exposure, and that is too high a price to pay for information." He rolled up the window and slowed down as a new Cadillac wove down the street toward him. "For now, I'll have to do all my inquiring as indirectly as possible."

"It sounds time-consuming and aggravating," she said, and laughed at herself. "When I was younger, I would have found such a prospect exciting. Age really is creeping up on me."

He held her hand briefly, then shifted down into second gear. "That driver is too drunk to be out on the street," he said as the Cadillac swerved past him.

"It's New—" she began, and stopped herself. "You're right," she agreed as she swung around in her seat to follow the Cadillac's erratic progress down the street.

"Not that matters were much better during Prohibition, from what Oscar King has told me," Saint-Germain said.

"I wish it weren't so," she said, and settled in the seat again. "But I saw more drunkenness during Prohibition than before, or since." She twiddled her key in her fingers. "Have you made up your mind about what you're going to do?"

"About Cenere, you mean?" he guessed.

"Yes."

"No, not yet, not entirely," he said. "But I will shortly."

"If you decide to leave, will you tell me where you're going?" She sounded forlorn.

"I don't plan on leaving," he said. "Not for a while, in any case."

"But you could change your mind," she murmured.

"That is the prerogative of all humankind, vampires included." He rolled down his window again to signal for Taylor Street. "You might change your mind, as well. You may decide you would rather not spend time with me, or you'd like to go north for a time, to do more drawings, or you could accept the offer from the gallery in New York and travel there for a one-woman show."

She shook her head. "You make it seem so . . . so uncertain."

"Because it is: the uncertainty is the one sure thing in life," he said as he pulled into a parking place, set the brake, and turned off the motor and the headlights. He opened the door, preparing to go around to the passenger side to help her out.

For the moment she gave up quibbling with him, and allowed him to offer her his arm as she stepped out of the silver car. "At least we have tonight."

"What's left of it," he said, glancing at his watch. "Luckily this is winter, and the sun won't be up for hours yet."

"And we can turn that time to good use," she said as she climbed up to her front door and slipped her key into the lock.

"Yes." He paused, looking back at his car. "But if you don't mind, I'll join you shortly. I think it would be wise to park somewhere else, a block or two away."

She shivered, speaking in irritation to conceal the sudden dread that gripped her. "Do you think we might have been followed?"

"No, I don't think it, but it is a possibility, and I believe it would be best to proceed on the assumption that it could be happening." He took her hand and kissed it. "I'll be with you in five minutes." With that, he turned and went back to his Pierce-Arrow.

Rowena watched him go, struggling with the fear that had formed under her ribs in a cold, hard lump. Try as she would, she could not dislodge it, and for the first time since he came to San Francisco, she had a hint of apprehension about their affaire that even her awakened desire could not banish.

TEXT OF A LETTER FROM ENID CURTIS AT LAKE TAHOE, CALIFORNIA, TO J. HAROLD BISHOP OF HORNER BISHOP BEATIE WENTWORTH & CULPEPPER IN CHICAGO, ILLINOIS.

PONDEROSA LODGE
LAKE TAHOE, CALIFORNIA

February 1, 1937

J. Harold Bishop, Esq.
Horner Bishop Beatie Wentworth & Culpepper
Atttorneys-at-Law
7571 Michigan Ave.
Suite 602
Chicago, Illinois

Dear Mr. Horner,

I have had my attorney, James G. Avery of Sacramento, review the contracts you have supplied regarding the silent partnership proposed by Lord Weldon, who, I understand, is an associate of Ferenc Ragoczy, who stayed here at the end of last summer. I have read the contract carefully and I understand its terms, and I have had the advantage of good counsel on this matter.

Mr. Avery advises me that so long as the terms of the guarantee of autonomy are strictly enforced, he sees no reason I should not sign it. He has suggested this addition to Paragraph 9, Clause 6, of the contract regarding the guarantee of autonomy for me: that shall not be revoked without cause as stipulated in Paragraph 8, Clause 4, Dissolving the Partnership. If this is satisfactory to you, please let me know, I will insert the language and initial it, and return the contract to you as quickly as airmail will bring it to you. If you would prefer to make the amendment yourself, and send a new draft back to me, I will return you this copy of the contract with the pertinent addition penciled in for your perusal. I would appreciate hearing from you in this regard at your earliest convenience.

I am still amazed that this Lord Weldon should make such a generous offer. The money promised is beyond our current expectations regarding income, but now that there are people coming to Reno for gambling, we resort owners around Tahoe are seeing the first signs that this region might also enjoy something of a surge in business. If Lord Weldon does not mind waiting for at least a decade to see any significant return on his investment, then I hope to justify his faith in Ponderosa Lodge.

While I realize the autonomy clause does not require it, I will keep complete records of all repairs, improvements, and additions to Ponderosa Lodge and I'll be happy to present him notarized copies of any and all of these records if he should ever wish to review them. And in any case, I will keep you informed of any and all changes undertaken here.

Please extend my gratitude to Lord Weldon, and assure him he will always be welcome here. I look forward to the day I can shake his hand and give him a full tour of the place. The same goes for you; if you should ever wish for a Sierra vacation, I will reserve my best cabin for you and your family.

Sincerely yours,

(Mrs.) Enid Curtis

~

chapter two

C arlo Pietragnelli was waiting in the circular driveway, an umbrella raised over his head as Saint-Germain brought the Pierce-Arrow to a halt and got out.

"Thank God and all the Saints! Pieta di me!" he exclaimed. "Grazie, grazie, Signor Ragoczy. And you, Signor Rogers."

"What on earth is wrong?" Ragoczy asked as he hurried into the shelter of the porch, his raincoat flapping around him, Rogerio a foot behind him. It was not quite noon, and the weather was early February foul, spitting rain on gusts of cutting, icy winds interspersed with twenty-minute stretches of drenching downpour; the storm had arrived shortly after midnight and was expected to linger for three days. "We left as soon as you called."

"It's my neighbor, Hiro Yoshimura. You met him, if you will recollect." He was hastening to open the front door.

"Yes; the Japanese farmer," said Saint-Germain, shaking the water from his hat. "What is the trouble, for I assume there must be trouble. You said the situation was urgent."

"He's dead," said Pietragnelli, and crossed himself.

"How?" Saint-Germain asked, shocked by this announcement.

Pietragnelli took a deep breath and launched into his account as if afraid to stop. "It was the White Legion, of course. It had to have been. They have been after him, and the rest of us, for months. But Yoshimura had the brunt of it. This time they struck directly, and worse, far worse than before. He was beaten early yesterday evening, between five and six, from what we can establish. His hands left at five and I found him—he was supposed to come by for supper, and when he didn't arrive and there was no answer on his telephone, I went to his farm—a short while after six. It had to happen in that time he was alone. Thank God it wasn't raining, for that would have chilled Yoshimura, to say nothing of what the mud might have done. When I got to his farm, I searched his house, and discovered he wasn't in it, so I looked more widely—chicken coops, duck pond, the storage shed—and finally came upon him by the pump-house, blood everywhere, and three of his chickens, out of the coop, were beginning to peck at him. He was not really conscious, just moaning. It was hideous. There was blood coming out of his nose and ears. I got him into my car and drove him into Santa Rosa, to the hospital." His eyes filled with tears. "He was not himself most of the time, saying little bits of things, and then fading out; I didn't understand most of it—it must have been in Japanese. From the cursory examination I did before I lifted him into my backseat, I was sure he had a broken arm, and ribs, and bruises everywhere, but that wasn't the worst of it: he had a terrible injury on the side of his head."

"When did he die?" Saint-Germain asked, his voice as kindly as his question was blunt.

"Around eight this morning; the hospital called me just as I was going out the door to start the morning chores; I start late in the winter and early in the summer. And it was raining, and Mrs. Barringstone hadn't come to work yet; she was waiting for the school bus with her children, down at the front gate. The nurse who called told me that the doctor worked on him all night, and when he was as patched up as they could make him, they put a nurse on duty to watch him, which is the best they can do for anyone. He stopped breathing, and that was the end of it. I called you as soon as I heard, and then I called Will Sutton and told him that he and the sheriff have to do something; he was shocked to hear about this. And doubtless he isn't the only one, the word is all over the area, thanks to our telephone operator. Of all of them, Violet is the worst, and she has been on duty this morning, which is the same as issuing a public announcement. She listens in to everything, and passes it on whenever anyone makes a call. I know she heard the hospital's report, and mine to you and Will Sutton, and that would be enough for her to start telling all the subscribers on the line." He made a gesture to ward off the Evil Eye before he dropped into the nearest chair in the parlor. "I was so sure we had them on the run. They had stopped coming into Geyserville to recruit, and I thought that meant progress."

"You mean the White Legion?" Saint-Germain asked, wanting to be sure he was following Pietragnelli.

"Yes. Not even the Leonardis were making a show of themselves, and I thought that was a good sign." He sighed. "You should have seen what they did to him. I was almost sick when I found him. He had broken skin on his hands and face, and all that blood . . ."

"I know this must be a great loss to you," said Saint-Germain. "He was your friend."

"It was the White Legion. Yoshimura said it, but only I heard him; the doctor didn't bother asking him who had hurt him; he was too busy trying to treat his injuries and once they gave him an injection for the pain, he didn't say anything. It might be good medicine, but it was irresponsible. They could have waited long enough to hear him name the Leonardis, or the White Legion. They didn't let me stay with him more than half-an-hour, while they got information about him and what had happened, though I said I was willing to stay there. They told me to go home. I'm not a relative, and that made it wrong for me to be with him," Pietragnelli exclaimed, then ducked his head and lowered his voice. "I think I should call his wife and family."

"The hospital will do that," said Rogerio, certain they had already done so.

"I still should call them; I know them slightly, and I was with him; they will want to know how it was; I can tell them," said Pietragnelli. "They must be suffering just now. I ought to tell them about what happened."

"And what was that; do you know?" Saint-Germain asked gently. "You found him, beaten and half-conscious. Will that give them any solace?"

"I know more than that: I know that the White Legion came and beat him again, of course. They wanted him out of the area, along with many of us. It isn't just that he's Japanese; they're after others. I told you about it. And the more I look into it, the more I think it's a land-grab, because when someone leaves, a member of the White Legion takes over the property for a smidgen of its value," said Pietragnelli, growing angry as he spoke. "I spent some time in the County Clerk's office, looking up deed transfers, and there's a real pattern, if you take the time to look for it. I don't know who among them did this, but I know the Leonardi boys are behind this particular attack, not only because they don't like anyone not white enough for them, they want to expand their family holdings again, and this is a good way to do it."

"Do you think this will bring the Yoshimuras any comfort?" Saint-Germain kept his voice level and there was sympathy in his dark eyes. "Or will it make their burden greater."

"It will tell them who is responsible," Pietragnelli insisted, paying no attention to his tears. "They will want to know that."

"They will, in time, and beyond all cavil." Saint-Germain pulled up a straight-backed chair and faced Pietragnelli. "Is your assertion actual knowledge or reasonable conjecture?"

"Who else would do it? Oh, there are many who are not happy about the Orientals coming here, but none of them would go so far as to kill, except the White Legion. Why should I doubt what is so obvious?" Pietragnelli asked. "I know what's going on. They painted his mailbox yellow four times in the last six weeks, and they've named him among those they plan to drive out. I'm on their list, as well."

"Being on a list, no matter how disgusting, isn't proof they killed Yoshimura," said Saint-Germain, thinking of the many times he had been on lists, and what repercussion they had had. "It means that he knew he was in danger, and so did many others. His wife must be aware of that, too. But how can you accuse the White Legion, or the Leonardis, with only that to go on? He could have been killed by someone else who took advantage of the threats to act, confident that any investigation would turn toward the White Legion first." He had experienced more than one such attack, the worst sixteen centuries ago; the criminal who had tried to kill him had almost got away with his deed because no one but Saint-Germain suspected him.

"That's very unlikely," said Pietragnelli.

"Yes it is, but it's not impossible. This isn't a time to embroider the truth, for it will only cloud the work to be done. Did Yoshimura say who it was? Did he identify the Leonardis specifically?" Saint-Germain waited for Pietragnelli's answer, aware it was a difficult one.

"No," he said at last. "He said it was the White Legion. He said there were two of them and they wore hoods, with a chess knight on them, just as they have on all their pamphlets."

"They could be recognized, which means Yoshimura must have known them on sight," Rogerio said. "The hoods prevented recognition."

"So I think. I am sure Yoshimura knew his assailants. And the Leonardis have been the most vocal of those speaking against Yoshimura." Pietragnelli buried his head in his hands. "I brought this on him. It is my fault, mine."

"How do you come to that?" Saint-Germain inquired.

"I was the one who made him stay and fight. I said I could lend him protection. I promised him that we would put an end to the White Legion in Sonoma County." He had begun to weep. "Oh, God. I should have seen this coming. I could have prevented it."

"You did send guards to him, didn't you?" Saint-Germain knew the answer. "You had men keep watch on his farm. He was aware of the danger." It was no comfort, and he knew it. "But it is a terrible loss."

"And it is on my soul," said Pietragnelli heavily.

"I hope not, for it is not your burden," said Saint-Germain, continuing, "Would you like to talk to a priest about this?"

"What good would that do? Neither Father Boncuore nor Father Bryce like Orientals. They would tell me to pray, and I can do that without their help." He shook his head. "No. I am accountable for this, and no amount of Ave Marias will change that. I encouraged Hiro to stand against the White Legion. Had he gone to his wife in South San Francisco, he would still be alive: I persuaded him to stay."

Saint-Germain regarded Pietragnelli compassionately. "If you had sent the White Legion to attack him, then I might agree with you, but you took reasonable measures to prevent just this kind of brutality, and that should absolve you of all blame."

Rogerio took it upon himself to build up the fire, for the room was chilly and the logs in the fireplace were almost reduced to ashes. He used the poker to break down the charred wood, then reached into the copper washtub, where wood was stacked, took three sections of a split oak trunk and laid them on the glowing embers, fanning the wood with yesterday's newspaper. He sat back on his heels and waited for the logs to catch, the poker resting on his knees in case the logs needed to be shifted.

"You are a kind man, Signor Ragoczy, and you are seeking to cheer me," said Pietragnelli. "But I know what I know, and nothing you tell me can change that. I was the one who took up the challenge. Those who joined me did so at my instigation. Yoshimura has paid for my recklessness and I must answer for it. He defied the White Legion because I convinced him to." He rubbed his face to wipe away his tears. "And it is for me to see that justice is done. If I fail in that, then I am truly among the damned."

"I think you may be too severe; you need not make yourself the villain of the piece. If you heap disdain upon yourself, you may alleviate some of your self-imposed guilt, but it will do little to gain justice for Yoshimura, or to bring any of his attackers to answer in a court of law. If, on the other hand, you are determined to bring his attackers in, you may wish to find a way to accomplish your ends that will also bring respect to Yoshimura's memory," Saint-Germain proposed at his most bracing.

"And how am I to do this?" Pietragnelli wondered aloud. "I am at a stand-still."

"Making accusations without strong foundations will not do it," Saint-Germain observed, knowing how much Pietragnelli felt the need to do something to help his murdered neighbor. "You may vent your spleen, but it will not bring about the ends you seek. You have to have proof that the White Legion is responsible."

"But I *know* they must have done it," Pietragnelli protested.

"I do not doubt you, but a court of law would have to, and once the culprits are tried, if they are acquitted, they cannot be tried again, even if their guilt is shown beyond all question." He saw Pietragnelli prepare to argue. "That is the law in this country, and it will prevail. You know that as well as I, if not better. If you seek to circumvent it, you will be doing the very thing you deplore." Saint-Germain waited until he had all Pietragnelli's attention, and then he went on, "Have you any evidence—not supposition or conviction, but evidence—that the Leonardis were the ones responsible for killing Yoshimura?"

"No," Pietragnelli admitted, adding, "but there was a note in my mailbox this morning. It said *you're next*, with a skull-and-crossbones at the bottom of the page, and a chess knight. That, I believe, identifies the Leonardis."

"It may," said Saint-Germain, alarmed at this information. "Do you have the note still, or did you dispose of it?"

"I kept it. I plan to give it to Will Sutton when he comes here. He's supposed to stop by around three." He lifted his head as if it weighed ten pounds. "I have been trying to decide how to face him."

"Do you expect difficulties?" Rogerio came from the fireplace to hear the answer.

"Not from Sutton, no. He is a good man, but his hands have been tied, for there are those above him who support the White Legion—in fact, it is rumored that some of them are members—and they will discourage any investigation that works against the White Legion or its interests. If Sutton can make headway, it will surprise me very much." Pietragnelli closed his eyes as if to shut out all he was thinking. "It is going to be a long time before those of us who oppose the White Legion will feel safe again."

"Small wonder," Rogerio remarked.

"And, unfortunately, it is probably wise for those of you who are targets of the White Legion to be on guard more than you have already been, and to be prepared for more trouble." Saint-Germain held up his hand to stop any outbursts from Pietragnelli. "I know what it is to be hunted, and the need for care in all things when you are. This is not a time for posturing, but wariness."

"But we're men with crops to tend and fields to care for. It was one thing when we had to keep the midnight harvesters from making off with our crops, but this—this is much worse, isn't it? This is an assault, not just theft." Pietragnelli was beginning to get angry. "What are we supposed to do—hire armed men to escort us to the grocery store and build high walls around our lands, with guns atop them?"

"No; that would be bad for farming," said Saint-Germain, hoping for an easing in the tension which was building up in the parlor.

Pietragnelli smiled in spite of himself. "You're right, Signor Ragoczy. So high walls are out of the question." He rubbed his lower lip. "Then what are we to do? You have made recommendations before—give me the benefit of your experience again." There was a trace of mulish anger in this, but not enough to keep Saint-Germain from answering.

"By killing Yoshimura, the men who attacked him—whoever they may be—have made a crucial mistake. They have now committed a serious crime, something that cannot easily be ignored, and that is likely to arouse public sympathy for the victim, Oriental or not. It is one thing to threaten and bully, for many will tolerate and even endorse such tactics; it is another matter entirely to take a life. The law may turn a blind eye toward the former, but it cannot afford to disregard the latter. And you have the attention of the press, which can be a formidable ally." He paused a moment, his demeanor deceptively mild; his dark eyes were luminous with purpose. "On the drive up here, I imagined all manner of trouble that might have befallen you, but this wasn't one of the possibilities that crossed my mind."

"Then you didn't appreciate the problems we face," said Pietragnelli.

"No, I didn't." He regarded Pietragnelli steadily. "And for that, I apologize, although that is insufficient."

"As you say," Pietragnelli allowed.

Saint-Germain rose and walked down the room. "I can't tell you how much I had hoped—" He broke off. "But I underestimated the matter."

Pietragnelli shook his head. "You weren't the only one. I never thought it would come to this. I doubt that any of our neighbors did, either, except the Leonardi boys. I wanted to believe that my notice in the *Press-Democrat* would keep the White Legion at bay. It seemed to be working. I knew many of my neighbors were laughing about it, and that the ridicule was doing some good. No one in Geyserville was boasting about being in the White Legion the way they were doing last summer, and that gave me courage to go on—because I thought I was making headway, and I even hoped that we could put an end to the White Legion in Geyserville. But that might have been what made the Leonardis angry, and goaded them into killing Yoshimura." He got to his feet and walked to the fireplace where the logs were just starting to burn. "I should have been the one they attacked. Not Hiro Yoshimura."

"But you have workers living on your land, and guards as well," Saint-Germain pointed out. "You have defenders, and Yoshimura didn't, not as you did." He could read the distress in Pietragnelli's eyes. "Your men did what they could for him, but it wasn't enough, and it didn't keep him from harm."

"And for that, he's dead," said Pietragnelli, stifling a sob.

Saint-Germain came up to Pietragnelli and laid his hand on his shoulder. "You are exhausted. Why don't you get a little sleep now, before Deputy Sutton comes? You'll be more ready to talk to him if you've rested."

"How can I sleep at a time like this?" Pietragnelli asked indignantly. "What do you take me for—an uncaring fool?"

"You need sleep so you will be ready to take up the fight again. If you're worn out, Sutton will not be inclined to listen to you, and you will not make a strong case to him. You must prepare your campaign, and Deputy Sutton is your first skirmish in it," said Saint-Germain reasonably. "The time will not be lost. While you rest, Mr. Rogers and I will speak with your men, to find out if any of them noticed anything going on last evening, or during the day. If any of your men saw anyone going to or leaving the Yoshimura farm, that could help the police. Or if there was anything unusual that caught their attention, they may be willing to tell me about it, and Deputy Sutton, as well. And I'll speak with the guards. They should have been alert to trouble." As he said this, he was puzzled why no one had come forward.

Pietragnelli shrugged his big shoulders. "I don't know; I could drink two cups of strong coffee. That would restore me." He turned and started toward the kitchen. "It wouldn't take long to make."

Rogerio stopped him. "Then you will be up two nights in a row, and that will help no one."

Saint-Germain looked toward the kitchen. "Where is Mrs. Barringstone? I haven't heard any noise from the kitchen."

"She's taken hot bread out to the men in the winery, for their dinner. They stop work for an hour, to have their dinner. When they've finished eating, she'll be in to start work on supper. If you want to speak with her, she'll be in the kitchen shortly." Pietragnelli said this remotely, as if these ordinary events were entirely foreign to him.

"Is there any chance she might have seen something, or her children?" Saint-Germain asked.

"I don't think so," Pietragnelli said. "She was in the kitchen when I left for Yoshimura's farm, and was back in her cabin with her family by the time I returned."

"And Mr. Barringstone? What of him?" Rogerio inquired.

"He's at the winery from eight-thirty until six," said Pietragnelli. "I can't imagine he'd know anything."

Saint-Germain managed an understanding nod. "Well, go have a nap. Let yourself rest. You need it. You know, sometimes a little sleep will bring details into the mind that were overlooked before."

"True enough," Pietragnelli allowed, and managed to hide a yawn by turning away and hunching his shoulder. "All right, you've convinced me. I'll do it. But I mustn't nap for more than an hour."

"We'll have you up before Deputy Sutton arrives," said Rogerio. "And a cup of coffee will be waiting for you."

"Sta bene," said Pietragnelli, making for the stairs and plodding upward.

"He's exhausted," Rogerio said to Saint-Germain as soon as the door to Pietragnelli's room closed.

"And it's doing him no good," Saint-Germain concurred. "Let him rest until two-thirty. It's not enough, but it's better than nothing."

"Yes," said Rogerio. "Do you plan to talk to the men while they're eating?"

"It seems as good a time as any," said Saint-Germain.

"Do you think any of them actually saw anything of use?" Rogerio looked toward the kitchen. "Or Mrs. Barringstone?"

"I don't know. There are other wives who live in the cabins, and some of them have children in school. We should speak with them, as well." Saint-Germain paused, deliberating inwardly. "It will probably be best to ask the women to come into the house. If we speak to them one by one, the men won't like it."

"No, probably not," Rogerio said, and glanced toward the window. "You know, for a state with a reputation for sunshine, we've seen a great deal of rain and fog."

"Peculiarities of the region," Saint-Germain said, dismissing it. "We'd best go out to the winery first, and talk to the men."

"Shall I fetch your hat?" Rogerio offered.

"No, I'll do it," Saint-Germain responded. "But you might want to get an extra tub of butter from the kitchen, to be able to offer the men something they'll appreciate." He went and plucked his hat from the rack by the front door and resisted the urge to grin. "We might as well get this done."

Rogerio nodded and went with him through the kitchen, on to the pantry, where he took a tub of butter from the cooler, and went out the back door into the storm, Saint-Germain half-a-step in front of him. Holding their hats, they walked quickly across the yard toward the winery and ducked into the main door to find Pietragnelli's workers gathered around three picnic tables, most of them with partially eaten plates of food in front of them. At the far side of the room Mrs. Barringstone was deep in conversation with a man in an old, quilted-denim jacket. Behind them rose three columns of two-story-high barrels; the odor of fermentation pervaded the huge room.

"Good day to you," Saint-Germain said, looking about at the startled faces; he moved aside so Rogerio could put the tub of butter on the central table. "Please; don't let me stop you eating. I'm here on Mr. Pietragnelli's behalf. My name is Ragoczy." He nodded to Mrs. Barringstone. "A pleasure to see you again, ma'am."

She offered a disapproving look and went back to her quiet discussion.

Saint-Germain endured the snub with urbanity. "As I'm sure you all know by now, Mr. Yoshimura was severely beaten last night and died this morning at the hospital in Santa Rosa." He saw the men exchange glances; some of them nodded. "The beating appears to have taken place yesterday evening, between five and six. Deputy Sheriff Sutton is going to be calling here later in the day, and will probably want to take statements from all of you. What I am asking you to do is to cast your minds back and see if you can recall anything that might assist in the identification of the men who beat Mr. Yoshimura." He noticed another flurry of sidelong glances, and knew that these men had been talking about the murder of Mr. Yoshimura already. "If any of you has anything you'd like to say, either here or privately, I'm willing to listen. If you would prefer to save your comments for Deputy Sutton, well and good. But please, if you know anything, don't keep it to yourself."

"The man was a damned Nip," said one of the workers seated at the middle table, and was supported by a mutter of endorsement.

"Yes, he was. But that's hardly reason enough to beat him to death," said Saint-Germain, outwardly unruffled. "You may not like Orientals, but how would you feel if Mr. Pietragnelli were attacked?"

"That couldn't happen," said the man Saint-Germain assumed was Mr. Barringstone.

"Do you think not?" Saint-Germain asked, and let the question hang. "You know he has been threatened. Why else are there guards here at the winery?"

"They just want him to shut up," said another man. "That's all."

"He's making the White Legion look bad," said a third.

Saint-Germain listened, and when the men fell silent, he said, "From what I can tell, the White Legion doesn't need Mr. Pietragnelli or anyone else to do that."

"Hey! They're sticking up for white men, making sure we don't get drowned in a sea of foreigners." This was the third man again.

"Sounds like the usual rhetoric: those other persons—not like us—are taking what rightfully belongs to us as birthright. But who among you was born here in Geyserville? Or Sonoma County? Or California?" Saint-Germain said, managing to sound slightly disinterested. "It's nothing new. When there are hard times, it's easy to point fingers at outsiders and blame them for all misfortune. Look what's happening in Spain and Germany." He wondered if any of these men knew about the German situation, for America had done its best to ignore Europe since the end of the Great War.

"Bunch of European generals," said a man of about forty, and spat.

"Yeah," said Mr. Barringstone. "The men are working, and the country's on the way to recovery." This assertion was met by another round of approving grumbles.

"Some of them are," said Saint-Germain. "Others have had everything taken from them in the name of recovery, and their losses cannot be restored." He looked directly at Mr. Barringstone. "That isn't how Americans are supposed to deal with problems. And Mr. Yoshimura was an American citizen, as hard-working as any of you."

Two men laughed; the rest shushed them, and one, slightly younger than the rest, said, "I'll give you he worked hard. But what right did he have to be here?"

"The same right you do, I expect," said Saint-Germain. "As I understand it, all Americans came from elsewhere, except the Indians."

"What are you—some kind of hoity-toity liberal?" The third man made no apology for his manner or his question.

"I'm an exile who has lost all his land and his people," said Saint-Germain quietly. "So I know what it is to be a stranger among strangers."

"Looks like you've done all right for yourself," grumbled the oldest man at the tables.

"Eventually I managed to," Saint-Germain said, and went on, "Consider for a moment if the situation were reversed, and you had a small farm in Japan, one you had paid for and worked yourself, hoping to better yourself and your family, and some of the locals didn't like having a white man working their land, and decided to put an end to it—what then?"

"That's different," Mr. Barringstone said.

"Is it? In what way?" Saint-Germain said. "Well, all I ask is that you consider Mr. Yoshimura not as an Oriental but a neighbor while you make up your minds what you intend to tell the deputy sheriff."

"Sure," said the third man sarcastically.

"Well, you were willing to eat his vegetables," said Mrs. Barringstone suddenly. "The kitchen garden here isn't big enough to feed us all, and you know Mr. Pietragnelli bought produce from him." The men shuffled awkwardly, and her husband ordered her to be quiet. "Well, I won't," she announced. "You act as if you're so much better than he was, but at least he had land to call his own."

"No drought drove him off," the third man reminded them all.

"No, but the White Legion sure tried, and you know it as well as I do," she said, and gathered up the two big bread-baskets she had brought out to the men forty minutes ago. "They had to kill him to get rid of him, and you all sit here pretending it doesn't matter. I'm ashamed of you, all of you—even you, Virgil Barringstone." She stumped off to the door and let herself out.

"Uppity woman," said the third man, but there was no echo of his complaint.

"She's made dinner for you for over a year, Warton," Mr. Barringstone said forcefully.

"And she's done a good job, but that doesn't give her the right to—" Warton began, only to be interrupted by the youngest of the men.

"I think it does." He lifted his jaw and looked at Saint-Germain. "We'll think over what you said, and when that deputy comes, we'll talk to him. Mind you, we might not have much to say, but it could be . . ." He looked over at Warton.

Saint-Germain gave a single nod. "Thank you, gentlemen. I know you'll give this the serious attention it deserves." He met all of their eyes in turn, and went on in his most cordial tone, "We'll be speaking with your wives as well, in the main house, too. If you want to send someone along to listen to their reports, he'll be welcome." He stepped back toward the door, Rogerio opening it for both of them.

"Hey!" the youngest man called out.

"Yes?" Saint-Germain stopped to listen, the rain already soaking the shoulders of his raincoat.

"Did you mean it, about talking to you or the deputy privately?" There was a quality of defiance in his question.

"Yes," Saint-Germain said, not letting himself become hopeful.

"That's good," the young man said, and was about to go on when there was the sharp crack of a rifle-shot and the sound of breaking glass. Three more shots followed, each accompanied by breaking glass.

The men in the winery were shocked to stillness, and then shouting erupted as they all got to their feet and made for the door, where Saint-Germain and Rogerio were standing; in a disorganized wedge they shoved through out of the winery and rushed toward the house, where Pietragnelli was bellowing.

"Stay back!" Saint-Germain shouted with such an air of command that the workers obeyed him at once. "You don't know where the shots are coming from."

The men came to a halt, four of them ducking down in a belated attempt to cover themselves against more fire, one turning back for the winery door.

A fifth shot cracked, and one of the dining-room windows shattered.

"It's coming from over there!" Barringstone shouted, pointing to a clump of trees on a small knoll off to the left. His jacket flapping around him, he ran toward the gate that would lead him to the shooter.

"Esecrazione! Codardo!" shouted Pietragnelli, standing at his ruined window. He continued to curse in Italian.

Mrs. Barringstone and two other women had come out of their cabins, all looking frightened and angry.

"Don't bother," Saint-Germain called after Barringstone. "He's leaving." The sound of a revving engine was loud enough to hear over the jumble of shouts and the spatter of rain.

"How did he get onto the land?" the oldest worker yelled.

"The south gate!" Warton shouted.

"Where are the guards?" Rogerio asked Saint-Germain.

"I don't know, and that is very troubling," he said. "Come. We'd better get into the house and see what sort of damage was done." He started toward the kitchen door. "Barringstone! Get back here! You can't catch him. He's gone."

Barringstone stood in the rain, swinging his arms in a frenzy of futility. "How! Why!"

"That is what we must determine, including who," said Saint-Germain, and resumed walking, preparing to help Pietragnelli assess the damage.

TEXT OF A REPORT FROM INSPECTOR JOHN SMITH TO ASSISTANT
COMMISSIONER DAVIS B. NAUGHTON; DELIVERED CONFIDENTIALLY BY HAND.

13 February, 1937

Davis B. Naughton
Assistant Police Commissioner
Room 311
City Hall, San Francisco

Assistant Commissioner,

In accordance with your instructions, I am providing you this report prior
to filing one officially, and I trust you will keep this private between us, as
you have indicated you would.

The five incidents of theft at major hotels is nearly solved, and we hope to
conclude the case before they can strike again. We lack a few critical pieces of
evidence to make an arrest, but we have determined that the gang involved
is comprised of three men and a woman, and they have committed similar
thefts in Seattle and Portland. I have reports from both police departments,
and two confirmed identifications for fingerprints found at those scenes that
were also found in these burglaries.

We have obtained a warrant to search the apartment of one Leon Paul
Holland. He and his sister, Neola, arrived from Portland in October and have
been associating with Andrew Dare and William Reever, both of whom
have records for breaking-and-entering. The Hollands have been arrested on
suspicion of burglary but never held over for trial, due to lack of evidence.
Andrew Dare has served time for robbery in Washington State, and William
Reever may be an alias.

The reason we are narrowing in on these four is that Ferdinand Pinkly, a
known fence, has been approached by Holland, who was offering a number
of uncut gemstones, and who had no proof of ownership. Since one of the
thefts included fourteen uncut gems taken from the Commodore Suite at the
Saint Francis, we brought one of the stones to Ferenc Ragoczy for identification. He had an accurate description of the stone and proof of ownership (he
had purchased the stones from a Lord Weldon), which indicates to me that
the Hollands are either directly or indirectly involved in these crimes.

Incidentally, Ragoczy has been cooperative in this investigation, and has
provided us with a great deal of specific information about the items taken
from the suite, and has made himself available to answer questions. I have
some questions about the man himself, but I must say he has been forthcom-

ing with me when I have spoken to him, in a reserved sort of way, as many rich folk are. The other victims are no longer in San Francisco, but Ragoczy has purchased a house here and has been useful to us.

If the search of their apartment turns up anything of use in making a case against them, the Hollands, Dare, and Reever will be arrested and charged. The theft at the Palace Hotel was so recent that I haven't had time to alert all the pawnbrokers and fences yet, but I'm working on it, and I am confident that the thieves haven't disposed of all their loot yet, so if we can find where they've hidden the pelf, we should be able to make our case stick in court.

I realize these thefts have been embarrassing to the department and the Mayor, and I will do all that I can to put an end to them as quickly as possible. Rest assured that the suspects I mentioned are quite likely our culprits, so our chances of nailing them are good, and once they're incarcerated, we can all heave a sigh of relief. Theft may not be as bad as murder, but it's mortifying for cops, no matter how trivial it may appear to others.

When the arrest is made, you can release the information on these crooks to the press, but I ask you to hold off until we have them in custody, because otherwise they might leave the jurisdiction, and catching them will be much more difficult, to say nothing of bringing them back to San Francisco for trial.

If you decide to inform the Commissioner, I'd recommend you hold off until our search is complete. No reason to raise hopes until we have real evidence in our hands.

Sincerely,

John Smith

chapter three

Cenere prided himself on his patience, and once again he knew why. He had been watching Oscar King's offices for more than six weeks and finally his wait had paid off, for he now saw Ferenc Ragoczy enter the building shortly after one p.m. and make for the bank of elevators. Cenere slipped into the lobby of

630 Kearny, went to the newsstand, and purchased a copy of the *Call-Bulletin*, opening it at random, dawdling, in anticipation of his quarry's return.

It was almost twenty minutes later that Saint-Germain left Oscar King's office and took the elevator down to the main floor, his brow knit in thought; he carried a leather briefcase and an umbrella, and he made his way through the crowded lobby quickly and efficiently. On the street he went toward Waverly Place, with its warren of shops and back doors, most with Chinese signs on them, where his Pierce-Arrow was parked, a note on the windshield in Chinese; he removed this and tucked it into his overcoat pocket; then he let himself in on the driver's side and started the engine, checking the gauges before he pulled out of his parking place, driving slowly toward Sacramento Street. He looked in his rearview mirror and noticed a tall, thin man standing at the corner, staring after him. Ordinarily he would have assumed it was the car that interested the watcher, but it struck him that this might be the man Oscar King had mentioned at his New Year's party. Or it might have been someone hired by the White Legion—his last meeting with Carlo Pietragnelli had revealed more specific threats to the vintner and any who helped him. Saint-Germain had a brief series of recollections—Sidney Reilly in England and Russia, Helmut Rauch in Munich—that reminded him how much the twentieth century depended on political scrutiny; not even Delhi or Rome had been as relentless in pursuing its outsiders.

Chiding himself for being overly cautious, he continued to look in his mirror until he reached the corner and turned right, and into the flow of traffic. At least, he thought, the man is on foot, and he won't be able to follow me once I'm through the intersection. Close upon that realization came the worry that the man might have made note of his license plate number, and could trace him through the Department of Motor Vehicles, where such information was a matter of public record, which anyone could seek out. The Pierce-Arrow was registered to the Clarendon Court address, which meant that the man following him—if he was following him—could find him with minimal effort. That prospect bothered him and he had to resist the urge to try to speed, for the traffic was congested, cars working their way between double-parked delivery vans and trucks; Saint-Germain fretted at his slow progress, and took the first turn, going left, away from Chinatown.

From his vantage-point on the corner, Cenere made note of the make and model of car Saint-Germain drove, and the license plate number, committing the information to memory. He was almost disappointed that it was going to be so easy. He had been looking forward to getting the truth from Oscar King, one way or another. Still, he reminded himself, Ragoczy would not be on guard if his attorney remained unscathed, and that would be strategically useful. This way, there was little chance the man would flee before Cenere could find him and arrange the *lamentable accident* Colonel Morales had ordered. Turning on his heel, he went down the hill toward the streetcar line, already making plans.

A chorus of cars' horns warned Saint-Germain of impediments ahead, and a moment later, the blare of a siren strove to clear the way for an ambulance bound for Stockton Street. A uniformed policeman was in the street directing cars away from the path of the ambulance, using his arms and whistle to signal the traffic. At the corner, two cars—a Ford Model Y and a Lincoln tourer—were angled into each other, the Ford showing much more damage than the Lincoln; glass was all over the street, and the Ford was belching white smoke from its radiator. By the time he had made it past the accident, Saint-Germain was deeply uncomfortable; he had been mulling over all he and King had discussed and was unsettled by where his ruminations took him. He pulled over at a Hancock service station and went to the telephone booth next to the service bay. He dropped in his nickle and gave Rowena's number to the operator, listening to the ringing on the line. "Rowena?" he said when she answered.

"Saint-Germain," she said, and heard something in his voice that troubled her. "Is anything wrong?"

"I'm not sure. I hope not." He looked over his shoulder, half-expecting to see the tall, thin man watching him from across the street, although he knew this was virtually impossible, given the difficulty of pursuit.

"You sound"—she tried to find the word: upset was too overwrought, worried was too passive—"startled."

"Ah." He hesitated an instant. "That is an apt description. I'm not coming to your house as we planned, in case I am being followed."

"Followed?" She was shocked, but made as quick a recovery as she could. "What makes you think so? Why would anyone follow you?" Before he could speak: "Is it that man Oscar King mentioned at New Year's?"

"It may be. Or I may be jumping at shadows, for which I apologize, if I am."

"Is it about . . . what you are?" She coughed gently, an unnecessary warning for discretion.

"No, I don't think so. I doubt any of those interested in me would care about . . . that aspect of my nature." He paused. "After talking to Oscar King about Carlo Pietragnelli's situation, and all the White Legion has been doing to him, it could be that I'm ready to find conspirators everywhere, of any stripe, all of whom would want—at the least—to discredit me, and at the most to be rid of me." It was an odd admission, and one he found disconcerting, another way in which the twentieth century had imposed itself upon him; all the precautions he had developed over four millennia no longer seemed to apply, and that contributed to his perturbation. "In any case, I don't want to lead the man to you." He paused. "Will you meet me at Julius' Castle at five? I'm going to park my car out on California or one of those side-streets out near the Presidio, and I'll come in to meet you there. Come by taxi. I'll pay for it, and I'll see you get home safely."

"Are you sure it's safe to meet in such a public place?" she asked.

"Unless the man is psychic, yes. We can be easily lost in a crowd, and protected by numbers. Once we're isolated, then he can hunt us with relative impunity." Saint-Germain had a brief impression of the many times that had happened to him, and he made himself banish those painful memories.

"Julius' Castle at five. I'll be there," she said.

"If I'm being foolish, we can enjoy the view. If this is something more, then we'll be in a good place to observe." He managed a rueful chuckle. "You like Julius' Castle, or so you've said."

"Yes. I do. Thank you," she said.

"I'm sorry about dragging you into this, but I think it would be best if we are in accord on how to deal with this—if there is anything to deal with." He added the last to ease the tension he felt increasing between them. He sought to lessen it, saying, "I don't want you to get caught in anything again."

"This isn't going to turn ugly, is it?" she asked.

"Not if I can stop it," said Saint-Germain. "There may be nothing that should be stopped, but I am troubled by what Oscar King told us."

There was a brief silence between them. "You got me out of that cabin in the Alps. I'll assume you'll get me out of this."

"If there is anything to be got out of," he appended. "I hope I am being too wary, but better this than not careful enough."

"I suppose you're right," said Rowena.

"I would prefer to be wrong," he conceded.

"We'll talk about this later," she said. "I'll be there."

"Thank you," he said as he heard her hang up. After he broke the connection, he dropped another nickle in the slot and gave the number of his Clarendon Court house to the operator.

"Good afternoon," said Rogerio, picking up on the second ring.

"And to you, old friend," said Saint-Germain in the Latin of Imperial Rome.

"I gather something is wrong?" Rogerio said in the same language.

"It seems so," Saint-Germain answered.

Rogerio was silent an instant. "Shall I make preparations to leave?"

"Not just yet," said Saint-Germain. "I hope it won't come to that. But there is a man who is perhaps following me. Tall, slender, mid-thirties or a trifle older, perhaps. He's seen my car and probably has the license number. It won't take him too long to get the address from the state."

"If he knows to look for the address there," said Rogerio.

"We must assume that he will do so," said Saint-Germain. "If he is any kind of a professional, he will know how to find me."

"Yes, I imagine so." Rogerio sounded unruffled, but Saint-Germain knew him well enough to be aware of his dismay.

"You know how to deal with this," said Saint-Germain.

"Of course," said Rogerio.

"I have implicit trust in you," Saint-Germain said. "You know how to handle these problems."

"And so I shall," said Rogerio. "Thank you for alerting me."

"Thank you for preparing the house," said Saint-Germain. "I'm not going to be back until later tonight; if my plans change, I'll let you know."

"Very good," said Rogerio.

"By all the forgotten gods, I hope so," said Saint-Germain, and finished in English. "Be careful."

"I will. And you."

As he got back into his car, Saint-Germain checked the mirrors with extra care, and then drove toward California Street. He turned off in three blocks, driving parallel to California Street on Sacramento, and then returning to California, finally crossing on Arguello to Clement, where he found a parking place on a cross-street, and then walked over to Clement, making his way west on the south side of the street. Three blocks along the street he went into a bookstore, asking the clerk, "Do you have a public telephone?"

The clerk pointed to the rear of the store. "It's a pay phone."

Saint-Germain went to the telephone booth and took up the directory, and looked up the number of a taxi company. "I'm going to be at Clement and Arguello and I want to go to Julius' Castle. Will you please send a taxi to pick me up here at four-thirty? I'll be on the southwest corner, if that will be satisfactory?" he asked as soon as the operator connected him.

"Four-thirty at Clement and Arguello, southwest corner, going to Julius' Castle. You got it," said the dispatcher.

"Thank you," said Saint-Germain. "The name is Weldon." It was an alias he had been using for two hundred years; he had found it convenient because it was in no way related to Ragoczy, Saint-Germain, or any form of Francis.

"Very good, Mr. Weldon," the dispatcher told him, and hung up.

Saint-Germain emerged from the telephone booth and began to peruse the shelves, his briefcase, hat, and umbrella giving him the appearance of an ordi-

nary customer; more than shopping, he was buying time, giving himself an opportunity to discover if anyone was paying attention to his actions. He looked at the
titles in the nonfiction section, selecting *Inside Europe* by John Gunther; he
thumbed through the pages, and decided it would be interesting to read, and
tucked it under his arm as he made his way to the recent-fiction shelves, where
he debated between Huxley's *Eyeless in Gaza* and Steinbeck's *In Dubious Battle*.
He finally took both of them and made his way up to the counter at the front of
the store. "I'll get these," he said, reaching for his wallet.

The clerk punched in the prices on the adding machine, cranking down for
each of the hardcover books, and adding the sales tax. "Nine seventy-six," he
said, sounding slightly bored.

Saint-Germain handed over a ten-dollar bill and accepted his twenty-four
cents' change, then watched while the clerk took a length of brown paper and
wrapped the books carefully, taping the package closed. "Thank you."

"They're costly," said the clerk as if he was used to hearing complaints.
"Especially the Gunther."

"But books are important," said Saint-Germain as he opened his briefcase
and put the books into it. "They're money well-spent."

"We like to think so," said the clerk, and lit a cigarette. "If you like buying
books so much, come back anytime."

"Thank you," Saint-Germain said as he went out of the shop. He ambled west
on Clement Street, needing to keep occupied until four-thirty. It was a blustery
afternoon with no hint of spring in it; lowering clouds and bad-
tempered fits of rain provided an excuse for him to keep his hat pulled low on his
brow, and his overcoat buttoned. From time to time he opened his umbrella
to shield him from the sudden squalls, and that provided him more anonym-
ity. It was hardly a disguise, but it made him like most of the men on the street,
except for those with hand-lettered signs advertising pencils, apples, matches,
and leather coin-purses, who were wrapped in ragged coats and looked out at
the world with pebble-flat eyes as they did their stoic best to be indifferent to
the miserable weather; these men were constant reminders of the country's
difficulties, and seemed to be a rebuke to everyone earning a living. Saint-
Germain bought a coin-purse, so as not to be wholly indifferent to these men,
and kept on walking. Eventually he found a coffee shop and went in. A
Wurlitzer jukebox in the front of the dining area was playing "I Got a Feelin'
You're Foolin'," which was followed by "A Fine Romance." Without being
too obvious, Saint-Germain sat down in a rear booth, ordered a ham sandwich
and a cup of coffee, opened his briefcase and took out the package of books.
He opened the Huxley and began to read, letting the writing engulf him; he

hardly looked up when the waitress—an angular woman in her mid-twenties—arrived with his coffee and food.

Twenty minutes later she returned and slapped down a bill for eighty-eight cents, noticed that neither the sandwich nor the coffee had been touched. "You want a warm-up for that? It'll be a nickle."

"No, thank you," he said, looking up from the page. "But if you don't mind, I'd like to have a little time to read. If you want to add that to the check, I'll be glad to pay for the space. I don't want to take advantage."

The waitress blinked in surprise. "No; it's okay," she said after a brief consideration. "We aren't busy right now. You can stay until we start to fill up, no charge, but if we get busy, then you'll have to buy something more or go." She blushed a little, and stopped to slip a quarter into the jukebox before she went back to her post behind the counter. Strains of "I've Got You Under My Skin" filled the diner.

Saint-Germain caught the young woman staring at him; he answered this with just enough of a smile to elicit one from the waitress, who later confided to the cook that the stranger in the expensive overcoat was a real gentleman. "He's got that air about him—you know, like Ronald Colman."

"How would you know?" the cook growled. "How many real gentlemen you seen come in here?"

"You can tell," she said knowingly.

"You and your movies and love songs," the cook scoffed, but he took advantage of a chance to look at the well-dressed stranger in the rear booth, and conceded that he looked classy. "Not like most of the guys we see in here."

By four o'clock, Saint-Germain was more than a hundred pages into *Eyeless in Gaza* and was almost sad to give up reading the book for the time being. He put the book back in his briefcase, wrapped the sandwich in two paper napkins and slipped it into his overcoat pocket, dropped a quarter on the table, and went to pay for his food.

The waitress took the dollar he gave her and offered him change, smiling as she did. "You come back, now," she said.

Saint-Germain strolled down Clement, pausing to give his sandwich to a youngster trying to sell pads of lined yellow paper for fifteen cents before continuing on to the southwest corner of the intersection with Arguello; he took up his position on the curb, hat pulled low, umbrella open, waiting for the cab to arrive.

Five minutes later one pulled up. "Weldon?" the driver asked. "Going to Julius' Castle?"

"Yes," said Saint-Germain, closing his umbrella and getting into the rear seat, placing his briefcase beside him.

"Some weather we're having," said the driver as he turned down Sacramento Street. "Makes you think winter'll last forever."

"I understand it's fairly usual at this time of year," said Saint-Germain, who had seen a winter that lasted all year, and who found the mild climate of this region only inconvenient, not dangerous, as Russian winters were.

"Not from around here?" The driver seemed determined to have a conversation, for he kept his eye on Saint-Germain's hat-brim in his rearview mirror.

"No," said Saint-Germain, not wanting to provide the man with any information he might recall about him later.

"You don't sound like it," said the driver, leaning on the horn to encourage an elderly Dodge Brothers sedan to get moving. "You follow the Seals at all?"

"Sorry; no," said Saint-Germain.

"You got your own teams at home, huh," the driver said, and shot ahead along the street.

"Yes."

"I know how it is. You like the home-teams best." All the rest of the way to Telegraph Hill, the driver kept up a running commentary on sports of all kinds, from various ball games to horse racing, interspersing his summaries with renditions of "I'm an Old Cowhand from the Rio Grande," all without protest from his passenger, so that by the time he dropped Saint-Germain at the foot of the walkway leading up to the restaurant, he was in a comradely state of mind. "Pleasure having you in the cab. That'll be a dollar even. Sorry we had to sit at that light on Van Ness, but when fire trucks are—"

Saint-Germain handed him a dollar and a quarter. "No problem."

"Thank *you*," said the driver, touching the brim of his cap in salute. "Wish more of my fares were as nice to drive as you." He glanced around to see if anyone was hailing him, then pulled off slowly down the narrow street.

Julius' Castle commanded a fine view of the Embarcadero, the Bay Bridge, Yerba Buena Island, and the East Bay hills. It was handsomely appointed, the furniture a tasteful mix of contemporary and traditional, the decorations tending toward the European. Glassware, flatware, linen, and napery were impeccable, comfortably elegant, all of these making the restaurant a very popular place. The maitre d' had shown Saint-Germain to a table by the large, rain-spattered window, proffering a menu, and saying, "The kitchen won't be serving for half-an-hour, if you don't mind waiting."

"I don't," said Saint-Germain. "I'm expecting a friend to join me, a Miss Saxon. She will probably ask for me."

"Very good, sir," said the maitre d', and withdrew.

Saint-Germain looked over the selections and the prices, and wondered momentarily what Rowena would choose for herself—the prices were high but not completely outrageous, and he could easily afford the best they had to offer. He had not long to wait to find out what Rowena would select; five minutes after he opened the menu, the maitre d' escorted Rowena to the table by the window. He rose to greet her, kissing her hand in greeting, then watching her shrug out of her red-fox coat and hang it over the back of her chair. "You look lovely," he told her.

"Thank you; I try," she answered lightly, knowing she was well-turned-out; she had on a cocktail suit with a trumpet-skirt and long, fitted jacket of dark green faille over a blouse of ivory lace. Her hair was newly cut and styled, rolled off her face and secured with three decorative combs; she wore a lapel-pin of yellow jade in the shape of the character *the creative*; her scent combined roses, jasmine, and amber. She carried a small purse of green snake-skin which she laid on the table between them. "I see you've been looking at the menu. Tell me, is there anything you recommend?" she asked, teasing him affectionately.

"Judging by the aromas from the kitchen, the pork roast and the lamb with rosemary should be quite good." He smiled at her. "Thank you for coming. I'm sorry to inconvenience you." As he said this, he thought again how much change the twentieth century had ushered in: three decades ago he would not have suggested to Rowena that she meet him anywhere in public without making sure she was chaperoned. Now it was only the very old-fashioned who thought twice about women going on their own to meet men they chose to know. He was about to say something of the sort when Rowena anticipated him.

"I was thinking how fast I would have been, had we done this when I first came here; and, given the state of the world at that time, I would have been. After the Great War it all changed," she said, leaning across the table enough to be heard as she lowered her voice. "But I'm older, too, and who thinks a woman of fifty-two is fast?"

"Who indeed?" Saint-Germain replied. "But you're right, of course. Manners are changing more quickly than I have ever seen happen, except in times of war or plague."

"What lovely dinnertime small talk," she marveled, and sat back in her chair.

The maitre d' led a party of four to a table on the other side of the dining room; they were chatting, holding drink glasses in their hands, the two women in formal gowns, the men in business suits.

"Still, I thank you for joining me," Saint-Germain said, his dark eyes resting on her. "I have no wish to inconvenience you."

"So you said. Coming here isn't inconvenient," she told him as she opened the menu. "I should warn you, I'm hungry."

"Have anything you like," he said.

"You can afford it." She glanced at him over the top of the menu.

"I can," he agreed.

She contemplated her choices and closed the menu, setting it aside and giving him her full attention. "I've had an excellent day. I've been working on two new canvases. So far they've been coming along well." Bracing her elbows on the table, she leaned toward him. "What on earth is happening?"

"I'll tell you while you eat. I don't want to be overheard," said Saint-Germain. "I know that it sounds absurd, but I am truly concerned."

"I trust you, even though I'm not sure I believe you; not completely," said Rowena. "If you say there is trouble, then I know there must be." She flashed him a brilliant smile. "In case anyone is watching us," she explained.

"I'm assuming we're safe here, at least for this evening," said Saint-Germain.

Rowena smiled and nodded. "Then I'll make the most of it," she announced, as if challenging someone in the restaurant to dissent.

As if taking this as a cue, one of the waiters came up to the table; he poured water into their goblets as he asked, "Do you have any questions? Would you like to order now?"

"Yes, please," said Saint-Germain, nodding to Rowena. "What would you like?"

"I'll have the rack of lamb with rosemary, medium, and the Green Goddess salad, with a lot of dressing, if you would. What's your soup tonight?" She reached for her napkin and opened it, dropping it into her lap.

"Cream of leeks," said the waiter.

"Oh, good. I'll have a bowl of that." Rowena held up the menu to the waiter. "I'll decide about dessert later."

The waiter nodded. "And for the gentleman?"

"Nothing, thank you. I fear—"

"He's recovering from an intestinal complaint," said Rowena, lowering her voice conspiratorially. "He's not quite ready for solid food."

The waiter took this awkward revelation as well as he could. "I'm sorry, sir. If you decide you want a bowl of . . . of broth, I'm sure our chef could make one for you."

"Thank you," said Saint-Germain. "But it might be wisest if I have nothing."

"You know best," said the waiter; he collected their menus, and went to place the order.

"Very deft," said Saint-Germain to Rowena.

"I do think on my feet," she said with a self-satisfied smile.

"Very good," said Saint-Germain, and glanced out the window. "You can see the cars moving on the bridge."

"And the electric trains on the lower deck, with the trucks," Rowena agreed. "I'm not saying it isn't a genuine accomplishment. It's making a difference in the city already, and it hasn't been open much more than three months."

"Isn't that what it's supposed to do?" Saint-Germain asked, taking his tone from her.

"Yes, so Mayor Rossi claims. Governor Merriam, too." She pursed her lips. "But some of it is a way to keep men working. I'm not saying it's not useful to have bridges instead of ferries, but their biggest benefit is the labor they require." With a tsk of chagrin, she looked away from him. "I didn't mean to go off on that. I've been re-reading FDR's second Inaugural Address, and it stirs up so many things."

"He has a great deal to contend with," said Saint-Germain.

"And no matter how he tries, it's an uphill fight for him, poor man," she said, and ran her finger around the rim of her water goblet. "I feel for him. I voted for him, the first and second times he ran, and I'd do it again, but I still feel for him."

"This is a very big country, and its problems are complex; what benefits one group or region is detrimental to another," said Saint-Germain, suiting his conversational tone to hers. "That may be stating the obvious, but it is nonetheless true. Look at the problems with the power companies in Oregon and Washington."

"Hiring movie stars to tell the voters that publicly owned power companies mean trouble," she said condemningly.

"And it does," said Saint-Germain sardonically.

"Yes, it does—for the private power companies." She dismissed this with a toss of her head. "That's hitting below the belt."

"That it is," said Saint-Germain.

"You might as well put Lucky Luciano in charge of the FBI," she said. "And he's in prison, thank God."

The waiter came back to the table bearing a tray with soup, a basket of bread, and a ramekin of butter, all of which he put down with ceremony. "Your Green Goddess salad—do you want it now, with the soup, or before your entree?"

"After the soup, if you please," Rowena said as she picked up her spoon. "Thank you."

The waiter went away to take the order of a couple who had been seated a few minutes ago.

"Is it to your liking?" Saint-Germain asked as she tasted the soup.

"It's fine," she said, without paying much attention to it. "I've had it before." She waited a moment, then prompted, "Are you going to tell me about what's going on?"

"Yes," he said, speaking softly once more. He was grateful that no jukebox blasted out popular tunes, or radio program penetrated the conversations at the tables in the dining room. "When I left Oscar King's office today, I'm fairly certain I was followed, as I told you."

"Yes?" she encouraged him.

"I wish it weren't the case, but I'm convinced that you should be on guard. If he is the man I think he may be, he is a very resourceful and ruthless piece of work, capable of horrible acts, and willing to employ all manner of methods to gain what he seeks. There's no telling what this man will find out about me, nor what use to which he'll put the information, or how he may obtain it." He saw her suppress a shiver. "He isn't von Wolgast, but he could be quite—"

"Dangerous?" she suggested, her golden eyes shining with angry tears. "No doubt. You wouldn't be warning me if you thought he was harmless, would you?"

"No." He took a long breath. "I don't know for certain what peril this man represents, but I'd like you to think about taking precautions. If you have a pistol and you know how to use it, you may wish to have it handy."

"I have a pistol and I know how to use it. I have a shotgun, as well. One of my father's over-and-unders; it was one of the things I inherited." She continued to eat her soup, saying nothing for a short while. "All right. I'll get them out of the attic, clean them, and load them. Anything else?"

"I hope I'm not crying wolf," he confessed. "At the same time, I very much want this to turn out to be a tempest in a teapot."

"Aphorisms for all occasions," she said, and then looked at him. "I'm sorry. I didn't mean that as it sounded."

"No harm if you did," said Saint-Germain.

"But I hate the notion of being frightened again," she grumbled. "I've had enough of that to last a lifetime."

"For which I am deeply contrite," Saint-Germain reminded her.

"Oh, it's not your fault, not entirely. I have not gone out of my way to avoid you, in spite of the trouble you attract. You see, I would rather have your company than not, and, it appears, you collect enemies." She sighed and worked some more on her soup. "Have you any more information about this fellow who may or may not be following you?"

"No, nothing more," Saint-Germain said. "I've had time to think about it, and I still can't tell if this is the man Oscar King mentioned, or if he is someone who is working for the White Legion."

"Do you intend to try to find out?" Rowena asked.

"Certainly. I don't want to be looking over my shoulder every waking minute."

He could see she was still upset; he went on, "If I find out that this could make you a target, then I'll keep away until I've—"

"But I don't want you to do that," said Rowena. "I want to spend as much time with you as I can, until you leave San Francisco. I know I'll miss you dreadfully when you're gone, and sooner or later, you will go." She set her spoon on the charger. "I know you aren't going to stay here, and not because you don't stay anywhere for very long. You're too caught up with what's happening in Europe to stay away from it, as much as you say you want to. You'll reach a point where you have to go back."

He could not bring himself to answer her; he was glad to see the waiter and bus-boy coming with her Green Goddess salad.

The soup-bowl was whisked away on the charger by the bus-boy and the salad-plate set in its place by the waiter, a perfect pas-de-deux. "Would you like pepper, ma'am?"

"No, thank you," said Rowena, and reached for her salad fork.

Saint-Germain waited until the waiter was gone, and then said, "It's not my intention to leave, at least not for a while."

"I know," she said.

"But if it is prudent for me to keep to myself for the time being, I'll do it, much as I would prefer to be with you," he went on.

"I know," she said.

"You may decide you'd prefer to leave the city for a time—go where you'll feel safe, where you can be protected, for as much as I wish it were otherwise, I cannot protect you now. My very presence creates the risk I am trying to help you to avoid." He leaned forward, his voice dropping still lower. "If I could spare you this and still remain close to you, I would, but, Rowena, it may not be possible."

"Yes; I know," she said patiently. "And I promise you, if it seems that I am in danger, I'll consider everything you've said. And find an appropriate means of dealing with it. But I'm not yet persuaded that I have anything to worry about. How can this man find me—and why should he wish to? Oh, I'll make sure I have new locks on my doors and windows, and I'll alert Clara Powell that no one unknown to her is to be admitted to the house, under any circumstances, but I'm not going to leave the city simply because you *suspect* an unknown man *might* be following you. What kind of paltry woman do you take me for? I'm not going to fall apart because there's a hint of sinister activities taking place around you."

"It seems a remote possibility, on the surface." Saint-Germain wished he could convey to her the nature of the trepidation he felt. "But such unlikely possibilities have a way of materializing, and I don't want you exposed to anything that might . . . disrupt your life."

"Having to change the locks disrupts my life," she observed, jabbing her fork into the lettuce. "Having to protect myself disrupts my life."

"For which I am sorry, but it is a small price to pay for safety," he said, thinking he sounded far too prim. "You shouldn't have any of this touch you."

"But it touches you, and through you, it touches me. So I'll resign myself to dealing with the potential consequences." She moved her salad-plate aside, half of it uneaten.

"A good beginning," said Saint-Germain, doing his best to look relieved. "I appreciate your candor, no matter what happens."

"You're very adroit," she said, and signaled to the waiter to bring her main course; she dabbed her mouth with her napkin, and returned it to her lap. "I'm not easily scared off, Comte. I might have been when I was younger, but no more."

Saint-Germain reached across the table and took her hand, his dark eyes fixed on her golden ones. "You humble me, Rowena."

At that she laughed. "Why don't I believe you?" she asked, expecting no answer. "That's the last thing I'd want to do."

"Ah." Saint-Germain rubbed her hand once and released it. "I won't embarrass you by making an effusive display in public."

"No, certainly not," she agreed. "You can do that later, when you take me home."

TEXT OF A LETTER FROM MILES SUNBURY IN LONDON TO DOÑA ISABEL INEZ VEDANCHO Y NUÑEZ AT COPSEHOWE IN HAMPSHIRE.

43C Siddons Lane
City of Westminster
9 March, 1937

Doña Isabel Inez Vedancho y Nuñez
Copsehowe
nr. Briarcopse
Hampshire

My most dear Doña Isis,
I cannot thank you enough for the many kindnesses you have done me since my dreadful assault. Your presence has sustained me far more than anything the medicos have accomplished on my behalf. I am grateful to you for all you have done for me, your attention, and your help in my long weeks of recovery. It has been a terrible burden you have taken upon yourself, and you have borne it easily, as if it were no imposition at all, but instead a most welcome pastime, which is more than I am prepared to believe.

I don't want you to feel that you must continue your ministrations—although I would be less than truthful if I didn't own that I would want them to continue—for you are a married woman, and I would repay you most shamefully if I allowed you to damage your reputation or compromise your conjugality through any act of mine. So, if you deem it proper that we discontinue our friendship, I will understand and respect your decision. A man in my profession too often sees how even the most innocent good-will can seem dalliance to those with such inclinations, and for that reason alone, I would urge you to reconsider your frequent visits and other signs of distinction you have been so good as to extend to me.

It has been one of the delights of my life to have you so diligent in your regards in my time of greatest need. Many another would have been willing to turn away, or not make any effort beyond a card or telephone call, but you have visited, have brought me delicious meals, have tended me, have sympathized with me, have bolstered me when I was discouraged, have comforted me when I was in pain. No one else has done so much for me, nor has anyone been so caring. I hope not to read more into this than your concern, but it has been more than simple courtesy, at least to me, that you have been willing to spend so much time with me. In such times as this has been, I realize I might be more inclined to become attached than I would under other occurrences, but I would be less than honest if I didn't acknowledge that my emotions are now engaged in a way I never thought would be the case. If I have misconstrued your objectives in attending to me, I apologize and plead exigencies of circumstances to account for it.

The street in which I live was named for a famous actress. In her day, the King of England was asked if it offended him to see Sarah Siddons playing Queens, since she was a commoner, to which Charles replied that Mrs. Siddons was the only real Queen: all the others were imitations. I tell you this because I believe those sentiments can also be ascribed to you. I am very much taken by the nobility of soul that frames your character. And, beyond all doubt, you are the most beautiful woman I have ever met. I will be bereft to have you gone from my life, but it must be, or I will bring such rumors upon you as must eventually reach your husband's ears and lead to a crisis in your marriage that not even my skills in court could mitigate.

It is difficult for me to discuss this, for I am very much confused. I am aware that you may not realize the extent of my affection for you. I may be laboring under a misapprehension in assuming that there is any connection beyond altruism between us; however I am certain that you will not continue to give me hope where none can possibly exist.

I have thought long and hard about this aspect of our relationship, and I am convinced that you have been unaware how our companionship might be interpreted by those with small minds and an inclination to create scandal. Before you put yourself in a more conspicuous situation, I think it would be most prudent for us to discontinue our luncheons and long afternoons together; I have progressed with my walking because of all you have done, yet it is just this generosity of spirit that has led to the environment of aspersion that has attached to our meetings. It is most distressing to me to contemplate the hours I will miss you, but I can see no other way to do you the honor you deserve than to sever our dealings now, much as I would prefer not to have to do so. I know you may not understand why I do this, but I assure you, it is for the best, for I would regret more than I could say bringing you any pain or opprobrium through any actions or words of mine.

Let me tell you that I am afraid some of the damage may have already been done. One of the men in chambers with me told me that his wife was very much shocked to hear I have been entertaining a married woman alone in my rooms. Try as I might to explain what you have done for me, and why, it meant nothing to him, nor, I must suppose, did anything he deigned to pass on to his wife. I am cognizant of how this is seen in chambers, but I know it would be inexcusable to have such calumnies go beyond this place.

I'm sorry that I have exposed you to such controversy as must accompany this letter. I would never injure you in any way, were it in my power to prevent it. I am appalled that your generous acts on my behalf have redounded to your discredit, and I assure you I will do all in my power to minimize the impact of my imprudence. It would be the most wonderful thing in my life to be able to continue our association, but I fear that is no longer possible, so I ask you to forgive me for addressing you in this way when I would so much rather talk to you face-to-face. But that, sadly, would lead to more speculation that can only bring you damage, which I am determined not to do.

Believe me,

Your most devoted,

Miles Sunbury

～

chapter four

Oscar King looked out of place in Carlo Pietragnelli's damaged house; his three-piece pin-striped suit and meticulous linen shirt were strong contrasts to Pietragnelli's work-clothes and heavy Hudson's Bay jacket worn against the bustling winds; the living room was a patchwork of light and dark shadows, marking the destruction of the windows. The attorney surveyed the cardboard covering the shot-out panes, and shook his head. "Truly horrendous. I can see how you must be frightened. I would be, were I in your position. How many have you lost this way?"

"To this day?" Pietragnelli asked. "Seventeen in this house, nine in my workers' cabins. I must suppose there will be more." He put his hands on his hips and took up a pugnacious stance. "I will find them! I will make them pay!"

"And so you shall," said Oscar King, glancing over at Saint-Germain. "You're right; this is a most serious situation. The police are not doing their job in tracking down the culprits, from what you told me, Ragoczy."

"No; apparently there are those in the Sheriff's Department who are in sympathy with the assumed perpetrators, if not actually among their numbers, and as such, they are disinclined to act." Saint-Germain saw Pietragnelli nod, confirming his remarks.

"My workers are being threatened now, as well. It isn't just the shot-out windows. Two couples have taken their children out of school, because they are afraid they are no longer safe. That troubles me very much." Pietragnelli indicated the parlor beyond the double-doors of the living room. There was a small fireplace on the far wall, and two settees facing each other in front of the hearth. "If you'll come in and sit down, Signor King? And you, Signor Ragoczy?"

"Grazie," said Saint-Germain, and went into the parlor immediately behind Pietragnelli.

King took a little more time to look over the damage he saw, and shook his head; when he spoke, his manner was slightly pedantic, as if he were laying out a case to a jury instead of speaking to an abused property owner. "Such a fine old house, to be treated this way. This building is historically important in the region and legitimately beautiful on its own account. Whoever is doing this has no regard for things of value, that is quite demonstrable."

"It is an insult," said Pietragnelli indignantly. "It should never happen. I am ashamed."

"You have nothing to be ashamed of," said Saint-Germain. "You haven't shot out your windows, nor have you done anything that deserves this."

"Someone thinks I have, and I must know who it is, and put an end to it, or it all comes to me," Pietragnelli countered, his face darkening. He pointed to four missing panes in the French doors, with cardboard taped in place of the missing glass. "I am appalled at this."

"It is a horrible thing," said King, coming to take a seat by the fire in the parlor, which crackled merrily, driving out the cold that rode on a biting north wind polishing the clear sky and setting the new leaves and grasses straining at their fragile bonds. "Ragoczy told me about your trouble, but I wasn't truly prepared for this."

"They no longer pretend they do not wish to be rid of me; they are blatant in their purpose, and make no effort to conceal their intentions," said Pietragnelli. "The Leonardis want my land. They think I owe it to them, because I bought some of their plantations when their vineyard was failing, and they seek to serve the same turn they are convinced I served them. They resent me for being able to do it, and they want la vendetta—revenge upon me. They masquerade behind the White Legion—which is reprehensible enough—but it disguises their true intent."

"You must forgive me if I find that a trifle unlikely," said King, sinking down on the settee. "I know that men often find gratitude an intolerable burden, but still—to go to all this trouble, to deliberately ruin you . . ." He shook his head.

"They killed my neighbor, Mr. Yoshimura. And now the Leonardis are purchasing his farm from his widow. They're paying the lowest possible price, and Mrs. Yoshimura is in no position to refuse, nor is she inclined to hold out for a better price; she's been scared by the way Yoshimura died. I have offered to pay her more than she has been offered by members of the White Legion, and to share ownership with her, so that she and her children can continue to earn money from it, but she's too frightened. I've asked her to consider for another two months. I've even sent my men over to work the fields, so that she won't have to take an even greater loss on the land." He clapped his hands twice. "I can't think of anything else to do that can help her."

"If, as you say, she is frightened," King began in a measured way, "then it must be supposed she is being coerced, and any contract entered into as a result of coercion can be declared null and void. She has the right to repudiate the agreement made." He stared at the fire as if he could read secrets in it. "But she would have to be willing to bring a civil action against the Leonardis, and it may be she would not want to do it."

"A Japanese widow might not get a fair hearing in any court in this county," said Pietragnelli. "Even Italians have difficulty being accorded the same rights as the Protestants; it's ten times worse for Orientals."

"That is a pattern encountered everywhere," King said in agreement. "But that doesn't mean that the favoritism is right, or cannot be challenged." He coughed. "Of course, it is expensive to fight such prejudice."

"But not impossible or hopeless," said Saint-Germain, giving King an incisive glance.

"No, neither of those," said King. "But Mr. Pietragnelli is right—many Americans are biased against Italians, because of men like Al Capone and Frank Nitti."

"Not all Italians are gangsters," said Pietragnelli firmly. "Even most Siciliani are farmers and fishermen, not Mafiosi."

"Yes, Italians do many things in America beyond breaking the law, as any person of common sense will know. For example: one is mayor of San Francisco, and Rossi is not alone," said King, understanding Pietragnelli's point, going on in his courtroom style. "Italians have been crucial in restoring the California wine business; and not all are agriculturalists, some cultivate other fields; the Bank of America is led by an Italian. And Italians are inclined to support all manner of Italian ventures. Giannini dines at Fior d'Italia once a week, and thus makes the restaurant famous and well-patronized."

"That is all very well in San Francisco, but this is Sonoma County." Pietragnelli glared up at the ceiling. "In many ways, more than Marin County separates us from San Francisco."

King nodded twice. "Exactly. That is one of the reasons we're having this discussion. I am interested in dealing with this problem in terms that apply here."

"Do you think it can be done?" Pietragnelli came as close to feeling defeated as it was possible for him to be. "I don't see how."

"I must suppose that we will find a way," said King. "The law doesn't support the terrorizing of American citizens, not officially." He said the last carefully. "We know this is more an ideal than a reality, but it is the spirit of the Constitution, to protect all citizens from manipulation or exploitation."

"If they are of European descent, certainly it is more likely to occur," said Saint-Germain, his voice deliberately neutral.

"And not all Europeans," added Pietragnelli. "The Puritans were Protestants, and many Americans distrust Catholics almost as much as they mistrust Jews and Orientals. They are afraid of the Pope." He slapped his thighs with both hands. "It is a most frustrating state of affairs. I know that what is happening to me isn't legal, but I cannot invoke the law for protection because the officers of the law are supporting criminals." His exasperation increased with each word so that at the end he was almost shouting.

"I know we will find a way to protect you," said King. "If we have to go to Sacramento and file an action there, we will."

"I hope it won't come to that," said Pietragnelli.

"For Lord's sake, why?" King asked, looking up as the sound of the Pierce-Arrow's horn cut through their conversation.

"Mr. Rogers has seen something," said Saint-Germain, glad now that he had left Rogerio on guard duty. He looked at Pietragnelli. "Are you expecting anyone?"

"My children. My daughter and son-in-law, in any case. Not Angelina or Massimo. Perhaps Adrianna. I asked Sophia and Ethan to join us and I warned them that they might have to deal with—" He stopped as a rifle-shot barked from a short distance away, followed at once by a squeal of brakes.

"I can tell you want to be inclusive, Mr. Pietragnelli," said King, "but mightn't this be too much of a risk for your family?"

"Davvero. If those . . . those vile tapini—" He made himself be still until he had regained control of his temper. "I'm sorry. My tongue outruns my mind. I shouldn't speak so to the likes of you, Mr. King."

"It's understandable, and I've heard much worse with far less provocation," said King, in a cultivated combination of geniality and hauteur; it had served him well in front of juries, and it did so now.

"You're a kind man," said Pietragnelli.

"You should be glad I'm not; you don't want an advocate who will not go to the limit of the law on your behalf," said King. "Ragoczy is a kind man, so I needn't be. Nor should I be, not if you want me to take care of your case effectively."

Pietragnelli made a sign of understanding, his face canny. "Capisco, Signor Re, I do understand you," he said grandly. "Undoubtedly you are right; I know your advice is well-considered and many men seek it, so I will listen to you and I will—" He rose as he heard a car door slam, and less than a minute later, a young man and a heavily pregnant young woman wrapped in a camel-hair coat hurried into the house.

"Someone shot out our windshield! It's ruined!" the woman exclaimed, and rushed toward Pietragnelli, who had made it into the living room and was standing with his arms extended. "Ah, Papà! Che farai?"

"It is what we talked about last night, Sophia," he said as he took his daughter in his arms, holding her carefully. "As you see, their efforts continue. It is an affront to me that anyone should do anything to harm you." He patted her shoulder before he released her and hugged his son-in-law. "Ethan. I'll see to the repair of your car."

Ethan Carmody stepped back. "It was damned scary," he said, making no excuse for his language. "I thought Sophia might get hurt, and that was . . . unthinkable."

Pietragnelli took both Sophia and Ethan by the hand, and led them into the parlor, where Saint-Germain and Oscar King were standing to receive them. "This is my daughter Sophia, and my son-in-law, Ethan Carmody. His mother is a Constantino, which accounts for his good looks. Miei figli, this is Ferenc Ragoczy, who has been so good to us for so long, and Oscar King from San Francisco, who is a noted attorney."

Ethan held out his hand to Saint-Germain. "A pleasure, sir. Who is the gentleman outside? I must assume he is with you."

"That is my longtime associate, Mr. Rogers," Saint-Germain confirmed, noting that Ethan's handshake was nearly a contest of strength, or a test of which of them had the more powerful grip. "He is there to keep an eye out for any trouble."

"Yes," said Sophia. "He took off in the direction of where the shot came from. He was wholly unafraid."

"Actually," said Saint-Germain as he kissed Sophia's hand, "he probably is frightened, as any sensible person would be. But fear doesn't keep him from acting."

"Then he is a very remarkable man," said Ethan, and looked over at Pietragnelli. "Is this what you meant when you said there had been some trouble here?"

"Essentially, yes," said Pietragnelli. "I didn't want to tell you about this, because I wouldn't want you to get caught up in this. I wanted to spare you the worry you would have, and keep you from having to deal with the interruptions the attacks bring into my life. But these evil men have extended their malice to my workers and now I begin to fear they will attempt something with you, and Angelina, and Massimo, which would distress me more than I can say. So I want you to help me consider the various possibilities open to me." He looked at his daughter and son-in-law. "I called Angelina and Massimo, on the telephone, but neither of them can be here today, nor can Adrianna, it being a work-day, but they have said they will abide by your decisions in that regard, and they will take the precautions Signor Ragoczy recommends."

"Precautions can be expensive," said Ethan.

"So they can," Saint-Germain said, cutting off Pietragnelli's remarks. "But that is something I will cover."

"Why should you?" Ethan challenged, doing his best to maintain a courteous demeanor. "Why should it matter to you? Are you hoping to trade on my father-in-law's indebtedness to you to oblige him to do your bidding?"

"It has happened before," said Pietragnelli. "But nothing Mr. Ragoczy has done in the last decade would lead me to believe that he would do anything of the sort."

Saint-Germain directed his answer to Ethan. "My participation in this business has contributed to the problems you are currently enduring, so it is appropriate that I should bear some of the cost. How can I expect any of you to take on the trouble and expense that is not of your making? Your family has a business in peril, and I have an investment in that business. So it would be better if I covered the price of your being guarded than if you are left to shoulder the whole."

"I concur," said King. "Ordinarily I would not, but given the peculiar nature of this situation, I think Mr. Ragoczy is right." He took a cigarette from the silver case in his waistcoat pocket, and used the lighter built into the top of it. "It is a fortunate thing that Mr. Ragoczy has such probity. Many lesser men would not be inclined to extend themselves." He blew out a stream of smoke, staring at the far wall.

"Didn't you pay for guards here already?" Ethan asked. "And look where we are now."

"Yes, I did. But I underestimated the damage that could be done, and the guards were given too many tasks to do. As a result, this house has broken windows and the guards are exhausted, trying to do at least twice the work we anticipated," said Saint-Germain. "Another reason to manage this crisis more strategically."

"Is it possible the guards agree with the White Legion?" Sophia asked, and held her breath for the answer.

"It is possible but highly unlikely," said Saint-Germain. "The men are of Russian descent and would not be inclined to support the White Legion, which wouldn't want them, in any case."

"And so you vouch for them?" Ethan accused.

"I can vouch for the reputation of the company for which they work," said Saint-Germain.

"He was very precise in his instructions," said Oscar King.

"We'll agree he's a prince among men and a model of integrity," said Ethan, finally bringing his fraying temper under control; Saint-Germain said nothing and so, after an awkward silence, Ethan went on, "I shouldn't have taken it out on you. But that bullet through the windshield, I have to tell you, would have done the same to you."

"Oh, beyond question," said Saint-Germain. "I can understand your fury. You have a pregnant wife and she could have been hurt."

"Well, she could!" Ethan burst out.

Pietragnelli touched Ethan's arm. "If you are angry, you should be angry with me," he said sadly. "All this is ultimately my fault."

"No," Oscar King announced, cutting into Pietragnelli's self-denunciation. "It isn't your fault, Mr. Pietragnelli, nor is it Ragoczy's. It is the fault of the White Legion and the Leonardis, if Mr. Pietragnelli is right and they are the ones at the forefront of this assault. The man pulling the trigger is the one who is responsible for the shot through your windshield, Mr. Carmody. The men who beat Mr. Yoshimura are the ones who are guilty of his death. You do not have to answer for what happened. You have not done anything that justifies men shooting out your windows. Make sure you understand this, all of you, or you will not get through this ordeal. And it is an ordeal; do not underestimate it."

Pietragnelli sighed. "We'll find a way. My family is strong. We do not flee at the first sign of trouble, and we don't desert one another."

Saint-Germain saw Sophia stand a little straighter, although she was still clearly shaken; after a long moment, she said, "We'll find a way."

"Is that what you mean?" King asked. "For men often promise full cooperation, and then refuse to do the sensible things offered to them. In your case, I hope you will not reject any proposition put to you, but will give it thoughtful deliberation."

"You seem worried that we will not be acquiescent; that we will not do as you recommend," said Pietragnelli.

"When men are under pressure, it is not an easy thing for them to see the advantage of a plan not of their own making, let alone one that might cause them to give the appearance of capitulation. I wouldn't want to leave Geyserville, were I in your shoes," said King. "I'm not the least surprised that you dislike the proposition Mr. Ragoczy has to put before you. But your situation is still very risky, and potentially more hazardous. I say this in the hope that you will be able to evaluate the recommendation we have settled upon, instead of turning it down without giving it your full attention and attentive reflection."

"You may not like what I have to propose," Saint-Germain said before King could expound any longer. "But it is the one way I have hit upon that can ensure your safety and still take the measures necessary to protect your winery and vineyard." He took a couple seconds to gather his thoughts. "Mr. King is right: I want you to consider what I propose to you; do not respond without careful thought."

"This sounds drastic," said Ethan, trying to joke.

"It will be more disruptive than you will like, I reckon, but it is as cautious as anything I've been able to come up with." He glanced at King. "We discussed this on the way up here, and Mr. King is in general agreement with me. We have reviewed all the options, and we want you to do the same."

"Swell," said Sophia dryly.

"There is one other factor here that I hope you will include in your discussion." He looked at Pietragnelli. "You want a fair fight over this, don't you?"

"Well, of course," said Pietragnelli. "What else could I want? If the fight isn't fair, the victory is a lie."

"Admirable sentiments," said Oscar King. "But sadly, your opponents don't see matters that way. And they will use your fairness against you if they can." He nodded to Saint-Germain. "That was your point, I believe."

Saint-Germain went back into the parlor, going up to the fireplace and resting his arm on the marble-fronted mantel. "First, I can assure you that what I put forth to you will not cost you a cent," he said, waiting while Pietragnelli led Sophia and Ethan to the pair of settees, indicating they should sit down; Oscar King brought up the rear and pulled a maharaja's wicker chair nearer to the fire. "I don't know how this will sound to you."

The front door opened and Rogerio's impatient step indicated he was agitated. "I couldn't see him," he said as he hurried into the parlor. "I saw where he had been standing, but he was gone well before I got close. There was only one set of footprints."

"Leading south," Saint-Germain said.

"Yes. Off toward the south gate. I didn't see any car or truck parked at the fence, but that doesn't mean . . ." He faltered, aware that Pietragnelli was becoming restive. "I wish I could tell you I had seen two young men who headed toward the Leonardi vineyard, but I can't."

"They will show themselves," said Pietragnelli, his ire returning. "And when they do, I will carve their hearts from their breasts."

"Now, now, now," King soothed. "Nothing so vituperative, if you please; not that I cannot understand your impulses. Intemperate remarks can return to haunt you, especially if this case goes to court. Not that anyone here would want to testify that you made threats, but if an opposing attorney should ask if anyone in this room heard you threaten to cut out the Leonardis' hearts, they would have to say they had, and that would put you in a very bad light. If you feel these things, well and good, but, for your own protection, keep them to yourself." He let the people in the room cogitate for the better part of a minute. "Let me advise you to be particularly careful around your workmen, Mr. Pietragnelli, until this problem is resolved."

"If someone had taken a shot at your daughter, would you say the same thing?" Pietragnelli dared him to speak against him.

"I would have the same emotions you do, but I would do my utmost not to voice them, for fear of having them twisted to the advantage of my foes," said King. "Now, if you will listen to what Mr. Ragoczy has to say, we can proceed with our plans."

Saint-Germain glanced at his watch. "I won't take any longer than I must to explain this to you. I made a telephone call this morning, to Lake Tahoe. There is a Ponderosa Lodge in the woods on the north shore, run by a Mrs. Curtis who is called Mrs. Curt. The lodge is fairly isolated without being remote; it is surrounded by cabins, and just now, most of them are empty, so she would be glad of any business that could come her way."

"I take your meaning, but am not leaving my vineyard," Pietragnelli said with the full weight of his determination.

"I realize you don't want to, and I know you don't want to make the situation more dangerous than it is, so I ask you: just take an evening to think about this, and try not to let yourself believe what you want to believe because it is how you would like matters to be. You don't have to concern yourself with how this will be done. I will pay for guards to keep watch over your property, and make sure your workmen and their families are safe," Saint-Germain went on, his manner deferential. "Your vines will be tended, and—"

"You provided guards already, and the windows are still being shot out," said Pietragnelli, unwilling to grant any concession to Saint-Germain.

"True enough. The men had to divide their attention between the riflemen and the raids on Yoshimura's farm. I have already admitted that there have been too few of them to do the work properly. If I had hired more guards, you would not have had this trouble," said Saint-Germain. "I would like to think that I can ensure the protection of your property more easily if I don't also have to defend you as well."

"So you propose to send me and my family to a resort at Lake Tahoe, leaving my hands to continue to risk their lives to tend my vines?" Pietragnelli demanded.

"I believe your absence will lessen the risks the workmen face," Saint-Germain said, determined not to be goaded into argument. "Let them think that you have been frightened off. The guards will apprehend the culprits and then they can bring them to the law. It won't be as easy for the sheriff to ignore professionals as it is to dismiss the complaints of a vintner."

"And what about us?" Sophia asked. "What do you—?"

"Mrs. Curt has room for all of you, and it will not cost you anything to go there. I'll have other guards at your home in Calistoga. They'll look after the mare you have there." Saint-Germain saw the ghost of a smile form on Sophia's lips.

"Where do you plan to find these guards?" Pietragnelli asked, his curiosity increasing.

"There are any number of men eager for work who were soldiers in the Great War and haven't been able to use the skills they learned in the army; given the state of the country, they will be inclined to give superior service," said King. "I have discussed this with an employment agency that usually supplies guards for banks and factories and grand events, and he is confident that he can provide more than a dozen competent men within a week, if you decide to go along with this plan."

"Soldiers on my land," Pietragnelli lamented. "What are we coming to?"

"You will find that they can do the work you need, and in a proficient manner, with a minimum of disruption to the necessary work of the vineyard," said King. "You will have some respite, which you will need, for once the miscreants are apprehended, you will, of course, return at once to participate in their prosecution." He paused. "If the political climate is as . . . narrow as you have said, it may be that the court may prefer not to litigate, but we will have the kind of witnesses they dare not ignore, and that will work to our advantage."

"It sounds to me as if you think this is the best way to deal with our problem," said Ethan, still a bit defensive.

"Yes, I do. I think so long as you are here, the White Legion, or whoever is behind this attack, will continue to escalate the offensive against you; it is possible they may attempt something far worse than shooting out windows, such as setting the house or the winery on fire," said King in a very measured way.

"You're trying to frighten us," said Ethan belligerently.

"No; you're already frightened, and well you should be; I would be, were I in your situation," said Saint-Germain. "I am certain that you will do well to go to Ponderosa Lodge so that the guards can handle this. If you insist on remaining here, it will be more difficult to protect you, and your workmen, and their families."

Pietragnelli pressed his lips together, and tried to sort out his emotions. "I will need at least one night to ruminate."

"By all means, do," said Saint-Germain. "I hope you will discuss it at length, and examine any and all alternatives that may be open to you." He shifted his stance so his lower shoulders rested against the mantel, and thrust his hands into his trouser-pockets. "No matter what, you will have disruption in your life; it is only a question to what extent you have upheaval, and how you decide to address it."

"You say that easily enough," Ethan accused.

"Hardly easily," said Saint-Germain.

"You're a powerful and wealthy man, and you have undoubtedly found ways to avoid the intrusions of life." Ethan sat forward on the settee. "You can buy your peace, if you must."

Before Saint-Germain could think of a response, Rogerio spoke. "Mr. Ragoczy left Spain less than a year ago with a price on his head. There is no reason to believe that has changed. He had to leave his businesses behind, to have them confiscated by the military insurgents. And that wasn't the first time he has had to leave everything behind. If you think he is recommending this move to you as a cavalier gesture, you have underestimated him and his regard for you and this place. He is trying to ensure your safety, and the safety of this vineyard, if he can." He noticed the frown on Saint-Germain's face, and said, "I have no wish to embarrass you, but this impetuous young man doesn't know what you've been through, and unless he does, he'll make assumptions that are . . . ill-considered." He looked directly at Ethan Carmody. "If Mr. Ragoczy advises you to make a strategic retreat, you may be confident that he recommends it to your benefit."

"These men are trying to lay claim to my vineyards," Pietragnelli stated with as much emphasis as he could summon.

"Which we are trying to prevent," said Oscar King. "If you are willing to spend a week or two in the Sierra Nevada, you give us the opportunity to take a more active role in protecting this place."

"So you say," said Pietragnelli, doing his best not to be resentful.

"I'm on my father's side, whatever it may be," said Sophia, taking Pietragnelli's hand in hers.

"An admirable sentiment," said King, "but it may not be very practical in the long run." He pointed to the cardboard over one of the French door window-panes. "So far they have used rifles and shotguns, but there are other weapons—Molotov cocktails, dynamite, or something equally destructive—that could be used. Usually threats increase in severity as long as there is resistance to them. I do think there is reason to be unsettled about your vulnerability. Your workmen aren't trained to deal with such things, but the men I have had recommended are. They would prefer not to have to look after you as well as your lands."

"You've done so much without a word to me," Pietragnelli said, glowering.

"I have no wish to alert your enemies," said Saint-Germain, "and if your operators do listen to your conversations as much as you say they do, I would not do you a good turn by revealing too much on the telephone."

Pietragnelli managed a single nod. "Yes. You're right to be careful about that." He leaned over and gave Sophia's shoulder a squeeze before letting her go. "I know how conscientious you are, and I honor your rectitude, but I don't like having decisions forced upon me."

"I do understand," said Saint-Germain, "little though you may think so."

"I hate having to leave my vineyard. It smacks of cowardice, and that galls me. What does it say to my neighbors if I retreat in the face of trouble? It may be as you say, and being here makes the chance for more destruction all the greater, but I do not want to abandon this vineyard, not for vicious bigots." Pietragnelli got up and began to pace the length of the parlor, going as far as the door to the dining room, then back to the French doors. "I cannot see the use of going away, though I know you mean well by making the offer. If the men you say you can hire are as capable as you say, they must be able to—" He stopped. "But if you're right, and our presence makes the danger worse, what am I to do?"

"Go to Ponderosa Lodge," said King. "You can have daily reports, if you like, so long as they go through my office. I don't want anyone telephoning directly, to keep your location as secret as we can. If the operators gossip, you must be careful not to give them any grist for their mills."

"It still seems like running away," said Pietragnelli.

"It must," said Saint-Germain. "And I realize how much you would rather stay and fight. But if your vineyard is destroyed and your house wrecked, wouldn't that be a Pyrrhic victory?"

"It might be," Pietragnelli allowed.

"So you have much to gain in doing those things that are inclined to minimize the potential for damage to your business and property," said King. "In the meantime, there are any number of things I can do that might not stop the White Legion or the Leonardis, but can make it more difficult for them to act." He looked at Pietragnelli. "It will be easier for me to make my case if you are not here, for that would help me to show a credible threat to life and property."

Ethan was intrigued. "What sort of things can you do?"

"We can file a cease-and-desist order to begin with, a reasonable thing to do," said King, ticking the possibilities off on his fingers. "Then I could prepare a lawsuit alleging that the White Legion has undertaken a campaign of assaults with the intention of coercing certain farmers and vintners to sell their lands to avoid further attacks. Some of your neighbors would probably be willing to support that, but it may be a bit more difficult to prevail in court. On the favorable side, it would draw attention to the pattern of intimidation, and that will be of interest to the Attorney General in Sacramento. I'm sure the White Legion wouldn't like having their activities in the spotlight. Nor would your sheriff, for it might lead to demands for his resignation. Then I could—"

"Never mind. I get the picture," said Ethan, and went on, "I suppose you know the White Legion has men in Napa County, too, from one end of the valley to the other. I've seen their pamphlets in Calistoga, where we live."

"I want to say no, absolutely no," said Pietragnelli. "But I will do as you ask, and take the evening to discuss it with Sophia and Ethan. It may be more complicated than I first thought." He glanced at Ethan. "Why didn't you say anything about the pamphlets?"

Ethan shrugged. "I supposed you knew. I didn't see any point in talking about the obvious, not where the operators might listen in."

"I understand," said Pietragnelli, doing his best to keep his anxiety in check. "But it puts all of this in a different light, unfortunately."

King nodded. "You let me do what I have to do, and make the most of your time away from Geyserville."

"What about the Yoshimura farm? The Leonardis won't take it over for another month, if their offer is accepted by the family; that is still not certain. And there are still things there the midnight harvesters want. I wouldn't like to leave the farm unguarded. If you're going to protect my vineyard, you should take care of the Yoshimura farm as well."

"If that is what I must do to satisfy you, then I will," said Saint-Germain.

Pietragnelli shook his head. "I haven't made up my mind yet."

"Nor do I expect you to," said Saint-Germain. "But I want you to know that I am willing to make many concessions if only it will help you to go to Lake Tahoe."

"It is so far away," said Pietragnelli.

"You can drive it in a day—I did." Saint-Germain nodded toward Oscar King. "He can make arrangements to have a car at your disposal, or an open ticket for the train—you can catch it at Truckee and ride it down to Davis and come on from there with your son, or in a hired car, whichever suits you more."

"You're being very magnanimous," said Pietragnelli. "I should comply with your requests—I could catch up on my reading and have property under guard— but I am still not sanguine about going away while my vineyard is under siege."

"All I ask is that you'll consider my offer, and what could happen if you decide to remain here." Saint-Germain lowered his eyes.

"Will you still supply us with guards and this attorney and all the rest if we don't leave?" Pietragnelli demanded.

"Certainly," said Saint-Germain. "I wouldn't leave you without any additional support when you will need it more urgently than ever."

"So you say," Ethan challenged. "But why shouldn't you compel us to do as you wish?"

"Because then you would resent the whole, and you would not cooperate with the plans Mr. King will outline to you." He moved away from the mantel. "I think you have enough to think about. We'll leave you to your deliberations; I will contact you tomorrow morning to learn your decision." He went to the door into the living room. "Incidentally, if you change your minds later on, we can always find ways to deal with your new decision, whatever it may be."

"You're so very reasonable," Ethan flung at him as if trying to force Saint-Germain to rescind his offers and leave them alone.

"You see, it is easier for Mr. King, Mr. Rogers, and me. This isn't our family business and our home, so it behooves us to be willing to accommodate you, for you have so much to lose." Saint-Germain executed a little bow, and then went directly to the front door, holding it open for Rogerio and Oscar King; they went out into the windy spring day.

TEXT OF A LETTER FROM MORETON GUARDIAN SERVICE IN SACRAMENTO
TO OSCAR KING IN SAN FRANCISCO.

MORETON GUARDIAN SERVICE
1108 D STREET
SACRAMENTO, CALIFORNIA

March 26, 1937

Oscar King
King Lowenthal Taylor & Frost
630 Kearny Street
San Francisco, California

Dear Mr. King,

I am in receipt of your check for $4,000.00 dollars drawn on an account on the San Francisco Bank of America for one month of guard services to be provided at three plantations of the Pietragnelli Vineyards, of Geyserville and Calistoga, and the farm of the late Hiro Yoshimura. This will provide you the services of thirty-two men at the Geyserville properties, all proficient in the use of small arms and experienced in patrol, entry and exit inspections, border maintenance and monitoring. They will work in twelve-hour shifts of sixteen. A total of eight will be assigned to the Calistoga vineyard, and will work in shifts of four. All shifts will report in at the end of their shifts with a complete report of incidents. If any specific infractions of the law are observed, they will be duly reported in writing to the proper authorities as well as to you for the perusal of your client. I will also submit written summaries to you at the end of each week.

I realize our services are very costly, but I make no apology for it, because we deliver precisely what we pledge. I have never lost anything or anyone we have been hired to protect. We have patrolled at San Simeon and Spreckles mansion, and protected the most gaudy of Hollywood premieres.

I have taken the maps you submitted to me and I have reviewed them with my senior employees. We have arranged our patrols in overlapping patterns, which I will, if your client insists, explain to you. I would prefer to keep such information among my own workers, for the patrols are less likely to be breached if only we know what they are. If the client should insist on being provided this information, I will tender it, but under protest, for I do not think it advisable to let our plans beyond our immediate control.

My patrol leaders at Geyserville are Hill and Morgenstern, at Calistoga Parker and Scott. I will give them any names you designate for permission to enter the Pietragnelli properties, and the Yoshimura farm. As soon as I have these names and a description of the persons in question we will begin our work.

It is a pleasure doing business with you. If there is anything you or your client need to discuss with me, you have only to telephone and I will do my utmost to answer your questions promptly.

Sincere regards,

J. D. Moreton

Founder, Moreton Guardian Service

⌒

chapter five

Rowena could not identify the sound that had brought her awake, but it had jarred her out of a sound sleep as surely as an earthquake would have done. For several seconds she lay still, breathing through her mouth, trying to decide what she had heard; she turned on her bedside lamp and squinted at her alarm clock: one-seventeen. When she had retired a little after ten, she had read for half-an-hour before turning out the light, and fallen asleep fairly quickly. For a moment she considered calling out, but then all the warnings Saint-Germain had given her over the last five weeks stifled the cry in her throat. She did not know what might be in the house. Things she had dismissed so easily in the day now were more troublesome than when she had once again discussed them with Saint-Germain earlier in the day.

There was another rolling click, as if a furtive step moved upward, and this time she knew beyond a doubt what it was: someone was climbing the stairs. She sat up, prepared to call out, hoping Saint-Germain had changed his mind and was going to spend the night with her after all. But there was no greeting, and the movements she heard so faintly seemed more stealthy than romantic. On impulse, she turned out the light and lay still, listening. There were two other bedrooms on this floor and both were nearer the stairs than hers; if the person on the stairs was unfamiliar with the layout, she would have a little time. She would make the most of it.

Very slowly she eased herself out of bed, flinching at every hint of sound she made, from the sigh of the shifting blankets to the soft groan of the springs; as she perceived it, every whisper was magnified, and the house amplified all sounds to the level of honks and bellows. As she set her foot on the floor, she held still, wanting to be certain before she made her next move, for once she left the bed, she would have to be prepared to act. How much she wanted to rush, but she forced herself to wad her pillows under the covers in what she hoped would look like a sleeping shape, then inched her way to her armoire, gingerly pulling the mirrored door open and reaching inside for her father's over-and-under shotgun. She had loaded it over a week ago, and felt foolish while she did; now she took great comfort in the metal barrels and the beautiful rosewood stock. She moved warily, bringing the stock to her shoulder, the barrels still pointed toward the floor, even as she closed the armoire door and crept into the niche between the end of the armoire and the wall where she waited, ready to bring up the barrels and fire.

There was a quiet footfall in the corridor, and the faint squeak of a hinge: the person in the house had opened the bathroom door. Clearly he did not know his way around, which struck Rowena as being increasingly ominous with every passing second her alarm clock measured off in ticks that seemed as loud as firecrackers. Waiting was nerve-wracking, making her acutely aware of how isolated she was here. She had to resist the urge to burst out of her bedroom door and confront the invader. But that would mean making noise, and noise would alert the culprit, and that could lead to her losing what little advantage she might have. If only she had decided on a second telephone and had it installed in her bedroom! But there was no point in lamenting over sins of omission, not here and not now. She made herself concentrate on everything around her, obstinately refusing to let her attention slip away to less frightening things than hiding here in the dark with a shotgun in her hands.

Finally her door-knob twisted, and the door began to swing inward.

Rowena sank back as far as she could even while she tried to make out the figure in the doorway; she pressed against the side of the armoire as if to be absorbed by its mass into just another shadow in her dark room. She watched, acutely sensitive to every nuance of movement he revealed. The man was tall and slender, in dark clothing with an alpine mask over his face. He held a pistol in his gloved hand, and he very slowly advanced on the bed, his slow progress supremely confident; Rowena could almost smell malice emanating from him, and it frightened her. Suddenly her protected niche felt more like a trap than a haven.

The tall man bent over the bed, bringing the gun up toward the pillow.

How much Rowena wanted to scream! It was all she could do to remain quiet. She tightened her grip on the shotgun as the thin man started to draw back the covers, uttering an oath as he did. Rowena lifted the upper barrel of the shotgun and fired, the blast deafening in the small room. She staggered and almost fell back against the wall.

Cenere slewed about, aiming his pistol while hissing a string of obscenities in a language that sounded not-quite-Italian. He fired twice.

Now Rowena let out a high-pitched shriek and fired the lower barrel; she had the satisfaction of seeing the thin man lurch while clapping his arm against his side. She pushed out of her hiding-place and struck at him, knocking him backward onto the bed; he let go of his pistol and clapped his hand to the wound in a more concentrated effort to stop the bleeding.

"What—? Buckshot?" he gasped.

"Yes," she said, panting, astonished that she had gained the advantage. She grabbed his pistol and let go of the shotgun. "Now you lie back there. Do you understand me?" Her words were rapid and breathless, but her hands did not shake as she aimed his pistol directly at his head. "I don't suppose I'll miss at this range."

Cenere had a low opinion of women's ability to handle firearms, but he was unwilling to put this to the test, not while he lay there bleeding and she held his own pistol aimed at him. "I'm wounded."

"Good Lord, I should hope so," Rowena exclaimed. "I'm only sorry it wasn't worse."

"Well, help me," he ordered.

"Why should I?" she countered. "Lie there, mister. I'm going to tie you up."

"With what?" He did his best to laugh and ended coughing, each jolt sending pain through his body.

"Silk scarves, if I must," she said grimly, and, still aiming the pistol at him, went to rummage with one hand in her chest-of-drawers. At last she pulled out three lengths of silk and stuffed them into the neckline of her peignoir, all the while watching him.

From his place on the bed, Cenere could tell that his wounds, while painful, were not truly serious; he was in more danger from blood-loss. He studied the middle-aged woman who held his pistol and decided he had been mistaken to try to reach Ragoczy through her. She was not the kind of female who would be frightened into giving up any and all information he wanted, and as much as he might enjoy forcing her to talk at another time, he could not risk killing her; she was just the sort who would lie to him and expire. He promised himself another time with Miss Rowena Saxon—once Ragoczy was out of the way, he would reward himself with slowly killing her.

"Hold out your arm," she said as she came nearer to the bed.

"I'm bleeding," he complained.

"Whose fault is that? Put out your arm." She lifted the pistol a little higher. She was feeling light-headed and knew that it was distress that caused her giddiness.

"I'm hurt, don't you understand, you cow?" He hoped to goad her into doing something rash.

"I can shoot you again and tie you up at my leisure," she said at her most measured.

Sighing, he flung out his right arm. "Very well. There you are."

She approached him carefully, pulling out a scarf and making a loop in it. "Lift your hand."

"For God's sake—!" he protested. "Do you use them on that degenerate you sleep with?"

She fired again, and saw a portion of her upholstered headboard spray splinters and bits of fabric and stuffing. "Next time I'll hit you. I'll aim for your shoulder, but I might get your jaw or your neck."

Cenere lifted his hand, wanting to seem defeated; he would have to move quickly, and the way he was bleeding, he might not be able to overwhelm her. "There. Is this what you wanted?"

She slipped the loop over his wrist and drew it tight. In that moment, he rolled and fell into her, knocking her backward. "Damn!" she yelled, and fired.

This time the bullet clipped his shoulder, just a flesh wound, but enough to make it impossible for him to attack her beyond one emphatic blow with his fist that glanced off her cheek but was still strong enough to knock her over. Instead of continuing his assault, he lunged for the door and struggled to get out of the bedroom. He tugged the door closed behind him as he heard her trying to get to her feet. Rushing as much as he could, he stumbled down the corridor to the stairs. He had to grip the bannister with both hands in order to descend without falling, and he tottered four times, losing precious time to hold himself erect. His blood was leaving a trail anyone could follow, and he knew he would have to get away quickly or he would have every policeman on duty looking for him. As he caught sight of the telephone, he took a few precious seconds to tug its wire from the wall, hoping this would slow her reporting of this incident. Banging his way through the kitchen, he made for the back porch as if seeking deliverance. He reached the rear door and bumbled out into the tiny yard. There was still the fence to climb, which had not been more than a minor obstacle when he had come here forty minutes ago; it now loomed high as the towers of the unfinished Golden Gate Bridge. He struggled over it, grunting and sweating, and dropped into the other yard on rubbery legs. This was not good, he knew, as he made himself keep going toward the street where his motorcycle waited. If he could manage to ride it for an hour he could reach help beyond San Francisco, where he would not be found. This conviction drove him on even as his vision began to waver as shock started to take its toll.

Rowena pulled herself to her feet using the bed-stead. Her head rang from being hit, and she could feel a patch of blood on her face. She was mildly disoriented, and made an effort to keep standing, and finally managed to get her feet squarely under her. She knew the man was gone, for she had heard him slam out the back door. She would have liked to sit down and cry, but she was aware that would only help the criminal, so she marshaled her resolve, turned on the lights—the mess was appalling: blood everywhere, and gouges from buckshot and bullets marring her walls and furniture—and went out into the hall. Following the trail of blood down to the first floor, she went to the telephone stand at the foot of the stairs. She picked up the receiver and heard only silence; she dialed the operator with the same result. For an instant she felt tears well, but she strove to contain her rocky emotions; her ordeal was not over yet. As she took a step back, she saw that the telephone was not connected to its box, and she stifled a sob. She turned on more lights and tried not to step in any of the blood on her floors and carpets. With a sigh, she took her raincoat from the coat-closet across from the front door, picked up her purse, checked it for keys and her change-purse, then went to her garage, raised the door, and got into her Chancellor Miller Speedster. As she drove out in search of a pay telephone, she kept alert for a tall, lean man in dark clothes who would probably be limping now, or at least moving slowly.

On Hyde Street she found what she sought, and made a call to the police, giving her name and address and a brief summary of what had happened. She also told the duty officer that she was afraid to return to the house until the police arrived. He promised they would come soon, and hung up. She waited almost a full minute before she called Saint-Germain.

"Ferenc Ragoczy speaking," he said as if he were used to telephone calls in the middle of the night.

"Oh, Good Lord," Rowena said, and to her intense chagrin, burst into tears, unable to say any of the prudent, cordial things she had intended.

"Rowena," he said, suddenly very worried. "What's happened? Are you all right? Where are you?"

"I'm in a telephone booth at Hyde and California just now," she said, trying to regain some composure.

"Why on earth?" he asked, such anguish in his voice that it almost took her breath away.

"Someone broke into my house," she said, and began to sob once more.

"When did this happen?" There was no hint of blame in his question, which somehow made it harder for her to bear.

"This evening. Not quite an hour ago. He had a pistol. I just called the police. I have to get back." She was about to hang up. "I think he was after you."

"Do you want me to come?" He paused. "Whatever you want, I will do."

"Oh, yes, please," she said, and dropped the receiver back into the cradle before she started to weep in earnest. There was some relief in tears, but she was unwilling to indulge herself for more than a couple minutes. She leaned on the telephone booth door, shaking so violently she wondered if she could trust herself to drive back to her house. Telling herself it had to be done, she got back into her car and returned the way she came. As she reached the corner of Taylor Street, she thought her neighbors must surely have noticed something, and that slowed her down; she wanted their help, not to make a spectacle of herself. As she parked in the space just in front of her door, she finally let go of the steering wheel, not realizing until then how tightly she had been holding on to it. She sat for several minutes, unable to make herself get out of the car, let alone enter her home. Finally she saw a police car pulling in across the street, and she stared in relief. A moment later two uniformed officers came across the street, one of them pausing by her car window.

"You the lady who called?" the man asked.

"Miss Saxon. Yes, I called. I wanted to report a break-in. Of an occupied house. This one." She began trembling again. "I told your Sergeant Brady what happened." It amazed her that she remembered the man's name.

"Yes, ma'am. He passed it on to us." He opened the car door. "What say you let us in so we can take a look around? Just to see how things are?"

She found his tone more condescending than reassuring, but she did as he recommended, only then aware that under her raincoat her peignoir was bloody. "The man had a pistol. I think it's still in my bedroom somewhere; he's gone," she said, and saw the two policemen exchange glances.

"A pistol. Are you sure?" the second cop asked.

"Yes; of course I am. I can't tell you what make it was. I hardly had any time to examine it. But it isn't a revolver, if that is what you're wondering," she said, glad to be angry instead of weepy. She unlocked the door and stepped inside. "The telephone cord is pulled out of the wall. I would have called from here if he hadn't done that."

"Sounds pretty bad, all right," said the first policeman, his manner patronizing. "We'll check it out for—" He went silent as he saw the spatters of blood on the stairs and floor. "Jesus," he exclaimed softly.

Rowena removed her raincoat deliberately and hung it up, then turned around, certain she would command their attention now. "The bedroom is much worse."

"I couldn't see your face, out there; you really got hit. That's one hell of a bruise," said the first officer. "And your . . . your bathrobe. God."

This sympathy almost unnerved her. "How do you want to manage this?" she demanded in her most imposing manner.

"We've got to make sure this place is safe, and then we'll radio in for help," said the first policeman. "I can't let you go upstairs, not yet. In case the criminal's still here."

"He left," said Rowena, hugging her elbows with her bloody hands.

"He might have come back. He's been hurt. Unless you're cut up." The second policeman came up to her.

"Just this, on my face," she said brusquely. "I think the man has buckshot in him, and a crease in his shoulder."

"Your doing?" the second officer asked.

"No one else was here," she said, and was shocked at how shaken she sounded.

"You let us do our job, ma'am," said the first officer. "You go sit down, try to calm yourself. You have anyone who can come help you?" He had one foot on the stairs, but hesitated, his hand on his revolver.

"I called a friend. He should be here shortly." She could hardly admit to herself how much she wanted to see Saint-Germain.

"Okay," said the officer, and began to climb, taking care not to step in the splotches of blood. "You, Snyder, you stay down here. Just in case."

"Okay, Baxter," said Snyder, taking up a stance at the foot of the stairs.

"I tell you, he's gone," Rowena said, increasingly shaky and tired.

"We got to make sure, ma'am. Then we'll get back-up over here, and someone will take your statement." Snyder looked around. "Nice house."

"You're not seeing it at its best," she said as cuttingly as she could.

"I can tell," said Snyder, keeping his attention on the stairs. "The guy must be hurt. He sure is bleeding, since you say you aren't."

"I do hope so; I hope he bleeds until he's dry," said Rowena in hushed fury, and clasped her hands together to prevent them shaking. Strange, she thought in a remote part of her mind, *my hands weren't shaking earlier; you'd think, with what was going on, I would have been nervous then, not now.*

A bell sounded two-thirty; Snyder cleared his throat. "Saint Anselm's."

"Probably." Rowena sighed. Her face was starting to hurt in that stubborn, throbbing way that meant deep bruising, and she had a headache.

The sound of the knocker made Rowena jump. She hoped she had not yelped; she glanced at Snyder. "I think it's my friend," she said.

"I'll open the door," said Snyder, and called up to his partner. "Hey, Baxter. Someone's here. What do you want me to do?"

"Answer the door," came Baxter's reply. He sounded depleted, and from the echo, he was in the bathroom. As if in confirmation, the toilet flushed.

Snyder went cautiously to the door, drew his revolver, and eased the door open, ready to shoot. "Who are you?"

"Ferenc Ragoczy; Miss Saxon called me from the telephone booth at California and Hyde. I came over as quickly as I could," said the newcomer, keeping his manner cool and his voice level. "Inspector John Smith can identify me, if you require this." He remained on the porch, letting the policeman make up his mind.

Rowena ended it for him: she rushed out of the living room and threw open the front door. "Thank goodness you're here!" she clamored, flinging herself into his arms and letting herself cry; her sobs were deep, wrenched from the heart, and much as she felt abashed, she realized that comfort was more important than decorum. "Let him in!" She hung on to him, relieved he had arrived and distressed by the ferocity of her need for him.

"You can come in," said Snyder, moving aside to admit him.

Saint-Germain supported Rowena with his arm and got her back inside, taking her into her studio and sinking her down onto her rolled-arm chair. "Don't give yourself trouble, Rowena. You're safe now. Do you need a wrap for your shoulders? Would you like to change clothes?"

"No," she said, taking hold of his hands. "Just stay close, will you?"

"If that's what you want," he promised, and sat on the arm of her chair. "Are you cold?"

"Yes; inside, not outside," she said.

"Let me pour you a brandy," he offered.

"Sorry, sir," said Snyder. "No brandy. You don't want her forgetting anything. She hasn't made a statement to an investigating officer yet."

"I don't think a little brandy will blot the night out of her memory, much as she might wish it would," said Saint-Germain. "It will steady her, and that will help her to give her statement. Or don't you want her to relax?" He opened the cabinet where she kept her liquor, and brought out the brandy and a snifter.

Snyder was troubled. "I don't know. You know how it looks, a woman drinking. They won't put much stock in what she says."

Baxter appeared on the stairs; he was pale and dismayed. "Oh, let her have a drink. And get me one, too."

"You're on duty," said Snyder.

"You go upstairs and tell me that afterward," said Baxter, and sat down heavily on a bench under the front window, fanning his brow with his hand. "God, it's awful up there. You can't imagine."

Snyder watched while Saint-Germain prepared two snifters of brandy and handed the first to Rowena, then gave the other to Baxter. "You might as well make the most of this. The other policemen will be here soon."

"And welcome," said Baxter, and drank down half the brandy in his snifter. "That room is a shambles—literally."

"What happened up there?" Snyder asked. He glanced up the stairs again. "How bad is it? Why can't I check it out?"

"Because it has to be gone over by the inspectors, and I have to make sure the scene isn't contaminated. I can tell you: someone tried to kill Miss Saxon, no doubt about it. It's real plain." He blew out a lungful of air as if he had run up a steep hill. "She was cool-headed enough to stop him, though Jesus knows how. That bed is ruined, and so is the rug. And there's blood all over the place. They'll need the rug and bed, and photos, in case there's a trial, to show how the room looked, and match the blood type of the man who attacked you with what's on the bedspread. You'll have to do something about the walls; not paint, but paint and then paper. You'll need a strong cleaner to get rid of the smell." Baxter took another drink and finished his brandy. Setting the snifter aside, he shook his head. "I don't want to upchuck again."

"If you think you're going to," said Rowena, "the kitchen is that way. Just try not to make a mess. Things are bad enough already. My housekeeper will be here at ten. She has a dentist appointment at eight." She had a second sip of brandy, and was glad of the fiery track it drew down her throat to her stomach.

"Did you know the man?" asked Snyder.

"No. And to anticipate your next question, I didn't see his face—he was wearing a skier's mask. He seemed to know what he was about, as if he'd done it before—that much was obvious. And the lights were off, so I can't tell you what color his eyes are, or his hair, or anything else about him beyond that he is tall and slim, except that I shot him." Her voice rose sharply, and she made herself stop.

Saint-Germain put his hand on her shoulder. "Do you want to say this now? You'll only have to say it again when the other police arrive."

"I don't know," Rowena began only to be interrupted.

"We got to get the story as soon as possible," said Baxter. "Sorry, ma'am. You've had one hell of a night, but—" He rose from the bench. "We got to start following that blood, just in case the guy's fallen on the street somewhere around here."

"You're assuming he was alone," said Saint-Germain. "He might have had an accomplice, or perhaps a driver."

"Then we'll find out where the blood stops, and maybe someone saw something," said Baxter. "A man on the run with buckshot in him is hard to miss."

"At two in the morning," said Rowena sardonically. "Who'd tell the police about that?"

Snyder shrugged. "We won't know until we go looking; we could turn up something useful. We have before. We'll be checking out local residents tomorrow, in case anyone was up and looking out the window. It happens," he insisted.

"We got to do everything." Baxter looked over at Rowena. "And we will. But take it from me—I wouldn't go up into that room again, Miss Saxon. Have your housekeeper clean it, down to the wood, and then hire someone to paint and paper it for you."

"I've already seen the room," Rowena pointed out as she put the snifter down more emphatically than she had intended. The loud clatter of the glass demanded the attention of everyone in the two rooms.

"But not the way it's gonna be," said Baxter. "You think it's bad now, it'll be worse in the morning. Crime scenes are messy."

"How am I supposed to live in my house?" Rowena demanded, almost knocking over her brandy snifter.

"You might want to find a hotel," said Snyder. "You must have friends you can stay with. I think that would be best."

"There's a man out there who wants to kill me," said Rowena, her voice soft with rage. "What hotel would want me? And wouldn't I be a welcome guest, with a killer after me?"

Snyder had begun his protest when there was a sharp knock on the door, and a voice announced, "Inspector Porter. We got four cops out here needing to come in."

Baxter lumbered to the door. "Just a sec, Inspector. Tell your men to be careful coming in. There's a blood trail we don't want to mess up."

From outside Porter relayed this message: "Open up."

Baxter pulled the door wide and pointed down at the blood. "See what I'm talking about?"

"Gad," said Porter, taking stock of the situation. "Some kind of attempted murder or rape, is that the case?"

Baxter made a series of signs intended to get Porter to mitigate his language. "Miss Saxon is right here, sir, and I don't know as you want to—"

But Rowena had risen and went toward the newly arrived police. "I don't know about the rape," she said, "but I wouldn't put it past him." She held out her hand. "You're Inspector Porter?"

"Abel Porter, at your service," he said, taking her hand even as he stared at her bloody peignoir. He was nearing forty and doing it with as much panache as he could manage; he was well-dressed for a cop, and his manner had a hint of flamboyance. "Has either of these men taken your statement?"

"Not officially, no," said Rowena, beginning to shake again.

"Come, Miss Saxon. Sit down. I'll take your statement while my men do their work. I'm sure you'd like us out of here as soon as possible." He took her by the elbow and guided her back into her studio, where he found himself staring at Ferenc Ragoczy. "And who might you be?"

Saint-Germain was tempted to give a flip answer, but instead held out his hand. "Ferenc Ragoczy. Miss Saxon called me and asked me to lend her my support, which I did."

"Um," said Porter. "All right. Perhaps you should sit down, Miss Saxon." He released his hold on her. "If you want to—"

She went back to her favorite chair and picked up her snifter. "It's been a difficult evening, Inspector Porter."

"No doubt it has." He was doing his best to be soothing, which only irked Rowena.

"A man got into my house tonight, with a pistol and, it would seem, the intention of murdering me. Don't talk to me as if you think I'm hysterical. Under the circumstances, I am a model of self-possession." She drank a little more brandy.

Before Porter could speak, Baxter tugged at his sleeve. "You should go upstairs, Inspector. Have a look in the bedroom before the other johnnies get there."

Porter looked mildly surprised, but after a moment, did as Baxter asked, saying, "I'll be back directly, Miss Saxon. Don't have too much of that brandy."

"No, I won't," she promised, and turned her gaze on Saint-Germain. "This is a madhouse."

"It is," Saint-Germain said, "and you know, I've been thinking: perhaps you'd be willing to come to my house for a day or two, while the police go about their business here. You'll get no quiet here, you know. You could pack a bag, and no one would have to know where you are unless you chose to tell him."

She drank another bit of brandy. "I don't want to go into the room," she said in a small voice. "I think Baxter may be right about that."

"Then you need not," he said. "Tell me what you need and where I may find them, and I'll attend to it for you." He saw that Snyder was about to protest, so he added hurriedly, "Not just now, but in an hour or so."

"It would suit me, I guess," she said, wanting to be rid of all the demands being made on her.

"Then, when Inspector Porter returns, I will broach the matter with him," said Saint-Germain, watching two uniformed policemen beginning to measure and mark the blood-trail, working from the stairs to the main floor, using chalk and a ruler to mark the locations of all the dribbles and spatters they could see.

"They're going to need some time to get this done," said Baxter. "We probably won't be out of here until after dawn."

Saint-Germain could see how distressing this was to Rowena. "You come with me tonight, Miss Saxon. You'll be welcome for as long as you'd like. My house-man will make up the guest room for you, and you can rest all day, if you like."

Baxter joined in. "He's right. Cops can make a real rat's nest. Get away for a couple of days, until you can put this place to rights again."

"I'll consider it," said Rowena, determined not to capitulate too quickly or too readily.

"You do that," said Baxter. "It'll buck you up to get away from here. You won't be reminded all the time of what has happened. And you can be protected. If we need anything from you, we can come to you."

"I said I'll consider it," Rowena said peremptorily.

Saint-Germain dropped down on his knee next to her chair. "As soon as you talk with the inspector, you can decide what you want to do," he told her. "In the meantime, finish your brandy. I'll get you more if you want it."

"Oh, I want it," she said. "But I'd better not have it. I'm so jittery that I'll probably fall asleep in a minute as soon as all the pressure is off me."

"Very good," said Saint-Germain, and rose to his feet again.

Inspector Porter returned from the upper level much chastened. "That was . . . pretty bad."

"It's probably worse with the lights on," said Rowena, not trusting herself to laugh at her intended jest.

"You say that the blood is his?" Porter asked.

"There's a little of mine. But I clipped his side with my shotgun, and I gave him a flesh wound in the shoulder. It wasn't really bad. The blood didn't . . . you know . . . spurt, so I didn't hit any important blood vessels. Still, he bled a lot." She could feel her bravado slipping, and went on, "I don't know what to say, all things considered." As she finished up her brandy, she held the snifter out to Saint-Germain. "I've changed my mind. Give me a splash more."

He took the snifter and went to her cabinet. "The Mattei again?"

"Yes, please." She made herself look squarely at Inspector Porter. "How are we supposed to do this?"

"I need to ask you some questions," said Porter, falling into the automatic habits of his profession; he took a notebook and pencil from his inner jacket pocket. "Tell me as much as you can remember."

She took the snifter back from Saint-Germain—he had put in rather more than a splash—and held it, looking over the rim as if to ensure protection. "Where would you like me to start?"

This sensible question took Porter aback. He frowned, then said, "Start, if you would, at the time you went to bed."

Rowena cocked her head. "I had a quiet evening; I dined alone about seven, and cleared up after myself. I listened to the radio—to the news, and then the concert from Cleveland—and then spent some time working on sketches. Beethoven helps me think, as Brahms helps me feel. It was a good concert, I think; Beethoven's *Pastoral*, and the third and fourth *Brandenburg Concerti*." She sipped her brandy. "I went to bed around ten, or a little after. I came up, washed my face and brushed my hair, then got ready for sleep. I have been reading *The Dream Life of Balso Snell*, and I managed another dozen pages before the sentences began to blur, and I turned off the light. When I woke up again, I went for my shotgun." Although she had been speaking easily enough, her throat now felt tight. "When I was in my twenties, I was kidnapped," she said. "I have tended to keep weapons near at hand ever since."

"Oh, dear. Were you ransomed?" Porter asked.

"No; I was rescued." She volunteered nothing more.

"You were very fortunate," said Porter, thinking of the most recent kidnappings to command public attention; he shuddered. "I can see why you might have a gun or two in the house."

"In my armoire," she said. "When I woke—it was one-seventeen, according to my bedside clock—I think it was because I heard something untoward, and it warned me."

"What kind of thing?" Porter inquired, his pencil poised.

"I don't know," she answered. "Something that was wrong enough to wake me. I listened for a while, and then I took a chance and got out of bed so I'd have my shotgun. It should be up in the bedroom."

"It is, and a German pistol," said Inspector Porter.

Rowena took a long, shaky breath. "I hid, and waited for the man to try to find me. I could hear him in the corridor, opening one door and then another. I did my best to keep track of where he was by the sounds he made. I recognized the bathroom door because it has a squeaky hinge. I think he even opened the linen closet. My room is at the end of the corridor, and that gave me time to get ready."

"Your telephone is on this floor?" Porter asked, although he knew the answer.

"I have a twenty-foot cord and can bring it upstairs, but not as far as my bedroom." Rowena quivered. "I should have ordered a thirty-foot cord."

"He might have cut it in any case," said Porter. "We'll contact the telephone company to get your line fixed." He flipped his notebook to the next page. "What happened when he reached your room?"

She told him haltingly, trying to be precise but put off by the shock that held her. From time to time he asked her to repeat some part of a response, or to clarify what she had said. It took almost an hour for her to answer all the questions Inspector Porter put to her, and when he closed his notebook and put away his pencil, she said, "Do you require anything else of me tonight?" She was still feeling rattled, and she was almost sure she had forgotten something important that the man had said to her, but she could not call it to mind.

"I don't think so, not right now," said Porter, glancing at the policemen coming in from the back door. "Anything?"

"He's gone," said one of the officers. "I think he had a car parked on Mason. The blood stops there, on the sidewalk. First thing in the morning, we'll start canvassing."

"Good," said Porter. He looked at Rowena. "You might want to go with your friend tonight, Miss Saxon. We got a lot to do here still."

She nodded mutely and turned to Saint-Germain, trying to find the words to ask him to help her. "I . . . If you . . ."

"I'll go pack your bag for you. If you need to get new clothes, Mr. Rogers can take you shopping," said Saint-Germain. "Do you mind if I pack for her?" he asked Inspector Porter.

"Go ahead. I'll go up with you." Inspector Porter watched Rowena for several seconds. "You're either very lucky or very resourceful, Miss Saxon. If you hadn't kept your composure, this evening might have had a very different outcome."

Rowena folded her arms. "Yes, Inspector," she said, too exhausted to shiver any longer. "I know."

TEXT OF A LETTER FROM CARLO PIETRAGNELLI AT PONDEROSA LODGE TO FERENC RAGOCZY IN SAN FRANCISCO.

PONDEROSA LODGE
LAKE TAHOE, CALIFORNIA

April 13, 1937

Ferenc Ragoczy
c/o Oscar King
King Lowenthal Taylor & Frost
630 Kearny Street
San Francisco, California

Dear Mr. Ragoczy,
Only my son has refused to stay here with me, and I have therefore decided to accept your offer of a guard for him. He is in Davis, and the White Legion must surely know it. With Sophia and Ethan here, and Angelina, I am beginning to understand that you were right, and there is an advantage in being away from the winery, though I am still vexed by having to be gone

during this onerous time, and I am worried for Adrianna, I am sorry to have to admit it, but I am a fair man, and so I will acknowledge that we are better-off for taking your advice.

The reports I have received from the guards have been encouraging. I begin to think the culprits will be apprehended, and once that has happened, we may return and help the law to take its course. I am relieved to have such diligent men looking after the plantations, because I can be tranquil in the certainty that they will do their utmost to maintain the land and the vines as well as the men who work for me. The guards are truly meticulous in their duties, and I know that from Will Sutton's letters as well as the guards' reports, which is most reassuring. It is comforting to have the evaluations of sensible persons at times like these.

Mrs. Curt has been a wonderful hostess to all of us, putting us in her best cabins, and making us feel like we're on vacation instead of hiding out. That's probably why I have asked her to put me to work while I am here, for I am not accustomed to staying idle, and I don't want to be left with nothing to do but contemplate the worst. Also, from what I can see, she could use a little help around the place. I've told her that I can do all manner of repairs as well as painting and the like. This is a beautiful place and it's a shame to let it get run-down.

One of the pleasures of being here has been the opportunity to catch up on my reading. I hadn't realized how little I have been doing in the last months; here I can spend an hour or two a day reading various volumes of fiction and nonfiction, and have the chance to think about what I am reading. I have also been browsing through the dictionaries Mrs. Curt has here. I have always liked dipping into dictionaries—you find the most amazing things in them. Yesterday I came upon laniate (to rend, tear) and oenomancy (telling fortunes with wine); I was especially taken with the latter, as you might believe. To the extent that I am making the most of this time, I am very glad to be given it, without the constant worry of shattering windows.

Agreeable as my time here is, I don't want to have to be here many more weeks, so anything you can do to help along our resolution, I'll be more grateful than I am already. I can tell it would be almost too easy to let everything drag on, and I would not have a good harvest, and my workers would be annoyed for being left to face the risks without me there to share them. Letting this procrastination continue, unless it's absolutely necessary, in which case it isn't really procrastination, will only make it harder to resume our old way of life when matters are finally settled. At the same time, I do want them settled so we will not have to take measures of this sort again. Not that I would object to coming here again, for I would not, if it were truly to have a vacation and not as an escape from danger. Keep that in mind while you go on trying to stop the White Legion and the Leonardis. My family has endured a lot—I don't want them to suffer any more than necessary.

It's not that I'm unmindful of what you have done, for that isn't true. I might have succumbed to the attacks if I hadn't had the staunch sponsorship you have given me. But you have learned to live as an exile, which, I fear, it isn't in me to do. My vineyard, my winery, are as much a part of me as my blood, and any loss of it is like bleeding, and it will be as deadly as an open vein. That may mean I am lacking in flexibility of character, in which case, so be it.

I look forward to hearing from you. It is consoling to have your telephone calls, and I thank you for sustaining the expense, as you have sustained so many others.

Cordially and appreciatively,

Carlo Pietragnelli

chapter six

Oscar King studied the man on the other side of the desk: the two men were about the same age and similar build, with the kind of studied demeanor that came from years in front of juries; the judge cleared his throat and shook his head, and King said, "*You* called *me*, Your Honor; I'm here at your request. Having nothing else to go on, I take it this is about the two young men the guards at the Pietragnelli Vineyards brought in."

"Yep," said the Honorable George Cavendish. His official robe hung on a coat-rack in the corner, a subtle reminder of his status.

"I have been told they aren't being held in the jail; that you've released them to their parents, no bond. Is that correct?"

"It seemed the best way to handle things," said Cavendish.

"And I assume, since you endorse that policy, that you are going to explain your position on the case?" King asked.

"It's more of an approach than a position," said Cavendish with careful reserve.

"You're going to outline your approach, then? For my benefit?" King duly modified his inquiry, doing his best to be cooperative without conceding anything to Judge Cavendish beyond what civility demanded.

Cavendish fingered his white mustache. "Up here in Santa Rosa, things work a little differently than they do in San Francisco. We're trying to keep the situation from erupting."

"So I've been told," said King, waiting for what he supposed was coming. "How does this tie into the Leonardi boys, or Hiro Yoshimura?"

"Our bucolic appearance is deceptive," Cavendish went on, refusing to be hurried. "I have to tell you that this . . . arrest is potentially very . . . embarrassing throughout the county. It could have repercussions for some of our most prominent citizens."

"Who support the White Legion," King interjected.

"I didn't say that," the judge pointed out sternly. "Only that it could be embarrassing."

"Yes: murder can be embarrassing," said King with heavy sarcasm. "So can attempted murder, if it comes to that."

"What do you mean, murder? If you go about making accusations like that, you may have to answer for it." Cavendish drew himself up in his leather chair. "Nothing the Leonard boys have said links them in any way to Mr. Yoshimura's death."

"Murder," King corrected him.

"If you insist on calling it that," Cavendish said sourly.

"What else would you call it?" King demanded. "He didn't die of natural causes, that's sure."

"It may be manslaughter, you know," said Cavendish, trying not to incite King further. "The coroner wasn't convinced the beating was premeditated."

"Oh, wasn't he? Did he happen to say why not?" Oscar King asked, and looked toward the window of Judge Cavendish's office; it was a lovely spring day, getting warm, promising an early summer. "A man with several broken bones and bad bruises got them by misadventure, or through the oversight of a person or persons unknown. But you're right: all that damage could be nothing more than accidental." He snapped his finger as if with sudden inspiration. "And Mr. Yoshimura was a farmer. He may have fallen off a large cabbage."

"You watch your tongue in here, Counselor," warned Cavendish. "I'm giving you a lot of leeway on Pietragnelli's behalf, but my patience isn't inexhaustible."

"Goodness no; that's apparent by the alacrity with which you pursue justice," said King with blatantly assumed contrition. "I would never presume to disrespect any man charged with upholding the nation's laws."

"I could tell you to leave, King," Cavendish grumbled.

"But you won't, because you want to keep this inside these walls if you can. That's why we're talking unofficially. You're afraid of the attention a trial would bring, and so you want to arrange something a bit more private." King coughed diplomatically. "It's never amusing to have to admit you have organizations like the White Legion operating with impunity, is it?" He was unwilling to let the judge dodge the issues.

"We have to be careful; it isn't worth having it all blow up in our faces. The incidents are all out of proportion already," said Judge Cavendish.

"I don't suppose Mr. Pietragnelli would agree—or Mr. Yoshimura," said King musingly.

Judge Cavendish struggled to regain the momentum he had wanted to achieve. "It's always a question of whose ox is gored, isn't it? There's more at stake here than grapes and windows, and even you must know it. This is systematic action, for several reasons. There have been all kinds of union organizers trying to get the hands to follow them, and in these days, who can afford what the unions demand? You know what kind of trouble they can make: how many of those organizers are Communists? That isn't what any of us want, is it? . . . Well, most people would rather let the White Legion clean house than risk making the Communists more powerful."

"Carlo Pietragnelli isn't encouraging Communism, and everyone in Geyserville knows it. He's a shrewd businessman, and he's reliable as anyone in the valley. He kept going all through Prohibition, and he's done a lot to help his neighbors, as most of them know. He pays good wages and offers his workers the best he can afford, which is more than many another does," said King. "This isn't about Communists, Your Honor, and you know it. This is about running off people from profitable lands. Anyone who thinks otherwise is a fool."

"It can look that way," said Cavendish unhappily. "Which is why it's so potentially explosive to have the Leonard boys in jail." He folded his hands. "They don't like being called Leonardi, you know."

"They were caught on the Pietragnelli land with a rifle," said King, "no matter what they call themselves. The cartridges from the rifle match those dug out of the walls at Carlo Pietragnelli's house, and we're not talking about a standard .22 or anything else light. This is nothing particularly significant in and of itself, but the report Deputy Sutton filed indicated the weapon was an older rifle, and the bullets had to be specially ordered. The only person ordering such bullets was Thomas Leonardi. It may not be conclusive evidence, but it is indicative, don't you think? It increases the likelihood that someone in that household fired those shots. Somehow I can't see Thomas doing it, can you?"

"It's . . . troubling about the rifle," Cavendish allowed. "The Leonard boys deny having any intention to do harm to anything or anyone at the Pietragnelli vineyard."

"They have a damn strange way of showing it," said King, making no apology for his language.

"You know how young men are—they get notions, they don't think about the consequences of their acts, and the next thing you know, there's trouble. Young men are impulsive, and they don't stop to reflect, as older men do." He laid his hand over his watch-pocket. "It's not as if you can prove otherwise, not enough to get a conviction."

"Are you saying the District Attorney isn't going to take the case," said King.

"I'm saying he hasn't enough evidence—hard evidence—to take before a jury, and given the nature of the case, he doesn't want to start anything that could backfire on him. There's too much supposition and not enough real, provable facts." Judge Cavendish frowned. "Ordinarily I wouldn't agree with him, but just now, I do."

"Which is why we're having this charming tête-à-tête in your office where no one can hear our exchange of opinions," said Oscar King.

"We'd like to make sure Carlo Pietragnelli doesn't have to sacrifice too much on account of what the Leonard boys might—and we must say *might*—have done." Cavendish opened the humidor on his desk and offered the contents to Oscar King. "Real Havanas, rolled on the thighs of pretty girls and soaked in rum."

King took one and tested it between his fingers. "Must be fifty cents apiece."

"Sixty, but worth every penny," the judge boasted, still holding out the humidor. "Take one home with you, for later."

"Thanks, but no," said King. "It might look like a bribe."

Cavendish had a rich, plummy chuckle. "Lawyers like you cost a lot more than a couple cigars."

"Just the same," said King. "I'll join you for now, but that's all." He sniffed the cigar. "Very good."

"They'd better be." He picked up a large lighter with a built-in nipper. "If you want to snip the end." He demonstrated on his own cigar, then worked the lighter and puffed the cigar into glowing embers. Satisfied with the smoke, he handed the lighter to Oscar King. "Go on."

After the minutest hesitation, King took the lighter and clipped the end of his cigar, then lit up. He loved the aroma of the smoke, and felt a sniggle of guilt as he inhaled. "All right. What are we talking about?"

"What do you think would be fair for Pietragnelli?" Judge Cavendish asked, avoiding a direct response. "Given that we can't take this case to trial."

"A trial that could identify his attackers and send them to prison. It would fix responsibility and provide some peace for the Pietragnellis," said Oscar King promptly. "But since—as you say—that isn't going to happen, you had best tell me what the county is prepared to do, and I'll submit the offer and terms to my client."

"Who is where?" the judge asked, much too casually.

"Out of the area," said Oscar King with equal nonchalance. "When and if your offer is accepted and the documentation is completed—"

"Nothing in writing," said Judge Cavendish hastily.

King pounced on this. "Oh, yes, in writing, with provisions of confidentiality, and terms under which the confidentiality must be kept as well as terms under which it can be breached, such as if the Leonardis are released from jail."

"You can't make such demands," the judge blustered.

"Of course I can. And I will. You want this swept under the political carpet for reasons I don't know, nor do I want to be told, this is murky enough without that. It doesn't change the facts: Pietragnelli and his family need assurances that they will be protected, and the only way to guarantee their safety is a contract—a written contract—that will make it possible for them to have some leverage." He took a long drag on the cigar. "You can't seriously expect Carlo Pietragnelli to be willing to give away that leverage simply because you would prefer it, now can you?" He gave a predatory grin. "What do you take me for?"

"You listen to me, sonny boy," said Judge Cavendish, his hand gathered into a fist. "I'm not going to have you blowing the lid off Sonoma County because it gets you airtime and a fancier office down in the big, dangerous city. You're a spoiler, King, out to wreck what you can't loot, coming in here for a little while and leaving all of us to clean up the hash you make. Don't think we haven't seen your kind before." He lifted his finger to underscore his words. "And I'm not going to have you running off to Sacramento to the Attorney General, getting the state all riled up about a couple isolated incidents. It won't be allowed."

"Fine thing for a judge, making threats," said King, doing his best not to be angry; he knew that was Cavendish's intention, a way to keep him off-guard. "If you don't want the Attorney General dragged into this, then you better start coming up with something worthwhile, or I'm leaving and driving back to San Francisco, and I'm going to report our entire conversation to Mr. Pietragnelli, no matter what. Then he and I will decide what to do next, whether you like it or not." He held out the cigar. "This is very good."

Cavendish glowered at the ceiling. "You're not going to make this easy, are you?"

"Why should I? It hasn't been easy for my client," King pointed out. "It's his interests I'm obliged to represent."

"I don't deny that, but I have to remind you that we can't conclusively tie the Leonards to the troubles Pietragnelli has been having." He tapped his broad expanse of blotting paper and tried to seem above it all, as he often did on the bench.

"And you aren't going to make any effort to find the link, are you?" Oscar King asked. "I won't require an answer. Think of my question as rhetorical."

"If you won't discuss this in good faith," Judge Cavendish said, his disgust obvious, "we have nothing more to say to each other, and I'm just taking up your valuable time for no good reason. I'd be sorry to have that happen, but if you think it would serve your client's interests to throw the whole shebang away . . ." He opened his hands to show his helplessness.

"Until you offer something substantial, this can go nowhere. I won't let my client be victimized by a fast shuffle." Oscar King tapped off the ash at the end of his cigar into the empty waste-basket beside the judge's desk. "What kind of an attorney would I be if I left my clients exposed to all manner of retribution with no fall-back to keep them safe? The agreement must be written, with confidentiality clauses and provision to break them. I can't bring Pietragnelli any agreement that does not contain such language."

"All right. The sheriff won't like it, but I can see your point. I'll explain it to him. He's not as unreasonable as you seem to think he is." He knocked the ash off his cigar into his large copper ashtray. "But that confidentiality provision will have to be ironclad, with forfeiture of all awards and grants if it isn't kept to the letter."

"There will be no punitive actions taken against Pietragnelli, his family, his workers, or his neighbors. This is absolute. No sideways actions, either. No zoning games, no water-rights disputes, no tax changes, no road or dam development, no eminent domain that would compromise his vineyards. I know all the tricks, Judge, and I'll be watching you. Pietragnelli has adequate financial backing, so banks aren't an issue, but suppliers and transportation is. None of those aspects of his business is to be compromised in any way, or those of his employees. If that happens, the confidentiality terms will be terminated." He leaned forward. "Also, there will be no whispering campaigns, no rumor-mongering, no hints and innuendos that can destroy a man's reputation. Pietragnelli is to resume his wine-making without any nasty repercussions from this case. Is that clear?"

"How am I supposed to enforce such terms?" Judge Cavendish asked innocently. "I can't keep people from talking. The First Amendment says so."

"That isn't my concern; it has to be done; you know how to do it, so I leave it up to you. And the Leonardi boys are not to be allowed to stay in this area," King went on. "They're not to get off scot-free for all they've done."

"There I agree," said the judge unexpectedly. "Well, we both know they're out of hand. It would make things easier if they didn't stick around—who knows what they might get up to next? What do you suggest?"

"The army and navy. One boy to each service. They shouldn't serve together," said King, who had thought about this on the long drive up from San Rafael. "They have to be on their own."

"Their parents won't like it," said Judge Cavendish.

"They would like public notoriety even less," said King.

"You have a point there," said Judge Cavendish. "I'll see what I can do."

"Not good enough," said King. "You get it done, or I head for Sacramento."

"You're driving a hard bargain," Cavendish complained.

"There's reason to do so, wouldn't you agree?" King asked with a suggestion of a smile. "You'd do the same thing in my place, wouldn't you?"

"All right. The boys go into the service—not the same service; one army, one navy—for what? Two years?"

"Five. Make it a minium of five years. You can set up enlistment terms for that long, can't you? I know you can pull the right strings to make that stick, and get it in writing, so there's no shift later on. That'll keep them off the streets until 1942, and that should teach them a thing or two about the world, if nothing else." King rubbed his hands together. "It's little enough for either boy, considering what they've done."

"I'll try," said Judge Cavendish.

"Convince them, Your Honor, or the deal won't hold," said King. "Now, about restitution."

"Oh, Lord," the judge said, addressing the ceiling.

"The house and workers' cabins are to be restored completely. No skimping, no half-measures, no delays. The windows will be replaced, the buildings painted, and any secondary damage repaired. All of it, even if it's only a scratch on a fence-post." King held up his hand, indicating he was not through yet. "The county is to pay the family a thousand dollars for each month they have been under siege, and for each month until the work is finished." It was an outrageous amount, but he wanted to find out how serious Judge Cavendish was in regard to making this case vanish.

"That's a hefty chunk from the county budget," said the judge, scowling portentously.

"A trial would cost more, wouldn't it? The publicity alone would be costly, to say nothing of the potential for civil claims afterward." King was beginning to enjoy himself, for he could see Cavendish squirm.

"Let's say I could get the Board of Supervisors to authorize the payments—

would that be an end to it or would you have more tricks up your sleeve?" Cavendish was still trying to menace King, but his heart was no longer in it.

"That would depend on my client, of course," said King. "But if all these conditions are met, and met promptly, then I think we could have the whole thing resolved in short order."

"Pietragnelli will have to have his signature notarized if he doesn't come here to the courthouse to sign," Cavendish said, once again fishing.

"He can reach a notary where he is, and you needn't worry about it being authentic; you can have verification of all sorts, so long as you don't require Mr. Pietragnelli to return to Sonoma County until this is settled." King drew on his cigar once more, thinking its flavor had improved in the last several minutes. "If you require it, his notarized signature could be witnessed by a judge, like yourself."

"We'll . . . decide upon that when the terms are agreed upon," said Cavendish, his gaze held by the contents of the bookshelves on the other side of his office.

"I want you to understand that Pietragnelli won't come back to Geyserville until the contract is signed and sealed," said King, making the most of his momentary advantage. "It isn't that there's any distrust of you, Your Honor, but since the White Legion operates in secrecy, it's not wise for him to come here without real protection, and that means more than hired guards at his house. Although those will continue on duty for as long as Mr. Pietragnelli and I deem them to be necessary." He had been assured by Ferenc Ragoczy that the guards would be paid for as long as a year if it seemed reasonable to keep them on.

"I'll keep that in mind," said Judge Cavendish; he was growing weary of their talk, which was not going the way he intended.

"If there were some way to address members of the White Legion directly, I might be able to get a restraining order for them, and that would save us a great deal of minutiae, but since the organization remains secret and its membership undisclosed, I'm going to have to make all kinds of clauses and conditions for person or persons unknown."

"Do you really think all that is necessary?" Judge Cavendish asked, and went on, "Of course you do. And you're determined to wring as much blood from this turnip as you can."

"I wouldn't put it that way," said King. "You're planning to abrogate my client's right to test his injury in a court of law, and if he is going to do that, it is going to be for something more than a tip of the hat and a ticket to the movies."

Cavendish looked annoyed. "Sure. You don't have to be re-elected by the voters, and you don't live in this county."

"Good thing, too," said King. "You may have your problems, but at least a portion of them are your responsibility. You have become . . ." He trailed off, seeing that he had overstepped. "I'll wait to hear from you about how you will arrange the specifics, but I'll relay the basic issues—as we've discussed them—to my client, and let you know what his position is." He stubbed out his half-smoked cigar and prepared to rise.

"Understand me, King," said Cavendish in the same voice he used to hand down the stiff sentences for which he was famous, "I won't have you playing with me. You're going to have to hold up your end of the bargain. I want you to get your client to end this, or neither you nor I will be able to answer for what happens."

"Another oblique threat," said King. He shoved up from his chair.

"More a word to the wise. The White Legion has big plans for this region," said Judge Cavendish.

"I figured that out," said King, making for the door.

"I need an answer by Monday," said Judge Cavendish.

"You'll have it," said King, as if this weren't rushing him. He usually did not work on the weekend, but this being Thursday, he realized he would probably have to. "Shall I telephone, or would you rather have another private discussion?"

"It's best if we meet face-to-face. But we shouldn't be seen together again; it wouldn't be wise. If you want to join me in San Rafael at the Fisherman's Net, next Monday afternoon at . . . shall we say two? . . . we can resume our talk. I'll reserve a curtained booth." The judge did his best to regain his dignity and very nearly succeeded.

"So you're afraid of them, too," said King quietly. "The Fisherman's Net, next Monday, two in the afternoon. I'll be there, and we can conclude our work, I trust, Your Honor." So saying, he let himself out. He took the stairs down one floor to street level and stepped out into the shining afternoon, going along to the side-street where his Lincoln was parked. He had a lot to think about, and as he swung onto US Route 101, south-bound, he felt mildly distracted. There was so much for him to evaluate, so much he would have to report to Pietragnelli later that evening. He was going to Ragoczy's house, to make his telephone calls from his house in the hope of avoiding too many eavesdroppers.

The ferry from San Rafael was almost full; King spent the time out on the upper deck, looking at the Golden Gate Bridge. In another month it would be open, and Oscar King could drive to Santa Rosa without having to use the ferry. It was a glorious sight, he thought, something grand to welcome the world to the Golden State. When the horn sounded to alert the passengers to return to their cars, King went slowly, wanting a last look at the two red towers and the graceful suspension cables.

From the Ferry Building he drove up Market Street to Buchanan, and turned west between the U.S. Mint and San Francisco State College, going out to Stanyan at the head of Golden Gate Park; he turned left and drove up the hill to Clarendon Court. By the time he reached Ragoczy's house, it was almost dark, and the windows of all the houses shone with electric lights; Ragoczy's house was no exception, and behind the draperies the rooms were bright. He parked across the street from the house, taking his briefcase from the backseat before going onto the porch.

Mr. Rogers admitted him to the house, saying, "Mr. Ragoczy and Miss Saxon are in his labo—study on the third floor."

"The converted attic?" said King. "Thank you, Mr. Rogers." He glanced at the beautifully furnished living room—done in a tasteful combination of Art Nouveau and Oriental motifs—then made for the stairs.

"Would you like something to eat?" Rogerio called up after him.

"Yes, if you would," King called down. He continued up to the third floor and was about to knock on the door when Saint-Germain opened it from the inside.

"Do come in, Mr. King," he said. "You know Miss Saxon."

King nodded. "Good evening, Miss Saxon."

She smiled from her brocaded love seat, where she was reclining in dull-brick crepe de chine trousers and a blouse of ivory silk broadcloth. She was as elegant as Irene Dunne and as composed as Myrna Loy. "It is a pleasure to see you again, Mr. King."

The attic now looked like a cross between a library and a chemical laboratory, for there were retorts, alembics, scales on a long trestle table, and two chests with strong, locked doors. Most puzzling to King was a beehive-like structure made of fine white brick that stood at the far end of the room.

"My athanor," said Saint-Germain, following King's gaze. "It's a kind of oven."

"For chemical experiments?" asked King.

"I have a fair number of patents for chemical formulae," said Saint-Germain. "I like to keep my hand in."

"Yes," said King. "Sunbury said something about fuels."

"Among other things," said Saint-Germain in a tone that did not encourage more discussion.

"Well," said King, pulling up a chair from its place by the trestle table, "let me tell you how things turned out today." He coughed. "You can decide what we're to tell Pietragnelli."

"Why, everything," said Saint-Germain. "It is his right to know what is going on, and to make decisions based on as much information as we can provide."

King nodded at once. "Yes. I do understand."

"I hope so," said Saint-Germain. "You serve me poorly if you don't do your utmost for him."

There was a long silence. Finally Rowena said, "Should this be a private conversation? Do you want me to leave you alone?"

"It would be best," said King with a slight nod of apology. "Ragoczy is Pietragnelli's business partner, and he must be part of all binding agreements that have bearing on the business. But you aren't part of the business, so it wouldn't be appropriate for you to participate in our discussion." He looked away. "I'm sorry."

"I do understand," she said, getting up and going to the door to the lower part of the house. "Let me know when it's safe to come back." With a provocative scroop of her trouser-legs, she left the attic, closing the door behind her.

"It's a pity to send such a remarkable woman away, but given the nature of our discussion, I have to tell you that we need our confidentiality maintained." He sat down in the chair he had chosen. "I don't know what to tell you about this offer. It's most irregular."

"I'm not surprised," said Saint-Germain.

"Do you mean you were expecting something like this?" King demanded. "I thought it was damned odd."

"No doubt," said Saint-Germain. "Tell me what happened."

More slowly than he intended, Oscar King did as Saint-Germain asked. He was interrupted only once, when Rogerio came in with a tray that had a bowl of ox-tail soup and a thick, multilayered sandwich of chicken, ham, cheese, onions, lettuce, and an array of condiments. It took King almost forty minutes to review everything Judge George Cavendish had said while he made sallies at his meal. At the conclusion, he said, "I think his offer is genuine. I wish I knew whom it is really coming from."

"That would be useful," Saint-Germain concurred. "But he isn't going to tell you. Carlo Pietragnelli may have some ideas about it." He had been sitting on a drafting stool, but now he got up and went to the love seat. "You should call Pietragnelli shortly. He'll have finished dinner and he'll be going off to his cabin shortly. Tell him everything, and let him know I will support any decision he makes, so long as I know what it is." He lowered his head. "I don't want to try to make up his mind for him."

"You may not like what he chooses," King cautioned.

"I may not. But my interest is financial, and his is deeply personal. It would be high-handed of me to put my earnings above his livelihood." Saint-Germain went to open the door. "If you want to use the telephone in my study, you know where it is."

"Are you sure you don't want to talk to him?" King asked, a bit nonplussed.

"He and I will talk another time. He doesn't need to hear my opinion yet." He studied Mr. King. "You are doing an excellent job, Mr. King. I am more than satisfied with your advice and I have a high regard for your opinions. But tonight your primary obligation is to Pietragnelli. I will talk to him on Sunday, after he's had a chance to ponder his options."

"All right," said King. "But there is something on your mind. You're preoccupied; I can tell, though you hide it well. If it isn't Pietragnelli's situation, then what is it?"

"Ah, that," said Saint-Germain. "You are a most observant man, Mr. King. I am concerned. I am fairly certain that the man who broke into Miss Saxon's house was intending to use her to gain some advantage with me."

"Why would you think that?" King wondered.

"I have a price on my head still in Spain," said Saint-Germain.

"Why should that follow you here?" King had masked his sense of alarm quickly, but not fast enough for Saint-Germain to be unaware of it.

"I'm not imagining this," Saint-Germain said with uncanny calm. "As you may recall, Miles Sunbury, my attorney in London—the man who referred me to you?— was badly beaten by a man seeking information about me with the apparent intention of pursuing me. There is a lot at stake for General Franco—and wasn't it fortunate for him that General Mola had that tragic accident?—and the men around him. They can't afford any loose ends, and I am one such."

"Isn't that a little far-fetched?" King wanted to make light of the possibility.

"I would like to think so. But, if you will recollect, you had someone call at your offices and ask for me, someone from Spain," said Saint-Germain. "You warned me about him at New Year."

"But that would mean you have been followed for . . . for months!" King exclaimed.

"So it does," said Saint-Germain, then shrugged. "Well, there's nothing I can do now. Go call Pietragnelli. At least we can make some progress on that front."

"All right," said King, feeling disquieted. He started for the door, then hesitated. "You don't think this White Legion situation has anything to do with the man who might be following you, do you?"

Saint-Germain managed a swift, ironic smile. "I'm not completely paranoid, Mr. King. No, I do not think the two are connected. Nor do I think the government is reading my mail." He could see the guarded relief on King's face. "But I would hate to have any of my friends come to grief on my account."

"Um," said King, setting his foot on the first step down. "It is very shocking about Miss Saxon. I could hardly believe it when you telephoned me about it."

"Yes; it is shocking," said Saint-Germain.

"I'll talk to Mr. Pietragnelli," said King, recovering himself. "It may take some time to review the whole with him."

"I'm not worried about the telephone bill," said Saint-Germain. "Take as long as you need."

King nodded and turned to go down the stairs.

Saint-Germain watched him go, for the first time feeling that a practicable solution was possible for Carlo Pietragnelli—not the justice the vintner sought, but a resolution that would be tolerable for everyone caught up in the case. But Rowena's intruder still bothered him, and the more he deliberated on the attack, the more he believed that the man was not finished yet.

TEXT OF A REPORT FROM INSPECTOR ABEL PORTER TO INSPECTOR JOHN SMITH.

May 14, 1937

Inspector John Smith
Columbus Avenue Station
San Francisco, California

Dear John,

Thank you for your report on Ferenc Ragoczy. I have found it most interesting reading, and I am beginning to share your conviction that he is connected to the attack on Miss Rowena Saxon, little though it appears to be so. I find only very trivial incidents in her past that would suggest she could become the target of such an attempt as the one made upon her, but in regard to Ragoczy, there are many more questions, most with inadequate answers.

You say that in your investigation of the thefts at his hotel suite one of the items stolen was a collection of uncut gems, and that they were appraised as very valuable stones. Is it possible that Ragoczy gave some of those stones to Miss Saxon? Their relationship appears to be a close one, going back a number of years. If she has a collection of these stones, and someone—maybe the thieves from the Saint Francis—suspects it, it could be that she would be attacked in order to get the jewels. Being uncut, they can be especially valuable in the clandestine market, for once they're cut, they will be completely untraceable.

Your report indicates that Ragoczy was some kind of industrialist in Spain, and lost his business at the onset of their Civil War. But he isn't Spanish, as you and I have both ascertained, and we know he travels on a Hungarian passport. That makes him something of a puzzle. You have information that he has been in diplomatic service, but it appears he is avoiding the consulates and foreign communities in San Francisco, which is hard to understand, unless he might be recognized. I agree with you that he is very likely an agent of one kind or another, but for whom, and why? What is his mission here? And, assuming he is here in that capacity, the attack on Miss Saxon becomes more sinister, for it suggests that he is actively involved in a mission that is important enough for someone to want to stop it. If Miss Saxon is not part of his mission—and I am satisfied that she is not—then she is in great danger from him. What I haven't determined is if he knows about it, and what he plans to do to deal with it.

Your recommendation that we hold off sending his fingerprints to the FBI for a while is well-taken. I don't want those grandstanding G-men coming in and tromping all over our work. If this is as big a case as I think it may be, the last thing either of us needs is that dandy, J. Edgar, barging in here like Ahab after his whale, blowing his own horn, and splattering pictures of himself all over the front pages of The Chronicle and the Call-Bulletin.

I have made an inquiry with Ragoczy's attorney, Oscar King, in the hope of filling in some of the blanks about the man, but I don't expect much from him. You know how lawyers are. Tight as clams about their clients. But if Ragoczy is a spy, then King should be willing to tell us what he knows. A man in his position cannot be seen to help enemies of his country, now can he?

In terms of getting other information on the attack, our interviews with neighbors haven't turned up much useful. One man on Mason Street said he thought he heard an engine starting the night Miss Saxon was attacked, at around one-forty, which could be in the time-frame of the escape. He said it didn't sound like a car starting, so I don't know what to make of it. No one mentioned seeing a motorcycle, and that is about the only thing I could imagine making the noise described. In that neighborhood, a motorcycle would certainly be noticed, so I have to decide whether or not the man on Mason was mistaken, or a motorcycle went unnoticed.

If only the Golden Gate Bridge weren't opening on the 27th, we'd be able to assign more men to this investigation instead of turning half the police in San Francisco into escorts for all the swells coming into the city. But since that's the way it is, we'll have to make the most of what we've got, so any help you can give me will be much appreciated. I can see this is going to be a real knot of a case, and it isn't one I should be able to unravel on my own, especially not now. I'm glad to share the credit with you if you'll lend your expertise to the investigation.

Many thanks,

Abel Porter

chapter seven

At the head of the line waiting to drive over the splendid span were the most impressive automobiles in San Francisco, all gathered for the great occasion: a Stutz Black Hawk, a Rolls-Royce Silver Ghost, a Triumph Dolomite Roadster, a Bugatti Royale, an Hispano-Suiza Sport Boulogne, a Zeppelin Roadster, and an Alfa-Romeo Monza were among the first cars across the bridge; they were laden with reporters and dignitaries, all of them flighty as children at this astonishing function. The day before pedestrians had been allowed on the bridge, and that had been a glorious celebration, but today, May 28, vehicles were going to claim their roadway. With police escorts, the pack of automobiles crossed the bridge, drove into the vista point, turned around, and drove back the other way. There was no foot-traffic on the bridge today but pedestrians lined both ends of it, waving and cheering, and pointing out the most famous persons and the grandest cars.

Saint-Germain and Rowena were on the Marin County side of the bridge, ambling through the crowd at the edge of the roadway, taking stock of everything going on around them. Rowena was wearing jodhpurs and field boots as much to keep warm as to look sporting; her hacking jacket was expensive tweed and her shirt was pale green silk. She carried a small, dark brown, cartridge-style bag slung from her shoulder, and her gloves were of matching leather. This was the first day out since the break-in at her house that she had truly enjoyed herself, and she was determined to make the most of it.

"Thank you, thank you, thank you," she exclaimed. "I know I said I didn't want to come, that it would be too vulgar and crowded, but you were right: I would have hated to miss this. I'm going to write to my nephews tonight, to tell them all about it. Yesterday would have been too much, official opening or not, but today, with all the cars—" She pointed to the Zeppelin Roadster, one of the largest of the cars, with a front end reminiscent of the diesel engine of the Santa Fe Chief and a body like a Trailways bus. "Isn't that impressive?"

"Not as much as the driver would like it to be, I would think," said Saint-Germain.

She laughed almost merrily. "Your Pierce-Arrow is nice enough for me."

"You have the gift of tact, Rowena, and you use it well. I'm glad today is going as you would like, with all you have been through, and all the memories that have been stirred up. If you reach a surfeit of crowds, we will leave, but as long as you're enjoying yourself, we'll remain. Remember, you have a chance to spend some time in the countryside when we're finished here," said Saint-Germain. "We can go over the mountain to the ocean when this is over."

She clung to his arm more from enthusiasm than apprehension. "I think that would be lovely. We'd get time alone together." Her expression became more serious. "There are some things I want to discuss with you."

"I realize that, and we'll have a fine opportunity a little later on," he said. "At the end of the afternoon, shall we go back by ferry, as we came, or do you want to drive over the bridge?"

"I want to drive over the bridge, but since the traffic is going to be hideous, I think it would be wiser to take the ferry back, because it will be half-empty, I expect. To see the bridge in use from the deck of the ferry! Sort of hail and farewell, don't you think? Out with the old, in with the new?" She leaned her head on his shoulder. "Is it my imagination, or do things change faster than when I was a child?"

"They do change faster; I've been noticing it for the last four hundred years," said Saint-Germain. "And the changes will continue to accelerate, unless something intervenes to stop them. This Great Depression here in the United States has certainly slowed change down."

"How can you say that, here, at this bridge?" She turned away from the towering structure, gazing out toward the east and the hills of Alameda County. "The Bay Bridge is new. Treasure Island isn't even complete yet. They're going to have a permanent port for the China Clipper in place. And yet you say change has gone more slowly."

"Oh, this is impressive enough, but, useful though these bridges are, they are an artificial change in many ways, imposed to make it possible for people to earn enough to live by building them, and using them to make earning a living easier. This is not the result of—" He stopped. "Never mind. I won't impose my economic theories on you."

"Why not? All the pundits are doing it all the time in the papers and on the radio; you, at least, have some perspective on the problem." She sighed. "But you're right. Not today. Today we are tourists, aren't we?" She pointed toward the bay. "All those sailboats. They must be having a wonderful time."

"On the water," said Saint-Germain sardonically.

"Oh, I don't mean that *you* would, I only mean that it would be fun to see this bridge from down there, with the sails singing in the wind." She laughed, a bit tentatively. "Is crossing running water so far above it any easier for you?"

"No," he said, a frown forming between his fine brows.

She glanced at him and changed the subject. "Where did you finally park your car?"

"Half-way into Sausalito," he said.

"It might be a good idea to get out of here in a while," she said, admitting in a lowered voice, "I'm beginning to feel as if I'm being watched again."

"We'll go," he said, putting a reassuring hand on her shoulder. "Don't worry. I won't make you come with me to get the car. I'll find a spot where you can rest and I'll go fetch it. Then you can decide where we might go next."

"All right," she said, not wanting to wear herself out hiking back to the car. The last few weeks she had been worn out, and little as she wanted to acknowledge it, she had to conserve her energy, at least until the strain of her attack passed, and the nightmares it had spawned. She was thankful for the many times Saint-Germain had come to her room and held her so she could sleep, yet she was disgusted that she should need such coddling. An independent woman like her, bothered by bad dreams! For the first time in her life she began to feel age pluck at her, and the experience chilled her more than the salt-scented wind.

They made their way through the throngs of reveling people; loudspeakers magnified the voices of officials and bands as several of each took turns in front of the microphones. It was almost impossible to hear what was being said, for the people gathered at either end of the bridge were boisterous. A family with three children was pushing through the crowd ahead of them, trying to stay together, for it was apparent that if they were separated, they would have an extremely difficult task to find one another again. Those swarming around them jostled and rejoiced, making the most of this day for which they had waited so long.

"It's not as bad as yesterday," said Saint-Germain. "There aren't nearly so many people."

"That's unnerving," said Rowena, laughing a bit self-consciously. "Your three best friends could be in this mob and you might never see them." They were on the footpath down to Bunker Road, with people moving up toward the vista point. "Are you on the Lateral Road?"

"Just up the hill from Alexander Avenue, actually—inside the city of Sausalito, on Sausalito Boulevard." He nodded to a well-dressed couple struggling up the steepest part of the slope.

"That's a fair distance." She was a bit ashamed at how glad she was not to have to walk it for herself. "I'll watch the people. There must be faces I'd like to sketch."

"That isn't the only thing that might be in the crowd," said Saint-Germain, and felt her falter at his side. "I don't mean to frighten you, not with all you've been through. But it is best to be alert in such a place as this."

"I understand," she said, the merriment gone from her voice and her eyes. "And I know you're right. I wish you weren't, but you are."

"So if you will let me find you a place to sit a little out of the ebb and flow . . ." He nodded toward the curving road. "I shouldn't be long. Traffic isn't piling up yet."

"We could take the ferry from Sausalito," she pointed out.

"Then you wouldn't get your afternoon in the countryside. But we'll do whatever you choose." Saint-Germain indicated a line of thick posts made from broad tree-trunks. "Take one of those for your chair, and give yourself twenty minutes or so to relax. I won't need much more time than that."

She put her hands to her hair. "I'm going to look a fright."

"Never," he said, and chose the broadest of the posts that marked the edge of the road. "Be careful. Remember, these are here to stop cars from going off the pavement. Keep an eye on the traffic, and don't take any chances."

As she sat on the broad post, Rowena said, "I'll make every effort." She kissed her fingers in his direction as he strode off down the curving hillside. "And I'll study faces."

"Very good," he answered, and lengthened his stride, using the footpaths to cut over to the Sausalito Lateral Road, his deceptively easy stride covering ground more rapidly than most people could run. It was a windy day, which took most of the warmth away. The chill did not bother him, but the hazy sunlight did, making his skin prickle.

Rowena shielded her eyes so she could watch Saint-Germain as he slipped through the crowd on the road. The way he moved fascinated her—lithe, swift, and powerful, like watching a gifted dancer, although Saint-Germain did not dance—and she wished she had a camera so she could freeze his movement and paint it later, to remind her of this day when he was gone, providing he photographed at all. Eventually she lost sight of him as he went around the bulge of the hillside. She had left her watch on her dresser, so there was no way to keep track of the length of time Saint-Germain had been gone. If she had had cigarettes with her, she would have smoked, but as it was, she contented herself with studying the faces of people going by her. Occasionally she could hear music blaring from the loudspeakers at the vista point above her, but for the most part, she let her thoughts drift; it was a wonderful time to sit in the sun and feel the crisp breeze snapping around her. It was easy to half-doze in the sporadic warmth and let the excitement of the day eddy around her.

The sound of a siren cut into her reverie, and she got up from her tree-stump post, slightly disoriented. How long had she been lethargic? It seemed more than twenty minutes. She was suddenly worried. Where was Saint-Germain? Shouldn't he have returned by now? She listened to the wail of the siren with increasing alarm, all the while telling herself that she was borrowing trouble, that the chances were that the siren had nothing to do with her. She noticed that many others were watching the police car as it rushed down the Lateral Road, and that bothered her, as well. She wanted to know what had happened that the police had been summoned. Who could tell her? Impulsively she began to walk along the road, going the direction Saint-Germain had.

Another police car bawled past her, the faces of the two men inside grim; Rowena felt a cold mass solidify in her solar plexus, her fear made physical; whatever was the cause of the police being summoned, she saw that the officers thought it was dire. She resisted the urge to run, telling herself that the reason Saint-Germain was taking so long to reach her was that the emergency that had summoned the police had delayed him. How much she wanted to believe it and how much she dreaded what might have happened. Her head was starting to ache, another manifestation of her dawning panic. She could not think of anything more to do than go toward the place where the police cars were going, all the while hoping to see Saint-Germain's Pierce-Arrow coming down the road in her direction.

She had gone more than half-a-mile when she found a white-faced man approaching her, occasionally looking back over his shoulder. "What is it? What's happened?" she asked the man as he staggered up to her.

"It's . . . pretty bad. You don't want to go look, lady, you really don't," said the man.

"What—?" she asked. "Tell me what happened?"

He shook his head. "A fancy silver car lost its brakes, they think. It came down the hill, crashed across Alexander, and went over the retaining wall and bounced down the side of the hill below, into the bay." As he spoke, his skin took on a greenish tinge, and when he finished talking, he flung away from her and went off into the dry grass to vomit.

"A silver car?" Rowena repeated, aghast at the emotions that took hold of her.

The man could not answer her; he stood bent over, his hands on his knees, his elbows akimbo as his guts lurched again.

Rowena began to run, her thoughts blurred by all the awful possibilities jumbling through her. She forced herself not to break into a run, but she walked rapidly, and occasionally dashed the tears from her eyes, trying to convince herself that she was being foolish to worry so. As she rounded the hill, she saw two police cars drawn up at the side of the narrow road near a break in the metal railing above the concrete retaining wall, three of the officers standing at the break, looking down the steep incline toward the edge of the water. "Oh, Good Lord," she burst out.

One of the policemen caught sight of her and bustled toward her. "Sorry, ma'am. You shouldn't be here. This isn't the kind of thing ladies should see."

But she would not be turned away. "Tell me what kind of car it is."

"It don't make any difference," said the policeman. "It's a wreck, in any case. The doors on the left side are off, and the roof looks like crumpled paper." He regarded her with that official menace that police often employ to discourage onlookers.

"Let me see," she insisted. "I have been waiting for my friend, who went to get his car so we could leave." She met his eyes with the upper-class imperiousness she had learned in her youth; status won, and the officer looked away first. "My friend drives a Pierce Silver Arrow, three years old, as I recall."

The officer coughed. "Do you know where he was parked?"

"He said he was on Sausalito Boulevard," Rowena answered, making herself sound unafraid.

"Um." The policeman now avoided her stare deliberately. "Would your friend be a middle-aged man, on the shortish side, in a black suit with a striped tie?"

"Yes," said Rowena, holding her breath.

"Sorry, ma'am. I don't know how to break it to you. They're fishing him out of the bay right now. He got tossed out of the car when the doors came off, and I'm afraid he bounced down the cliff pretty hard. His suit caught on the bumper, or he'd've landed next to the Benson house, not in the bay." He pointed to the sixty-year-old structure that stood at the edge of the water, backed up against the cliff, built on piles that were lapped by high tide. "As it is, he's . . . well, there's an ambulance coming. We'll have to let them—"

Rowena felt a single idea go through her. "He can't die."

"We all hope so, ma'am," said the officer in a manner that revealed he thought otherwise.

"No," she said. "He can't die." She looked about her. "I need to make a telephone call. To his house."

"You might want us to do that, ma'am, after he's out of the water," said the policeman with rough sympathy.

"I need to do it. Now." She stared down the road. "Where is there a telephone?"

The policeman looked disquieted. "Well, there is the Red Slipper, just down the way, off of Second. The sign's pretty discreet, but you can see it when you get to Richardson Street."

"All right," said Rowena, determined to do her utmost for Saint-Germain. "Don't take him away until I get back," she warned.

"We might have to, ma'am, if he's—"

"I'm his blood relative, and I am ordering you to wait for me. I have some arrangements I have to make for him." She was already walking, feeling strength coming back into her body as she walked down the hill. Much as she wanted to know what had happened, she would not let herself dwell on the dreadful possibilities. She had to call Rogerio and begin making arrangements for getting Saint-Germain back to his house, for once in the hospital, he would be in as much danger as he was when his car had plunged over the cliff. At Richardson Street, she turned away from the bay and began looking for the Red Slipper. This turned out to be a fifty-year-old three-story house with widow's walks and two cupolas, painted pink and white. A valentine-shaped sign identified it as the Red Slipper, and Rowena realized that this was one of Sausalito's famous-but-discreet bordellos. She faltered, then went up onto the broad piazza-porch and knocked on the door.

"Yes?" The man who opened the door was a big mulatto with cauliflower ears and a mashed nose.

She was determined not to be embarrassed. "I'm sorry, but my friend was just in a car accident, and I'd like to use your telephone to notify his—"

"Come on in," said the man, regarding her with curiosity. "The telephone's over there, next to the cloakroom. It's pay."

"That's fine," she said, and hurried in the direction he pointed; she had a vague impression of glossy cherry wainscoting and burgundy wallpaper, and there was a perfume in the air that was spicy and flowery. The telephone was in an alcove with a sliding door, and she slipped into it quickly, taking change from her purse and dropping a nickle into the coin slot. "Operator. I need a San Francisco number," she said when asked what number she wanted.

"That'll be fifteen cents for the first three minutes," the operator informed her, and took the number while Rowena deposited a dime.

"Ragoczy household," said Rogerio after four rings.

"Thank God you're home," Rowena said without greeting. "Rogers, there's been an accident. A bad accident."

"Indeed, Miss Saxon," he said, so coolly that Rowena knew he was upset.

"In Sausalito. The car is wrecked. And the police will be taking him to the hospital." She spoke in rapid spurts.

"The hospital? Which hospital?"

"I plan to ask them to take him to one in San Francisco," said Rowena. "Which do you recommend?"

"The Affiliated Colleges of the University of California are just down on Parnassus, which is convenient to this location, and the hospital is considered excellent." He paused. "I'll call and make arrangements to meet his ambulance."

"Good," said Rowena. "I'll see if they'll let me go with him." She did her best to keep from dwelling on what might happen to Saint-Germain.

"Very good," said Rogerio. "And I wouldn't fret. He's come through much worse than this, and survived." He had a brief impression of Saint-Germain hanging from a crucifix, the sun burning him almost beyond recognition; that had been in Mexico, three centuries ago, but he banished it from his thoughts.

"Thank you, Rogers," said Rowena, and hung up. For several seconds she hung on to the telephone and shook, but then she told herself she had no time to waste this way. As she came out of the alcove, she found the man who had admitted her standing nearby. "That was very kind of you," she said to him.

He gave her a half-smile. "You sure you don't want to stay for a while?"

She achieved a shaky laugh. "No, thank you." On impulse, she held out fifty cents to him.

He waved the money away. "This wasn't business. I don't want a tip." He led her back to the door and held it open for her. "I hope your friend's okay."

"Thank you. So do I," she said, and turned away, heading back toward the place where Saint-Germain's car had crashed through the barrier and down the cliff.

Two more policemen were at the scene, one of them of higher rank than the others. He eyed Rowena with suspicion. "You the lady with him?"

"I am," she said, comprehending the imprecise question. "I want to ride with him in the ambulance."

"It might be pretty messy," he warned, but with less concern than the first officer had shown.

"I'm prepared," she said. "I have spoken to his business colleague, and he instructed me to have him taken to the hospital at the Affiliated College of the University of California on Parnassus."

"Oh, did you?" The officer put his hands on his hips. "It costs extra, doing that. And you may have to pay up front."

"I have enough with me, I'm almost certain," said Rowena, certain the ambulance could not cost more than a taxi-ride to Mills Field, which was three dollars; she had thirty-five with her, a lavish sum, which made her feel protected: she could stay in a hotel and have a good meal for much less; she could surely afford the ambulance charges.

"Well, we'll see what the ambulance driver has to say," the officer proclaimed. He looked down toward the water. "They got him out. They say he hasn't breathed."

"He could be in shock," said Rowena.

The officer gave her a pitying glance. "Yes. That's it, ma'am."

Rowena ignored this. "Let me see him."

"He's pretty badly banged up," said the officer.

"Don't worry about me, Officer," said Rowena. "I'm not going to faint or do anything unseemly."

"So you may think, ma'am, but—"

Rowena interrupted him ruthlessly. "I am going down to the water's edge, and I am going to remain with my relative. It's what he'd do for me."

The officer heaved a put-upon sigh. "There's steps over there. Damned steep, but they'll take you right down to the back of the Benson house. The ambulance will pull in on the other side of the house."

She stared at him. "You were going to take Ragoczy away without letting me know, weren't you?"

He hitched his shoulder. "Something like that."

It would have been tremendously gratifying to yell at the officer, to heap all her worry and tension on him, but she stopped herself; she needed this man's good opinion or she might lose Saint-Germain. "You were wrong, Sergeant," she said before she went to the steep wooden stairs leading down the cliff to the shore. Grasping the railings tightly, she went down as quickly as she could, glad of her field boots that protected her shins from the whipping berry vines that slapped at her as she passed.

Four policemen were gathered around a still figure lying on the shore, his sodden clothing badly ripped, the side of his face skinned to the bone. His right arm and shoulder were severely abraded, and there were pebbles and other debris in the torn flesh; blood ran sluggishly from the grisly injuries. Two of the policemen were wet, mute testimony to their rescue efforts. As Rowena approached, one of the officers knelt down and took Saint-Germain's wrist again, trying to find a pulse. He shook his head, and was about to speak up, when he caught sight of Rowena, and he released his hold on the wrist and got up.

"Excuse me," said Rowena as she came up to the policemen. "This man is my blood relative. I want to look at him."

Slowly the police moved aside; one of the men whose clothes were wet said, "You don't want to do that. I'm afraid he's gone."

Rowena was shaken at the extent of the damage she saw, but she reminded herself that no matter how bad it looked, if Saint-Germain's spine was unbroken, he would recover, if she could keep him away from the doctors, so she knelt down next to him and leaned over him, trying not to see the shredded skin and exposed tissue. "You have to breathe," she whispered urgently. "They'll call the coroner if you don't breathe." She was tempted to shake him, to force him to respond, but she knew the police would stop her if she tried; she repeated her plea, and was finally rewarded with a rough sigh, and a twitch in his hand.

"Jesus! Will you look at that?" the tallest of the officers exclaimed. "I would have sworn he was—" He silenced himself.

Taking his undamaged left hand in hers, Rowena said, "You have to send him to the University Hospital," she said to the police. "He has a condition that needs special attention."

"If he's come through that, you're damned right it's special," said another one of the officers, his voice higher-pitched than usual. "I'll tell the ambulance driver where to take you."

Rowena brought her gaze back to the ruin of Saint-Germain's face. "Your beautiful clothes are wrecked," she said inconsequentially, unable to bring herself to speak of anything more afflicting than that as she stroked his small, well-proportioned hand.

Saint-Germain moved slightly; a hint of sound came from him. "No accident."

She put her finger on his lips. "Shush," she whispered. "Not here." She glanced at the police, afraid they might have heard him. For some reason she could not define, she could not bring herself to trust the police. "We'll get you to the University of California Hospital, you know, the one on Parnassus, by Sutro Forest."

His fingers twitched in hers to show he heard her. "Saw him," he gasped. "Saw him."

A whooping siren cut through the desultory conversation among the policemen, and the tallest one leaned over, taking Rowena by the arm. "You gotta let the ambulance attendants through, ma'am. We'll arrange for you to ride with him."

Rowena allowed herself to be lifted, but she stood where she was. "I appreciate it, Officer."

"I sure thought he was . . ."

"Dead," she finished for him. "Those of his blood sometimes have . . . catalepsy. Some of them have even been buried because a mistake was made. Fortunately they . . . were restored."

"Good God," the other wet policeman said. "What a terrible thing. No wonder you're so worried."

The necessity of having to say anything more was lost as two ambulance attendants came rushing toward the group of policemen, a stretcher held between them.

"Where's the patient?" the attendant in the lead asked.

The policemen moved aside, but Rowena stayed where she was. "This is my kinsman. I am coming with you."

Before the attendants could refuse, the tallest officer said, "Yeah. The guy's got some kind of seizure condition. Don't ask me but it's creepy." He pointed to Rowena. "She'll explain it."

The attendants were not pleased, but they offered no argument, moving to

Saint-Germain's left side to load him onto the stretcher. Saint-Germain moaned, which shocked the attendants so that they almost dropped the stretcher. "He's gonna need blood," said the rear attendant.

"Undoubtedly," said Rowena. "But his type is very rare, and he needs his own physician. That's one of the reasons he has to go to the University of California Hospital in San Francisco. I'm sure you know where it is."

"It'll cost you fifteen dollars," said the lead attendant as he and his partner lifted the stretcher with Saint-Germain on it.

"I can afford it," said Rowena as she fell in beside the stretcher.

The ambulance was ready for them and they loaded it quickly. One attendant remained in the back with Saint-Germain and Rowena, the other got into the front with the driver and turned on the siren.

"You're lucky," said the driver as the attendant gave him their destination. "The bridge is open. You couldn't have done this a day ago."

"A day ago we wouldn't have been here," said Rowena, sitting on the pull-down chair on the rear door. She stared at him anxiously. "Is there anything you can do?"

"We'd take off his clothes, if you weren't here," said the attendant in the rear with her. "It has to be done."

"Don't let me stop you," she said. "I'm an artist; I've seen any number of naked bodies." But not Saint-Germain's, she reminded herself, not entirely.

"If you're sure? He's not going to be pretty," said the attendant even as he reached for heavy shears.

"Go ahead," said Rowena, and steeled herself for what she would see; it had been a long time since she had seen him without a shirt or a robe on.

The attendant began to cut Saint-Germain's trouser-leg, taking care not to touch the wounds. "It's amazing he doesn't have any broken bones, not that I can see. A fall like that should mean fractures everywhere."

"The car must have protected him," said Rowena, feeling the ambulance swaying. How strange, she thought, to be crossing the Golden Gate Bridge for the first time and not be able to see anything.

"We must be the first ambulance over the bridge," said the attendant as he dropped the cloth into a paper sack and began on the jacket; where he was not battered and bloody, Saint-Germain was very, very pale, his skin seeming almost translucent.

"I guess so," said Rowena.

"He's in pretty good shape, I'll say that," the attendant went on as he tossed the right side of the jacket into the sack and started on the shirt. "Silk. Don't see too many silk shirts."

"He dresses well," said Rowena.

The attendant had cut the shirt and undershirt; he caught sight of the wide swath of scars on Saint-Germain's torso, running from the base of his sternum to the top of his underdrawers. "Will you look at that?" he marveled. "He must've been in the Great War."

"He was in Europe before the war," said Rowena truthfully enough.

"Someone sure got him." The attendant kept on at his task as the ambulance slowed for the tollbooths. "Those are old scars."

"Yes; they are," said Rowena. She bit her lower lip to keep from crying, all the while wishing she were stronger, more able to maintain a proper deportment under pressure. Her headache was getting worse and she felt herself growing hot, a symptom of her change-of-life. This was hardly the time for such nonsense, she thought as she felt a finger of sweat slide down her neck.

"You all right?" the attendant asked.

"I'm upset," said Rowena.

The attendant nodded. "Small wonder." He moved the paper sack aside.

She rubbed her hands together. "How much longer?"

"Fifteen minutes, maybe less," said the attendant. "We're running the siren, and the cops won't stop us."

"Is that really an advantage?" She could feel the ambulance rock as it sped along the street that led to the passage through Golden Gate Park.

"We'll go up to Ninth Avenue, probably, then up the hill." The attendant had taken out a towel and was cleaning his hands.

"The driver must know the best way; the fastest," said Rowena as if to convince herself.

"He sure does." He took out a white drape and spread it over Saint-Germain, taking care not to do anything to make his injuries worse. The fine cotton was soon spotted with red. "It's gonna be hard to clean him up. There's sand and rock and glass in his wounds. And shock is always a problem when you're dealing with an accident."

"I'm sure his doctor will know how to manage it; he will meet us there; I know he will," said Rowena. She would have liked to hold Saint-Germain's hand, to care for him herself, but that would not be possible yet.

"They'll take care of him in Emergency," said the attendant. "They have a good staff, and they're hard workers."

"I'll keep that in mind," said Rowena, hoping that Rogerio would be there to meet them.

"He's gonna need blood," said the attendant.

"Oh, yes," said Rowena.

The attendant found a jar of saline solution and an intravenous needle and line. "I should try to get this started."

"It might be better to wait," said Rowena. "I think his physician will want to do it. He's supposed to be coming to the hospital."

"Did you talk to him?" The attendant hesitated.

"No; I spoke to his associate, who assured me he would call Ragoczy's physician." She mustered all the authority she could. "I don't want to do anything that could compromise his recovery."

"Makes sense to me," said the attendant, and moved back from the stretcher to sit down next to Rowena. "My name's Holmond, Walter Holmond," he said.

"It's good to meet you, Walter Holmond. I'm Miss Saxon," she said, offering her hand.

His handshake was firm but not so tight that it hurt. "You're a real trouper, Miss Saxon. Not many women could do this," he said, and fell silent.

Rowena sat back, longing for an aspirin. She would be so glad to have this day behind her, to have Saint-Germain safe once more; that was her biggest worry now, that she would be unable to protect him from the kind of scrutiny he most dreaded. As the ambulance turned left, she hung on to the side of the seat, her queasiness increasing, not all of it from the motion of the vehicle.

"He's a good man?" Holmond asked, jutting his chin in Saint-Germain's direction.

"The best I've ever known," Rowena said.

"Then I hope for your sake he pulls through," said Holmond, adding, "We're almost there." He coughed. "You'll have to pay the driver."

"Fifteen dollars," said Rowena. "Yes; I will."

The ambulance slewed to the right and barreled across the intersection, then sped up Ninth Avenue.

"Maybe three minutes more," said Holmond.

Let Rogerio be there, let Rogerio be there, Rowena repeated silently. "Hang on," she murmured to Saint-Germain, and thought she saw him nod, trusting it was something more than the motion of the ambulance that caused it.

TEXT OF A LETTER FROM COLONEL ANDREAS MORALES IN SEVILLA TO
CENERE IN SAN FRANCISCO; SENT AIRMAIL.

88, Calle de los Obreros
Sevilla, España
11 June, 1937

Cenere
North Point Hotel
901 North Point Street
San Francisco, California, USA

My dear Cenere,
Your telegram has finally caught up with me, and I am grateful to you for
keeping me informed of your activities, although I cannot entirely call it
progress; I am also surprised you should spend so much on a telegram when
an airmail letter would have been less than twenty percent of the cost of the
telegram. Still, you were obeying my instructions and what's done is done.
The same cannot be said of your mission. I will agree your attempts on
Ragoczy's life should have succeeded, and that they have not is hardly to your
discredit, but I also agree with you that to act again soon would be a great
risk that is likely to be too problematic to contemplate, at least for the next
month or so; Ragoczy must be on the alert, and he has shown himself to be a
formidable opponent, and for that reason alone, circumspection is called for.
Let me tell you now, however, that your failure to kill Ragoczy is not
acceptable. You will remain where you are until this mission is complete.
And you will not threaten me again in regard to informing my superiors. I
may have exceeded my authority, but you have taken the most flagrant
advantage of my desire to see this Ragoczy removed. Consider all you have
done and you will be grateful that you are being permitted to do the work
you have been so handsomely paid to do, rather than suffer the same fate as
Ragoczy must—I say must advisedly, certain that you will not miss my
meaning. If you should fail to kill him, do not return to España, or you will
find that you will have to answer for your failure before a firing squad.
I cannot recommend another attack on the artist-woman, no matter how
closely associated she may be to Ragoczy. She is a noted personage, and
attacks on her could bring about the very scrutiny your work is supposed to
evade. The police have investigated the break-in, you tell me, and have not
closed their case. This situation can too easily turn against you; bide your
time if you must. As much as I want Ragoczy dead, I want more to have no

connection, directly or indirectly, to that so-called accident or the break-in at Miss Saxon's house, not with the police taking such an interest in the matter. I want you to keep that in mind as you make your next plans as you undertake to fulfill your pledge to see Ragoczy dead.

You say you tampered with his brakes and the steering-linkage on his automobile, which is totally wrecked due to the fall the auto took into the water. Had matters gone only a bit more in our favor, Ragoczy would be dead now and you would be returning to Europe, where there is more work waiting for you. But such is the perversity of fate that your best efforts succeeded only in causing severe injuries, and the destruction of the vehicle. In regard to the latter, I am assuming that the damage you inflicted on the auto could not be easily identified as artificial rather than unfortunate; if your role in the accident can be determined, then you must reevaluate your task and determine if it is prudent to continue as you have done. It may be that another approach is called for, and it is up to you to discover it and put it to the most careful use. Under no circumstances are you to be arrested; if that should happen, you will be utterly on your own, for your apprehension by the police would undo all the advantages you have so carefully achieved.

You also inform me that Ragoczy has been in the care of a private physician from the time he was injured until now, making it impossible for you to reach him through hospital personnel, a most distressing development, and one you must factor into your next plans. I will not support any action that will expose your purpose, and that includes more attempts on those close to Ragoczy, for that makes for complications that may lead to the sort of discovery you are sworn to evade.

Another two thousand dollars has been wired to you, as per your request. I cannot imagine how you contrive to spend so much. For most Americans, two thousand dollars would be a handsome salary for a year, and you claim to need five times that amount to do your work, which, on the face of it, is a simple thing to accomplish. You may be very good at what you do, but it doesn't change the fact that you are expensive to maintain. This is the last money I will vouchsafe you until I have word from you that you have succeeded. I have been patient, but I expect results, discreetly achieved. I will pay you your price, but I also ask that you do this with as much dispatch as you can without risking discovery. Be certain that any prevarication will only be held against you, and any revelation to the local authorities will bring swift reprisals. If you are identified as what you are, you must leave or assure your silence. I know I make myself clear.

Should anything bring a compromise upon me, or any project to which I have been assigned, I will see that you answer for it. Now that General Franco is advancing so successfully, it is essential that nothing interfere with the triumph of our cause. With all you have demanded, it will go badly for you if anything you have done comes to light. You will have to answer for your failure, and if I must, I will make a public display of you; I will disgrace you and see you stand before a firing squad. So if you are losing determination on this mission, let me assure you it will be far worse for you, should you attempt to make a bargain with Ragoczy or the American authorities. You are not the only assassin known to me, and I will not hesitate to silence you if it is necessary. If you continue to threaten me with exposure, I will break off all ties with you and consider our association at an end. Do the work you have contracted to do and I will see you appropriately rewarded.

You may continue to use this address for the next four months, for I will be supervising General Franco's supporters here in Sevilla. Our cause is gaining momentum every day, and coordinating the actions of those who are willing to join with us is increasingly important, so it is also crucial just now that no nefarious deeds be attributed to us. You must know that my strictures on this point apply to you as well as to our fighters here. I look forward to your telegram informing me of your completion of your commission, and your plans for a prompt return to España to answer for all you have accomplished.

Andreas Morales, Colonel

~

chapter eight

"What a beautiful day to visit the winery. Why must we discuss your leaving in the midst of all this?" Rowena said as she and Saint-Germain motored out of Petaluma on their way to Geyserville; the September morning was hot and the traffic on Route 101 was crawling; up ahead about a mile a maroon DeSoto was pulled onto the shoulder, the driver sweating at the task of changing a tire as the rest of the north-bound cars inched by, stately as a parade.

"There are only a few minor matters to clear up, including the automobiles. Oscar King has all the paperwork done to arrange the transfer to you. The Auburn isn't your Chancellor Miller Speedster, but it is a very nice machine, for all of that," said Saint-Germain. "I think you'll enjoy it; if you don't, sell it." He was in his black tropical-weight summer suit, a crisp linen shirt beneath and a red-and-black foulard tie; he had not worn a hat.

She turned to him, watching his profile as he concentrated on the road ahead. "I wish you'd let me pay you for it. I can easily afford it."

"I'd just as soon not," said Saint-Germain.

"Do you think you might come back?" Her question was wistful, and she made no apology for it. She played with the ruffled peplum of her mallard silk blouse and brushed imaginary dust off her khaki twill skirt.

"We've been over this already." He smiled swiftly. "I can't bring any more misfortune upon you: I won't."

She put her hand on his arm, touching him lightly so as not to interfere with his steering. "I've thought about that, and I've decided I wouldn't mind."

"I would," he said, and eased his Duesenberg SJ around the DeSoto. "I've done enough to you—perhaps too much."

"I don't think so," she said. "You have given me so much more than you have received from me."

"You haven't died yet," he reminded her. "When you do—"

She leaned back on the seat again. "When I do, I'll sort it out. Today I think it would be delightful to live for decades and decades more. But when I actually get there, I may decide I have had enough of life."

"I don't want to cause you any more heartache than you already have had," he persisted. "And I know whereof I speak."

"No doubt," she said, deliberately imitating him. "But you're still alive, at least in your own way." She noticed the small stand of redwoods up ahead on the left, a quaintly decorated restaurant and gift shop standing in its shadow. "Sportsmen like to come here, I'm told. They fish in the Petaluma and Santa Rosa Rivers. There's some duck-hunting in the hills around here."

"But no fox-hunting," said Saint-Germain.

"No. Nothing like that; California doesn't seem like hunt country," said Rowena. "I don't miss that nearly as much as I thought I might. Not that I was ever fond of fox-hunting as such, though the riding was invigorating." She stretched a little.

He lowered his arm out the window to signal his slowing down for an intersection, stopping carefully. He put the Duesenberg in first gear and continued across the intersection slowly, shifting into second as he reached the other side. "You can ride in California."

"At Ponderosa Lodge, if nowhere else," she said, trying to smile.

"Yes. You can ride there."

She nodded, and spent half-a-mile looking out the window. "I love the end of summer. It's not just the harvest, it's the drawing in of the year. You can feel it start. The light changes, somehow. This year it changed last month—a bit early. In spring, it's a gradual change, hardly perceptible from one day to the next, but autumn arrives on a specific day, when the light changes. It's easier to see here, in California, than it is in England, but I've seen it there, too, now that I know what to look for."

Saint-Germain glanced out at the sky. "The light does change," he said; he did not often notice it as the years flickered by, but he recognized what she was describing.

They drove through Santa Rosa in silence, and went on north, the traffic remaining dense, and providing an excuse for their stillness. As they reached the outskirts of Healdsburg, she spoke up as if they had been conversing all along. "Are you really expecting trouble at the winery?"

"Trouble now would do the most harm; so yes, I think there is an opportunity to do real damage, and it will have to come before the crush is over. Little as he admits it, Carlo Pietragnelli believes the White Legion will strike, and strike soon. So does Oscar King."

"So this is more than a farewell visit?" For the first time that day she was uneasy.

"It is possible." He continued to drive, his demeanor unconcerned. "I do share their concern; the crush is almost over."

"You know something, don't you?" she asked sharply.

"Let us say I suspect," said Saint-Germain. "There are rumors, little more than that. But these rumors are consistent and specific, and that makes them worrisome."

"You won't tell me what they are, will you?" Suddenly she laughed, tossing her head. "I wish I could be angry with you, but I can't. I've been trying to, but—" She shrugged.

"If you would prefer to argue, tell me and I'll attempt to oblige you," he said, managing a wry smile.

"It's no good if you agree to argue," she said ruefully. "Oh, Comte, I know I'm going to miss you."

"And I you." He braked to allow a truck laden with crates of produce to cross the road; he moved on. "How do you plan to spend the holidays this year?"

"I don't know. They're still a couple months away, and Thanksgiving is in November." She sighed. "I have thought of asking Penelope to come for Christmas. She could fly to New York and come across the country by train or airplane. I could see my nephews and . . ."

"Yet you hesitate," he said.

She faltered, wanting to explain herself clearly. "It's difficult with Penelope. Ever since she became a widow, she has set her life in stone, a monument to her mourning. Not that she sees it that way: she lives at Longacres with a staff of nine, and she thinks of herself as deprived because Rupert Bowen is dead. I don't make light of her loss, but it isn't the catastrophe she seems to believe it is. He wasn't a saint, and his death, while it was very sad, didn't mean that the world stopped. Penelope expects everyone to share her grief. I find this . . . trying. I'm sure she finds my lack of commiseration upsetting, too. But she's my last immediate relative. She has her sons, but I don't. I'd like to feel more contact with them, and with her, but . . ."

"But you find this compelling, the desire to keep in touch with your own continuity." He reached out and brushed her hand.

"It must be hard for you, not having that," she said, a bit self-consciously.

"Ah, but I have the Blood Bond with those who have loved me knowingly, and that sustains me. Blood is blood, one way and another, and it is the sum of all we are." He put both hands back on the steering wheel.

She considered this. "I hadn't thought of it that way."

He kept on toward Geyserville; Saint-Germain mused for a few miles. "Don't let too much time go by without seeing your nephews," he recommended. "The years can slip away so quickly. I know."

"I'll keep that in mind," said Rowena, sincerely.

They had reached the turnoff. "Carlo Pietragnelli can provide you some sense of balance, if you begin to feel a lack."

"You're not matchmaking, are you?" She pulled at the small strand of pearls around her neck.

Saint-Germain shook his head. "No. But the man has a family and he is as tied to his earth as I am to mine, and you may find solace in this."

"England is my native earth," she reminded him.

"Have some crates of it sent to you, or I'll arrange it. I'll go along to Chalfont Saint Giles and load up sacks for shipping to you." He chuckled and his face softened. "I'll be a midnight harvester, if I have to be."

Her laugh was a bit shaky. "I'll arrange it with Penelope. You won't have to sneak in at midnight."

"I'd appreciate that," said Saint-Germain. "I wouldn't like to have to explain what I'm doing. I'll leave that to you."

They were following the telephone poles along the graveled road that led to the entrance to the Pietragnelli Winery; Rowena rolled up her window to keep the dust out, and remarked, "Look how dry the hills are. They must be looking forward to rain."

"As soon as the grapes are in, I should think so," Saint-Germain agreed. "But they won't want it until the picking is done." As they slowed down for the gate, he said, "Pietragnelli would be quite delighted to have you paint his winery. He'd never ask you himself—he'd consider it too intrusive—but I know he wishes you'd do something more than sketches."

"I have my sketch pad with me," Rowena reminded him.

"I think he would like to see a painting eventually." He turned and drew up at the gate to the winery; pulling on the brake and putting the gears in neutral, Saint-Germain got out of the Duesenberg to open the gate. As soon as he had it pulled back, he returned to drive through, then stopped and went to close the gate again, looking around carefully as he did, scanning the goat-farm and the vegetable plantations across the road as well as Pietragnelli's vineyards. He noticed that two guards were keeping to their posts, each about fifty feet from the gate, and each held a rifle. When he was back in the car again, he said, "Thank you for coming with me today. I know this isn't what you had in mind as a farewell—"

"It's always a pleasure to visit the winery," she said with automatic good manners. "Even though it looks more like an armed camp. You really are expecting trouble, aren't you?"

"Preparing for it, in any case. The guards have been here a week." Saint-Germain started down the road, dust rising behind him. "The harvest is when the winery is most vulnerable; the work is demanding and must be done swiftly—if the harvest is lost, the winery loses more than work hours."

"You needn't apologize for taking care of Pietragnelli," said Rowena. "I would be surprised if you didn't make the effort."

"What can I be but grateful?" Saint-Germain said as he stopped the Duesenberg in the curve of the drive at the front of the house. He set the brake, put the transmission in neutral, and turned off the ignition.

"How can I reach you once you leave?" Rowena asked.

"You can write to me in care of Miles Sunbury, as you have done in the past; he'll know where to find me. As soon as I am established at a location, I will send you the address, if it is prudent to do so." Saint-Germain got out of the car and went to open her door. As she stepped out, he kissed her cheek. "Don't decide that I am no longer interested in you. You are a wonderful woman. Never doubt it."

"You're a shameless flatterer—and I love it," said Rowena playfully to cover the rush of emotion that threatened to overwhelm her.

Saint-Germain regarded her seriously. "I don't flatter you. I am praising you, and deservedly, Rowena. You may not be accustomed to it, but you merit it, and more. I hope you won't dismiss this when I'm gone as my good manners, for your character isn't an issue for politesse."

She blinked, and when she spoke, she stammered. "I—I'm not, you know. Deserving."

"You will pardon me for disagreeing," said Saint-Germain, and stepped back from her, taking her hand and tucking it through the crook of his arm.

"You've tasted my blood," she said just above a whisper as they started toward the front door. "You say you know me."

"I do," Saint-Germain assured her as he rapped on the screen door.

"Momento!" Carlo Pietragnelli called from inside. "Mrs. Barringstone! They have come!" A few seconds later the front door came open and Pietragnelli barreled out to greet his guests. "In buon' punto!" he exclaimed. "Today is almost the end of the crush. Most of the grapes are in, and we can be joyous. You can join us in our festivities, in spite of all the difficulties we have faced this harvest. My workers are out bringing in the last of the whites. Tomorrow we do the red plantation on the eastern slope of our second vineyard, and it will be finished until next year." He clapped Saint-Germain on the shoulder. "We'll open a bottle of the best to drink to the new wine. If you don't want to drink with me, then so be it, but the rest of us will have our celebrations."

"I should hope so," said Saint-Germain.

Pietragnelli turned to Rowena and grinned. "You do me honor to return, signora. I am delighted to have you here!" He kissed her hand. "La qualità," he announced. "I can always tell."

"If that means what I think it means," said Rowena, "many thanks. Mille grazie."

"Come in. Come in," Pietragnelli effused, making more room for them and half-bowing to allow them to enter his house. "Mrs. Barringstone! My guests are here!"

"I am coming, Mr. Pietragnelli," she called from the kitchen.

"She is bringing a treat," said Pietragnelli confidentially. "She and I have been baking all morning, making harvest pugliese with walnuts, olives, garlic, and Asiago cheese, for the workmen and for you, Signora Saxon." He stood aside in the entry-hall so Mrs. Barringstone could approach with a loaf wrapped in a blue-and-white towel set in a flat-bottomed basket. "There is butter in the covered tub. This is just out of the oven, quite fresh, as it should be. Mrs. Barringstone, cut a slice for Signora Saxon."

Mrs. Barringstone did as Carlo Pietragnelli asked, making sure the slice was on the generous side. "You eat it all, it's very good." She waited, watching while Rowena buttered and tasted her slice of the newly baked loaf.

"Excellent," said Rowena around a partial mouthful of bread. "This is delicious."

"Jut as it should be," said Pietragnelli. "We'll have a proper dinner at four, so the men can have a break before we finish the crush."

"It's a good dinner," said Mrs. Barringstone. "If I say so myself."

"She is getting better at the herbs and spices," said Pietragnelli. "In another year, she will not need my recipes for pasta or minestrone."

"Mr. Pietragnelli has told my husband that he's going to keep us on for another year at least, and he's promoted my man. It makes everything so much easier for us." Her lips quirked in what might have been a smile.

Saint-Germain took advantage of the moment. "Are we going out to the winery? I know you don't want to be away from the workers for long."

"No, I don't; you're right," Pietragnelli said as he went to the kitchen door and opened it, the aroma of crushed grapes hung on the air, a disturbing, delicious presence that seemed to permeate even the ground. Half-a-dozen men were standing around a crushing machine—a huge funnel with a deep trough at the bottom of it that ran half-way across the yard; a long Archimedes' screw turned in the trough, crushing the grapes and sluicing the juice toward a huge vat standing in the doorway of the winery.

"Mr. Pietragnelli," said Warton, then nodded at Saint-Germain.

"How is it going?" Pietragnelli asked as he bustled over to the crushing machine. "The smell is very good. Keep on."

Rowena looked at the work going on and blinked. Flustered, she turned to Saint-Germain. "I thought . . ."

"You assumed they crushed the grapes with their feet in a vat, signora, as they did in the past," said Pietragnelli. "Some of the vintners still do, but they are few and far between, and they do not live on the wines they make, nor do they employ as many men as I do. These days we use machines, those of us who want to prosper, and who have more than a dozen acres in vines. These machines work much faster than human feet, and they separate out the stems and seeds better than the old strainers did. Not that you want to lose all the seeds and skins—they affect the color and the taste. Here, you can see how the first state of the wine is; I will test it for sugar this evening."

Saint-Germain noticed Virgil Barringstone standing aside from the rest, looking awkward; he could see the anxious glance he exchanged with a young, freckle-faced boy of high-school age, and wondered what the two were up to. He made a mental note to keep an eye on the two of them, and turned back to Rowena. "This winery is very modern."

"That is why we are thriving," said Pietragnelli. "I have already arranged with Mrs. Curtis at Ponderosa Lodge to serve our wines exclusively. That is a good beginning, and one that benefits both of us. I have it in mind to approach other resorts and hotels, to make exclusivity agreements for our wines. I have a good range of wines—not just so-called Burgundy and Chablis—and that will stand me in good stead, if I am able to make the most of this harvest." He was all but bouncing with excitement. "I am filled with plans."

"I gather so," said Saint-Germain, and watched while Mrs. Barringstone began to pass out large sections of pugliese-loaves; he noticed that neither the boy nor Mr. Barringstone came forward to get their allocation of bread.

"Let us all enjoy the bounty of the earth, in wine and bread, the soul of nourishment." Pietragnelli took a large bite of the bread, chewed vigorously. "The wine of other years we will have later, when our labors are finished for the day."

Warton took his slab of bread and sniffed it. "Dago bread. But it's good."

Rowena had only a sliver of her slice left, and she was considering if it would be polite to ask for a little more when Pietragnelli came up to her. "You must have another piece, signora. We cannot have so fine a guest go hungry."

"I am not going hungry," said Rowena, "I could not do so as your guest, and the bread is superb." She accompanied him to the plank table, where Mrs. Barringstone had set out her baskets of pugliese and tubs of butter.

Saint-Germain moved back from the yard, and into the shade of a stand of oaks, where he knew another pair of guards was posted. "Which of you is Howe, and which is Beckworth?" he asked as he approached the two.

"I'm Howe," said the fair-haired man with the scar on his jaw. "He's Beckworth."

"I'm—" Saint-Germain began.

"—Ragoczy. We know who you are," said Howe smartly. "I appreciate working for you, Mr. Ragoczy."

"You're working for Mr. Pietragnelli," said Saint-Germain.

"Your lawyer signs the checks, on your account," said Beckworth. "That makes you the employer, the way I see it."

"You still work for Mr. Pietragnelli," said Saint-Germain.

"Anything you say, boss," said Howe, with a wink.

Saint-Germain looked from Beckworth to Howe and back again. "Let me make this clear to you: your job is to guard Mr. Pietragnelli and his vineyards and his workers and his family. Their safety is your responsibility." Although he had not raised his voice, his authority gathered around him as an all but visible presence. "I expect you to be diligent in your duty: if you want to continue to be paid."

Howe took a deep breath and came to attention, revealing the soldier he had once been. "Yes, sir."

"Very good," said Saint-Germain. "I want you to pay special attention to Virgil Barringstone, and to that youngster with the freckles. They're up to something. Whatever it is, be sure it doesn't get out of hand."

"Any idea what it could be?" Beckworth asked when Howe hesitated.

"None at all, but they are planning something. They are behaving questionably. " Saint-Germain met Beckworth's gaze. "It would be better if nothing happens than if something starts and is stopped."

"No more broken windows, you mean," said Beckworth.

"That is the least of it," said Saint-Germain. "But think of that as a starting-place."

The guards exchanged glances. "The White Legion?"

"I have no proof. But it wouldn't surprise me, given all that has happened here. They're far from gone from this area, no matter what the courts may want to think: in spite of all the mediation done, I very much doubt that all the White Legion is willing to remain peaceful. They've attempted to kill more than one of the growers in this region. Keep that in mind while you watch," said Saint-Germain, then strode off back toward the winery yard, where the workers were finishing up their bread and drifting back to their labors.

"The last shift is due in from the vineyards," said Pietragnelli. "When you have crushed the grapes they are bringing, then we are done for the day, and we will toast the new vintage as we should." He beamed. "Tonight we have roasted pork with herbs and sweet onions—everyone will share!"

Rowena was sitting on the bench at the plank table; she finished her bread and stood up. "Thank you, Mrs. Barringstone," she said, "and Mr. Pietragnelli."

"You're welcome, I'm sure," said Mrs. Barringstone, and very nearly ducked her head. She began gathering up her baskets and butter-tub in preparation for returning to the kitchen.

Pietragnelli went back to the crusher, to the end of the long trough, where the juice ran into the vat. He stuck his hand in the stream and caught a palmful of the liquid, drawing it back and sipping it. "This is going to be a good year." Then he addressed Rowena. "You would not like to drink this. It tastes raw and bitter, and its first fermentation makes it rough. But in three years, it will be nectar, if all goes well."

A few of the men cheered, and one of them whooped merrily; Virgil Barringstone and the freckled young man withdrew to the winery, standing together in the shadow of the vat, their heads together, their expressions somber; Saint-Germain watched them from his vantage-point across the yard, and his brow drew down in worry.

Warton went to supervise the dropping of bunches of grapes into the large hopper at the top of the funnel. He looked into it, taking care not to get his hands anywhere near the mechanism. "We're ready for the last load for the day," he announced.

"Good thing," said one of the older workers.

"Everyone will have to put in a few hours of hard work, but we're close to the end of the harvest, and at the end of it, we'll have something to be proud of," said Pietragnelli. "When I was gone from this place, I fretted every day, fearing that we would have to lose the entire vintage for the year. Fortunately, that wasn't how it turned out, and I was able to return in plenty of time to supervise the crush."

"And a very promising one it has been," said Warton.

"That it has," said Pietragnelli, deeply satisfied. "My daughter Sophia has said the harvest is going well in Calistoga, as well, which makes this year a very fortunate one. Sophia hasn't supervised this year, of course." He strutted along the trough. "Her twins are doing very well; she is exhausted, but as proud as a woman can be: a girl and a strapping boy."

His workers were used to hearing his boast, and so they paid little attention to him, but Rowena exclaimed, "You must be thrilled. These are your first grandchildren, aren't they?"

"They are," he said. "The boy—he was born second, but no matter—is named Alexander Carlo, for his grandfathers, and his sister is Louise Angelina, after her aunts. It is all to the good, all to the good."

"Your daughter is doing well?" Rowena asked.

"Tired, as I said, but radiant as I have ever seen her." Pietragnelli winked. "You know how women are when they become mothers."

Rowena found this remark a bit awkward, but she said, "I have seen how motherhood changes women, yes."

"Then you must know that my girl is flourishing." Pietragnelli came to her side. "Someday you must see Sophia and her children. Before she has more of them." He laughed aloud, and was about to go on when the honk of a car's horn claimed his attention.

Saint-Germain was already moving toward the house and the parking-circle beyond; he recognized Rogerio's Auburn and sensed that the urgency in this summons was crucial. He lengthened his stride, rushing up to the driver's door just as Rogerio got out. "What is it?"

Rogerio was bothered but not panicked. "Nothing, I hope. But best to be careful. There is a large group of men gathering down near the Yoshimura farm; most of them have shotguns or rifles, and three of their vehicles, at least, have a white chess knight painted on them."

"Did you alert the guards at the gate?" Saint-Germain asked.

"Yes. And I told them to notify the deputy sheriff in Healdsburg. They have access to a telephone just across the road at the Stackpole goat-farm—in case the men at the Yoshimura farm try to cut the lines here, or the operators don't pick up rings from this place. It could come to that, you know." Rogerio rubbed his hands together. "It might not be a bad idea to make sure the workers here are aware there could be trouble coming."

"Two of them already do, I think," said Saint-Germain, and quickly summarized his observations to Rogerio while Pietragnelli and Warton came up to the front of the house. "Pietragnelli, I need your attention for my associate," he said, firmly and courteously at once.

"Good day to you, signor," said Rogerio. "I'm sorry to arrive with ill-tidings, but I think you might want to prepare for trouble."

"Com'è?" asked Pietragnelli, indignation flooding through him.

"I think you may be under attack," said Rogerio bluntly. "More than a dozen men are gathering near here, in trucks, and I doubt it is for good."

Pietragnelli cursed fulsomely in Italian, then controlled himself enough to remark, "I hoped this was taken care of. I prayed your guards were unnecessary, that the settlements would hold, and finally we would have no reason to worry."

"If you mean your out-of-court agreement," said Saint-Germain, "it may be that not everyone is satisfied with it."

"Then they are fools, for this action will bring the full weight of the courts down on them." He swung around to face his workers who were straggling up behind him. "It has happened. We are going to have to defend this vineyard, this winery, from arrogant fools!" He held out his arms as he turned to address Saint-Germain. "The rest of my men will be in from the fields shortly. They will have the last of the grapes for the crusher. We must work quickly or lose much of the harvest. How can we crush and fight?"

"That may be the very thing they are counting on," said Saint-Germain. "Let me talk to the guards, to see what can be done." He tugged at Pietragnelli's sleeve, pulling him a few steps to the side and lowering his voice. "Be careful of Virgil Barringstone and that freckle-faced boy: they know more about this than they should."

"Are you certain?" Pietragnelli asked, astonished.

"Certain enough to mention it to you," said Saint-Germain.

Pietragnelli nodded. "Yes. Yes. Capisco." He swung back to speak to his workers. "Most of the men coming in from the fields will be here shortly. Two of you here will keep on with the crush, helping the workers who bring the grapes; the rest will come with me, and we will prepare to face whatever it is we must."

The men seemed confused, and Warton finally spoke up for all of them. "Which of us should do what?"

"Ah!" Pietragnelli burst out. "Sta' bene! You—Barringstone and Gibbs stay with the crush, and make sure it is done. Keep at your tasks. The rest of you, go to the guards, and do as they tell you." He glanced at Saint-Germain. "What do you think?"

"It seems sensible to me," said Saint-Germain, who could see how anxious the workers were becoming. He saw Virgil Barringstone shy a rock at the nearest guard. "Better to do something than nothing."

"È vero," said Pietragnelli. "It is fitting that we make ready." He raised his voice. "Mrs. Barringstone! Take the women and children into the house, into the parlor." He motioned to Rowena, saying grandly, "You go with them, signora. It will give them courage to have you with them."

"Let me have a gun, Mr. Pietragnelli. I know how to shoot, and I won't waste bullets on shadows," said Rowena.

"She can be trusted with a gun," said Saint-Germain. "As can I, and Mr. Rogers."

"You don't have to do this," said Pietragnelli.

"But I want to," said Rowena with heat. "I want to do something more than huddle in a shuttered room. I am not so lacking in moral fiber."

"I would not think so, ever, signora," said Pietragnelli. "All right. I have a shotgun I can give you. It is loaded with grapeshot." If he found any humor in this, he did not betray it, but addressed his men. "Come! Make ready! Barringstone, Gibbs, go back to the crusher at once. The last of the harvest for today will arrive shortly. Keep on with your work as long as you can. I don't want to ruin this crush. Don't interrupt your work unless you are directly attacked. The rest of you, come with me to the barn. I'll hand out weapons." As he prepared to bustle away, he turned back to Saint-Germain. "I thought I managed that well."

"It was adept," said Saint-Germain. "What about the workers coming in? The men outside may be waiting for them to come, so you will be distracted."

"They will be wrong, if they suppose so," said Pietragnelli as he broke into an energetic jog.

Saint-Germain signaled to Rogerio. "Have we weapons?"

"Your sportsman's case has two revolvers, .38s. I chose them because they're small. They're in their holsters."

"Good," said Saint-Germain. "Fetch them."

"Do you want to fight with Pietragnelli?" Rogerio asked, a bit surprised.

"If I must, I will. But I want you to drive into Healdsburg and be sure the deputy is bringing men to stop this. If you cannot find him, search him out. You will do more good that way than with a gun." Saint-Germain managed a hard smile.

"Do you think they'll let me go?" Rogerio asked, cocking his head in the direction of the front gate. "They're very near already."

"Use the south gate," Saint-Germain recommended. "Go out that way, the same way the harvesters will come. I doubt anyone will pay much attention to you."

Rogerio ducked his head. "As you say. How soon?"

"Now, if you would; as soon as you've got my revolvers. Take one for yourself; give one to me." He saw Mrs. Barringstone crossing the yard, four women and eleven children gathered around her. "She's an admirable woman. A pity her husband isn't her equal."

"You seem convinced that he is with the opposition," said Rogerio as he pulled his keyring from his trouser-pocket.

"I think it's likely," Saint-Germain said quietly. "Deal with the deputy as you think best, but make sure he comes out here, and that he doesn't come alone."

"All right," said Rogerio, opening the trunk of the Duesenberg and pulling out an oblong leather duffel. "Your revolver," he said as he opened the case and drew out two holstered .38s.

"Thank you," said Saint-Germain, taking one from him. "Cartridges?"

Rogerio pulled out a small box of them. "Here. You may need these more than I."

A shout from the knoll beyond the winery yard brought both Saint-Germain and Rogerio into the yard. "The pickers are coming!"

Howe emerged from the trees. "Six men, in a single truck."

"Let them come," said Saint-Germain. "But watch the gate. One of us is going out." He gestured to Rogerio. "Opportunity knocks, old friend."

Rogerio managed an encouraging look. "I won't be long."

"Very good," said Saint-Germain, and moved away as Rogerio got into his Auburn and started the engine. As soon as Rogerio had pulled away, Saint-Germain hurried to join Pietragnelli, and found him in the barn, handing out the last of his shotguns and rifles. "The workers are coming in with the last of the day's picking."

"Then we must prepare," said Pietragnelli. "Come, my men. Tonight you fight for your dinner. If you succeed you will have more than the harvest to celebrate. We go to join the guards. Let them order you." He paused to look at Rowena. "Are you sure you want that shotgun, signora?"

"Much more than I want to be without it," she said, hefting the weapon.

"Then God protect you, and the Saints preserve you from harm," said Pietragnelli with an expression of concern.

"And you, Signor Pietragnelli," said Rowena before she turned and started back for the house.

"Nothing must happen to her," Pietragnelli declared softly. Then he shook off his mood, and motioned to those around him to follow him. "We go toward the front of the vineyard, the main gate. That is the way they must come."

The men formed a ragged line behind Pietragnelli and trudged out along the drive, many of them sweating, and not entirely from heat. As they came over the rise, the two guards from the front of the property rushed up to them. "There are seventeen men at the Yoshimura farm, and they've started this way in four trucks."

"How do we deploy?" asked Warton. "Where do you want us to stand, or lie?"

"There are three clusters of brush," said Pietragnelli. "We can hide in them."

"Brush can't stop many bullets," the guard warned. "I could go get Howe and Beckworth, and a truck."

"No time," said Saint-Germain, shading his eyes and pointing in the direction of the Yoshimura farm to the rising dust. "They're coming."

"Get behind something—anything. They mustn't see us," said Pietragnelli, choosing a clump of berry vines near the fence and bringing his rifle up to his shoulder. "Don't shoot until I tell you to."

The workers scrambled to obey him, but the guards hesitated. "Where's Beckworth and Howe?" one asked.

"On duty. Watching the side gate," said Saint-Germain. "As they should be. There could be a second attack coming. If this is a diversionary tactic, we must be prepared to fight a second skirmish."

"Right," said the guard, and went back to his post.

Saint-Germain dropped down behind a tussock, thinking of the many times over the centuries that he had faced enemy forces; from the days of his living youth to the Medes and Hitties, to the Greeks, the Huns, the Moors, the Mongols, the Turks, the Germans. More recently he had faced the Russian Army and the army in Spain; for the last thirty-five-hundred years he had striven to end the conflicts around him, abashed by what he had done in the first five centuries of vampiric life. This encounter struck him as no stranger than most of the battles he had survived, and he feared it would not be the last one he would fight. He held his revolver at the ready and watched as the line of trucks turned onto the county road and headed for the gate to the Pietragnelli Winery, the men in the trucks already brandishing their weapons as the first of the four trucks roared onto the entry road.

One of the men in the trucks fired a volley of shots toward the winery gates and a minute later the lead truck smashed through it, the men riding in its bed shouldering their weapons, getting ready to fire.

"*Now!*" Pietragnelli shouted, and his men began to shoot.

Saint-Germain aimed for the tires and was able to flatten the front tire of the lead truck before one of Pietragnelli's men screamed and broke out of cover, blood pumping from a wound in his neck; in the next instant, confusion turned to chaos as the lead truck slewed off the drive and lurched onto its side and the other trucks were forced to stop, becoming easier targets.

One of Pietragnelli's men broke from cover and ran, throwing his shotgun away as he ran.

"*Cerdo! Coward! Execrato!*" Pietragnelli shouted after him.

"Let him go," Saint-Germain called out. "We have—"

"Shoot them! *Fuore! Fuore!*" Pietragnelli shouted to his men. "No quarter!"

A few of his men answered his orders, rising up in their positions, guns at the ready. Two of the men actually fired, and one of the bullets struck the front right tire of the second truck. The vehicle swerved and lurched, throwing the men in the back off their feet; a rifle fired as the man holding it fell.

More shots spattered, and another of Pietragnelli's men broke and ran.

"Get between the trucks!" Pietragnelli shouted, and rushed to occupy the breach. "Shoot out the tires! Now!"

Six men answered his cry and rushed out onto the road, firing toward the tires, most of them yelling as they shot.

Then, very faintly, came the shriek of a siren, then two, then three. The last truck began to back up, but was halted as one of the guards shot its tires flat. Three men jumped out of the vehicle and began to run as five sheriff's cars came racing down the road, Rogerio's Auburn bringing up the rear.

"Stop! Stop!" Pietragnelli bellowed, springing out from behind his berry-patch. "No more shooting. Basta!"

One of the men in the second truck, halted now on the side of the road, took aim at Pietragnelli, and would have shot him, but was stopped by his nearest companion, who shoved the gun-barrel upward.

Warton had gone to the wounded man and was attempting to administer first aid, but most of the men stayed in their protected spots, unwilling to expose themselves to danger.

The first sheriff's car swung into the drive, bumping across the ruined gate, and moments later a bullhorn blared, "Put down your weapons! All of you! Put them down! Now!"

A few of the men on the trucks obeyed, setting their guns aside and raising their hands, although five of them seemed prepared to fire on the deputies.

"Down!" the bullhorn screeched, and was punctuated by a single shot fired into the air.

"Shit," said one of the drivers as he climbed out of the truck cab, lifting his hands. This seemed to be a signal, for all the rest lost their bravado and obeyed the bullhorn's imperative.

Pietragnelli surged toward the deputy, calling on God to thank him. "Come, my workers. My guards. It is over. At last." He looked over at Saint-Germain. "We've prevailed."

A deputy strode around the front of his Ford, snapping his fingers to the men with him. "Get the guns and lock them in the trunk. They're evidence." He glanced toward Pietragnelli. "Looks like you got 'em dead to rights this time."

"And so the judge will know," said Pietragnelli, a fierce grin masking his genial features.

Saint-Germain got to his feet, brushing himself off and holstering his revolver. "Yes; luckily we have," he said, and mentally added *for now* as he went to join the men gathering around the police cars.

The deputy in charge was unknown to Saint-Germain, a big man with a meaty, flushed face and a receding hairline under his peaked cap. He glowered at the well-dressed stranger, then looked directly at Carlo Pietragnelli. "You gonna press charges?"

"Most certainly," said Pietragnelli, wiping his brow with a huge, blue handkerchief. "There was an agreement. They signed it."

"These men?" The deputy cocked his jaw in the direction of the men the other deputies were rounding up.

"Perhaps not them specifically," said Pietragnelli as he stuffed his handkerchief back in his pocket. "But their superiors, most certainly. And these men are bound by the terms, no matter what they may think." He turned away and shouted to his men, "Tell the police what they need to know and get back to work if you are unhurt!"

"The attack is unjustifiable, in any case," Saint-Germain added as Pietragnelli bustled away.

"Yeah," said the deputy. "That's so." He drew a battered notebook and stubby pencil from his breast-pocket. "So tell me what this is all about."

"I'd ask a man named Virgil Barringstone that question," said Saint-Germain. "I believe he has more to do with it than he cares to admit."

The deputy wrote down the name, but his expression was skeptical. "What makes you think the fellow has anything to do with this?"

"He was behaving oddly earlier today, shortly before the attack," said Saint-Germain. "I noticed him because he and one young worker were holding themselves apart from the rest, having conversation that was certainly private."

"There might be any number of reasons for that," said the deputy, looking a bit bored and preparing to walk away.

"Then speak to Mrs. Barringstone," Saint-Germain recommended. "She is the cook here, and she may not like speaking against her husband, but she will if she thinks he is in violation of the mediation of the courts of this county."

The deputy paused. "Sounds damned peculiar, Mr.—?"

"Ferenc Ragoczy," he answered, holding out his hand. "I'm one of Carlo Pietragnelli's investors. I came to see this year's harvest."

"Oh, yeah," said the deputy, and scribbled a note to himself.

Saint-Germain sighed. "If you take the time to check with the court in Santa Rosa, you'll soon discover—"

"I know about the White Legion," said the deputy. "Everyone from Eureka to Salinas knows about them."

"Then this should be a simple matter for you," said Saint-Germain, self-possessed and calm. "Speak to Judge Cavendish in Santa Rosa about this incident, and you'll find that there is an agreement on file that this assault clearly violates."

"The agreement the Dago mentioned?" the deputy asked.

Saint-Germain took a deep breath. "Yes. Judge Cavendish will explain it."

"Cavendish?" said the deputy, interested for the first time.

"Yes; and Deputy Will Sutton," said Saint-Germain. "He has a number of reports that are likely to be useful to you."

"I'll ask Pietragnelli about this," said the deputy.

"Very good," said Saint-Germain, and stood aside as the deputy lumbered off toward Carlo Pietragnelli, his notebook and pencil at the ready.

Rogerio came up to Saint-Germain, saying, "What do you think Oscar King will make of this?"

"He'll tear into it with dogged determination," said Saint-Germain with visible relief. "And he'll keep at it until it's ended." He gave a one-sided smile. "To protect my investment."

"Of course," said Rogerio.

Saint-Germain nodded. "Let's return to the house. This is going to take a long time, and Mrs. Barringstone will be worried."

"And Virgil Barringstone may attempt to leave," Rogerio added.

"Exactly," said Saint-Germain, and began to walk up the dusty road toward the winery.

TEXT OF A LETTER FROM DRUZE SVINY IN WINNIPEG, MANITOBA, CANADA, TO FERENC RAGOCZY IN SAN FRANCISCO.

13-251 Churchill Road
Winnipeg, Manitoba
28 September, 1937

Ferenc Ragoczy
c/o Oscar King
King Lowenthal Taylor & Frost
630 Kearny Street
San Francisco, California, USA

Dear Mr. Ragoczy,

I was delighted to hear from you after so much change in both of our lives. It relieved me to learn that you are well and still doing business through Eclipse Shipping. So many other industrialists from Spain are not so fortunate, as I am sure you know.

Of course I'll make the arrangements you request; in fact, I wish there were more I could do. But since this is all you ask me to do, you may rest assured that I will attend to this promptly. I will obtain schedules tomorrow and plan from there. To make sure I understand your intention, I gather that you and your associate wish to take a train from Calgary to Montreal, stopping here in Winnipeg for a day or so before going on. And the two of you want to fly to Amsterdam from Montreal, stopping in Iceland for two days en route. I will make the appropriate reservations by the day after tomorrow, and, as you request, I will send you a telegram with the information on what and when for your journey. You tell me that you will drive to Calgary from California, weather permitting, and that you will arrive there on or before October 25, which will mean that you would want to travel no earlier than the 26th. If any of this is incorrect, please let me know as soon as possible. If I hear nothing from you in ten days, I will assume this is your wish, and I will finalize the reservations with the recommended deposits on sleeping compartments and space in the baggage car.

You are kind to ask: of course I am pleased to be here at Manitoba Chemical, Ltd. The company is a growing one, the staff has welcomed me graciously, and my salary is very, very generous. I have a nice home with more room than I've ever had to myself before, and I've been asked to do occasional lecturing at the local university on mathematics, which I am told will not conflict with my work here. I have two dogs and a cat, and I can even afford a maid once a week! Who would have thought that the daughter of a butcher would come so far in the world? I have money in a time when many do not, I have a nice place to live, and I am allowed to do the work I like best. I think myself most fortunate.

There is one cloud on the horizon, and that is news I have had from home. I have very few relatives left, as you know. The Great War demanded a high price of my family. And now I learn that my second cousin, Carel, who was studying in Berlin, is missing, and no one seems to know where he is. I wrote to his landlord, who has informed me that Carel went out one evening and never returned. For some reason, the landlord is reluctant to report him missing, though he has been a tenant for more than six years and has always been reliable. Had I not been strenuously advised against it, I might go to Berlin to look for him, but from what I have learned from newly arrived Europeans, asking such questions can be very dangerous. I have decided to insert an advertisement in the papers of Berlin asking for information about my second cousin, and see what I can learn that way. If I discover nothing, then I may have to reassess my plans. I have been promised that there is a place for me with this company if I wish to take a leave of absence to look for Carel, and that strengthens me.

I am so looking forward to seeing you again. I will pick you up at the station, of course. I have an automobile of my own, and I anticipate entertaining you to the limits you will allow. I cannot tell you how touched I am that you will allow me to do this for you, and I once again extend my regards to you.

Most truly,

Druze Sviny

chapter nine

Rowena tossed the last of the Holland covers over her dining table, fussed with it enough to square it; she tugged on the securing cord, tied it in a bow-knot, then turned away. "That's it, then, at least for now," she said a bit distractedly and hugged her arms, holding the sleeves of her jacket tightly enough to crush the heavy silk fabric. Her elegant ensemble—a narrow-skirted suit with a nip-waisted jacket in a clear cobalt blue over a blouse of amber lace—seemed out of place amid the covered furniture, as if she were an interloper. At three-fifteen it was still warm, but the first snout of fog was poking through the Golden Gate, all but obliterating the splendid bridge and sapping the warmth from the setting sun.

Around them, the house was chilly, a reminder from mercurial October that winter was coming. With all the furniture shrouded, it made the place appear haunted by objects. In the fading light the vacant walls where pictures had hung looked like blank windows.

"Is there anything else to do? What chores are left? I'm almost done here, so what would you like me to do?" Saint-Germain asked from the entry-hall, where he was completing the task of removing all the chalk marks the police had left behind; most of it was gone, but little bits remained in the grain of the wood on the stairs, and he worked at these with a soft cloth soaked in linseed oil, removing every trace of it. He finished this pursuit and tossed the rag into a woven wastepaper basket near the telephone.

"I have to make sure all the windows are closed, and that the back door is securely locked," she said, a bit of tension coming into her voice. "The Realtor is coming tomorrow, and I want it to be ready to sell."

"You might find a tenant more readily than a buyer, especially now, with the country in such economic straits," he pointed out. His charcoal suit and black roll-top pullover were elegant but subtly disquieting, making him one with the deepening shadows, his features seeming paler by contrast, the injury from his dreadful accident still apparent on the left side of his face, like a malign shadow; his small, beautiful hands as disembodied as a magician's. "That way, you wouldn't have to give it up entirely."

"But I want to be rid of it," she said with sudden intensity. "How can I ever feel safe here again?"

"You might, in time," he said, concern softening his tone. "Or you may decide that you want to deal with what happened here, after a while. If you still have the house, you'll find it easier to return to it."

"I can see the advantage," she conceded. "But not enough to make me want to hang on to this house. It might as well be haunted, with a ghost that can't be exorcized." She looked up at the ceiling. "It served me quite well, but no more."

Saint-Germain came up to her in the dining room and rested his hands on her shoulders. "Are you truly certain you want to sell it?"

"I'm certain," she said firmly. "I would want to in any case, but since you're letting me have your house, I'm anxious to move. I don't need the reminder of that night—I remember well enough without the house." Turning around, she looked directly into his eyes. "I meant it: I won't feel safe here."

"Do you think that may change? not now, but in the future?" he ventured, thinking of the many places he had given up in the past, convinced he would never want them again, and now would have liked to own.

"It might, but I doubt it. I don't want any reminders," she repeated, more emphatically than before. "It's hard enough being here."

"Rowena," he said, with such sadness that she could not bring herself to speak for several seconds.

"Don't do that," she said, turning away from him.

"Do what?" There was no challenge in the question, only concern.

"Soften the blow," she accused.

"I hadn't intended to; that would not be true consideration of you," he told her.

"But you think I'm wrong," she pursued.

He shook his head. "No, not wrong; I know what seems certain now will change over time, and you will see it in another light."

"When I have lived four thousand years as you have, perhaps. For now, and for the decades to come that I am here, in this city, I want no part of this house. It's too fresh, the attack. It's salt in a wound." She shook her head. "Try to understand—I'm not able to step back from the assault and I may never be. I'm not as resilient as I thought I was, and that's as hard to accept as anything." Her voice was small and tight and she pulled a short bit away from him, enough to put a little distance between them, but not out of reach. "You are philosophical, and that's admirable, but I haven't achieved your perspective."

"It took me centuries to come to it," Saint-Germain said in a voice that caressed her as surely as his hands touched her neck.

"So you can understand why I am not ready to keep this house," she said.

"Of course," he responded. "I wish it were otherwise, for your sake; it would mean that you had begun to heal."

"There is something else," she admitted. "With you gone, I'd like to have a link with you. Living in your house would provide that."

"You have it already," he promised her as he turned her toward him. "And it is more than wood and plaster." His dark eyes held her gaze for a short while.

"The Blood Bond?" she asked just above a whisper.

"That will endure as long as you are alive in your life or mine." He traced the line of her jaw with a single finger. "Only the True Death will end it."

"Sustained on memories," she said, not quite mordantly.

"On intimacy," he corrected her, as conciliating as possible.

"Yes; on intimacy."

She frowned. "Is that enough?"

"It is all I have, my dear," he said, thinking back to Berlin, a decade ago, and Madelaine de Montalia. "I have found that it suffices." His wry smile came and went quickly.

"Say what you will," she murmured. "You're leaving."

"Not just at once," he reminded her.

"No, but in a week or a month, you'll be gone."

"As you knew I would," he said, his tone musical and plaintive.

"All right, I knew. And I don't want to harp on things. From the first, I understood this was only a brief stopover in your travels, and I know there's no point in arguing about it. According to you, all stopovers are brief, whether they last two days or two decades," she said, and put her arms around his waist. "But that doesn't mean I have to like it. Or that I comprehend it all yet."

"No; it doesn't mean either of those things," he told her as he smoothed one strand of her wayward hair back into place; his touch was as kind as his voice.

"So," she said, the word catching a bit in her throat.

He held her close, his dark eyes on her golden ones. "We've parted before."

"And it took us a quarter century to reunite, in case you had forgot," she said brusquely, going on less peremptorily. "And a war kept us apart for much longer than either of us had anticipated. That could happen again." She leaned her head on his shoulder. "I doubt I have another twenty-five years to spare."

"That needn't concern you if you decide to come to my life; you'll have an opportunity for many, many things, if you want it," he said as he stroked her back through the soft crepe jacket of burnt sienna that draped her shoulders.

"I may do that, and I may decide against it. Or I may try it and discover it doesn't suit me." She pressed her lips together, then asked, "Would it bother you very much if I decided against your life?"

"Yes," he said. "But it would bother me even more if you felt you had to remain a vampire for my sake when you would rather not be undead. Not everyone who comes to this life is willing to embrace it, and if you cannot embrace it, you will come to abhor it, and with it, me. I'd prefer that not happen." He recalled Nicoris and Demetrice, Avasa Dani and Tulsi Kil, Heugenet and Gynethe Mehaut, and experienced a pang of grief for all of them. "If vampiric existence is what you want, then make the most of it; it will delight me to have you among those of my blood. If it turns out not to be a life you can abide, then deal with it as you must. I will not fault you for any choice you make: believe this."

"Would you miss me then?" The question perplexed her as she heard herself ask. "If I chose to die the True Death?"

Out in the bay the first foghorn moaned, its forlorn notes sounding a mournful clarion to the bank of thickening mist that was beginning to roll over the city.

"I will miss you when I am driving to Canada. I will miss you when I return to Europe. I will miss you every day we are not together." His embrace tightened a little, reassuring her.

"Then why must you go? Doesn't it make more sense to remain here? I can't go with you, not now, but you could remain here; not in the city, but somewhere—at the winery, or Ponderosa Lodge, or someplace not too far away. That's possible, isn't it?" Abruptly she stepped back out of his arms. "No, of course it isn't," she said, answering her own question before he could speak. "I'm being unreasonable. I know it."

"I wish it were otherwise," he said. "I must go because my being here puts you into danger. I must go because I cannot be sure who next will come after me, or what he might do to you to get to me, and that is unbearable. I must go because I've garnered too much attention, which will soon lead to the kinds of investigations that I cannot easily endure. And there is trouble brewing, and not the trouble of the White Legion: no, it is their aims carried out on a grand scale."

"You can't mean that you think war will start again, so soon?" She was appalled.

"In a year, or two at the most, yes, the war will resume." He reached out and took her hands in his. "It will not be contained in Spain. War is in the air as surely as rain. The Germans are too eager for it, smarting under their defeat in the Great War, and the French are daring them to attempt it, certain they will easily prevail. The Italians are already harrying Ethiopia, and they will not be content with that. Mussolini may be a popinjay, but his generals are determined men, resolved to re-establish Italy as a power in the world. Germany is worse, with their supposed alliances. Hitler is being cordial with Mussolini so that he need not fear that the South will come against him, and he will have unchallenged access to the Balkans and Greece."

"Are you certain of this?" Rowena paled.

"Not as certain as I would be if it were writ in stone, but given what has been happening, I believe that everything points that way," he responded.

For a long moment, both were silent. "This isn't a good subject for parting," Rowena said at last, and shivered. "Wasn't that all settled before? Didn't enough men die?"

"Enough men died to stop the fighting, but there are more now, and the same issues still rankle." He looked at her somberly. "That was the trouble. The war never reached resolution. Everyone ran out of men to fight, and materiel to fight with, and so the war halted. But it didn't end."

"You say that there is more of the Great War to be fought?" Even as she asked, she could feel the answer within her, and she had a terrible vision of her nephews going over the top onto no-man's-land.

"It seems so," said Saint-Germain gravely. "Everything points to it."

"You're not very comforting," she charged him.

"If that's what you want, I'll say it will be avoided, that the national leaders learned their lessons back in 1918, and it truly was the war to end all wars." He held her gaze with his own, and spoke to her in a low, steady voice. "But such condescension would insult your intelligence, and it would peeve you."

She pulled free of him again, turning on her heel to put more distance between them. "Oh, why are we talking about this? It's horrid." She rounded on him once more. "Can't we talk about something pleasant?"

"Certainly; whatever you wish," he said, remaining still as she began to pace from the dining room, through the entry-hall, then into the studio and back again. "What would you like to talk about?"

"Do you think that you can put all that behind you?" she exclaimed. "If the situation is as bad as you say, can you ignore it?"

"No, I can't, not for long." He held his hand out to her, which she ignored.

"You're vexing, Saint-Germain." She clicked her tongue in exasperation, then gave a brittle little titter, her golden eyes sharp with misery. "There are times I wish you weren't quite so understanding, Comte."

"Do you want to argue?" He was acutely aware that she did not, that she was dejected and hoped to relieve her despondency with anger. "If this would make parting easier for you, then I am willing to wrangle for as long as you like."

"I want *something*, but not your indulgence," she challenged. She began another circuit of the three rooms.

"I wasn't indulging you," he said without heat.

"How can you—" She stopped her outburst. "I don't want to think about war, or loss, or loneliness, or anything unpleasant. It's hard enough to think about losing you."

"You needn't," he said mildly. "Shall we talk about painting? Or art? Or books? Or music? You have only to tell me."

Her eyes snapped. "Don't be so reasonable!" Then she stood still. "I'm sorry. I'm being beastly."

"No, not beastly: you're distressed," he said. "I don't mean to presume, Rowena; I know you, and that brings comprehension."

"You think you know me," she countered, appalled at her lack of manners. "How many men know women? Most of you don't even listen to us, or take us seriously!"

"Ah, but I am not quite a man, and I learned more than three thousand years ago to listen," he said without a hint of apology.

"Vampire makes a difference? Is that it?" Her outburst upset her even as it filled her with a kind of excitement. Recklessly she went on, "Is it because of my blood?" Her straight stance warned him that she would not accept any half-answer.

"Yes, because of that, and because I have seen your work, and you have done me the honor of admitting me to your confidence." His dark, enigmatic eyes rested on her for the greater part of a minute while the foghorn uttered its two-note warning to ships. "I do love you, Rowena. Time and distance will not change that."

"And you will love others," she said, so suddenly that she astonished herself. "With the same passion and the same—the same totality?"

"Yes, I will love others, but not quite as I love you, for no one else is you. Love is our life, and we are bound to pursue it. As will you." He gave her a little time to consider this. "That won't diminish my love for you, nor yours for me."

"You keep saying that, but are you so sure?" She had dared to approach him and now stood a little more than an arm's length away from him. Astonished, she said, "I'm jealous. Of no one I know."

"You have no need to be. You cannot be supplanted in my heart: not now, not anytime." He spoke equably.

"Are you making light of me?" she demanded, wishing she could stop this confrontation and not knowing how to do it.

He refused to rise to her bait. With his dark, enigmatic eyes on hers, he closed the distance between them. "You haven't experienced my nature in yourself. When you do, you'll realize that we are drawn to life, and the totality of those to whom we're drawn."

"What a nice way to think of prey," she said, deliberately caustic.

"Hardly prey; we're not tigers, or sharks, and what we require is more complex than a meal," he chided her with such gentleness that she felt tears well in her eyes. "Oh, you can hunt for living men, and their terror will suffice to feed you in the most basic way. I've had such . . . an actuality before now, and I'm still aghast at what I did then, millennia ago. It is a dreadful experience." He tried to shut out the recollections of the oubliette in Nineveh, and the abased feeding of his captivity; he pushed the memory away. "If you want to continue to know the joys and grief of living, if you want nourishment rather than subsistence, you must search for those who can knowingly accept you, and take on the risks that intimacy brings. Blood is the most essential, most truly personal manifestation of life, and to use it as nothing more than liquid is ultimately disrespectful to both you and those whose blood you take. Even those we visit in sleep give up their dreams to us; those who receive us as what we are do us great honor, for it is through that knowing, that love, that we live rather than simply survive."

She glared at him. "How can you tell me this? Are you trying to convince me that you give all those you love everything you have given me?"

"No, and yes." He went into the studio and sat down on one of the covered chairs, leaning back on the overstuffed cushion under the muslin drape. "Each of you is different, and all of you have courage and passion, or none of you would countenance what I am. Few women are willing to know my love for what it is. You did, and others have as well, but there are not many of them, and I treasure each of them as I treasure you. The rest, those for whom I am a pleasant dream, to them I am grateful, but it is the gratitude of loneliness." The memory of Csimenae made him flinch. "Still, I treasure all but one of them."

"All but one," she mused, approaching him reluctantly, as though compelled to do so. "Why should you want me to be one of those women?"

"Because you are a capable, remarkable woman." Aware that he had her attention, he went on, "You are capable of making your way in the world as not many women are, and you want to make your way—you don't resent your freedom as many others are apt to do. You have defined yourself, which is what I most admire about you: that you are utterly Rowena, that you have remained true to your soul is what I love." He spoke directly, no tinge of seduction in his words. "The vampire life has many benefits to offer those strong enough to endure it, but it demands understanding and compassion—of one's self as well as those loved. You have that capacity, if you are willing to accept it."

She stared down at him. "Thank you. I think."

"You asked me: that is my answer," he said to her softly.

"Damn you," she muttered.

He was neither angry nor hurt. "Why?"

"Because you disarm me," she said, and sat down on the arm of the chair. "If I could convince myself that you were unreasonable or unkind or self-centered, or that you would become indifferent to me, I wouldn't have to listen to you, and you wouldn't have to repeat yourself. I could dismiss it all as your self-indulgence, as the kind of male arrogance that is all around us. But I can't; you saved me, all those years ago, and when the family regarded me with shock and dismay, you sent me your encouragement, although you suffered the terrible loss of your ward, and you have never shown me anything but generous concern. How can I pretend to have no tie to you now, when you've been my staunch support for so long? Had there been no Blood Bond, I would esteem you, and love you. I admit that at present I feel some ambivalence about my emotions, but I have no doubt about my love for you." For more than a minute she was silent; she seemed almost defeated as she stared out the window at the advancing fog. "I thought we'd have rain before now."

"Is it unusual for the autumn to be dry?" Saint-Germain asked, following her conversational lead.

"There have been dry autumns," she said slowly, and fell silent again.

Saint-Germain laid his hand on her leg, the silk of her hose a slick beneath his fingers. "How much longer do you want to stay here?"

Rowena sighed. "I don't know. Until it's dark." She leaned toward him, her eyes pensive. "I have lived here a long time, and I feel as if an old friend had betrayed me. I'm sad that it ended this way."

"The house can't change what happened. A man did that, not the home," Saint-Germain reminded her.

"It's not sensible, I know," said Rowena. "But that's how it seems to me." She moved so that she could put her arm along his shoulder.

"Then that's how it must be," said Saint-Germain, almost apologetically.

She kissed his brow. "I wish I could keep you here, but I know that I can't. You're right, and that's obvious. But . . ."

His eyes held warmth and grief in their dark depths. "You understand. Understanding isn't always an easy burden to bear."

"To have so much end at once—living here, in this house, your company, the conviction that I could not be hurt . . ." Again her voice trailed off.

"Such matters are never easy," he said, turning to kiss her fingers that lay on his shoulder.

"Still . . ." She sighed. "I don't know. I feel as if I'm losing my sense of direction, or my orientation. I don't know where I am, or where I'm going—not all the time, but enough to fash me." She looked toward the window. "Fog's getting thicker. It must have been warm inland today."

"That would make a difference, wouldn't it?" Saint-Germain said, and felt her nod.

"Um-hum." Rowena said nothing more until the dining-room clock chimed four. "Teatime," she said remotely, then a bit more directly, "Or it would be, back in England. Here, for the women who go to the Saint Francis, it is. But the rest of us . . ." Her words drifted off again. "My mother used to chide me for not being more accommodating, for not acquiescing to the men I knew. She warned me that I would end my life alone. She'd probably think I had proven her right, and she would expect me to be chagrined."

Saint-Germain looked up at her. "And are you chagrined?"

"Occasionally," she admitted slowly. "Not the way my mother intended, but chagrined, nonetheless."

"Why?" he asked with genuine interest.

"For not doing enough; isn't it obvious?" she said at once. "For being too frightened to take more chances on myself. I told you that I'm disappointed with myself, didn't I? Well, that hasn't changed just because you've been here. I know what I could have done, and won't do, and it shames me." Moving suddenly so that she could face him fully, she said, "If you could persuade me that becoming a vampire would end that for me, I'd be glad of it."

"I can't promise you that," he said. "All I can promise is more time—how much is never certain, but the chances are that you will have a century or two at least, if you want."

She laughed, for the first time without nervousness or hidden anger. "All right. I won't press you again." Rising from the arm of the chair, she took his hand and urged him to rise. "Come with me."

He followed her to the stairs and up to the guest room at the front of the house over the dining room. "This isn't your room," he said as she opened the door.

"That man tried to kill me in my bedroom," she answered, and went through.

On the threshold, he paused. "Are you sure this is what you want?"

"Yes. It is," she said as she kicked off her shoes and began to unbutton her jacket. "I want to say good-bye to this place with something better than an attack."

Saint-Germain came into the room and drew the curtains closed, then came to her side, taking the jacket from her. "Let me do this."

She shivered and handed the jacket to him, which he laid over the back of the grandmother's chair next to the dresser. "Go ahead," she murmured, and stood to allow him to unbutton her blouse, which he put atop the jacket before he tugged her silk-and-lace slip out of her skirt's waistband and over her head, then dropped it on the chair.

"You are a very beautiful woman, Rowena," he said as he reached around her to unfasten her white brassiere; he put it on the seat of the chair, and turned back to her, and touched her arms, and then her breasts, taking his time in rousing her.

"I'm getting old," she said, looking down at her exposed flesh.

"That doesn't mean you're not beautiful," he said, and kissed her nipples as he knelt before her and unfastened her skirt.

"How do you suppose I'll feel, if I live to seventy or more? My grandfather lived a long, long time, so I might, too." She put her hand on his head, pulling her fingers through the loose, dark waves. "I wish I could come to your life as I was twenty years ago, or thirty, like a butterfly emerging from a wizened cocoon. But if I have to wander the world an old, old woman—"

"I'm a very, very old man," Saint-Germain reminded her as he unzipped her skirt and helped her to step out of it.

"We've been through this before: you don't look much older than forty: that's the difference," she said, watching him unfasten her hose from her garter-belt and roll each one down her leg. He bent to kiss the swell of her left calf and trailed kisses down to her ankle, then did the same with her right, enjoying her anticipatory shudder. "How do you know what to do?" she marveled, then said, "No, don't tell me."

He undid her garter-belt, so now all she had on were her panties. "Do you want to take those off, or shall I do it?"

"I'll take them off," she said. "While you take off your jacket." She paused. "I saw your scars, when they were taking you into the hospital."

"Some women find them . . . intrusive," said Saint-Germain, laying his hand at the base of his ribs, the wool of his roll-top pullover seeming as insubstantial as gossamer.

"You know my scars," she said. "Why won't you let me see yours?"

He looked up at her. "Does it matter to you?"

"God, yes!" she exclaimed. "I don't want to feel like a bird with a broken wing while you soar. I don't want to dwell on my lackings. If I can see that you, too, have had deep wounds—"

"They killed me," he said with a hint of irony.

"Well, those are deep wounds," she responded reasonably, plucking on the shoulders of his jacket to convince him to rise. "I need this from you, Saint-Germain."

The room seemed suspended in silence; the distant baying of the foghorn was muted, and the traffic in the street was little more than a mutter.

"Then you shall have it," he said as he straightened up, and shrugged out of his jacket, putting it over the arm of the grandmother's chair.

His compliance startled her, and for a moment she could think of nothing to say. "Thank you," she finally told him. She watched him carefully as he took off his roll-top pullover and dropped it on the jacket. The white swath of scars spread from the base of his ribs to his belt. "The trousers, too," she told him, staring at him in fascination mixed with revulsion. Seeing the scars in the hospital was some- how different than here, and she made an effort not to look away, though she had to swallow hard against the sudden tightness in her throat.

He unbuckled his belt and opened his fly; he let the garment drop, then crouched to untie his shoes and remove them, and his socks. As he stood up, he gathered up his trousers and folded them before putting them over the arm of the chair atop his jacket.

"What on earth did they do to you?" she could not keep from asking. "What kind of execution does that?"

"They disemboweled me," he answered. "A very long time ago."

"With what? The edges look so jagged."

"A wide-bladed bronze knife," he said, holding up his hands to indicate its length. "About sixteen inches long. It took a long time: hours."

She winced in spite of herself. "Why did they kill you?"

"Because I won a battle," he answered, and did not elaborate.

"You'll be cold," said Rowena as she threw back the comforter; she sat on the side of the bed and slipped out of her panties, then lay back, naked.

"I'm never cold," he said, coming to her side.

"Well, *I* am," she said, holding out her arms. "Get out of those shorts and get under the covers."

He complied, watching her as he did. As he pulled the comforter up over them, he gathered her into his arms. "Rowena, Rowena," he whispered before he kissed her. "What do you want of me?"

"I don't want anything *of* you—I want you," she said simply, and guided his hand to her breast.

"You will have me always," he vowed, following her lead in caressing her, aware that she was seeking something more than stimulation.

"How will that happen?" she asked, half-combative, half-pleading.

"You are one of my blood," he said, kissing the line of her brows, so lightly that snowflakes would be heavier.

She wrapped her arms around him. "Oh, pay no attention to me. I'm being a fool. Just love me."

His kisses became more ardent, at last finding her lips, all the while tantalizing her with his gentle touch, now on her arms, now on her back, now on her flank, now on her breasts, his hands possessing an insight all their own that led them to the secrets of her body, opening and exciting her. He explored her body, discovering sensations that heightened her pleasure beyond anything she had known before, thrilling sensitivities that sounded her to the depths of her being and elicited emotions as potent as her physical responses. When she was breathing luxuriously, his mouth expanded on what his hands had done, beginning with her shoulders and slowly, rapturously making his way to her breasts, then over her abdomen to the tufted folds between her legs.

Rowena sighed ecstatically, whispering his name. "So good," she breathed.

Gradually Saint-Germain sought out her most profound transports, the sorcery of his mouth and hands eliciting a depth of response that she had not thought possible. As her first surge of consummation shook her, he moved up her body to nuzzle her neck, sharing her passion and her transports, his esurience as gratified as she was, cradling her as she drifted into sleep.

Chimes from the kitchen clock announced that it was six-thirty, and the sound woke her. "Oh," she said as she looked about the dark room. "I must have dozed off."

"Not for very long," he said, and kissed her.

"We should probably leave," she said when they had ended the kiss.

"As you wish," said Saint-Germain, not yet moving to leave the bed.

"It's going to be cold, getting dressed," she said, and without warning tossed back the comforter and sheet. "It is!" She bustled up and went to reclaim her clothes.

They dressed with companionable haste, saying almost nothing to one another, and then they stripped the bed. "What do you want done with these?" he asked, indicating the sheets, comforter, and pillowcases.

"Put the sheets in the laundry hamper in the bathroom. I'll fold up the comforter and put it on the end of the bed."

Saint-Germain bent to retrieve the sheets and prepared to leave the bedroom. He was almost out the door when Rowena stopped him.

"Thank you," she said as she began to fold the comforter.

"It is I who should thank you," said Saint-Germain.

"No; you made this a wonderfully memorable good-bye," she said.

"I'm not leaving for a while," he reminded her, feeling her emotion with gratitude.

"This was good-bye, no matter when you go," she said, motioning him away from her. "And we both know it," she added before he closed the door.

TEXT OF A LETTER FROM DOÑA ISABEL INEZ VEDANCHO Y NUÑEZ IN HAMPSHIRE, ENGLAND, TO FERENC RAGOCZY IN SAN FRANCISCO, CALIFORNIA, SENT VIA AIRMAIL AND IN CARE OF OSCAR KING.

> *Copsehowe*
> *nr. Briarcopse*
> *Hampshire*
> *England*
> *17 October, 1937*

Ferenc Ragoczy
le Comte de Saint-Germain
c/o Oscar King
King Lowenthal Taylor & Frost
630 Kearny Street
San Francisco, California
United States of America

My dear Comte,
    It seems too long since I've written to you that I hardly know where to

start; I trust you will not be troubled that I address you through your San Francisco attorney rather than your English one. I assure you this is not mere caprice but something more appropriate. I suppose it would be most apt to start with that which is most important to me, since I cannot determine that which is most important to you: in the last month, Miles Sunbury and I have finally become lovers, over his initial objection. Such scruples that man has! I had to show him three of Ponce's letters before he comprehended that our estrangement is total and irreparable. I have wanted this for some time, as I assume you perceived, and so I am happier about this deepening expression of our affections than Miles is at present, but in time he will resign himself to our affaire. Since he brought me my two lurchers, I have known he is the very man for me, but it took his being badly hurt for him to be willing to unbend enough to accept my attachment to him. He attempted to dissuade me from the course on which we're now embarked, but I would not be deterred, especially not now, when my country is falling more deeply into the hands of the Fascists. I have accepted that if I ever return to my home, it will be years from now.

It should be obvious that I have been following the news from Spain, all of which has been most troubling. I learned recently that three of my friends from Cádiz have died in prison, the rumor being that they were murdered—starved or beaten, depending on whom you believe—and I, for one, believe that they did not die natural deaths, if they are actually dead, and this report is reliable. This is the most pressing reason that I know I may never go back to my native land. This is a most sobering realization, for it puts me more certainly in England for decades to come. Depending on how things may turn out with Miles, I will have to decide if Copsehowe is the place I truly want to make my home. So far I am inclined to like this life, even with the guards you have provided me, but in five years, or ten, rural peace and tranquility may pall.

What troubles me still more is that I cannot be sanguine about the world at large, and I would hate to begin to travel only to find myself stranded, or in deeper inconvenience than that which I have already escaped. You have intimated that such things have happened before, and so I hope you can tell me what I should regard as a dangerous indication in international developments. The current situation in eastern Europe worries me very much, but I have been told that my apprehensions are alarmist, no doubt because of the losses I have endured, and the unfortunate circumstances presently obtaining in Spain. I hear all the drums of war getting louder and louder, and all Europe pretending not to hear them! Tell me: does this new Prime Minister

Chamberlain's policies seem prudent to you, or do they look too malleable? Am I being frightened by nothing more than my own anxiety, or do you see danger in any of this? I have been thinking in circles for so long that I cannot find a balance point, and, as much as I would enjoy it, I cannot put these questions to Miles, for he would see criticism in them that I do not intend.

Let me have the advantage of your observations as soon as you are in a position to provide them. I can see the usefulness of travel, and if I must, I will leave England and find another place to adopt as a home. It may be that I am looking for something that cannot be found, and in pursuing it, might I not lose all I have made for myself here? It would mean giving up Miles Sunbury, and I would rather not do that, yet it may be that I will have to; in which case, the sooner I depart, the better for both of us. I am very much consumed with inner discord even at a time when I have newly discovered such contentment that I can hardly express it. I rely upon you, with all your experience and compassion, to provide me the insight and wisdom I cannot find for myself, and which I have found nowhere else.

There are so many debts I owe you that I would hesitate to add them up, but I can think of no other counsel I would trust more, and so I add to my obligation to you in the hope of finding some deliverance for myself. Without you, I would probably be dead by now; my life is in your hands in many, many ways, including my current happiness, which is entirely to your credit, as well. So pardon my continuing requests for your good advice—in that regard, you have only yourself to blame for my reliance upon you.

Devotedly yours,

Isis

chapter ten

There was no sign of permanent scarring from his injuries lingering on Saint-Germain's skin, nor would there be; since he had risen after death, no wound, no matter how severe, had left a lasting mark on his body. He was wearing a black silk smoking jacket over black wool trousers, no shirt to cling to his healing flesh; his dark hair had been close-clipped to make the abrasions to his scalp less apparent, and the stiffness that had marked his movements through the summer was finally, now in late October, gone. He sat in his study, his attention on the windows and the fading light beyond. It would soon be dark, and then he would have business to do. He looked over at his visitor and smiled. "I appreciate you coming by, Inspector Smith. I realize the police are under no obligation to keep victims of crime abreast of the progress you have made."

"It's always good when there is progress, Mr. Ragoczy; this case didn't look at all promising at first, and not just because of when it happened," Inspector John Smith said. "And with this case, it's been especially difficult to put the pieces together—no slighting to the Sausalito force, or the Marin County Sheriff," he added conscientiously.

"I can well understand why." Saint-Germain pointed to the coffee-cup Smith balanced on his knee. "Would you like a refill?"

"No, thanks. Two cups're plenty for me." He closed his notebook and slipped it back into his breast-pocket. "Good thing you saw the man who cut your brake-lines. You noticed him next to your car, and paid attention to him."

"I only wish I had realized what he was doing. But why should I? I had assumed he was attempting to steal the car. On a day like that, I suppose thieves are everywhere. I recall him plainly: tall, thin, with ears flat to the head. I should have realized he had something more on his mind." He was still upset with himself for being so careless that day. Only when he had pulled away from the curb had he realized the true intention of the sinister man in the longshoreman's clothing, and then it was too late.

"It's a mistake we could all make," said Inspector Smith neutrally. "There are more car thefts than there are attempted murders from cut brake-lines and steering-linkage. But there's no question of what happened to you."

"I still should have been more cautious. I had reason to suppose that there was a man attempting to do me—or those close to me—harm." He shrugged. "Well, I won't burden you with my self-recriminations."

"I don't think you have cause to have any," said Inspector Smith. "But we've talked about this before."

"So we have," said Saint-Germain. "And you have been kind enough to put up with my railing." He touched his eclipse-device signet ring, which he wore on the little finger of his right hand, and said, "Do you find these multijurisdictional arrests are difficult?"

"They can be, and this one is probably going to be trickier than most; the man isn't an American, and he may go to his consulate, or demand representation from his own country. He could find a loophole that would keep us from putting him on trial, or even charging him. Stranger things have happened." Smith looked as if he had a number of stories of just such complications, and only restrained himself from telling them with an effort.

"I have no doubt. The law has so many permutations," said Saint-Germain, thinking of what he had been told of the arrangements that had been made between Sonoma County, the Leonardis, and Carlo Pietragnelli, apparently to the satisfaction of all; at least the White Legion had turned its attentions away from Geyserville, preferring to center its activities in Cotati and south into Marin County. It had been a victory of sorts.

"And more twists and turns than a snake down a rat-hole," said Smith. "I'll be glad once the culprit's in custody. I got a feeling you're right about him, and he's a dangerous customer."

"I would like to be mistaken," Saint-Germain said.

"Who wouldn't, in a situation like this?" Smith took a deep breath. "Well, I'm sorry you had to go through so much, but at least the man'll be in jail tomorrow. And then it's up to the courts." He prepared to rise. "I'll let you know when the arraignment is, and any preliminary appearances he has to make."

"You're sure this is the right man," said Saint-Germain.

"As sure as I can be without admissible evidence," said Smith. "I'd stake my pension on it."

"You say the man has been in San Francisco all along?" Saint-Germain asked as if only mildly interested.

"It seems so. He arrived last winter," Smith answered.

"Ah."

"Inspector Porter's looking into any connection he might have to the break-in at Miss Saxon's place, but the link is hardly even circumstantial." He offered this without much zeal. "I don't think they'll be able to make a case, even if they can show probability; blood type would help, but it isn't conclusive, only indicative."

"Especially if he's type O. Do you recall the type of the blood found at Miss Saxon's house?" He maintained the same manner of mild curiosity.

"I think it was B, as I recall," said Smith. "I have a note about it somewhere if you want me to look."

"Not necessary. Type B could narrow the field. A pity you found no useful fingerprints. And footprints in blood may not be good evidence." He waved his hand in dismissal. "Never mind. I'm sure you'll do your utmost."

"Within the limits of the law," said Smith, putting his cup aside and getting to his feet. "It's all the police can do."

Saint-Germain rose with him. "Of course. Within the limits of the law." He shook hands with Smith. "It is disquieting to think he has been in the city for so many months. Did he move around?"

"You'd think he would, wouldn't you?" said Smith. "Nope. He stayed in the same hotel, over near the Ghirardelli Chocolate Factory, a nice, inconspicuous location, nothing obvious or flashy. He leased a motorcycle to travel on; he disappeared for ten days after Miss Saxon's house was broken into, but that isn't anything beyond suspicious. We don't know for a fact that he was out of the city at that time, just that he wasn't at his hotel."

"She shot him, as you'll recall," said Saint-Germain, going toward the door. "He had to get medical help somewhere—I doubt very much he removed the buckshot himself."

Smith chuckled. "No, probably not. But we can't prove any of it, more's the pity." He went across the entry-hall to the front door. "Will you tell Miss Saxon that I'm sorry we haven't any better news to impart to her?"

"Yes, I will, and thank you for your kindness to her." Saint-Germain opened the door, and revealed his 1932 Duesenberg SJ parked at the curb.

"You liking your Duessy?" asked Smith, a touch of envy in his question.

"It's a very powerful car, and it handles nicely. It's a shame the Depression has damaged the automobile industry as much as it has." Saint-Germain gave Inspector Smith a firm smile. "Thank you for all you've done, Inspector. I am more grateful than I can say. You have been most forthcoming about your progress."

"You've been a lot of help, too," said Smith, glancing toward the car again. "It was very useful that you found out so much about the fellow."

"Useful for a man you held in some suspicion, you mean; I am grateful that you finally exonerated me in your mind," Saint-Germain said genially. "Oh, you needn't deny it: in your position I should have been most uncertain about me."

"I didn't think we were that obvious," said Smith, stepping out onto the porch. "We certainly didn't want to be."

"You weren't," said Saint-Germain. "But I have been hunted by experts and I am more . . . sensitive to it than most." He nodded toward the inspector's Ford opera coupe across the street. "I wish you good fortune tomorrow."

"Thank you," said Smith with genuine respect. "I'll call you in the evening, to tell you how it all went."

"That's most welcome." He looked toward the dark mass of Sutro Forest as Inspector Smith turned away and crossed the street. As soon as the inspector pulled away, Saint-Germain went back into the house, closing the door with purpose. "Rogerio," he called out.

"We're in the kitchen," Rogerio answered. "Miss Saxon is showing me how to make Mongolian Beef. It will be useful for dinner parties to come."

Saint-Germain went back through the living room and dining room to the kitchen, where he found Rowena wielding a Chinese cleaver with artful expertise.

"The beef has to be thin-sliced, or it won't cook properly. If you don't have a curved Chinese sauté pan, you can use a cast-iron frying pan. The scallions have to be slivered, too. Nothing too thick." She demonstrated. "You know enough about Chinese cooking to realize the importance of fine chopping."

"Did you learn this from Clara Powell?" Rogerio asked, imitating her technique.

"No; Clara isn't much interested in Chinese cooking. I learned from Lin Yao-Soo, who was the master-chef at the Golden Pheasant. He was a genius at his work." She stepped back from the counter, wiping her hands on her apron.

"And you an apt pupil, I should think," said Saint-Germain. "That is half the secret in teaching, an apt pupil." He regarded Rowena for a long moment. "Are you still determined to lease your house on Taylor Street?"

"Oh, yes. My mind's made up." She untied the apron and hung it over the hook by the sink. "Even after we . . . I won't feel truly safe there, particularly after you've gone."

"And you have made arrangements for Mrs. Powell?" Saint-Germain asked. "Do you want her to continue to work for you?"

"I have spoken to Mrs. King about her. She must earn a living, you know; her husband won't be out of prison for another six years at the earliest." Rowena frowned. "This isn't entirely because of the attack, you know. Mostly, but not completely."

Saint-Germain accepted this. "Would it make any difference if the man who attacked you was arrested?"

"Arrested?" She swung around to stare at him. "Are you sure?"

"It seems possible," he answered carefully.

"Is that what Inspector Smith came to tell you?" she asked.

"Among other things," said Saint-Germain. "Would that be enough for you?"

She pressed her lips together. "I don't know. You told me that they probably couldn't prove he was the man in my house, and that bothers me."

"Will this be enough for your dinner?" Rogerio interrupted. "Pardon me, but I should start cooking."

"With the rice and the Hunan-style chicken, more than enough; all we have to do is cook the beef and the chicken," she said, then stared at the far wall. "If they are able to lock him up for a good long time for your attempted murder, it would not be entirely satisfying, but it would be acceptable. How likely is that to happen?"

"Inspector Smith seemed a bit unsure on that point," said Saint-Germain. "Not that I blame him: there are so many factors to take into consideration."

Rowena nodded. "You expect something along the lines of the agreement reached about the Leonardis, don't you?"

"I think it's likely," Saint-Germain replied.

"That's what I was afraid of," she said. "That wouldn't reassure me at all. They might repatriate him to wherever he comes from, but he wouldn't have to answer for what he has done, would he?"

"Perhaps not," said Saint-Germain. "I may be wrong, but I had the distinct impression that Smith was preparing me for legal disappointments."

"Does he know something, or is he only guessing?" Rowena asked as Rogerio turned on the stove and selected a cast-iron frying pan in which to pour hot sesame oil.

"I suspect it's an educated guess," said Saint-Germain.

"That's what I'm afraid of," said Rowena.

"And you would not want that outcome?" Saint-Germain asked.

"Would you?" she countered.

"No, I would not," he said. "The man is too dangerous."

Rogerio checked the rice cooking in a covered pot on a back burner. "You'll have to act quickly."

"Yes," said Saint-Germain, touching the lapel of his smoking jacket. "I should go change. This is too casual for this evening."

"I'll be at your disposal in half-an-hour," said Rogerio.

"You needn't come with me, you know," said Saint-Germain.

Rogerio ignored this. "I suppose we'll go in my car."

"It would be wiser," said Saint-Germain, looking around toward Rowena.

"All right," said Rowena a bit nervously, "what are you up to?"

"Something that needs to be done; I'll tell you about it when I come back," said Saint-Germain, and left them alone in the kitchen.

In his private apartment, Saint-Germain dressed quickly in a black turtleneck sweater under a black sports jacket. He changed his shoes from soft house-slippers to short jodhpur-boots with thick soles that were lined with his native earth, preparation to being away from the house; for even at night, his native earth strengthened him. A black watch-cap completed his ensemble and provided some protection for his damaged face, which was still sensitive. As he left his room, he twitched the cap a bit lower on his head; the skin on the right side of his face was not so obvious that it could be too readily noticed, but he felt more secure with his features hidden. The only things he carried were a keyring and a money-clip with four 5-dollar bills and a 20 in it.

Rogerio was waiting at the base of the stairs. "Miss Saxon will be sitting down to dinner in a few minutes. She's changing, as she often does."

"Fine," said Saint-Germain. "Then let's go out now. The less she sees, the better for all concerned."

"I wonder if she would agree?" said Rogerio as he opened the door.

"I don't think I'll ask her," said Saint-Germain, and stepped out, going along to the Auburn, parked near the end of the block.

Rogerio locked the door and went after Saint-Germain, car-keys in his hand. "Where are we going?"

"To a hotel near the Ghirardelli Chocolate Factory on North Point," said Saint-Germain.

"Do you know which one?" asked Rogerio as he headed down the hill.

"I have a general idea where it has to be. I can probably narrow it down to three blocks, perhaps four, and that means four possible places." Saint-Germain fell silent for several blocks. "I want you to drop me about four blocks from the area, and I'll walk the rest of the way. If you'll drive over to the Hyde Street Pier and take a walk along the waterfront there, I'll join you when I'm done. Return to your car when forty minutes have gone by. If I'm not there, walk for another twenty minutes and come back to the car again. If I'm still not there, drive home and wait for me until morning. If you hear nothing from me, take Rowena out of the city—to Pietragnelli's winery, if nothing else seems advisable." He looked straight ahead. "I know you would prefer I didn't do this, old friend, but if I don't, I'll have to accept the necessity of looking over my shoulder for the next ten years. I don't want to have to answer any more questions that might prove troublesome."

"I understand all that, but if this man has truly been sent to kill you, how can you be sure another won't take his place?" Rogerio asked, feeling worried.

"I can't. But if this man disappears and then I leave, it may take time to find me, and I can turn that to advantage." Saint-Germain put his gloved hands up. "I have no obvious weapon with me, and I can be searched by anyone, assuming there is any reason to search me."

"You're still taking a chance," said Rogerio.

"As you did when you spirited me out of the hospital and through Sutro Forest to the house," said Saint-Germain with kindness.

"That—you will agree—was a very different case," said Rogerio, then nodded once. "All right. I'll do as you ask."

"Thank you," said Saint-Germain, and glanced out at the fog, which was blanketing the city; he achieved an ironic chuckle. "I would never have thought I would be glad of San Francisco's miserable fogs."

"It is very chilly tonight," said Rogerio. "No one will wonder at your jacket or your gloves. Or your watch-cap."

"Precisely," said Saint-Germain, once again falling silent.

"You could have used the telephone to find him; the directory has addresses," said Rogerio.

"That is hit and miss, assuming I could get accurate information, and telephone calls could cause my target to bolt," said Saint-Germain. "The police wouldn't like that."

"Do you think they'll like what you're planning to do?" Rogerio asked neutrally.

"Not officially, certainly," said Saint-Germain.

"Aren't you afraid he'll recognize you?" Rogerio could not conceal his surge of worry.

"On the contrary: I'm counting on it. I will know I have the right man if he does." He looked out at the cars maneuvering around them. "What's the reason for all this?"

"I have no idea. I'll try to go around it." Traffic was unexpectedly heavy on Van Ness, and so Rogerio turned off it before he reached Bay, driving north on Larkin to Chestnut, where he pulled over to the curb. "I'm going on to the Hyde Street Pier. I'll get a parking place on Beach Street, between Hyde and Polk."

"I'll find you, either there or at the house. Don't come near the warehouse on the pier, whatever you do. That must be kept apart from the rest." Saint-Germain let himself out of the car and stepped onto the sidewalk, moving quickly away from the intersection. He went toward the looming mass of the Ghirardelli Chocolate Factory, looking along the buildings on the street for a sign for a hotel; the first he tried, on Hyde, had nothing useful to tell him, and said that there weren't very many hotels between Fisherman's Wharf and Lombard Street. Saint-Germain thanked the clerk for the information and went out onto the street once more to look for another hotel. He finally spotted one near the corner of North Point and Leavenworth, a short distance from Columbus, which looked more promising. The place was ordinary, not run-down, but more utilitarian than luxurious, intended for commercial travelers, journalists, and those needing a place to stay for a few months but not wanting to try to rent a room or apartment. It was the sort of hostelry that rarely had trouble—no robbery, no visible prostitution—the kind of establishment the police did not worry about. Since this was the only hotel Saint-Germain had seen in the immediate area, he decided to inquire at the desk. He had formulated a story that was credible and would not alert any but the most distrustful of clerks; he went into the small lobby and up to the registration desk.

"Can I help you?" asked a young clerk with scarred cheeks and lank hair.

"I am looking for someone." Saint-Germain spoke with a heavy Russian accent as he focused his attention on the clerk. "I am looking for someone, possibly a European, someone who can serve as a translator for an associate of mine who is just now visiting the city and has need of someone who can perform this task. So.

I need to find someone who is skilled and discreet who can help us for a short time. I was told—by the police—you might have such a man here; he was described to me as tall, thin, about thirty-five. I am hopeful that you may be able to direct me to him. This is important to my associate, whose time here is short and whose need is great. The man I have been told of may have been here as long as eight months, from what I have learned, and so will be especially valuable to my associate." He slipped a folded twenty-dollar bill under the edge of the registration blotter. "It would be very helpful to my associate to have this man help him."

The clerk stared at the money. "I think we may have the man you're looking for," he said at last as if his tongue were dry.

"Very good. Tell me about him," said Saint-Germain with an affable smile.

"Well, his passport is Italian, but he might not be from there," said the clerk with a confidential smile. "He seems to talk a lot of languages, or he says he does. He has a fair amount of money, or he seems to. He's paid up till the end of November." He frowned. "There's something strange about him."

"You're saying he might not be interested in more work," said Saint-Germain.

"He might not," the clerk said, one finger coming to rest on the twenty.

"Is he in his room tonight?" Saint-Germain asked, his eyes on the bill.

"I think so." The clerk took the money. "Room 414."

"And what is the man's name?" Saint-Germain asked as an afterthought.

"Cenere. He said it's Italian, as I mentioned," the clerk told him, adding, "Do you want me to ring his room and tell him you're on the way up?"

"If you want to," said Saint-Germain as if that did not interest him one way or the other. "It makes no difference to me."

The clerk blinked. "The elevator's on your right."

"Thanks," Saint-Germain said, going in that direction but selecting to take the stairs that ran up immediately behind the elevator. He did not bother to see whether or not the clerk called to warn Cenere; for once he was beyond the lobby, he moved far faster than most men could run, climbing to the fourth floor at a sprint and stepping into the corridor, which was softly lit by shell-shaped sconces on the walls between the doors. He took stock of his surroundings quickly; 414 was at the other end of the corridor, and Saint-Germain approached it carefully, for he could hear the telephone in the room ringing.

"Yes?" said the voice on the other side of the door. "Who? . . . On the way up? . . . Thanks."

So Cenere was warned now, and would make himself ready; just as well. Saint-Germain acted quickly, going directly to the door and knocking twice. "Signor Cenere," he said, still affecting a Russian accent. "I have a proposition to put to you."

"What might that be?" Cenere asked.

"My associate is seeking a translator. The work would not be long, and the pay would be generous." He waited for a response.

"Who is your associate?" Cenere demanded; he made no offer to open the door.

"An expatriate Russian currently working with Italians. We are engaged in some . . . delicate negotiations that need real skill in translation beyond our capacity to accomplish." Saint-Germain supposed this indirect answer would intrigue a man like Cenere. "He's not without means, and his need is urgent."

"How much are we talking about?" Cenere asked.

"Five hundred now and five hundred at the end of the week, when the work is done," said Saint-Germain.

"Fifteen hundred, all of it now," Cenere countered promptly.

"Nyet," said Saint-Germain.

"Then we have nothing to say to one another," said Cenere.

Saint-Germain paused. "I'll call my associate and see what can be arranged. I will have to go down to the lobby to use the pay telephone."

"I can wait," said Cenere. "You're the one who came to me."

There was an edge to his tone that Saint-Germain heard clearly. "I will make a telephone call and return."

"Go ahead," said Cenere.

"I'll return shortly." Saint-Germain retraced his steps down the hall, hit the button to summon the elevator, and then slipped into an alcove near the entrance to the stairs. As he had anticipated, he had not long to wait: as soon as the elevator came, waited, and descended, Cenere's door opened and the man stepped cautiously out, a pistol in his hands, and he came down the hall, glancing over his shoulder as he moved. From his hiding-place, Saint-Germain watched Cenere hurry to the elevator, shoving his pistol into his trouser's waistband at the small of his back. There was a shine of sweat on his forehead. He was very much the man Saint-Germain remembered seeing, the man he had described to the police, and for an instant, he had a flicker of wrath that very nearly precipitated impetuous action, but he was able to restore his composure and purpose, keeping to his place of ambush.

Cenere tapped the button to summon the elevator and began to pace, his body tense and his face hard. He halted in front of the elevator, and stood, tapping his toe while he glanced at the unmoving floor indicator. Growing impatient, he looked about for the access to the stairs, and started toward the door with a quickly muttered oath in a language not English. As he stepped through the door onto the landing, he was too annoyed to notice the swift motion behind him, until a small, powerful hand closed on his neck.

"Mr. Cenere, if you try to fight, or to aim your pistol, I will have to break your neck; please believe that I will," said Saint-Germain as softly as if he spoke to a good friend.

Cenere stood very still, trying to take stock of the situation; he knew at once that this was Ragoczy, and that he should still be incapacitated by the injuries he had received in May. Carefully his eyes slid to the side in an effort to see his attacker for himself, to confirm his impression and to assess the man's condition. "So it is you. Whatever you're going to try, it won't work."

"Do you think so?" Saint-Germain said, vindication giving force to his purpose as he tightened his grip enough to restrict the flow of air to Cenere's lungs and blood to his brain, holding on with unexpected strength until the taller, thinner man wobbled on his feet in a near-faint; Saint-Germain removed Cenere's pistol, took out the ammunition clip, and dropped it and the pistol down the stairwell, hearing them fall all the way to the basement, as he had intended. The clatter attracted no attention, and Saint-Germain continued, "Do you think you can make it down to the ground floor?" He knew better than to expect an answer; he shoved his shoulder under Cenere's, as if to prop up a man too far-gone in drink to manage for himself, and then began his descent to the main floor. Occasionally he spoke to Cenere in his heavy Russian accent as he applied more pressure to Cenere's neck, to give the illusion that the man was inebriated. "You should stay away from schnapps, my friend. It always goes to your head. Schnapps is the very devil."

They reached the main floor, and after a brief perusal of the place, Saint-Germain saw a door leading to the side of the building, away from the front desk; no one was paying any attention to this secondary exit. He lugged Cenere in this direction, still providing occasional exhortations about schnapps. As he worked the door open, he had to release his hold on Cenere's throat; almost at once Cenere began to struggle, his arms flopping in a feeble attempt to strike at his captor. All his efforts were useless, having no apparent impact on Saint-Germain, and for the first time Cenere began to wonder if he could deal with the man at all. Once the door was open, Saint-Germain renewed his grip on the man's neck and this time he held him until Cenere's body drooped, unconscious. Slinging the tall man over his shoulder without any apparent effort, Saint-Germain went out into the alley and made his way toward the street. Holding Cenere as if he were a seaman's large duffel, he kept to the shadows as he made his way toward the waterfront and Fisherman's Wharf and the bristling commercial piers beyond it.

There were fishing boats riding in their berths, the lines holding them to their berths moaning as the rise and fall of the water shifted the strain on them; a few had lights on, and men working at cleaning the rigging. Hurrying on, Saint-

Germain passed beneath the restaurants, going on to the long piers giving access to the ships and the warehouses beyond. Saint-Germain could feel the movement of the bay beneath the wharf pull at him, sapping his strength, but he kept on, even as he realized Cenere was regaining consciousness, and was aware he would have to go more quickly, or risk having to subdue the man again. He turned along the waterfront, making for the pier on which stood a warehouse with his winged-disk device on the doors and the name *Eclipse Shipping* beneath each one. Going to the office door, Saint-Germain pulled a key from his jacket-pocket and opened the lock, then slipped through the door and gratefully dropped Cenere into a wooden chair.

"Where are we?" Cenere muttered as he strove to take in his surroundings; the dim light made him blink in an effort to see.

"We're at a shipping office, Mr. Cenere," said Saint-Germain.

"How do you—" Cenere surged to his feet, his head lowered as he rushed at Saint-Germain.

Saint-Germain swung aside, took hold of Cenere's jacket and used the man's own momentum to bash him into the solid-oak desk that faced the door; Cenere staggered and slumped. "That was foolish, Mr. Cenere."

Cenere could hardly focus his eyes, but he spat to show his contempt. "What are you up to?" His speech was slurred.

"I am dealing with a man who likes to hurt people; you wanted to kill me, which is one thing, but you tried to harm Rowena Saxon, which is another matter entirely," said Saint-Germain levelly. "I am putting a stop to your antics."

This last word stung Cenere to the quick. "You underestimate me, Ragoczy."

Saint-Germain laughed. "Do you think so?" He nodded toward the side of the warehouse. "No one but I knows where you are."

"You can't keep me here," Cenere said contemptuously.

"You think not?" Saint-Germain studied his prisoner. "Now, why would you do that?"

"You're a dead man, Ragoczy," Cenere accused.

Saint-Germain offered him a slight, ironic bow. "As you see."

"If I don't kill you, someone else will," Cenere told him defiantly.

"Very likely. But not today, I think. And not here." He made a gesture encompassing the office. "This pier is owned by Eclipse Shipping, and there is a merchant ship loading for Europe—Spanish ports among them—just beyond the warehouse doors."

"All very interesting," said Cenere with an air of boredom while he tried to think of how he could attack Saint-Germain.

"It should be," said Saint-Germain. "You're going to stow away on it."

"And how am I going to do that?" Cenere asked, but no longer as daring as he intended.

"You'll be in a crate, of course. You'll be able to get out of it, at least you should be able to—in about twenty-four hours. Consider it as my way of returning you to the men who sent you." Saint-Germain shook his head. "I wouldn't recommend you attempt to pull my legs out from under me, or to slam something against my knees. If you try anything, I will be obliged to give you a concussion, and that could be dangerous for a man going into a crate."

"In fact, you're concerned for my welfare," said Cenere, heavily sarcastic.

"No, nothing quite so altruistic," said Saint-Germain. "I'm being pragmatic."

"You mean you're going to kill me," said Cenere in disgust.

Saint-Germain shook his head. "I think I'll let your employers take care of that."

"How do you reckon that?" Cenere asked.

"If you remain here, you will cause more trouble. If you are . . . sent back to your employers, they will deal with you in their own way. As I suspect you already know." Saint-Germain had no expression in his voice.

"Do your dirty work for you, in other words," Cenere accused.

"I should think that would be up to you," Saint-Germain responded.

"I'd think you'd want to kill me yourself," said Cenere. "To be rid of me for good. To be sure."

"Because that's what you'd do to me if you could?" Saint-Germain did not wait for an answer. "I'm a good deal harder to kill than you imagine, although you came closer than many who have attempted it." This admission gave him a trying moment as he recalled many close calls he had endured before: Cenere had been more potentially deadly than many others. In this preoccupied state, he sensed more than saw Cenere make a swipe at his leg; he kicked out twice—once on Cenere's ribs and once on his jaw, and had the satisfaction of seeing the man double over and lie still. He checked the pulse in Cenere's neck, and assured he was still alive, Saint-Germain went to fetch the packing-crate he had set aside for this use; a box of crackers and a quart of water were in the crate already, along with a rough blanket—little enough for a man who was going to spend at least twelve hours encased. He had a hammer, four-inch-long nails, and a customs label near to hand as he went to work, making sure that the crate could be opened with a good deal of effort from the inside.

It was almost two hours later when Saint-Germain let himself out the warehouse office door and went along the waterfront. He was fairly certain that since it was well after their appointed time to meet, that Rogerio had returned to Clarendon Court. Saint-Germain set out for Broadway, where he would be able to find a taxi. He thought about his efforts of the evening, and was generally pleased. Cenere would disappear: his crate was addressed to Carpathian International Traders in Barcelona and was part of a stack of crates the stevedores would begin loading at six in the morning. He had no doubt that Cenere would be discovered well before Spain was reached, but he knew the *Eclipse Corona* was not scheduled into another port-of-call until Acapulco, which ensured his escape from the United States, the very thing Saint-Germain most wanted.

By the time the taxi let him off at Frederick and Cole, Saint-Germain had considered all the ramifications of what he had done, and had narrowed his plans down to three, which he would present to Rogerio and Rowena for their consideration. Walking the last half-mile uphill to Clarendon Court, he gave himself a little time to enjoy the city around him. It was so unlike the place that Madelaine de Montalia had described to him in her letters, about eighty years ago, and yet most of what she had found charming in the place remained, although somewhat changed, as it would continue to change. As he let himself into the house, he found Rogerio seated at the dining-room table, an account ledger spread out in front of him.

"I noticed that Eclipse Shipping has been improving its profits," Rogerio observed as if they had been discussing this only moments before.

"Its profits are going into the restoration work at Ponderosa Lodge," said Saint-Germain. He noticed the clock on the mantel was about to chime one. "Is there some reason to be doing accounts at this hour?"

"It's time for the monthly review," said Rogerio.

"And that, my friend, is not an answer," said Saint-Germain, coming to take his seat opposite Rogerio. "How long did you wait?"

"Ninety minutes, all told. Miss Saxon was worried when I came home without you. I tried to comfort her, but she was disinclined to accept it."

"I'm sorry she had any distress on my account," said Saint-Germain.

"I told her you would be all right, that you had come through far worse, and not so long ago," he said with a suggestion of a smile. "She acted as if she almost believed me by the time she went off to bed, but I could see she was still apprehensive." He paused to turn one of the ledger pages. "She would be glad of your company, now you're back."

"Then perhaps I should go up to her and let her see I'm safe." Saint-Germain waited for Rogerio to object; when he said nothing, Saint-Germain went on, "I surmise we can deal with the other considerations in the morning, when we leave." He rose. "Thank you for all you've done."

Rogerio looked slightly astounded. "You have nothing for which to thank me. I am always at your service."

"You'll permit me to disagree, on both points," said Saint-Germain as he started to climb the stairs; he heard Rogerio chortle as he continued up to the guest room to wish Rowena good night, and then to finish his packing.

TEXT OF A LETTER FROM OSCAR KING IN SAN FRANCISCO TO FERENC RAGOCZY, SENT IN CARE OF MILES SUNBURY IN LONDON VIA AIRMAIL.

KING LOWENTHAL TAYLOR & FROST
ATTORNEYS-AT-LAW
630 KEARNY STREET
SAN FRANCISCO, CALIFORNIA

November 29, 1937

Ferenc Ragoczy
c/o Miles Sunbury, Esq.
Sunbury Draughton Hollis & Carnford
Solicitors and Barristers
New Court
City of London, England

My dear Ragoczy,

I understand you reached London from Canada more than a week ago and may already have left England for wherever your next residence may be. This will catch up with you, I am certain, for Mr. Sunbury will forward it to you. I, for one, am sorry to see you go, but I can understand the reasons you felt you had to depart.

This is to bring you up-to-date on your affairs in California: the title of your house on Clarendon Court has been transferred without condition to Miss Rowena Saxon for the sum of one dollar ($1.00), and she is now in residence there. The title to the Auburn driven by Mr. Rogers has also been completed, and Miss Saxon is now the duly registered owner of the car, in accordance with your instructions to me.

The sums you have set aside for the Pietragnelli Winery have been conveyed to Carlo Pietragnelli, who expresses his gratitude to you most effusively. His remedies, provided by the settlement that was negotiated before the incidents of September, have been put into motion, with regular judicial review. The Attorney General of the State of California is going to investigate the White Legion, and will vigorously prosecute any infractions of the law that may be laid at their door. With the strong likelihood of Culbert Olson winning against Frank Merriam, the political climate will tend to support that kind of inquiry. It has been more than forty years since a Democrat occupied the Governor's Mansion, and it strikes me that this is a good time for such a change, at least when it comes to putting a stop to this kind of trouble.

I have been visited by Inspector Porter twice since you left; I have said nothing of your whereabouts, which I am ethically bound to do, being your counsel of record in California and therefore required to keep total confidentiality in your regard—not that the Inspector has anything beyond suspicions that you have been party to the apparent disappearance of a reputed European assassin, yet I know he is eager to settle the matter, at least in his mind. Without an actual complaint, his hands are legally tied. I have indicated to him that I will release to him only such material as you provide me written authorization so to do, and he must abide by this, since, little as he may like it, it is completely in accord with the law and the ethics of my profession.

The management of your Ponderosa Lodge contracts has been transferred from J. Harold Bishop of Horner Bishop Beatie Wentworth & Culpepper to this office. Both Bishop and I agree that it is sensible for all those matters to remain in California, and since Mrs. Curtis is amenable, I have filed the necessary forms. I have enclosed copies of all the applicable paperwork, with an amended contract for your signature. Please initial where indicated, sign in the presence of a notary or of three witnesses, and return it to me as soon as is convenient for you.

It has been an honor to know you and to represent you: I will continue to execute your orders to the limit of the law, for as long as you require. I thank you for conveying your power-of-attorney to me for the purposes of filing tax returns. That will simplify my ongoing work for you, and maintaining your various accounts at Bank of America, the details and balances of which are included in the rest of the enclosures.

The investigation in regard to the failure of the brakes on your Pierce-Arrow Silver Arrow has not made any progress, although there is some indication that the steering-linkage was actually cut. What cannot be determined is whether this was the result of the impact of the car's fall, or due to prior mischief. The Marin County Sheriff has declared the case no longer active, and neither the District Attorney nor the police are inclined to do anything further. Should the case be reopened, I will inform you, but as things stand, I would suggest you accept that it will not be possible to bring the incident to the conclusion for which you had hoped, and I am sorry to say that *without an identified culprit, not even a civil suit would prosper; all my avenues for remedy are exhausted.*

May I say that I look forward to seeing you in San Francisco one of these days again? This goes beyond the courtesy of professional representation: my wife and I have truly enjoyed your company; you will be welcome in my house at any time. I wish you safe travel and success in all your ventures.

Sincerely at your service,

Oscar King

enclosures as indicated
OK/jmm

EPILOGUE

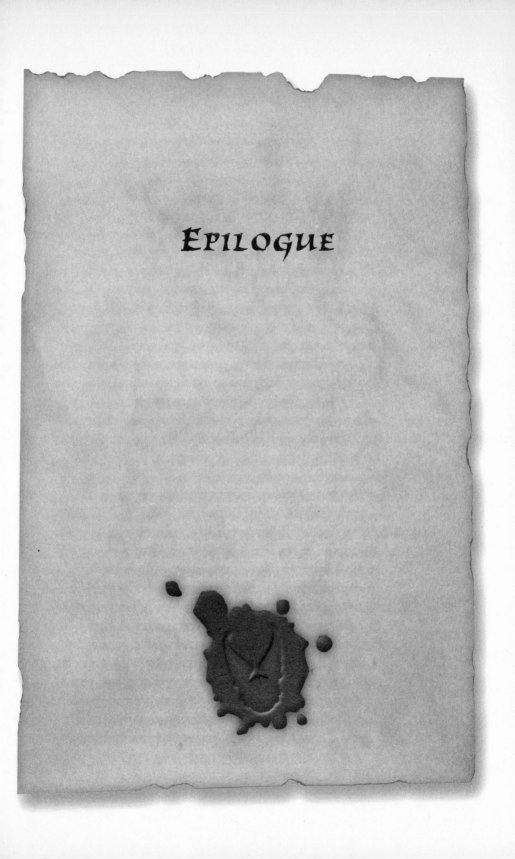

Text of a letter from Madelaine de Montalia in Caracas,
Venezuela, to le Comte de Saint-Germain at Montalia, Provence,
France, sent by airmail.

Hotel Los Ingleses
Avenida Ancho
Caracas, Venezuela
22 January, 1938

le Comte de Saint-Germain
Chateau Montalia
nr. Saint-Jacques-sur-Crete
Provence, France

My most cherished Comte,
I cannot thank you enough for being willing to take up residence at
Montalia, for I am not going to be able to leave my work here for at least
two more years, and I am very reluctant to cut my dig short, considering all I
have had to do to get here. It took me almost eight years to get the necessary
permissions to undertake this exploration, and I fear if I leave now, I will be
unable to return for perhaps a decade, and the sites are already in a compro-
mised condition—another decade and the destruction may be too extensive
for anything beyond the most elementary recoveries, which would please
none of the sponsors of the dig, to say nothing of the loss it would mean to
the records of human experience it would represent.

At the same time, I hear the rumors of war growing louder and louder; I
share your apprehension and I dread what is to come. I am helpless to stem
the tide that is rising, much as I may deplore it. And I fear for what I have,
and while that may be callous, I find that my homes are one of the few
things I can protect from the havoc that is coming. Without a dependable
friend at Montalia, I fear it will suffer as Monbussy-sur-Marne did in the
Great War. The armies never intend the wreckage they cause, but it happens,
in any case, and I believe it will not be long until more than Spain is up in
arms and guns are pounding again. You have seen the signs many times
before, and you know how quickly peace can erode once the generals begin to
tell the government what has to be done. I look at Europe and I despair.

It is probably very wrong to ask you to put yourself in harm's way by liv-
ing at Montalia, and it may be that I should abandon this dig and return to

face whatever is in store for France, but I cannot bring myself to do that, and not only because the prospect of war is so pervasive—it is also because I have come so far to do this expedition, and I would rather not give up the prize, which is finally within my grasp, for no more purpose than to be shot at in my own home. What benefit the world would derive from having me endure another war, I cannot imagine, but if you tell me it is worthwhile, I'll do as you advise. Yet I must admit I would prefer to remain here, doing the work I love, and for which I have labored so long to bring within my grasp. I hope that you will not hold my decision against me, and if you think it is too cowardly, tell me so, and I will return to Montalia for the duration of whatever is to come.

Paradoxical as it may seem, I do so long to see you, although I also recognize how difficult it is to be with you, to love you as I love no one else, and yet have no means to express it beyond the sense of the Blood Bond. If only there were a way that those of our blood could impart life to one another! But to do that, we would have to be living, and so the longing will remain unfulfilled and our intimacy as intense as it is unrepeatable. I will treasure you and all we have had together even while I cherish the living who accept my love knowingly, as you taught me to do almost two hundred years ago.

Always your

Madelaine